Praise for Joyce Gee and The Altira Series

"A compelling, well thought out story which leaves you wanting more."
—*Early Reader Review*

"*Magic of Lies* is fast-paced, witty, and was instantly my new favorite fantasy series. Joyce Gee built a beautifully rich and diverse world. *The Altira Series* deserves a home on any fantasy lovers' bookshelf alongside George R.R. Martin, J.R.R. Tolkien, and Sarah J. Maas. With so many enchanting characters, you'll be rooting for them all. I highly recommend reading it!" —*Alex Williams, editor*

"Magical and exciting! Can't wait for the rest of the series!"
—*Starred Review, 5/5*

"I loved Joyce Gee's debut, MAGIC OF LIES. Princess Eirian is sent away after her birth and returns to her father's kingdom twenty years later with the expectation that she will become queen. But she is a magic user in a kingdom that does not like magic users, and her father Nolan suffers from a terrible disease that is robbing him of his memory. I loved the tension in this fantasy novel, with war looming, with the questions about King Nolan, about Eirian's magic and her worries about ascending the throne. I also really liked the friend group, and the tension with the various romantic leads, Aidan the captain of the guard and Celian. I am looking forward to book two!" —*Starred Review, 5/5*

"Magical and exciting! I can't wait for the rest of the series!"
—*Cori Nevruz, thriller and suspense author*

About the author Joyce Gee

Joyce Gee is an Australian author based in Mandurah, Western Australia. Growing up among the rainforests of Far North Queensland, she loved to vanish into the other worlds hidden within the trees. When she isn't writing, she enjoys drinking tea, pottering around the garden with husband and their two children, or escaping with her camera to capture the beautiful landscape of Western Australia.

Her latest release is *The Altira Series*, composed by *Magic of Lies, Blood of Husks, Grave of Dandelions, Shadows of Life, Game of Gods,* and *Fires of Unmaking.*

The Altira Series

When Princess Eirian returned home after decades away, she thought it would be a fresh start. Born with magic, she struggles to balance her ability to give life with the desire to kill. Raised a mage in a distant city, she struggles to adjust to life as a princess in a court where magic is undesired.

With assassination attempts and rumors of war, Eirian proves to those around her that she is not one to hide from confrontation. Even when it risks her life.

The Kingdom of Endara is at war and Eirian refuses to be the soft-hearted queen the enemy expects. Among her growing collection of secrets is one that can help turn the tide of battle, even if it means that her people might turn on her.

She knows she can buy the precious time needed for reinforcements to arrive, but she will have to break her promises to the ones closest to her.

With nightmares clawing at her fragile mind, Eirian embraces the whispers that have followed her for as long as she can remember. In the aftermath of the real enemy revealing herself, Eirian retreats from the allied armies to seek answers.

Accompanied by Aiden, Celiaen, and Galameyvin, they are determined to confront the spirit of the last mage and face the dark god seeking their destruction. The price for victory is one that Eirian is willing to pay, even if her friends are not.

The Altira Series (continued)

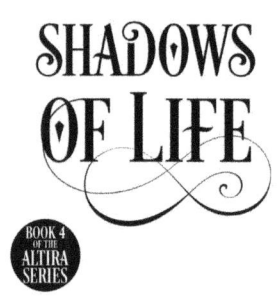	Tormented by her mother's memories, Eirian fears what she will become if she accepts her duty. The gods of Death and War have waited patiently for Eirian to make her move. Willing to do whatever they must to ensure the enemy is destroyed and reborn, the gods of War and Death must risk Eirian turning Tir into dust to keep her on their path.
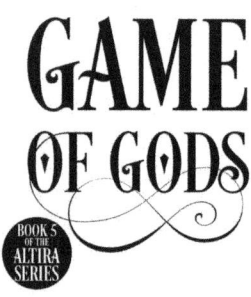	There is a thin line between saving the world or destroying it, and Eirian finds staying on the right side harder with each passing day. Determined to bring down Annawyn, Eirian returns to where she grew up. No longer hiding the truth, she knows her presence will cause disruption across the land. But with increasing attacks from the Unseelie army, Eirian cannot stand by while innocent lives are destroyed because of her mistakes.
	Faced with distrust, Eirian tries to protect the ones she loves with the help of War and Death. All she needs to do is find a way to force the mad god to pass over before her manipulations destroy Endara. But unraveling the darkness woven throughout the people she once ruled is not an easy task. They know that if they do not stop the enemy's forces, countless innocent lives will be lost.

BLOOD OF HUSKS

BOOK 2 OF THE ALTIRA SERIES

JOYCE GEE

BLOOD OF HUSKS

BOOK 2 OF THE ALTIRA SERIES

JOYCE GEE

5310 PUBLISHING Published by
5310 Publishing Company
Go to 5310publishing.com for more great books!

SCAN ME

This is a work of fiction. The situations, names, characters, places, incidents, and scenes described are all imaginary. None of the characters portrayed are based on real people but were created from the imagination of the author. Any similarity to any living or dead persons, business establishments, events, or locations is entirely coincidental.

Copyright © 2022-2023 by Joyce Gee and 5310 Publishing Company. All rights reserved, except for use in any review, including the right to reproduce this book or portions thereof in any form whatsoever. Reproducing, scanning, uploading, and distributing this book in whole or in part without permission from the publisher is a theft of the author's intellectual property.

Our books may be purchased in bulk for promotional, educational, or business purposes. Please contact your local bookseller or 5310 Publishing at sales@5310publishing.com or refer to our website at 5310PUBLISHING.COM.

BLOOD OF HUSKS (1st Edition) - ISBNs:
Hardcover: 9781998839063
Paperback: 9781998839056
Ebook/Kindle: 9781998839070

Author: Joyce Gee
Editor: Alex Williams
Cover Design: Eric Williams
Map Illustrator: Dewi Hargreaves

BLOOD OF HUSKS (1st Edition) was released in September 2023.

ADULT FICTION (with Young Adult interest; it can be categorized as New Adult 16+)
Fantasy / Epic
Fantasy / Action & Adventure
Fantasy / General

Themes explored include: Epic fantasy; Adventure fiction; Love and relationships; Coming of age; Death, grief, loss; Interior life; Identity / belonging; Politics; Narrative theme: Social issues; Mythical creatures: elves.

For Anita,

*Who never stopped dreaming of
what this story could become.*

Acknowledgements

I'd like to begin by acknowledging the Traditional Owners of Australia and pay my respects to Elders past and present.

To my amazing husband, Beau, aka The Chef, thank you for your unending support. You are my rock, and I could never have done this without you. To my children, always dream of the stars and have the courage to reach for them. I'll always hold you up. And to the rest of my family, near and far, who have supported my dreams, thank you. Especially you, Kyle, for arguing over getting a signed copy of the first book for free. Your support means the world.

To Freya, I hope you're watching on and laughing at me. Every story I write is for you. Always. I miss you every day. To Barbara, I hope you're proud of me. It's been a long time coming.

Once again, I could not have done this without the support of Anita and Meghan, my fabulous alpha readers. The two of you have seen this story unfold in so many ways. And Callai, my crazy Callai, the source of too many laughs and endless hours of friendship, you have helped keep me somewhat sane all these years. I don't know what I would do without you. To Grace, Dana, Ben, and all the others who have cheered me on all these years, I cannot thank you enough.

To the ladies of the TMT. You still know who you are. Thank you for being the incredible people you are.

Lastly, the writing community on Twitter. You guys are fantastic! The support I've found among you never ceases to amaze me.

—*Joyce Gee, author*

CAST OF CHARACTERS

Kingdom of Endara
Eirian Altira: Princess of Endara, purple mage
Nolan Altira: Eirian's father, King of Endara
Dowager Duchess Amira Altira: Nolan's sister, mother to Llewellyn
Duke Everett Altira: Eirian's cousin, next in line to the throne, Duke of Tamantal
Duke Llewellyn Altira: Eirian's cousin, third in line to the throne, Duke of Onaorbaen
Duke Marcellus: Nolan's cousin, Duke of Raellwynt
Duchess Brenna: Marcellus's wife, chief of Eirian's ladies in waiting
Countess Elena: Countess of Caerwel
Earl Alastair: Elena's husband
Countess Elyse: Countess of Periyit
Earl Craig: Elyse's husband
Earl Baeddan: Earl of Nareen
Countess Caraf: Baeddan's wife
Earl Adalardo: Earl of Gerygaen
Earl Gallagher: Earl of Jurien
Dowager Countess Kaie: Gallagher's mother
Countess Kathleen: Countess of Kaban
Earl Kendall: Kathleen's husband
Chancellor Ulric: Endaran small council
Treasure Sabine: Endaran small council
Chamberlain Wendel: Endaran small council
Justiciar Ollier: Endaran small council
General Cameron: Endaran small council, commander of the Endaran military
Lady Isabella: Eirian's lady in waiting, daughter of Countess Kathleen
Lady Romana: Eirian's lady in waiting, Elke's sister, daughter of Earl Baeddan
Lady Elke: Eirian's lady in waiting, Romana's sister, daughter of Earl Baeddan
Lady Bea: Eirian's lady in waiting, Earl Gallagher's sister
Captain Gunter: Captain of Everett's guard

Kingdom of Endara – Eirian's guards
Captain Aiden Cathasaigh: Captain of Eirian's guard
Merle: Aiden's second in command
Devin: Merle's squad
Fox: Merle's squad
John: Merle's squad
Sid: Merle's squad
Tobin: Merle's squad
Fionn: Squad leader

Kyson: Fionn's squad
Paxton: Fionn's squad
Geoff: Fionn's squad
Zack: Fionn's squad
Tyler: Fionn's squad
Fisk: Aiden's squad
Gram: Aiden's squad
Lyle: Aiden's squad
Randolph: Aiden's squad
David: Aiden's squad
Mac: Aiden's squad
Gabe: Squad leader
Jack: Gabe's squad
Layne: Gabe's squad
Kip: Gabe's squad
Wade: Gabe's squad
Andrew: Gabe's squad

Kingdom of Ensaycal
King Paienven Kaetiel: King of Ensaycal, red mage
Queen Sannaeh Zarthein: Paienven's wife, sister of Archmage Baenlin Zarthein, red mage
Princess Awena Kaetiel: Princess of Ensaycal, daughter of Paienven and Sannaeh, blue mage
Princess Nadinna Kaetiel: Princess of Ensaycal, daughter of Paienven and Sannaeh, blue mage

Kingdom of Ensaycal – Princes of Ensaycal
Prince Galameyvin Kaetiel: Prince of Ensaycal, Celiaen's cousin, blue mage
Prince Celiaen Kaetiel: Crown Prince of Ensaycal, son of Paienven and Sannaeh, red mage
Prince Yaernan: Paienven's brother, blue mage
Prince Selagan: Paienven's brother, blue mage

Kingdom of Ensaycal – Celiaen's companions
Tara: Red mage in charge
Alyse: Tara's assigned blue mage
Tynan: Blue mage assigned to Celiaen
Kenna: Red mage
Ianto: Blue mage assigned to Kenna
Lydia: Green mage
Harlow: Yellow mage

CAST OF CHARACTERS

Link: Yellow mage
Tully: Red mage
Cai: Blue mage assigned to Tully
Darcie: Blue mage assigned to Imogen
Osric: Blue mage assigned to Mabel

Mages of Riane
Archmage Baenlin Zarthein: First red archmage of the high council
Archmage Azina: First green archmage of the high council
Fayleen: Yellow mage, Eirian's best friend
Soren: Blue mage assigned to Baenlin
Jaren Valkera: Red mage, friend of Eirian
Rylee: Red mage, friend of Eirian
Luke: Blue mage assigned to Rylee
Master Howell: Green mage

Kingdom of Telmia
King Neriwyn: King of Telmia
Prince Emlyn: Neriwyn's son
Lord Vartan: Neriwyn's lover and general
Lord Faolan: Telmian envoy to Eirian
Lady Saoirse: Faolan's twin sister, part of Telmian delegation
Lord Tharen: Part of Telmian delegation

Kingdom of Athnaral
King Aeyren: King of Athnaral
Ambassador Darryl: Athnaralan ambassador

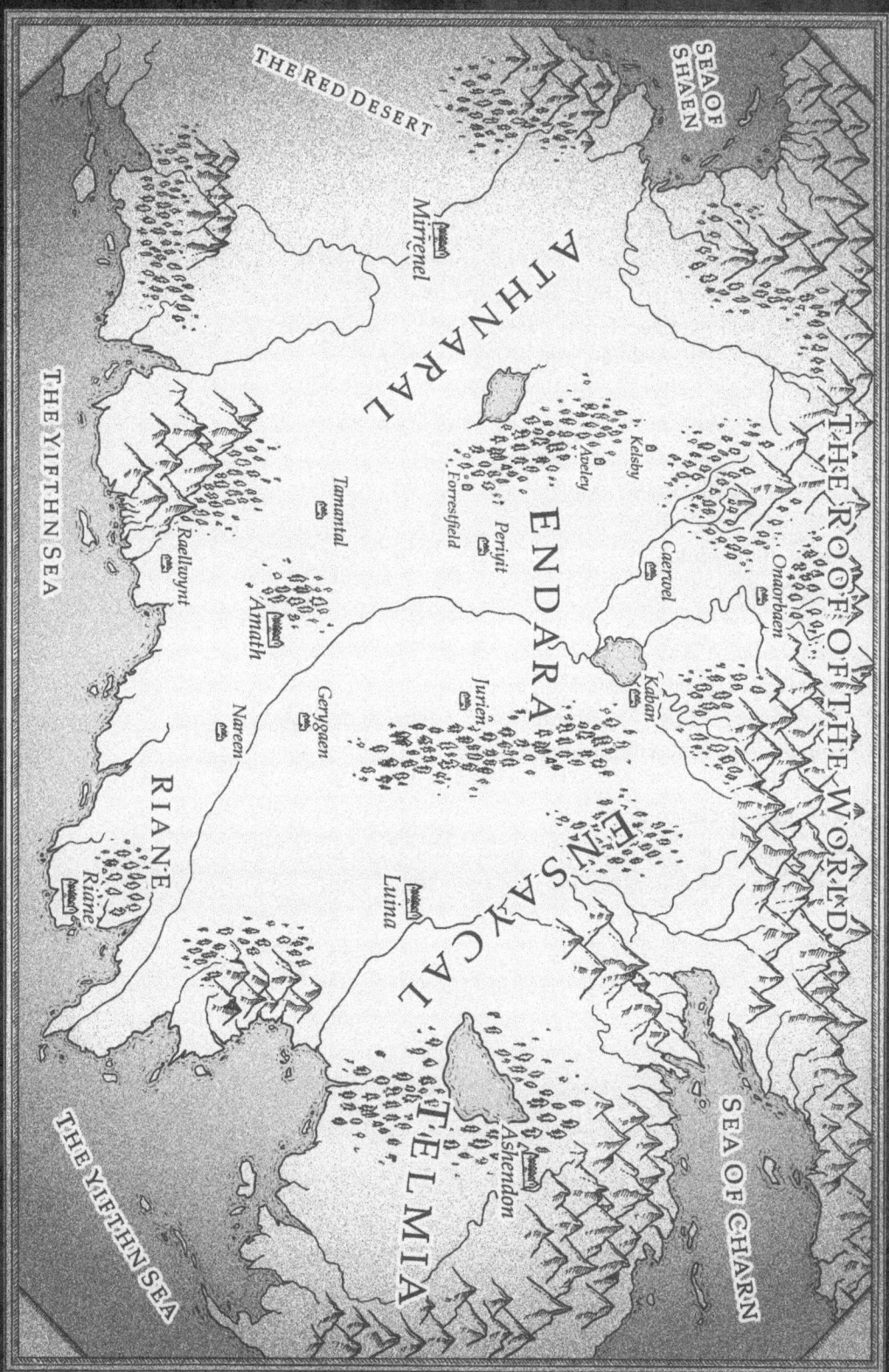

ONE

Gazing at the pile of things on the bed, Galameyvin chewed on his lip and contemplated his choices. Next to them, the pack he had stolen provided an interesting puzzle. He had to keep it light, only taking essential items. His plan was risky, and he did not know his chances of success. Trying to take a horse would gain attention too quickly, and what advantage of speed it could provide was not worth how fast the hunt would come after him.

He needed to escape Ashendon and flee Telmia before he lost his mind. All the days of pointless nothing were wearing him down, and Galameyvin feared he would become as frivolous as the daoine if he remained. It had reached the point where he suspected he was losing days. There were periods when everything was a fog, his memories fading into gray and taking his resolve with them. If he did not leave soon, he would never want to go.

"I need you," he muttered to his armor and weapons.

Shoving them to the side, he discounted them as items to go into the pack. Then, reminding himself that time was short, Galameyvin made his selections and threw them in the bag. It would be a long walk to the border, but he only needed to make it to the first town on the other side. Once in Ensaycal, he would be safe to buy a horse, ride for Endara, and find Eirian. Wherever she was.

Pulling on his armor, Galameyvin adjusted it before adding his belts and weapons. It was not the gleaming plate Celiaen wore in battle, but the quality of the leatherwork and wards were the best Riane could craft. As a prince of Ensaycal, he had access to the best crafters for anything he could want. Most blue mages went without armor, but he was rarely willing to stay out of the fight.

"Right, I think that's everything."

While taking the last rummage around his chamber to make sure he had not left behind anything important, Galameyvin ran through his plan. He would take advantage of the daoine being busy with another one of their feasts. While they occupied themselves with food, wine, and each other, the gardens were empty, and he could run for the forest bordering the western side. From there, he had to make his way through the towering jarrah trees without being caught, cross farmland, avoid towns, and reach Ensaycal.

Satisfied he had everything he needed in the pack, Galameyvin hoisted it onto his back. Crossing to the door, he hesitated with his hand on the knob, a voice whispering to him it was not too late to change his mind. He could stay. Neriwyn had assured him they would leave Telmia to lend help to Endara. There was no reason not to believe it. If he stayed, the journey would be far more straightforward than what he was planning. His hand dropped away from the knob, and he shifted around.

Catching sight of the tapestry adorning the wall opposite the bed, Galameyvin shook his head and banished the voice. He stared at it, admiring the image of a lake framed by mountain peaks. Blinking, he reminded himself of what he was doing and put his hand back on the door. As he turned it, he felt a flash of concern that it seemed locked. The feeling faded when a second attempt was successful, and the door opened into the silent hallway.

Galameyvin had memorized his intended route, carefully noting markers that would guide him out. Doing his best to keep quiet and move fast, he recounted the map in his mind and followed the twisting hallways through the castle. Holding his magic close, he reminded himself not to hesitate if he encountered one of the daoine. Most of them were suggestible, and those he struggled against would be close to Neriwyn or attending to court matters. It was a relief when the door to the garden appeared.

Pausing mid-stride, Galameyvin stared at the carved timber in surprise. The door was open, lit torches secured in sconces on either side. Beyond, the garden beckoned, shrouded in darkness. He had expected the door to be shut with the current feast happening in another part of the castle. Figuring that someone must have slipped out into the garden with companions to find a pleasant spot for their own enjoyment, Galameyvin went through and left it open. It was best to leave it as it was and avoid alerting whoever might be around to his presence.

No one had lit the torches and lanterns that adorned the pathways and pergolas of the garden. Even the weeping tea tree grove near the castle, a popular nighttime location, was unlit. They strung delicate hanging lanterns through the branches, illuminating them and creating a beautiful space for midnight picnics. In the dark, the garden made Galameyvin nervous, the shifting shadows mixed with the shapes of plants casting intimidating forms.

A hand found the hilt of a sword for reassurance. The cold metal and leather gave him something solid to focus on. His feet followed the map in his mind, and the light of the full moon was enough to double-check the directions on signs to ensure he was still going the right way. When he eventually reached the edge of the garden where it gave way to wilderness, Galameyvin stopped and questioned his sanity.

The jarrah trees towered high above, the canopy of leaves blotting out the sky. Beneath them, darkness reigned, and the sounds of nocturnal creatures reached Galameyvin's ears. He knew what lurked out there. Swallowing his nerves, he wished he had Eirian's ability to read the land. There were snakes out there. Deadly ones that he would not stand a chance at surviving the bite of. Not only them, but spiders. Thankfully, only the small varieties, not the giant ones, occupy the Dinaden forest.

"You idiot," he grumbled in frustration. "You should've grabbed a torch."

Angry with himself for making a mistake, Galameyvin turned and looked back over the gardens and wondered if it was worth the extra time to go back. The forest was a sprawling mass of trees that would take too long to go around. Rubbing his face, he considered if it was worth staying on the outskirts until daybreak and then going in at a different location. There was a chance it would throw off anyone following him. They might assume Galameyvin had gone for the most direct path through the trees.

Going over the maps he had memorized, he decided that going south along the forest would be better. It would take him toward younger growth and the chance of a thinner canopy. No matter what he decided on, the forest would take days to cross. The daytime was only marginally safer than night, but at least he could see the danger coming. Treading heavily, Galameyvin hoped the teachings about snakes were correct.

Keeping on the edge of the tree line, he watched everything as he walked. The shadows twisting in reflection of the movements of branches made his nervousness increase. Galameyvin attempted to squash the feelings, clinging to his magic. He did not want to embrace the calmness it could provide him but the lingering bloodlust that set him apart from most of his fellow blues. It helped him stay alert and prepared.

"If you cut in now, there's a creek that runs in the right direction and isn't too deep."

Freezing at the sound of Emlyn's voice, Galameyvin peered around in the moonlight to find where he was standing. When his searches provided nothing, he waited. He wanted to believe he imagined it, and he had not heard Emlyn speak.

"It's the shadows getting to you," he muttered.

Emlyn chuckled, "My apologies."

The shadows shifted, and Galameyvin watched Emlyn emerge from a cluster of trees on the garden side of his path. Whatever wards he had been using had masked the taste of his magic, and Galameyvin felt the impact of it against him like a shield strike.

"Prince Emlyn, I can explain."

"I'm sure you can, but there's no need. As I said, if you cut in now, you'll find that creek. It's shallow enough to walk in, and if you stay in it long enough, it should mask your scent to throw off some of the hounds."

Adjusting the way the pack sat on his shoulders, Galameyvin stared at Emlyn in shock. He did not know if he could believe what was being said. Doubt flickered through his magic, and Emlyn snorted.

"I'm telling the truth."

Galameyvin asked, his uncertainty obvious in his tone, "Maybe you are, but why? Why would you help me abandon the job my king set me? Especially when your father has instructed me to remain here when I've asked to leave."

Shrugging, Emlyn waved dismissively at the forest. "Because you want to go. I doubt you'll get far, and I'll deny any suggestions I helped. You're not a prisoner."

"I need to go."

"You want to be with her."

"Yes."

"That wasn't a question," Emlyn replied. "I don't need you to tell me where you're going. I figured that out. My father will find you before you reach the other side of the forest, but there is a slight chance he might not."

Licking his lips, Galameyvin looked at the looming trees. The presence of another person did not make them any less formidable, but Emlyn had given him some hope.

"What do I need to do?"

"For a start, make it to the creek. You'd be walking against the current, but that has its advantages. If you reach the point where it deepens past your knees, you're almost at the waterfall. That's where you want to get out."

"If?"

In the moonlight, there was the ghost of a smirk on Emlyn's face. Galameyvin felt the voice of doubt return. The same voice had urged him not to leave his chamber earlier. Despite the guise of offering help, Emlyn did not come across as hopeful. Which made Galameyvin wonder if his suggestions were simply to make it a more challenging game for Neriwyn.

"Emlyn, what will King Neriwyn do to me?"

Tilting his head to the side, Emlyn peeked in the castle's direction. "A lot of things. You might be an elf, but unless King Paienven requests your return, you're governed by the same laws of Telmia as the rest of us. As far as my father is concerned, you belong to him."

"I don't belong to anyone!" Galameyvin snapped. "As you said, I'm not a prisoner. If I want to leave—"

"You'll sneak out like a thief in the night? Yes, that makes perfect sense."

"I've asked nicely. Repeatedly."

"Yes, you have. I understand you feel the need to go to Eirian, but my father has promised that you'll accompany him to Endara when he leaves."

Frowning, Galameyvin turned away from Emlyn to stare into the dark forest. His words were the truth. Neriwyn had made those promises. It was only his impatience that was driving him to attempt a feat that few daoine had ever managed. Crossing his arms, Galameyvin contemplated the choice in front of him.

"After I make it to the waterfall?"

Emlyn was silent. He glowed like all daoine did, the sheen of magic giving his skin its own light. The first time Galameyvin had seen it in the dark, he had remembered all the times Eirian had appeared similarly. All of them knew the stories of how powerful mages had been before the mage wars, and Galameyvin wondered if the daoine glowed because they embraced their power.

"You don't expect me to make it that far at all."

Lips twitching, Emlyn shuffled his feet and glanced over his shoulder at the castle, saying, "I don't expect you to make it into the forest."

Inhaling sharply, Galameyvin asked, "Has he already discovered my departure?"

"No, not yet. He's busy with Vartan for the moment."

"So I have at least the night?"

Snorting, Emlyn specified. "They're making plans. He'll discover your departure as soon as they're finished, and he comes to find you."

The words had Galameyvin moving toward Emlyn. Stopping a short distance away, he stared in expectation.

"Why would he?"

"Why do you think?"

"Endara."

"Indeed. If you really want to continue on this path, I'll give you help." He pressed his lips together before adding, "However, I strongly suggest you don't."

Running a hand through his gold curls, Galameyvin wanted to believe Emlyn was telling him the truth. If Neriwyn and Vartan were making plans to depart Telmia for Endara, it suggested the war with Athnaral was close. They faced a slow journey, but it would be easier than he could expect on foot.

Dragging his bottom lip through his teeth in uncertainty, Galameyvin said, "I want to trust you're telling me the truth. All I desire is to be with Eirian."

"Then come back to the castle. I'll make sure Neriwyn doesn't find out about this little adventure, and you won't have to worry that he might decide not to let you go with him."

"He wouldn't, would he?"

Lifting a shoulder, Emlyn's mouth twisted, and he gave Galameyvin a look that suggested Neriwyn might decide to leave him behind. Around him, the shadows twisted as the breeze picked up and shook the branches high above. They stood in silence while Galameyvin considered what choice to make. It had not occurred to him that Neriwyn might punish him for his actions by denying him what he wanted most.

"But if I go now, he will, won't he? Neriwyn would order me to remain here in Ashendon."

Emlyn nodded. "My father has a temper. He wouldn't take this well, and yes, he would lash out. You don't want to find out what happens to those who displease King Neriwyn."

"How did you know where to find me?"

"I have foresight, Prince Galameyvin."

Reminded of the powers Emlyn wielded, Galameyvin sighed. He was unsure how foresight worked, but he knew enough to believe what he was told. Wrapping his hands around the shoulder straps of the pack, he gazed into the darkness. Lost in the shadows of the night, the castle was a distant monument waiting to reclaim him.

"What did you see?"

"I saw you trying to flee my father through the forest. After I had my vision, I started watching you closely. I didn't know when you might try to escape the city, just that you would."

It was difficult to grasp why Emlyn would have a vision about him trying to leave, and he said, "What else?"

"You mean, why would I bother? Perhaps I wanted to protect you from his wrath?"

Galameyvin could not argue with the sentiment. "I suspect there is a lot more to it than that. Even so, my thanks."

"We can walk and talk at the same time. The longer we linger out here, the greater the chance of Neriwyn discovering your absence," Emlyn commented with a wave.

Following him, Galameyvin kept his eyes down and remained close. The pace Emlyn set was quick. It demonstrated his confidence in knowing where they were in the garden. Which was something he could admit to being clueless about. Left to find his own way back to the castle, he would have wandered aimlessly for hours. He was not sure he had been in that section, and without light, there was no way to tell.

"Tell me, how would King Paienven have reacted to the news you abandoned the duty he set you?"

Flinching, he admitted, "Not well. He'd view it as a betrayal."

Casting a look over his shoulder, Emlyn arched a brow. "And yet, despite the potential wrath of two kings, you'd risk it for her?"

"Always."

"Good."

"Really?" Galameyvin sounded uncertain. "I'm not sure it's a good thing."

"You're not wrong in your belief Eirian needs you."

"I'm not? Then why keep me here? Aren't I better off by her side?"

"Can you force an image and the associated emotions on a large group of people?" Making a sudden turn down a different path, Emlyn said, "As a defensive measure, of course."

Mulling over the question, he wondered how many people Emlyn was talking about. It was something Galameyvin had done on a small scale during a fight. He hated twisting perception, but they taught blues trained to accompany reds how to do it.

"Well, I suppose it depends on how many are in the group. I've done it to about a dozen in one hit."

"At least you know how it's done. Riane didn't fail in that regard. You're a powerful mage, Galameyvin, and your willingness to tread the line will come in useful in war."

"What do you mean?"

Emlyn did not answer, holding up a hand to silence Galameyvin. Feeling the ripple of magic surround them, he suspected the silence was because of some daoine nearby that Emlyn had sensed. They continued to walk, with the wards muffling any sounds their feet might make. As they got closer to the castle, he noticed torches had been lit and caught the sound of laughter.

Gazing at the back of Emlyn's head, he realized the wards were blocking out the magic and emotions of the others they had passed. He did not know if it was for his benefit or theirs, but Galameyvin was thankful. Ahead of them, the open doors waited, flickering torches making the shadows dance across the stone. The hallway beyond appeared like a chasm to swallow them.

"You're the one who left the doors open and the gardens unlit," Galameyvin whispered. "I thought it was a little odd."

Chuckling, Emlyn shrugged. "I wanted to see what you would do."

"If I had decided to go into the forest and risk it, would you have told the king?"

"I wouldn't have needed to."

"What aren't you telling me?"

"No one leaves Ashendon without my father knowing. I lied when I said there was a slight chance you'd make it. Neriwyn has wards layered through the forest, and he knows when someone crosses them."

Galameyvin was familiar with those types of wards and huffed in annoyance. He imagined they were likely coupled with ones discouraging people from crossing them. It was the sort of trick Celiaen liked to pull. Most masters and the archmages used similar ones in their offices when they were absent. More powerful mages could easily dismiss them if they wanted to. Neriwyn had magic far greater than he did, and Galameyvin doubted he would have gotten past them.

"How do you stand it?"

They reached the door to the chamber assigned to him, and Galameyvin stared at it in resignation. Emlyn leaned against the wall beside it, studying him thoughtfully. His hand closed around the doorknob, reluctantly turning it and pushing the door open. Waiting until he went through, Emlyn followed. The click of closing made him clench his fists in frustration.

"The days all blur into each other. It's endless nothing. No one seems to have a purpose other than to eat, drink, fight, and fuck."

Emlyn arched a brow and said, "We're immortal."

"The daoine waste their own potential!"

Shrugging the pack off, Galameyvin dumped it on the bed and turned to face Emlyn. He was staring at the tapestry of the lake, grief crossing his face like a shadow. Sensing Galameyvin's magic twisting around him, Emlyn shook his head and rubbed his face.

"It's not that simple."

"Isn't it? I've heard a lot about how Riane has failed to teach things, but I don't see your people doing anything about it."

"There's a lot you don't understand, Galameyvin." Crossing his arms, Emlyn asked, "Would you have us overruling your laws and dictating how things are to be done?"

Waving vaguely, Galameyvin argued, "No, I'd have you teaching us! You've had the blessing of thousands of years to learn. Teach us to be better! When you know better, you do better."

Eyes darting to the pack, Emlyn shook his head. Seeing a flicker of concern in his eyes, Galameyvin understood the message with no words. Knowing Neriwyn would question his armor and weapons, he removed them while Emlyn crossed to the bed and unbuckled the bag.

"I'm sure by now you've worked out that daoine magic is not the same as the magic elves and humans wield." Shaking out the pack, Emlyn muttered, "At least you thought this through."

Placing his weapons on the rack provided, Galameyvin glanced at the piles of things scattered over the bed while Emlyn sorted them out. It was a strange sight, but he was thankful for the help. They needed to make sure Neriwyn had no reason to suspect he had planned to leave. Urgency had his fingers swiftly undoing the buckles of his armor, the leather falling away from Galameyvin's body. It joined the weapons on the rack before he approached Emlyn at the bed.

"It's not so different that you can't teach us."

Taking a pile of folded clothes to the wardrobe, Emlyn said, "Maybe things have happened for precisely the right reasons. It's not so much that we've failed to teach, but that you've failed to remember."

"I don't understand."

Placing his notebooks and writing equipment on the desk, Galameyvin stroked the spines tenderly. He rarely went without them, enjoying the privilege of recording his observations and experiences. The echo of Celiaen teasing him about it played out in the corner of his mind while he turned back to the bed. Emlyn focused on his clothes, leaving the other things for him to deal with.

"You of all people should understand." Waving at the desk, Emlyn finished putting the clothes away. "I've seen you writing every day. You like to record things."

It clicked into place, and Galameyvin shook his head. Images of the extensive network of catacombs carved into the ground beneath Riane came to his mind, and he understood. He had seen the dusty rooms filled with boxes. There were chambers filled with books that no one bothered to look at. They placed things in the catacombs and ignored them until forgetfulness claimed their existence.

"We've done this to ourselves."

Emlyn picked up the midnight blue silk coat from the bed and tossed it over the back of a chair haphazardly. His fingers traced over the embroidery of the triple sword emblem of the Kaetiel family. Glancing at Galameyvin while he carried the bundle of fruit to the table in the opposite corner of the room, Emlyn sighed.

"Laws shouldn't govern magic."

"I'm not sure I agree. Without laws, what is to stop mages from taking advantage of their superior power?" Galameyvin asked, placing the fruit in the bowl he had taken it from.

Huffing, Emlyn rolled his eyes and answered, "You're misunderstanding my point on purpose. I said magic, not people. Laws help guide people down the path of acceptable behavior. Magic knows no right or wrong. That is wholly on the user."

Looking around the chamber, Galameyvin thought it looked normal. The only sign of his attempt to leave was the pack. Hurrying to pick it up, he went to place it in the wardrobe. Stopping him, Emlyn took it from his hands with a faint smile.

"I'll take it. Better it doesn't stay here to tempt you to try again."

"How far off is King Neriwyn?"

"Don't worry. He won't learn anything from me."

Winking, Emlyn ran a hand through his dark brown hair and turned to the door. Galameyvin did not stop him. He knew if Emlyn was leaving, it meant Neriwyn was on his way.

"You never told me why you had a vision about me leaving."

Emlyn paused at the door and glanced back. "You need to be with Eirian for the fight. I couldn't let you put it in jeopardy. That's all."

"Would my absence make that much of a difference to the war?"

"It would make a difference to Eirian."

Pressing his lips together, Galameyvin thought about what she was capable of. Celiaen could not stop Eirian if she slipped over the edge and let her power go on a rampage. She would fall and take him with her. Together, they were a storm of destruction.

"Because I can stop her?"

"Yes."

Scratching the back of his hand, Galameyvin said, "I hope I don't have to."

"So do I."

Opening the door, Emlyn slipped through and shut it, leaving Galameyvin alone in the room. Shoulders slumping, he covered his face and thought about what he would do while he waited for Neriwyn to appear. Digging his nails into his forehead, the slight pain was a distraction from his nerves. Hands falling away from his face, he glanced at the stack of books on the desk.

Crossing to it, he selected one and carried it to the bed. Sitting on the edge, he let the tome rest while removing his boots. Piling the cushions up, Galameyvin made himself comfortable and settled in. He would spend the time productively if he had to wait for Neriwyn. Opening the book, he studied the first page and frowned. It was not a book he remembered selecting from the library. There was a knock at the door, and the sense of Neriwyn's magic made Galameyvin look up from the page.

It took a moment for his eyes to adjust before he called, "Enter!"

Neriwyn stepped into the room, leaving the door open while he took in the sight of Galameyvin propped up in bed. Chuckling, he turned and closed it, his hands pressed to the timber while he listened to the sound of Galameyvin snapping the book shut.

"How can I help you, Your Majesty?"

Keeping the book in his lap, Galameyvin peered at Neriwyn patiently. He hoped that the anxious beat of his heart was not apparent. Against most people, the calmness of his magic would hide it, but Neriwyn was a far more powerful opponent. Pushing away from the door, he turned and looked at Galameyvin with a faint smile.

"Have you already gotten so bored with us that you'd rather read a book than enjoy the delights of our feasts?"

Eyes darting to the book, Galameyvin tentatively replied, "I wasn't in the mood for it tonight."

"I have news for you."

"Really?"

"Queen Eirian has left Amath. All reports coming in say that King Aeyren has his armies mustering for war. In expectation of that happening, I'm issuing the call for my warriors to prepare." Neriwyn ambled over to the chair and sat. "Which means you'll get your wish soon."

Nodding solemnly, Galameyvin did not feign surprise. It was easier to show his genuine response, one of resignation and concern. As much as he wanted to be with Eirian and Celiaen again, the prospect of war made his heart sink.

"Thank you for letting me know. It will be good to see my friends and family, even if the circumstances aren't ideal."

Raising a brow, Neriwyn asked, "Is that it? No demands to know when we'll depart?"

"I'm well versed in the logistics of war, sire, and I know you can't say when we'll leave. It all depends on how long it takes for your army to be ready. Not just the warriors, but everything else that goes with it."

"Yes, I suppose you are. Let me remind you, Your Highness, that until King Paienven commands otherwise, you remain in my service."

"Have I displeased you?" Stroking the book in his lap, Galameyvin said, "I hope not. If I have, I didn't intend to."

He looked around, cocking his head to the side. Nothing seemed out of place, and Galameyvin felt confident that between them, he and Emlyn had put everything back where it went. Following his glance around the room, Neriwyn sniffed at the air and chuckled.

"Something is bothering you, sweet boy."

"Nothing to be concerned about, Your Majesty. I'm worried about war and what it will mean for all of us. Especially Eirian."

Rising to his feet, Neriwyn let Galameyvin think he believed him. He had smelled the lingering scent of Emlyn in the room and knew he had been there not long beforehand.

"Have a little faith in your beloved. Eirian possesses strengths she isn't aware she has."

"It's not her strength to fight that concerns me."

"Then what?"

Galameyvin's eyes were downcast as he replied, "It's what she'll do to win that worries me."

Two

Crouching next to a tree, Eirian peered at the small stream running through the gully. Beside her, Marcellus was silent as they watched the soldiers filling their flasks from the water. They were in a forest between the lands of Periyit and Caerwel, with Athnaral barely half a day's ride away. Scouts had continued to report Athnaralan soldiers crossing the border, but Eirian had not expected to see them.

"There aren't many. We could easily dispatch them." The colonel accompanying them glanced at the bow in Eirian's hands. "I presume you can use that half as well as I've heard."

Glancing at him sideways, Eirian replied, "They haven't spotted us, but I imagine they have friends. If they don't return, said friends will realize something happened."

"They haven't spotted us because of your magic." Marcellus stroked his chin thoughtfully, adding, "I suggest we back off quietly and return to Forrestfield. We know they're here, and our scouts suggest they're moving north."

"But why northward and not east?"

Shrugging, the colonel turned, keeping low to the ground. "Well, they might try the old come down the river trick."

Marcellus grimaced. "They might try to take Onaorbaen because they know your father is there. Maybe they think if they capture the former king and the rest of the royal family, you'll surrender to their demands."

"No one has ever taken Onaorbaen. If they tried moving on Llewellyn's home, they'd end up trapped against the Roof of the World," she pointed out.

Taking another look at the soldiers, Eirian estimated the distance to them.

She cocked her head, glancing at the light filtering through the trees while watching the movement of leaves to judge the breeze.

"I could take out half of them easily before they could scramble up the slope."

It was an easy lie. Eirian knew she could kill all of them without touching her bow.

"You're confident." The woodsman's words were barely audible.

"She's that good," Marcellus said and touched her arm with a nod in the direction they had left their horses.

Fox agreed, "It's true."

Almost crawling, the five of them scrambled back to the rest of their group waiting in the trees. Once out of sight, they could walk properly, carefully picking their way through the undergrowth. The woodsman guided them, and it relieved Eirian to see the rest of the party, her guards watching their approach.

"Was the view pretty?" Gabe asked.

He looked out of place in the forest, and Eirian noticed a patch of decaying greenery beside him. It reminded her of the day in the garden after discovering the truth about her mother. Dismissing the observation, Eirian told herself she imagined it.

"The view was an eye-opener," she replied, her tone making his eyes narrow.

"I won't get in trouble with the captain, will I?"

Scoffing, Eirian shook her head and shared a look with Marcellus. "Let's get back. I want to find out why no one reported them using that spot."

"Chances are they're using different spots each day to lessen the possibility of being spotted. When we get back, I'll order scouts to keep watch along the stream." Sounding tired, the colonel shook his head. "This is an unpleasant business."

"Too many steep slopes. A man would break his neck before you'd get the chance to separate his head from it," a local soldier commented and slapped the trunk of a tree.

Rolling her eyes, Eirian assured them. "Don't worry, we won't be engaging here."

"That was a neat trick back there," the woodsman said.

It had surprised Eirian when he did not flinch at her magic. Chuckling, she peered through the trees as she walked, her magic sensing Faolan hidden out of sight.

"Thank you, I have many neat tricks up my sleeve."

Sighing, Eirian twisted her braid in her hands and tried to dismiss her concerns about the Athnaralans. Observing the men, Eirian noticed Fox was the most confident of them. The way he moved through the forest betrayed his upbringing on the edge of the Fingers. Fox had asked to come along despite being off duty. Watching him made Eirian feel ungraceful, and he smirked every time she stumbled.

"You're not on your game today, Your Majesty," Fox said mockingly.

Eirian flinched when she caught another root hidden under a thick layer of dead leaves. "Don't start, Fox."

Gabe arched an eyebrow and looked over his shoulder at Eirian. "She's not using her magic. I've noticed you're using it less, Your Majesty. Ever since you played in the rain."

Pursing her lips, Eirian glanced at where she had sensed Faolan and said, "I don't want to frighten people."

"What do you mean, frighten people?" the woodsman asked from the front of the line.

"I'm a mage, and people fear mages."

"Don't know who told you that, Your Majesty. Mages be mighty useful. Can't say I know anyone who wouldn't like to have one living near."

Frowning, Eirian mulled over his words. Staying quiet, the group focused on returning to the horses. The forest was denser than the woods close to Amath. A thick roof of foliage above their heads cast an eerie light as the rays from the sun battled to make it to the ground. Reaching out, she stroked her fingers over a clump of hanging lichen, the tendrils soft against her skin. Something about the tree pulled Eirian, and her gaze caught on a mage ward carved into the trunk. It made her stop, dropping to a knee to brush the plant away.

"What have you found?" Marcellus called.

Tracing the long-healed injury to the trunk, Eirian frowned at the tingle of magic that remained. It pulled her, and she pressed her hands against the mark, letting the power flow between them.

"It's an old ward carved into the tree."

"Lots of them in the forest. We can't cut the buggers down," the woodsman muttered.

Closing her eyes, Eirian concentrated on the tree and her magic spread. As it went, more trees flared into her awareness, the wards carved into them linked. Realizing it worked to sense other presences in the forest, she pictured the prowling wolf. He felt what she was doing, and Eirian pulled her hands from the tree to break the connection.

Dusting her hands off, Eirian stood and told the group, "Let's keep moving."

Curious, Marcellus strode along beside her. "So, what do they do?"

"I'm not sure, honestly. It's like when I read the land, except the trees acted like sentinels. They're linked in a network and took some of the power requirement out of the action."

Her mind held a map of the trees, and Eirian fought back a shiver whenever they drew close to one. It struck her as an odd reaction, but she did not know how they created the network. For all she knew, her response was typical.

"Did you sense anything?"

"Only what I already knew. Lord Faolan is following us." Eirian watched Marcellus stiffen and shake his head in disapproval.

"I don't like the way they watch you. Not to mention the indecency when they transform in public. I know they're different, but they could at least respect our ways and not parade around naked where everyone can see them."

"I've worked a lot of magic naked." Eirian's lips twitched at his horrified expression, and she added, "I've killed while naked."

"Is that why it doesn't bother you or the elves?"

"Most definitely. If what you're doing will ruin clothing, do it naked. Some healing requires a great deal of skin-to-skin contact, for example."

Marcellus gave her a sideways look, muttering, "You can't heal."

"I used it as an example."

"Then what can you do that is better done naked?"

Arching an eyebrow, Eirian gave a predatory smile. "I don't think you want to know the answer, Your Grace."

A scoff from Gabe drew her attention to the guard, and he pointed at the edge of the forest. Eirian caught a hint of amusement in his eyes, but it faded quickly.

"The horses," Gabe said.

Feeling mischievous, Eirian crouched and lay her hands against the damp soil. Glancing to where she sensed Faolan, she sent her power snaking through the ground and into the tree roots surrounding him. His surprise when the roots lifted and tangled him made her laugh. Confused, her companions did not question when Eirian signaled for them to mount. Turning the horses toward Forrestfield, Eirian glanced over her shoulder to wave at the wolf watching from the tree line.

It was not long before the garrison keep rose above them against the blue sky, the guards on the wall alerting the occupants of their return. A constant bustle of noise and life greeted them, soldiers going about their duties as though royalty were not visiting. Men were waiting to take their horses, and the colonel ordered the woodsman to remain with them so he could share the location of the Athnaralans. Eirian retreated to the keep, and her guards kept close, fearful of their captain if they let her out of their sight.

Eirian found Everett with General Cameron and a group of officers. They gathered around a table with maps spread everywhere, and she slipped between them.

"We saw Athnaralans while we were out." The conversation cut off, and they stared at Eirian. "I counted a neat dozen but couldn't sense any others close."

Shuffling through maps, Cameron pointed at one. "Where?"

Squinting at it, Eirian attempted to work out any landmarks. She ran a finger over it and tapped on a location.

"The stream, they were fetching water. I think it was about here."

"Did they see you?" Everett demanded.

"Of course not. I'm handy like that."

Barking orders, Cameron turned to his aides, saying, "That's closer than previous reports."

She smiled patiently. "I know."

"We'll increase the watches and scouts. Someone might think it a good idea to capture you here."

"I wish them luck," Eirian chuckled. "I don't think they'd enjoy the attempt."

"We should move to the next stop sooner," an officer said. "We have more troops north, but we have to go through the forest."

Everett grew concerned and glanced at the map in front of him. "I don't like that prospect. The forest is an ambush waiting to happen."

Holding up a finger, Eirian pursed her lips. She considered the network of trees and the possibility of using them.

"I discovered something in the forest. I'd need to investigate it, but I suspect I could use it to our advantage while moving along the forest road."

"I presume you mean a magical advantage?" Cameron questioned, his curiosity apparent.

"Yes, but I can't make any promises. At the very least, I can use it to give us a heads-up if they attempt to ambush us."

"What is it exactly?" an officer asked.

Shrugging, Eirian held her hands apart and gestured to the maps. "I don't know for certain. There are trees with wards carved into their trunks, and they're linked. I used my magic on them and saw the entire forest."

"This is an original keep from before Endara. One of the oldest, and there are many of them up and down the border. In fact, they set the border where it is because of them. Perhaps our Telmian friends know something," Everett said.

Cringing at his words, Eirian replied, "I had the same thought."

"You're avoiding them."

"I'm going to stare at the countryside from the roof. While I do that, I'll contemplate approaching the daoine about this. I need information."

Those gathered around the table bowed as Eirian left. Grumbling as they escorted her up the hundreds of steps, her guards did not engage her in conversation, sensing her desire for silence. The roof was almost empty, only a pair of soldiers patrolling. When they saw her, they bowed and huddled in a corner out of the way. Crossing to the edge facing the forest, Eirian leaned on the wall and chewed her lip.

"Your Majesty," Gabe called.

She caught sight of Tharen standing in the doorway. "He's fine, Gabe."

Turning back to the view, Eirian listened to him walking toward her. Tharen was a calmer presence than Faolan. His power reminded her of gently swaying grass, and it possessed a calming warmth. He stopped out of reach, touching a hand to the low walling of the roof. Standing in silence, she watched him from the corner of her eye, admiring the way he shimmered like silver in the sunlight.

"Faolan suggested you wouldn't wish to speak to him."

"He'd be right. Why did he send you?"

Eirian continued to watch from the corner of her eyes, not wanting to meet his gaze. Tharen respected her choice and stared at the forest. They stood in silence, neither willing to discuss why she had been avoiding them.

"Mages were a lot more powerful. I don't know when it changed, but you're all less than you were," Tharen said quietly.

Mulling over his comment, Eirian replied, "Could it be you remember mages as more than what they are?"

"No, I remember correctly." He waved at the rooftop. "A long time ago, at least for your kind, mages built everything. Magic was in everything."

"Do you know what changed it?"

"War, it's always war. After the gods vanished, those with magic tried to fill the void. Magic warred with magic. It allowed the darkness to creep in and take hold. After we pushed the darkness back, unity became important, and they created Riane. We thought having them working and learning together would mean magic would grow."

"It makes sense. Sharing knowledge should promote growth." Curious, Eirian glanced over her shoulder. "But knowledge doesn't change raw power, does it?"

Tharen agreed, "It's the raw power that seems less. I wonder if our king hopes you're a sign of it returning. However, your power is extraordinary, even by the standards of the past. You've barely scratched the surface of what you're capable of."

Breathing deeply, Eirian clutched her right arm to her abdomen and pushed thoughts of her mother away. Tharen waited for a response, aware something was bothering her.

Eirian murmured, "I've heard it before. All I can do is make the best of the time I have to be the best I can be."

"While your magic gives me hope, I question it. What you did in the storm, I've only seen one other capable of doing it. And she was not human. You have power beyond mine, and I'm one of the most powerful daoine alive."

His words did not help keep her focus from her secret, and Eirian wondered if he knew. Tharen's gray eyes betrayed nothing when she met them.

"I know. I've put a lot of effort into keeping much of my power secret. I fear Riane's reaction if they knew everything."

"You're a child leading the deaf and blind."

The words stung more than Eirian expected, and she said, "Is that insult called for?"

Waving at the roof, Tharen gave her a condescending stare. "Are you aware of what you're standing on?"

"I'm standing on a keep?" Uncertain, Eirian looked where he was pointing and squinted. "No, I'm clueless."

"At least you can admit it. Faolan said you encountered the guardian trees. They once connected fortresses up and down the lands. Those with the ability to do so could stand on the roof and link, pulling power from their fellow mages."

Gasping, Eirian's mind whirled with the enormity of his explanation. "They could create massive barriers around entire regions of land."

"Or kill with it."

"Using the trees?"

"You know exactly what I mean. You can do it with no help on a smaller scale. These towers act as a conduit, amplifying the power poured into them by the users. Or user, if a single mage possesses enough power," Tharen explained and gave her a pointed look.

Stepping away from the wall, Eirian paced across the roof until she sensed the ward built into it. Dropping to her knees, she ran her hand around the mark and noticed the difference. Everyone watched in silence. Flicking her gaze at Tharen, Eirian frowned before pulling her hands from the stone.

"I've never heard of anything like this. Surely there'd be books in Riane about constructing these sorts of things."

"Forgetfulness is a plague upon history, even among my people. We never stop regretting the actions of those who came before us. We hope our penance will change what happened when all it does is prevent growth. I imagine in some dusty corner of the city, you'll find many long-forgotten things."

A light breeze caught his pale hair. Eirian stared at Tharen from her position and admired his ethereal appearance. She half expected him to dissolve into the sunlight.

Looking down at the floor, Eirian muttered, "You're right. What makes it worse is we've forgotten what drove us to penance. We settled into a constant circle of peace and combat over the same stretch of land. Familiarity became our cage, while the mages withdrew and grew fearful of those without magic."

"Even my people forget and grow complacent. We became these frivolous creatures because it was easier than pretending."

"I feel you're trying to lead me to something." Glancing at her guards, Eirian noticed the dark way Gabe was watching. "Perhaps you should save us time and tell me what it is."

Smirking, Tharen shrugged and said, "Honestly, I'm not trying to tell you anything so much as to garner what you've learned and kept to yourself."

Her stomach clenched with fear, and Eirian avoided his stare by leaning forward to run her hands over the worn stone.

"I keep many things to myself."

"I'm glad you spared me your protests. They're as much confirmation as saying nothing. You intrigue Faolan. He wants to discover your secrets, but I only care if they prevent you from being useful."

Staying silent, Eirian did not answer. She dragged her hands over the mark and caught her palm on a sharp edge. Turning it over, she watched the blood bead and sighed.

"Powers forbid I cease to be useful."

"I'm sure someone will always find you useful. Power drives the world, and you have a lot. I can smell the blood. Do you need my help?"

"No, it's nothing, just a scrape."

Pressing her hand into the fabric covering her thigh, Eirian glanced at him over her shoulder to find he was standing behind her. Holding his hand out, Tharen stared at her with a hint of amusement.

"Show me, and I'll decide. I'm not the chief healer among my people for no reason."

Refusing to give him her hand, Eirian ignored the way his magic urged her to do as he commanded. "I don't need your help for a small nick."

"Do you understand that you have given this place your blood? The lingering magic of its creators has tasted the power in you."

"What do you mean?"

"Blood holds magic, and as the Altira, you must know this. I'm curious what you and Celiaen could do with this keep and its twin. Perhaps there's hope for magic."

Reminded that they forbid blood magics in Riane, Eirian stared at her hands in horror. "Did mages die to make things like this keep?"

"Not mages. The balance was the lives of those they used the magic against. Don't deny the power you use to kill finds balance in your living and the other dying." Ignoring her protests, Tharen squatted and grabbed Eirian's hand, turning it over to study the thin cut at the base of her thumb. "If you leave this, it'll be sore for days."

"One death can save many others," Eirian murmured.

Snorting, Tharen gave her a sideways look and ran a fingertip over the cut, his power sending shivers down Eirian's spine. Greens had healed her many times, but his magic felt different. It was familiar, stirring the memories at the back of her mind.

"You can't be sure the lives you saved were worth saving. Killing you would cause countless deaths, which would mean many who deserved to die would live. The thing about death is every life has a reason."

Watching her skin knit together, Eirian lost herself in thinking over his statement and wondered what those she had killed in the past might have done if they had lived. She felt the urge to glance at her guards, and she met Gabe's gaze. He winked, and she looked at Tharen.

"Everyone is, at the very least, a son or a daughter. How am I to know if they're worth leaving alive when they're trying to kill?"

"Have all deaths at your hand been trying to kill? What of the death sentences your justiciar issues? They've borne your signature, and the recipients' families would blame you. You killed them as surely as if you'd struck the blow."

"Why do you seek to cast insecurities on me? I understand the repercussions, and I understand if I linger on these thoughts for too long, it will cause more harm than good."

Tharen smiled and told her, "I'm pleased you understand. So many don't. They can't own their feelings. You should get a sense for this keep because it might come in useful."

"How do you know?" Her tone was accusatory.

"Did you think he missed the Athnaralans you espied? We know they're there, and they know you're here. Their king knows you're here."

"Will he come?"

Shrugging, Tharen looked skywards. "I doubt it. This land is not in their favor, but the network means it is in yours. Not that they'd be any more aware of it than your people are. You could've ridden on and never realized."

"But instinct drew me to it. I could have touched any tree, but I touched one within the network. It called to me."

"It called to you like storms do. We've not missed that even the sunrise calls to you. You draw energy from the world. You're a most singular woman," Tharen said.

"I didn't draw power from those trees," Eirian replied.

"Didn't you? Now you know they exist, you'll be on the lookout. Perhaps you'll find another, and it'll be of great use to you. Or perhaps they'll never be of use to you other than as something you help your fellow mages rediscover. In a drive of curiosity, they'll cast open forgotten tomes of knowledge. Magic will grow again."

"Do you think the decline of magic is because the gods left?" Watching Tharen's face freeze at her question, Eirian closed her hand into a fist and felt a slight tug at where the cut had been.

Turning his pale gaze toward her, Tharen frowned, admitting, "I've considered it. Surely they never expected their creations to only thrive so long as they remained among us."

"What?"

"I'd like to think the gods didn't create us to depend on them as a source of life and power."

Running a hand through her hair, Eirian asked, "Then where does our magic come from?"

"The earth, the sky, every fiber of life that exists, has ever existed, and will ever exist. I dread to imagine our world if magic stopped."

"I think we'd be okay. Humans anyway, we're less dependent on it."

Tharen grabbed her hand and slammed it against the floor. His power flowed into the mark and encouraged Eirian to reach out to the connection her blood had unwittingly forged.

"Feel the beat. Do you think we'd be okay? Magic is life."

Unresistant, Eirian maintained eye contact with him as she felt the network struggle to flare to life. He saw a hint of amusement in her eyes, and Tharen frowned.

"Magic is death as well," she said. "We'd adapt. We always adapt. We must adapt, or we will perish. That is survival."

"Life and death are opposite sides of the same coin. You cannot have one without the other."

"Your people do."

He replied, "Death can claim us. In the meantime, we serve our purpose."

Reminded of her mother, Eirian murmured, "I understand existing purely for a purpose. I understand how it feels to resent your life because you know it can never be your own."

"Yes, I suppose you do." Letting go of her hand, Tharen peered at the anxious guards. "I'll leave you alone to think."

"Thank you. Please tell Faolan to stop shadowing me."

Keeping her hand to the stone, Eirian did not shut down her connection, staring at Tharen with a hint of anger. The ghost of a smirk appeared as he rose and looked at the sky.

"I'll tell him, but he'll disregard my suggestion. Faolan desires to know many things about you, including the secret that weighs heavily on your mind."

"There's no secret."

"So you claim. Don't let it overwhelm you. No secret is worth that."

Eirian let her stare linger before cocking her head to look pointedly at the door. "I'll keep it in mind."

Bowing stiffly, Tharen spun and strode away, giving Gabe a wide grin as he tilted his chin in challenge. Left in silence, Eirian placed her other hand on the stone and bowed forward to rest her forehead between them. Eyes closed, she focused on the link between the building and the trees. It was a strange sensation, feeling the power run through the ancient keep's outer walls, following prepared pathways.

The images in her mind were more precise than they had been earlier. The wards in the keep amplified the link, as Tharen said. Around her, time slowed as Eirian felt her magic touch on everything living in the forest, the tendrils of power reaching out to the tower on the other side. Lips parting, she felt her heartbeat and breath slow, sharing a beat in time with the forest.

In the corner of her mind, she felt Celiaen's power against hers. Welcoming it, Eirian basked in the pleasure of their bond. It shifted as she realized everyone with magic was aware of her outpouring. She felt their feet touching the ground as her magic flooded through it. Their lungs drew breath from the air she shared. Their fear that she could draw on them tasted strong on her tongue, and Eirian felt the temptation, knowing they could not stop her from commanding their magic.

Celiaen's fear was the strongest, their link making him the easiest to draw from. His pleading thoughts echoed in her mind, and Eirian smiled, letting her power caress and wrap around him reassuringly. Only the daoine felt unconcerned, confident in their ability to stop her drawing from them, and pleased with the demonstration. The confidence they radiated made her want to prove them wrong. She could touch their magic, and she knew if she tugged at it, it was hers to command.

Eirian turned her focus to the forest, and she relished the life there. Her mind flitted with birds from branch to branch, the feathered creatures undisturbed by the magic. Leaves rustling in the wind felt like they were brushing against her skin. Rabbits hurried from burrow to burrow, paws barely touching the ground as they moved. They made her feel small and alert. She tasted the pounding heartbeats of scouting parties and woodsmen.

As strongly as Eirian felt the life, the darker side of her magic rumbled with a desire to destroy it. The fear she could feel from the humans within proximity of her power fed it. It whispered along the edges of her mind, reminding her how easy it would be to draw that life into herself, to turn it into withered decay. She had done it before, and it would be easy to do it again.

Gasping, she pulled back and yanked her hands from the stone. Lifting her head, Eirian met Gabe's dark gaze as he crouched in front of her while the rest of her guards huddled at the doorway with the two soldiers. Magic flickered around her vision, and she saw shadows around him, inky black lines marking Gabe's skin. He did not reach out, remaining still as he regarded her.

Feeling drained, Eirian struggled to move into a seated position with her legs stretched out in front of her. Her knees protested the most, the stone an unforgiving surface to kneel upon for so long. The whispers of her magic continued to linger, the power within reach. It told Eirian she knew the man in front of her, and all she needed to do was remember him.

"What was that?" Gabe asked, his voice a low hiss.

"I was exploring." Stretching, Eirian groaned, "How long was I kneeling?"

He cocked his head to the side. "I don't know. Everything got odd after the silver one left. You've never done magic like that before."

"You sound angry and fearful."

"Doubt I'm the only one feeling out of sorts. They certainly aren't feeling themselves."

Gabe ran a hand through his short hair before letting it drop, waving over his shoulder at the others. Eirian looked away, guilt filling her. She saw the fear on their faces.

"I'm sorry. I didn't know what would happen. In hindsight, I should've left it for another time and warned everyone. I didn't expect that side of my power to surface."

"It's done now. Did you learn anything useful?" he said, sitting in front of her.

"Well, I didn't sense any Athnaralans. So, I suppose there's some benefit to my actions."

"You know you're going to get yelled at for this."

Understanding who Gabe was referring to, Eirian clenched her jaw. Seeing the stubborn look on her face, he chuckled.

"You know how he gets about your magic sometimes. He'll consider what you did as a danger to everyone."

"He'd be right. It was. If I had a fraction less control, I fear what I might've done." Sighing, Eirian slumped and said, "Gabe, if I ever look like I'm going to lose control, please knock me out. I promise you there will be no repercussions."

Gabe glanced away, and Eirian saw his hand slip to his knife as he admitted, "We have those orders."

"You were going to do that when I stopped."

"I was the least affected. My self-control is substantial enough that I could approach you with only the thought of knocking you out."

Eyes wide, Eirian looked past him to the group. Kip felt enough like himself to flash her a grin. She understood what he was implying.

"You would've killed them."

"If you hadn't stopped, and if I hadn't made the call to stop you. However, I wonder if I could have turned my blade on you."

There was a darkness in Gabe's eyes that felt familiar to her, the whisper of memory begging at the edge of her mind.

"You think you couldn't because you like how I make you feel. If you hurt me, it stops, and you'd regret my death," she said.

Gabe pursed his lips. "I'd miss you."

Exhaustion was beckoning, and Eirian knew she needed to move. "I need to return to my chamber, and I need food. This was enough to exhaust me."

"I see the tiredness in your eyes. Can you stand on your own?"

Eirian coaxed her arms and legs to move, each limb protesting the actions. Struggling to stand, she envied the way he got to his feet. Gabe chuckled and threw her arm across his shoulders. He slipped his own around her, lifting her to her feet. Feeling her lean heavily against him, he looked at his squad.

"You'd be useless on a battlefield doing things like this."

"Using my magic in a fight with blades doesn't drain me. I poured my magic into the earth and touched every living thing within a greater distance than I've ever done before. My power is raging and ready to go. The exhaustion is physical only."

Layne was quick to slip in on her other side, his arm joining Gabe's across her back, and he asked, "You mean everyone felt what we did?"

"I'm sorry," Eirian replied. "When I say every living thing, I mean it. Animals, birds, insects, moss growing on rocks, the worms."

Her guards stared, and Gabe growled, "Move your asses. We need to get her to her chamber before the captain comes."

Reminded of Aiden, the men were quick to head down the stairs. It forced Layne to let go and trudge behind. Eirian was thankful for Gabe's support. Her head grew foggier as tiredness threatened to overwhelm her. Despite the urge to shut her eyes and sleep, she focused on keeping her feet moving and not stumbling. It startled soldiers patrolling through the keep, and her guards quickly explained it.

"Gabe?" Eirian muttered.

"Yes, My Queen?"

"If I promoted you to captain, who would Aiden kill first?"

His gaze flickered to hers in amusement, and he said, "Presuming you gave me a choice, I'd turn you down, and he wouldn't kill either of us."

"He keeps pushing my limits. I don't know how much more I can tolerate him."

Reaching her chamber, Kane knocked on the door before pushing it open and checking the room. "No one is here. Should we fetch her lady and the duchess?"

Staring at her bed, Eirian said, "Help me get my boots and belt off. I don't think I can wait much longer before I pass out."

Holding her up while Kip quickly unlaced her boots, Gabe shifted slightly so Wade could undo her belt and carry the weapons to the rack in the corner.

"The captain takes his job seriously. You're the focus of his life," Gabe said.

"He confuses me," she admitted as he helped her to the bed. "Some days I want to kill him and others..."

Shooing the other guards out, Gabe remained beside the bed until he was sure Eirian was asleep. Sighing, he unfolded the blanket and covered her with it.

"You confuse him as well, but it's not your fault or his."

Moving silently back out of the room, Gabe shut the door and turned to the rest of his troop. They shared looks, each man nodding in silent agreement before he opened his mouth to remind them not to speak of what they had witnessed on the rooftop. Leaning against the door, Gabe crossed his arms. He waited for the inevitable flurry of fury that was on the way.

"What about the captain?" Wade asked softly.

"He doesn't go in there, not until she wakes. No one goes in."

Kip agreed, "Merle is on duty next. He'll respect it. You know they're going to demand to know what we saw."

"We tell them the Queen did magic, and we're not mages."

"What about those locals?" Layne asked, and his hand slipped to the knife in the small of his back.

Gabe scowled. "I know. They're two frightened men. Everyone felt the Queen use her powers, but we don't speak of how exhausted it left her."

"It's a weakness, that's for sure."

Wade said, "We keep her safe."

"We keep her safe," Gabe confirmed.

Looking puzzled, Kane asked, "It's why she's always eating, isn't it? Why you give her fruit all the time."

"It is. I'll get some after the captain has been," Gabe chuckled.

Three

Angry voices competing made the volume in the chamber rise. Rubbing her temple, Eirian watched on in horror. Then, considering the options, she reached into the middle of the table to pick up the reports that had triggered the arguments. Reading each one quietly, she frequently glanced at the map. Most of the people arguing ignored her, and she was thankful for it.

"This is what we'll do," Eirian said without raising her voice. "Everett will accompany the bulk of our people through the forest road and to the next garrison."

Everett looked at her when he heard her words. His change caused others to stop, and soon all eyes were on Eirian.

"What do you mean I'll accompany the bulk?" he demanded.

"I mean exactly what I said. Celiaen and his companions will go with you. I'll remain here with my guards and the Telmians, where we will use the tools available to us to cover your movements. It'll be easy to follow once you're clear."

"No!" Marcellus crossed his arms, shaking his head. "I'm sorry, Your Majesty, but no."

Nodding, Cameron supported him, but there was a hesitation in his response. "He's right. We can't leave you here with so little protection."

"Little protection?" Scoffing, Eirian shrugged. "I'm not sure I'd consider myself and the daoine as little protection."

"We felt what you did the other day, and we heard how exhausted it left you. You'd be vulnerable," said one of the general's assistants, glancing at her commander.

Rubbing his chin, the right hand to the general said thoughtfully, "I think the plan has merit, but you haven't told us the catch."

Eirian flinched. "Yes, Daniel, there is a catch. I'd need to convince the daoine to help. My thought is to survey the forest to ensure there are no ambushes. Then make repeated sweeps at intervals. Prince Celiaen can interpret my warnings."

"While what you're suggesting you do with your magic is wonderful, we cannot risk you like that." Everett crossed his arms and looked around the chamber, taking in the looks of agreement.

Marcellus made a counter suggestion. "I was with you in the forest the other day. Can't you check for ambushes along the way? You don't need to do it from here."

"Unless you planned on doing something to any Athnaralans you found?" Cameron voiced his suspicions.

"It crossed my mind."

Her admission sent them into an uproar, voices shouting as they argued their thoughts on using her powers. Closing her eyes, Eirian sighed and waited for them to stop. Her magic warned of Celiaen's approach, and she wondered if he would agree with her plan. She heard a door hitting stone through the shouting, and his magic surrounded them.

"What do you think you're doing?" His voice silenced them, and the Endarans stared in shock. "By the powers, I thought you were a bunch of squabbling hens."

"Your Highness, this doesn't involve you." A nobleman attempted to dismiss him.

Celiaen stood inside the door, his arms crossed as he looked at them. "We have a treaty. Anything that might cause a war between Athnaral and Endara involves me."

Staring, Eirian wondered how long it had taken him to perfect the voice he was using on her nobles and said, "The Prince is right; this involves him."

"Does he know of your plan?" Everett asked.

"What plan?" Celiaen growled, and Eirian felt his suspicion over the bond.

Taking advantage of a potential ally, Marcellus explained, "She wants us to go through the forest and leave her behind with the Telmians and some guards."

"No." Celiaen dismissed the idea without a second thought.

"That's what I said."

"The risk of you losing control is too high, Ree." Meeting her gaze, Celiaen said, "You'd put yourself and the people you were trying to protect in danger. I felt how close you came."

"I considered it and was hoping the daoine could help prevent it," Eirian replied.

"You can't risk it. It's that simple. Think about what you're asking."

Her thoughts went to the secret they kept between them. Eirian knew he was telling her it would risk revealing her heritage.

"What do you suggest?"

"We've been investigating the trees, and we can all use them. If we spread ourselves along the line, we can check each time we pass one of those trees. We'd have enough warning, and you'd be safe among your people."

Celiaen turned away from Eirian to look at her traveling council. There were a variety of expressions on their faces. Behind him, Tara snorted, sharing a look with Tynan and Alyse.

"Are you sure you can use them?" Eirian asked.

"Some of us easier than others. There are also such things as scouts. This is a well-traveled road we're talking about. It's not some random trail in a backwood."

Weighing in, the garrison commander added, "We keep the underbrush cleared as a firebreak. So there isn't much cover for anyone to lie in wait."

Cameron nodded, pleased with the alternative plan. "Magic or not, we go that road. We decided that crossing at the ford and going inland wasn't worth the extra time it would take to double back."

"Yes, but when we made that choice, there weren't large numbers of Athnaralans mustering on the border," Gallagher grumbled.

"Actually, there was," an aide said. "You had the reports."

Fed up, Eirian banged the table and stood. "Fine, we do it Celiaen's way! I want everyone ready to go tomorrow."

"Yes, Your Majesty," Cameron said, bowing his head.

Eirian approached Celiaen. "I want you to show me you can use the trees, so we're going for a ride."

With a glance over his shoulder at his companions, Celiaen replied, "We can do that."

Huffing, Eirian brushed past him and nodded at Tynan and Tara as they stepped out of her way. Outside the room, her guards were waiting, chatting among themselves, while Aiden watched them seriously. Catching sight of him, she paused, her heart sinking at the reality that he would accompany her to the forest. Deciding to ignore him, she continued on her way.

Keeping her head down, Eirian did not respond to Aiden's demands to know what was going on, leaving it to Celiaen to deal with him. When she reached the stables, the men quickly saddled Halcyon and the mounts for her guards. While they waited, the elves split from the group, going off to sort out their horses.

"Are you going to continue to ignore me?" Aiden growled.

Taking the reins from the soldier who had saddled her horse, Aiden held tight. Looking at him over Halcyon's back, Eirian's eyes narrowed. After the incident on the rooftop, he had been driving her crazy with his overbearing attitude. It seemed like he was taking any chance he got to berate her for her slip.

"Are you going to continue to be a pig-headed ass?"

There were coughs as her other guards pretended not to hear what Eirian had called their captain. Eyes narrowing, Aiden shot them a look that promised they would suffer if they repeated her words. Huffing, she snatched the reins from his hand and tossed them over Halcyon's neck before hauling herself into the saddle.

Checking her weapons, Eirian shook her head and nudged the horse into a trot, heading to the gate. They had camped most nobles and soldiers outside the town because the garrison was not big enough to house everyone. Celiaen was waiting with his companions, a hand shading his eyes as he watched the sky. Finally, she spotted Tharen, and he smiled when she acknowledged him.

"You were fast," Eirian said.

Turning to the forest, Celiaen replied, "Let's say I had an idea you'd want us to prove it."

"You had your horses ready and waiting?"

Tharen approached, leaning forward in his saddle as he asked, "You're going to look at the trees?"

"We are. Celi said they can use them." Cocking her head, she studied Tharen. "Are you coming?"

"Anyone with magic can use them. Of course, not to the same extent as you, but then, you are rather unique," Tharen replied.

Something in his voice made Eirian and Celiaen exchange worried looks.

"Was I right? The wards depend on power and not the inclination?" Curious, Tynan brought his horse up on the other side of Tharen.

Looking at him, Tharen nodded. "Indeed. Anyone with magic, but what they can use them for depends on how much power they have."

They fell silent when Eirian nudged her horse into a canter. It was a brief ride, the map in her mind guiding her to the nearest ward. She sensed the network, like the shadows ever-present in the corner of her vision. Knowing it was because of her connection with the tower, Eirian wondered how easy it would be to reach out and link without touching a tree. Her magic wanted to connect, and she felt giddy at the prospect. They dismounted at the edge of the forest, and she pointed at the tree.

"How did you know it was there?" Celiaen asked, glancing between Eirian and the tree. "We didn't find that one when we went looking."

"How, indeed?" Tharen sounded perplexed.

Running a hand over her head, Eirian explained, "I can feel them, like a map of the forest in my mind. One day, when we're at peace, you and I can come back here and experiment with the system. Preferably with a team of yellows assisting… and Tessa, this would be the perfect project for her."

Approaching the tree, Eirian ran a hand over the trunk and avoided touching the ward. It sang wordless promises of what it could do with a taste of her power. Standing on the other side, Celiaen watched her with a hand on the hilt of a sword. Her guards remained at the edge of the trees with the horses, keeping distance between them and the magic. Aiden joined the mages, finding a spot to watch from. He had no intention of letting Eirian out of his sight.

Stepping back, she nodded to Tynan, signaling that he should show her what he could do. He crouched by the ward, placing a hand against it, and his power was like the cold wash of a stream. It amazed Eirian to sense how far Tynan's reach extended, but she also felt how much it cost him.

"That was amazing!" She knew she sounded breathless and looked at Tharen. "Did you know I could sense them using it?"

He frowned. "No, I didn't. Are you sure it's not because you have shared power with him?"

Curious, Eirian called another of Celiaen's companions, "Lydia."

Lydia knelt where Tynan had been and ran her hands over the ward before looking up at her prince. Celiaen nodded, and Eirian felt the same cold wash of magic. Looking at her hand, Eirian studied the green band. She had expected it to feel different depending on the order each belonged to, but it did not. Eirian worked her way through each waiting mage until Celiaen was the last one left. Then, locking eyes with him, she grinned.

"Well, what are you waiting for? On your knees."

His lips curled into a smirk, and Celiaen glanced at Aiden. He was leaning against a tree, glaring at them with a hand on the hilt of his sword.

"You know I'm always willing to get on my knees for you, Ree. You just have to ask nicely," Celiaen said, taking a step closer to her.

Eirian stared in amusement. "Keep dreaming, Celi. That's the only place you'll hear me ask."

"Oh, dear heart, in my dreams, you beg."

Making a show of kneeling at the base of the tree, Celiaen watched Eirian's face as he placed his hands on the ward. He had watched her as the others used their magic, noting how she reacted to whatever it was she felt. It left him uneasy that she was so affected when the rest of them sensed nothing. Even Tharen was watching her in concern.

Taking a deep breath, Celiaen let his magic flood into the ward and kept his eyes locked on hers. He knew the moment Eirian felt it, her eyes wide and her power flaring furiously. It pulled at their bond, and he thought she would reach for him. He hoped she would.

"Stop!" Tharen shouted, and he grabbed Eirian's arm to turn her toward him. "Focus, Eirian, focus."

Pulling his hand from the tree, Celiaen cursed. "It won't work. Ree's too affected by whatever connects her to the trees."

Shaking her head, Eirian kept breathing deeply, staring at Celiaen hungrily.

She wanted to feel the rush of his power through the network again.

"I'm sorry! I didn't know that would happen," she told them.

"Why did she react to the Prince like that and not to everyone else?" Aiden asked.

Exchanging looks, those who knew of their bond waited for a suggestion.

Celiaen responded, "My guess is because Ree and I have shared our magic a lot."

"I agree. The next question is if Eirian can use the network without affecting the rest of you. If she can, then it's only Celiaen. If she can't..." Tharen looked at Eirian.

"Then neither of us can use it. But what about you and your people?" Eirian stared at him before flickering her gaze to the tree and asking, "Dare we risk it?"

Rubbing his arms, Tharen pursed his lips. "Before we do anything else, I want you to do it. Don't reach out to the entire network. Just focus on that tree."

Eirian carefully reached out and touched the ward. The link pulled, and she struggled not to let go, forcing herself to focus on the closest handful of trees. It took more effort than she expected, and feeling a sliver of fear, she yanked her hand away from the trunk and shivered. Looking at her in concern, Celiaen wanted to suggest that she stay away from the wards, but Tharen beat him to it.

"That took far more effort than it should have. I don't know what's going on, but I don't think you should use it. Going from the lack of reactions in the others, it's your closeness to the Prince that's an issue."

Scratching the stubble on his chin, Celiaen agreed, "I felt nothing I didn't feel with everyone else. So why are you affected when the rest of us aren't?"

Mulling over it, Eirian hugged her arms around herself and stared at the tree. Going over what happened on the rooftop, she remembered the cut to her hand.

"Blood."

"What?"

"No..." Realizing what she referred to, Tharen frowned. "Surely not? I would have to discuss this with the others to see what they think."

Confused, Celiaen asked, "Would one of you explain?"

"I cut my hand on the rooftop. Tharen said I'd given my blood, and it would know my magic. I assumed he meant it would be easier for me to use the wards," Eirian told them, holding out the hand she had cut.

"Altira blood? Was this network of guardian trees made by her ancestors?" Tynan said, "I think I can help."

"Really? How?" Aiden scoffed.

"I can help Ree focus."

"No!" Celiaen was quick to protest. "It's too risky. What if Ree overwhelms you? I think both of us should avoid touching the trees. She can do it her normal way."

"You don't understand, Celi. Even standing here, I can feel the network without touching it. I think it's because of my ability to feel the land, to connect to it. Perhaps someone with Altira blood helped create it, and the old magic recognized that part of me." Groaning, Eirian wanted to hit something in frustration.

Still baffled, Tharen looked between them. "What if you did it together?"

"That's a terrible idea!" Tara shook her head. "I've seen what happens when they lose control together, and it isn't pretty. We've cleaned up after them."

Throwing her hands in the air, Eirian stepped away from the tree, grumbling, "Celi and I will be useless tomorrow."

"It won't kill you," Aiden muttered. "You can let us do our jobs for a change."

Tara laughed. "You don't know your queen very well, do you, Captain? She's worse than he is."

The other red mages among Celiaen's companions looked at each other with grins before agreeing with their commander.

Celiaen shrugged and said, "I'm happy not to use these trees. There's too much at stake to risk Ree losing control."

"Do you think I should shield my magic until we are away from the forest?" she asked seriously.

"No, you can use it as an opportunity to practice control. I'll stay with you and step in if it gets too much." Tharen frowned at the tree. "This is most peculiar."

Meeting Celiaen's worried stare, Eirian wondered if the same question was on his mind. It occurred to her that her duine blood was why her magic reacted the way it had to the link with the guardian trees. Wishing Tharen had not introduced her to the tower, she sighed and turned to look at their horses.

Eirian told them, "We may as well head back. Everyone needs an early night. It's going to be a long day tomorrow."

No one protested, and they returned to the horses. While the others mounted, Eirian lingered a moment under the trees. Celiaen stood beside her, observing the agitation in her movements.

"I'm worried about your magic, Ree," he murmured, leaning closer.

Turning to him, Eirian met his gaze. "So am I."

"Do you think?"

Eyes flickering to Tharen, Celiaen knew she understood.

"That's my worry. Promise me you'll tell me if you feel anything is changing with your powers because of the bond," she whispered.

Celiaen smiled and cupped her face. He rubbed her cheek with his thumb, the feeling of his skin against hers stirring their bond more than usual. Eirian turned her head slightly, her lips brushing over his palm.

"Ree," Celiaen breathed her name.

Knowing the rest of the group was waiting, and her control was weak,

Eirian stepped back. He saw her hesitation, grabbing her hand to make her turn around.

"We had better not keep this lot waiting. Everyone has much to do."

"Eirian." Celiaen said, "Please be careful."

"I will be."

"We're waiting for you," Aiden called.

Letting go, Celiaen walked with Eirian to the horses. They rode back to the town slowly, taking the time to discuss how the mages would spread themselves through the convoy. Looking at the white clouds scattered across the sky, she hoped their concerns would come to nothing. She did not think the Athnaralans would risk it. The terrain was not in their favor, and it would be too difficult to get in and out again. Ahead of them, the sprawling camp surrounding the town was a hive of activity as they prepared to leave the following day.

Standing alone a short distance from the camp, Faolan watched them approach, and Tharen said, "He wants to talk to you."

"I don't think I'll ever get used to you lot being able to communicate without speaking." She shuddered, turning Halcyon toward Faolan. "The rest of you can wait here or go on your merry way."

Nudging the gelding into a trot, Eirian crossed the small distance to meet Faolan. Hearing others follow, she growled in frustration and glanced over her shoulder to confirm her suspicions. She had known Tharen would accompany her to speak to Faolan, but Aiden and Celiaen were close behind. Faolan glanced at the additions and rolled his eyes in amusement as she dismounted.

"How bad is it?" he asked Tharen.

Running a hand through his hair, Tharen replied, "I don't know what to think."

"I presume you speak of my connection to the trees?" Leaning against Halcyon, Eirian scratched his neck and smiled at his twitching ears.

Faolan stared at her thoughtfully, a hand on his chin. "I can't give you an answer. You're a mystery, Eirian Altira, and I fear what it means."

Her lips twitched, and sharing a look with Celiaen, Eirian ignored Aiden's presence. "You don't think it's because of my bond with Celi? You said his bloodline is as important."

"It's possible. You're descended from the first magical children of the gods. His Majesty would know better than I. There's only one I've ever seen who could pull the magic of those around and disperse it into the ground." There was a flicker of grief in Faolan's eyes, and he turned to Tharen. "Do you remember?"

"I do. It's not possible, though," Tharen replied. "My only suggestion is they intended this, and she hasn't been able to explore the true extent of what she can do or learn to control it."

Celiaen scoffed, "We spend years working on our control in Riane."

"Yes, Riane, where they teach that your magic should follow rigid rules.

Tell me, little Queen, did you struggle with their restrictions?" Faolan questioned, cocking his head to the side.

Reluctant, Eirian gave Celiaen an apologetic look. "I'm sorry, Celi, you know it's the truth. I struggled a lot."

"You struggled in the beginning because you hated having magic!" he argued. "You didn't want to be there."

Her brown eyes were sad, and Eirian shook her head. "It was more than that. I kept most of what I could do a secret from the masters. I don't think I realized until recently what the issue was."

"Your magic was telling you that their restrictions were unnatural. Perhaps that's why you took so well to the blade. It presented the least restriction and encouraged a more natural flow of magic." Faolan looked at the camp as he said, "We should've realized. If we can't help her relearn her magic, it could cripple her in the fight against the darkness."

"Relearn my magic? Surely it wouldn't be that hard." Eirian pushed away from Halcyon and took a step toward Faolan as he turned to her.

"Harder than you think. First, we'd need to teach you to forget their teachings. This must be why our king insisted you come with us, Tharen."

Aiden was unamused and asked, "When exactly do you propose to teach her? We're traveling Endara and preparing for war. She's hardly drowning in free time."

"That's just it. I am." Eirian's eyes went wide when the thought struck. "I don't have to forget what I know. It's not either-or. I can work magic instinctively. Correct me if I'm wrong, but you want me to do what my magic is telling me to do."

"In a way," Tharen answered, slightly dubious. "It's not that simple."

"But it is. You keep saying the teachings of Riane restrict magic instead of allowing it to be. Do you want to see what happens if I let my magic be?"

"Eirian!" Celiaen protested, worried that she might reveal something more.

Intrigued, Faolan said, "Show us."

The four men stared as she let go of Halcyon's rein and walked away, stopping when she was clear. Eirian tilted her head back and let go of her magic. She felt the beat of life as the power rolled out like a lazy fog. There was no need to direct it into the plant life it touched, and Eirian heard the distant shouts of surprise as everything grew. It was as natural as breathing to her.

In the corner of her perception, Eirian felt the trees absorbing the magic that entered the forest. Eyes seeking the sun, she drank in the warmth and fed it into her power. Each breath she took became part of the air, and she sensed the life drawing on it. The feelings were ones she could get lost in, another reason she never let go completely. It did not take long for the whispers to begin, the desire to turn it all to ash.

"This isn't news to us. We're aware you can make things grow," Tharen muttered.

A loud, piercing cry sounded from the sky, and they looked up at the huge eagle hurtling toward them. Saoirse landed in front of Eirian, transforming back to her duine form.

"How are you able to do that?" she demanded.

"What do you mean?" Confused, Faolan started toward the two women.

Smiling at the naked lady in front of her, Eirian asked, "How far away were you?"

"The river and making my way back. I felt you in the air. How? You're not pulling magic from your mate."

She glanced at Celiaen, who stared back blankly. It was more than the growth that Saoirse felt. Eirian's magic had filled her, replenishing her energy. They had all noticed her ability to do it to those close, but she had been nowhere near Eirian when it happened.

"She made things grow that far away?" Mouth open, Tharen was wide-eyed with shock.

"I told you, I know how to go with the flow of my power. I keep it restrained constantly because things keep growing if I don't. Do you have any idea how annoying it is to have flowers following you everywhere? When I fight, I let go because the magic is happy to kill."

Her magic was still unrestrained, and Eirian watched the horses reaching for the thick green grass conveniently growing toward their mouths.

Rubbing his face, Tharen sighed. "While I admire your reach, you're like a one-trick jester."

"One trick?" Eirian's mouth twisted, a dark gleam in her eye as she said, "Would you like me to show you the other side?"

"No, that's enough," he replied quickly, understanding what she was suggesting.

Pulling her power back, Eirian explained, "When I release my control, it likes to make things grow. I hold my power back because of that."

"Besides giving livestock extra grazing, what purpose did your display serve?" Crossing her arms, Saoirse looked at those around her.

"Her Majesty is struggling with control of her magic." Aiden sounded fed up.

Rolling her eyes, Saoirse chuckled before pointing at Celiaen and Eirian. "I can make one suggestion that would help. You two need to complete your bond."

"No!" Eirian protested, shaking her head vehemently. "Absolutely not."

Celiaen's mouth twisted in frustration. "I've said it a few times."

Silent, the three daoine stared at them before exchanging looks.

Faolan was the first to speak. "My sister has a point. Your bond being incomplete is a distraction. It wants to be complete."

"It might explain why you reacted so much more to Celiaen using the tree. That you haven't completed it after so many years is amazing." Glancing sideways at Aiden, Tharen chuckled, "What's the matter, Captain? You're not keen on your precious queen bedding someone else?"

Aiden growled, "This is inappropriate."

"Until Ree's willing to complete it, we'll have to work around the bond," Celiaen informed them.

Throwing her hands in the air, Eirian huffed. "Do you all-knowing daoine know of a way to undo the bond?"

"No. It's unusual among our kind because we can't undo it. I don't know why you won't just fuck him," Saoirse answered scornfully.

"Sister," Faolan murmured.

Saoirse rolled her eyes and stepped back, shifting into her bird form.

"Thank you for your help," Eirian muttered as the bird took off, and she moved toward Halcyon.

Rolling his shoulders, Faolan followed and said, "Saoirse speaks the truth, and it's your choice not to heed it. You need to complete the bond before it forces you."

Turning, Eirian startled Faolan by pushing him back. Magic surrounded her, fury rippling through it.

"I will not be told who I should bed because of some stupid mistake I made when I was too young to grasp the consequences! I'll regret this bond until the day I die."

Celiaen stared at her in shock, and beside him, Aiden gave him a sympathetic look. He did not know what they were talking about, but the devastation on Celiaen's face told him plenty.

"Thank you, Your Majesty. You've made my position in your life undeniably clear," Celiaen said.

Realizing the implications of her words, Eirian turned to him. "Celi, I didn't mean—"

"No, don't bother."

"Celi!"

Shaking his head, Celiaen pulled his horse around, saying dismissively, "By the way, explain to the good captain here what exactly we're talking about."

Covering her mouth with both hands, Eirian watched him nudge his horse into a canter away from the camp. Tharen grimaced, refusing to meet her eyes as she glanced at them.

"Now that you've upset the Prince, you probably should take his advice and tell me what the fuck you've done this time." Leaning forward in his saddle, Aiden stared at her.

Faolan answered, "They bound their magic. It's a link between their life force. So if one died... well, fortunately, they're powerful enough that they should withstand the backlash of the bond breaking."

"It's forbidden in Riane for many reasons." Rubbing her face, Eirian stared in the direction Celiaen had ridden and whispered, "I didn't mean to hurt him."

"And yet, you keep on hurting him. One day, he may decide waiting for you isn't worth it. Or is that what you want? For him to turn his back on you so you can live in denial?" Tharen said, "You say you don't love him, yet how were you able to forge the bond in the first place? There's a reason it's a magical marriage."

"I love him, but not like that," she lied.

Putting a hand on her shoulder, Faolan shook his head. "If I were you, I'd reconsider because what you describe is not enough."

Aiden was staring at her, and Eirian saw the anger in his eyes. But there was more than anger, and her heart clenched at the betrayal in his gaze.

"How could you think this isn't a serious issue we should know about? I don't care what they say about your ability to survive if he died. We should have known there is always a possibility!"

"Aiden," Eirian sighed. "You don't understand how forbidden it is. If Riane knew—"

"Fuck Riane! You're the queen of Endara! What stupid girl risks her life by doing something so fucking idiotic? Maybe you should've turned down the throne and gone with that blasted archmage back to Riane." His voice was bitter, and Aiden pointed at her. "You need to tell the dukes. They should bloody know that if someone kills the elf, you'll die."

Astounded, Eirian opened her mouth to speak, but no words came out. She felt cold as she replayed Aiden's words in her head, forced to acknowledge that he had a valid point. The bond with Celiaen had never crossed her mind when accepting the throne. Groaning, she bowed her head and covered her face. His hand still on her shoulder, Faolan offered her some reassurance and squeezed it.

"You can only go forward and make the best of the consequences. We still need to work on your control."

Her eyes narrowed, and Eirian said, "You know what? My control is fine! It was fine before you came along and interfered. It will continue to be fine. If it wasn't, I'd have killed you by now. This hiccup with the trees is because it's new, and if I had the time to become accustomed to it, there'd be no issue."

"I disagree," Tharen replied.

"I don't fucking care if you disagree!" Yanking her shoulder from Faolan's grasp, Eirian lifted her foot into the stirrup and pulled herself onto Halcyon's back. "We're done."

"I think you should listen to them," Aiden said, and moved his horse to block her way.

Magic surrounded Eirian like a dark presence, and Halcyon shied slightly, his rider barely flinching with his movement. "Don't you dare."

"I'll always dare, darling. That's my fucking job."

Aiden ignored the magic surrounding them and stared at her with a challenging look. The two daoine watched in concern as Eirian drew herself further upright.

Eirian growled, "Captain, I'm ordering you to get out of my way."

"No, Eirian, you need to shut up and listen. Don't you think you've endangered yourself enough? If they can help you, then let them before you do any more damage."

"I haven't done any damage."

Arching a brow, Aiden disagreed, "You've done a lot of damage, but you don't want to see it. Do you think Everett will trust you when he finds out about the bond? What about the damage you did to your relationship with the Prince?"

"That is none of your business!"

"How many times do you think he's going to let you stomp all over his feelings? I wouldn't put up with it. No one is worth that sort of treatment. He should turn his back on you and tell his father to leave Endara to Athnaral out of spite. I sure as fuck wouldn't blame him."

"Prince Celiaen wouldn't do that to spite me. He cares about the people," Eirian replied.

"If either of you gave a shit about your people, you wouldn't be in this situation. You're both intended to rule a kingdom, and of all the stupid, impulsive things you could have done! I expected better of you, but now it's clear I was wrong!"

Feeling her magic deflate, Faolan told Aiden, "You've made your point."

"Have I?" Aiden asked coldly.

Remembering the daoine, Eirian swallowed nervously. "You're right, Aiden. I'm stupid and impulsive. I don't always think about the consequences. However, I can't tell Everett and the others about my bond with Celi. If Riane found out, it could cost us both our heads."

"Excuse me?"

"The laws are the laws; this bond is potentially a death sentence."

Tharen shifted his horse to face her and asked, "Surely they wouldn't execute you? You're powerful mages and leaders among your people. For them to make a move against either of you would be perilous."

Keeping her eyes on Aiden, Eirian watched the warring thoughts cross his face. "Is it worth the risk?"

"You say the bond is incomplete. If something were to happen to one of them with it like it is now, are they more at risk?" Aiden questioned, weighing his options.

Shrugging, Faolan looked to the sky. "It's hard to say. I don't know anyone who has started the bond and not finished it. If it's forbidden in Riane, how did you end up bonded?"

"By blood and blade, the power took over. That's all we recall. It wasn't intentional. We'd have completed it, we were so lost in the magic and the lust, but Gal stopped us. The next day he made Celi return to Ensaycal, and we didn't see each other for two years."

"Galameyvin stopped it?" Tharen frowned.

"Yes. By the time Celi returned, I'd learned to banish the urges from the bond. So, my ability to control my magic is fine. So long as I have the time to master it," Eirian told them.

Thinking about the bond reminded her of the look on Celiaen's face, and Eirian brushed her mind against the link between them, hoping he could feel how sorry she was. It was no surprise when he did not respond.

"I'm not entirely sure what to make of it. I've never heard of magic forging a bond of its own accord," Faolan said.

Tharen agreed, "Neither have I. But, unfortunately, we don't have a few years for you to master changes to your magic."

"Fine," Eirian replied crankily. "I'll do my best to learn what you can teach me."

FOUR

Sitting on a pile of rocks, Eirian gazed out over the green hills. She had never seen a landscape like it and could not get over the way it seemed to roll on forever. There was a violence to it that made her think the gods had reached into the ground and ripped out the rocky spine of the land. Dotted about were small clusters of trees and the white spots of sheep grazing. Out of sight, the forest they had crossed through seemed like a gateway to another place. Eirian was glad they had left it behind.

Merle perched on a rock, watching her in boredom. "How long do you want to sit there?"

"For as long as I can. How can you not appreciate this view?"

Stretching his arms, he shrugged. "I suppose because I was born here."

Chuckling, Fox held up a little woven flower he had crafted out of grass seed stalks. It received jokes from the other men.

"Further north, and we'll be on my turf. If you want amazing, wait until you see the Fingers."

Letting her gaze sweep over the hills, Eirian smiled and said, "Let me have my peace, Merle, because it may be some time before I can admire this beauty again."

"If I could, I'd take you to see this one spot. It's a lovely waterfall set into a valley," Merle told her.

"A waterfall?" John asked.

A smile tugged at Merle's lips, and he stared into the distance, remembering the carefree days of his youth. "Yes, a waterfall. We'd sneak off during the summer before dawn to avoid work and come back at dusk."

The men chuckled.

Devin wriggled his fingers at him. "Bet you swam with some lovely girls from neighboring farms."

"Well, there was one lass."

Watching the guards laugh and joke, Eirian relaxed and pulled her legs up, wrapping her arms around them so she could rest her chin on her knees. She wanted to stare at the landscape all day and memorize every bit. Bird calls caught her attention, and she watched the brightly colored flock of lorikeets wing their way from one cluster of trees to the next. They circled in the air a few times before they settled into the trees, and she heard them chattering away.

Eirian let go of her legs and leaned back with her face turned to the sun. She desperately needed these moments. They allowed her to energize herself when the stress of being on the verge of war became too much. Sometimes, they made up for the frequently terrible nights of sleep plagued by nightmares. However, they did not make up for the pangs of loneliness and regret every time Celiaen refused to speak to her.

"You look more at ease than you have for a while," Tobin said.

Fox laughed, "It helps that she's not at the boss man's throat constantly. Whatever fixed that, we're grateful. He's been in a slightly better mood."

Grunting, Eirian chose not to acknowledge his comment about Aiden. "Merle, are we going to be anywhere near this waterfall of yours?"

"Maybe. Why?" He sounded wary.

Turning to look at him, Eirian smiled slowly. "It sounds lovely. I'd like to see it, perhaps tomorrow or the day after?"

Exchanging looks with Fox, Merle replied, "We can run it past the boss man. Are you sure you can spare the time?"

"I'm touring my kingdom. Making time to see local spots is exactly what I'm supposed to be doing. Unfortunately, I won't be able to make time once we're back on the flats."

"Not with the reports of Athnaral troops mustering near the border," Fox muttered, flicking his next grass creation at one of his companions.

She agreed, "Precisely. Let's take the chance to enjoy ourselves before things get worse."

John rolled his eyes at Fox and flicked the little grass ball back. "I miss Amath. All this open countryside gives me the creeps."

"I bet you give it the creeps right back, John!" Howling with laughter, Sid hopped off his rock and slapped Devin on the shoulder. "What do you say? Should we push the city boy down the hill?"

Devin held up his hands and snorted. "Don't involve me in this! I might not be a city boy, but I was born in the south. It's flatter land there."

"What is Riane like?" Fox asked curiously. "I've never been that far south."

Letting her gaze sweep over the land again, Eirian sighed. "Spectacular. They built the city right on the cliffs overlooking the Yifthn Sea. It's flat and sparse for miles before the land becomes farmable. They say the original builders didn't want to take land away from farmers. The mage towers are taller than the main keep in Amath, great glistening white towers that dominate everything around them."

Tobin looked unimpressed. "Why would you build on a cliff? Wouldn't it be at risk of eventual collapse?"

"Mages built it, and they worked wards deep into the cliff to prevent collapse. They built a wall along the cliff line with wards to stop people from going over the edge. I imagine if you threw yourself off, you'd think you were flying before you died on the rocks below."

Closing her eyes, Eirian pictured the cliffs and sea in her mind as though she were there. Then, for a moment, the smell of it came to her.

"You can hear the constant roar of waves crashing into the cliffs, and there is always a breeze that carries salt from the water. I've seen nothing that comes close to the color of the sea. It's so vibrant. When you go further along the cliff, you realize how small you are."

The six men stared at her.

Merle cleared his throat. "I always thought that of here. You can stand on one of these hills, look out at the rolling sameness and realize how easily you could get swallowed up. It's one reason I joined the army and then the guard. I didn't want to get swallowed up."

"An odd choice," Fox muttered. "I've been up into the Fingers and stood among the peaks looking across a sea of more peaks, and you realize why they call it the Roof of the World."

John laughed, "Well, I've stood in a river of shit, wash water, and watered-down ale, listening to men brawl and wished I were somewhere else in the world. Now I'm somewhere else in the world, and I miss my city."

Even Eirian had to laugh at his comment.

"I love all of it," she informed them.

The sound of horns blaring in the distance made them turn. Reluctantly sliding off her perch, she approached Halcyon. He did his best to grab as much grass as possible before his time ran out. Eirian observed her guards moving quickly from the corner of her eyes, and with a shrug, scratched the horse behind his ear. She did not want her peace to end, her lack of enthusiasm showing in every slow movement.

"Your Majesty." Merle prompted her to move.

"I know."

Double-checking her tack before she hauled herself into the saddle, Eirian rolled her eyes where he could not see it. Merle led the group to the main track that made its way through the hills to the town of Aveley. Like all the towns they had stopped in, local people had welcomed them warmly, and it amazed Eirian how willing they were to share what they had. They treated Merle like a hero, the townsfolk proud to have one of their own guarding their queen.

When they reached Aveley, there was activity everywhere, and Aiden was waiting with a fresh squad of guards. Dismounting while he held Halcyon, Eirian watched the bustle of soldiers and townsfolk.

"What is going on?"

Aiden told her, "Scouts returned with reports the Athnaralans are moving."

Rubbing her face, Eirian sighed, and held up a finger to silence Aiden until she was better prepared to hear what he had to say. "Thank you for the ride, Merle."

"No problem, ma'am. Let me know if we're going to the waterfall," Merle replied, signaling to his men. "We'll see to the horses."

Eirian let Aiden lead her to the central garrison building. It was a hive of activity, soldiers rushing everywhere. A deep breath helped clear her mind in preparation.

"It's not good news, is it?"

"I don't know yet. I was only told there is movement. The Duke of Raellwynt wanted you informed as soon as possible," Aiden replied.

Men saluted as they strode past, concern showing on their faces. Pausing outside the entrance to the building, Eirian gave him a pained look.

"We don't have enough numbers."

"No, we don't."

Squaring her shoulders, Eirian pushed through the door and into the crowded room. People moved out of her way, letting her cross to where Everett stood. Aiden ordered his men to remain outside. Touching her arm, Everett gave her a worried smile before turning her to greet the scout.

"I don't need all the details," she told the man.

Looking thankful, he bowed. "I watched them breaking camp, waited to see what direction they would go. They're making their way toward the pass. My partner went ahead to Kelsby to inform them."

"How many?"

"Your Majesty—" Cameron went to distract her, but Eirian held a hand in his direction while pointing at the scout.

"How many?" she asked again, her tone hard.

"At least a legion."

Glancing at Cameron, the scout gave him an apologetic look, and the general shook his head in response. The silent communication reassured the young man that he understood it was impossible not to answer Eirian. She took a deep breath and stared into space blankly while processing the numbers.

"We don't have a legion in this region. We're waiting on troops out of Onaorbaen to bolster numbers. If Athnaral has a legion worth of men here, how many have they mustered to the south?" Eirian asked quietly.

"Athnaral outnumbers us three to one. We know that," Marcellus replied.

She waved dismissively. "I'm aware of the basics of population. I'm worried about drawing more of our troops northward if the bulk is south. We need to know if this is all of them up here."

Putting a hand on the scout's shoulder, Cameron said, "Our scouts are doing their best."

"I know, and they are doing a fine job. But, we need more information and quicker."

"How do you propose we do that?" The garrison commander asked.

Frowning, Eirian glanced at the door. "I'm going to ask the Telmians. Lady Saoirse has proven to be a useful set of eyes, and Athnaral is hardly going to pay attention to a bird drifting overhead. It is time we use all the resources available to us."

"They won't make a move in this direction because the terrain is too difficult to engage," Everett commented.

"I know. We keep ourselves holed up here until we know what's going on. Most of the land between us and the Fingers is farmland. The nearest large town is Kelsby, correct? Over a day's ride. We warn them, and then, if Athnaral makes a move over the border, we make ourselves as annoying as we bloody well can."

Seeing where she was going, Cameron said, "We do what we can to slow them down."

"What are our numbers?" Aiden asked.

"We have a full cohort here in Aveley and in Kelsby and a full cohort behind us in Hills Edge. Plus, the cohort traveling with us," Cameron's second-in-command answered. "That's not including all the guards."

Frowning, Eirian glanced over the room. "What about the elves?"

"There's only about thirty of them." Gallagher shrugged, saying, "They won't make a difference against the numbers we face."

"No, not the ones with us. I mean their armies." Tugging her braid, Eirian said, "Right, this is what I'm going to do. I'll beg Lady Saoirse to take a flight and scout out what we're facing. We need to know if they have more than a legion."

Marcellus agreed, "We will work on strategies for dealing with them when they push past the border. Which will happen at Kelsby."

Turning to leave, Eirian paused. "Have there been any more reports of crops dying?"

"A few." Everett gave her a puzzled look. "But no signs of Athnaralan involvement."

"Anything near here?"

Crossing his arms, the local commander told her, "The garrison inland at

Preston has been investigating the livestock theft. The nearest crop deaths are a good two-day ride toward the river."

"Thank you."

Eirian let Aiden open the door so she could leave. Outside the building, she turned to him, and he arched his brows. He could tell the news bothered her.

"I need to find the Telmians. Does anyone know where they are?" Ignoring the look on his face, Eirian turned to the rest of the squad.

Mac answered, "I believe they've camped near the elves."

The door opened again, and Eirian turned to look at Everett as he joined them.

"Eirian, we need to talk."

"What about?" she asked, letting Everett draw her away from the building.

Everett gave her a concerned look before saying, "Everyone knows there's trouble between you and Celiaen. He informed me earlier they're returning to Ensaycal."

Disappointment filled her, and Eirian did her best to hide it. "How soon?"

"Within days. What happened?"

Her eyes flickered to Aiden, watching the anger smoldering in the stare he directed at her. Eirian did not need to ask what he wanted her to tell Everett.

"We had a disagreement."

Shaking his head, Everett muttered in frustration, "Remember what the council ordered. We can't risk the alliance with the elves. You better fix it and try to avoid leveling the town while you do it."

"Don't worry, we'll take it away from here to fight it out." Winking, Eirian reached up and ruffled his hair. "Go back inside. I'll see the daoine and work my charms on the lovely lady."

"I'm more worried she'll work her charms on you."

"Not for lack of trying on her part."

Turning on her heel, Eirian did not see the indignant look Everett directed at her. Matching her stride, Aiden signaled to his men to stay further back. The townspeople watched as she headed to the sprawling camp, the tents taking up much of the free flat land. Smiling at a group of children that ran in front of them, Eirian glanced at Aiden.

"What are you waiting for?"

"I don't know," he admitted. "I'm not sure what else I have to say on the issue. I want to go behind your back and tell Everett, but I respect why you've ordered me not to. It would be a disaster if Riane held the two of you accountable."

"Thank you, Aiden," she said in relief.

"How are you going to fix things with the Prince?"

Falling silent as they walked, Eirian considered her options. Celiaen was avoiding her, and none of his companions would speak to her other than Tara. She had come to her the night before they left Forrestfield to yell about Eirian's treatment of Celiaen.

"You won't like my idea, but I need you to agree to it. I need to fix things with Celi."

Remembering the sight of them in the woods outside Amath, Aiden growled, "No."

"You don't even know what I'm going to do!" Scolding him, Eirian paused when she felt the magic of the daoine.

"I have a fair idea, and it involves leaving your guard. Why don't you try talking to him like a normal person?"

Closing her eyes, Eirian smiled sadly. "I don't want to leave you. Just make it look like I have. You can't deny I've been behaving myself."

Spotting Tharen, Aiden pointed at him and replied, "Go speak to the Telmians. That's what you need to think about right now."

Nodding, Eirian touched a sword hilt for reassurance and made her way to Tharen. He regarded her in silence before leading her into a large tent. Behind her, the guards split up and surrounded the spot. Sprawled out on a pile of furs with Faolan opposite, Saoirse stared at a board covered in small round disks that Eirian had not seen for years.

"What can we do for you, little Queen?"

Faolan did not look up at her as he spoke, his eyes following the move Saoirse made. Watching them curiously, Eirian tried to remember the rules of the game.

"I was hoping to beg a favor of an eagle."

Saoirse paused her move. "You're presumptuous, but what exactly do you want?"

"We need to know how many troops are in position over the border. Our scouts are reporting an entire legion has packed up and moved toward the pass into Endara."

The siblings stared at each other over the board before Faolan nodded.

"Isn't that what scouts are for?" he asked.

"Yes, it is, but they can't get the information we need as easily or quickly as Saoirse. It would be of great use to us, but I understand if you don't want to do it."

Keeping her eyes on the pair, she rubbed her thumb against the rings on her fingers nervously. Saoirse turned to Eirian, her eyes narrowing mischievously.

"But what would be in it for me?"

Arching a brow, Eirian said, "If they outnumber us, we're less likely to engage, and therefore I won't die in battle. Yet."

Tharen stood beside Eirian and chuckled, "She has a point. This isn't a time to trade favors, Saoirse. I'd offer my help in the matter, but my animal form isn't much use for surveying troop movement."

"Wait, you can shapeshift as well?" Eirian questioned, turning to him.

"Tharen is one of the most beautiful among our people." Moving some pieces on the board, Faolan mocked his sister. "Once again, I've defeated you."

Saoirse got to her feet and grumbled, "I'll beat you next time, brother."

"You say that every time!"

"What is your animal form?" Eirian asked Tharen.

"Not relevant to the situation." Tharen smiled, amused by her irritation. "You aren't here for me. Direct your focus to the one you're here for."

Stepping up to Eirian, Saoirse dragged a fingertip over her cheek. She arched her brows, ignoring Faolan watching them.

"You and your prince are still at odds with each other," Saoirse said.

"What does that have to do with what I'm asking?"

"Nothing, but I'm curious. I'll do this scouting for you, but I offer you this in return. Fix things, or when I get back, I won't play nice. You might be off-limits, but Celiaen is not."

"Sister," Faolan growled.

"No, Faolan, it's only fair. I haven't touched him out of respect for this foolish girl."

"Faolan is right," Tharen said.

Turning back to Eirian, Saoirse smiled and stepped in closer, their eyes level as she informed Eirian, "Repair what you broke, or I'll have him."

Maintaining a blank expression, Eirian struggled not to let the pang of jealousy she felt show. Her effort failed, and Saoirse smirked.

"I intend to fix things with Celi. You're more than welcome to try your charms."

"These games are beneath you, Saoirse. You should prepare for your journey instead of trying to anger Eirian."

Tharen sounded bored and turned away from them, moving to a small table with a jug on it. He held it up, and Faolan nodded.

Saoirse cupped Eirian's cheek, murmuring, "You can deny it all you like, but you consider him yours."

Eirian refused to respond to the taunt and asked, "Do you need to see any maps?"

"You said you were looking for a legion. I don't think a blind man could miss over five thousand men." Saoirse huffed, "I'm going to get something to eat."

The two men watched her flounce out of the tent before returning their focus to Eirian. Holding out a cup, Tharen offered her a drink, and she accepted, inhaling the rich scent of the wine it contained. Cocking her head to the side, she peered at him thoughtfully, but did not take a sip.

"How long will it take her to get the information we need?"

Faolan replied, "At least a day, I'd say. She's a swift flyer, but it's a distance to travel, and her energy is not limitless."

Tightening her grip on the cup, Eirian considered drinking the wine. "We're outnumbered."

"Perhaps you are, but you'll do what's needed." Tharen sipped his wine. "I suspect you have some tricks to even the odds."

"Indeed. Where you can give life, you can take it," Faolan said as he approached Eirian to put his hand on the base of her cup. "Drink deeply, Your Majesty. It will help."

"What will it help with?"

He smiled slowly. "It helps with many things. Clarity, courage, a dash of recklessness, and a lowering of inhibitions in the most reserved of people."

Meeting his gaze, Eirian sipped at the wine tentatively, letting the taste fill her mouth. It was not like the wines she was used to, and she closed her eyes, inhaling the smell of it.

"It's Telmian wine, isn't it?"

"We've used our supply sparingly. You're the only one we've shared with."

"I'm most fortunate then. A sip is more than enough for me," Eirian murmured, holding the cup out for Faolan to take.

Faolan regarded her but did not take the cup. "Why is that? It would help you relax."

"That's why I don't drink. I worry I could do harm if I'm too relaxed. It dulls my ability to control myself."

Tharen took the cup and said, "A valid reason. Have you been working on those exercises I gave you?"

"Daily," she answered.

"Your dear captain is feeling increasingly agitated." Looking at the flap of the tent, Faolan added, "He's a very conflicted man, but like you, he puts his duty first and his heart second."

Following his gaze, Eirian sighed. "I know. I sometimes fear it's a mistake to let him remain as the captain of my guard."

"You enjoy being at odds with him. It's obvious how the two of you dance around each other. You attempt to hide attraction behind pointless arguments as though fighting will disguise what you feel," Tharen said with a shake of his head.

Snorting, Faolan drained his cup. "She enjoys fighting with everyone. Perhaps that's why you've only let yourself relax with Galameyvin. He calms your urge to fight and your trust in his abilities to do so makes you direct your feelings toward him."

"Saoirse?" Tharen asked.

"No, that one is mine. Saoirse is a lover, not a fighter. She doesn't always understand what goes through the mind of a warrior."

Rolling her eyes, Eirian turned to leave. "Thank you for your unrequested observations, but I should return to the garrison."

"You have a plan for dealing with your prince, don't you?" Faolan stopped her with a hand on her arm. "I'd happily lend you some wine if it will help matters along."

"I suspect I'll spend the rest of our lives begging Celi for his forgiveness. So yes, I have a plan, but no, I'll not complete the bond."

Baffled, Tharen asked, "Why not? You can only gain from it."

"Because if you're right and we stand a better chance of surviving the death of the other with the bond incomplete, then I owe it to Celi to give him that chance." Eirian added, "You should be the ones who can respect that. After all, you're here to ensure I fight the darkness."

"Do you think he'd appreciate your decision? What if you need the bond to defeat the darkness? Do you know if he'd want to live on in a world where you've died to save everyone?" Chuckling, Faolan let go of her arm and stepped back. "I sound like a romantic fool, but it's the truth."

Shrugging, she replied, "He already knows he'll have to deal with a world without me."

"Give him the chance to make his own decision."

Tharen took Saoirse's spot and started clearing the game board. Looking at the men before leaving, Eirian frowned. Mulling over their words, she did not glance at her guards. Picking her way through, she barely acknowledged the soldiers' calls as she passed, her mind far away. A cool breeze whipped through the camp, the banners fluttering enough to catch her attention.

Halting, Eirian stared at a flag bearing her family crest as it flapped back and forth. Then, instinctively, she turned and faced north, peering into the distance as though she could see the towering peaks of the mountains she knew were far away. Mountains that she hoped to see at least once. Her guards watched her in confusion.

"They want us to spread out."

Aiden frowned. "What?"

"Athnaral wants us to spread out. I mean, why wouldn't you spread out an enemy you outnumber? Spread them, then sweep down the line, watching them tumble like stones on a hill."

"Are you suggesting what I think you are?"

Nodding, Eirian glanced at him. "If I had remained in Amath, we'd have centralized the army and moved to meet his. The elves would have marched to meet us there. But we split our numbers."

"What makes you think that?"

"Why one legion? The scouts could tell if it was more. If you were going to invade, you wouldn't split your numbers up, would you?" Running a hand over her head, Eirian muttered, "I wouldn't. That would defeat the purpose of superior numbers."

Chuckling, Aiden said, "You're a fighter, not a strategist. The general and his people have considered what you are suggesting and have a plan."

"I know. I suppose they smile and nod when I say things because I'm the queen. But, sometimes, I like to think that maybe all the time we spend studying strategy in Riane is useful."

"Yes, but this is their job. It's what they dedicate their time to, all they have trained to do. You're the queen. You have to focus on a lot of things they don't," Lyle said, and Eirian turned to him.

"Thank you for the reminder. Is that your way of telling me I should focus on being the queen and let everyone else do their jobs?"

Aiden started laughing, and his men stared at him, the group halting. He waved at Eirian, knowing it would frustrate her.

"I tell you that, and you don't listen to me, but Lyle makes an observation, and you come to the same conclusion," he said.

"I listen to you, sometimes. However, when someone who rarely makes such comments speaks up, it's a refreshing reminder!" Crossing her arms, she glared at him.

"Perhaps I should get all of my men to tell you these things instead. Then you might pay more attention to me."

Lyle glanced between them nervously and held up his hands. "Hey now, look, I meant nothing by it! Please leave the rest of us out of this."

"What he said." Fisk pointed a thumb at Lyle.

The other four guards agreed. Stepping toward Aiden, Eirian let her arms drop and tilted her head back to meet his stare.

"It's almost as though they expect us to fight."

"Would they be wrong?" he asked.

"No."

Aiden dropped his gaze to where Eirian's hand was creeping toward her knives. She caught the look and stopped moving. The flicker of frustration in her eyes made him chuckle.

"If you want to play, we can go to the training yard. Perhaps today is the day I'll finally knock some sense into you."

"Only if I let you!"

He smirked and said, "Until you stop restraining your magic in fights against me, I'll always be on top."

Fisk rolled his eyes, muttering, "The day he lets her be on top will be the day he gets what he wants."

"I heard that, Fisk," Aiden growled, not taking his eyes off Eirian.

Stepping back, she told him, "I have things to do, and you're distracting me."

"Things like fixing everything with your prince?"

"Yes, like that." She turned to the garrison. "You're infuriating, Captain."

"Not as much as you are, Your Majesty. Yet, no matter how much we lament it, neither of us will change."

Matching her stride, Aiden remained at her side. Sighing, Eirian ran her hand over the hilt of a sword and glanced down thoughtfully. Their weight was a comfort and a constant reminder.

"If my plan doesn't work, he might never forgive me."

"Never is a long time," Aiden replied, giving her a sideways look.

Biting her lip, Eirian admitted, "A lot longer than you know. I'd like to go back into the hills tomorrow."

"You know I can't let you be alone out there."

"But you can give me the illusion of it."

Shrugging, he agreed, "That's true. How's it going to help with your problem?"

Tightening her grip on the hilt of her sword, Eirian said grimly, "Because while I'm out there enjoying the view, you're going to make a delivery for me."

"I'm not sure I like where you're going with this. Delivery of what and to whom?" Eyes narrowing, Aiden glanced around the town.

"I need to make Celi come to me, and I don't think he will if I ask. I mean, he's refusing to see or speak to me. So, first thing in the morning, I'll go out for a ride with Merle and his men, and you'll return a gift to Prince Celiaen for me."

Realizing what Eirian meant, Aiden grabbed her arm and forced her to stop walking. The men of his squad gave them a circle of space.

"You can't mean what I think you do. That would add insult to injury, and only a fool would think it could help you fix things," Aiden said.

Letting her gaze flicker to where his hand gripped her arm, Eirian smiled. "Good thing I'm a fool."

"What if he keeps them and leaves without speaking to you?"

"Then you find me a new sword, and we hope his father sides with the alliance."

Aiden ran his free hand through his hair. "Fuck. I really should say no."

"And yet you won't. Because you don't like Celi, and you're going to take great delight in handing him those swords," Eirian murmured.

His eyes darted to hers, and he said, "I don't know what you're talking about."

Eirian smiled knowingly. "Don't presume I don't know. I pretend not to notice, for both our benefit and for theirs."

"Eirian—"

"Don't mistake my disregard for innocence. I'm not a sheltered and clueless girl. You think you know the extent of the things I've done—"

Tightening his grip on her arm, Aiden said, "Don't mistake my disregard for ignorance. I'm not one of your lords! I don't choose to not hear the things you say to maintain an illusion. I don't miss what is between us, and I've told you before—"

"Oh, wonderful! Mother and Father are fighting again," Merle said cheerily.

The two squads exchanged looks. Letting go of her arm when Eirian stepped back, Aiden did not take his eyes off her.

"Her Majesty would like to go back into the hills tomorrow morning."

Clasping his arms behind his back, Merle maintained a broad smile. Judging from the tense air between Aiden and Eirian, as well as the nervous looks from others in the squad, he knew he had interrupted something that needed to be interrupted.

"We could visit the waterfall."

"First light," Eirian replied. "The captain has duties and won't be coming."

"That's a pity. I think the captain could use just as much a cooling off as you, ma'am," he said in amusement, ignoring the angry look sent his way.

"Take Fionn's squad as well. I don't want Her Majesty leaving this town without two full squads at any point." Aiden smirked at the look on Eirian's face and informed her, "Don't worry, ma'am, you'll have plenty of protection."

Clearing his throat, Fox said, "If we have to be out at dawn, maybe we should find Fionn and let him know."

"That's a great idea. We'll let the stables know as well," Devin added.

"Hey, boss man, it seems like Merle and his gang want to escape the two of you. Can we go to?" Laughing, Fisk winked when she turned to look at him.

Eirian rolled her eyes and turned her back on them. Undoing the binds that secured the two scabbards to her belt, she held the twin blades in her hands. Turning back to Aiden, she shoved them into his grasp. Refusing to look at any of them, Eirian kept her gaze on the hilts as he held them. Stepping back, she took herself out of reach, hoping it would help control her desire to snatch the weapons from him. It felt wrong to hand them over.

She met Aiden's stare and said, "You know what to do."

"Your Majesty?" It dumbfounded Merle to see Eirian surrender her swords. "I don't think any of us understand what is going on."

Aiden said, "Your queen, in her great wisdom, thinks she can lure Prince Celiaen into speaking to her if she sends his gifts back to him."

John snorted. "I've seen ladies do that, and it doesn't end well. Men don't like their love tokens being sent back."

"Speaking from experience?" Gram goaded.

"Well, there was this one time." The men laughed nervously as John attempted to break the tension.

Eirian sighed. "Just do it, Captain. That's an order. I know you prefer to be the one giving them, but I'm still your queen."

"Is there anything in particular you want me to say to him?" Remaining serious, Aiden ignored the uncomfortable banter of his men.

"I don't know. I haven't thought that part through."

Holding back a laugh, Aiden mockingly said, "Why doesn't that surprise me? Honestly, you've thought none of this through. I'll tell the Prince you don't want them anymore because they're a constant reminder of your stupidity."

"Don't you dare, Captain!"

Letting her magic seep into her threat, Eirian itched to grab her weapons back, and she could tell Aiden knew it. He was not the only one, the other guards taking steps back.

Aiden tilted his chin up, taunting. "Always with the daring! One day, you might follow through. See Her Majesty back to her chamber while I secure these."

The guards exchanged looks before Gram replied, "Yes, sir. Your Majesty."

Reluctantly letting the men usher her away, Eirian shot Aiden a look. "Perhaps tomorrow I will dare."

Saluting Eirian with her swords, Aiden gave a smile she recognized. "I look forward to it."

FIVE

Aiden stood in the middle of the camp and stared at the sky. The glittering stars were giving way to the pale light of dawn, and he heard horns calling for the change of watch. He admired the sky and its beauty, a small pleasure he always enjoyed. His hands grasped the twin swords that had brought him to this part of the camp. The prospect of what he was about to do gave Aiden the delight Eirian had said it would. Thinking about her, he smiled coldly and glanced at the beautifully crafted hilts, tightening his grip on the scabbards.

It was impossible to deny that he hoped Celiaen would keep them. He dreamed of giving Eirian new swords, of seeing her wear and wield weapons he had chosen for her. Pushing away from the thought and the possessive urge it brought out, Aiden relaxed his grip slightly. Feeling the familiar brush of magic, he turned to spot Tynan standing a short distance away, watching him. Tynan dropped his gaze to the swords, and a look of horror crossed his face.

"What are you doing with those? Is Ree okay?"

"Her Majesty is fine." Nodding his head at the tent, Aiden tried to sound unhappy as he asked, "Is your prince awake?"

Crossing his arms, Tynan frowned and replied, "He is. You didn't answer my question. What are you doing with her weapons?"

"I'm here on orders from my queen. I have business with Prince Celiaen. Will you please inform him I'm here?"

"Where is she?"

"For the sake of maintaining the pretense of touring the kingdom, she's out riding."

Tynan took a deep breath and sighed. "I see. Without her weapons. I'll let Prince Celiaen know you wish to see him."

"Thank you."

With a smile, Aiden looked at the sky and wondered how far Eirian had gotten. Merle had told him of the place they were going to, and he was sorry to miss it. Realizing he would get nothing more from Aiden, Tynan turned on his heel and strode into the tent. Celiaen was tightening the laces on his boots when he looked up in annoyance.

"What is it?"

"Captain Aiden is outside and would like to speak to you. He said Eirian ordered it."

Feeling the anger flare in Celiaen's magic, Tynan grimaced. He did not look forward to telling him about the swords.

"Tell him to go back to his mistress."

"He has her swords."

"What?" Sitting upright, Celiaen stared at him. "What do you mean, he has her swords?"

Tynan said, "I'm sorry, Celi, it's her captain. He wouldn't tell me more than he needed to. Do you want me to send him in?"

He stared into space while he touched the bond linking him to Eirian. Anxiety rippled across it, a feeling that had become increasingly familiar. There was a thread of hope in response to him reaching out, but Celiaen chose not to respond to it. The anger he had experienced in the days since her words remained, and he would not give her the satisfaction of hope.

"She's okay, anxious, but unharmed. I'd have felt it if something had happened."

"Aiden said she's gone out riding. It's only just first light."

"She sent him and left before he spoke to me. I know what Ree is doing. This is her way of trying to confront me. Bring him in, and I'll hear what she's told him to say."

Nodding, Tynan slipped out to find Aiden where he had left him. He grinned, tucking the swords under his arm as he made his way to Tynan. Celiaen was standing with his hands clasped behind his back by the time they stepped into the tent. Aiden bowed before pulling the two swords from where he had them held. Then, with a hand around both hilts and his other hand cradling the tips of the scabbards, he held them out as an offering.

"Good morning, Prince Celiaen. My queen sends her regards."

Swallowing back his fury at the delight in his voice, Celiaen did not move. He wanted to remove the smug look from Aiden's face, but he knew what would happen if his control slipped. Sensing the other blues of his company outside, Celiaen suspected they had seen Aiden with the swords and were preparing to intervene.

"Odd that she sends them via you. Is it a punishment or a reward?"

"Oh, definitely a reward. My queen knew I'd like it."

The flicker of anger that escaped Celiaen's iron control made Aiden smirk. Knowing he could shake his composure was pure pleasure. There were similarities between Celiaen and Eirian's reactions when he pushed them. Which was something Aiden prided himself on knowing how to do.

"So you've stopped fighting with each other. Ree doesn't like to fight with too many people at once. I think you should thank me for the opportunity to be in her good graces."

Returning the smirk, Celiaen did not move. Instead, they regarded each other impassively, and Tynan cleared his throat nervously. He felt tempted to call Osric and Ianto in for support. Between the three of them, they could stop anything from happening.

Aiden replied, "I'll take what graces she gives me. At least I get to spend my years at her side."

His stare dropped to the swords, and Celiaen asked, "Why do you have her weapons?"

"She sends her regards. These are her regards."

Moving quicker than he expected, Celiaen drew a sword from the scabbard in his hand. He pressed the tip to Aiden's chest, the magic surrounding them a match for the fury that showed on his face. Tynan stepped toward them with his hands out, but he did not press his calming influence. The temptation to call out for the others remained strong.

"If you think I'm clueless as to her intention," Celiaen growled, taking the second sheathed blade with his free hand.

"On the contrary, I expected you to see right through this charade. I'm sure Eirian did as well, but she often exhibits clouded judgment about you, so perhaps not." Aiden ignored the press of the blade to his chest and said, "You're welcome to chase after her as she expects."

"No, not this time."

Chuckling, Aiden batted the blade away dismissively. "Good, perhaps she'll learn something from this."

"You want me to call her bluff?"

Surprised, Celiaen slid the blade back into the scabbard and turned, tossing the pair onto his bed. It gave him a chance to regain his composure. He needed to take a deep breath and clamp down on his magic. Enough of his rage had flickered over the bond to make Eirian aware Aiden had delivered her message.

"Just this time. Otherwise, calling Eirian's bluff is my job."

"You take great delight in that aspect of your job," Tynan commented, stepping away.

Aiden smiled and replied, "One day, she might mean it."

Running a hand through his hair, Celiaen closed his eyes and muttered, "I suppose Ree told you to tell me she's sorry."

"She didn't tell me to say anything because she didn't think this through. My orders were to deliver the swords and nothing else. She's out in the hills waiting for you to chase her. I heard something about a waterfall," Aiden told him.

"Really?"

"Her plan is probably for you to wrestle and yell at each other, maybe roll around on the ground a bit before dusting yourselves off. Eirian wants to pretend she didn't say she wished your bond had never happened."

"She told you. I suppose she had little choice after what I said."

"You didn't tell me you ousted your bond to him!" Tynan stared, wide-eyed with shock.

Nodding, Celiaen confirmed, "I did."

"I'm curious. Who has Eirian been rolling around in the hay with if you've never completed the bond?"

The two elves looked at Aiden, faces blank as he glanced from one to the other with an arched eyebrow. He admired their desire to protect Eirian, but his curiosity demanded an answer.

"Don't bother denying it. She has all but said it outright in front of us. Unlike her cousins and ladies, we don't live in a world of denial."

"Who it was is none of your business," Celiaen said.

Shrugging, Aiden put a hand on his knife. "I didn't fancy gutting a man thinking he was trying to do her harm when he was only sneaking out of her bed."

"Don't worry, you won't be mistakenly gutting him when he is in Telmia." Tynan snorted and shot Celiaen a dark look.

"Ah, so it was the other prince. That explains so much. I bet it burned every time you saw them sneak off together." Chuckling, Aiden did not hide his enjoyment. "Do you think she let him be on top like she lets us?"

Snarling, Celiaen swung a fist at Aiden, but he dodged it and resisted the desire to take a swing back. He was itching for a valid excuse to punch Celiaen, but did not want to be the one who started the fight. Tynan quickly got between them with his calming power, questioning why he had not gone with his instincts and called the others in.

Tynan said, "Celi, he's trying to goad you."

"Damn right I am! You make her weak."

"I do not make Ree weak!" Celiaen did not need to raise his voice, the thundering anger of his magic surrounding them.

Looking at his fingernails, Aiden shrugged. "Yes, you do. You're her weakness, just as she is yours. Do everyone a favor, don't repair your friendship. Follow through with your plans to return to your father and free yourself of what you feel for her."

"Captain," Tynan cautioned.

"She'll hurt for a while, but in the end, she'll be better for it. Or she'll realize she loves you, abandon her throne and run away to find the happy ending you wish you could have."

Celiaen declared, "You will never get what you want from Ree! She would never marry the illegitimate son of her father's friend, the bastard half-brother of her most beloved cousin."

"Oh, she doesn't need to marry me. Of course, Eirian gets to feel me often. There isn't a curve of hers that I'm not familiar with." Aiden smiled, adding, "No one has as much access to her as me, and it's only a matter of time. I'm a very patient man."

Tynan's magic was quicker than Celiaen, and he stood between them, a hand aimed at each man as he glared at Aiden. Neither attempted to push him out of the way, and he breathed a sigh of relief when Aiden took a step back. It baffled him that Aiden did not seem overly affected by Celiaen's rage, but he did not care. All that mattered was that they were not attempting to kill each other.

"Enough! This is the Queen of Endara you're making jealous, crude comments about, not some cheap whore!" Tynan snapped.

"You're right." Celiaen reminded himself that he knew more about Eirian than Aiden did and said, "Thank you, Captain, for returning these weapons to me."

"Are you going to chase her?" Aiden asked.

Running a hand over the hilt of one of his swords with a smile, Celiaen replied, "Don't worry, I'll make sure my sword finds your queen. Our friendship will endure this, as it will endure anything else that crosses in our way. As you said, it's only a matter of time."

"Celiaen!" Tynan scolded.

Giving him a curt bow, Aiden turned to leave, but stopped short of the exit. Gazing at the sliver of pale sunlight visible through the gap, he considered what else he wanted to say. The taste of his magic lingered on Aiden's tongue like a familiar flavor that belonged there. It was one reason Eirian's magic often unsettled him, and he wondered if his reaction to Celiaen was because of the bond.

"I will always do what's required to protect Eirian. Serving her is my only duty, but you can never say the same."

Silence filled the tent as Aiden left the two elves alone. Looking over at his bed, Celiaen narrowed his eyes at the sight of the two swords he had tossed there. Tynan's shuffling movements drew his attention back to his companion, and Celiaen met his worried gaze. Without Aiden present, his rage faded and left a hollowness behind.

"What are you going to do?"

"I don't know. Half of me wants to do what Ree expects, to go charging after her and fight it out. The other half finds it frustrating. Where do I draw the line?"

Tynan looked at the ground. "I can't answer that. Only you know what your limits are."

Groaning, Celiaen walked over to the bed and sat, picking up the blades to rest them in his lap. His hand ran across the scabbards tenderly while he stared at the chest of his belongings. Tucked away safely between layers of clothing were the two rings he had intended to give Eirian for her birthday. Every time he thought about giving them to her, he hesitated, and now he understood why.

"Between this and what Ree said about our bond? I think I'm at my limit. It's always her mistakes but me fighting for forgiveness."

"I suspect you might find she'll come to you. Her people have concerns for the alliance, and they're pressuring her to repair your relationship."

"Maybe the bastard is right, and it would be better for us if we didn't. I love Ree, but I wonder if it is worth all of this."

Chuckling, Tynan gave him an understanding look. Like the others, he had witnessed the progress of Celiaen's affections for Eirian over the last twenty years. It started as a protective friend before somewhere in the previous ten years, it had shifted to love. A completely unwavering devotion to Eirian that never faltered, no matter what happened. Tynan almost envied what Celiaen felt, but was thankful he had so far avoided losing his mind over another person.

"The story of your father's pursuit of your mother is legendary. Maybe you're more like him than you realize. Right down to your taste in women."

Opening his mouth, Celiaen struggled to find an argument. There was a grain of truth in what Tynan had said. When he was a child, he had loved hearing Sannaeh recount the story of Paienven's pursuit of her. Baenlin had told Celiaen that half the reason Paienven had scraped through as a red mage instead of a blue like his brothers was out of determination to pursue Sannaeh.

"I wonder what my uncle would say about your comparison."

"Yeah, no, I don't want to think about Baenlin. He gives me nightmares."

"I think I might spend the day training." Lifting the swords from his lap, Celiaen put them down and stood. "It's definitely a day to stay close to camp."

Tynan pursed his lips, waving at Eirian's weapons. Understanding the unspoken question, Celiaen considered what he would do with them. Two options stood out. He could slip them into her chamber to be found when she returned. Or he could keep them and make Eirian plead for their return when she came to her senses. Chuckling, Celiaen suspected she was more likely to go straight for him, and he could make the most of both options.

"Let's take a detour and return them to her chamber before I take out my frustrations on someone. Kenna has been in a mood recently. She might be up for a round or two."

"Not Tara?" Tynan questioned in amusement.

Celiaen flinched and said, "I don't think so. I've had enough of her lectures for now. Do you know where she is?"

He had seen Tara and Alyse leave the camp early and suspected they were in the garrison liaising with the Endarans. Tara had fought in two wars and helped put down multiple rebellions in Ensaycal. Her expertise garnered her respect from General Cameron and the commanders of the Endaran army.

"I think she's with the Endarans."

"Good. They humor me, but they take Tara seriously. I don't blame them. She has more experience than the rest of us, and no amount of study can replace that."

While Celiaen gathered what he needed, Tynan commented, "Are you sure you want to track down the king?"

"Yes."

"But why?"

"Because I need to prove myself."

"To who?"

Muttering curses under his breath, Celiaen marched over to the tent door with Eirian's swords tucked under his arm, hand grasping the hilts securely. The sun had risen fully, the brightness casting a slightly hazy glow. Tynan spotted his fellow blues hovering close and nodded to them. Aiden might have left, but they had stuck around in case Celiaen got out of hand.

"Are those what I think they are?" Ianto asked, slipping in to walk next to Tynan.

"If you think they're Ree's swords, then yes, they are."

His eyes widened, and he let out a low whistle. The others had noticed the bundle Celiaen was carrying, exchanging concerned looks while they trailed after him. Thanks to the news delivered the day before, the camp was bustling. Soldiers were dismantling anything they could get away with packing. Everything was being scaled back to basics to prepare for a sudden order to leave Aveley.

Ianto murmured, "What happened?"

"Ree sent them as a message." Sensing Ianto's confusion, Tynan explained, "She wants to lure Celi into their usual shit. Figured giving him her swords would do the trick."

"Wait..."

Waving at Celiaen's back, Ianto pulled faces while he attempted to make sense of what was going on. Behind them, Cai chuckled.

They commented, "We're going the wrong way."

"I know, right! The horses are in the other direction."

Snorting, Tynan said, "He won't do it."

"Did I hear you correctly?" Cai asked.

"You did."

Disbelieving, Ianto declared, "Tara hit his head too hard yesterday."

"That's not—"

"We should get Kels to check him."

Covering his face with a groan, Tynan listened to Cai laughing and considered telling Ianto to return to his tent. If Celiaen had not wanted to train with Kenna, he would have followed through with his idea.

"Or maybe he's finally growing up? Why should Celi go to Ree when she's in the wrong?"

Huffing, Ianto dismissed the question and said, "I don't get what the big deal is? What did Ree do to Celi that's got you, Tara, and Alyse so upset? Everything seemed okay when we were playing with the trees, and then those fucking daoine got involved."

"Does it matter what she did?" Cai added, "It hurt Celi, and that's all that concerns us. They're both our friends, but our loyalty belongs to him."

Ahead of them, the garrison loomed, and Celiaen halted abruptly. It was early enough in the day that most of the nobles had not appeared, and the army officers were taking advantage of the peace to get on with what they needed to do. They were not the reason Celiaen had stopped. His gaze was on two of his companions hurrying toward them.

"Link, Lydia," he greeted them. "What's going on?"

Waving over his shoulder, Link explained, "We went with Tara this morning. Lady Saoirse has been in contact with Lord Faolan, and the scouts were right."

"We were on our way to find you," Lydia added.

"They're talking about leaving Aveley tomorrow or the day after."

"Fuck," Celiaen muttered.

Running a hand through his hair, Tynan turned to look out at the hills and wondered where Eirian was. He doubted she knew what was going on with how early she had departed. Glancing at Cai, Tynan pointed at the two swords Celiaen carried and received a nod.

"Let Cai take Ree's swords to her room. You need to find out what's going on."

Lydia realized what Celiaen was holding and asked, "Where's Ree? We hadn't seen her and figured they hadn't sent for her yet."

Turning, Celiaen handed the weapons to Cai. "Take them directly to her room. Do not give them to anyone else. Put them in her chest. You know which one I mean."

"I will," Cai murmured, taking the swords.

"Right, let's go."

Matching his pace, Link filled Celiaen in. "Apparently, the legion is far enough ahead that it's unlikely this lot could reach Kelsby before the Athnaralans do."

Clicking his tongue, Celiaen considered the options available to the Endarans. He knew what Eirian would do. She would insist on rushing to Kelsby to slow the Athnaralan legion. If forced to do battle, she would dive into the thick of it and reveal what she could do.

"It'll be a slaughter if they attempt to stop a legion with their current numbers," Lydia commented.

"Not unless Ree does something," Tynan muttered.

Shaking his head, Celiaen said, "We don't say a word about Ree's abilities. If she reveals them, that's her choice, but we won't betray her secret without her permission."

"Letting her loose on the Athnaralans would be a massacre."

Ianto agreed, "In the right situation, she could turn the tide."

"She could also lose her head for it," Lydia said. "Which is why we've always kept it secret. No one knows outside of Fay and us. Not even Rylee or Jaren."

Before entering the building that served as a command center, Celiaen lifted a hand and bid them stop. Endaran officers watched from a distance as they scurried about their tasks. For most, the novelty of having Ensaycalan royalty around had worn off, but for the Aveley soldiers, Celiaen remained an unexpected sight.

"Tynan and I will go in and join Tara. Ianto, let Kenna know I want to get some training in after we're done here. Link, grab Harlow and find Captain Aiden. I don't care what the laws of Riane state. I want the two of you to go over the armor and weapons of every single one of Ree's guards."

Nodding, Link asked, "What if the captain refuses?"

"Tell him it's for her protection. It'll help keep them alive to protect her."

"Alright, we'll do our best."

Lydia waved vaguely at Ianto, and Celiaen shrugged. He turned back to the building, taking a deep breath while preparing to face what was happening inside. Tynan relaxed his hold over his magic, maintaining a calmness that affected those within range. When they entered the room where Cameron was overseeing discussions, it was not a surprise that Alyse was exercising her influence over the Endarans.

"Prince Celiaen, glad you could join us," Marcellus spoke first.

"How bad is it?"

Cameron shook his head. "They're days away from Kelsby. Even if we leave first thing tomorrow, we won't make it before them."

"Any word from Onaorbaen?" Celiaen asked hopefully. "I know you've been expecting a legion from there."

"They're pulling together, but a lot of them have been on your side of the fence."

Clearing her throat, Tara commented, "Remember that pesky rebellion Awena asked to sort out?"

Pinching the bridge of his nose, Celiaen recalled the meetings Paienven had held before he left Luina. They had argued over letting it simmer while the focus was on Athnaral, but Awena had used it as an opportunity to prove her ruthlessness. If he had not asked for permission to pursue Eirian, Celiaen would have done it himself to deny her the chance. That Awena had convinced Endaran commanders to assist her was frustrating, but not unusual. The treaty worked both ways.

Marcellus stated, "I hate to say it, but do we think there's the possibility your northern rebellion had help from Athnaral?"

"Aeyren hates the elves," Daniel said. "What would be the point? Paienven wouldn't throw his entire army at a rebellion."

Celiaen shook his head, replying, "My father has gotten proficient at dealing with uprisings. Besides, he had already given the order for the bulk of the army to move to the Endaran border before he approved Awena heading north."

"A good thing he did. Reports have him moving into position further south in Tamantal and Raellwynt. Periyit won't be far behind." Tapping a finger on a map, Cameron added, "We need his help up here."

"I'm planning to ride to locate him and bring a legion north. You might lose the town for a while, but we'll take it back."

"Our job in the meantime is slowing Athnaral down as they press inland."

"Is Kelsby going to evacuate?" Tara inquired, frowning as she studied the reports. "Remaining to be slaughtered is a waste of valuable resources."

Sharing a look with Daniel, Cameron answered, "The garrison is remaining in place. They'll try to buy time for the people inland to escape. Evasive measures are something farms and villages in the north know. Raiding parties from Athnaral aren't uncommon up here."

"I've dealt with a few myself," Aiden spoke from behind Celiaen. "They like to keep us on our toes. As far as Athnaral is concerned, we had nothing formal in place, and they could cross the border as they pleased to do what they wanted."

"You get around," Tara chuckled.

"I'm good at what I do. I'm not called the bastard of Tamantal just because of my birth."

Previously silent, Everett said, "What my brother means is that he has a reputation for his ruthlessness in dealing with Athnaralan incursions."

Celiaen turned to stare at Aiden, forgetting about Eirian for the time being. He had seen the reports of what Aiden had done to a group of Ensaycalan rebels hiding in an Endaran town. The results had pleased Paienven, and he rewarded him and his company of soldiers well. It reminded Celiaen of his admiration for Aiden. Something that was frequently lost beneath his jealousy over Eirian.

"Don't worry, Your Grace. I'm very aware of the captain's reputation for ruthlessness. It earned him an invitation to my father's court, if I recall correctly. One he declined."

"After I took care of your minor problem, I had other jobs to do and no time to spend flirting around Luina," Aiden said.

Inclining his head, Celiaen did not argue with Aiden, and turned back to the table. Their animosity did not matter when there was a war to focus on. Meeting Tara's gaze, his mouth twisted in uncertainty, but she shook her head.

"We can't stay here and hope His Majesty sends a legion north," Tara stated. "He might assume you lot have it under control because Eirian is here."

"That's true. My father is never in a location with less than a legion accompanying him." Glancing at Aiden, Celiaen asked, "Have you sent someone to bring her back?"

"No," he answered with a faint smirk.

Chuckling, Celiaen worked out what Aiden was thinking. They both knew Eirian would fret while she waited for him to show up. If she found out about what was going on, it would distract her from fixing things with him. Aiden intended to prolong her torment.

"Where is our queen?" Cameron inquired.

"Not here. I'll update Her Majesty when she finishes with her current task."

Everett looked from Aiden to Celiaen. "Can we continue to count on Ensaycal for help?"

"Of course," Celiaen said.

"Even though?"

With a snort, Tara commented, "Fear not, Ensaycal won't abandon Endara."

"Do we leave tomorrow or?" Cameron did not finish his question.

The people in the room looked at each other, keeping their thoughts to themselves while they waited for someone else to speak. They knew the chances of winning a battle at Kelsby with their current numbers were next to nothing. Staring at each other across the table, Celiaen and Tara silently argued over what to do. What Eirian might do to protect her people filled both of them with fear.

"Leave tomorrow!" Marcellus declared.

Daniel agreed, "Either we get there on time, or we don't. If we don't, we pull back and wait for reinforcements."

"Do we wait for Her Majesty to agree before we give the orders?" Everett asked.

Shaking her head, Tara replied, "She'll agree. Don't worry about that. Just get the orders out there, and everyone ready to go. I'll let our people know we're leaving in the morning, Celi. We'll pack light and aim to ride fast."

"I'll prepare letters you can give to the garrisons, and they'll provide fresh mounts as needed," Cameron informed her. "It's the least we can do."

Tynan said, "Lend us your queen, and we'll get there in no time."

The Endarans stared at him.

"She can replenish energy for small groups with little need for rest," he explained.

Clearing his throat, Aiden prepared to ask a question they all wanted to know. He hoped the elves would be more honest than Eirian about it, but he had his suspicions. There were too many secrets about what she could do, and Aiden hated it.

"Should we be concerned about Queen Eirian if we encounter combat?"

"She's more than capable of fighting," Celiaen was quick to reply.

Crossing his arms, Aiden elaborated. "Does she have more surprises for us?"

Alyse smiled sweetly and said, "Eirian is as dangerous as any red on a battlefield. Left unchecked, she'll kill until there's nothing left to kill. Keep her away from the battle, and you have nothing to worry about."

"She might slow down smaller numbers. She can use her ability to grow things as a trap. We've all been entangled in roots." Tara laughed, adding, "I wouldn't mind watching her do that to a cohort or two."

While he appreciated their attempts to cover the darker truth, Celiaen turned to Aiden and said, "Just keep her from the battle. She doesn't have a blue, so letting her engage with any number of the enemy is dangerous. You don't have any protection from her influence."

"Could you leave Tynan?" he asked.

Choking on his surprise, Tynan answered, "I'm afraid I don't have the power to stop her. Not without the help of every other blue with us. It's safer and simpler if you keep her away from the battle."

Marcellus agreed, "We'll keep her from the battle. She's the queen of Endara. Her place is not on a battlefield."

"Magic or not, the Duke is correct," Daniel said.

Frowning, Cameron studied Celiaen. "Well, let's get on with this. There's no time to delay. War is upon us."

SIX

Eirian wrung water out of her hair and looked around the stream. She sensed her guards scattered around, but not a hint of Celiaen. Looking over to where they had tethered the horses, she gave Fionn a hard stare as he waved his knife in a mock greeting. The sun was warm, and slapping a hand to her arm, she grumbled at the sight of blood where the biting insect had gotten her. They had been a constant bother, and she itched a red lump from an earlier bite.

"Let's go back," she called, bending to pull her boots on.

"Sorry, ma'am, I should've warned you about the mozzies. I didn't think they'd be this bad," Merle apologized from his perch on a rock near the waterfall.

Turning to look at the falls, Eirian reminded herself that it was a beautiful spot despite her plan's failure. It was not a large waterfall. The rock face it poured over was only slightly taller than she was when she stood on the bank. Crystal clear water tumbled over the rocks, pooling at the bottom where it was deep enough to swim in before it continued its way down through the narrow band of trees between the hills.

"It's okay, Merle. I've experienced worse. Thank you for bringing me here."

Finished with her boots, Eirian grabbed her belt and knives and returned them to her waist. Other guards appeared out of the trees, making their way to the horses. None of them had taken a dip in the water, and she regretted they had not enjoyed the visit as much as she had. Fionn approached, a long cloak draped over his arm that he held out in offering. Arching a brow, Eirian shrugged and took it, shaking it out before she secured it around her shoulders.

"You look cold," he chuckled, winking.

"Don't be a lecher. You don't want the boss man to flog you again!" Geoff called.

Eirian stared at Fionn with her head cocked. "What did you do this time?"

Fionn grinned. "He caught me getting handsy with a lovely lass. You know how it is."

"Why don't we pretend Her Majesty doesn't know how it is," Merle grumbled, picking his way along the bank toward them. "And you won't be telling her."

"There's no fun in—" Eirian chuckled, but stopped when Merle gave her a look.

"Come on, it'll be afternoon by the time we're back. The captain will wonder how it went."

Laughing, Fox brought Halcyon over and said, "He'll be happy to hear your plan went tits up like he said it would. Pity, he's more difficult to live with when he thinks he's right."

Frowning, Eirian checked over Halcyon's tack. "I suspect I was wrong to entrust the job to him. I should've gotten Gabe to return the swords to Celi. I can trust him."

Appearing at her side, Merle offered a hand and replied, "You can trust the captain to always do what he believes is the best thing for you."

"I need to learn to be harder on him."

Hearing laughter from the other guards, Eirian shot a look at them and frowned, but Merle drew her attention back.

"Do you think your relationship with us is out of the ordinary? Do you think your father wasn't friends with his men? He used to drink with them and share stories. Confided in them, and so on."

"I know, but Aiden pushes boundaries."

Merle cocked a finger, and Eirian leaned down to hear him murmur, "It's because he's at least half in love with you."

"What?" Startled, Eirian tightened her grip on the reins.

"Well, okay, not half. That was a slight under exaggeration. You're expected to be friends with us. We're with you more than anyone else, even your ladies. Imagine how much harder it'd be if you weren't friendly." Patting the big brown gelding on his neck, Merle smiled grimly and said, "Think about it."

Shaking her head, Eirian glanced at the other guards. They were doing their best to look everywhere but at her.

"Everett doesn't—"

"Yes, he does. I know Gunter, and they're firm friends. The Duke is bad at cards."

"Really?"

"I bet you never thought twice about how you act with the Prince's companions. You see them as equals, so you don't think your behavior is inappropriate," Merle pointed out. "You know bits and pieces about us when you bother to learn. Don't tell the captain I told you this, but he's not like the rest of us. He has noble blood. His father—"

"Merle!" Sid shook his head.

Fox also shook his head and said, "He won't appreciate you telling."

Looking at each of them and noting the serious looks they wore, Eirian's eyes narrowed. "I could order you to."

Eirian scolded herself for missing the obvious. She had been suspicious, but never asked Aiden about his background. The signs had been there.

"No, they're right. Ask your cousin why he chose Aiden to be your captain." Merle hurried to his horse.

Letting Merle guide them out of the area, Eirian slumped in her saddle. Lost in her thoughts, she barely noticed the guards chatting as they picked their way through the hills. Reaching out with her magic, she tried to sense where Celiaen was. The tug of their bond told Eirian that he had not left the town. His lack of action left her infuriated, and she wondered what Aiden had said to him.

"Who are you maddest at?" Fox asked.

"Myself. You told me it wouldn't work, but I was too stubborn to think it would be any different from in the past. I hope I didn't make it worse."

Giving her a sideways look, Fionn chuckled, "Personally, if a woman returned my tokens of affection, I wouldn't be chasing after her to give them back."

"Most men wouldn't give the woman they love a set of swords as a symbol of their affection," John said, laughing.

Waving at Eirian, Fionn argued, "We're not talking about most men or women. I don't think Her Majesty would've appreciated some jewelry, furs, or whatnot as much as she does those swords or her pretty haubergeon."

Fox replied jokingly, "Fairly sure both of them want to cover Her Majesty with furs."

Eirian rolled her eyes and asked, "What should I do?"

Laughter greeted her question, and Merle sighed. He doubted he could control the group and questioned if it bothered him.

He told her, "I'm not sure you should ask us. You'll get nothing but crude answers."

"I doubt they'd say anything I haven't heard before."

"Well, I'd suggest following through on all that foreplay you've got going on with him."

"Which him?" Tobin mocked.

"What foreplay?" Eirian asked in confusion.

Merle gave her an amused look while the others started laughing again. Grinding her teeth, Eirian glared at them, unamused by the laughter.

"We obviously have different notions of what foreplay is."

"You're the unmarried queen of Endara," Tyler muttered. "You shouldn't have any notion of foreplay."

Fionn winked and commented, "Has it ever occurred to you that for some people, like yourself, your training might be a bit of... you know."

"We've all watched you. It gets very heated," Sid added.

Fox snorted. "My pa likes it when Ma helps him out with the skinning."

"That's disturbing and not exactly helpful." Giving Fox a disgusted look, John shook his head and asked, "Who are we talking about?"

"It is helpful if she gets the point!" Fox huffed.

"Pretty sure that's what we're telling her to do!" Chuckling, Fionn glanced at his comrades. "Look, Your Majesty, you're a warrior, and he's a warrior. Pretend his sword represents his... you know. Don't you get all hot and bothered during a good sparring session?"

"Again, who are we talking about? The prince or the captain?" John grumbled.

Feeling her face burn, Eirian looked to the side in embarrassment. "I see where you're going. Besides letting him sheath his sword, have you got any useful suggestions?"

"Oh, Your Majesty, how rude! Our poor sensibilities!" Fionn mocked.

The guards howled with laughter.

"Cut it out, Fionn." Rolling his eyes, Merle pointed at the town. "We're almost back."

"You should talk to him. No fighting, no magic, just talk to him," Paxton said.

He was the first to stop laughing, and when Eirian glanced over her shoulder at him, he was staring at her thoughtfully.

"You're right, I should, but I don't know how to. We've always beaten our disagreements out of each other," Eirian replied, looking at her hands resting on Halcyon's neck.

Snorting, Merle gave her a look. "I want to say typical men, but I'm not sure that applies."

Glancing at the sky, she shrugged. "I know."

"What do you want to do?"

"I'm going to go to him and try talking. There's a first for everything."

"Fionn and his men can head back in and let the captain know where you are. I'll stay with you until whoever takes over shows up. No doubt it'll be him."

Silence fell on the group as they approached the outskirts of the town. Bringing their horses to a halt, they dismounted, and Fionn took Halcyon's reins from Eirian, leading the horse away. Watching them go, she wanted to grab the reins and race off to avoid the conversation she knew she had to have.

Touching a hand to the knife on her belt, Eirian drew a deep breath and let Merle lead the way through the sprawling city of tents to where the elves were situated. She felt the magic in the air, but did not dare pay attention to her bond. Spotting Tynan hovering in front of a tent, she balked, and Merle touched her shoulder.

"You're a queen. Just pretend this is politics."

"I don't think it can ever just be politics," she whispered nervously.

He muttered, "Then fuck him."

"Merle! I thought you wanted to help me?"

"I am helping you. Those are your choices if you want to fix things with your prince. Either talk to him and negotiate a solution or give him what he wants." Shrugging, Merle pushed her forward and said, "Just go do it."

Clinging to the cloak, Eirian approached the tent slowly. Tynan watched, his calming aura of power washing over her. Welcoming it, she pushed her magic down and contemplated shielding, so it did not become involved in the conversation.

"Was it a pleasant ride?" There was a hint of amusement in his voice as Tynan grinned at her.

"Hello, Tynan. Where is he? Is he free?"

Cocking his head to the side, Tynan pursed his lips and said, "I don't know. Celi might be somewhere comparing weapons with your captain. He'll be along shortly."

She muttered, "I shouldn't have sent Aiden."

"Perhaps, but if you had sent another errand boy, Celi might have chased after you. Go on in. He's expecting you, so I doubt he'll mind if you're in there waiting."

Pulling the tent open, Tynan bowed and waved her in. Glancing over her shoulder at her guards, it didn't surprise Eirian when they didn't push to follow.

"Does he hate me?"

Frowning, Tynan told her, "He could never hate you."

Taking a deep breath, Eirian stepped into the confines of the tent. Crossing to his bed, she sat on the edge. Waiting for Celiaen to appear was not helping her anxiety, and she covered her face. Trying to count the heartbeats she heard echoing from all directions, she attempted to push her nerves away. It was difficult, but digging her nails into her forehead, Eirian used the pain to focus.

A brush of magic alerted her to his arrival. Peeking between her fingers, she saw Celiaen standing in front of her with his arms crossed. He stared, and his dark eyes were black in the strange glow caused by light filtering through the tent's fabric. The coldness in his gaze made her freeze.

"If you planned to greet me with the sight of you in my bed, you're not doing it right," Celiaen said. "And it's a bold assumption it would work."

Dropping her hands to her lap, Eirian replied, "I doubt it's a bold assumption if it's what you want."

Celiaen arched a brow, unfolding his arms to wave. "You're welcome to prove it. I suggest removing your clothes, and if you wish, I'll go back outside so we can start again."

Remaining frozen, Eirian gazed at him. "Celiaen."

"I didn't think so. What are you doing here, Eirian?"

"I came to tell you I'm sorry."

"You might need to be more specific. There's a lot that you need to apologize for," he informed her.

Slumping, she looked down at her lap sadly. "You're right. I have a lot to apologize for. What I said that day… I need you to know I don't regret our bond."

"Liar."

"I'm not!"

Turning his back on her, Celiaen began unbuckling his weapons as he said, "Yes, you are. You regret it, and unless you change how you feel about me, you'll always regret it. You can't deny you wish it were Gal."

Not trusting herself to respond, Eirian watched him toss his swords to the side, eyes lingering on the blades as his knives and belt joined them. Turning her gaze to Celiaen, she noticed his hair had grown while they traveled. She wanted to run her hands through it to see if it was as silky as she remembered. While his fingers worked at the laces of his jerkin, he turned to stare at her.

Shrugging the leather off, Celiaen tossed it onto the pile with his weapons before moving his attention to his bracers. Getting to her feet, Eirian stilled his hands and unlaced them, sliding the leather off his wrists when they were loose enough. She threw them and flinched when they missed the pile, not looking at him. Growling, Celiaen pushed her away, and she staggered backward, catching the edge of the bed and landing on it.

"You're wrong, Eirian."

"About what?"

"Everything! You think a hollow apology and offering yourself to me will solve this, but it won't because you think you're in love with Gal."

"I'll always love Gal! Don't you still have feelings for your first love?"

Celiaen whispered, "You are my first and only love. I have never felt for anyone what I do for you."

Covering her face, Eirian shook her head and asked, "Tell me how to fix this?"

"What did you hope to achieve by sending your swords back to me?"

"I expected you to come charging after me, thundering rage letting you beat me as you always do."

He arched a brow in amusement. "I beat you because I'm better than you. So, after I beat you, then what?"

Waving dismissively at his comment, Eirian rolled her eyes. "I don't know. We'd argue, roll around on the ground, throw some comments about, and things would be okay again. Like we've done in the past."

"I'm sorry, Ree, but that's not good enough. We're not children anymore."

Studying him, Eirian felt a pang of hope at her nickname. "What is good enough?"

"Why should I tell you?"

Celiaen studied her back, taking in the lack of armor and the cloak he knew was not hers. There was the fragment of a twig tangled in her hair. It made him wonder what Eirian had done while out riding.

"Because I hate the situation we're in! I hate being at odds with you. I need you," she admitted.

"Do you?"

Groaning, Eirian remembered what the two daoine men had said. She could not bring herself to admit the truth, and she suspected he would throw it back in her face if she did. All she could do was dance around it like she had for years.

"Our bond exists despite what I claim I feel, and I know, deep down, it's true."

Pointing at the ground, Celiaen wanted to challenge her. "What if I said begging at my feet would be a good place to start?"

Pushing herself off the bed, Eirian dropped to her knees in front of him and looked up, returning his challenging stare with her own. She would do whatever she had to.

"Then I'd call your bluff."

"What if it wasn't a bluff?"

Celiaen stared down at her, clenching his hands into fists. She cocked her head, lips twitching with a hint of amusement. The longer he stared, the less confident Eirian felt he was toying with her.

"Then I suppose I should grab the front of your tunic and tearfully beg your forgiveness. Would telling you I'm an idiot help?"

"You don't cry and beg. You're not that kind of woman, and you never could be."

Reaching up, Eirian grabbed his tunic. "Why don't we find out?"

Pulling away, Celiaen sat on the bed and said, "No, you're not, and you insult us by trying to be. Forcing yourself to complete the bond isn't what we want. I don't want you in my bed because you think there's no other way. By the powers, I don't want you if you don't believe you love me."

"What are we doing, Celi?" Eirian asked, not turning to look at him.

"I'm going to return to my father. I know he's in Endara with the bulk of our army. I'll see this war through as the heir to the throne of Ensaycal, and then I'll step aside and go to Riane. My uncle has told me he'd groom me to take the seat beside him as an archmage. Calhoun is getting old, and his fading won't be far off."

Going cold, Eirian turned and stared at him in shock. She could not believe he would make such a suggestion. Not when it would make Awena next in line for the Ensaycalan throne.

"You can't be serious? Why would you do that?"

Directing a look that told Eirian all she needed to know, he continued,

"You can't remain the queen, not with your duine blood. When you abdicate, I'll be waiting in Riane for you."

"You'd have me choose between you and freedom?"

"No, I'd give it to you. If you still think your path lies with Gal, you can run away to Telmia and be with your mother's people. Or perhaps by then, you'll have realized you love me as much as I love you."

Rubbing her face, Eirian felt drained and said, "I can't let you make that mistake."

"You assume you're the reason I want to do this. I've been thinking about it for at least the last forty years. I've long suspected my path lies with my magic and not a throne."

Celiaen smiled at her and patted the bed beside him. He enjoyed the exasperated expression Eirian wore.

"You wouldn't lie to me about this?"

Arching a brow, his smile faded, and he replied, "No, I wouldn't. I hope you can support my decision."

"How will your father react?"

"I imagine he'll be furious, but my mother will support me. Are you going to stay sitting in the dirt?"

Glancing down, Eirian snorted and lifted her hands to undo the clasp holding the cloak. Releasing it, she let the wool pool around her and made a note to return it to Fionn.

"I'm only in the dirt because you told me to be."

Cocking a finger, Celiaen pointed at his feet and said, "I told you to be at my feet."

"Imagine the scandal," Eirian chuckled, rising to stand.

"Did I say you could walk? I think crawling would be a better demonstration of your desperation for my forgiveness."

Meeting his eyes, Eirian could not tell if he was joking. Her smirk faded, and she dropped back onto her knees. Putting her hands to the floor, she crept over the short distance to Celiaen. Stopping at his feet, she looked up, and the desire she felt through their bond startled her. She was not sure which of them it belonged to. Leaning forward, he cupped her cheeks, stroking a thumb over her lips.

"I can't forgive you."

"What?"

Moving to pull back, Eirian stopped when his grip on her face tightened. Celiaen clicked his tongue at her, discouraging any further attempts to remove herself from his hold.

"There's only one thing that will make me forgive you, and you're not ready for it."

"I don't understand."

"That's why I know you're not ready. When you open those pretty eyes to the truth, that's when I'll forgive you. But you need to reach that on your own. No one can tell you what to do," Celiaen said as he let go of her face and sat back.

She did not move, muttering, "Does that mean I can get up off the floor?"

Unable to hold back his laugh, Celiaen nodded. "If you want to. Though I'm rather enjoying the sight of you like that."

"Of course you are."

Giving Celiaen a cranky look as she scrambled to her feet, Eirian rolled her shoulders and glanced at the pile of leather, mail, and weapons. It provided her with something to focus on while composing herself.

"I've never seen you toss your swords aside like that."

"Perhaps I did it to distract myself from the thought of what I want to do to you. Or perhaps it was to remind me of what you did to my swords."

"I did nothing to your swords."

Reminded of the conversation with her guards, Eirian blushed and turned away. Celiaen grinned and grabbed her hand to pull her onto the bed. Holding her down, he gazed at the lingering redness of her cheeks.

"Why, Ree, is that a blush?"

"No!" Eirian protested and pushed at him.

"Don't lie to me." Pinning her hands to her chest, Celiaen kept grinning and asked, "Why did a comment about swords make you blush?"

"It was just a silly conversation with my guards earlier."

Eyes narrowing, he chuckled and let go, flopping onto the bed beside her. Celiaen wondered what Aiden would have to say if he heard. It almost tempted him to let the other man know, just to feel the rage it would inspire. If not for the punishment the guards would face, Celiaen would make a point of telling him.

"I suspect I know. It's been a day for sword innuendo."

"Are you sure of that?"

"Yes."

Taking a chance, Eirian rolled over to straddle him. She placed a hand on either side of Celiaen's head while carefully tucking her knees into his sides. They were in an awkward position on the bed, and it left her with little room to maneuver. Licking her lips, she smirked when he groaned.

"Really sure?"

"I'm sure you're testing my self-control," he replied.

Relaxing his hold on his magic, Celiaen watched Eirian take a deep breath when the bond tugged at her, eyelids fluttering. Biting back a gasp, she shook her head and did her best to deny the pull. They needed to keep their minds clear.

"Celi."

Lifting his hands to her hips, Celiaen pushed her back, the action unbalancing Eirian, and she fell forward onto her elbows. Raising his brows, he gave her a challenging look. It was clear she was struggling with the bond; he felt it too, but he wanted to torment her more.

"Yes, Ree? Is my sword too much for you? I thought it's what you came for."

"Oh, I don't know about being too much for me," she replied.

Wriggling on purpose, Eirian smirked when he groaned, digging his fingers into her hips. She knew what Celiaen was trying to do and was happy to return the favor.

"Of course, it might be too much for you."

"Eirian, I meant what I said. I don't want to do this."

Leaning down, Eirian gave him a doubtful look, saying, "And yet you do. You've waited for how long for me to say yes?"

Sliding a hand along her back, Celiaen grasped her braid and turned Eirian's ear to his mouth to murmur, "And I'll keep waiting. Until you stop regretting our bond, I won't be slipping my sword into your sheath. Do you understand, or do I need to explain in greater detail?"

"I don't think I'm going to look at swords the same way for a while."

She was careful when Celiaen let go of her head and pushed off him. Amused, he propped his head up to watch her.

"Did your guards actually tell you to come in here and seduce me?"

Eirian gave him a dirty look. "What do you think? They said our sparring is foreplay."

"Isn't it? Particularly when our arguments end the way you planned to end this one. If we didn't get interrupted every time, this whole situation might not have happened."

"You don't need to agree with them."

"I'm only a man, Ree. When I knock those blades from your hands and have you pinned beneath me, our magic filling the air..." Celiaen sighed and ran a hand through his hair.

"I hope you don't believe I was rejecting your gift," Eirian said.

"Don't worry. They're already in your quarters. You might be an idiot, but you're not callous. Even without your captain spilling your plans to me, I figured it out."

Sitting next to Celiaen, she nudged and chuckled, "And you didn't fall for it."

"I thought it was time I rejected you, and you came chasing after me. I hope the feeling is uncomfortable and drives you to distraction." Glancing sideways at her, he grinned.

"Why are you leaving me?"

The sadness in her voice made his grin fade, and Celiaen took one of her hands in his, squeezing it. It was a comfort.

"Because war is here, and I need to make sure my father does the right thing."

"I'm scared. I don't want war, and I fear the darkness the Telmians speak of. I fear madness is spreading over the land, and I can't stop it. I fear I might prevail against Athnaral and the darkness, only to have them drag me away because of my blood. I fear my magic is changing." Shaking her head, Eirian did not look at him and admitted, "I fear losing you. That something might happen, and I never get to see you again."

Celiaen lifted his free hand to her face and leaned in, resting his forehead against hers. "I promise you, no matter what happens, I'll always be there for you. I'll always find you again. Only death could stop me."

"I don't deserve your loyalty."

Closing her eyes, Eirian enjoyed the peace his touch gave her. The bond whispered that Celiaen's lips were right there. All she had to do was kiss him and stop fighting.

"I disagree, but do me a favor and don't make me wait for fifty years."

Giggling, Eirian pulled back and said, "Like your mother did to your father?"

"Indeed." Smirking, Celiaen glanced at the tent door. "I suppose you should leave."

"I know, but I don't want to. I want to find a spot with a view of the sky where we can lie and talk like we used to. I don't want to face the days to come."

Knowing she spoke of the war, Celiaen murmured, "I'm sorry, Ree. You couldn't have prevented this war, you know that. I wish we could do exactly as you suggest."

He pulled Eirian into a hug and felt her press her lips to his neck. Tightening his arms around her, Celiaen thought he heard her whisper something against his skin. Then she shrugged off his hold, standing and stroked his hair gently.

"I just hoped," she admitted.

"We all did."

Celiaen caught her hand, kissing her palm before she turned. Watching Eirian walk away reminded him of his vision of her when she was a child. For a moment, he considered changing his mind and stopping her. The sad look she cast over her shoulder before slipping out of the tent made Celiaen remain seated. He could not stop her from leaving. He knew they would do something they would regret if he did.

Rubbing her face, Eirian hesitated once she was outside. Her magic begged her not to walk away from Celiaen. A hand on her shoulder caused her to look up, and she stared at Aiden. His mouth twisted in concern, eyes darting to the door of the tent behind her.

"Ma'am, I have news to deliver."

"What?" Surprised, Eirian asked, "What news?"

Aiden hoped delivering the news of the decision to leave Aveley for Kelsby would work to distract Eirian from whatever had happened between her and Celiaen. It was why he had asked Celiaen not to mention anything to her.

"While you were out frolicking in—"

"Frolicking?"

"Do you want the news or not?"

She grumbled, "I was not frolicking."

"Well, while you weren't here, General Cameron held a meeting with a few others, and they decided that we'll be departing tomorrow."

It had precisely the effect he was hoping for. Aiden watched the emotions flicker across her face. A mixture of confusion, anger, and fear.

"Why?"

"The bird has been in contact, and the Athnaralan—"

"We won't reach Kelsby before them," Eirian whispered in despair.

He shook his head, squeezing her shoulder. "No, we won't. But we're going to try. That's all we can do, Eirian. Try."

SEVEN

Eirian watched the lines of soldiers making their way along the road. Swallowing her anxiety, she tugged at the reins and turned Halcyon to make her way toward the party of elves. She did not hurry, though she knew everyone was keen to leave. Spotting Celiaen a short distance away from his company, Eirian dismounted and led her horse across the last few paces to greet him.

"It's a fair day."

"Indeed, it is." He smiled sadly, "You don't have to pretend to be okay."

Glancing over her shoulder at her guards, Eirian muttered, "I'm not sure you're right."

Closing the distance between them, Celiaen reached out and took one of Eirian's hands, gripping it tightly as he leaned in and rested his forehead against hers.

"Look at the dawn and remember, I'm always thinking of you, no matter how far apart we are," Celiaen whispered.

"Celi." She let go of the reins and touched his face with her free hand.

"I'm not stupid, Ree. I know what you're riding into, and I know what you'll do if pushed. Don't get killed before I can sweep in and save the day like the gallant prince I am."

Laughing, Eirian ruffled his hair. "That'd be fine if I wasn't a queen already."

Smiling back, Celiaen instructed, "I mean it, don't get yourself killed. Promise me if things aren't in your favor, you'll get on your horse and run. We can rebuild Endara. What you can do is not worth the cost on any level."

"You know I can't make such a promise," she replied quietly.

"But there is someone who can, and I know he'll do it." Looking at Aiden, Celiaen lifted his unoccupied hand and waved. "A moment of your time, please, Captain."

Frowning, Aiden dismounted and tossed his reins to Merle before he walked over to the pair of royals. He did not know why Celiaen summoned him, but he was keen to find out.

"I'm surprised you're inviting me into your cozy farewell."

Arching a brow at Celiaen, Eirian did not glance in Aiden's direction. "I know what you're doing, Celi. Do you think—"

"Ree, shush and let me have my satisfaction."

Celiaen shook his head at her, and she fell silent, turning to face Aiden, who scowled as he watched them.

"So, how can I satisfy you, Your Highness?" Aiden asked, continuing to frown as he stared at Eirian.

"There is so much you can do to satisfy me, Captain," Celiaen chuckled. "I've told you before."

"Celi—"

With a squeeze of their joined hands, Celiaen cut Eirian off and said, "This foolish woman won't promise me she'll stay out of the fight. You, however, I know you'll do whatever is needed to keep her alive."

"That's hardly a secret."

"I'm giving you my blessing to knock Ree out, tie her to the back of your horse, and run for anywhere east so long as it's not a battlefield. Whatever you have to do to keep her alive at any cost."

Eirian rolled her eyes and huffed, "Honestly! I'm quite capable of looking after myself, and you know it better than anyone, Celi."

Aiden bowed his head to Celiaen and said, "You have my word that I'll do that, and if I can't, someone else will. We know our duty. Protect her, even from herself if needs be."

"Thank you, Captain." Returning his focus to Eirian, Celiaen grinned. "Don't be mad, Ree. You know why I have to ask. Besides, he's not intimidated by you."

Sighing, she shrugged, magic surrounding them. It was a reminder and a threat.

"Just don't forget what I can do. I won't cower from a fight."

Turning away, Aiden chuckled, "I think we're aware you don't cower from a fight. Have a swift journey, Your Highness. Don't get killed because I can't protect her from that."

Watching Aiden stride back to the others, Celiaen shook his head. "I know I can trust him to look after you. That matters more to me than anything else."

"I don't need looking after."

"Yes, you do. Otherwise, you're likely to get some stupid idea that'll end up with you dead. You're the queen, not a foot soldier. You sit on your horse with your guards, nobles, and generals, directing the troops. You don't fight."

Glancing at the swords he had given her, Eirian drew in a deep breath before saying, "I'll try, but you know I can't sit back and let others die. Not when I could turn the tide."

"You're one mage, Ree, regardless of how much power you have, no matter what you can do. I know what Saoirse reported, but a single legion is too many for you to take on. You'd be stupid to try," Celiaen said and returned his hand to her face, leaning in.

Feeling his magic join hers in surrounding them, Eirian took comfort in it. She missed it when they were apart.

"I know I'm only one mage, but I'm not just any mage."

"When we reunite and have my father's armies at our back, we'll fight together. You know it will be worth the wait."

"Don't go."

Celiaen released her hand to pull Eirian to him, his arm around her waist. She placed her hands on his chest, knowing what was coming.

"One for the road," he murmured, and lowered his lips to hers.

Eirian smiled sadly when he let go and stepped back. She felt the gulf between them and held out her hand. He did not take it, and meeting her gaze, let her see the conflict he felt.

"Celi."

"Don't, Ree. I'll come back to you like always. First, I need to get you a bigger army."

He turned and walked toward his companions. Hurrying after him, Eirian grabbed his arm and surprised Celiaen with a second kiss. A desperate promise for the future.

"You better!"

Grinning, Celiaen brushed her cheek gently. "Nothing could stop me from coming for you every time."

Watching Celiaen accept his reins from Harlow, she waved farewell to the group. She had known them most of her life. They were her friends, and Eirian would miss their company. Lingering, she waited for Celiaen to turn and look at her. Meeting his gaze across the distance, she nodded and felt the pull of their bond. Hearing the creak of a saddle and the thud of hooves, Eirian realized Aiden had collected Halcyon. Accepting the reins, she hoisted herself into the saddle, carefully avoiding her bow.

"For a woman who claims she doesn't love him, you certainly have everyone fooled. The first kiss was his, but the second?" Aiden gave her a pointed look.

"Maybe I'm the one being fooled."

"Sometimes you have to look elsewhere to discover what you wanted was right in front of you the whole time."

Looking at Aiden in surprise, she turned Halcyon's head. "I can't say I expected that sort of insight from you."

He nudged his horse to follow, chuckling, "Well, you spend more time picking fights than listening to me."

"I deserve that."

Joining her guards, Eirian avoided the grins directed at her and did her best not to flinch at the whistles that earned glares from Aiden. Glancing them over, she noticed they were more heavily armed than usual. She was not the only one riding with a strung bow at the ready. Turning her attention in the direction the elves had gone, Eirian clung to the lingering brush of Celiaen's power. Once they were out of her reach, it would be some time before she felt the familiar comfort of his magic.

"Are you ready?" Merle asked, exchanging a look with Aiden.

"No, not really," Eirian sighed. "But the day is getting on, and we need to move."

"Let her take a moment to make sure her head is where it needs to be." Fionn chuckled, "Don't worry, Your Majesty. None of us think any worse of you for feeling what you feel."

"I do," she muttered.

Eirian shook her head and turned Halcyon in the road's direction. Nudging him into a canter without warning, she let him pick his way over the uneven ground. She intended to slip into the line, away from the nobles. The soldiers gave them glances, the sight of their queen armed and mounted riding alongside them no longer a novelty. Throughout the journey, most of the soldiers had seen Eirian in training. She enjoyed the ripple of respect they afforded her, and giving Aiden a knowing smile, she let Halcyon drop to a walk.

"Is this a strategic placing?" Aiden rechecked his sword for assurance.

"We look like a group of officers."

"Should something happen, I'd appreciate it if you made use of your most excellent archery abilities."

"I'll do my best, but no promises. Unfortunately, my quiver isn't a magical arrow-producing one, and there's only so much I can do before I run out."

"That would be a handy trick!" Fox laughed, glancing at his bow.

Laughing with him, Eirian shot a grin over her shoulder at the best archer in her guard. "I'd give it to you if I had one. I'm sure there are yellows in Riane trying to make it happen. Given how long we've been warring with each other, you'd think they'd have succeeded by now."

"Self-cleaning armor would be my request," someone grumbled, earning laughter from all around.

Joining in the banter, a soldier called out, "That's what a wife is for!"

"They're royal guards, mate. They're not allowed to have wives!" the person in front of them commented, more laughter rippling through the soldiers.

"Neither are you lot when on the march!" Devin replied, making a rude gesture.

"I think you mean husband! Got to make him earn his keep!" a woman joked.

Other women within earshot echoed her sentiments. Giggling, Eirian smirked at Merle, his sour expression fueling her amusement.

"Oh, come on, it's funny! I'll try to change the law after we do this. I think it's outdated."

Merle shook his head and said, "If you think it bothers us, you'd be wrong. No one forced us to become royal guards. The conditions of the job are no secret. They haven't changed in hundreds of years. We know what we sign up for."

"I appreciate that. It's not like I'm desperate for the same." She ignored the continuing banter. "Quite the opposite. It's the last thing I want."

Aiden asked, "If you think the rules for royal guards are outdated, does that include excluding women from applying?"

Nodding, Eirian did not look at Aiden and replied, "I do. I understand what they're trying to do, and I disagree because I know how I feel. Not all women want to have children and make families. I mean, you feel that way now, but, in a few years, you might realize you want a family and a life that isn't about serving some entitled royal."

"We could say the same about you."

Shooting Aiden an unreadable look, Eirian did not respond straight away. She mulled over the topic.

"If the chance arises, you mean. I doubt any amount of time will change how I feel about having children. It's something I've felt for as long as I can remember," she finally said.

"Don't worry, I'll make sure the chance arises. I'm not letting you die on my watch."

Aiden expected her to reply with something sarcastic, but Eirian shrugged and looked ahead. Toying with Halcyon's mane, she went over the information she had gathered about the crops dying. There was a growing concern over how it would affect winter stores, and the war with Athnaral would worsen the situation. That they were happening simultaneously bothered Eirian. Snorting, Halcyon tossed his head and shied, startling her from her thoughts.

"You looked like you might fall asleep in the saddle," Aiden commented, reaching out and patting her horse on the rump. "Perhaps he thought he'd wake you before you fell."

"I was mulling over the crops. Thought it would be better than mulling over war."

"I can't see how that is a better subject than war. Either way, you're going to worry."

"Maybe I was being positive and thinking about what I need to deal with after we defeat Athnaral?" Glancing at Aiden, Eirian noticed his amused smile.

"You should also consider how it affects feeding your troops. There will be a decrease in yield due to combat destroying crops. As well as the inevitable death of innocent bystanders who are the people doing the farming."

Eirian knew his observation should not surprise her. Contemplating briefly if she should ask Aiden about his father, she glanced at the sky.

"It sounds like you know more than you let on."

"I know a lot more than you give me credit for." Aiden shrugged.

"So, you're not just a pretty face." Eirian looked at Merle and grinned. "Is there anything you want to tell me?"

"I'm not sure I'd call the boss man a pretty face." Gabe leaned forward to meet her gaze and said, "That's Fionn's job."

Fionn brought his horse forward in line with the other two and asked, "What's my job?"

"Being a pretty face," Gabe informed him.

Merle smiled, understanding what Gabe was trying to do. The other guards joked at Fionn's expense, and he grinned at them.

"Oh, definitely! I'm the prettiest face around."

Aiden shook his head, muttering, "And I trust you to protect the Queen."

Holding his hands in the air, Merle struggled to keep a straight face. "He has such a modest ego as well."

Eirian rolled her eyes, laughing, "Thank you for trying to distract me, but surely there are other topics you could joke about?"

"It's not a joke topic, but my older sister had another baby while we were in Aveley. It was nice to see my family." Merle smiled sadly, glancing over his shoulder.

"Why didn't you introduce me? I'd have liked to meet them, Merle," Eirian said.

Staring at Aiden, Merle replied, "I know you mean it. I asked my mother, but the suggestion I bring the Queen to our farm when she'd just had a baby mortified my sister."

"I wonder what she'd have said if you had told her I've attended not only a goat giving birth but a mare and a human woman. Not all at the same time, of course, though that would be a brilliant tale to tell."

Fionn choked. "A goat?"

"You've done what?" Aiden demanded.

"It's part of our training in Riane. The goat was a funny story. I haven't thought about it in years." Grinning, Eirian remembered the day it happened.

"Oh, this I have to hear. Tell us, please," Fionn pleaded.

Fionn was too curious to let it go, attempting to push in between her and Merle. Merle did not budge, giving him a dark look and bringing his horse closer to Eirian.

Merle told him, "I think we all want to hear this."

Eirian waved and said, "Well, things like that happen when we're young, before they determine our order. It's part of figuring out where our gifts are. They took us to a farm for a few weeks during birthing season. We had to work around the farm and attend births. I've mucked out more stables than I care to remember."

"You know how to muck out a stable?" John asked in surprise.

"I know how to do lots of things that would shock you."

Making a strangled noise, Fionn demanded, "Back to the story!"

"Fay was with me, and they gave us a nanny to watch. As you'd expect for a pair of girls, we took it seriously. Fay had seen lots of sheep give birth, but this was her first goat. I'd only seen drawings in books, so the entire process fascinated me," Eirian told them.

"How old were you?" Aiden asked.

"Ten."

Merle chuckled, "I remember what girls are like. I have too many sisters."

"Anyway, another pair of novices joined us, and this poor nanny had four of us watching her every move. When she started, we were very enthusiastic. Our orders were to observe with our eyes and magic only and get help if we thought things weren't going well," Eirian continued.

The guards watched intently, and Fionn impatiently encouraged her to continue her story. "And?"

She shrugged. "The nanny knew what she was doing. It was the idiot children watching her who didn't. Our group's only boy was so completely horrified when she popped the kid out that he vomited all over Fay. She screamed and fell off a fence rail, breaking her arm. He started sobbing and bolted. His partner went running to get the master. They left me standing there without a clue what to do. Poor Fay was groaning on the ground, covered in vomit and cradling a broken arm."

"What did you do?" Gabe asked.

"I tried to help Fay, but even then, I wasn't a healer. When we met up with the master, she assumed it was me who'd vomited, clearly a princess wouldn't be able to handle watching a goat birth. I stormed off in a huff to find the boy and dumped him at her feet while she healed Fay's arm. He never lived it down, and I took great delight in kicking his ass whenever I could." Chuckling darkly, Eirian shook her head and admitted, "In hindsight, I probably tormented him more than he deserved."

Aiden snorted. "I bet it wasn't funny at the time."

"Oh, no, I thought it was hilarious. I helped Fay to her feet and laughed the entire way to camp. Wearing a little vomit didn't bother me. It was a big, hilarious, why me moment. But Fay was cranky with me for ages."

Fionn leaned forward and asked, "Have you ever seen anything that has disgusted you so much you vomited?"

"I've come close." Frowning, she shuddered at the memory.

"First time you killed someone?" Gabe guessed.

Brushing his suspicion off, Eirian replied, "You'd think so, but no. I once broke my leg badly enough to see the bone. The sight of my broken bone made me feel things..."

Her revelation stunned them.

Gabe broke the silence and asked, "You broke your leg?"

"Fell out of a tree and broke a rather nice bow by landing on it." Sighing, she shrugged. "And my pride, but it was the bow that upset me."

Aiden admitted, "It should surprise me. I want to know why you were in a tree with a bow, but I won't ask right now."

"I will!" Merle declared.

"The Duke of Raellwynt is approaching."

He pointed at the group of riders heading toward them. Eirian pushed her reluctance aside and waved at Marcellus.

"Greetings, Your Grace," she said.

Marcellus returned her wave, looking over the cluster of guards surrounding her as they came to a halt. The two groups regarded each other while the soldiers continued on.

"So, this is where you've been hiding, Your Majesty. I was expecting you to be at the front, champing at the bit for action," Marcellus said.

Arching a brow, Eirian replied, "You'd be pleased to hear that I put myself in the middle somewhere, thinking it would be safer."

"My wife is beside herself that she has misplaced you."

"Brenna worries too much. I had to bid farewell to Prince Celiaen before I joined the convoy. By the time I did, this was the easiest place to slip in."

Looking around, Eirian realized they had crossed into flatter land. Instead of rocky hills covered in green, she viewed an expanse of rolling green fields broken only by the odd patch where crops grew. In the distance, the shadowy form of more hills broke the horizon. Eirian wondered how long it would be before she caught her first glimpse of the Fingers. Turning to Marcellus and his companions, she waited for him to speak.

"I hope His Highness has a swift journey. We need his father's help."

"Indeed, we do. They'll ride as fast as they can," Eirian said awkwardly.

Nodding slowly, Marcellus sighed. "I know they will."

Eirian looked at Halcyon's neck. "You want me to join you."

"It would make everyone more comfortable if we could see you. Besides, wouldn't you rather be where the reports are coming to?" Playing on Eirian's need for information, Marcellus looked to Aiden for support.

Aiden shrugged, saying, "While Your Majesty is safer here, there are benefits to being with the commanders of your army."

Conceding to his suggestion, Eirian reached back and ran a hand along her bow to ensure her sword was not interfering with it. Her action received a smile from many of her guards.

"We should get a move on to catch up with the front of the line," Aiden prompted.

Chuckling in agreement, Marcellus signaled for his men to turn and waited for Eirian to join him. "It won't be that bad."

"I know, and I'm sorry you feel you need to make such reassurances," Eirian replied.

Soldiers glanced at the riders as they went past, barely registering that it was their queen. Eirian did not stand out from her guards, her armor helping her blend in and affording her anonymity. Aiden had admitted he appreciated her being a challenging target to spot. They suspected any Athnaralan spies would look for a woman in a dress and not one who looked like another soldier. The horses slowed, and Eirian tightened her grip on Halcyon's reins.

"Honestly, I don't know how we could be a bigger target!" she declared.

Flapping in the breeze above them, flags bearing the Endaran crest were the least of what Eirian took issue with. She was not the only one.

Aiden's mouth twisted. "I hope you're okay with your ladies being mistaken for you."

"You're paranoid," Marcellus said disapprovingly.

"You know exactly what we mean, Marcellus. I think any pretense that this is a casual tour of the kingdom has vanished. We're likely to see a battle within days."

Eirian ground her teeth and glanced around for Everett. Guessing who she was looking for, Marcellus waved over his shoulder.

"I think he's somewhere near the back of the line."

Uncomfortable about how obvious they were, Eirian rechecked her weapons and noticed many of her guards were doing the same.

"Everett's a grown man and capable of keeping himself safe. If not, he has a lot of guards to do it for him."

Eyeing her in amusement, Merle signaled to his squad. The five men understood what he was directing them to do.

Merle said to Aiden, "We'll keep to the outer line. Fionn can take the other side."

"Gabe and I will remain with Her Majesty." Aiden nodded, and when Eirian chuckled, he asked, "Is something amusing?"

"No, nothing at all," she replied.

Eirian watched the two squads of guards split off from the group and smiled in amusement. Grunting, Aiden's eyes narrowed, and he looked at the guards surrounding the nobles, his mind constantly assessing the situation.

He told her, "Try to stay close to the outside and the back. Any potential attackers should overlook you."

"Do you think there is a risk?" Marcellus scoffed. "They wouldn't be able to hide their approach."

"A single accurate shot could take out Her Majesty and plunge us into chaos."

"He's right. It's not like they'd have to cover much of an area. There is only one road we could take to get to where we're going," Eirian said.

Negotiating her way through the lines, Brenna glared at Aiden until he gave her space to come up beside Halcyon. Eirian tried not to laugh at the frustrated look on his face.

Brenna demanded, "Where have you been, Your Majesty?"

"I've been boosting the morale of my troops."

"Really?"

"No, I was taking some time to clear my head," Eirian admitted, glancing east.

"She said goodbye to her prince." Smiling at Brenna, Marcellus waved to someone a short distance away.

"Honestly, the two of you!" Brenna muttered, "One day, they're going to tell stories making fun of your love."

"I'll be glad to provide future generations with some amusement."

Eirian slumped in her saddle and contemplated the reality of being around to see those future generations. Looking at Brenna and Marcellus, she felt deep sorrow. The prospect of seeing their descendants live and die made her hope she would not see the other side of the confrontation with the darkness. Grief must have shown on her face, because Brenna reached out and touched her arm.

"I'm sure everything will work out if you have a little faith."

She could not correct the assumption. "Thank you, Brenna. I'm full of worries and fears, and I wish you and Isabella weren't here. If something happens to you."

"We won't be anywhere near a battlefield, and neither will you!" Shooting a look at Marcellus, Brenna informed her, "First sign of conflict, we're running."

"I can't abandon my people."

Sighing, Brenna shook her head disapprovingly. "You're the queen. No one will think any worse of you for retreating to safety."

Putting a hand to the hilt of one of her swords, Eirian partially drew it free. The steel of the blade flashed in the sunlight, and Aiden snorted.

Eirian said, "I have more experience in combat than most of the soldiers behind us."

"It's not a matter of experience. It's a matter of keeping you alive. Dead in a ditch is of no use to Endara. You forget you're more than a sword. You're a symbol. If Athnaral was to win, you become the shining light of hope to inspire Endarans to fight back." Taking a deep breath, Brenna ignored the looks on the faces of those around her. "Stop being a stubborn man and do what is best for your kingdom."

"She has a point," Aiden muttered, shrugging at Eirian's scornful look.

Rubbing her thumb over the engravings worked into the hilt, Eirian replied, "I understand what you're saying."

"It just wouldn't be you to do it." Marcellus chuckled, "Which we appreciate."

Meeting Gabe's gaze, Eirian waved at the line of riders ahead of them. "I wouldn't mind knowing the latest reports."

Gabe nodded. "I'll find out for you."

Watching him go, Brenna huffed, "I don't understand how you can be so easy around him. Sometimes he makes my skin crawl."

"He makes your skin crawl, yet you enjoy my company?" Laughing, Eirian did not hide her amusement.

Aiden interrupted the argument before it began, asking, "Are we planning on losing those before we reach Kelsby?"

He pointed at the flags, and Eirian scowled. She let go of her sword to pat Halcyon. Thankful for Aiden's quick intervention, Marcellus smiled at Brenna.

"I imagine so. They're a bit of a nuisance," Eirian answered.

"They're part of the illusion," Marcellus commented. "An illusion you suggested. Just to remind you that this entire journey was your idea."

"The illusion is moot when we can't be sure we'll make it to the garrison before the Athnaralan legion." Aiden shifted in his saddle to look around. "Kelsby may be under siege when we get there."

Not bothering to contribute to the conversation, Eirian watched the constant shift of the nobles. She sensed the daoine, but a glance at the sky told her Saoirse was not circling above them. Letting their magic linger in her mind, Eirian decided she was thankful for their presence. It meant that she was not alone. Remembering her reluctance, she chuckled and questioned when she had warmed up to them.

"What are you thinking about?" Brenna asked, smiling faintly at the obvious amusement on her face.

"Oddly enough, I'm thinking about the Telmians."

Aiden replied, "Lord Tharen has been a helpful teacher. Don't you feel it's remiss of Riane not to teach you the things he has been?"

Eirian frowned. The question she asked daily lingered unspoken on her tongue. She did not know how much difference her duine blood made to what she could do.

"I think Riane has grown complacent over the years."

"Maybe the high council needs Telmia to give them a wake-up call."

"You may be right. I hope when this war with the darkness comes, the neglect that Riane has gone through will not cost us," Eirian said grimly.

Marcellus looked over at the nobles in front of them. "Most of them claim it's nonsense, and I'm not sure I believe in this darkness. Yet you do, and Llewellyn and Everett believe you. How do we fight against a shadow threat that we don't understand?"

"Clearly with magic. Otherwise, why would it be so important that I be there to fight it? The Telmians don't talk about great armies, just a mage with Altira blood." Eirian was pensive, turning her gaze to the sky.

Brenna shook her head. "I think we should focus on the enemy at hand."

Spotting Gabe, Aiden said, "I think we can oblige you there, Your Grace.

Gabe is on his way back."

"Excellent. He should have something to report," Marcellus said.

Eirian located him and followed his track through the other riders. "Back already, Gabe?"

Saluting her, Gabe informed them, "Scout reports are coming and going rather often. Athnaral has not changed direction. They're still going straight to Kelsby."

Eyes narrowing in suspicion, Aiden asked, "There is more, isn't there?"

"A messenger from the south caught up with the convoy. There are reports of legions along the border."

"Any word where the elves are?" Eirian questioned.

"Nothing new." Gabe shook his head.

Cursing, Marcellus slapped a hand against his leg in frustration. "Aeyren is planning to spread us out and cull our numbers."

"Paienven is already in Endara with his army," Eirian pointed out. "However, I think you're right. Aeyren wants us to spread out."

Feeling out of her depth, Brenna waved at Eirian. "Have any of the scouts reported where King Aeyren is?"

"What?" Frowning, Marcellus cocked his head to the side.

"Well, if I was Aeyren and serious about taking over Endara, I'd aim to be with the part of my army closest to the enemy queen."

Eirian agreed, "You can't fault that logic. He offered marriage as a peaceful solution. Perhaps we could still negotiate peace. Surely Aeyren doesn't want to condemn thousands to death for a war that his kingdom has never won."

Angry, Marcellus glared at her. "The time for peaceful solutions has passed. They've crossed the border to march on one of your towns."

"I understand, Your Grace. Believe me, I do. However, I'd be remiss if I didn't try for peace and buy us more time. Avoiding war is my priority."

"Would you back down on your earlier decision and marry him?"

She shook her head. "No, I wouldn't, because it wouldn't bring peace. Paienven would invade instead, and he wouldn't put me back on the throne. He'd have a nice little cage someplace to keep me."

Aiden cleared his throat. "He wouldn't kill you, but Aeyren might if he captured you."

Thoughtful, Eirian glanced at Gabe. She met his stony gaze and saw the question he was thinking.

Putting it into words, Eirian said, "We need to find out where the King of Athnaral is. There is no point speculating with no facts to back it up."

"Speculation is how we prepare. What do you think strategies are? I thought you spent a lot of time studying them in Riane?" Aiden replied.

Marcellus nodded in agreement. "Aiden is right. We have to speculate. But tell me, what does your gut say?"

Eirian leaned forward with her wrists resting on the pommel and peered at the sky to take a gauge of the sun's movements. She pondered his question.

"For all it's worth, my gut agrees with Brenna. I'd want to engage directly with the leader of my enemy. He'd know of my relationship with Celiaen," Eirian finally answered. "What better way to force Ensaycal to back down than to have me as a hostage. Celiaen wouldn't risk my death."

"Paienven is unlikely to care about what his son feels for you," Marcellus said.

The response made Eirian glance at Aiden, her hard stare warning him to remain silent about his knowledge. His cheek twitched, the only sign of his anger.

"We can't know what Paienven would do for his son."

"If Aeyren had you as his hostage, do you think it would inspire Riane to action?" Brenna asked.

Gabe spoke up, his voice emotionless, "If she was a hostage, I'd deal with the situation."

They looked at him, and Eirian smiled. "I know you would, Gabe. None of them would see you coming."

Pale with shock, Brenna said, "Are you saying you'd kill your queen if they took her hostage?"

"No, I wouldn't need to. Just a few of those around her, and once she had a weapon or two in her hands, she'd help me finish them. Then we'd stroll on out of there." Gabe smiled coldly. "It would be good fun."

Marcellus muttered, "The terrifying part is I suspect Her Majesty thinks it would be good fun as well."

Eirian cackled, "You know me so well."

EIGHT

Cameron stared at the lines of Athnaralan troops. The men lined up neatly as they stood a distance from the town. It was not the view they expected to see. They had prepared themselves to face Kelsby under siege. Or occupied.

Eirian glanced at Cameron nervously. "Why are they sitting there?"

"It appears they're waiting, Your Majesty," he answered.

Looking over her shoulder, Eirian hoped Brenna and the others were safely away. "Dare we approach the town?"

"That might be what they're waiting for. You should think about retreating." Thinly lipped, Cameron shook his head and looked at Marcellus. "Don't you agree?"

"Her Majesty will do what is needed," Marcellus replied.

Closing her eyes, Eirian released her magic and let it spread across the land. Other than the daoine, she sensed no other mages, and she felt relief. It was short-lived, tempered by the feeling of shadows chasing along the edge of her power. Opening her eyes, Eirian shook her head at Cameron, choosing to only tell him what she knew for sure.

"I can't feel any mages with them."

He looked relieved by the information. "Well, at least we have a minor advantage."

Shifting in the saddle, Eirian looked at her soldiers. The smaller numbers were more apparent now that she had seen the Athnaralan legion they faced.

"Should we send out a white flag? Perhaps they're waiting for us to open communication."

"We should," Marcellus said.

Cameron commented, "We have nothing to lose. If we can open negotiations with them, it might buy us time for more troops to arrive."

Letting Cameron make the arrangements, Eirian resumed studying the army. "Please tell me Kelsby completed their evacuation?"

Marcellus nodded gravely. "Everyone who isn't necessary for the defense of the town has left."

"Good. We don't need innocent deaths here."

Turning Halcyon, Eirian pushed him back through the lines, her guards surrounding her. Aiden was at her side, a spot he rarely left.

"What are you thinking?"

"If we must engage, I plan to be with the archers for as long as possible."

"You don't want to wait here?" Aiden shared a look with Merle.

Shaking her head, Eirian pointed to where she saw the lines of archers waiting. "I'll come back, but right now, I can't sit and wait."

The group made their way to the archers, bringing their horses up behind the line. Several soldiers looked at them, anxious faces staring as Eirian sat on her horse, assessing their position. Frowning at the sky, Fox licked a finger and held it up, shaking his head.

"Wind isn't in our favor. Don't suppose you have a trick up your sleeve for that?" He nodded at the lines. "One that will work for all of us."

Eirian shook her head. "I don't, but the Telmians might."

Approaching, a woman saluted and asked, "Can I help you, Your Majesty?"

"Are you the captain?" Aiden looked her over.

She replied, "Captain Olivia. I know who you are, Captain Aiden of the Queen's Guard."

Smiling, Eirian turned her mount to show her bow. "I'm here to familiarize myself with the location so I can be of use."

Olivia dropped her gaze to the bow before looking back up at Eirian. Other archers watched on in silence.

"I won't have time to look after anyone. Especially not well-meaning royalty who think they can kill an armored man over two hundred yards because they can hit a target."

"Two hundred yards with a moving target is easy. I expected a bigger distance. I could show you, but we're in a precarious situation, so you'll have to take my word. Don't worry, I won't be endangering your company," Eirian informed Olivia.

"I've seen her drop an enemy in a forest without sighting him, thanks to her powers. You don't have to worry about us getting in your way," Aiden said.

Winking, Eirian grinned. "It's okay, Captain. I understand your concern. We'll stay out of your way, and you can pretend we're not here. My safety is their job."

"If you and any other archers among your guard aren't holding up, you will get out of my line," Olivia stated.

"You have my word."

Turning on her heel, Olivia returned to her position and ignored the following eyes. Eirian pulled an arrow from her quiver and handed it to a runner at the wagons behind them. Holding it up, the young man nodded and tapped it against a barrel before handing it back. Satisfied, she turned to her guards and inclined her head in the direction they had come. As the horses picked their way along, Merle gave Eirian a puzzled look.

"Why did you give one of your arrows to the boy?"

Eirian stroked her bow gently and explained, "I use a recurve. It takes slightly lighter arrows, so I needed to be sure there were more available."

"I've always wondered why you don't use a long like the rest of us," Fox said, eyeing her bow.

Snorting, Aiden commented, "Because she can't use a long from the back of a horse like she can the bow she has."

"Pretty much. Recurves are easier to use in close combat. You should see what some of the best red archers can do. They're amazing." Leaning forward in the saddle, Eirian peered at the cluster of nobles and sighed.

"I don't like this," Aiden muttered.

"You and me both. Something is wrong with this. I feel a shadow."

He grabbed her reins and pulled Halcyon to a halt. "Then let me get you to safety, Eirian."

Gazing at him sadly, Eirian shook her head. "I can't yet, Aiden, but I'll go with you when the time comes."

The screech of the massive eagle that was Saoirse drew their stares to the sky to watch the circling form.

Aiden informed her, "I'll hold you to that, else I'll force you from the field. You can't turn the tide."

"I hope the Athnaralans don't realize what she is," Eirian murmured.

"She knows what she's doing." Merle frowned at the circling bird.

Spotting Everett waving at her, Eirian sighed. Halcyon sensed her reluctance and tossed his head, tugging at his bit as though he agreed with Aiden that she should leave. Scattered over the sky, white clouds lingered like an audience, casting the occasional shadow as they drifted between the land and the sun. There was a dryness to the air, and licking her lips, she felt the cracked skin sting a little.

Dropping a hand to the hilt of her swords, Eirian rubbed her thumb over the engravings and wondered where Celiaen and his party were, how much ground they had covered. She missed him far more than she would admit out loud. Shaking her head, she reminded herself not to think of him when she was staring at the enemy that wanted to take her kingdom from her. Thinking of

Celiaen would not help.

"He's waiting for you. It might be important." Aiden nodded at Everett.

She replied, "I know. By the powers, Aiden, I dread what this day will bring us."

Gathering her nerves, Eirian glanced at the two rings she wore and forced herself to square her shoulders, nudging Halcyon forward. Reserved, Aiden stared at the back of her head before he followed.

"Don't we all."

"Good call trying to open the lines of communication." Everett skipped the greetings and asked, "What were you up to?"

"Surveying the archers. I thought it would allow me to satisfy my need to help in battle but also allow me an easier route to get away." Smiling tensely, Eirian turned to Cameron.

He nodded at the waiting lines of soldiers. "Nothing yet, ma'am."

"I hate this."

"You're not alone, Eirian. None of us wants to be here." Running a hand through his hair, Everett shook his head sadly.

"Hopefully, the fact they haven't attacked Kelsby upon arrival is a sign they'll negotiate. Surely if they were invading, they'd have wiped them out before we arrived?"

They stared at Eirian's hopeful expression. Feeling the Telmians, she turned to look for them. She spotted Faolan and Tharen riding toward her, with the rest of their party remaining a distance away. Eyes wide, she took in their armor, and her eyes dropped to their swords. It was the first time anyone had seen them dressed for a fight. Joining her, they looked past the Endarans and frowned at the Athnaralan lines. Everyone was silent, staring at them.

"There's something off," Faolan spoke, glancing at Eirian. "Can you feel it?"

"It's an uncomfortable itch," she replied, nodding. "Shadows lingering in the corners of my mind."

Marcellus cocked his head and asked, "I thought you said they didn't have any mages?"

Tharen scowled. "They don't."

"Then what do you feel that the rest of us can't?" Cameron looked between them. "If it's not enemy mages, then what?"

Staring at Eirian, Aiden remembered the hunt. "Can you read the land?"

The Telmians looked at her, and Eirian replied, "I have, but I don't know what I'm looking for. Honestly, I thought this off feeling was because of the emotions broadcast by the two thousand people surrounding me. What else could it be?"

"It's been many years since we experienced this, but there is a familiarity to it that makes me worry." Looking up at his sister, Faolan's eyes narrowed.

"I'm worried about her." Flicking her hand, Eirian did not follow his stare.

Dropping his gaze, Faolan regarded her, and his horse stomped a hoof impatiently. "She knows what she's doing."

Staring back at Faolan blankly, Eirian blinked slowly, drawing a deep breath. He was not the only one who felt a familiarity with the situation. She wanted to deny the shadows and the whisper of memories pulling at her mind.

"I'm sure she does, probably better than the rest of us," Eirian said. "That doesn't mean I can't worry about her."

"Well, if things go badly, at least she can get away the easiest," Gabe chuckled, sharing a look with Merle.

"If things go badly, Saoirse has her instructions," Tharen replied coldly.

Waving at the other Telmians, Everett asked Faolan, "Where do you intend to put your legendary skills to use?"

"We'll be wherever your queen is. King Neriwyn sent us to protect her, and that is exactly what we will be doing."

"Good. Between your lot and Aiden, she'll find it hard to argue when it's time to go."

Before Eirian could respond, shouts from the front of the line drew their attention. The messengers were riding back, the white flag fluttering above their heads. Their progress across the field was swift. She felt like her heart would beat its way out of her chest. Dread filled her, nausea lingering as she swallowed nervously. Separating their ranks to let the messengers through, the cavalry and nobles watched the Athnaralans.

"Well?" Cameron demanded.

Taking a deep breath, the officer saluted Eirian first. "They were waiting for us to arrive and want to meet with Your Majesty."

"That's good news." Frowning, Eirian glanced at Cameron and asked, "Could we use those orders against them? Could we delay the meeting for as long as possible to give our reinforcements more time to arrive?"

"We can't. They have orders to attack if we do not hold a meeting on the day we arrive," the officer replied.

Faces fell in frustration, telling Eirian she was not the only one who had thought to delay. Crossing her arms over her saddle's pommel, she leaned forward and nodded at Faolan. He understood what she was communicating and looked at Tharen, inclining his head back to their party. The two lords left to prepare their people for the task ahead. Turning her gaze to Cameron and Marcellus next, Eirian pursed her lips.

Everett realized what she was communicating and declared, "I'm coming with you."

"No, Your Grace, you're not, and that is an order." Eirian looked at him and said, "They want to meet with the Queen of Endara, but only a fool would let them get close to both the Queen and the Prince."

Beside him, Gunter muttered, "She's right. You can't go out there."

"But you'll take the daoine with you?" Everett argued.

"Yes, because they make an impression. I'm using them as a reminder that we have formidable allies. We can hope they're an effective deterrent." Eirian returned her focus to the messenger. "How much time do we have?"

"They're waiting to see you set foot out there, and then they'll meet us in the middle. If you haven't approached by nightfall, they will attack."

Signaling to some of his aides, Cameron began preparing. "No time like the present."

"Indeed, let's get on with this," Marcellus agreed.

Turning Halcyon to the party of daoine, Eirian led her guards over to them. Marcellus and the nobles he had selected joined soon after, followed by Cameron and his aides. The officer was among the group, still carrying the white flag. Looking at the gathered party, Eirian took in the array of weapons and breathed deeply, tightening the grip on her magic. Meeting Tharen's concerned gaze, she chewed on her bottom lip and watched understanding flicker through his eyes.

Eirian did not argue when they surrounded her, letting the officer lead the way. The tension rose when a group of riders left the other force. Bringing their horses to a halt in the middle of the field, they waited for the enemy party to reach them. With Marcellus and Cameron to one side, and Faolan and Tharen on the other, Eirian sat upright in her saddle, hands nestled together on the pommel. She watched the approach of the people who would decide if they would be at war.

The dozens of guards, Telmians, and officers spread out around them like a comforting blanket. But it was Aiden and Merle at her back that reassured Eirian, the cold calm of Gabe that gave her confidence. The Athnaralan party stopped a few feet away, and a broad, heavily armed older man pushed his horse to the front of the group. His scornful gaze swept over the Endarans before coming to rest on Eirian, a sneer turning the corner of his mouth.

"I suppose you're the woman who thinks she's the queen of Endara." He let his gaze travel over her and scoffed, "You don't look like a queen."

Eyes narrowing, Eirian mirrored his action and let her gaze drift over him. "Appearances are frequently disappointing. I am Eirian Altira, Queen of Endara. You are?"

"General Tomas," Cameron greeted the other man coldly.

He smiled, and Eirian felt like someone had dunked her in icy cold water. She heard mutters from others.

Tomas sneered in disgust. "Still going, old man? I'm not surprised a woman doesn't know when to replace the old and useless."

"What I want to know, General, is why you've invaded my lands? Our kingdoms have maintained peace for many years now, and it has served profitably," Eirian said.

There was something about Tomas that made her want to drive a blade straight into his throat, and it was taking more effort than Eirian expected to suppress the urge.

"We're here to liberate Endara from your unlawful rule."

Lifting her left hand to rub her chin, Eirian smiled as his gaze dropped to the two rings she wore. They were precisely what she had intended for him to notice.

"What upsets you more? That I'm a woman or that I'm a mage? Athnaralan laws do not apply to Endara; therefore, there is nothing unlawful about my rule."

He nodded at the two lords beside her and asked mockingly, "Are these supposed to be your Telmian friends?"

Watching a predatory smile form on Faolan's lips, Eirian bit back a chuckle.

Faolan replied, "Yes, I suppose we are. I'm Lord Faolan, Telmian envoy to Endara."

"I see none of your elven masters here. Have they abandoned you already?" Dismissing Faolan, Tomas returned his stare to Eirian.

"I have no masters, only servants. Now, if you could please get on with telling me why you're in my kingdom."

His sneer returned, and Tomas said, "Women should not rule! Only weak men would let a woman overstep boundaries."

Fluttering her eyes at him, Eirian replied sardonically, "And yet the grand mage is a woman, and she rules over all of us. I don't see Athnaral invading Riane to tell them it's unlawful for a woman to rule. You've had ample time to do so. She's been the grand mage for several hundred years, after all."

"The mages will get what is coming for them."

"Will they?" Eirian purred. "I beg to differ."

Her magic surrounded her, a crackling cloud of sensation giving away her anger, though her smile remained. None of the Endarans flinched. They had become accustomed to her displays. Watching the Athnaralans shift nervously at the overwhelming feeling of her power, Marcellus could not resist his desire to grin.

Marcellus told her, "I think we're wasting our time here. Once again, Athnaral is overstepping its boundaries."

"I agree."

Tomas glared at Eirian, tilting his head back and dropping a hand to the hilt of his sword. "I have a message from my king. And a gift."

"Well then, get on with it." Eirian arched a brow impatiently.

"He wants you to know his original offer is still available. Marry him, unite Endara with Athnaral as it should be, and he'll protect you from the interference of Ensaycal. Refuse, and we'll take Endara. If you refuse, he cannot guarantee your safety." Leering at her despite the magic surrounding them, Tomas chuckled.

Eirian did not spare it a thought, and before he finished laughing, she answered, "No."

"Think about your people."

"Believe me, I am. That is all I think about. But I will not marry King Aeyren."

Frowning, Tomas held up a hand and signaled for one of his men to ride forward. There was a box balanced on his saddle.

"Take this gift. Open it when you're back with your nobles. Hopefully, it will give you some perspective of what to expect should you not do the wise thing and accept my king's most generous offer."

Watching one of Cameron's officers accept the box, Eirian turned back to Tomas, the desire to kill him making her hand itch for the feel of a blade in it.

"There is nothing that will make me change my mind. Endara is, and always will be, independent."

"Don't fool yourself thinking you have the stomach for war. You're a woman. I think you'll change your tune soon enough."

"No, General, it is you who is fooling himself. You don't know what I'm capable of, and I suggest you beg the powers you never find out."

A coldness to her tone made Tomas shift, showing the first sign of uncertainty. Her magic carried the whisper of her threat and the promise of a painful death.

"We're done here."

"You dare dismiss me?" The moment he spoke, Tomas knew he would regret it.

Eirian's fury filled the air. Bow in her hands, she had an arrow nocked and drawn before anyone registered her actions. The rage accompanying the move was different to the cold threat her magic had carried moments before.

"Give me a good reason not to kill you! I am the queen of Endara!" Eirian spat at him. "You're nothing but an invader in my lands. Killing you wouldn't make me pause, just another dead man by my hand."

"Your Majesty," Cameron cautioned her.

"If I say we're done, we're done, so scurry back to your master like the rat you are!"

Lowering the bow, Eirian returned it and the arrow to their places before turning Halcyon around and kicking him into a canter. Not giving the Athnaralans a chance to respond, the Endaran party followed. She dismounted and tossed the reins to a startled Fionn when she was safely behind her soldiers. Pacing, she rubbed her arms and shook her head repeatedly, her magic a turbulent force surrounding her.

Remaining a distance away, the daoine watched in curiosity while her guards dismounted to wait cautiously. General Cameron also dismounted, signaling his aides to bring the box over and place it on the ground while observing Eirian. Those who had not been part of the meeting asked questions among themselves. Everyone was curious to know what had happened.

"That could have gone better," Marcellus grumbled.

Cameron disagreed, "No, that was as good as it was going to get. The moment I saw who it was... Aeyren must be here."

"What?" Eyes wide, Everett caught his words and halted in front of them. "What do you mean Aeyren must be here?"

"General Tomas is his most trusted general. He's rarely far from his king these days. Tomas served Aeyren's father and earned a reputation for being ruthless. I've seen his work, and I don't want to think about what he would do to Eirian if he got his hands on her. Ask Aiden what he knows when you get the chance."

Sharing a disturbed look, the two dukes glanced at the box wearily.

"I take it things were tense?" Everett asked.

Shrugging, Marcellus waved at Eirian. "Well, I don't see us avoiding this war. The options given were to marry their king, or they will invade."

"Marrying Aeyren won't avoid a war." Cameron nodded at Eirian as she stopped pacing and turned to the box.

Eirian stated, "Let's find out what the gift from our neighbors is."

Hovering at her side, Aiden reached out and stopped Eirian before she crouched in front of the box. "I don't think you should open it. Let someone else. General Tomas is cunning and spiteful. I wouldn't trust it."

Forming a half-circle around the box, Cameron and his aides nodded in agreement.

"Your captain is right, ma'am."

Signaling to an aide, Cameron watched the frustration cross her face as the man crouched behind the chest. Eirian waited for him to reach over and unlatch the lid, pulling it open quickly so they could see the contents. It took her a moment to register what she was seeing, the sound of a younger noble retching filling the ears of everyone within hearing. Taking a deep breath, Eirian stepped up to the chest and knelt, peering at the head of the ambassador who had attended her coronation.

No one spoke, eyes darting between Eirian and the chest as they waited for her to react. Approaching, Faolan stood a few steps away, with Gabe beside him, and watched. Closing her eyes, she took another deep breath and exhaled slowly before she pushed away from the ground and stood. Her magic surrounded her, and they felt the rage. Waving at the aide holding the lid open, Eirian stared at the Athnaralan troops.

"Show the man some respect. Bury the head," she instructed.

"Your Majesty?" Everett prompted.

"I told him he could return to Endara, and we'd provide him with safety." Her voice was bitter, and Everett flinched. "Ambassador Darrell was a good man."

Watching the aide shut the lid before another picked it up, Cameron said,

"Tomas would have tortured him."

"They'd hope the sight of his head would scare you and make you agree to their terms," Faolan spoke quietly.

"They betrayed him. Why else would they torture Darrell and present his head?"

Eirian continued to stare into the distance, not seeing her people's lines in front of her. Stepping closer, Everett reached out and grasped her arm.

"His death is not your fault. They want you to think you can't protect your people because you couldn't protect him."

Turning to look at Everett, Eirian's gaze dropped to the hand on her arm, and he let go, stepping back as though scolded. "Don't tell me what I already know. Darrell was a dead man the moment they chose him. Perhaps Aeyren suspected his wavering loyalties. We can assume his wife and children are dead. If they're lucky."

Everett realized he had not known the ambassador had a wife and children. "General, if we attack first, do you think the surprise will give us an advantage?"

Cameron screwed up his face and said, "It might if we assume they expect you to be distraught by their gift. However, they're still at least five thousand, and we're barely half that. I don't see how we can win this."

"You want me to buy time?" Eirian frowned with concern.

"Make them think you're considering the offer. We play on their assumption you're a delicate woman, and their gift has shaken you. You need time to recover from the shock while you reconcile what might be in everyone's best interest."

Everett looked at Marcellus. "It might work, but how much time would it buy us?"

"You're putting a lot of faith in my ability to pretend I'm shaken. They'll probably attack us anyway and attempt to capture me, thinking that once in their hands, we'll decide in their favor." She smiled wryly. "And if not, killing me will be easier."

Cocking his head to the side, Faolan regarded her thoughtfully. "You wanted to slit the general's throat. I felt how strong the urge was."

Eirian admitted, "From the moment he drew close, something about him... he was wrong."

"Was it just him?"

The Endarans stared at Faolan in confusion before looking at Eirian.

"Yes, it was. It took a lot of effort not to let that arrow fly."

Grunting, Faolan turned on his heel and strode back to his people, leaving Eirian perplexed.

Even more confused, Everett asked, "What happened?"

"Her Majesty threatened to kill Tomas. She aimed an arrow at his throat,"

Cameron explained. "It would have been far less than he deserves and struck a costly blow to Aeyren."

"Why would it be a costly blow to their king?" Eirian queried.

Marcellus inclined his head. "Of course, you probably didn't catch the revelation from the good general here. That man you want to kill is close to his king. So close, in fact, Cameron thinks Aeyren is with that legion."

Her eyes narrowed, a hand unconsciously reaching for a blade at her waist. "How long before our reinforcements arrive?"

"At least a week," one of Cameron's aides replied.

"We could end all of this with one blow. Kill Aeyren, and they're without a king. They'd need to retreat, establish who is in control. He has no sons and no brothers, all he has is a sister." Eirian smirked, looking at Everett.

Everett stared at her, horrified. "I see where your mind is going, and it's a bad idea."

"They have no mages, and it wouldn't be hard for me to get in there and find him."

"You want to assassinate the King of Athnaral and then propose I marry his sister?"

Exchanging looks with an aide, Cameron murmured, "That could be a viable option. I'm not sure how many options there are to inherit the throne, but they might see reason if we point out it will unite Endara and Athnaral."

"They want Endara under their rule, not the other way around!" Everett countered.

"Can I point out a flaw in this idea?" Gallagher spoke up from behind the dukes.

They turned to look at him, and Eirian nodded. "Go ahead."

"Ensaycal might not appreciate unification between Endara and Athnaral, regardless of who is in control. No matter which way it goes, we become a threat to them."

"You have a point," Eirian agreed. "The status quo needs to remain as it is to avoid an all-out war between humans and elves."

Rubbing his head, Everett gave Eirian a pained look. "But you suggested—"

"No, I didn't. You all jumped before I finished. You marry the sister, become King of Athnaral. Llewellyn becomes my heir. You reform Athnaral from within. Our family rules both kingdoms in peace with each other."

"They wouldn't agree to that."

"We don't have to tell them."

Waving over his shoulder at their enemy, Marcellus shook his head. "You're talking about assassinating a king."

"Yes, and?" She shrugged, not bothered by the idea, adding, "He tried to assassinate me."

"We're supposed to be the honorable ones!"

Eirian gave Marcellus a bemused smile, chuckling as she held her hands out. "While I appreciate the sentiment, Your Grace, I disagree. I've never considered myself a particularly honorable person. I've killed too many and not always cleanly. But I am practical."

"I can do it. You don't have to give me the order." Gabe moved to stand beside Aiden, adding, "If no one gives me the order, you can pretend that Endara had nothing to do with it."

"I'm sorry, Gabe, but I can't let you do it." Eirian smiled at him.

Dropping to a knee, Gabe saluted her and bowed his head. "You're my queen, you'll always be my queen, and my job is to protect you."

Aiden nudged Gabe's knee with his foot. "Get up."

"While I have no doubts over your abilities, Gabe, I think this task is above someone without magic." Reaching out, Eirian brushed her fingers over his hair. "If I thought otherwise, you know I'd let you."

Covering his face with his hand, Marcellus groaned, "Everett, can't you make her see sense? We're openly discussing killing the King of Athnaral!"

Everett stared at Eirian before answering, "Yes, we are."

"And you don't see the problem with this?"

"I'm not completely sure, to be honest." Shaking his head, Everett stared at Eirian.

"I need you to trust me," Eirian said.

"General, send a messenger to the Athnaralans and tell them the Queen is in shock over her gift and needs the night to recover and weigh her options," Everett instructed.

Glancing between them, Cameron shrugged. "I don't know what is going on, but I agree with that messenger. Consider it done."

Eirian walked to her horse and took the reins from Fionn. "I need to think."

Unwilling to argue, they let Eirian mount Halcyon, guards surrounding her. Her gaze swept over the Telmians before she turned toward the back of the Endaran lines and nudged Halcyon into a canter. She did not slow until they were past the soldiers, easing to a walk once clear. Glancing sideways at Aiden, she waited for him to speak, knowing he would demand answers to the questions clearly on his mind.

"What was that back there?" Aiden asked softly, not looking at her.

"A diversion. Tell me, do you trust everyone back there?"

"No, I don't. Are you suggesting one of them might be a spy?"

Shrugging, Eirian sighed. "I don't know. Do you trust me?"

"Why are you asking me that?"

"Because a moment will come that I need you to trust me and do what I tell you, even though all your instincts will tell you not to."

Aiden pulled his horse to a halt, his men stopping in surprise as Eirian turned Halcyon to face him. "You can't expect me to agree."

"Yes, I can, and you'll do it. You'll do it because, you know, deep down,

I wouldn't be asking if it wasn't necessary. I'm asking because it would devastate me to kill any of you, and I can't guarantee you'd be safe from me. I'm asking because someone will need to pick up the pieces." Rubbing her chin, Eirian regarded him sadly and said, "I'm asking because you swore you'd protect me."

"What's going to happen?"

"I can't tell you what tomorrow will bring. Perhaps only the gods know. But by the powers, I'll do what I must. I only hope you don't hate me. Remember, where I can give life, I can take it."

Fionn stared at her and said, "You have some wild plan in your mind that you don't know will work, but you won't tell anyone."

"With every passing day, I find reasons I shouldn't have accepted the crown."

"You're our queen. We serve you," Paxton commented. "Whatever you do."

"I'm not worthy of your loyalty. So please, believe me when I say you'll know when the time comes, and I ask you to trust me."

She regarded each man, meeting their eyes. One by one, they dropped their gazes.

Aiden said, "You know more than you're letting on."

She saved him for last and smiled wryly. "Always. I have suspicions at the back of my mind. An accumulation of snippets of information has led me here. A realization that some secrets can't stay buried forever. The truth will out."

"You fear you might turn on us in battle?"

"It has crossed my mind, but I remind myself I've never turned on an ally in a fight. Then again, this is different. Promise me this, and I'll promise I'll follow your commands when it is over. For as long as I'm the queen."

His eyes narrowed suspiciously, and Aiden said, "That feels like an empty promise. As though you don't expect to be queen when it's over."

"You have nothing to lose in making this promise," she countered.

"I disagree. I could lose everything that matters to me."

Going for a different route, Eirian nodded. "I understand. Can you promise me when the time comes and I ask you for this favor, you'll look me in the eye and decide then if you trust me? I'll trust you to make the right judgment."

"One day, you'll spill all of those secrets you keep. That will be the price you pay for this." Sighing, Aiden ran a hand through his hair and looked at his men. "Let's get back."

NINE

Flames danced, sparks drifting into the air as the logs collapsed in on themselves. It was a fascinating swirl of colors, and the longer Eirian stared into it, the more mesmerizing it was. Her thoughts faded as she focused on the fire, letting the crackle fill her ears and drown out the nearby nervous chatter. They were close enough to the Roof that the nights were chill, even though summer had months left. She welcomed it as another distraction from the thousands of enemy troops a stone's throw away.

"You should try to sleep."

Aiden stared at her from the other side of the fire, his face shadowed in the darkness. Turning her gaze upward, Eirian took in how many stars there were in the sky. They called to her, summoning a distant longing from the depths of her memories.

"Even if I try, I doubt it would happen. I've gone longer without sleep, don't worry about me," Eirian replied.

"We don't know how long Athnaral will give us for you to recover from your shock before deciding on their offer. You need rest."

Smiling faintly, Eirian glanced to either side and noticed some of her guards had settled back and drifted off. She almost envied them.

"They expect to see me by mid-morning. I'll do what I can to buy time."

Grunting, Aiden stretched his legs out as he watched her through the dancing flames. He sat in silence, and Eirian returned to staring at the stars.

"You could bend the truth a little. Tell them you can't marry Aeyren because you're married already," he suggested.

"How is that bending the truth?"

"The Telmians said your bond is marriage. Just don't tell them it's with the elf. Be vague. Imply someone unoffensive to the Athnaralans."

Eirian shook her head, chuckling, "I don't think that'd work. No matter what decision I make, there'll be a war."

"Even if you had refused the throne and let Everett become king?" Aiden asked, and there was something in his voice that made her frown.

"I believe so. Something is driving them to destroy years of peace."

A niggling at the back of her mind told Eirian she had forgotten something, and she gazed into the flames. Aiden crossed his arms and cocked his head to the side, watching her.

"What do you mean?"

"I don't know. It feels like there is something out of reach, a shadow. I mean, I've always felt it, but it's getting worse."

"You think it involves the darkness the daoine speak of?"

"I half think the darkness is all the bad things we're capable of. I mean, short of it being a god, what could be so powerful it takes alliances of magic to overcome?"

"But the gods abandoned us. That's what they teach. We don't even know their names," Merle grumbled from where he had been dozing next to her. "We're on the brink of war, and you're going to theorize if the gods left? Do we look like mages to you? What would we know of the gods? We're guards."

"No, that wasn't my intention." Eirian looked at him in amusement.

Merle arched a brow, rolling his eyes. "That's not how it sounded to me."

"I was throwing ideas out there."

"Maybe the gods have problems of their own." On the other side of Merle, Gabe muttered, "Things aren't always as they seem."

Shuffling footsteps alerted them to the approach of another, and Everett joined the circle around the fire, sitting next to Aiden. Peering at Eirian, he nodded and covered his mouth as he yawned. Giving him an amused look, Aiden glanced at her and saw the curious way she stared. She looked like she wanted to say something, and Aiden wondered if she had caught on. He had considered telling her so many times to prompt her to remember him.

"Can't sleep either?" Everett ignored the way her gaze flickered between them.

"I haven't tried. I'm too agitated."

Merle shuffled around, sitting and rolling his shoulders, giving up on the sleep he wanted. Next to him, Gabe grunted and moved, remaining quiet and watchful.

"You owe us a story about a broken leg, and now is a good time," Merle stated.

"What?" Everett asked in confusion.

Eirian laughed, "I suppose I do. It'll keep us amused for a time."

"Yes, it will."

Stretching her arms into the air, Eirian crossed her legs and leaned forward into the heat of the fire. She glanced at Merle.

"Are you sure you want that story? I have many."

"Absolutely. I need to know what led to your leg getting broken," Aiden said.

Waving his hands about, Everett hushed them to ask, "What are you talking about?"

"If you shut up and listen to the story, you'll know as much as they do." Chuckling, Eirian smiled at his flustered look.

Aiden told him, "She has a point."

Scratching her head, Eirian pulled a face as she thought about where to start. "So, as you learned last time, as novices, we enjoyed a rather vast range of learning experiences."

"Yeah, that's an understatement," Merle chuckled.

"Shush you," she scolded. "This happened when I was fourteen. They sent those of us showing an inclination to the red into a forest for a few days. They gave us a bow, a quiver with six arrows, and a knife. The last one back to Riane was the winner."

"Wait, you had to hunt each other?" Aiden leaned forward and stared at Eirian in horror. "For what purpose?"

"No quarry is as devious as a person who knows they're being hunted. We aren't to kill each other. The arrows had little bags of colored powder that burst on impact and stained everything. The knives were dull. Masters surrounded the forest and supervised the entire time."

Everett looked mortified. "Are you serious?"

"You should've heard the story about the goat." Merle laughed.

Eirian crinkled her nose in amusement, enjoying the laughter of those listening.

"Goat?"

"Oh yeah, she attended a goat giving birth."

"Stop teasing him, Merle. I'm sure Everett can tell you stories about me as a little girl that would be just as amusing," Eirian pointed out.

Everett continued to stare at her in shock.

"Anyway. I've always enjoyed climbing, and I had spent a lot of time in those woods. Enough to know convenient hiding spots for someone lying in wait."

"That's true. You were always a climber," Everett said in agreement.

Nodding, Eirian grinned. "As usual, you'd say I was a little too confident."

"You slipped and fell out of the tree?" Aiden looked disappointed. "That's it?"

"Oh, no, no, I wish! No, I climbed up and disturbed a snake."

Those listening laughed.

"Hey, I bet all of you would panic as well if you were merrily climbing a tree only to put your hand on a snake."

Gabe chuckled, "I can't say I blame you for disliking snakes."

"I like snakes, fascinating creatures."

Curious about how her leg came into the story, Everett said, "So, what happened?"

"I put my hand on the snake, not realizing it was there. It moved. I panicked and let go of the branch, falling to the ground. On my way, I caught my leg and landed on it awkwardly, breaking it below the knee."

There were groans around the fire.

"Thankfully, the snake didn't follow because that would've been the final straw. I mean, laying on the ground at the base of a tree with a broken leg and the bone sticking out was enough for me. Landing on my bow was an added insult. They had to pick fragments out of my back."

"That would've been a serious break. How did you get help?" Aiden chuckled at the look on Everett's face.

She arched her brows in amusement. "Magic."

"No, really."

"I'm serious! I used magic. It's easy enough to alert other mages when we need help."

Everett shook his head. "Why, by the powers, would the high council put the heir of a kingdom in danger like that?"

"In Riane, you constantly battle to prove that you're better, stronger, more capable than your peers. The archmages and the masters encourage it. Nearly every mage aspires to earn the title of master," Eirian replied.

There was a note of disdain in her voice, and Aiden pursed his lips, regarding her curiously. "Except you?"

"I knew I'd be a queen one day. Or perhaps it was because I was born with so much power that the competition was unfair. I was a princess, and often I felt the need to do better than everyone else."

"You worked harder to prove yourself," Merle commented.

"Yes. Sometimes I'd hear them whispering I didn't deserve my power. It's unfair that I'm so powerful and destined to rule a kingdom. I suppose they're right, but things are rarely what they seem, and nothing is ever fair." Bitter, Eirian shrugged and looked at her hands, watching how the dancing fire cast shadows over them.

Considering her words, Everett asked, "Did Celiaen suffer the same issues?"

Smiling wryly, she nodded. "The pressure on Celi was more than on me. His uncle is an archmage, and his mother is a renowned master. The Zarthein family is powerful in Riane. Let's not go into the fact that his father is Paienven Kaetiel. There has never been much room for mistakes on his part."

"I don't know about that," Aiden snapped. "I think they gave both of you plenty of room to make mistakes with no regard for the future."

Her smile faded, and Eirian glared at Aiden across the fire, ignoring the baffled expression on Everett's face. Shuffled movements and cleared throats told her that the rest of her guards were preparing for an argument between their captain and the queen they served.

"Don't start this again, Captain."

"You can't deny they should've shown a little more responsibility for your actions! What do they do about pregnancies, for example? How would they have explained it if your dalliances with the other prince had resulted in a child?"

"Aiden!" Everett choked.

His mouth was open in horror as he stared at the man beside him. Pointing at Eirian, Aiden shook his head.

"I'm sorry, little brother, but not all of us enjoy the same ignorance as you want to have about her. You were lucky. I remember the tears my mother shed over our situation."

"It doesn't work like that for mages!" Eirian hissed angrily before she realized what Aiden had said. "Wait, did you say, brother?"

"Don't change the subject!"

Rubbing his face, Everett could not decide who to look at and said, "He's right. One subject at a time. What do you mean it doesn't work like that for mages?"

"They teach us preventative measures from early on because youths will be youths, and nothing can stop that. With the right education, there is no interruption to training," she explained. "There are simple wards we can use to prevent the spark of life occurring."

"You could marry and choose not to have children?" Everett looked mortified.

Rolling her eyes, Eirian sighed. "I know my duty. If I got married, then I wouldn't prevent pregnancy. Not unless it was a strategic move."

"Could you use the ward on non-mages?" Merle asked.

"No, like a lot of things, it can only be self-cast. There are other options for women that don't require magic. They teach us those as well, just in case. The wards are only preventative. They don't take care of any mistakes."

Everett admitted, "I don't know how I feel."

Her eyes narrowed. "You're not a woman. You don't get to feel anything. Nor are you a green who has seen what hazards pregnancy can wreak on the body. Now, topic change?"

Aiden inclined his head at Everett. "She has a point. Men don't suffer the same repercussions. You and I know that all too well."

"Aiden is my brother. We share a father." Meeting Eirian's gaze, Everett sighed.

She looked at them in disbelief before turning to Merle. "What?"

Merle said, "I told you to ask your cousin why he appointed the captain."

"Brothers? How did I not know? I mean, I had my suspicions that you were more than you seemed, Aiden. Merle said your father was noble, and your familiarity with Everett made me think of a distant cousin or someone who served his father."

"My mother was a younger daughter of a viscount in Tamantal. She made the mistake of falling in love with a married man. He had no issues keeping her as his mistress since his royal wife hadn't produced an heir. He frequently paraded me in front of your aunt as a reminder that it was her failing he didn't have a legitimate heir." Aiden did not look at Everett, knowing he felt guilt over their father's actions.

Pursing her lips, Eirian nodded slowly. "I'm not surprised, but why?"

"Our father trained him from the start to not just be the future captain of my guard, but an earl in case your father never had a child," Everett admitted. "Then you came along, and it looked as though his ambition was for nothing. Everything changed when you showed your powers. Suddenly, the possibility of me being king returned. Our father always said that once I was king, all I needed to do was legitimize Aiden, and he could take over Tamantal."

"You're a bastard, a completely noble one with no direct claim to the throne but ample to the title of Earl of Tamantal." Eirian exhaled heavily. "I suppose everyone knows. How did I miss it? It seems so obvious now."

"I did point out that you don't always pay attention to us," Merle muttered, chuckling at the exasperated look she gave him.

Resting a hand on Aiden's shoulder, Everett offered an apologetic look. "Deciding to make Aiden the captain of your guard was purely selfish on my part. Besides the fact that he is undeniably one of the best swordsmen in Endara, I knew there was no one I could trust more to protect you. His loyalty is unparalleled. Besides, if I didn't get the throne, then what better position of power could I secure him?"

Aiden shot him a look and grumbled, "You hoped I'd keep you informed on her."

His comment made Eirian smile faintly, glancing at the sky to track the moon's progress.

"You haven't done that. Oddly enough, my brother is more loyal to you than I expected." Chuckling, Everett shrugged. "I won't complain. It's how it should be."

"We're talking about the little girl who used to find rabbits in snares and sneak them into the castle to care for them. I've never forgotten how sweet she was. Powers know, sometimes it's the only thing keeping me from strangling her."

Eirian stared at Aiden. "You knew me as a child? I don't remember you."

Everett laughed. "I remember that! You used to take the blame, so father didn't flog her or me. Wild animals—"

"Don't belong in castles unless they're on the table!" Aiden finished, and they laughed.

"This is unbelievable!" Eirian huffed.

Merle leaned in closer to murmur, "Don't worry, he's not your cousin. You can keep fighting with him as per usual."

Growling at him in frustration, Eirian clenched her fists. Her response made Merle laugh.

"Honestly, Everett, tell me why I shouldn't dismiss Aiden and get a new captain?"

"Honestly? I always thought you knew and were being polite. Aiden's parentage isn't a secret." Everett shrugged and said, "How was I to know you're forgetful and oblivious?"

Flashing her the challenging look she had grown to expect from him, Aiden smiled. "Who my parents were changes little. I'm still the same person you enjoy fighting with every other breath. I'm still the person who won't hesitate to knock you out to make sure you don't get yourself killed on the battlefield."

"You'd do that?" Everett asked.

"Absolutely. I even promised the Prince I'd do it."

"Fair enough, I won't argue."

Opening her mouth to respond, Eirian halted when she felt the familiar prickle of magic across her skin. Turning her focus in the direction it was approaching, she waited for Faolan to appear out of the darkness. When she caught sight of him, she frowned at his clothes.

"They're not planning on waiting for you to approach them to continue negotiating." Not sitting, Faolan informed them, "They're preparing to attack at dawn."

"How do you know this?" Everett asked in alarm.

"Are you sure?" Eirian spoke at the same time.

Looking between them, he nodded. "Funny thing about being a magical wolf in the night, you can get places unnoticed. Hear things that human ears would not hear."

Everett stood, cursing. "Powers! They want to take us unaware and capture you."

"Did you discover if their king is with them?" Eirian's face was blank as she tried to keep her thoughts from showing.

Faolan shook his head. "I'm sorry, but I'm not that unnoticeable. I could only skirt around the edges of their camp and listen."

Aiden nodded, saying, "It's better than nothing. I imagine we'll have scouts reporting the same thing. Best we prepare."

Remaining silent, Eirian did not look at any of them, lost in her thoughts. The clearing of a throat brought her attention back to the men staring at her, and she blinked.

"We had better prepare. Quietly, though," Eirian commanded.

"I'll alert Cameron and Marcellus." Everett looked at Aiden and told him, "If we don't cross paths before it starts, look after her."

"Always." Nodding, Aiden did not smile. "Don't get yourself killed, little brother."

Arching a brow, Faolan pointed at Everett's back and looked at Eirian. "Did you finally figure it out?"

She sucked in a deep breath. "You can worry about that later. Go back to your people, put some more clothes on."

"At least I left myself some basics before I went for my hunt," he commented, glancing at the thin tunic and trousers he wore.

"Yes, we thank you for not walking around naked in the middle of the night in a camp full of nervous soldiers." Merle saluted him.

Gabe looked at Faolan with a slow smile. "Your confidence doesn't threaten all of us."

Eirian saw the appreciative look Faolan gave Gabe and what he received in return. She cocked her head to the side, pursing her lips.

Catching the exchange, Merle muttered, "This is not the time."

"Her Majesty is right there," Aiden agreed.

"Her Majesty." Eirian chuckled and said, "Doesn't mind at all."

Laughing, Faolan gave her a slight bow before turning and retreating into the darkness. Left alone with the guards, Eirian turned her gaze to the fire and felt apprehension filling her. None of them moved, those aware of what was coming dwelling in their thoughts. Aiden sat watching her with an unreadable expression, and Eirian glanced at him, knowing he expected her to say something. Mustering the nerve to speak, she ran a hand over her head and down the messy braid hanging over her shoulder.

"What do we do now?"

"Nothing. We wait until the order comes to move into position. Then we pray to the powers we survive this day."

Eirian replied quietly, "Perhaps the powers aren't the ones to pray to."

Looking to the eastern horizon, she searched for the glow that preceded dawn but could not find it. It reminded her of Celiaen's words, and Eirian clenched her eyes shut, reaching out through their bond to sense where he was. She desperately wished she could feel something from him. Hearing movement, she stared at Aiden crouched in front of her. Reaching out, he gathered her hands in his and cocked his head to the side, nodding at Merle.

"Just say the word. We'll get the horses ready and vanish into the night. You don't have to stay here for this. No one will think any worse of you."

She shook her head and told him, "They might not, but I will, and the guilt would be... I can't, Aiden. Just remember what I asked of you."

"I won't abandon you on the battlefield because you order me to. My life is not worth more than yours."

"I'd ask the same of Celi."

Conceding her point, Aiden asked, "Would he do it?"

"Yes, but he knows why."

Before he could press further, they heard the sounds of movement as officers began organizing their people. The conscious members of the guard roused their sleeping comrades, and Aiden gave her hands a last squeeze, letting them drop into her lap as Eirian stared at him.

"We need to locate the captain from earlier, Olivia?" he said to Gabe.

Gabe nodded before he got to his feet and slipped into the shadows. Eirian rubbed her thumb over the purple band, looking down at her left hand. It no longer felt like it belonged there, but she knew it was a reminder.

She murmured, "That's a good thought. We'll move when she does."

Following her gaze, Aiden said, "I notice you fiddle with those when anxious."

"How many must die to ensure a balance?"

"Them or us?"

"Both. The value of a single life is not the same for each person." Pulling both rings from her fingers, Eirian held them out and asked, "Will you keep them safe for me?"

Holding out a hand, Aiden watched the bands drop into his palm. It surprised him to feel nothing except their weight. Closing his fist, he slipped them into the pouch he always wore around his neck. Eirian watched him tuck the small leather bag back beneath his tunic and mail. Her brow furrowed as she brought her gaze back to his face.

"I've never asked what is in that."

He shrugged. "It belonged to my mother. You probably wouldn't remember her. She served as a lady to your aunt."

"Why don't I remember you?" Puzzled, Eirian sighed. "When this is over, we're going to have a serious discussion about certain things."

"I'll hold you to that."

Aiden stood and offered her a hand. Staring for a moment, Eirian slapped hers against it and let him haul her to her feet.

"Perhaps it'll be the time I don't hold back on you. You would deserve it for what you did before. You know how funny Everett gets."

Not letting go of her hand, he grinned. "Don't make promises you won't keep."

"Who said I was?"

Aiden purred, "Why, darling, are you finally going to put me in my place?"

Grinding her teeth, Eirian gave him a look that he could not decide was thankful or annoyed. "Ask me again on the other side of this."

Watching her step away to face Merle, Aiden wondered how different things would have been if she had never possessed magic. It was not the first time he had contemplated it, and he knew it would not be the last. They would have grown up together, and he suspected his father's ambitions for him would have changed from earl to king. The same aspirations that members of the court whispered in his ear. Fionn stepped in beside him, the fair-haired guard unsmiling as he tracked Eirian's movements.

"You know that was an idiotic move earlier." Giving Aiden a disappointed look, Fionn muttered, "I'm amazed she didn't kill you."

"So am I."

"Why did you do it?"

Glancing at him, Aiden admitted, "Because it's going to play on her mind, and when she looks at me, she is going to remember she's angry. I don't know if you've noticed, but our queen thrives on anger."

Turning his gaze back to Eirian, he nodded. "That's true. Maybe you also wanted her to understand why you get the way you do. You know, in case there isn't an after. You realize you're never going to end up in her bed now?"

"Don't make me flog you."

"I'm just saying, Captain!" Holding his hands up, Fionn stepped away and started looking for the men of his squad.

Rubbing her arms, Eirian waited for a moment before she crouched to pick up her things. Her haubergeon sat folded and stacked with her jerkin and bracers, the leather belt Fayleen had crafted wrapped around them, and knives sitting on top. The twin swords were separate, and she wrapped her hands around the hilts for reassurance.

Sliding the jerkin out of the way, she ignored the movements around her as her guards prepared themselves. Heavy in her hands, Eirian lifted the haubergeon over her head and slipped her arms through the sleeves. Shaking herself to help it settle, she turned to her jerkin and pulled it over the top. By the light of the fire, she began tightening the laces.

"Here."

Aiden batted her hands away and tugged at the leather cords that secured the garment, alternating between that and making sure the mail sat correctly beneath the leather. He tightened it more than Eirian had planned to.

"You don't want it slipping."

"Don't tell me you want to replace my ladies," Eirian said teasingly.

Turning to pick up the last part of the mail he had commissioned for her and her belt, Aiden continued to assist. Giving Eirian the belt to hold while he placed the hood over her head, he did not smile.

"I don't think I'd look as good in a dress as they do."

"I wouldn't be so sure."

She let him take the belt from her without an argument, seeing a glint of amusement in his eyes. Tightening the belt around her waist, Aiden let his hands linger on her hips when he adjusted the armor.

"That isn't too tight, is it?"

"It's fine." Twisting and stretching, Eirian made sure she could move and watched Aiden pick up her bracers. "You know I'm capable of dressing."

"I know."

Rubbing his fingers over the leather of her bracers, Aiden wondered why he could not feel the magic worked into them. Pursing her lips, Eirian held her hands out and glanced to the sky while he slid the leather over her wrists.

"I don't think dawn is far off," she commented.

"I agree."

"Two-word answers. I like this version of you."

Aiden smiled faintly, finishing the second bracer. "You can manage your weapons."

"I don't know about that, Cap'n," Kip laughed, appearing beside them. "She might appreciate your hands on her swords."

Rolling her eyes, Eirian picked up her knives, muttering, "Incorrigible."

While she secured the knives to her belt, Aiden picked up the two swords and held them with the hilts in front of his face. He chuckled, knowing exactly how to frustrate Eirian further.

"Don't want to disappoint the children." Aiden held them out of her reach before tossing them to Merle.

"What did you do that for?"

"No! No, don't involve me!" Merle protested.

He quickly passed the weapons to the guard next to him. Putting her hands on her hips, Eirian glared at Devin. Looking at the swords in his hands, Devin shifted his gaze to Aiden.

Eirian said, "Devin, think about what you're doing."

"Sorry, Your Majesty." Tossing the swords to Aiden, Devin shrugged. "Got to avoid the tension somehow."

"You're not trying very hard to get them back," Aiden mocked, waving them at her.

Meeting Merle's concerned gaze, Eirian smirked. He did not get the chance to warn Aiden before she spun. Her foot caught Aiden behind his knee as she snatched the swords from his grasp and shoved him to the ground. Surprised, he glanced at the fire, thankful she had knocked him away from it. Lifting her left foot, Eirian put it on his chest and stared down at Aiden while she secured the swords to her belt.

"I didn't need to try very hard."

Eirian removed her foot and offered a hand. He grabbed it, intending to get up.

She added, "You should've seen that coming."

Her jibe made Aiden change his mind. Pulling Eirian down, he rolled to make sure she did not get close to the fire.

"So should've you," he murmured.

Laughing, Eirian lay on the ground beneath him. She did not move, gazing up at Aiden and his triumphant smirk.

"Yes, I should."

Shaking his head, Merle held out a hand to them. "We're preparing for battle, and you're playing like we aren't possibly going to die today."

Aiden rolled off Eirian and waited until she was on her feet before he let

Merle help him up. "That's exactly why, and you know it. Need to break the tension somehow so she doesn't send us insane with her magic."

"I have more control than that." Dusting off, Eirian shot Aiden an annoyed look.

"I'm sure you do, but let's not risk it, yeah? Did you find her, Gabe?" Aiden looked past her at the returning man.

Nodding, Gabe frowned at them. "I did indeed. Do I want to know?"

Clapping a hand to his back, Fionn waved and said, "Mother got Father on his back for a change. It didn't last, and he corrected the slip."

"It's disturbing when you call them that." Gabe sighed, shrugging off the hand.

"Merle started it!"

"Why me?" Rolling his eyes, Merle signaled to the guards behind him. "I'm taking Fionn, and we're going to prepare the horses. Don't forget your bow, ma'am."

Watching the men disappear into the night, Eirian felt her nerves return. She glanced at Aiden and said, "I take it we should start moving."

Securing his weapons, Aiden replied, "You still have time to change your mind."

"The time to change my mind passed months ago."

"I don't think that's what he meant," Gabe muttered, tossing an apple to Eirian. Catching it, she nodded to him. "Thanks, Gabe."

Falling silent, Eirian shifted and looked to the horizon while she ate, not seeing the glow that would tell them the sun was dawning. Gabe hovered close, his demeanor suggesting he was feeling out of his element. Giving him an understanding look, she picked up the last of her weapons. She had unstrung the bow and now regretted it.

Deciding it was time, Aiden nodded, and they picked their way toward where the archers were gathering. People were preparing themselves, everyone trying to make as little noise as possible to avoid giving away their plans. The anticipation in the air tugged at her magic, and Eirian appreciated Aiden's concern. The wagons with their barrels of arrows told her when they reached their destination, and she peered at the glowing campfires of the enemy.

Crouching with the quivers propped against her, Eirian fished the string from its pocket and pulled the bow out. Others were doing the same, and her fingers moved deftly as she worked to prepare her bow. Aiden and Gabe stood above her, watching the sky as the glow finally appeared. Runners delivered arrows along the lines as the archers drove them into the ground in front of them, preparing their supplies within easy reach. Passing her bow to Gabe, Eirian lifted the quivers and strung them over her shoulders, adjusting the straps.

"Really?" Aiden asked.

"If I need to move fast, I'm going to want to have my hands free," Eirian explained. "Saves hassle to do it now."

Signaling to a runner to bring her arrows from the wagons, Eirian nocked one and drew back briefly to make sure she had strung the bow correctly.

Creeping in beside her, Fisk pointed at the other archers, then to the stacks of arrows in front of them.

"Just in case you didn't realize, we're not here to aim. Nock, draw, loose. The more you can release, the more chances of hitting some of them as they advance. This isn't a hunt, and it isn't target practice."

Frowning, Eirian ignored the looks directed their way and said, "But with my magic?"

"Don't aim. You don't have time. Nock, draw, loose. Just keep repeating it as you go." Fisk showed her without an arrow and glanced up as the archers' captain strode over.

"You know what you're talking about." Olivia regarded him thoughtfully.

"My father was an archer. I had different ambitions."

Turning to leave, she said, "Just make sure you don't get in our way."

Eirian replied, "Don't worry, we won't. You might even appreciate some of my gifts."

Feeling the approach of the daoine, Eirian turned and saw them. The sky was getting lighter, casting their faces into shadow, but they stood out with an ethereal glow. It was as though they had absorbed the light of the moon. Beside them, Merle and Fionn led their men and the horses, Halcyon's reins firmly in Merle's grasp as the gelding paced calmly. Aiden went with them to tether the horses and find out what information they had gathered.

Half of the Telmians carried bows of their own, but not Faolan or Tharen. Positioned between them, Saoirse clasped a cloak around herself, and Eirian chuckled, suspecting the woman wore nothing beneath it.

"It won't be long now," Faolan commented, standing behind Eirian.

Nodding to Saoirse, Eirian winked and asked, "Are you our eyes?"

Saoirse admitted, "I'm not much of a fighter. Best I keep to the wing."

"You could've gone with Brenna and the others."

"I might not be a fighter, but I have my uses."

Chuckling, Faolan offered a hand to Eirian. "She's our scout. Before anyone else can spot it, she'll let us know it's time to get you away."

"We'll not die this day," Eirian informed them.

Rolling her shoulders, she rested the tip of her bow on her boot and looked around at them. People stared at her.

"You have my word."

Tharen's eyes narrowed, and he studied her. "You speak as though you know something the rest of us don't."

Glancing away, Eirian watched Aiden and Merle returning with their heads close together as they conversed. "Just have a little faith in me."

The sun appeared above the horizon, and Eirian let her thoughts drift to Celiaen as his words came to mind. She wished he were by her side. Thankful for the direction they were facing, she knew the Athnaralans would face into the dawning light, and it would give her forces an advantage. The breeze had shifted from the day before, and Eirian could hear the grumbles of the archers. Messengers hurried, carrying orders between commanders. As she stared at the Endaran soldiers, she wondered where Everett and Marcellus were. She hoped they were with the general and his staff at the back.

"There." Aiden pointed as they watched the Athnaralans move into position. "Looks like you were right, wolf."

Faolan rolled his eyes. "As if there was any doubt."

Walking away, Saoirse let go of her cloak and undid the clasp at her throat. Allowing it to drop to the ground, she winked at those watching.

"Have fun. I'll keep out of the firing line."

Watching her shape change, Eirian asked, "What's it like, changing your form?"

"Hard to explain, but in the beginning, it's quite painful." Faolan watched Saoirse glide over the Endarans before she began circling higher.

Grunting, Aiden settled behind Eirian and murmured, "Everything is ready. It's not too late to leave."

Closing her eyes, Eirian let her magic flow out over the land between them and the enemy, familiarizing her mind with the life there. She sensed every root, every ground-dwelling creature, every insect creeping through the grass. Dew on the grass was droplets on her skin. Opening her eyes, she turned to look at Aiden with a sad smile.

"Don't worry, Aiden."

"I think you're planning something stupid."

They heard the horns echoing from the opposing force, and Eirian did not answer. There was a stillness over the Endarans, anticipation as they watched their enemy advance. No volleys had flown from either side, but she watched the archers picking up their bows, arrows held loose at the ready. Her magic prickled over her skin, and she tasted the bloodlust, knowing it was eager for release. Tightening her grip on her bow, she cast a knowing smile at Tharen. His stare told Eirian he suspected what she had planned.

A whisper spread along the line, and Fisk lifted his bow, saying, "Remember, nock, draw, loose. Then do it again, and again, and again."

Olivia called out, "Archers! Ready!"

Eirian pulled three arrows from the ground and nocked the first while holding the others ready. She watched from the corner of her eye and saw Fisk do the same. A screech from Saoirse came moments before Olivia issued the command.

"Loose!"

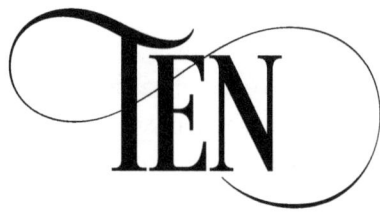

TEN

She heard shouts as officers prepared the infantry, but Eirian kept her focus on the rhythm she had established. Nock an arrow, draw, and loose. It had not taken long to realize she was not as prepared as expected. The advantage she thought her magic would give turned out to be the opposite. Archery was not satisfying the bloodlust, and Eirian spent half her concentration keeping it under control. Biting down on her bottom lip as she kept releasing arrows, she tasted blood.

"Your Majesty!"

Aiden's concerned voice broke through her focus, but Eirian did not dare stop her motions. She feared that if she stopped, the bloodlust would take over. Blocking out the whispers at the edge of her mind was bordering on impossible. They constantly reminded her of what she could do if she let go. Looking at the ground beneath her, Aiden frowned at the sight of dead grass. It was the opposite of what he was accustomed to seeing around her.

"We need to get you away!"

"Not yet," she replied.

Shaking her head, Eirian did not take her eyes from the lines. Her refusal caused frustration among her guards. They saw the advancing Athnaralan infantry lines and their threat to the smaller Endaran numbers. There was only so much they could do before being overwhelmed. By then, it would be too late to get Eirian away safely. Aiden growled, turning to Faolan in frustration.

"Are your people staying here to fight or coming with us?"

"We go where she goes. We're prepared to leave the moment you give the order, Captain." Faolan watched the infantry and muttered, "This is futile. It'll be a slaughter."

"What are we supposed to do?" she asked softly.

Speaking was a mistake, and Eirian's motions faltered. Her control dropped, the magic guiding her hands to lower her aim to the lines. Holding her breath while it chose, she closed her eyes. As the arrow left the bow, she let go of her breath and nocked another. Beside her, Fisk realized what she was doing and cursed, breaking his rhythm to reach over and grab her arm, forcing Eirian to stop.

"You're going to hit one of ours!"

"No, I'm not."

"You can't tell me your magic can guarantee your shot remains clear. I don't doubt your aim, but they're moving. A step in either direction means one of ours will take the arrow."

Fisk did not let go of her arm, and Eirian tossed her head, glaring at him. Around them, the other archers continued to shoot, their focus remaining on the battle. They would keep on until ordered to stop. Merle saw doubt creep into her eyes and supported Fisk.

"He's right."

Eirian looked at the arrows in front of her and huffed. "Fine, you're right."

Taking the chance to push departing, Aiden signaled to Fisk to hold off. Nodding, he drove the arrows into the ground and waited. Those daoine assisting the archers followed suit, waiting for instruction from Faolan to continue or retreat.

"It's time to go," Aiden declared. "The longer we remain, the higher the chance of them coming for us. They'll want to break our lines quickly."

Faolan reached out and touched her shoulder. "You know he's right, little Queen."

She watched the lines meet, and the desire to be among them was an overwhelming pull. Eirian knew she could stop the battle. That was her plan, and the magic whispered instructions in her ear. All she needed was to break free of those holding her back and make her way into the fight. Licking her lips, she shook her head and clung to her bow for focus.

"So many unnecessary deaths," Eirian murmured.

"I can feel your magic. If we don't get you away, you'll be a danger to all of us."

Startled, Aiden shared a fearful look with Merle. All of them were aware of the thrum of her power and the urges it stirred. It affected everyone within reach, making him recall the day Baenlin had played with the guards in Amath. Celiaen had told him to keep Eirian away from the fight, and he suspected why.

"What do you mean?"

"It might seem like a strange analogy, but she's a fox in a henhouse. Her magic wants to join the battle. But the longer she fights to control it, the harder it's going to get." Shrugging, Tharen looked up at Saoirse as he spoke.

"Then that confirms it. We're leaving now. That's an order!"

Signaling, Aiden observed the archers among his men setting down their bows while the daoine did the same. Eirian did not move, her gaze remaining locked on the fight. She had one hand wrapped around the shaft of her bow while another hesitated with arrows positioned between her fingers. Frustrated by her lack of action, Aiden moved to yank her bow away.

He snarled, "Your Majesty, do you understand?"

Eirian gripped her bow tightly and replied, "I understand."

"Then move your ass before I pick you up and chuck you over my shoulder."

Chuckling, Faolan inclined his head. "I'd like to see that, but not today."

Lifting her bow over her shoulder, Eirian slipped it into the quiver and glanced at the men. None of them were laughing. They watched like she was a threat they would have to overcome. Pursing her lips, Eirian did her best not to let the guards realize they were right. The shadows whispered and mocked her attempts to control the magic. She promised them blood if only they would wait.

"I'm sure the captain is disappointed he wouldn't be the first of my guards to do it," Eirian told Faolan.

"I won't be as gentle as Fionn," Aiden growled. "I can promise you that."

He waited for her to turn before believing she was going to leave the field. Rolling her eyes, Eirian cast a glance at Saoirse. The bird was closer to the Athnaralan lines than she had expected, and her gut clenched in fear. A small voice in the back of her mind screamed that the Telmian was in great danger. It was loud enough to break through the other whispers. Meeting Faolan's gaze, she gestured at Saoirse and hoped he understood her concerns. Squinting, Faolan peered at the circling form.

"Tell her to come back."

"She knows what she's doing." He shook his head doubtfully. "This isn't her first battle."

"I'm telling you, something isn't right. She's in danger."

Meeting her gaze, Faolan said, "You believe that."

"I wouldn't be saying it if I didn't! Can't you feel it?" Eirian replied in exasperation.

"No, I can't, but I'm going to trust your instincts."

Turning to stare at Saoirse, Faolan's mouth twisted in concern. Thankful he was taking her seriously, Eirian shifted her focus to Aiden. There was tension in his stance, mirrored by the rest of the guards. Twenty-five pairs of eyes watched her every move, prepared to do what they needed to make her leave. A swift glance at the Telmians showed a similar situation. If she was going to follow through with her plan, she had to think of something to get free of them.

Whatever it was, it needed to be quick.

"Don't even think about it, Eirian," Aiden said, cutting into her train of thought.

She peered at him in surprise and asked, "Think about what?"

Aiden flicked his gaze to where her hands grasped her swords, giving Eirian a knowing look. She let go of the hilts and bowed her head. Clasping her hands behind her back, she hid the first signs of her control slipping. She knew the shakes would worsen the longer she held back from the fight. Eyes narrowing, Aiden did not trust the look on her face. It made him want to pick Eirian up and carry her to the horses.

"You know what. Sometimes you fail miserably at hiding your thoughts."

Swallowing back her initial response, Eirian said, "You're right. Shall we?"

"After you, Your Majesty."

Understanding that Aiden would not make the first move toward the horses, Eirian started in their direction. Her magic protested, her control continuing to struggle with keeping it under grips. It wanted to turn, push past her guards, and join the fray. She reiterated her promise that the time was coming. Spotting Halcyon, Eirian forced herself to count each step she took, hoping that it would help.

Faolan grabbed her arm as she gripped the saddle and murmured, "You're shaking."

Looking at him sideways, Eirian saw the way her hands trembled in the corner of her vision. It was taking everything she could muster to keep a shred of command over her magic. The whispers were persistent. She wanted to tell Faolan how difficult it was and to plead with him to help her break free of those who would stop her, but she shook her head.

"I don't have the luxury of your years of control."

Around them, her guards were undoing the tethers securing their mounts. The sun was moving higher into the sky, but the only song heralding its progress was the sound of battle. Horns blared, louder than the screams of soldiers fighting. Eirian knew it signaled that the cohort stationed in the town had left the walls to join. When Faolan let go of her, she hauled herself into the saddle and gathered the reins. Watching as the others mounted, she kept counting, using every distraction technique she had ever learned to keep her bloodlust at bay.

Blinking, Eirian suddenly felt winded, and something made her look at the sky. Her eyes sought Saoirse's location, finding her circling above the battle. Fear crawled over her skin, and she knew that her instincts had been right. There was a threat to Saoirse that she could do nothing to prevent.

She called out in warning, "Saoirse!"

The Telmians turned, looking at the distant group member as Saoirse let out a piercing shriek. Screaming, Faolan kicked his horse into motion. His only thought was to get to his sister while she plummeted from the sky. Ignoring the shouts and grabbing hands of her guards, Eirian urged Halcyon forward, chasing him. It was not the distraction she wanted, but she would not miss her chance. Or let Saoirse die. Trusting the gelding to get her where she needed to go, she tracked the bird's progress as it struggled to control its descent.

Eirian reached out with her magic, doing her best to slow Saoirse's fall and to guide her in a direction to meet Faolan. The shadows retreated from the corner of her vision, giving way to a glimmer of something else. Using her power to see, she gathered the pale threads in the air surrounding Saoirse. At the back of her mind, she registered her guards and the Telmians in close pursuit. She heard their names screamed as they approached the battle.

"Get your sister!" she shouted to Faolan, knowing he was not in any state to fight. "Take my horse and get her away! I did what I could to slow her, and now it's up to you."

Glancing up at the huge eagle as she drew closer to the ground, Eirian threw herself from the saddle and pulled the twin blades. Halcyon snorted, tossing his head as he pranced away from his mistress. He felt her suggestion, heading to Faolan.

Seeing her guards closing in, Eirian snarled and pushed through the lines of Endaran infantry. Releasing her control, the bloodlust roared to life and spread through the soldiers. She smelled the blood spilled, feeling the way it seeped into the ground. The magic sang, telling Eirian where to go. It guided her to where the enemy was, whispering what attacks would come.

"Eirian!" Aiden screamed, pushing after her.

Her magic encouraged the soldiers forward so she could slip through the lines. She ducked and dodged, her every action guided by the power. Finally catching up before she reached the line of fighting, Aiden flung himself forward and grabbed her arm, pulling her around to face him. Snarling, Eirian barely resisted the urge to raise her sword against him. Whispers chased through her mind, reminding her Aiden was a friend the magic liked and not an enemy.

"Please," he pleaded, staring at the approaching Athnaralan line.

Merle was close, calling out as he shouldered his way through. "Captain! She's sending everyone around us into a frenzy."

Closing her eyes, Eirian felt the approaching swing of a sword and pushed him back so she could pirouette to meet the strike. Aiden pulled his sword free and prepared to defend her. He did not know if the Telmians had rescued Saoirse, but he trusted the bloodlust projected through the field had not overcome them. It was more intense than he had previously felt, and he suspected it was only fear that kept it from overwhelming him. Glancing at Merle, Aiden saw him battling with an enemy soldier and hoped that he was not the only member of the guard who was barely resisting the magic.

Turning his focus back to Eirian, Aiden stared in shock at how she moved forward into the Athnaralan line. Her blades sliced through anyone who got in her way like they were nothing but air. In all the months he had spent training with her, Aiden had never seen her move the way she was dancing through the enemy. He felt remiss in his gloating over every time he had defeated her. Eirian's constant warning that she was holding back, fully sank in.

"By the powers!"

Aiden took a deep breath and went after her. Gabe was there, moving to get as close to his commander as he could. He carried a pike in one hand, the shaft of it coated in blood, and an equally bloody sword in the other.

"Captain!" he shouted.

Nodding, Aiden blocked a swing as he struggled to monitor Eirian. He was thankful when Gabe drove the pike through the Athnaralan, and his sword blocked a fresh attack. As much as he trusted Gabe's abilities, Aiden had not expected him to follow them into battle.

"We need to get her out of here."

Letting the body drop, Gabe asked, "How? I suspect her magic won't let us."

"I thought I'd prepared for her…"

Glancing at Eirian while he yanked the pike free, Gabe said, "We knew she was holding back."

Aiden started forward and cursed, "Damn those fucking daoine."

"It wasn't them, Captain. She had a plan. You know she did. She was playing along until she had the opportunity."

"I have to stop her!"

"What if you don't?"

Halting, he turned to stare at Gabe in shock. His eyes caught sight of the odd charm he wore around his neck, and Aiden felt a whisper urging him to walk away from the battle. Death surrounded them, but nothing approached while Gabe waited for a response.

"If she dies—"

Cutting Aiden off, Gabe said, "Do you really think it's going to be easy to kill her?"

Shaking his head, Aiden was not willing to risk it. Banishing the whispers, he focused on Eirian's magic and followed. Gabe could do whatever he wanted, but Aiden knew what his purpose was. He had promised to protect her, and nothing short of death would stop him.

Eirian felt every drop of blood rolling over her blades, her magic embracing the way the steel slid through flesh like it was nothing. Her power was in control, but a corner of her mind begged her to stop. To fight for control and to remember the plan. It was hard to care when the smell of death filled her senses, fueling the darkness she harbored. There was no thought required. Her body was in the grasp of the magic as Eirian cut her way through her enemies like they were nothing more than hay.

Echoing along the edges of her power, she felt the bloodlust of the daoine battling. They had not succumbed to her influence, and she sensed their desire to get to her. Occasionally, Eirian heard her name called as her guards struggled against her magic. She felt Aiden closing in, her power recognizing him. The whispers welcomed his presence, telling her he could help. Unwilling to risk his life, she snarled when he blocked a blow aimed at her.

"Get out of here, Captain!"

"Not without you."

Aiden dodged out of her way as Eirian brought a blade around to finish the man he had parried. Meeting his gaze, she saw his panic and shook her head. No matter what the power whispered to her, she refused to listen. She wanted him to walk away and live. Taking a deep breath, she flexed her magic, pushing past the bloodlust to raise a ward around them. It would keep everyone else out for as long as she could hold it.

"I'm sorry, Aiden."

Staring at her, Aiden felt like they were in the eye of a storm that she controlled. While he could not see the magic, the effects of her ward were noticeable. People slammed into it like it was a wall, and Eirian flinched each time. He stepped toward her, watching the power dancing over her skin.

"I don't want you to die."

Feeling the pull of her magic, Eirian clung to the moment. It would not last, and she only needed enough time to convince Aiden to leave. Her ability to hold the ward was faltering, cracks appearing in it.

"I told you, you don't know what I'm capable of. I need you to trust me like I asked you to. Get your men and go, please, Aiden. I don't want to kill you too."

"Eirian, what are you planning?"

Reaching out for her, Aiden grunted when she darted away. The ward failed completely, allowing the advancing enemy to enter the space Eirian had claimed for them to speak. She held her swords ready, back to the Athnaralans, and gave him an apologetic look.

"I'm so sorry, Aiden, but I have to save my people in any way that I can."

Diving back into the fray, Eirian surrendered to her magic. Watching her cut her way through the enemy line, Aiden felt like he had failed. It made him want to let the bloodlust take over, to throw himself into the fight without care. Feeling a hand on his shoulder, Aiden spun to defend himself and found Tharen at his side. Exchanging a look, Tharen shook his head and tightened his grip.

"There's nothing we can do. I failed my task. She's lost to her magic."

"Not yet, she isn't," Tharen said. "But I don't know how we can stop her."

Angry, Aiden shoved him and yelled, "You said you're here to keep her alive! We wouldn't be in this mess if you kept that bloody woman on the ground!"

Unmoved, Tharen sighed. "I suspect she's going to keep us alive. Eirian said we wouldn't die. It's glaringly obvious she knows something we don't. This was her plan all along, and Saoirse being shot was simply in her favor."

"That's hardly a reassurance right now!"

"Unless you trust in her, there's nothing I can say to reassure you."

"She told me to trust her," Aiden whispered.

"So do it. Trust in Eirian." Placing a hand on Aiden's arm, Tharen added, "Your death will serve no purpose. She's going to need you, Captain."

Aiden remembered what Eirian had said to him the day before. Turning to stare into the battle raging around them, he realized Tharen had erected a similar ward to the one Eirian had used. Unlike Eirian, he was not struggling to maintain it. Shifting back to Tharen, Aiden looked at the sword he held with a frown.

"How are you able?"

"I can hold my own, but I'm a healer, not a warrior. My task is to protect you for—"

His voice faltered, and Tharen stared into the distance, where he felt Eirian battling. Concerned, Aiden followed his gaze, wondering what was going on. The whispers of her power reached them, the note carried in them different from the bloodlust. It was darker, Aiden's instincts screaming at him to run, but there was a familiarity to them. Tharen closed his eyes, his lips pressed together.

"What's going on?"

"You're about to find out."

Sucking a deep breath through his teeth, Aiden suspected he would not like what was coming. "How bad?"

Tharen flinched, murmuring, "It won't be pretty."

The magic told Eirian to keep going, and she obeyed, letting it guide her through the mass of invading forces. She needed to clear a space, and the bodies of her victims littered the ground. Her arms barely felt the impact as she parried the blows aimed at her. Blood was everywhere, and Eirian tasted it on her tongue, felt it on her skin as it mixed with sweat. A faint sting on her arm told her that someone had gotten a lucky blow, her blood running down her arm to join the blood of the dead as it dripped from her swords.

"Here," Eirian breathed the word.

Holding the blades extended to each side, she gathered her power and reached into the earth. It welcomed the blood of the slain. Eirian accepted what she was about to do, rekindling her familiarity with the land. Every heartbeat sounded in her ears as her magic coursed through them, human and otherwise. There was a sliver of control in her possession that had Eirian focusing forward and not back toward her people. Her magic elicited fear in those it touched. The Athnaralans realized danger was among them and scrambled to escape.

"Oh no, don't run," she whispered. "Please, it's easier if you don't."

The whispers of her power called for them to surrender. Instinct railed against it, fear driving them to flee. Eirian felt each life and the potential that went with them. She connected to them by shimmering threads no one else could see. Siphoning the vitality from the soldiers, she fed it to the ground. There were screams of terror when men crumbled, life sucked from them, wild growth covering the bodies. Distributing it, she kept none for herself, even though her physical strength was fading. It flowed into her people, giving them energy where they had been waning.

Her body cried out for some of the energy she was drawing from her victims, but she refused to take it for herself. Instead, Eirian latched on to the Telmians and sensed their horror as she drew from them to fuel her efforts. With their power, she bolstered her failing physical strength. The whispers laughed at her reluctance to use the life she was taking, making Eirian doubt her choice. Strengthening her resolve, she pushed to keep going.

As more fell to the magic, confusion grew, and the Athnaralans fled back on themselves. Those that ran forward died on the waiting swords of the Endarans. With each body that fell, her people surveyed what was going on. Horror and amazement spread as Eirian became a lone figure standing among the dead and the flowers covering them. Horns sounded from both sides of the field, commanding a retreat.

Pushing their way through the scrambling Endarans, Aiden was thankful for the ward Tharen was providing. It kept them from being knocked over as they went against the flow of people. Soldiers shouted at them to flee. Most of their words made no sense to Aiden, but he saw understanding in his expression when he glanced at Tharen. Whatever was happening, whatever the strange magic was, Tharen knew.

Opening her eyes, Eirian stared out at the corpses and the uncontrolled growth of every plant in the area. The bloodlust faded, more satisfied than it had ever been before, and she struggled to reconcile what she was seeing without the magic controlling her. The retreating Athnaralan army was a mess. She did not need to turn around to know the Endaran forces were in a similar situation. Horns continued to ring out, the sound harsh to her ears without the whispers drowning it out.

Taking in the view of hundreds of withered corpses, Eirian dropped her swords and covered her mouth. The smell of the blood on her hands made her want to vomit, and she pulled them away, but the scent remained. She doubted she would ever be free of it, no matter how many baths she took. It would cling to a corner of her mind to torment her whenever it got the chance, just like the memories of previous massacres at her hand.

"By the powers, what have I done?"

Taking a deep breath, Eirian struggled to remain calm as horror, grief, and remorse filled her. It was the emotional price for what she had done, the pieces that she had told Aiden to pick up. Sensing others approaching, she turned and stared at Tharen and Aiden as they stopped a distance away. They watched her warily, and Eirian saw them judging if it was safe. A cut was dripping blood down the side of Aiden's face, and he lifted a hand, wiping it away from his eye before shaking his head.

"How?"

Aiden looked around at the remains, horrified, and her heart broke. What little strength she had wavered.

Beside him, Tharen was ashen and said, "You pulled power from us to help you do this. Do you know what you have done?"

"I…" Eirian looked down, fighting the urge to be sick.

"You shouldn't have been able to use us."

Aiden frowned in confusion, asking, "What do you mean?"

"She didn't have enough strength on her own to do this, so she pulled power from us and twisted it to her purpose. We don't share power with anyone who is not of our people. To have it stolen from us and used like this?"

Waving at the dead, Tharen looked back at the lines of watching Endarans. He had seen similar things happen in the past, and while he hated the death, his horror focused on what Eirian had done to his people.

"She shouldn't be able to use our power."

"Did you know you could do this?" Demanding, Aiden took a step toward Eirian.

Flinching, Eirian closed her eyes and fought the wave of fatigue that threatened. It took her a moment to respond.

"Yes, I've done it before, but never on a scale like this."

Taking a step back, Aiden regarded her coldly and asked, "What did you hope to gain?"

"This isn't the time or place. She's going to collapse. We need to get Eirian away from here. She's used more magic than her body had the strength to handle," Tharen told Aiden.

He bent to pick up the swords from where she had dropped them. Seeing the reluctance in Aiden's stare, Eirian reached for the blades in Tharen's grasp. Her hands trembled, betraying how much she was struggling. It was an effort to move, but she forced herself to keep going.

"Here, let's put them away. We'll worry about cleaning later," she mumbled.

Tharen glared at Aiden while helping her slide them into their scabbards. He slipped an arm around Eirian's waist and let her sling one of her own over his shoulders.

"So much for doing whatever you needed to do to protect your queen!"

"It's alright, Tharen, I understand."

Her nails dug into his shoulder, and she felt the way his armor caught them, causing her pain. It was a welcome feeling, enough to help her focus as she staggered along beside Tharen. She did not blame Aiden for his reaction to what she had done. Eirian believed her response would be much the same if another mage had done what she had.

"Saoirse is safe," Tharen said, wondering if Eirian remembered.

Nodding, she rasped, "I know. I felt her. Tharen, I don't think I'm going to make it back to what's left of my forces before I pass out."

Catching her words, Aiden scolded himself and turned from where he stood. Tharen's words echoed in his mind, reminding him that Eirian was his queen, and he had sworn to protect her no matter what. He would get her to safety before letting his emotions get the better of him. Striding up to the pair, he stopped them.

"Let me," Aiden told Tharen.

Squealing in surprise when Aiden scooped her up, Eirian flung an arm around his neck and said, "What are you doing?"

"Getting you off this battlefield before you collapse. I'd rather not pick you up out of the bloody mud, and I'm sure you wouldn't like being covered in it."

"I'm sorry."

Eirian rested her head on his shoulder and felt his grip tighten. The whispers returned, mocking her for being weak. She did not listen to them and pressed her nose against Aiden's armor, inhaling the scent of him. It was familiar and comforting and exactly what she needed. In his arms, she felt safe. Aiden glanced down and saw her eyes fluttering shut as the exhaustion overtook her.

"Fuck," he muttered.

ELEVEN

Picking his way across the battlefield with an unconscious Eirian in his grasp was not as straightforward as Aiden hoped. Corpses littered the ground, the covering of wildflowers hiding them well enough that it was difficult to negotiate around them. Tharen led the way, his magic able to pick up the lingering traces of her power. Neither wanted to desecrate the remains of her victims by standing on one.

Aiden could not bring himself to look at the bodies. He saw enough of what Eirian had done to last him a lifetime. Glancing at her, he made sure she remained asleep. She appeared peaceful, cheek pressed against his shoulder and lips parted. Tendrils of hair had escaped her braid, sticking out from beneath the mail hood. They curled slightly, and Aiden wanted to tuck them behind her ear, but the blood splatter on her skin made him banish the thought.

Beside him, Tharen shook his head, pointing at a cluster of people waiting. He sensed Aiden's shifting emotions and hoped they would not have an issue with him later. It would be easier on everyone if he worked with them to deal with Eirian, but sweeping his gaze over the guards, Tharen knew others would not hesitate.

"There are your men. Faolan's with them."

"How do we explain what she's done?"

"It has been a long time since I saw that done. I'd wondered if Eirian was capable, and she'd hinted as much, but I assumed her desire to protect life would prevent it. It takes a certain degree of... I'm not sure, to be honest. Desperation?" Glancing at Eirian, Tharen said, "I'm more perplexed about how she pulled power from us."

Recognizing Merle standing at the front of the group beside Faolan, Aiden was thankful he had survived. Looking them over as they approached, he fought back the desire to give Eirian an angry look when he realized several were missing. Hovering close behind Merle, Gabe was nursing an injured side, and the worry in his eyes explained why he was there.

"Is she?" Gabe stepped toward Aiden, peering at Eirian.

"She's alive, and mostly unharmed. But you need to be treated."

He glanced at his wound, admitting, "We didn't want to leave without her."

Faolan offered his arms to take Eirian. "You're not unharmed, Captain, so let me."

"It's a scratch." Refusing to let go of Eirian, Aiden nodded to his men as they crowded around. "Let's hurry before they recover and decide we're easy targets."

"We should take her into town. Hopefully, the general will order people to recoup behind the walls," Merle said, eyes flickering down to study Eirian.

Keeping Aiden in the middle, the guards escorted an unconscious Eirian from the battlefield. Endaran nobles waited with Cameron and his staff as they approached the town. People trickled in, primarily the injured. Marcellus was standing beside Cameron, and he hurried forward when he saw the royal guards. Fionn carefully pulled the hood from Eirian's head and nodded at Aiden.

"Where is she?" Marcellus demanded, not seeing Eirian cradled carefully in Aiden's grip.

"The captain has her," Devin replied, remaining in at the front. "She needs a bed."

Marcellus went pale. "Is she injured?"

Lifting a hand to Tharen's arm, Faolan shook his head and explained, "She's exhausted. Tharen, remain with them, take care of their wounds. I'll help our people gather horses and supplies to come within the walls."

Tharen nodded, remaining close to Aiden. "I won't let her out of my sight."

Cameron looked out at the carnage and asked, "Did I miss the meeting where she told us she could do that? It would've been good to know she could level the field in one hit."

Surprised by Cameron's apparent ease with what Eirian had done, Aiden stepped forward with her in his arms. "This is why! Now find me a fucking room to put her in because the longer we stand here, the longer we're all exposed."

Signaling to the garrison commander, Marcellus gave Aiden an appreciative nod. He nodded back, thankful for the support.

"I'll take care of things here. See to the Queen. Don't let anyone near her until Everett or I come," Marcellus instructed.

"He lives?" Realizing he had not thought of his brother, Aiden flinched.

"Unlike Her Majesty, his guards got him away."

The guards bristled at the insult, but Aiden bowed his head and started after the officer. Keeping his grip on Eirian, he looked nowhere except at the woman they followed. Soldiers watched with horror and respect as the group hurried through the quiet keep. Those uninjured were busy dealing with the dead and dying or helping the others move into the town. Leading the guards up a winding staircase, the officer brought them to a set of chambers.

"No one uses these. We keep them for such visits." The officer shrugged, her eyes flickering to Eirian. "We cleaned up when we found out the Queen was visiting."

"Thank you." Merle nodded and watched Aiden carry Eirian to the next room. "Captain, we need to get her weapons and armor off, or she'll cover the bed in muck."

"And I need to see to that cut on her arm." Tharen was barely a step behind Aiden.

Frowning, the officer said, "My chambers aren't far. I'll quickly fetch some clothes."

Opening the door to let Aiden through, Tharen looked at each guard standing in the chamber. He assessed their injuries, working out what he needed to heal each of them. Reaching out with his mind, Tharen requested Saoirse to bring supplies.

"Sort yourselves out, get cleaned up. Once I've healed the Queen and your captain, I'll get to the rest of you." Tharen pointed at Gabe, taking in the way the man was swaying, and told him, "Perhaps I'll see you first."

Glancing over his shoulder as he crossed to the bed, Aiden grunted. "That might be a good idea. Her Majesty is fond of him. Merle, help me out."

While Tharen attended to Gabe, the guards fussed with their weapons and armor. Those uninjured aided their comrades, the men barely uttering a word to each other. Returning, another woman followed the officer who had brought them, each carrying a bucket of water and a bundle of rags for cleaning up wounds. Giving thanks, they watched the two women cross to the next chamber.

Aiden lay Eirian on the bed, her weapons stripped away and dumped in a pile on the floor, while Merle stood with her haubergeon and jerkin in his hands. Nodding to her companion, the officer attempted to shoo Aiden away from the bed.

"I've some clean clothes for her. We'll take it from here. You two go join your men."

Crossing his arms, Aiden refused to move, and snarled, "I'm not going anywhere!"

Rolling her eyes, she asked, "Do you think the Queen would be happy to find out you've seen her naked?"

"She wouldn't care."

Coughing, Merle shifted uncomfortably. "Yes, but others would. Do you want the duchess screaming at you about it?"

The reminder about Brenna was enough to make Aiden slump and bend to pick up the weapons on the ground, muttering, "I'm glad she's not here."

Letting Merle lead him out, Aiden glanced over his shoulder at the two women tending to Eirian. Once the door shut, he turned his focus to his men and met their eyes as they regarded him. Devin approached, taking the weapons as Tharen glanced up from healing a wound on Fionn's leg.

"Who did we lose?" Finally mustering the words, Aiden ran a hand through his hair and cringed at how it had matted with blood.

"Geoff and Layne," Fox answered, staring at the window without truly seeing it. "Kip, Fisk, and Kyson are tracking down our horses. I think Mac and John went looking for them as well."

Relieved, Aiden let go of the breath he had held when Fox spoke. He had feared the death toll would be far higher.

He asked for confirmation, "Only two dead?"

Sid explained, "A few of us didn't go running after her. We didn't want the archers accidentally killing the Queen. Mac thought it was a good idea to go let the Duke know."

Appreciating their reasoning, Aiden grunted. "We're going to be lucky if the nobles don't demand all of us dismissed for incompetence at the very least."

"She won't let that happen," Gabe replied. "She'll be the first to argue it wasn't our fault. Everything was going well, and we almost had her leaving."

"You blame us." Tharen pushed away from Fionn.

Aiden agreed, "I do."

Getting to his feet, Tharen pulled a fresh cloth from the clean bucket and approached Aiden. Guilt flickered across his face, and he regretted not speaking out about his concerns before the battle began. He understood the anger felt by the guards, but thought it was important to remind them of what they knew.

"Perhaps you're right. However, Eirian was barely in control, and I think we all know she'd planned to escape no matter what."

"You think the result would've been the same without your bird lady getting hit and her brother going after her?" Devin asked.

"Think about the things she said. If there is one thing I have learned about your queen, she hints a lot to tell truths about herself that she dares not say directly. I should've known she was capable of what she did. I suspected it was possible and said nothing."

Staring into Aiden's eyes as he wiped the blood away from his face, Tharen did not flinch at the anger he saw. Yet, beneath the anger, fear lurked. Fear of what Eirian had done, what she could do, and of what might happen to her in response. It was more obvious than Aiden would admit that he feared losing Eirian.

Sighing, Merle watched Aiden closely. "How'd she do it? I mean, we thought when she talked about being able to kill with her magic, she meant with weapons like at the start."

"That was beautiful to watch," Fionn admitted. "I've seen nothing like it. It wasn't the same woman we see in the training yard. The way she flowed through them…"

Examining the cut that ran up into Aiden's hair, Tharen pursed his lips. "It's not too bad, but I should heal it for you."

"Do it. None of us can afford to be injured right now."

Concentrating on healing Aiden before he explained what Eirian had done, Tharen observed how he tensed up at the magic. It was not unexpected, but it was inconvenient when mending a cut.

Tharen said, "Relax, Captain, unless you want this to scar. It would be a shame if your queen lost a pretty face to admire."

Grunting, Aiden turned his eyes away. "Apologies, I've felt enough magic today to last me a long time."

"I understand." After finishing, he asked for confirmation, "Is that your only injury?"

"It is."

"Excellent. I'll tell you what Eirian did as best as I can. Any further explanations can come from her. You've seen the way she makes a field grow. Normally, she threatens the balance by forcing things to speed up when she does that. What the cycle of life would take a month, she makes happen in a blink of an eye."

Wade frowned, asking, "What'd she do that was different?"

Tharen looked at his hands sadly and sighed. "Nothing. She rushed the life cycles of those men, aged them, and took their energy to give to anything that could receive it. I imagine you don't feel as worn out as you'd expect, and slight injuries have faded. It was an offering of balance. All that life had to go somewhere."

Scratching his head, Tobin admitted, "I don't feel like I could sleep for a day."

"Can all mages do what she did?" Fionn looked frightened at the thought.

"No, and among us, there is only a handful. Magic isn't as terrible as her actions today may make it seem. It can do more good than bad. She can do far more good." Feeling the need to emphasize the point, Tharen sensed Saoirse's approach. "Unfortunately, we remember the bad."

"Captain, how are we going to deal with this?" Gram asked, a fearful look on his face.

"She is not to be alone." Glancing over his shoulder, Aiden wanted to check on her.

Nodding, Devin fingered his sword hilt. "You're worried people might turn on her?"

"If you didn't know her, wouldn't you demand her killed out of fear for what she can do?" Merle pursed his lips, voicing a thought that had crossed each of their minds.

The door opened, and the officer stepped through, followed by her assistant. "We've cleaned her up and changed her clothes. The cut on her arm isn't bad."

"Thank you." Aiden bowed his head.

"Lieutenant Ash." She eyed him contemplatively. "And don't worry about it. She saved all our collective asses today in an eye-opening introduction to our new queen."

Fox grinned and said, "You're right. She certainly did."

"A few more like her, and I doubt Athnaral would press their luck."

Her words received nods from several guards. But Aiden shook his head angrily because he understood how the nobility thought. They would fear Eirian more than ever, and the voices that had been against her from the start would scream louder, finding more support.

"I don't know how you can think what she did was good!" he snapped.

Ash crossed her arms and said, "Spoken like an entitled city boy who's spent no time living on the border."

Several of the men whistled, taking delight in how the two faced each other. They knew Aiden's record and what he had done in service of Endara. His past was no secret to the men who served under his command.

Unimpressed, Aiden sneered, "I grew up in Tamantal with a sword in my hand, and I've spent time on both sides of the border. So while tactically I appreciate the results of what she did, I'll remind all of you that this is not just any mage."

"He has a point. We're talking about the Queen of Endara." The second woman shrugged, saying, "That's an awful lot of power in the hands of a monarch."

Tharen was silent, watching them talk. It reminded him how things had changed since he had spent an extended time away from Telmia.

"She's not the first mage to do that," he reminded them.

"That might be the case, but it has been a long time." Merle shrugged as he voiced his observation, "I mean, I'd bet that since the mage wars, someone has, but they covered up."

Fionn glared at Tharen. "Riane didn't teach her how to do it, so how could she have known she could do it?"

Spreading his hands, Tharen said, "Eirian can do things Riane never taught her."

Cocking his head, Aiden frowned. His men were arguing among themselves, the two women adding their input when they saw fit. Crossing to the door, he opened it and checked on Eirian. Seeing her tossing about on the bed, he shot Merle a look before slipping through the door and shutting it. He realized she was crying, and approaching the bed, he perched on the side to stare at her. Tears ran down her face, and Aiden wiped them away with his thumb. Then, rubbing his chin, he took a deep breath and let it out in a huff, watching her toss again.

"What am I supposed to do with you?" Aiden asked. "I think you've made things worse."

Hearing the door open, he looked up and glared at Tharen. He crossed the room, coming to stand near the bed. Aiden resented the calmness radiating from him, wishing he would show some disgust over Eirian's actions. Or anger. Anything that did not make it seem like any other day.

Tharen explained, "It troubles her mind. Each life Eirian took today will weigh on her. It's part of the price she must pay. Don't hate her for what she can and has done."

"I want to hate her. It's hard to reconcile the memory of the woman standing among piles of corpses with the innocent girl cradling injured rabbits in her hands. Eirian was the girl who'd sneak me food when my father withheld it as punishment. I wonder where she changed and what happened to that innocence," Aiden admitted.

Covering his face, he struggled with his conflict, and Tharen did not offer any reassurances. His feelings were something Aiden needed to come to terms with on his own.

"The first time I experienced her bloodlust, she was being challenged by one I assumed far more dangerous. While she was a capable fighter, I thought she was inexperienced. It felt wrong that such a desire for death had come from her. Then I watched her kill men like they were nothing. She tortured one of them, and they weren't her first. That sweet little girl who had wanted to help—"

"Perhaps she can bring so much death out of a desire to protect and save lives."

"I..." Aiden's shoulders slumped as he thought it over.

"She is that sweet girl beneath the burden of what she can and must do. Trust me when I tell you no one understands the price of life better than she does."

Hearing Eirian cry out, Aiden uncovered his face and reached out to calm her. She struggled, batting away his hands without opening her eyes. Magic flared around them, and he glanced at Tharen with concern. He remembered Eirian's admission that her nightmares could occasionally cause her to lose control over her power.

He commented, "That seems like a twisted way to go about things."

"You care for her despite your desire to hate her for what she can do."

"Spend enough time with Eirian, and I don't think anyone could help but care for her."

"Think about what you said. You know how much she cares. How many would have died if Eirian hadn't killed those men, and we lost the fight today? Innocent people, children."

Shaking his head, Tharen put a hand on Aiden's shoulder. The anguish on Eirian's face told Aiden he was right. It made him want to forgive her for the lies and the choices she had made to hide her abilities from them all.

"She knows the value of death," Aiden murmured.

"Yes, she does."

"There'll be many who demand her head for it."

Tharen stepped away from the bed and said, "Worry about that tomorrow, because right now, Eirian needs comfort while her body recovers. No one will know if you hold her. It might help her mind if you do. I fear when she wakes, she'll be distraught. I've requested Saoirse bring some herbs that will help us keep her sedated."

Frowning, Aiden glanced at him. "I can't climb into bed with the Queen of Endara and hold her while she sleeps. I could lose my head."

"I'll guard the door, as will your men, and none of them will speak of it. If you won't, then another will be willing. Either way, Eirian needs someone to provide her with comfort. And since her prince is far from here, you're the best choice we have. She cares for you as much as you care for her."

Feeling Eirian shudder beneath his hands, Aiden looked at her and watched her lips move in a silent cry. At war with himself, he met Tharen's understanding gaze, deciding what he would do. He stood to undo his weapons belt, putting it on the ground before undoing the laces of his boots and kicking them off. Removing his armor next, Aiden let it join the pile on the floor. Climbing into the bed, he gathered Eirian and wrapped his arms around her. She struggled, and he wondered if Tharen was wrong, but she relaxed into his grasp.

"Sleep, Captain. You need it as much as she does," Tharen murmured as he slipped through the door. "Saoirse will remain outside while I prepare some herbs to help. Call her if Eirian's magic does anything."

Alone with Eirian, Aiden stroked her head gently, watching her burrow her face into his shirt. Her tears made the linen wet. Tharen's comments lingered in his mind, and he knew he was correct. When she cried out, he tightened his arms and felt the flare of magic.

"Shh, darling, I've got you. I've always got you," he whispered.

Leaning down, Aiden kissed the top of her head and closed his eyes. He did not like his chances of falling asleep, despite the tiredness plaguing him. Fear of what might happen if he let his guard down clawed at his mind. Thoughts of soldiers bursting in and dragging Eirian away for execution played out. No matter how many times he reminded himself that his men were on the other side of the door guarding them, the fear remained.

Every time Eirian struggled again, her hands pushing him away, Aiden's fear spiked. Her magic was an ever-present reminder of his concerns. It made him wish Celiaen was there. He suspected he would have a better chance at reaching Eirian because of their bond. But, tightening his hold on her, Aiden realized the real reason Celiaen had requested he do whatever was needed to keep Eirian from battle. He had made the request out of fear of what she could do to ensure the survival of others.

"You warned us."

Aiden sighed, shifting his position when Eirian stopped struggling. He was half tempted to drape himself on top of her to keep her pinned down. It was fine to provide comfort, but how she twisted and fought against his hold left him fearful of hurting her. There was no way to know how her magic might respond and if it might perceive attempts to restrain her as a threat.

"Damn it," muttering the curse, Aiden glanced at the door.

He did not want to call Saoirse in, but he needed reassurance that Eirian's power could be contained. When she began struggling again, he tried his best to calm her, hoping his voice would get through to Eirian. The flares grew stronger, and her eyes opened briefly, letting Aiden see the magic flickering in their depths.

"Saoirse!"

Bursting through the door at his shout, Saoirse hurried over to the bed. Gabe and Merle followed, prepared to lend any help they could. Glancing over her shoulder at them, Saoirse pointed at Gabe and signaled for him to join her.

"I admire your attempts, Captain, but I think you need a little help."

Gabe arched a brow, looking from Saoirse to where Aiden struggled with Eirian. Then, nodding, he moved quickly to shed his weapons while Merle remained at the door to make sure no one entered.

"What do you need me to do?" Gabe asked quietly.

She waved at Eirian, saying, "Take the other side. I'm going to see if I can calm her long enough for Tharen to finish mixing his concoction."

"Then what?"

While Gabe moved to the other side of the bed to grasp Eirian, Saoirse sat next to Aiden and waited. The men felt the effects of her magic. It soothed them, a whisper that wanted them to do whatever she asked. Aiden shook his head and exchanged a look with Gabe.

"Are you powerful enough?" he felt strange asking.

Doubt appeared on Saoirse's face.

"You're not, are you?"

Clearing his throat, Gabe pushed an arm beneath Eirian and partially lifted her against his chest, and Aiden took the chance to shift his hold. Her magic flared again.

"Tharen's sedative will work," Saoirse said.

Merle grumbled from his spot at the door, "Sure it will."

Eyes narrowing, Saoirse ignored him and placed her hands on either side of Eirian's face. Her power was soothing, reminding Aiden of the blue mages he had met, and it lacked the heat he had grown to associate with Eirian's magic. Yawning, he struggled to resist it and hoped it would not take long to calm Eirian.

"How far off is Tharen?" Gabe inquired, watching Aiden battle the urge to sleep.

"Not far."

Realizing he appeared unaffected, Saoirse frowned and glanced at Gabe briefly before returning her focus to Eirian. She had expected both men to feel the effects of her power.

"Not feeling tired?"

Chuckling, Gabe tightened his grasp on Eirian, replying, "A little, but I'll manage."

Screwing up his face, Aiden peered at Gabe in confusion. "How are you not?"

"I've gotten sleep recently, unlike you, Captain."

Shrugging, Saoirse muttered, "I'm focusing on Eirian, but that doesn't exclude you."

Eirian's struggles had lessened, providing Aiden with some hope they could keep her magic under control.

"Can you do anything else to make sure she doesn't send the garrison into a frenzy?" he asked.

"We'll ward the room and surrounding areas. Faolan plans to have a couple of us around to maintain them. I believe what Tharen intends will keep her sedated enough for her magic to settle."

There was a knock at the door, and Merle moved to open it. He let Tharen enter, Faolan at his heels. Carrying a cup carefully, Tharen approached the bed and sighed at the sight of the two guards holding Eirian as Saoirse worked her magic to keep her calm.

"We need to get this down her throat," he said.

Grunting, Gabe shifted and pulled Eirian with him, holding her in a position better suited to swallowing. His arms pinned hers down, wrapped tightly around her torso.

"I'll hold her up while you deal with getting her to swallow."

Appreciative of Gabe's quick thinking, Aiden moved his hands to Eirian's head and cradled it gently. Saoirse accepted the cup Tharen held out with one hand while the fingers of her other dug into Eirian's jaw. Aiden and Saoirse worked together to pry open Eirian's mouth and tip in some of the liquid.

"Small amounts," Tharen instructed. "Don't want to waste it if we can avoid it."

"It's going to knock me out, isn't it?" Saoirse grumbled, wiping her face on her arm after Eirian spluttered.

"Sorry."

Faolan concentrated on placing wards on the walls. He kept out of the way, confident the four people surrounding Eirian on the bed could manage their task without his help.

He commented, "Not for long. It's not like you're the one drinking it."

"Next round is yours, brother. We'll see how long you sleep for."

Merle laughed, "Sibling love."

Uncomfortable with what they were doing to Eirian, Aiden hoped she would forgive them when she woke. He doubted Everett or Marcellus would question the reasoning behind drugging her, but he did not look forward to the conversation.

"How long will she need?" Gabe asked.

Crossing his arms, Tharen watched Saoirse tip more sedative into Eirian's mouth and answered, "I don't know. We'll give her this, then see how she's going when it wears off."

"I'd say at least a day," Saoirse said. "Her mind is a mess."

"And this will stop her magic while she sleeps?" Aiden needed to know for sure.

"It should do," Tharen replied with more confidence than he felt.

Picking up on the hesitation Tharen felt, Faolan approached and stared at the people on the bed. They would do what they could to control the situation.

"It works that way on most of us," he told the guards.

"Most?" Merle scoffed.

Tharen admitted, "I wouldn't give it to King Neriwyn and expect much of a result."

Rolling his eyes, Gabe explained, "What they're saying is there no way to be sure how effective it'll be."

"We might need to keep doing this every few hours, or we might not. All we can do is wait it out while Eirian's body recovers and her mind comes to terms with her actions."

Holding her head tighter, Aiden looked away while Saoirse tipped the last of the sedative into Eirian's mouth. She quickly scrambled out of the way, tossing the cup to Tharen before wiping her face on Faolan's sleeve. Protesting, he pulled away and nodded at Gabe.

"You should be good to lay her down again."

The two men released Eirian, and Gabe gently laid her down while Aiden shifted out of the way. He met Merle's worried gaze across the room.

"I need you to make sure no one gets past that door except us."

Merle saluted. "Already given the order. What about the dukes?"

"No one. Not until the Queen is conscious and in control of herself."

Exchanging looks, the three daoine silently agreed. Faolan had issued orders to the warriors among their company to remain on guard outside the chambers. They could not afford for anything to happen to Eirian. Slipping from the bed, Gabe collected his weapons from where he had placed them and watched Aiden rearrange himself.

"We're right outside if you need us, Captain."

"As soon as we can organize it, we'll bring food," Merle added.

Aiden looked at them, nodding his thanks. Satisfied they were no longer needed, Gabe and Merle made their way out of the chamber, leaving the three daoine behind.

"I won't go far," Saoirse assured him. "Shout if you need me."

"I'm going to assist the wounded, but I'll leave more of the sedative. Saoirse can administer it," Tharen said, waving for the other two to leave.

"Thank you."

Glancing over his shoulder while Saoirse and Faolan exited, Tharen watched Aiden stroke Eirian's hair gently. The worried expression on his face brought a smile to Tharen's.

"Don't worry, Captain, your queen will be fine."

Kissing her forehead, Aiden murmured, "I hope so."

TWELVE

Groaning, Eirian shifted uncomfortably and tried to lift a hand to her face. Finding her arm blocked, her eyes flew open as she struggled to free herself, panic making her heart race. A grunt rewarded her efforts, the sound making Eirian freeze, magic lingering in reach. Turning, she met Aiden's amused gaze as he shifted, propping his head on his hand, and the sight of him calmed her. She glanced down and realized her arm was beneath him and his leg sprawled over hers, explaining why she had found herself unable to move.

"This wasn't how I expected you to get me into bed," Aiden chuckled.

He lifted himself enough for Eirian to pull her arm free. Memories of what happened on the battlefield filled her mind, and she rolled away, covering her mouth to hold back a sob.

"What have I done?"

Amusement fading, Aiden reached for her and said, "You did what you had to do."

"So many lives." Barely paying him attention, Eirian covered her face.

"Eirian! Darling, listen to me! You had to do it." Aiden hauled Eirian into his lap, wrapping his arms around her tightly as she struggled. "Think of the lives you saved."

"I'm the monster I feared. None of them deserved to die like that."

Pushing her hands against Aiden's chest, Eirian would not look him in the eye for fear of seeing revulsion. Working out what she was doing, he refused to let go.

"What about those they would've killed after they wiped out your forces here? Those men would've swept through the countryside, killing people, raping women, taking anything of value. They would've burned villages, farms, and slaughtered livestock. You stopped that."

He felt her struggles pause, his words reminding Eirian of what they faced. Taking the chance, Aiden unwrapped his arms and cupped her face, lifting it so he could see her. Tears were running down her cheeks, a sight he had seen more of in the last day than he had ever wanted to see. Witnessing the despair and guilt in her eyes confirmed what Tharen had said. Aiden saw the sweet girl who had wanted to rescue every creature that crossed her path.

"You're not a monster."

"I've ruined everything. Athnaral will retaliate. My people will want me dead. Riane will want me dead. I wouldn't blame you if you wanted me dead." Eirian began to sob.

"I won't deny I was angry and fearful after the battle yesterday. Or that I wanted to hate you. I'm sure many others felt the same way initially. Given time, however, like me, they'll realize you did it to save us. You may have ended the war completely," Aiden told her.

Wiping a thumb over her cheek, he frowned at the way she flinched.

Eirian stared at him, saying, "Six hundred and seventy-two."

"What?"

"That's how many I killed yesterday without turning my blades on them."

Shocked, Aiden asked, "How do you know the number?"

"I'm not sure. I don't know their names or their stories, just the feel of their heartbeats, the potential they held. It's not the same as killing with a sword. I don't feel those deaths, and I can't count them."

"How did you learn you could kill like that?"

She glanced away. "I've always been able to make a seed grow through its entire life cycle and die. The question would linger in my mind if I could give life, then could I also take it away? I experimented, alone, fearful of the council's reaction if they discovered what I could do. It wasn't until an attack that I confirmed I could do it to a person."

"I can't imagine how big a burden it must be to live with your power and all the secrets you keep to protect yourself."

Meeting Aiden's worried stare, Eirian swallowed, fighting the wave of grief that brought tears back to her eyes. "I didn't think I was capable of what I did. But, leading up to the battle, it was on my mind. It was a plan to save us if I could bring myself to do it."

"Did you plan on breaking your promise to leave the field before the fight began?" Seeing her guilt, Aiden ground his teeth and said, "No, don't answer."

"I'm sorry, Aiden, sorrier than you could ever know."

Regarding Eirian angrily, he shook his head. "I should have known I couldn't trust your promise. You wouldn't have been able to resist it."

"I tried." Her voice was soft. "For your sake, I tried."

"Shut up."

He resented the way Eirian looked like a scolded child. Her shoulders had slumped, and her gaze was downcast, leaving Aiden wanting to wrap his arms around her again.

"I watched you for a day and night. While you sobbed and fought in your sleep. I held you down so Tharen and Saoirse could force sedating concoctions down your throat."

Eirian's eyes widened, taking in the pain that crossed his face. The memories of what they had done to keep her calm troubled Aiden. While he would tell her what happened, he would not admit how it made him feel.

"They claimed you needed to sleep while your mind came to terms with your actions. So I've lain here holding you while you cried because they said comforting would help."

She rubbed her face, feeling the dampness of her skin, and said, "You didn't have to."

"Yes, I did. I'm sure the others would've done it in my place. Some offered to share the task. My job is to protect you, to keep you safe, and because of your choices, I failed yesterday. Because of your choices, two of my men are dead."

The anguish Eirian felt at his words was apparent, and Aiden took a deep breath, reminding himself that coddling was not what she needed. No matter how much he wanted to protect her from everything.

"Eirian, it's time to stop crying and own your fucking choices."

"Who did I kill?"

"Geoff and Layne. They fell to the Athnaralans," he replied.

Slumping, Eirian closed her eyes and took a deep breath, asking, "And the others?"

Aiden glanced at the door, knowing most of his men were beyond. "Making sure no one killed you. Most of them have barely left the room since we got here."

The irony of his statement made Eirian giggle, and she poked at his chest. "But they let you stay in here with me?"

"I doubt they worried about me killing you." Giving her a twisted smile, Aiden caught her hand and cautioned, "Be careful with your poking, darling."

"What do I do when people demand my death for what I've done?"

"Athnaral will. You're an even bigger threat to them now. Some of your nobility will. I'm a little uninformed, so I can't tell you what has occurred. As for Ensaycal and Riane, I don't know, but your prince won't let you die, and neither will the Telmians."

Thinking about the daoine reminded Eirian that she had pulled power from them, and she asked, "Are you sure about the Telmians?"

"Well, the dynamic trio has had ample opportunity to kill you. If they wanted you dead, I'm sure you would be. Tharen told me you're not the first to do such a thing. Some of them can," Aiden answered, looking at her hand in his.

Eirian knew she had to tell him. "Aiden, there's something else."

Freezing, Aiden tightened his grip on her hand and did not lift his gaze. "Why is there always something else? How many secrets do you keep?"

"I'm sorry I can't make you feel better about it, but I'll always have secrets. I hoped to never reveal this one, but I suspect the choice is out of my hands. You've done more for me than I deserve, and I'd rather face your look of disgust in private."

Pursing her lips, Eirian turned her face to the door, feeling the Telmians beyond it. It was easier than looking at him.

"What if I don't want to know?" Aiden said.

"I wish I didn't know, but I'm glad I do."

Annoyed, Aiden gripped her chin, forcing Eirian to look at him. She met his gaze.

"You make it sound like it's a recent thing."

Flinching at the way his fingers dug in, Eirian nodded. "I learned after my coronation. If I had known before—"

"What is it?"

"My mother was duine. Or so she told my father. Nolan planned to take the secret to his grave, but in one of his fits of madness, he mistook me for her and revealed it."

"The day Gabe told you his story. We knew something happened."

Nodding again despite his grip, Eirian said seriously, "Yes, you're right. If I'd known before, I wouldn't have accepted the crown. I was going to deal with this war and then give it some time to find a way out before my lack of aging became clear."

Blinking slowly, Aiden mulled, "My father was right. Everett belongs on the throne."

"That's the first thing you think of?"

"You're planning on abdicating if they don't kill you first?"

Flabbergasted, Eirian yanked her hand and face from his grip. "I don't know what I was expecting from you, but I'm pretty sure it wasn't this!"

"Well, if you're not the queen," Aiden murmured.

Catching her wrist, he pulled her back against him. She knew she should pull away, but Eirian could not. Cradling her face, Aiden leaned in to kiss her. It was slow, demanding, and she did not want him to stop.

"Aiden," Breathing his name, Eirian pulled away slightly and met his gaze before kissing him again.

"I'm going to pretend I'm not witnessing this!"

Everett's voice startled them, and Eirian struggled to move away. Aiden kept an arm slung around her, disrupting her efforts.

"How long were you there?" Eirian asked, her cheeks burning.

"Long enough to see you didn't resist him," Everett said coldly.

"Everett."

"I suggest you let go of the Queen, Captain."

Inclining his head, Aiden released his grip and let Eirian scramble to her feet. "Apologies."

Leaning against the door, Everett glared at them. "Your men and the daoine have barred us from seeing Her Majesty since you brought her here unconscious yesterday. I'm finally allowed in, and this is what I find?"

"It was a spur-of-the-moment decision. Don't blame Eirian for my actions."

Slipping from the bed, Aiden reached for his boots and dragged them toward him. His actions made Eirian look herself over, her eyes narrowing at the strange clothes she wore.

"What happened to my clothes?"

"A well-meaning lieutenant offered a set of her clothes in place of your bloody ones. She and another woman cleaned you up. Don't worry, I still haven't seen you naked."

Everett covered his face, groaning, "She's my cousin! And the Queen of Endara! He's my brother, Eirian! Don't think I didn't see you kiss him back."

"For now. Wait until our precious queen tells you her big secret. It's a shocker." Not looking up from his feet, Aiden quickly laced his boots up.

"Thank you, Captain!" Eirian snapped and gave him an angry look.

"By the powers, what else is there?" Fed up, Everett threw his hands in the air.

Walking over to the window, Eirian tugged at the drapes and let sunlight chase the shadows away. The glass was thick, and while a glance around the room told her they kept it clean, they had not extended it to the window. She pressed her face to the panes and peered down at the town, squinting to pick out the people hurrying about. There was a warmth brought about by the rising sun, and shifting her gaze upward, she knew it was mid-morning.

"The fight was only yesterday?"

Sharing a glance with Aiden, Everett responded, "It was."

Eirian turned to them, saying, "There was certainly something to the daoines' advice. Captain, if you could please fetch me something to eat and drink."

Arching a brow, Aiden replied, "Of course, ma'am."

Waiting until he left, Eirian ran through what she was going to say. Then, feeling Everett staring at her, she walked from the window and her bare feet on the floor made her crinkle her nose. Eirian sighed and gave the silent man a torn look, grasping her hands behind her back to hide the trembles.

"You're going to be angry. I was. My father had his reasons. I don't know why my mother made him keep this secret. They never intended for anyone to know."

"Should I sit for this?"

"Probably."

Crossing to the bed, Everett sat on the edge, leaning forward with his arms propped on his knees. "It must have been some secret between the former king and queen."

Eirian nodded and replied, "My mother told Nolan she was duine. Of course, no one was to find out, but in his madness, he revealed it."

"You're not joking, are you?"

"I wouldn't joke about this."

Exhaling loudly, Everett let his head hang as he processed what she had told him and asked, "What else do you know?"

Walking over, Eirian sat beside him. "Only a little. Siani came to Endara to marry King Nolan and have his child. Siani shared something about the future to convince him to marry her and keep this a secret. I assume it related to the darkness. I don't know who she was to the Telmians."

"I'd like to think Nolan was the sort of man who wouldn't have let you take the throne unless he knew it had to happen. You're right. She had to have revealed things to him that influenced his choices."

"They knew she'd die. They knew I'd have magic."

Everett looked at her, grief in his eyes, and Eirian nodded. "You're telling me your father knew you'd grow up motherless and sent away from your home, your family, your people? Nolan knew the mages would raise you?"

"Yes."

"All the things I thought I knew about him... When did you learn this?"

"After my coronation. It was the day before he left. I went one last time, and Nolan thought I was her. I couldn't help myself and pressed him for information. I half wish I hadn't, but it's better to know. Imagine the questions in a few years when I failed to age?"

Taking one of his hands in hers, Eirian squeezed it. Everett studied her face and sighed.

"You should've trusted me and said something sooner. You have no control over the choices they made before you were born. Do you think our visitors know?"

Shrugging, Eirian stared at the door, admitting, "I believe Neriwyn knows. However, after what I did yesterday? There's no way to avoid the truth coming out. I did something they think I shouldn't have been able to do."

"I saw the results of what you did. Eirian, even without the knowledge of your blood, you'll struggle to keep the throne."

"I assume you've been in council. How many want me dead?"

"Half. However, you have Cameron on your side, and he controls the army. I fear it would cause a civil war if they tried to remove you. You're a hero."

She blinked in confusion and said, "Say that again. I'm not sure I understood."

"The soldiers think you're a hero. You fought beside them, killed those trying to kill them. Then you, and you alone, struck a blow to stop the battle and send the Athnaralans running. Stories are already spreading across the kingdom," Everett informed her.

"What I did was terrible, desperate, but terrible. Even Riane is likely to want my head," Eirian said, still confused.

Merle knocked and entered, carrying a tray. "Captain said you were hungry."

Nodding, Eirian accepted the tray gladly. "Thank you, Merle."

"Do you need anything else? Lord Faolan is desperate to speak with you, and I'm not sure how much longer we can stall him."

Eirian lifted the cup and took a tentative sip. "Let him in. I need to speak to him before I face my nobles. Wouldn't you agree, Your Grace?"

Peering at the plate of food, Everett gave it a sneer. Hungry, Eirian picked at the bread and let the silence settle. Merle backed out of the room, aware he was not welcome to remain. Once they were alone again, she glanced at Everett.

"I'm sorry, Everett. In Riane, there have been questions asked about my parentage. More than a few people have suggested I wasn't entirely human. Now we know."

"Your existence confirms the truth of their claims. A duine left Telmia to marry the King of Endara and convinced him to keep it a secret. Why else would Nolan agree?"

"You're taking this better than I expected." Eirian pointed out, "This means you'll have to be king. I don't belong on the throne."

"After yesterday, I think nothing shocks me anymore when it involves you," Everett answered as Faolan burst through the door.

Faolan pointed at Eirian. "You can't refuse me an explanation!"

"A good day to you too, Lord Faolan."

Ripping a chunk of bread off, Eirian popped it in her mouth and stared at him. Faolan stared back, infuriated by her response.

"You shouldn't have been able to use our power."

"And I'm deeply sorry for doing so. I shouldn't have, especially without your permission. What I did was tantamount to rape," Eirian replied.

Passing the tray to Everett, she took another sip from the cup. Everett glanced between them, not willing to interrupt.

"Thank you for helping me through the night. I didn't deserve your aid or the kindness you've shown me in giving it."

Holding his hands up, Faolan said, "While I expected your apology, an explanation is what I'd rather receive."

"Remember our first meeting alone, and I asked if any of your people had ever gone missing? You said none. I'm evidence you were wrong."

Crossing over, Faolan bent down and stared into her eyes. He frowned and stepped back in confusion.

"That isn't possible."

Eirian shrugged. "Why would my mother tell my father that she was duine? She knew things, foresight sort of things, and used her knowledge to make my father keep it a secret. King Nolan wasn't a stupid man."

"That must be what Neriwyn meant when he claimed your father would know why we had come. But who was your mother? Why isn't it obvious to us?"

"You think your king knows what Eirian is?" Everett asked.

Frowning, Faolan nodded. "Yes, he's the most powerful of us. Only our queen was greater, and no one has seen her in a long time... oh."

"What is it?"

Eirian's eyes narrowed, and she reached over to the plate and took another piece of bread, murmuring, "You know something."

"It would explain a lot. You mentioned foresight?"

Turning away from Eirian, Faolan grasped his hands behind his back and stared at the door. He could not tell her his suspicions. Not without proof.

"I know nothing but the ramblings of my mad father mistaking me for my mother. He claimed Siani came to him because of it. They knew she'd die and that I'd have magic."

Rubbing his face, Everett sighed. "Can you confirm it? Was her mother a duine?"

Glancing over his shoulder, Faolan answered, "I feel that what Eirian did yesterday answers it for us. The daoine don't share power, and a human or elf could not draw it from us the way she did. It was her duine blood that allowed her to do so, her connection to us."

"Are you sure? I need you to be certain because we're talking about the Queen of Endara, and your answer will affect her ability to remain in power."

"Everett—"

He stopped her, saying, "No, Eirian, you know it's the truth. If you're human, you can hold on to your throne. It wouldn't be easy, but working together it's doable."

Faolan stepped over and squatted in front of Eirian. "I think I know who your mother might have been, and if I'm right? Well, it explains and changes everything."

Looking at him curiously while she considered what she would say next, Eirian pursed her lips and nodded. "I understand. However, we should focus on my actions yesterday rather than this. Surely that's a more important issue to deal with right now."

"Yes, I gather you caused quite a stir."

Putting the tray on the bed behind him, Everett stood and paced. He was silent, glancing at them several times while crossing the floor. Rubbing his face, he finally stopped at the window and regarded it, keeping his back to the others.

"You're right. We need to focus on that. I think we keep this information between us. Aiden won't tell anyone if we ask him not to. Your safety is his priority. Right now, your grip on the throne has weakened, and we're still at war. We can't destabilize the kingdom."

A fresh knocking on the door prevented Eirian from responding. Standing, Faolan crossed over and opened it, allowing Marcellus to enter. Marcellus stepped inside and looked to Everett at the window before turning to Eirian. His mouth thinned, and bowing, he waited until Everett turned to look at him.

"I'm pleased you're up and about, Your Majesty. We have little time, so I'll get straight to the point. Athnaral is demanding to see you. Your nobles are in distress, and your forces outside want to see their great queen. I fear they'll riot if not reassured you're alive," Marcellus said, resting a hand on the hilt of his sword.

Eirian dropped her gaze to his sword and sighed. "Which do I attend to first?"

"Well, the nobles might change their tunes once they see your soldiers cheering your name. You certainly have a dramatic way of winning over your people."

"I tried to tell you," Everett said, looking grim.

"I know you did," she murmured. "While I'm disgusted by what I did and struggle to understand any that don't feel the same way, I can grasp their reasoning."

Marcellus remained unsmiling, and Eirian saw a glimmer of determination. "You're a powerful queen, a formidable one who can defend her people with her own hands and will risk her own life to do so. That is what they see. That is what you are to them. We need to reassure the nobles you're in control, both of your magic and the kingdom."

"Aren't you appalled by what I did?" she asked curiously.

"No. I've seen far worse things by far worse people. You keep secrets from those you should trust, so answer me this. Have you ever seen the mutilated remains of babies killed by invaders? The bloody, beaten, and raped messes of the women assaulted? Corpses of farmers strung from the beams in their barns, left to hang while their killers rape their wives and daughters? Because I have."

Searching his face, Eirian shook her head. She had seen similar things.

"I haven't seen what you have, but I've seen my fair share. I grieve those deaths as I grieve all I kill, but I know the price. The price of yesterday is the lives they would've destroyed. Innocent lives who don't ask for war."

"You killed men who signed up to die. That is the price of war. If you don't want to die, don't become a soldier," Marcellus replied.

Everett watched them staring at each other before he looked at Faolan. Cocking his head to the side, Faolan smiled, nodding to the door as Saoirse and another duine woman entered. Surprised by the intrusion, Marcellus and Eirian turned to regard the women.

"If the men would please leave, we have a queen to dress," Saoirse informed them. "News is spreading that she's awake, and her people are gathering."

Marcellus said, "Eirian, we need you to be the queen. Take command of your nobles, don't show any regret, and make them believe it. Then do the same with the Athnaralans. You can grieve when the war is over, but until then, we need you to be fierce."

Glancing at the two women, Marcellus strode out. Following him, Everett and Faolan gave Eirian a look before they shut the door. Blinking at Saoirse, she cringed when the second woman unfolded the bundle in her hands to reveal a green dress. Giving them a pained look, Eirian held up her hands and sighed.

"It is one of hers. Your height is close enough. I thought you should make a statement." Saoirse continued to smile. "We'll make them fall in love with their beautiful queen. Now, strip. I see you've eaten. Good, you needed it. Your delicious captain did his best to feed you some broth, but you're going to be hungrier for a while."

"I know. I didn't eat enough beforehand either." Standing, Eirian pulled off the tunic. "As for my people, surely they'd rather see me being myself?"

Shaking her head, the other woman tucked a golden curl behind her ear delicately and passed the dress to Saoirse. "No. Yesterday, they saw you as ferocious and deadly. Today, show them you're beautiful, kind, and nurturing. A woman who understands."

"I'm sorry, I don't know your name."

"Apologies, little Queen, this is Muireann. She's a gifted healer, and Tharen claims she's his greatest student," Saoirse said.

Waiting until Eirian had stripped, Saoirse got the dress ready to slip over her head. Stepping out of the way as Saoirse helped Eirian into the dress, Muireann pulled a comb from the pouch at her waist.

"You flatter me, Saoirse. I'm sure that's not true. I'm one of many Tharen has trained," Muireann muttered.

They shared a look over Eirian's shoulder, and Saoirse finished lacing the dress before stepping back and saying, "It's a lovely color on you. Good call, Muireann."

Beginning her task of taming Eirian's hair, Muireann agreed, "It's this hair, such a lovely warm, earthy color. I'm curious. If you left Riane before the start of winter, how did you end up with your hair so long?"

"Side effect of my powers when I vent my frustrations. Out of respect for my ladies, I didn't have it cut short again," Eirian answered.

Closing her eyes, she took deep breaths each time Muireann tackled a knotty section of her hair, letting go of them when the painful tugging at her scalp ceased.

"I wouldn't mind being able to do that."

Saoirse flipped her hair over her shoulder and chuckled, "I'm happy with mine. But I'm not a queen who gets henpecked by a cluster of women whose purpose in life is to attend to her every need. I noticed your scar."

Eirian lifted a hand, brushing it across the bodice as she said, "A training accident."

The two shared a look, and Saoirse asked, "With a whip?"

Shrugging, Eirian said no more while Muireann finished combing out her hair. She was uncomfortable with the question, and neither of them pressed further. Leaving the mass of long brown hair down, Muireann tucked the comb back into her pouch and stepped away, moving to the door to open it.

"I need shoes." Eirian held up one of her feet, wriggling her toes. "Unless barefoot will help make a statement."

"Come through. I believe your men have your boots and some other items."

Nodding, Saoirse waved at Eirian. "Go on, we're in a hurry."

Huffing, Eirian strode through to the next chamber and stopped short when she came face-to-face with her guards. Everett leaned against the wall with Aiden, their heads bowed as they spoke in whispers. Merle stood waiting, her weapons and belt clasped in his hands and her boots on the ground at his feet. Twenty-four men stared at Eirian, barely any room to move as they saluted her, and she blinked at them, taking it in.

Pushing her boots forward with his foot, Merle grinned and said, "We can't have you going barefoot, Your Majesty."

Eirian moved to deal with her boots, but Aiden shoved his way through and stopped her. Watching him kneel at her feet while picking up one of her shoes, she blushed and glanced away, not wanting to meet his eyes. Letting him pull the boots on, she returned her focus to the men and tried to study each of them. Knowing that two had died, she let her sorrow show as she looked at the survivors. Then, feeling fingers stroke the back of her knee and thigh teasingly, Eirian glanced down to watch Aiden release her foot.

"Thank you, Captain," she murmured.

"I wouldn't want you to push yourself," Aiden chuckled, remaining at her feet.

Rolling her eyes, Eirian reached out and grabbed her belt from the bundle in Merle's hands, quickly draping it around her waist and buckling it up.

"You want to aggravate me."

"Oh, always."

Rising to his feet, he touched her hand. Looking down, Eirian saw the two rings she had entrusted to his care and nodded. Aiden slipped them onto her fingers, stroking her palm lightly as he did so. A slight flare of her nose confirmed his action had the desired effect.

"I'd forgotten. Thank you," Eirian said as she turned back to Merle.

Handing over the swords, Merle informed her, "We made sure we thoroughly cleaned them and the scabbards. Who thought it was a good idea to put bloody blades in there?"

"I did. We were in a hurry to get away before I collapsed." Not looking at any of them as she ensured the scabbards were secure, Eirian held her hand out for her knives. "I'll try to remember next time that my men worry about a little blood."

A ripple of laughter filled the room, and Eirian smiled. The laughter helped her to pretend she felt fine. Exchanging looks, Saoirse and Muireann pushed her forward while Everett opened the door. Taking the cue, the guards filed into the corridor. Allowing Aiden and Merle to guide her, she kept her eyes forward and her head high. She barely took in anything as they escorted her through the keep. People ran before the group, and she wondered if they were fleeing in fear or to alert the others to her arrival.

"Eirian." Everett grabbed her arm as he said, "Whatever happens—"

"I know I can count on your support."

"Well, yes, no matter what, I'll support you. I was going to say whatever happens out there, stay strong and calm. They're your people, don't give them a reason to turn on you."

Dragging a hand through her hair, Eirian took a deep breath and asked, "What do you expect me to find?"

"I honestly don't know, but we'll face it together."

Squeezing her hand, Everett hoped she felt reassured. Nodding, Eirian stepped toward the entrance. Several guards moved quickly to get the doors, and Aiden positioned himself in front as Devin pushed them open. Their approach had spread among the soldiers, and the lines of people gathered outside startled the group. The moment Eirian appeared, cheers rose throughout the ranks of Endarans.

Staring at the soldiers, Eirian signaled her guards to step out of the way and walked forward, stopping on the bottom step. Lifting her hands, she swept her gaze over the people. Turning to the walls, she took in how they packed tightly along the top, jostling to get an unobstructed view. They saw Eirian with her hands up and fell silent as they waited.

"Thank you. It warms my heart to see you. It makes everything we endured worth it."

Her words carried, and they began cheering again. Beaming, Eirian glanced over her shoulder at Everett and noticed many nobles had joined him. Marcellus stood at his side, watching her like a hawk with his arms crossed over his chest. Taking the last step down and bringing herself level with the crowd, she ignored the protests of her guards and walked closer to the front line. Hurrying to keep up, Aiden and Merle matched her stride. Stopping a few strides from the first of the soldiers, Eirian saluted and held her hand in place over her heart. Following suit, they began saluting in return, dropping to their knees as they did so.

"Everything I do is to protect you, your families, and your towns. I do it for Endara. I am your queen, and it is my duty and my pleasure! I don't ask you to do anything I'm unwilling to do. As you would give your lives to defend your homes, so would I."

Everett stared at her, wide-eyed. Her voice was loud and clear, carrying over the heads of the kneeling people. Everything about her stance and how she moved displayed an authority he was not used to seeing. The dress Eirian wore clung to her, the deep green fabric rippling in the sunlight with every movement. It made him wonder how much she had held back. Feeling movement at his side, he glanced at the man who had joined him. The viscount was one of the most outspoken against Eirian.

"It should be you," he muttered.

"You're wrong, Philip. I couldn't do what she has done, and it's her actions that won them over. If it wasn't for her, none of them would be here."

Philip glanced sideways at where Marcellus was glaring at him. "If it wasn't for her, we wouldn't be in this position."

"Don't be so sure. Athnaral has been preparing longer than she's been queen. Why would they stand down because I took the throne? At least she can provide us with something that'll make them think twice."

Stepping away from Philip, Everett met Cameron's gaze. Smiling at those watching, Eirian spread her hands wide. The magic stirred, and she released it, sharing her energy with them. She felt them embrace it, letting it chase away their fatigue. She lowered her arms and moved along the line until she reached Cameron, offering her hands to draw him to his feet.

"General," Eirian murmured.

She grasped his wrists, letting him close his hands around her own.

"My Queen," Cameron replied with a smile.

"You have my blessing to do whatever is required."

Cameron's eyes narrowed as he replied, "Of course, Your Majesty, thank you. We brought the majority within the town walls. Those outside are taking it in turns to patrol, switching with those within. I've sent messengers to nearby towns, preparing them and sending for supplies. I'm also attempting to locate the troops on their way to meet us."

"Excellent. Have the Athnaralans moved?"

"They've withdrawn a distance from the town and set out white flags. Your actions bought us much-needed time, but they're demanding to meet with you. Our suspicions have been confirmed. Aeyren is among them."

Bowing her head, Eirian said, "I'm sorry for ruining your strategies."

"Don't be. You saved our collective asses. Just wish we'd known you could do that beforehand. That way, we could have devised a plan."

Letting go of her hands, Cameron looked to the guards and nobles at the entrance to the keep. She followed his gaze.

"You have the loyalty of your forces here, and as the news of what you did spreads, you'll have the loyalty of more. Loyalty to you, not loyalty to the throne."

Stepping back, Eirian shouted, "To your feet, Endarans! Our fight is not over! It will not be over until Athnaral has left our land!"

They started cheering her name as they rose, and turning, Eirian stared at the nobles, a grim smile on her face. She could tell who among them was against her, their fearful expressions becoming obvious discomfort as she looked at each of them. The jubilant sounds gave Eirian confidence, and she knew she needed every shred she could muster.

"All hail Queen Eirian!" Cameron shouted, slamming a hand to his chest in salute.

The gathered forces behind him echoed the words. They became so loud that Eirian wondered if the enemy forces could hear the sound beyond the wall. Meeting Aiden's gaze, she cocked her head to the side and raised her brows, daring him to say anything. His head cocked in the opposite direction, lips curling slightly as he lifted his hand to salute her.

"All hail Queen Eirian!" his voice joined the rest.

Thirteen

Eirian regarded the nobles and said, "I know what many of you are thinking. You barely wanted me on the throne, and now you're certain I shouldn't be."

Hearing protests, she held up her hand with the royal seal on it and shook her head, speaking over them dismissively.

"No, don't bother denying it. I'm not a fool, and I know what some of you say about me. I'm a woman, a mage. I'm not Endaran. Those who doubt me, how many of you would put your lives on the line alongside our soldiers? How many of you will do it time and time again? Because I did, and I will."

Pointing at the doors to the hall, Eirian's eyes narrowed.

"And they know it. That's why they shout my name. Everett is a good and honorable man. I understand why you'd rather he was the king. However, he can't inspire loyalty among the people of Endara like I can."

No one spoke.

"I invite you to contemplate what would happen if you attempted to force me from the throne. Not only would you cause instability during a war, but you would upset those good people outside who recognize me as their queen."

At Eirian's back, her guards, the general, and his staff stood with hands on the hilts of their weapons. She watched her supporters creep through their fellow nobles toward where Everett stood with Gallagher and Marcellus. It pleased her those not moving were lesser nobles and not members of the council. Without support, they could not push her from the throne. Gesturing at the warriors, Eirian made a show of cautioning them.

"King Aeyren is waiting to meet me. I expect he wants me dead, and I know some of you agree. But, luckily for me, you don't get to decide. I think it would be best to maintain a united front, and powers forbid, we might need you to be useful."

Aiden chuckled, "They wouldn't be much use as anything other than a distraction."

She replied, "Now, Captain, I'm sure many of them know how to use their weapons. They just need to understand their lives aren't worth more than the people outside this hall."

Eirian watched the anger appear on the faces of those they spoke about, and her magic welcomed it, curling around her like a cloak.

Putting himself forward, Philip sneered, "You're an abomination. What is to stop you from using your magic to do to us what you did to the Athnaralans?"

Arching her brows in surprise, Eirian said, "I don't believe you're planning on invading your lands and killing your people. Or are you? In which case, I'm sure your comrades will kill you quicker than I would."

"That's not what I meant!" Philip spluttered, thrown by her words.

"It isn't? Oh my, that's my mistake then. I thought you implied you were a threat because that's the only reason I'd use my magic against you."

The handful of nobles behind Philip looked around uncomfortably, their lack of confidence showing. Looking over his shoulder at them, Philip knew he was losing their support. Frowning, he turned to Everett with narrowed eyes.

"How can you stand there and support her? You were there for King Nolan. He raised you to rule Endara, yet you rolled over like a whipped hound and let her take your throne. You even put your bastard brother in charge of protecting her. We all know what some people suggest!"

"It was never my throne. Perhaps you should have raised your concerns years ago with King Nolan," Everett replied.

Marcellus crossed his arms and said, "Far greater men and women than you support her, Lord Philip. Queen Eirian has won the commanders of the army. We're at war with Athnaral. Have you forgotten what that means? The army is separate from the nobility. General Cameron has a seat on the small council."

"He's right. Think about your position, Philip. Making an enemy of your queen, the army, and members of the small council is a foolish move. Yes, what Queen Eirian did was horrifying. But you know what? I'm thankful she can do what she did." Gallagher looked at Eirian, his face filled with adoration, and said, "I can't imagine what it cost or how it weighs on her heart. I doubt I'm the only one who wishes they could ease that weight for her."

Eirian tried not to show her discomfort as she replied, "Thank you, Earl Gallagher."

Gallagher saluted and said, "I'm honored to serve, Your Majesty."

Philip sneered at the earl. "You've always credited mages with more than their due, and you worship her like a fool. Everyone knows you asked the council for her hand."

"General, have your people escort Lord Philip to his room and make sure he remains." Everett spoke, "If any of you feel your decision to support him was a little hasty, you're welcome to step away from the viscount."

Almost as one, the nobles moved away from Philip, Everett's invitation giving them the excuse they had been looking for. Eirian suspected they were only removing themselves from the firing line. For the moment, it barely mattered. They only needed to stay in line until the war was over. Remaining silent as Gunter and several others approached Philip, Eirian faced Cameron.

"I want to meet with the Athnaralans as soon as possible. Can't let them have too much time to get over their shock."

He agreed, "Or for their reinforcements to arrive."

"Do you think it's wise, Your Majesty?" Marcellus asked seriously.

"I don't see what choice we have if we want to capitalize on their fear of me. A nice healthy level of fear could give us a better negotiating position."

She smoothed her hands over the strange fabric of the dress Muireann had loaned her, making a note in the back of her mind to ask them about it. Mixed with her guards, several of the Telmians exchanged looks.

"Your Majesty, you're barely this side of exhausted after your performance outside," one of them commented.

Glancing away, Eirian did not admit he was correct. It was a weakness she would not confirm to those whose loyalty she questioned.

"Make the arrangements, General," Eirian instructed.

"Yes, ma'am." Cameron signaled for his people to follow.

Walking around, Eirian looked the chamber over. The stone arches carved from whole stones felt older than the keep in Amath. Pillars held up the ceiling, and approaching them, she ran her hands over the cold stone. Eyes going wide, she felt the wards. It was a surprise. She focused on the feel of them so she could understand their purpose. They supported the entire structure, reinforcing the weight-bearing abilities of the stone.

"Another keep built by mages," she murmured.

Eirian sighed and glanced sideways at the two men, letting her hands fall away. Aiden arched a brow at her, and Everett stared at the pillars.

"When this is over, we should request a survey of older keeps to discover their secrets."

"I don't suppose you can tell if this one is hiding a tactical advantage?" Everett joked.

"Perhaps later. Better yet, it would be nice if the daoine would have a look for us. Just in case there's something like the trees. Don't want me accidentally setting anything off."

Her quip failed to amuse, and Aiden watched suspiciously as she resumed pacing.

"Ma'am, sit and have something else to eat while you wait for the general to make arrangements," he commented.

"I think that's an excellent idea," Marcellus agreed.

Approaching her, Everett held his hands out and coaxed, "Come on, Eirian, let's get you some more food."

Arching a brow, Eirian chuckled, "I'm not arguing. Why are you trying to soothe me like a skittish horse? Are you afraid I might run away at the mere suggestion I sit down, eat, and rest for a little while?"

"Honestly? Yes," Everett muttered, glancing around the hall.

Laughing, Eirian allowed Everett to guide her to a table. They had pushed it to the side to prepare for the hall being used post-combat for the injured. Sitting, she rubbed her face wearily and slumped. Then, with fewer eyes scrutinizing her, she allowed herself a moment to not only feel her exhaustion, but to allow the others to see it. Standing beside her, Everett brushed a hand over her head and sighed.

"I don't think it's a good idea for you to go out there and meet Aeyren today. You look like you'll struggle to remain standing for much longer."

"I must meet with Aeyren. We need to establish how much time we have."

Glancing at Everett as he towered over her, Eirian shrugged and closed her eyes. Gallagher had remained in the hall with Marcellus, and he peered at her from where the two of them stood a short distance away.

He asked, "Surely you can force them back like you did yesterday?"

"Are you serious?" Aiden growled, "Please tell me you're not serious."

"It's a fair question, Captain," Devin muttered.

Nodding, Fox waved at Eirian. "We don't know what Her Majesty can do."

Groaning, Eirian covered her ears and pleaded, "Please be quiet."

"But can you?" Gallagher prompted.

Feeling the discomfort of the Telmians at the suggestion, Eirian lifted her head and replied, "Not today, not tomorrow, and not the day after."

"What your queen means is the amount of power it took, and the strain on her magic, body, and mind was tremendous." The Telmian who had pointed out her exhaustion spoke, "She can do it again, but not for a few days. She needs rest."

"My magic is fine. The exhaustion is strictly physical." Looking at him, Eirian frowned, her mouth twisting. "I don't believe they introduced us."

"My Lord Faolan has kept interactions with you restricted. I'm Ilar." He bowed, smiling faintly. "I suspect we may have more in common than you do with the loyal wolf."

"Oh?"

"Yes, I can do what you can do."

The answer stunned her, and those who were not already looking at Ilar turned to stare as Eirian asked, "You can draw the life out of things?"

Nodding, Ilar glanced at the handful of others watching Eirian intently. "I can, and while I'm not the only one, it's an exceedingly rare ability. Our king can do it."

Speechless, Eirian continued to stare at him.

"Why did no one mention this during planning?" Marcellus huffed, looking thoroughly unimpressed. "How many of you can do it? Can we use it as a defense if desperate?"

"There's one other who can do it. Muireann. However, she's a healer, and asking her to take life in that manner would be a great insult. Neither of us could manage even half of what your queen did."

Food and drink arriving provided a distraction, and Eirian peered at the trays in the hope of a pastry and pouted when there were none. Instead, there was bread, cheeses, fruits, and slices of cold meat, and she scolded herself for hoping for more. Making herself eat a little of everything, she mulled over her food in silence and half-listened to the snatches of conversation. Leaning against the table, Aiden was equally silent. General Cameron had returned, standing with Marcellus and Everett as they spoke in whispers, throwing the occasional look at her.

Risking the use of a small amount of magic to raise a ward, Eirian wiped her hands on her skirt and looked at Aiden. "Captain."

"I know. Everett has already hissed it in my ears. I'm not to breathe a word of your half-blood nature to anyone," Aiden muttered in frustration.

"That wasn't what I was going to say, but yes, it's remaining a secret," Eirian replied.

"Because of the war."

"You understand, don't you?"

There was a hint of sadness in his eyes when Aiden glanced at her. "All too well. What were you going to say?"

"I was going to ask why you kissed me."

"You think now is a good time to ask? May I point out you kissed me back?"

Shrugging, Eirian waved at the surrounding people dismissively. "It seemed as good as any. No one is paying attention, and our words are muffled. Thankfully, because otherwise, you'd have told the room I'm half-human."

"I've learned to pay attention. Unfortunately, your little trick also muffles what we can hear." Aiden stuffed cheese in his mouth and hoped Eirian would forget the subject.

Eirian snorted. "You don't want to answer, do you?"

"Is it that obvious?"

"Fine, but we need to talk about it sometime."

Pushing off the table, Aiden said, "No, we don't."

Sucking her breath in through her teeth, Eirian let the ward drop and stood shakily. The food had helped, but the drain on her body was not easily fixed. Strolling over to Cameron and the dukes, she grasped her hands behind her back, hoping to hide the tremors.

"Any news?"

"Yes, ma'am, but I didn't want to stop you from eating. King Aeyren will meet with you in the field mid-afternoon. However, he has conditions," Cameron told her, his mouth twisted in frustration.

"What are they?"

"He wants to speak to you alone."

"How does he propose we do that?"

Marcellus grumbled, "I imagine leaving your people a distance away and meeting out of earshot."

"Perhaps Aeyren thinks getting you alone would give him an advantage?" Everett commented, "If I didn't know you, I'd think speaking to you alone would separate you from anyone prompting your decisions."

"Ah, the old puppet assumption." Eirian rolled her eyes. "She's a woman, and therefore, someone must control her."

Cameron chuckled, "He doesn't know you."

"For all we know, Aeyren could be a puppet, and this is his way of speaking to me without influence."

They blinked at her, and Eirian could see that they had not considered what she suggested. Behind her, Aiden snorted.

"It didn't occur to any of you because, once again, you're assuming things based on him being a man. Clearly, I'm the only one who could be someone's puppet."

"We considered the possibility!" Marcellus was quick to respond.

Everett agreed, "It's a matter of who could influence the King of Athnaral. Their accusations of you being a puppet for Ensaycal or Riane are at least understandable."

Regarding them coldly, Eirian ran through her options and let a smile curl the corners of her mouth. They had learned to dread that smile, knowing the suggestion was likely to be one they would not appreciate.

"General, are your people ready to meet with Athnaral?"

"Of course, ma'am. Why?" Cameron asked blankly.

"Because we're going. Aeyren thinks he can dictate terms to me? Well, I won't let him." Eirian signaled to Fionn, and he darted over. "We need the horses."

Saluting her, Fionn glanced at Aiden and asked hesitantly, "Captain?"

"Don't look at him! I gave you an order."

Her voice was icy, and Fionn stepped back, summoning his squad without further hesitation. Others followed him. Doubting the wisdom of Eirian's decision, Marcellus reached out to touch her arm.

"Are you sure you want to do this, Eirian?"

"Yes. Even if Aeyren makes me wait, it gives me time to face my actions. Do we want him to see how the results of what I did in battle affect me?"

They could not argue with Eirian's reasoning, and she knew it. Stepping around Aiden and Merle, she made her way toward the doors with all the determination she could gather. The trembles had subsided, but it was only a matter of time before they returned. Unfortunately, sheer willpower would only get her so far. Guards lingered outside the door, watching with curiosity as she left the hall.

Gabe and his men led the way, none daring to utter a word. Outside, the troops had vanished, returning to their duties or their rest. Shouts rang out along the wall as they sighted Eirian, and she sensed how the guards surrounding her became more alert than they had been inside. Aiden attempted to direct her, and she gave him an annoyed look.

"The horses are this way," he said. "Your boy was unharmed."

"I know."

Aiden muttered, "Of course you do."

Fionn and his squad had recruited the help of some soldiers, and their horses were ready. Approaching Halcyon, Eirian held her hands out and smiled happily when he nuzzled her and let out a nicker of greeting. The velvety feel of his muzzle against her skin was welcome, and she leaned forward, resting her head on his neck to draw on his warmth. Then, running her hands over him, Eirian reassured herself that he was unharmed.

"Let me help you." Aiden approached, offering his hands, and reminded her, "You know you're terrible in a dress."

Accepting his aid, Eirian did not speak until she had settled in the saddle. Conscious of the eyes watching, Aiden did not let his hands linger like he wanted. Stepping away, he hauled himself onto his mount. There was some surprise when Faolan appeared in his wolf form. Staring at him, she smiled knowingly, and he kept close as they moved off. Above them, the sun had hit its peak and was creeping toward the west. Feeling the warmth on her face, Eirian tilted her head back and drew energy from it.

A low growl from Faolan drew her attention away from the sky before they passed through the gate. He intended to warn Eirian to prepare for the sight that greeted them. Bracing, she took a long look at the field where they had battled. Her recollection of how things looked when she had finished matched what her eyes were seeing. Eirian realized they had removed many corpses, but left those who fell to her magic.

It was disconcerting, knowing the overgrown wildflowers and grass mostly hid the withered corpses that had nourished them. Eirian felt the waves of unease from the sight among the Endarans. It was almost as palatable as her despair. The horses approached, many of them growing skittish as they sensed something about the ground. Finally, a gentle tug on the reins brought Halcyon to a halt.

Tugging her skirts carefully, Eirian dismounted without making a fool of herself. The moment her feet touched down, she felt the traces of her magic lingering on the earth. Faolan was at her side, his nose finding her hand. Others dismounted as she stood beside her horse with the wolf sitting at her feet. Glancing down at him, she lifted her hand from his reach and frowned as she shifted sideways.

"Majesty?" Everett joined her.

Shaking her head, Eirian held up a hand and said, "I want you to remain here with the horses. King Aeyren wished to meet alone, and so we shall."

"But he's not here, and you can't be sure he won't make you wait."

Eirian unbuckled her belt, handing Everett her weapons. "He won't."

Aiden growled, "You can't go out there unarmed!"

"I'm never unarmed. Besides, Aeyren would be a right fool to try anything. So shut up, Captain, and let me do this. If Faolan comes, we can pretend he's my faithful pet."

Faolan whined, lifting a paw, giving the men a look that resembled gloating.

"What if they realize what he is? They shot the bird yesterday," Marcellus commented and peered at the Athnaralan camp. "But you're right. Aeyren did request to meet alone."

Cameron said, "I don't think we need to remind you what's at stake."

Giving her weapons a longing glance without responding, Eirian turned from the people who had accompanied her. Once a few steps away, she called to Faolan cheekily.

"Come on, boy, if you're good and don't bite anyone, I'll find you a nice, tasty cut of meat for dinner."

Laughter made Faolan growl as he padded over to join her. The grass Eirian had grown was long enough to brush over his face while they walked together toward the middle of the field. Fluffy dandelion seeds stuck in his fur, and he gave the occasional shake to dislodge them. Letting her fingertips touch the tops of the seeded stalks, Eirian stopped when they reached the first set of remains. She did not crouch for a closer look. If she had not known what happened, she would have assumed the man had been dead for a long time.

Sitting beside her, Faolan had his head cocked to the side, watching Eirian's face and the emotions that crossed it. Her mind warred with her feelings as she forced herself to remember what would have transpired if she had not killed them. While looking at the bodies scattered through the green, she recalled the taste of their fear. Whining, Faolan nudged her leg with his nose, and she took a deep breath, focusing on the group of riders that had left the enemy camp.

Their approach helped Eirian gather herself and step carefully past the body. She picked along with the odd glance over her shoulder until she was roughly halfway. The other riders had stopped, and a lone man left them to make his way over. Faolan did his best to appear harmless, just a faithful companion accompanying his mistress. A slight breeze had picked up, and she pushed tendrils of hair out of her face while assessing the lone figure crossing the field of his dead soldiers.

The man approaching struck Eirian as nothing outstanding. Dirty blond hair framed his face, and as he drew close, she noticed he was shorter. It made her realize she had built Aeyren up in her mind into a formidable man. Smoothing her hands over her skirts, Eirian tried not to let her disappointment show as Aeyren came to a stop.

An air of wrongness about him made her skin prickle, but it was not as bad as it had been around General Tomas. Aeyren stared at her with light blue eyes, and Eirian arched a brow as he made it obvious that he was assessing her. Unlike Eirian, he possessed his weapons, and she looked at his sword in amusement.

"There is something oddly romantic about meeting a woman in a field of flowers." Aeyren broke the silence and waved at the mixture of blooms that surrounded them. "Of course, it becomes less romantic when you consider they're covering corpses."

Her lips twitched, and Eirian tried not to smile as she said, "I'm dreadfully sorry about that. I don't take well to uninvited guests trying to kill my people."

Aeyren did not look amused. "How did you expect me to respond to a mage taking the throne of Endara?"

"No different to everyone else, since my being a mage changes nothing. I don't intend to do anything except rule my kingdom as my family has for a thousand years."

"So you say. Then when you've married? Or the elves put pressure on you? You're a woman. You'd have done what you were told."

Eirian crossed her arms, noting how it drew his eyes to her breasts. Beside her, Faolan nudged her leg.

"I've always been curious where you Athnaralans got your women-hating notions from. We're not weaker. We're not incapable, and we're certainly not less!"

"While I disagree, we're not here to debate philosophy. You're unnatural, a woman with a power she shouldn't have, in a position of authority she shouldn't be in." Aeyren glanced at the wolf at her feet. "Commanding forces she has no right to be commanding."

"And here I thought you said we wouldn't debate philosophy? All those things are only wrong to you. My people have no issues with it. But, of course, we don't expect women to remain in bed waiting for our men to come home."

Aeyren leered at her.

Shaking her head, Eirian said, "You've invaded my kingdom over a philosophical difference. For years, we've remained at relative peace. While there's been the odd border skirmish, Endara and Athnaral have left each other alone. Why destroy all that goodwill?"

"Because you're a threat to all of us!"

Eirian laughed and lifted a hand to cover her mouth, waving the other at him. "Oh, please! I'm not a threat to anyone. I'm answerable to the high council for every action I take as a mage. I'm answerable to the council of Endara for every action I take as the queen. Then there's always the risk of angering Ensaycal and yourself. Do you think I'd do anything to jeopardize my people?"

"Yes, I do. You wouldn't be able to help yourself."

"Because I'm a woman, no doubt."

She rolled her eyes, scoffing at the way Aeyren glared. Faolan lifted his head and bared his teeth, growling when he took a step toward her.

"Wouldn't you like to feel less burdened by duty? I can offer you that," Aeyren said.

Looking down at Faolan, Eirian recalled why the Telmians had come. "It gets overwhelming sometimes. So many people rely on me. The lives my decisions affect."

"The throne of Athnaral weighs on me. I can only guess how much harder it is for you."

Clueless about what she was saying, Aeyren took another step toward her and smiled. Meeting his gaze, Eirian knew he had assumed she agreed with him. She decided it could buy time if he thought she was amiable toward him. Sitting up, Faolan leaned against her legs and she stroked his head.

"I don't want a war. You can't win, and it's my people who'll pay."

"You're right. The Endaran people are the ones who'll pay the price. I can stop that. You don't have to be at war with us. You can end a thousand years of conflict."

"Ensaycal will never stand for it."

Aeyren said, "United, we could defeat them."

There was a gleam in his eye that told Eirian he was lapping up her words. Looking down again, her hair fell over her face, and she dug her fingers into Faolan's fur. She could count on Aeyren's ignorance.

"There are many red mages in Paienven's army. You've seen what I can do on my own. Imagine what hundreds, even thousands of mages could do, men with greater strength."

He looked over the land, contemplating her point. "You fear your fellow mages?"

"I do, and so should you. Maybe humans could overthrow the elves, but it won't happen until we can defeat the mages. I didn't ask to be born with magic, but I can't change it, and since I'm stuck with it, I'll accept its benefits, and I'll use it to do what I can to protect my people."

"Despite the heinousness of what you did yesterday, I can appreciate it. You don't want innocent people harmed. You're a mother defending her young."

Shifting uncomfortably at how Aeyren looked at her, Eirian said, "Our people don't want war. They want to live their lives as they've always done. We must give them that."

"I agree with you."

He turned to look at his people. Eirian bit her tongue, reminding herself to be polite. Her forces needed time.

Aeyren commented, "I'm pleasantly surprised at how sensible you are. I worried you wouldn't be willing to listen."

"They've taught me to listen and consider my options seriously."

Turning to her, Aeyren smiled, and Eirian forced herself to smile back.

"A sensible trait. I apologize for my gift, and I hope it didn't shock you too badly."

Pursing her lips, Eirian made a show of looking down, hoping it would hide how much she hated what she was saying. "It was rather shocking, but I suppose his willingness to turn on his king made it a deserved fate."

"Hopefully, it doesn't make you think worse of me. I'm not an evil man. I'm a king trying to do what is best for my people. You understand. My original offer stands. I want to unite our kingdoms peacefully through marriage."

"Your offer is worth consideration. Any peaceful solution is. However, I fear Ensaycal would see it as an act of aggression, and all humans would pay. I've already turned down the Crown Prince. I can't risk angering Paienven further. Having grown up in Riane, I know the high council would side with Ensaycal."

He grunted in acknowledgment.

Giving Aeyren her best attempt at a doe-eyed look, Eirian asked, "Are there no other options we can explore for a peaceful solution?"

Shaking his head, Aeyren replied, "No, there isn't. If you marry me, I'll protect you from the elves. Our people, united, can make a stand against them."

"How can you be sure?" Eirian asked, hoping he would provide information.

"You don't need to worry about that. I'll take care of everything, and you can be free of the burdens unfairly placed upon you by people who should've known better. Think about what it'd mean for the Endaran people. No more war with Athnaral."

Closing the gap between them, Aeyren lifted his hand and stroked her face. The feel of his touch made Eirian want to scream, and she fought hard not to shudder in disgust.

Instead, she said, "I'd need to convince my council. I'm not free to marry without their approval. They may feel it would be better to replace me and maintain the existing status quo. Many feel my cousin is the better choice."

"Well, he's a man. But he can't offer what you can. I only extend my offer of peace to you. Marry me, and we'll unite all humans, and our son will be born king of both kingdoms."

"You've thought of everything. I like it when people plan accordingly."

Reaching out, Aeyren took hold of her hand and lifted it to kiss the back. "I'm pleased the stories of your loveliness weren't an exaggeration. You are a fine woman."

"Thank you, Your Majesty. I'm very flattered. You're a handsome man, and I'm surprised you've not married already," Eirian replied.

"I've been waiting for the right woman. Royal blood deserves only the best, after all. Unfortunately, you're already so old, but I'm sure it wouldn't take us long."

Bristling at his comment about her age, Eirian carefully plucked her hand from his grasp. "I'm only twenty-six."

"You can't deny you're old to be marrying and producing heirs."

"I hadn't planned on marrying or having children. However, you've given me much to consider, and I may change my mind."

"Yes, you will," Aeyren replied.

Faolan bumped her leg with his head, whining, and Eirian glanced over her shoulder at the lines of watching people. "But I'll need to convince my council it's the right path."

"How long will it take?"

"Several are here, but it would need a majority. They'd want to negotiate terms to protect themselves. They wouldn't care what happened to me so long as their heads remained on their shoulders and they didn't find themselves without their lands."

"I wouldn't expect any less. Have your fastest riders sent to assemble your council, and we'll negotiate. You, of course, will remain. I'd like to get to know my future wife."

Eirian said, "While we wait, will you withdraw? We wouldn't want to misconstrue anything as an act of aggression. I won't win my council over if they think you'll attack."

A flicker of triumph crossed his face, and Aeyren assured her, "You have my word."

Dropping in a curtsy, Eirian smiled. Her magic whispered across her mind, screaming he spoke lies. She did not need her power to confirm what she knew. The rage chased the exhaustion away, and flickers of it escaped her grasp. Aware of it, she noticed wildflowers wilting.

"Thank you for being so magnanimous, King Aeyren, and I truly hope we can reach an arrangement that suits everyone."

"I'm sure we will. Send those riders, and I'll be in contact." Aeyren glanced at Faolan. "Next time, leave the beast behind. You'll need to get used to not having it following you around."

Clenching her teeth, Eirian waited for him to walk away before she ran her fingertips over Faolan's head, the wolf baring his teeth at the man. Once she was sure Aeyren would not turn back, she spun on her heels and gathered her skirts. She stomped her way to where her people waited. Magic slipped from Eirian's control, a trail of desiccated growth following in her wake. Faolan radiated anger that rivaled her own, and the moment they drew close to the Endarans, she could tell they felt it as well.

"You look happy," Everett observed, earning himself a furious glare.

"I convinced him to give us time. I don't know how much, but it's time." Shuddering, Eirian leaned against Halcyon and breathed in his scent. "I feel like I need to go drown myself in a river."

Marcellus looked concerned and turned to Faolan, saying, "If they weren't watching, I'd ask you to tell us what happened."

"I led that... brute... to believe I'm open to his offer, and I need to convene my entire council to convince the majority. The whole thing has left me feeling dirty."

"So why is he furious?" Pointing at Faolan, Aiden arched a brow.

"Probably because he got called a beast." Slumping, Eirian looked at Cameron and said, "I couldn't learn much. Aeyren said he'd withdraw, but I don't believe him."

"You're not seriously considering his offer, are you?" Everett asked with concern.

Sighing heavily, Eirian shook her head and said firmly, "Never! I'd sooner marry a random farmer than that man."

Merle studied her. "There's something about him that's left you unhappy."

"Besides the fact he's a condescending, presumptuous, misogynistic jackass, which I could tell without magic, there's something wrong with him."

Ilar nudged his way forward and spoke, "My lord says the human stunk of darkness."

Swallowing, Eirian agreed, "You could say that. He felt unnatural, and it made my skin crawl. It was almost as bad as his general."

"So, we won't have peace with Athnaral?" Cameron asked.

"I'll do what I can, but let's not waste time. Send our fastest riders, find those damn elves, and make sure the rest of our army is on the move to the border."

FOURTEEN

The weather had changed, and the skies were an ominous gray. Weeks of persistent downpours had turned Kelsby into mud. Those not lucky enough to have shelter within the buildings remained huddled in their tents when not on duty. Across the sodden field, the Athnaralans stayed in place. Daily messengers traipsed the short distance between them as King Aeyren kept the pressure on Eirian to accept his offer.

Determined to claw out some time for herself, she had made her way to the roof of the keep. Fionn and his squad watched in silent curiosity as she removed her weapons and boots, leaving them to one side. Standing in the middle of the roof, the cold of the stone soaking into her bones, her eyes closed and face to the sky, Eirian breathed in the damp air.

"What's she doing?" Kyson asked.

Their eyes tracked the way Eirian almost danced across the roof.

Fionn pointed, replying, "Looks like some sort of fancy fighting, but without an opponent. Watch, that's a blocking move, and that's an attack."

"I'm surprised she hasn't fallen flat on her face. She's barefoot! How's she doing it?" Shaking his head, Tyler rested his elbows against the wall and looked at the sky. "It's going to rain again. Powers take this blasted weather."

The door opened, the five men turned to face whoever was coming through. Relaxing at the sight of Aiden, they did not look back at Eirian. Instead, they exchanged looks as they observed his reaction. Fionn was the only one who glanced at her. Mainly to assure himself she remained as she had been, eyes closed and a peaceful expression on her face. Aiden stared before looking over the rest of the rooftop, eyes settling on the pile of her weapons.

"How long has she been at it?"

"Oh, I don't know, a little while," Fionn answered. "We're not sure what she's doing. I think it's some sort of fighting style."

"You could call it that. There was an old weapons master when I was a boy who would be out in the yard first and last light every day to do it. He learned from a mage, said it helped clear the mind." Aiden unbuckled his belt, his men staring in shock.

"And your father made you learn it."

Grimacing, Aiden put his weapons down next to hers and muttered, "No. The Earl thought it was foolishness. I learned because I wanted to prove otherwise. I can't promise I'll look as good doing it as she does, and I'm certainly not going to take off my boots."

"Oh, come on, Cap'n, take them off!" Paxton laughed.

He was not the only one laughing, each man earning himself a dark look from Aiden. "No. Now, all of you bugger off and go guard the stairs or something."

Fionn did not move. "We are guarding something. The Queen."

"Well, do it from the other side of the door. I need to talk to her."

"Uh-huh. Talk. Right. We believe you, don't we, boys?" They chuckled at each other, and Fionn nodded to the door. "Let's give our captain some space to… talk."

Scowling, Aiden crossed his arms while they left. Fionn ushered his squad through the door, giving him a sarcastic smile and wave. Shifting to watch Eirian, he counted her steps and motions until he was sure of her pattern. Then he cut in as she moved and brought an arm up to block a forward motion. Her eyes flew open, narrowing in anger when they flickered to look at where his arm met hers.

"What are you doing?"

"Allowing you to put me on my ass."

Dropping her stance, Eirian stepped back. "I don't want to spar with you right now. Besides, if we slipped and fell, the blow to our head could be fatal."

"You don't think you could best me?" Aiden goaded.

"I know I can, but I'd rather not break your pretty head. Your brother might be unhappy."

Arching a brow at her emphasis on brother, Aiden gave her a challenging look. "Everett would say I deserved it. He hasn't forgiven me for a few things recently. Trust a woman to come between brothers."

She turned away, scoffing, "Don't be stupid."

"You sound just like him. Though he shouted it along with things like beheaded, treason, she's the queen, she's my cousin, and you're her fucking guard."

Aiden grabbed her arm, knowing it would make her take a swing at him. Eirian moved with his pull and brought her other arm up, responding precisely as he predicted, and she snarled when he blocked it.

"You're an ass."

Smiling, he chuckled. "Yes, but until you remove me from my post, one of us dies, or you stop being the queen, I'm your ass."

Eirian moved quicker than he expected, and the force of her strikes was a surprise. Carefully defending himself, Aiden did not dare glance over his shoulder for fear of slipping. Her anger was icy, and he wondered if he had pushed at the wrong time. When his back hit the stone wall, he knew she had forced him to the edge of the roof. A flicker of triumph passed through her eyes, hand raised to strike. Watching it come toward him, Aiden flinched when she stopped short of his throat.

Growling in frustration, Eirian turned her back on him. "Why do you make me so bloody angry with just a few words?"

"Do you want me to answer that?"

"Fuck it."

Spinning, Eirian grabbed his tunic and yanked him toward her. Her kiss came as a shock, and before Aiden could respond, she was pulling away, taking the faint scent of flowers with her.

"Oh no you don't!" he growled.

Grabbing Eirian's hips, Aiden jerked her back. There was a sense of challenge in his kiss, and she buried a hand in his hair, pushing up on her toes for more height. Groaning, he let go of her hips and moved one hand to her behind, pressing her closer while the other cradled the back of her head. Surrounded by the intoxicating scent of flowers, he did not want to let go. When she withdrew slightly, Aiden tightened his hold, expecting her to fight him. Instead, the mix of anger and lust in Eirian's gaze startled him.

"Eirian."

"I shouldn't have done that, but when I'm angry with you, I can't explain it. I never know if I want to kill you or..."

Shrugging, Eirian let go of his hair, her hand resting on his shoulder. He did not move, watching the conflicting emotions cross her face.

"I know."

Sliding his hand from Eirian's neck down her back, Aiden felt her go tense, and he wondered if she would pull away.

"You do it on purpose, don't you?"

Aiden dug his fingers in and lifted her onto her toes, chuckling, "Not all the time. But fighting with you comes naturally. I even look forward to it."

"How old was I when you first met me?"

Her question made Aiden groan, his head falling back so he could stare at the heavy gray clouds above them. "I don't want to think about you as a child right now."

Smirking, Eirian wriggled free. "Too bad, I asked a question, Captain."

Giving her a disgruntled look, Aiden turned around and leaned against the wall, staring out. They were facing away from the Athnaralan camp, and he took in how peaceful the land appeared. He watched from the corner of his eye as Eirian joined him. She glanced at him sideways, lips still curled in a smirk and cheeks flushed.

"I remember you were barely a week old, and you screamed a lot. Ma said it was because you knew your mother was dead. Your aunt was strict, and my mother hated how Tegan dictated handling you. She wouldn't allow your wet nurses to hold you except to feed. They had to leave you in your crib, and she guarded you constantly. No one was to touch you."

Remembering Eirian as a baby forced Aiden to think about his mother, and his hand went to the pouch around his neck.

"You never speak nicely about my aunt," Eirian commented with a frown.

He did not look at her. "Tegan was a hard woman. I understand circumstances made her that way. She hated her husband, my mother for being the other woman, her brother for putting her in the situation, and you for taking away her chance at being the mother of the next king. But, most of all, she hated her sister for being happy with her marriage and hated me for existing. Everett was her one joy, her darling son who loved her above all others."

Eirian tried to imagine how she would have felt if she had been her aunt. "You sound like you pity her."

"I do pity her, but she didn't have to be such a bitter person."

"Maybe she couldn't be anything else. Changing how you feel is easier said than done."

"It was the middle of the night. You'd been screaming for powers know how long, and it frustrated Tegan. She woke my mother and ordered her to watch you. I suppose she thought it would be a punishment, but my mother was always glad to do it," Aiden told her.

Eirian waited for him to continue his story, not willing to interrupt.

"My mother snuck me into the nursery and picked you up, cradling you like you were the most precious thing in the world. I watched her walk around, rocking you in her arms and singing songs she sang for me. Finally, you calmed down, and she sat, calling me over."

Turning to look at her, Aiden smiled sadly.

"You were bald and funny looking, with these big black eyes that seemed to see everything. Mother got me to climb in her lap and helped me hold you, wrapping her arms around both of us."

"Aiden," Eirian murmured.

"She said to me, 'this is your queen, and you need to protect her like you protect your brother.' I've never forgotten what she said. 'Love her as you love him. She has no one else.' I stared at you, so tiny and innocent, and I promised her I would."

Arching a brow, Eirian said, "I hope you don't kiss Everett like that."

Aiden glared at her before chuckling, "I never planned on kissing you."

"What changed?"

"I wanted to do my job, to protect you, be your friend, maybe a brother. I thought you'd remember. I met you at the border, and instead of a reserved princess, you were you."

Eirian remembered the day at the border to Riane.

"I watched you race your horse, and you were carefree, and the smile you gave me when you looked at me was like coming home. I felt drawn to you," Aiden admitted. "I tried to be distant and stern, but it was as though you saw it as a challenge. When it became clear you didn't remember me, I decided not to remind you."

"You're right. I saw you as a challenge. A battle of wills because I thought you didn't like me. I hid the truth because I feared what everyone would think, but I constantly wanted to show you what I could do."

"It would have been easier for both of us if I didn't like you very much." Feeling a splash of water against his face, Aiden sighed. "We should go inside."

"I'm sorry you're in this predicament," Eirian murmured sadly.

"I wouldn't say it's a terrible predicament. My father was an earl and my mother a lady. I have royal blood in my heritage." Aiden stood behind her and leaned in to whisper, "Your blood is no better than mine."

Shivering, Eirian did not move and kept her eyes locked on the gray mist closing in, ignoring the chuckle her response elicited. "I suppose you're more Endaran than I am."

Reaching past, Aiden put both hands on the wall and pushed her against it, lips remaining close to her ear. They taunted her.

"I certainly am. It's a pity you have to give up the throne. I'm the perfect candidate for a husband, as many are planning. They respected my father, and they respect me. They think I could control you." Her squirm made him chuckle, "And maybe I could."

"Is that what you want? I've told you before I'd happily give you a title and lands if you wished to leave my service. I'd legitimize you," she replied, ignoring his comment.

"I'm not interested in lands or titles. That's not what I want from you. As for leaving your service? Not happening. You're stuck with me, darling."

Pressing his lips to her neck, Aiden smiled at the way her breath hitched. Hanging her head, Eirian closed her eyes and breathed deeply, forcing herself to focus on the rain.

"You need to find someone else to love. Someone who deserves it, who is free to return it."

"You say that as though it's easily done, as though you wouldn't have me right here in the rain. I want you to remember the feel of my lips on you every time you spar with someone else, and how I make you feel with a few words."

Letting go of the wall with one hand, Aiden tugged at the edge of her tunic until his fingers found skin. His fingers stroked across her stomach, and Eirian groaned. With his nose brushing her cheek, he thought he would drown in the aroma of flowers. It was heady, no longer the sweet scent he was used to smelling from her.

"Aiden."

"I might not be a prince, but I'm your equal in all the ways you care about. Until age robs me, I'll always be a match for you, darling."

A rumble of thunder heralded heavier rain. Tilting her head back, Eirian opened her eyes to stare at the clouds, watching for a flash of lightning despite the drops pelting her face. Aiden's fingers continued to stroke across her skin, taunting her as they slipped lower. She needed him to keep going. Hearing her whimper, he nipped at her ear, hand continuing down.

"Oi, Captain, don't you think you should come in?" Fionn yelled from the shelter of the stairway.

Growling in frustration, Aiden pulled away reluctantly and grumbled, "Fuck."

Flustered, Eirian rolled her shoulders. "He's right."

"I could order him back to the other side of the door. We didn't finish our spar, and the rain would make it more interesting."

Flashing a grin, he chuckled when she sneered.

Stalking to her boots and weapons, she said, "No, I finished the round, and you lost."

"That's not how I remember it."

Following closely, Aiden expected her to turn on him. Bending to pick up her weapons and boots, Eirian did not answer. Without him partially shielding her from the rain, the cold was setting in, and she wanted to get inside, dried off and warm. Glancing at her feet, she scowled in regret at the painful numbness. Hurrying over to Fionn, she met his worried gaze and hugged her things tightly. Behind her, Aiden was glaring, and Fionn gave him a mocking salute.

"You look like drowned rats. Did you have to stay out while it poured?"

"Get Her Majesty back to her room," Aiden ordered the waiting guards. "She's going to soak the stairs. Make sure she doesn't slip."

Glancing over her shoulder at him in surprise, Eirian asked, "You won't ensure I'm safely locked in my chambers?"

Smiling, Aiden replied, "I'm off duty."

Tyler offered his arm. "Come on, ma'am, you're turning blue."

Eirian wiped the water from her eyes. "Let's go."

Keeping her gaze focused on where she was walking, Eirian let them guide her down the stairs. The keep was busy, and her guards were on edge until they reached the chambers allocated to her. Merle and his men were sitting in the first room, a game of cards in progress. He quickly sent Devin to fetch towels when they saw her dripping wet and barefoot. The fire was lit in the corner, and Eirian hurried to stand in front of it before she surrendered her wet boots and weapons.

"What happened?" Merle asked, glancing at Fionn.

"I lost track of time and didn't notice it was raining until the thunder rolled in." Looking at the puddle forming at her feet, Eirian sighed heavily. "I'm going to dry off."

Not waiting for a comment, she headed across to the next door and went through, shutting it behind her. Turning to face Fionn, Merle held his hands in the air questioningly.

"She and the captain... talked. All cozy in the rain. I didn't want to interrupt, but then the thunder started."

Shrugging, Fionn looked slightly embarrassed at the admission he had let Eirian get soaked. Merle sighed, glancing at the door. He knew what Fionn had tried to hint.

"No, I suppose none of us would interrupt them unless we had to."

Peeling off her wet clothes, Eirian draped them over the back of the chair and dragged it closer to the fire. She was thankful her guards had kept it going. Standing as close to it as she dared, she bit her lip at the painful sensation of her feet thawing. While slowly warming up, she forced her fingers to cooperate and undid the cord binding her hair.

Dragging her hands through the tresses, Eirian shook her head and giggled at the tickling sensation of it brushing her back. It was a feeling she found amusing after years of short hair. Glancing over her shoulder, she looked at the door when she felt the familiar prickle of Faolan's magic. There was a knock on the door, and Eirian contemplated dressing, but decided she did not care enough to leave the heat of the fire.

"Come in, Faolan."

"Majesty—" Faolan stopped in surprise with the door partially open.

"Do shut the door. It's nice and warm in here, and I'm cold."

Staring for a moment, Faolan turned and shut the door, keeping his back to Eirian as he said, "I know we're casual with our state of dress."

"I'm a mage, Faolan. Besides, I'd rather be warm and dry before I put cold clothes on." Turning to the fire, Eirian wriggled her toes and cringed at the discomfort she felt.

"Well then, I won't complain. Just because my king has declared you forbidden to us doesn't mean I can't admire you when presented with the opportunity."

"Admire away," she commented. "It's only fair. I do the same to you and Saoirse."

Crossing the room to stand beside Eirian in front of the fire, Faolan smiled before sniffing at her with curiosity. She arched a brow, giving him a questioning look.

"Did you know those of us who can shift possess traits in our natural form that we have in our animal form?"

"Really?"

Looking at Faolan, she considered her questions about the ability. His eyes gleamed as he looked Eirian over in amusement.

"I possess my wolf's sense of smell."

"I imagine it could get overwhelming."

"It's rather useful." Stepping closer, Faolan leaned in and sniffed again, purring, "What have you and your rugged captain been doing?"

Flinching, Eirian asked, "You can smell that?"

Grinning, he wriggled his eyebrows in amusement. "Oh, yes, little Queen, I certainly smell that. Arousal has such a delightful scent. It's one of my favorites. And you—"

"Why are you here, Faolan?"

"I'll get to that. But, first, I'm curious, you and your captain?"

Crossing her arms, Eirian stared into the fire intently. "I'm not talking about it."

"Oh, come now, Eirian. I like to think we're friends. Duine, even half duine, are lustful." He frowned and asked, "Or is it that Galameyvin has been your only lover?"

"No, he wasn't!" Eirian snapped. "There've been others when Gal and Celi were away from Riane. He wasn't my first."

"Let me tell you, the greater the power, the greater the lust you feel, be it blood or flesh. That's normal among us. If your precious golden prince wasn't your first, who was?"

"Who it was is irrelevant."

Faolan huffed. "I don't care who, but I'm curious what sort of man he was? Or was it a woman? I've seen the way you look at my sister. Who you're drawn to tells us a lot about your magic. Like calls to like."

Eirian closed her eyes and thought of Rylee. "She's a red. We were sparring partners."

Walking away, it did not surprise Faolan, and he commented, "Your magic draws you to your fellow warriors. It wants nothing less than someone who can hold their own against you. This is a reason we rarely marry. We change over the years, and things change with us."

"I thought you didn't marry because you fear getting bored after a few hundred years?"

"That too. It doesn't surprise me you love Prince Galameyvin. He's incredibly powerful. His magic would calm yours, and the side of you that gives life would desire it. Celiaen is your storm, but Galameyvin is your eye."

"My magic doesn't draw me to any of you."

"I suspect it would, if given the opportunity. I've been strict with my people. King Neriwyn declared you off-limits, and I've done what I can to maintain that. But, even if your bond to Celiaen was complete, it wouldn't stop either of you from enjoying others."

Silent, Eirian left the fire and crossed to her chest of belongings. Crouching, she lifted the lid and rummaged through for dry clothes. Pulling out the warmest she could find, she stood and dressed. Faolan watched, respecting her silence. Leaving her hair down, she turned back to the chest to find a pair of shoes Brenna had insisted they pack. Slipping them on, Eirian breathed a sigh of relief at the cushion between her feet and the cool floor.

"I wanted to warn you," Faolan spoke, breaking the silence.

Arching a brow as she walked back to the fire, Eirian wished she had a warm fur to wrap herself in. "What about?"

"We had word King Neriwyn is coming."

Taking a slow breath, she exhaled, silently asking the powers for strength. "The King of Telmia is coming here? I'm not sure how that'll affect negotiations with Athnaral."

"It's because of the negotiations that I'm glad he's coming. What we felt from Aeyren concerns me greatly."

"Why use the word warn? Seems an odd choice."

"I suppose it seemed the right choice. Neriwyn is probably more powerful than you, and I worry about how you'll respond to him."

Eirian shook her head, chuckling, "Don't worry, wolf. I'm sure your king will control himself. I welcome his influence over the negotiations, and hopefully, he'll be enough to make Athnaral go home."

Sighing, Faolan returned to her side and touched her arm. "Don't you fear he'll drag you away from Endara? According to the laws of the daoine, you belong with us."

"I believe he's always known what I am. If Neriwyn is as powerful as you say, how could my mother have hidden from him? What I fear are the answers he'll give me."

"You love this land."

"I do. How could I not? I've had hours to contemplate and accept that I can't be the queen when this is over. Right now, however, I need to be. That's why you're here. Because whatever is coming, whatever the darkness is, victory requires me to be a queen," Eirian said.

"Queen, so you can unite armies," he muttered.

"Something whispers to me that the sacrifice of the greatest life will save all lives."

Her eyes caught the glow of the fire as Eirian looked at him, and Faolan took a step back. Staring at her, he flinched when a clap of thunder sent vibrations through the building.

"You think you'll die before this is over."

"Yes."

"Why do you think that?"

She smiled faintly. "I'm the Altira, and I can make the land obey me. But I'd give it away in a heartbeat to save a life."

Saddened, Faolan replied, "Nothing matters more to you than the lives of distant strangers you'll never know."

"Yes."

Lightning continued to flash outside.

"I wish I could've known you under different circumstances, Eirian."

"Different circumstances would've resulted in a different me." She chuckled, "Then where would we be?"

"You're allowed to be selfish sometimes, you know that."

Waiting for the thunder to quieten, they stared at each other. Then, turning to the window, Eirian noticed how it had grown darker since she left the rooftop. It told her the storm was in no hurry to move, and the night would be a long, restless one.

"I suppose it wouldn't be easy. You have at least double the expectations to live up to as the queen. Though, if you're going to be selfish, then your captain is perfect."

Eirian shrugged. "You're right, Aiden is. When I left Riane, I shut down my magic and tucked it so far behind shields that other mages struggled to feel me. From the first time I met Aiden, I desired him. There was no magic involved. But then he made himself a challenge. I can't help being drawn to him. I've tried not to be."

"He loves you."

"He believes he does. Love is a hard burden to cope with. At least I know what men like Aeyren want. I understand their motives and the way they think."

Nodding, Faolan pointed out, "You think of sex as a tool, but love and sex aren't the same. Love should never be a tool. You desire your captain, but you fear indulging in it will leave you wanting more of him."

"I think he'll always spark desire in me," Eirian admitted. "Sometimes my power calls to him. Like something is missing, and Aiden should have magic to match mine."

"You've thought about it."

"More than I care to admit."

"So, do it," he said, nodding at the bed. "No one has to know. Well, they'd probably notice something. Most of them notice things, the brief looks you share, and lingering touches when you spar. How he handles you. And he certainly wants to handle you."

Eirian answered in amusement, "No, I can't. I don't need any distractions, and neither does he. My focus must be on the war."

Pouting, Faolan whined, "But I want to know what he's like."

Chuckling, she knew what he was trying to do and held her hands apart with a wink. "I've gotten a few good feels."

"Would it help if I told you I've smelled satisfied women on him?"

Eirian remarked, "I find it disturbing you can smell those things."

Giving her a wolfish grin, Faolan said, "It's useful. It would amaze you what changes a person's scent."

"Still disturbing."

"You should tell Aiden how you feel."

"Besides warning me about your king, was there anything useful you came for?"

"Possibly, but I forgot it when I saw you naked and smelled your arousal."

Eirian shot a look at him in annoyance. The expression told him she had heard enough, and Faolan bowed.

"I'll leave you to your solitude and this question. If you were free to do so, do you believe you could love him?"

Scowling, Eirian grumbled, "Goodbye, Lord Faolan."

"I can't ask about the scar?"

"No." She crossed her arms, his question making her self-conscious.

"Suit yourself."

Laughing as he walked to the door, Faolan pulled it open and set his sights on the man they had been discussing. Then, shutting it firmly, he crossed to Aiden and stood face-to-face with him, smiling in amusement.

"It's not nice to leave a lady wanting."

Aiden's glare turned to confusion. "I don't know what you're on about."

Tapping his nose, Faolan winked and replied, "A wolf knows things. She's feeling talkative, and if you push, you might get some honesty. Or she might try to shut you up."

"You're one of the most insufferable men I've ever encountered."

"I've got a secret to tell you, Captain." Cocking a finger, Faolan leaned in, whispering, "She has a scar that curls around her rib cage and under her left breast. A thin raised red line that stands out against the creamy expanse of her skin."

He looked at the door, growling, "Why should I believe you?"

"I dare you to ask her."

"Captain, what did he say?" Merle asked, concerned by the anger on Aiden's face.

"Nothing that concerns you."

Walking to the door, he pulled it open without knocking and stepped through. Hearing the door, Eirian glanced away from the fire. She spotted Aiden, pursing her lips in annoyance, and turned her back to the heat.

"Captain, what can I do for you?"

"You could satisfy my curiosity and lift your tunic."

"Excuse me?" Startled, Eirian moved to the window to put distance between them.

"You heard me."

"You don't get to come in here and make demands like that!"

Following Eirian to the window, Aiden blocked her path as she tried to avoid him. "Then tell me how Lord Faolan knew about your scar?"

Grinding her teeth, Eirian lifted her chin and replied, "I have many scars, as I'm sure you do. It's the life of a warrior."

Closing the gap, Aiden pinned her against the wall. "Well then, one warrior to another, you won't mind me seeing this one."

"I mind! What's gotten into you?"

"I dare you."

Aiden caught the hem of her tunic. Snarling, Eirian pulled it from his grasp and over her head to throw it to the side. Squaring her shoulders, she held her breath in expectation of his reaction. Instead of saying anything, he stared at the angry red line before running his fingers over it. The scar was sensitive, and his touch made her hiss. Her magic sang familiar whispers that she pushed away from her mind. He knew exactly what had caused the scar.

Aiden took a step back, growling, "Who would dare whip the future queen of Endara?"

"A sparring partner who didn't pay enough attention."

"What happened?"

Resting her head against the wall, Eirian looked at the ceiling. "They taught us to use a variety of weapons. I was overconfident and showing off to Celi. Jaren was an idiot. As punishment, he has a matching scar. They left us to heal naturally as a lesson."

"How'd the wolf know it was there?"

"Faolan saw me naked." Eirian watched his jealousy surface. "And he told you about it, knowing you'd storm in here. Well played."

Aiden closed the gap, demanding, "How did he see you naked?"

"I was warming in front of the fire after some brute kept me in the rain. Knowing my lack of clothing wouldn't bother Faolan, I let him enter without dressing."

"He knew about… did you tell him?" Brushing a strand of Eirian's hair away from her face, Aiden smiled at the way her eyes narrowed.

"Apparently, in his natural form, he possesses a wolf's sense of smell. It means he can smell a lot more than we can."

Eirian shifted to move away, her eyes on her tunic. Blocking her with his arm, Aiden shook his head.

"He told me it wasn't nice to leave a lady unsatisfied, but I know you're no lady."

Pushing him, Eirian let a trickle of her magic add force to it, and Aiden staggered back in surprise. "No, I'm not a lady. I'm the queen. That means I don't have to indulge any demands you make. It also means that if I tell you no, you had damn well bloody obey."

"You know that's never going to happen," Aiden replied.

"It has to. I can't afford you distracting me. I must focus on this war and the darkness."

"Eirian."

Walking back to the fire, Eirian leaned a hand on the wall and stared at the flames. "My priority is saving Endara from Athnaral and then saving everyone and everything from the darkness. When it's over, I'll be free to fight you, to fight Celi, to fight anyone stupid enough to love me."

Aiden sighed, watching how the fire cast shadows over Eirian's skin. It reminded him of the first night away from Amath when he watched the lightning and magic dancing over her. He wanted to chase them with his fingers and his lips.

"Love isn't stupid. It gives meaning to the fight when you know you're fighting for the love of your partner, your family, your friends, and even your people. Love makes you want to win and come home alive. Love gives you strength."

She replied, "I know."

"You think I'm stupid for loving you? That your prince is stupid for loving you? Yet you claim to love the other one? So who's the bigger fool?"

Bending to pick up the tunic, Aiden moved over to her. Shrugging, Eirian glanced away from the fire and debated what she was about to offer him.

"You're right. I love Gal. I love Celi. I could love you. However, I must put those feelings aside to do what I need to do. Let me win these wars. Let me earn my freedom. Then you can try to convince me. If you can catch me."

Cocking his head to the side, Aiden murmured, "That sounds like a challenge."

"That's because it is. I offer you the promise of a challenge if you let me do what I must. I'll give Celi and Gal the same offer."

"Well then, that gives me an even greater incentive to protect you."

Holding the tunic out, Aiden felt a flicker of hope. Resisting the urge to snatch it, Eirian plucked it from his grasp and pulled it on.

"I don't know why my damn scar is so interesting to everyone. You should've heard Brenna the first time she saw it."

"Are you joking?" Aiden said. "You honestly can't grasp why any of us would find a whip scar like that on royalty a little concerning?"

Watching the linen cover her, Aiden wished the light had allowed him a better look. Her shoulders slumped, and Eirian turned to the fire.

"I suppose."

Taking a step closer, Aiden placed a hand on her hip and felt her shift in his direction. "I'm sorry if I upset you."

"You test my control constantly, Aiden, and this was no exception."

"Someone has to keep you on your toes."

Giving him a sideways look, she muttered, "You certainly rise to the challenge."

"Yes, darling, I do," he murmured in her ear. "But you know that."

"Aiden."

Kissing her cheek, Aiden dropped his hand before he did anything more to regret. Before they ended up in her bed with no regard for the consequences. He needed to put space and people between them.

"Do you fancy joining Merle and his men for a game of cards?" Her brows rose, and he added, "I sent someone to get food for you."

FIFTEEN

Celiaen stared at the lines of soldiers stretched along the horizon. His father's banners flapped in the air, the triple sword of Ensaycal a welcome sight. The unwelcome view was the Athnaralan lines they faced. Turning to Tara, he shook his head. She shrugged, her eyes not leaving the battle lines as horns alerted officers of their approach. They sensed the hyper-alert magic of the countless mages among the soldiers. Spotting Paienven's command tent, he headed toward it.

"Are you sure you want to speak to him right away?" Alyse asked quickly, stopping Celiaen before he got to the tent.

"We don't know how much time we have to get what we need."

Kenna agreed, "He's got a point."

"Yeah, we left Ree up there, and who knows what she might do." Running a hand through their hair, Cai added, "I still think a couple of us should've stayed with her."

While he dreaded seeing Paienven, Celiaen knew it had to be done. There was little time to spare if he wanted to save Eirian from whatever might happen in Kelsby. If the Athnaralans were already attacking in the south, the likelihood was they were doing the same everywhere else. Beside him, Tara was silent, her mouth twisted as she stared at the tent.

"Tara?"

"I don't know what else you expect me to say, Celi. The situation we left Ree in is precarious, and I know she's a big enough idiot to do something foolish."

Coughing, Tully said, "Come on, Ree's not that big an idiot. She wouldn't do anything to endanger Endara."

Tara shook her head, waving at Celiaen. "It's not Endara I'm worried about. We all know what Ree's like. She'd die for this bloody kingdom. It's what she'll do on the way down that worries me."

"You mean..." Kelsey's voice trailed off.

No one said a word. Each of them was aware of what Eirian could do when pushed far enough. Clenching his jaw, Celiaen lifted his gaze to the sky and considered what he would say to Paienven. Tara glanced at him before continuing, her voice quiet.

"I mean, if it'll save Endara, Ree will sign her own execution orders and take the Athnaralan army with her. One great big crumbling ruin covered in flowers."

Celiaen knew what she was not saying. If Eirian did something drastic that would cost her life, it could very well take him down with her. So far away from her, they would get no warning, nothing to prepare them for the possibility. Clenching his fist, Celiaen cursed himself for leaving Eirian behind. Despite his confidence that Aiden would do everything he could to keep her from combat, he knew the other man stood no chance against Eirian.

"We need rest before we turn around and go back—with or without reinforcements from my father. Tully, I want you to see to making camp for us and take care of the horses. After I deal with Paienven, all of us need to eat and sleep." Rubbing his hands on his coat, Celiaen nodded to Tynan and said, "Let's get this done."

"You sure?" Tynan asked.

"Of course."

Scoffing, Tara signaled for Alyse to accompany Celiaen with her and told the others, "Go with Tully and get sorted. No point in hanging around here waiting for us."

The four of them turned their focus to the tent, and Celiaen drew comfort from the presence of his friends. None of them would lift a finger to prevent Paienven and his behavior, but they were there. If there was one thing he looked forward to, it was the day Eirian and Paienven met. Guards surrounding the tent saluted, bowing as he approached. Nodding, he passed through the gap with his friends.

"Your Highness!" an officer greeted him.

In the open-sided tent filled with high-ranking officers, his father was in the middle, leaning over a table covered in maps. One of his aides alerted the king to his son, and Paienven turned to face Celiaen. Looking him over, Paienven clapped a hand to Celiaen's shoulder and pulled him into the hug that everyone expected to see.

"You look exhausted. What happened?"

Running a hand through the black hair he had inherited from his mother,

Celiaen regarded Paienven and asked, "Are you about to engage with Athnaralan troops?"

"Not for the first time. Athnaral hasn't been willing to withdraw, and I sent legions south to liberate several Endaran towns. Where's your beloved queen? Her forces are doing their best," Paienven informed him.

Rummaging through the papers, an officer pulled a map out to show the towns in question. Staring at it, Celiaen cursed, sharing a look with Tara. It confirmed what they feared and reinforced the conflict they each felt over leaving Eirian. He doubted his response about her location would be well received by the officers or Paienven.

"Eirian's north, on the border at Kelsby, and facing a legion of Athnaralans. When I left to find you, they outnumbered the Endarans."

Protests of disbelief sounded among the officers, and Paienven arched a brow. Alyse stepped closer to Tara, prepared to step in to keep her calm if needed. Similarly, Tynan avoided meeting Paienven's gaze, sticking to Celiaen's side.

"You're telling me the woman you begged to marry is miles away, facing a legion of the enemy with inferior numbers, and you left her? The Queen of Endara, the mage the high council wants to make the most powerful person in the lands."

"I know what I did, and I—"

"No excuses, boy!" Paienven held up a hand. "I'm sure you thought you were doing the right thing. You want to take some of my forces north to save the day. How heroic."

Tynan cleared his throat before saying, "Queen Eirian was expecting reinforcements from Onaorbaen. She has experienced people with her making strategic—"

Paienven clapped a hand to the table. "Did I ask you?"

"No, Your Majesty, but—"

"You've met my wife, haven't you? The queen and the mother of your prince? If this Endaran queen is half of what they say she is, I imagine very few people would argue with her. Just like they don't argue with Queen Sannaeh."

Staring at Paienven impassively, Tynan replied, "Having met both women, I can safely say you're right. The prince is very much his father's son, and like his father, he feels a deep-seated desire to show the woman he loves he has something to offer. You united three kingdoms to win your queen. Prince Celiaen just wants to save the kingdom of the woman he loves."

Eyes narrowing, Paienven regarded Tynan curiously. He thought little of the blue who had replaced his nephew, but he could admit that his assumptions had been wrong. Galameyvin had a ruthless streak he admired, and he wondered if Tynan could be useful. Unsettled by the silence, Celiaen looked around the tent, hoping to find his uncles among them. It was rare for Paienven to go on a military campaign without his brothers at his side. They were the only ones other than Queen Sannaeh who could exert some control over him.

"Are my uncles not here?"

"Yaernan is south with his forces, dealing with the Athnaralan scum. Selagan remains at home. Your aunt is due any day, and your mother threatened to cut off my balls if I took him away from his wife so close to giving birth."

His answer caused chuckles, everyone aware of how dangerous Sannaeh could be. Holding up a hand to silence them, Paienven nodded at Celiaen.

"I need to speak with the Prince. Remain and continue your work. We'll go for a walk."

Celiaen murmured, "As you wish, Your Majesty."

Bowing, he waited for Paienven, falling into step with him as they left the tent behind. They were quiet as they moved away from the gathering without looking at each other. Paienven's golden curls caught in the sunlight, blue eyes watching the lines. Celiaen often wondered how it would have been growing up if he had been more like his father and less like his mother. Putting an arm over his shoulders, Paienven waved at the soldiers.

"Last time Athnaral made a full-scale attempt at taking Endara, our numbers were less, but we still outnumbered them. Since then, we've easily doubled the army, and the number of loyal reds among them is in the thousands. Your bloody uncle doesn't control all of them."

"You had a glorious vision, sire, and you've made it a reality."

Celiaen did not smile. He knew what it had taken to build the empire Paienven had dreamed of, and he knew what sort of man his father was. Grunting, Paienven squeezed the shoulder his hand rested on.

"I hear your bid to become her consort fell short of your expectations. Your queen wishes to remain unwed and has declared the Duke of Tamantal her heir. What happened?"

"Eirian has her reasons. Perhaps I could've convinced her if not for the Telmians. But, Father, they warned us the madness is returning. The one from the stories."

"Yes, we've received those warnings. Galameyvin has kept us well informed, as per his orders. At least he gets it right. They also tell of the rise of the Altira mage. One could almost leap to the idea that perhaps she's the danger rather than the salvation the daoine claim."

Celiaen frowned. "You thought Eirian might be the darkness returned?"

Looking sideways at him, Paienven continued, "Except one would like to think that the entirety of Riane would see through any guises the madness might wear. Your uncle is no fool, though I can't always speak so of the rest of them."

"Eirian isn't the threat."

"I'm sure she isn't, but we know little beyond the stories. Why did she turn you down?"

"She has always feared childbirth after what happened to her mother. To her, not marrying is a way to avoid that fate. She doesn't wish to risk herself when she has male cousins to do it for her," he answered truthfully.

Paienven stepped away, chuckling, "Wise woman. As a mage, she can avoid the risk and still have fun. I presume you put yourself forth as a candidate. Do you plan to spend tens of years chasing her in the hope she throws you some crumbs? I raised you better than that. You're the future king of Ensaycal, and you take what you want. You don't wait for scraps."

Scoffing, Celiaen shook his head. "Don't worry, I won't be chasing for crumbs."

"But you wish to ride to her rescue? Do you hope she'll fall at your feet in gratitude? She's queen of Endara, and we have a long-standing alliance with her family. There will be no falling at your feet."

"Perhaps it isn't her I hope to rescue. I know what she can do. Perhaps I wish to save her people and the Athnaralans from her wrath."

Freezing, Paienven stared with suspicion and asked, "What do you speak of?"

Cursing himself, Celiaen ran a hand through his hair and turned away while he considered what to say. He had little time. Paienven was not a patient man, and while he had been strangely pleasant so far, it would not last.

"Eirian has so much power and can do things most believe to be stories. She can give life, and she can take it with her magic. When the Telmians speak of the Altira mage, they speak of a mage of immense power, and Eirian is that."

"You expect me to be surprised. I know the old stories, even if we rarely tell them. Why do you think we've fostered an alliance with Endara for so long? They speak of the Altira uniting the warring mages to defeat the darkness."

Walking a few steps, Paienven looked at the soldiers he commanded. They were preparing for the next Athnaralan attack. It was challenging to be sure when it would happen, but his spies were doing their best to determine when the orders would arrive. Paienven had found that the war with Athnaral was not as tidy as it had been in the past. Something was driving the enemy, and he was starting to believe the old stories for the first time in his life.

"Do you think I'd allow you to pursue a human woman for any other reason? The fact she was to be queen of Endara was less an incentive than her magic."

"I thought you hoped I'd get soundly rejected to teach me a lesson."

Laughing, Paienven gave him a knowing look. "I had my doubts in both directions. There is elven blood in Endara, plenty of it, even in the small council. There is just as much Endaran blood in Ensaycal because blood blurs borders."

"Her council supported my proposal. If you wanted to make a show of it, threatening to nullify the treaty with Endara would force her to accept me. They may have let her overrule them on the matter but not without conditions."

Celiaen did not tell his father that Eirian would give up her throne. The truth of her heritage was not his to share with anyone, particularly not a man he knew he could not trust.

"I won't force those conditions. You want Queen Eirian, then you take her. You want troops to go north to defend her position? You have them. Not so you can ride to her rescue, but so you can defeat the Athnaralans and earn your right to my throne by destroying their king."

"Your informants know where Aeyren is?" Celiaen gasped.

"He's north, where you should be. Aeyren wants to take the Queen himself because he wouldn't dare risk her safety to his men. I know I would be, and that is why you must be."

"You say it as though you intend for me to capture Eirian."

"I do," Paienven said matter-of-factly.

"Father?"

Celiaen did not want to believe what he was hearing. He had worried that Paienven would turn his ambitions to Endara but convinced himself it was a foolish fear. Now his concerns were becoming fact.

Grasping the hilt of a sword, Paienven's lips curled with a hint of maliciousness. "I'm weary of defending Endara with little reward. If we're going to come to their rescue, we may as well rewrite the borders ourselves. Which is easiest done when you control the current queen."

"But you just said you won't force the council's conditions. Now you say you wish to take Endara?"

"Do you grasp nothing of politics, boy? We can't force Endara if we want the people to accept us. If we threaten to withdraw our protection, they may decide to surrender. Athnaral has only ever shown one face to Endara, and it has served us to do the same."

His grip tightened on the hilt of his sword, and Paienven pushed back the urge to wipe the shocked look from Celiaen's face. His response was enough to remind him of how much he detested the younger man. All he needed was a reason to declare Celiaen a traitor, and he could get rid of the disappointment in line for his throne. Awena would be a better queen for Ensaycal. Better yet, the war with Athnaral would claim his life and make matters easier.

Celiaen said, "Riane would become involved."

"Riane will do what I tell them! You'll take soldiers, and you'll go north to play the part of the gallant defender. The council already supports your union. You will clarify what the benefits of overruling their queen would be. You want her? You take her."

"Yes, sire."

Paienven scowled, continuing, "Meanwhile, we'll be well-positioned around Endara, protecting their borders from Athnaral. We'll help rebuild farms, offer stock to those who lost theirs, replant crops, and so on, so forth.

We'll be the benevolent rescuers they see us as, and we'll win over the people. When you own the loyalty of the common folk, you command a greater power than those who would rule without it."

"This is Endara. It was one thing to unite our people, but you're talking about uniting humans and elves! And you expect me to convince Eirian to marry me and let you?"

Angry, Celiaen forced his magic down despite knowing he was more than a match for Paienven. Aware that he would not defend himself, Paienven grabbed his coat and clenched it. The silk bit into his neck, but he did his best not to respond. It was an effort, but Celiaen could not risk any more of Paienven's wrath if he wanted to help Eirian.

"I expect you to do what your king orders."

Not fighting back, Celiaen asked, "And what does my king order me to do?"

"Wed the Queen of Endara. Make yourself the king. I don't care if you get her with child, but you have years to establish yourself as the ruler. Then, when she dies, you can offer continuity of rule. On that thought, perhaps it's better if you don't have children."

"She'd still make her cousin and his children her heirs."

Paienven dismissed it with a scoff, "He is unwed. We'd find him a wife we control, one of your cousins. Now, I think a legion will be sufficient. Aeyren has spread himself out, divided his forces, and they're weaker for it."

Relieved when Paienven released his grasp on him, Celiaen rolled his shoulders, tugging at his cloak. He used the act of straightening himself to settle his rage. It simmered below the surface, the magic begging to be released. When he was away, he would take his frustration out on Tara and any of the other reds among his companions who were willing.

"As you wish, Your Majesty. I'll leave as soon as you order it."

Shaking his head, Paienven instructed coldly, "You leave in the morning. I'm sending General Darragh with you."

"Thank you, Your Majesty. By your leave, I'll inform my companions of our orders."

Bowing, Celiaen retreated, terrified by what he had heard and what it meant. He did not know what he would do or how he would tell Eirian what was going on. Spotting Tara and the other two lurking a distance away, he headed straight for them. They did not need him to speak to know something was wrong, and Tara ground her teeth, glaring in the direction Paienven had gone.

"What did the fucker do?" she growled.

"Not here," Celiaen muttered. "Let's find the others. I want some distance between us and anyone who will report back to the king."

Eyes darting around, Alyse flexed her fingers, and they felt the buffer of magic surround them. It was not as good as it would have been if one of the yellows had done it, but the ward would afford them some privacy. With the tension running through the camp, Alyse dismissed her concerns about questions. Her power worked to dampen the emotions' influence on Celiaen and Tara. An understandable excuse no one would argue with.

"How bad is it?" Tynan demanded. "Celi, I felt how badly you wanted to kill him."

Scratching his neck, Celiaen muttered, "He's sending Darragh to ensure I follow orders."

"What orders?"

"Capture Ree, kill Aeyren, marry Ree, take over Endara."

Choking, Alyse said, "Excuse me?"

"Did you say kill Aeyren? As in, King Aeyren of Athnaral?" Tara asked in between laughing. "He wants you to kill Aeyren?"

"Paienven claims he's with his forces in the north," he explained.

Puffing his cheeks out, Tynan thought about everything Celiaen had said. It explained why he had been so angry with Paienven. Then, sharing a look with Alyse, he skipped asking for details and went straight for the vital part.

"What are we going to do?"

Shaking his head, Celiaen admitted, "I'm not sure. First, I must tell Ree what Paienven has ordered me to do. Then we need to deal with Aeyren. After that, things get complicated."

"Are you and Ree keeping secrets from us again?" Tara demanded.

"Yes."

"Will your secrets get us killed?"

Alyse put a hand on Tara's arm and murmured, "Love, don't be like that. I'm sure they have a good reason."

Glancing up at the sky, Celiaen prayed to the powers that Eirian would understand. They could trust Tara, Alyse, and Tynan to keep the secret and protect her.

"It's about her mother."

His comment had the three of them exchanging looks. They all knew the subject of Eirian's mother was one that needed a delicate approach.

"Celiaen, what's going on?" Concerned, Tara kept her voice low. "How bad is it?"

"Queen Siani was a duine," he informed them quietly.

Covering her mouth, Alyse muttered, "That explains a lot."

"Fuck," Tynan grunted, eyes sweeping over the soldiers surrounding them. "When?"

"After the coronation. King Nolan mistook Ree for her mother and let the secret slip. He knew the entire time. Everything. Including that she'd be a mage and Siani would die."

Tara listened to him, anger growing as she grasped what Celiaen said. She considered herself the closest thing Eirian had to a mother, and it pained her to find out what Nolan had done. Alyse slung an arm around Tara's waist and squeezed, feeling her simmering rage.

"We can't let anyone find out," Tara stated. "We have to protect Ree."

Agreeing, Celiaen said, "No one else can know what I told you."

"Do you think Faolan and the rest are aware?"

"Are you planning to kill them, Tara?"

She sneered and shook her head. "Not unless I have to. It's my neck on the chopping block if the truth ever comes out. The high council might spare you and Gal, but the rest of us? Not fucking likely."

"I don't think they're aware. Ree has a theory that Neriwyn knows."

Eyes widening, Alyse said, "You suspect he arranged everything?"

Celiaen nodded. Staring in horror, his three companions did not know how to respond.

"Ree believes it was all planned. They created her to fight the darkness," he told them. "She might be right. I don't know. All I know is that we need to help her."

"How?" Tara asked. "How do we help her? We don't know what we're up against."

Alyse noticed someone waving at them and shifted to look. Squinting, she took in Ianto with both arms flapping in the air. Then, clearing her throat, Alyse nodded in his direction to draw the attention of the others.

"We should find out what he wants."

Dropping the surrounding wards, Alyse led the group over to Ianto. He took one look at their worried expressions and flinched.

"I guess it went well?"

"It could've been worse. I'm not dead," Celiaen said, keeping his tone jovial.

Ianto pulled a face and guided the way to where the rest of their group had set up camp. They had left most of their gear with Eirian's convoy, so it had taken little time to organize themselves. Looking over the neatly arranged bedrolls, Celiaen wondered what Paienven would say when he found out his heir was sleeping rough. However, most of his companions were present, only a couple missing, and he had a fair idea what they were doing.

"You might want to sit," Cai suggested quietly.

Holding out a plate with several chunks of meat, Owen waited for them to take a piece each before waving at the fire someone had built in the center of their camp. Tara took a bite of the meat and picked a spot to sit, arching a brow when Celiaen remained standing.

"What have you learned?" he asked.

Sharing a look, Kenna and Tully silently argued over who would tell them what they had discovered in passing from soldiers.

"It's the Athnaralans," Kenna commented. "I'm sure you know about the attacks."

Tara looked bored, waving her food about. "We're aware."

"Well, there's more to it. Apparently, they've gone insane."

"Insane wasn't the word used," Link muttered.

"Yeah, but it describes the situation perfectly."

Glancing sideways at Tara, Celiaen prompted, "What do you mean by insane?"

Scratching his head, Ianto explained, "They're attacking, even after they've lost. Just over and over, throwing themselves at Ensaycal and Endaran forces."

Blinking in confusion, Celiaen stared opened mouthed while Tara whispered curses under her breath. Looking at the ground, Tynan mulled over what Ianto had said. He suspected it had something to do with the darkness. The well-trod earth at his feet reminded him of Eirian, and taking a deep breath, he prepared to mention his concerns.

"What if it's related to the darkness?" Alyse said.

Tynan added, "I was going to say the same thing."

"It makes sense."

Scoffing, Tully waved their suggestion off. "Not you two, as well! It's bad enough that Ree believes that nonsense."

"It's not nonsense, Tully." Celiaen nodded slowly. "And yes, it makes sense. The great madness. Even my father suspects there is truth to the stories."

"So this mysterious enemy is driving the Athnaralans to suicide by the enemy sword?"

Licking her fingers, Tara asked, "Why? What purpose would it serve?"

Celiaen looked around, staring at each of his companions. He saw the mixed emotions they were experiencing. The doubt, the worry, the confusion. Alyse and Tynan were the only ones who appeared convinced by what they had suggested. It surprised him that Tara was showing hesitation. After what he had told her, Celiaen had expected her support.

"I don't know, but the sooner we get back to Ree, the better. The king said Aeyren is up north. If his army is being driven by the darkness, then he's working with it. Which means Ree is in danger."

"You know I adore Ree, but what if she's the danger?" Cai glanced away, embarrassed by their question.

Kenna agreed, "Yeah, we know what she can do."

"Celi is right," Tara stated, meeting his gaze. "The sooner we get back north, the better. I don't think Ree is the danger we should worry about, but she's definitely involved."

"We can't abandon her," Alyse declared.

Squinting at Celiaen, Harlow inquired, "If the Telmians are right about the darkness, how do we fight it? I mean, Ree is powerful as fuck, but…"

Watching him spread his hands wide, Celiaen sighed. He did not know how to battle against the darkness when they did not know what it was. If Galameyvin had been there, he would have come up with some inspiring speech about how they just had to work together and have a little faith.

Dropping his gaze to the half-eaten chunk of meat in his hand, Celiaen wished he had never told Paienven to send Galameyvin to Telmia.

"We try our best. If we work together, we'll figure it out."

"Oh yeah, that sounds so easy," Owen muttered.

"Gal would've said it differently," Kenna grumbled. "Sometimes, I think he's the only one of the three of them with any sense."

Ianto smiled at her patiently. "We don't expect reds to have any sense. That's why you need us blues."

"Fuck you."

Clenching his jaw, Celiaen said, "I know Gal isn't here, and it's my fault. No need to remind me. We're leaving tomorrow for Kelsby with a legion and the company of Darragh."

"Darragh? Fuck," Tully groaned.

Whistling, Lydia asked, "What did you do to upset the king?"

Deciding to come to his rescue, Tara answered, "King Aeyren is in the north, and Paienven wants to make sure he dies. Darragh will see it done."

Thoughts turning to Eirian, Cai said, "What if Ree has already done something about it? I doubt the Athnaralans waited for the Endarans to have equal numbers to attack Kelsby."

"They have a point. Ree might have taken care of the problem already." Looking hopeful, Harlow added, "I mean, how hard would it be for her to sneak into their camp and slit his throat in his sleep. Or, you know, make him dust."

Eyes darting around fearfully, Tynan hissed, "We don't mention that."

"Turned him into plant food?"

"Maybe Aeyren is a bit husky," Tully chuckled.

"Better than chunks of unidentifiable flesh," Lydia whispered.

Her words reminded them of what Eirian could do when her rage reached a certain point. Each of them had seen the results of her losing control. The blood-stained walls, the remains of men who had violated others. Fragments of bone lodged into ceiling beams that could not be pieced back together. For some of them, Eirian's victims' screams haunted their dreams.

Looking at each of them in concern, Tara stated, "We're the only ones who know what she can do. So let's try to keep it that way, yeah?"

"What if we can't?" Alyse said.

Shrugging, she met Celiaen's fearful gaze. "Then we do our best to keep Ree and ourselves alive long enough to defeat the darkness."

SIXTEEN

The sun shone brightly, but it only made the air slick with humidity. Still sodden from weeks of rain, the field had turned to mud. Glaring at her boots, Eirian cursed herself for agreeing to wear another dress to meet Aeyren. Her advisers had suggested that she continue the guise of a gullible woman. They hoped that the longer she could stall him, the better their chances. The weather held up their reinforcements, delaying further conflict at the border.

Gathering her skirts, Eirian made her way along the ridge that overlooked both camps. It was slightly drier than the flats, and Aeyren was waiting with his men a distance away as hers were behind her. She had allowed Faolan to follow in his wolf form, an argument prepared should Aeyren protest. He gave her a measure of comfort through his confidence in his magic and abilities to lend her strength if she needed it.

No wind blew. Nothing stirred in the stillness except the loud buzz of insects. Birds circled in the air, the occasional one daring to dart down to snatch an unsuspecting insect in its beak. Eirian could have watched them for hours, the swirl and swoop mesmerizing in the way they moved. In the distance, she heard the distinct laughter of kookaburras. Standing still, she stroked Faolan's head gently and stared at them, smiling faintly.

Aeyren had an easier time stepping through the mud than she did, and he approached, saying, "In my castle, we have great aviaries filled with birds."

Frowning, Eirian detested the thought of them caged for entertainment, but refused to let her distaste show. She had to play nice. The lives of her people depended on it.

"It's like they dance to music we can't hear and can only hope to catch a snippet of."

"What a whimsical notion! One day we'll have tailors create a beautiful gown for you to make you look like a bird, and you can dance for me."

"I'm afraid you'd be sorely disappointed. I don't dance."

He glanced at Faolan. "I thought I told you to leave the beast behind."

Running her fingers over the fur, Eirian murmured, "You can't expect me to go unprotected. My dear pet guards me well."

"I can't fault the argument. But don't worry, I'll protect you, and you won't need such a creature. Have you had word from your council?"

"Not yet, sire. Even with the fastest horses and regular changes, it'll be several more weeks before we have an answer. I beg your continued patience. I can't make distance disappear, or horses run faster."

Glancing down, Eirian did her best to look apologetic. Aeyren looked at the lines of her people watching them and smiled coldly.

"I'm sure that's true. However, I'm afraid I don't have the patience to wait so long."

Maintaining a straight face, Eirian said, "I understand your desire to have an answer, but we can't rush these things. You understand politics better than I do."

"You're right. I know politics. But don't mistake me as a fool for a pretty face. You hope continual delays will buy you enough time for reinforcements to arrive. You expect that with them, you'll defeat my forces."

Faolan whined, leaning against her leg. Taking the distraction, Eirian crouched and stroked him to calm herself. He was warm, his fur soft beneath her fingers. Concentrating on the sensation, she kept her magic under control.

"I only do what my advisors suggest. Would you not do the same?"

"Of course, and I have been. I also have reinforcements on their way, another legion. Meanwhile, I have legions along your border waiting for my word to take your kingdom. The choice of what I do next is entirely up to you."

"I see." Eirian glanced up, eyes narrowing as she asked, "You want me to risk the ire of my nobles and decide without them?"

"You are their queen, are you not?"

Draping her arm over Faolan's haunches, Eirian stared out at the lush green countryside and contemplated how to respond. Her control slipped, wildflowers creeping into existence, covering the mud. She sensed Aeyren's impatience, his foot tapping in the corner of her vision. Wriggling her fingers, she channeled her anger into the growth, counting the beat of Faolan's heart while she did it. Keeping the growth slight, she held the desire to kill Aeyren at bay.

Licking her lips, Eirian nodded. She gathered her magic to herself, letting the whispers assure her of her capabilities. Aeyren was not a threat to her. Squeezing Faolan, she rose as gracefully as she could manage with her skirts. Holding her head high, she squared her shoulders and reminded Aeyren of who was taller. Whining, Faolan sensed the shift in her mood and attempted to caution her.

"Yes, you're right. I am the queen, and I won't risk their disobedience for the sake of your impatience. If you truly wish to unite our kingdoms peacefully, civil war wouldn't make a good start. So, I ask you to give my messengers time to reach Amath, time to convene with my council, and time to return. A month."

Aeyren countered, "Two weeks."

"Two weeks is not enough."

"Two weeks to get a response from your nobles, or you decide without them. After that, either you agree to give me Endara by marriage, or I'll take it."

"If you try to take it, we'll fight you."

Aeyren smiled, and her skin prickled. There was something behind his eyes, a shadow that made Eirian's magic surround her like a shield. It whispered louder, dancing around the corner of her vision. Memories clambered for recollection, screaming from the darkest parts of her mind. They continuously had the worst timing, and Eirian wished they would go away.

"If you fight me, things will not go well for you. Marry me, and I'll protect you. Otherwise, General Tomas has expressed a particular interest in you. He has served me so loyally that I might reward him."

Baring his teeth, Faolan snarled at Aeyren, and Eirian chuckled. The words made her decide she had played nicely long enough. Her magic encouraged her, a hint of rage flickering through the control she wielded.

"I have a few people who are vying for just such a reward. They'd enjoy having General Tomas as a gift for their loyalty," Eirian stated, her thoughts going to Gabe. "You've seen what I can do on a whim. Imagine what I could do with a little preparation. Do not presume to threaten me. You don't know what I'm capable of."

Aeyren said, "And there's a flash of the claws. I thought the stories were about a different woman. Breaking you will be a pleasure."

Staring at him with a determined smirk, Eirian cocked her head to the side. She wanted to show Aeyren why he should fear her, but resisted. It would be almost too easy to kill him, and her magic urged her to do it.

"You're right, I have claws, but considering your delicate sensitivities, I've endeavored to put you at ease. There's a reason they want to make me the next grand mage, and it isn't because I'm a pampered little woman."

"My delicate sensitivities?"

"Yes, those of an entitled man who's been told all his life that he's better than everyone else, especially women. Now, I'm sure your people have informed you the Ensaycalan army has arrived in Endara. You can grasp what that means for your attempt at invasion. My Telmian ambassador has told me King Neriwyn is on his way with his army to uphold their side of our treaty. Did you really think I'd deign to marry you?" Eirian let her last words linger, enjoying the flickering emotions on Aeyren's face.

"I could signal to my men to kill you here and now."

"You could try, but you'd be dead first. I know Endara has a plan in place for the assumption of control. Does Athnaral? Killing me would get you nothing except the wrath of all the other kingdoms. Could Athnaral stand against that?"

There was a hint of fear in his eyes, and Eirian smirked. Her magic purred in delight at his discomfort. Sensing it, Faolan whined, bumping his head against her leg.

"King Paienven would be pleased to take your kingdom. Remember, Endara stands between the humans of Athnaral and elven domination. Do you want to be the king who caused the downfall of his kingdom?"

Squaring his shoulders, Aeyren stepped toward her with a defiant look, and Eirian's magic swirled threateningly. "You don't scare me! Underneath the words and the magic, you are nothing but a weak woman!"

Rubbing her chin thoughtfully, Eirian did not back down. She had no reason to.

"I'm Eirian Altira, the rightful queen of Endara. If you can't respect my right to rule, then why should we respect yours?"

"You'd encourage an alliance to invade Athnaral?"

"I'd encourage the overthrow of someone who threatens all of us and our continued way of life. If you question my right, what will stop people from asking about yours? Or Paienven's? We see what you're doing. You're using it as an excuse to take Endara. But that doesn't mean the people would see it that way."

Eirian stepped toward him, and Faolan leaped to his feet, remaining pinned to her side. There was hesitation in Aeyren's eyes, but stubbornness and pride would not let him back away from a woman.

"You don't know what you're talking about. Whatever lies your advisers are—"

"Don't make half-assed excuses as though I'm an idiot. Let me tell you the story of a hunting trip I took a few months ago. We stumbled upon the most enjoyable quarry. But it was an eye-opener to my nobles and the big men who think they need to protect me because I'm a woman. I killed our quarry, but first I made one sing, and he told me who sent them."

"I wouldn't order the assassination of royalty!" Aeyren replied, the hitch of his voice betraying his words and the lie within them.

"Did I say it was an assassination attempt? I enjoy killing, and the pleasure of dragging my blades through their flesh. Well, you know how it is."

Aeyren realized his mistake, but Eirian did not give him the chance to speak.

Throwing her hands up, she gasped dramatically. "No, of course you don't! Because you don't have magic. If you think threatening me with war will get you anywhere, then remember I'll be at the front of the Endaran lines with my magic and my blades, and your armies will fall to me. A woman and the most powerful mage born in generations."

Hearing the deep tones of horns in the distance behind her, Eirian did not need to turn around to know what they signaled. Aeyren's face told her everything, the rage twisting it into something ugly. What made him feel off grew in intensity, and her magic flared, Faolan's following suit like a smoldering fire. Her fingers itched to hold a blade, the temptation growing to use her powers to draw her swords to her from where Aiden had them.

His anger over the Endaran reinforcements emboldened him. Pulling a small knife from his back, Aeyren pointed it at Eirian. Faolan growled, but she sighed in boredom.

"I'm going to take great delight in teaching you your place," Aeyren hissed. "You'll be lucky if there is anything left to give Tomas."

Rolling her eyes, Eirian wriggled her fingers in his direction with a grin and used her magic to twist the blade from Aeyren's grasp. She caught the hilt as it came flying to her, not looking at it as the itch for a weapon faded. Startled, he looked at his hand before taking a step back. Her power whispered, reminding her what she could do with one small knife. It wanted to taste his blood and feel his pain.

She purred, "Oh, come now, I thought we were friends."

"We could never be friends!"

"I'm glad we've dispensed with the pretense. It was making me uncomfortable." Twirling the knife, Eirian admired the craftsmanship. "Perhaps now we can talk."

"I have nothing left to say to you."

"That's a pity. I have plenty to say. What is the real reason you destroyed years of peace?"

His eyes watched his knife as Eirian continued to twirl it in her hand. "Because who wants something like you in control of your enemy?"

"I've never understood why we must be enemies. Are we such bloodthirsty creatures that we must always have someone to war with? Imagine how we could prosper if only we worked together," Eirian sighed, shaking her head.

"Spoken like a foolish woman. There will always be war. Endara is fortunate that, for now, Ensaycal finds you useful. One day soon, things will change. You'll cease to be useful."

Mustering bravery, Aeyren lifted his eyes from his knife to meet her gaze. Letting her smile fade, Eirian wondered if he could see what she wanted to do to him. She hoped he could, because she wanted him to be afraid. It smelled delightful.

"You may be right, but damn the powers if I let you be the reason things change."

There were shouts from each group, and Eirian watched as a single person approached from the Athnaralans. Her eyes took in the looming figure of Tomas as he trudged through the mud and wildflowers. Something must have shown on her face, making Aeyren turn and spot Tomas. His approach gave Aeyren courage, a broad smile softening his features. It made Eirian wonder how much influence Tomas had over him.

"Your Majesty!" Tomas greeted Aeyren. "The bitch has reinforcements arriving."

Eirian chuckled, "General, please, get it right. It's Her Majesty, the queen bitch." Sneering, his eyes narrowed at the sight of Aeyren's knife. "How did you get that?"

"Oh, do you recognize this?"

Holding the blade up, Eirian tilted her head to the side and watched Tomas reach for his knife. Beside her, Faolan snarled in a warning.

"Now, now, don't be rash. Your king thought he'd make a point. But, unfortunately, his point eluded me, so I made my own. I'm only a woman, after all."

"I look forward to gutting you," Tomas said.

"Gutting you is the least I have in mind. If you wish, we could go a round now, and you can try your best. Maybe I'll even let you draw blood before I separate you from your… sword," Eirian replied.

Her eyes flickered to his crotch to convey her meaning. Less frightened of Eirian's magic, Tomas pushed toward her.

"I'm not afraid of you."

Eirian's magic surrounded them. The whispers told her to kill him and give his energy to the earth. She wanted to shred him, to paint the ground with his blood. It would be easy to tear him apart and leave nothing but chunks of flesh. Desire to destroy made her lick her lips, imagining the metallic tang of blood.

"You should be," she purred. "It would cost me nothing to kill you before you took another step. Just give me a reason."

"General!" Aeyren spoke in warning, reaching out to grab his arm. "I'm ordering you to stand down."

Ignoring Aeyren, Tomas continued to get closer to Eirian, and she let him, dropping her hands to her sides with the knife tucked in her grasp.

"You think you're that good."

"I know I am."

Stepping forward to meet him, Eirian smiled. His fist came flying at her, and she lifted her unarmed hand, blocking it without flinching. She felt Tomas preparing another swing, the move prompting her to close her fingers around his wrist and twist. He snarled in pain, his other hand clawing at her. Faolan crouched beside them, his fury feeding Eirian's, and he prepared to intervene if needed. Aeyren watched, wide-eyed and unwilling to aid Tomas. Bringing her hand up, Eirian shifted her grip on the knife and let Tomas see a flicker of her darkness.

"You really shouldn't play with your food, Your Majesty."

Aiden's voice reached them, and Eirian's magic welcomed his familiar anger like an old friend. Letting go of Tomas, she glanced over her shoulder at him.

"I wasn't playing. The general required a lesson in respect."

Unsmiling, Aiden replied, "While I don't doubt they needed it, now is not the time."

"I take it you're the Duke of Tamantal, the rightful king of Endara," Aeyren said.

Eirian saw the wheels turning as Aeyren looked over at Aiden. Hands grasped behind his back, he shook his head. His eyes darted to Tomas, narrowing briefly before shifting to the knife in her grasp.

"You'd be wrong."

"Then who are you to speak to us this way?"

"I'm Aiden Cathasaigh."

He did not give his rank, and Eirian realized Aiden did not need to when Tomas's face twisted in rage. It broke through the strangeness surrounding him, and she frowned.

Reaching for his sword, Tomas snarled, "You're the Bastard of Tamantal! The man who killed my son."

Unable to hide her shock, Eirian turned to Aiden and asked, "You killed his son?"

"Yes. He led a raiding party into Tamantal, and I did my duty as ordered by my lord father and our king," Aiden answered. "And I'd do it again."

"This meeting is over. You will withdraw, King Aeyren, or face the consequences!"

She gave Aeyren a last look before she tossed his knife at his feet. Then, turning her back on him, Eirian walked away with Faolan on one side and Aiden on the other. Rage lessened her control, dandelions blooming in her aftermath.

"She can't protect you, bastard! I'll have your head!" Tomas shouted.

Looking at the group of riders, Eirian was pleased to see the lines of soldiers behind them with banners hoisted. Not glancing at Aiden, she ground her teeth in frustration at the position he had put her in. He felt her anger and clenched his jaw. Whatever she threw at him, he would handle. There was no way it would be any worse than their previous disagreements.

"I suggest you stay away from me for the rest of the day, Captain. Because right now, I could strangle you."

"You know I can't do that, ma'am," Aiden replied. "You're welcome to strangle me, but I hardly think it would solve anything."

She dug her nails into her palm. "I think it would solve a lot of things. Your continued impertinence for a start."

There was amusement in his voice when he spoke, "You enjoy my impertinence too much to want it gone."

"You made me look like a fool! You should have informed me of your history with General Tomas. Right now, I think you have a bigger target on your back than I do, and that's saying something!" Eirian shouted. "Fuck, Aiden! You completely blindsided me."

They drew closer to the waiting horses, and Aiden did not reply. He understood her anger and regretted the situation he had put her in. Taking in the mix of horrified and concerned faces watching her pick through the mud, Eirian braced for the questions that were coming. Merle held Halcyon's reins, and she extended her hands to accept them from him.

"What went wrong?" Everett was the first to speak.

Eirian shrugged, exchanging a look with Faolan. "Nothing went wrong.

What would make you think that?"

Marcellus did not look at her and muttered, "That didn't look like it went to plan."

"Well, maybe not to your plan. However, mine went perfectly. But to answer Everett, Aeyren threatened me. Suggested he might give me as a gift to his pet general if we insisted on fighting them. I simply made it clear what I thought of the suggestion."

"He did what?" Gallagher asked, "Why would he suggest that?"

"Aeyren probably thought it would scare me into agreeing to marry him."

Cameron said, "Do we assume our tentative truce has ended?"

"I think we can safely assume that. However, Aeyren may withdraw until his reinforcements arrive. Therefore, we need to get the legion commanders into a meeting as soon as possible and plan."

Preparing to mount, Eirian gathered her skirts. Stepping in, Aiden ignored the angry look she gave him and lifted her onto Halcyon's back. His hand lingered on her leg, feeling the tensing of her muscles beneath the layers of fabric. Their eyes met briefly, and he hoped she saw how apologetic he felt.

He murmured, "General Tomas won't let his king order a retreat now, and those men answer to him."

"You think his desire for revenge is that great?" Eirian spat.

Everett understood what they were speaking of and groaned, covering his face as the others began mounting. "Aiden, please tell me you didn't goad Tomas?"

"I didn't goad the general. I only gave my name when asked. The rest was all Her Majesty. Tomas is lucky she didn't break his wrist." Aiden signaled to his men. "Or slit his throat."

"I should've known letting you negotiate alone would go badly, Eirian."

Unsure who he was more annoyed with, Everett huffed at Eirian while she looked at him in annoyance. She did not appreciate his public criticism, the comment redirecting part of her anger away from Aiden. Reining in her magic before it caused any more growth, she sneered.

"I think the negotiations went well. King Aeyren and I made our positions clear. He has a better understanding of what he faces if he insists on trying to take my kingdom."

"A strong-willed queen with bigger balls than his?" Gallagher chuckled, and several other nobles laughed with him.

Arching a brow, Eirian nudged Halcyon and replied, "I don't know why the size of my balls keeps coming up. It's hardly relevant!"

Sighing in frustration, Everett looked at Faolan. "I hope we can get more sense out of you than we can out of her."

Faolan gave a loud yip and chased Eirian. Waiting for Everett to mount, General Cameron watched the Athnaralan group withdraw. They were the only two left, and he took the chance to speak.

"Your brother is right. Now Tomas knows he's here, he won't easily withdraw. He'll want vengeance. We shouldn't have let Aiden go to the Queen."

"Aiden has a way with Eirian. You felt her magic. Did you want to risk sending someone else?"

Everett hoisted himself into the saddle and looked at the enemy. Birds darted down, snatching at insects drawn by the wildflowers. They had watched the color blanket the mud while Eirian spoke to Aeyren. It had been an uncomfortable reminder of what she had done to end the battle weeks earlier. Yet something odd about it did not sit right with him. As beautiful as it could be, he could never work out where the additional animals came from when she grew things.

"Do you worry about what's going on between them?" Cameron asked.

Shaking his head, Everett replied, "A little, and then I remind myself that the only issue is Aiden's illegitimacy. Something easily remedied. There are worse options, and I don't think any of us should complain if he can influence Eirian. Powers know none of us can."

"Your father was a dutiful man. He knew his job, but he was also an ambitious one. He'd be proud of his sons and the situation they find themselves in, one next in line to the throne, the other eyeing up being in bed with it. I respected him, and I respect both of you. Aiden is a fine warrior, a capable politician, and a leader who easily commands the loyalty of those who serve him. He is a good, Endaran man with royal blood on both sides."

"It sounds as though you have it all planned out, old man."

"I'm simply saying the army will support Aiden marrying the Queen. Which I've told you before. Only now, we have soldiers who witnessed him carrying her from the battlefield after she saved their lives." Turning his horse, Cameron nodded at the departed group. "We should catch up. Our glorious queen wants things done."

"She refused a man with whom she has a long-standing friendship. Do you think we could convince her to marry Aiden? Because I don't, and Eirian wouldn't risk it outside of marriage with the captain of her guard," Everett replied.

Cameron chuckled, "Boy, I might be old, but I'm not blind. If there isn't something going on between them, I doubt it'll be long. Reminds me of courting my wife. After this war, if Paienven keeps to the treaty, the council won't give Eirian a choice about Aiden."

"You know she doesn't want to marry."

"Do you think we care what she wants? Now move before some Athnaralan decides we'd make excellent target practice."

When they caught up with the rest outside the town gates, a group of officers argued with an exhausted woman. Eirian dismounted, her guards between her and the waiting group, while the officers and nobles milled about. Then, eyes sliding to take in Everett, she pointed at the woman, and the arguments stopped.

"As much as I want to hear from you, she looks like she's had a hard ride, and that suggests it's probably important news we all need to hear."

Smiling at the officers, Eirian signaled her guards to let the woman through. Quickly dismounting, Everett and Cameron joined Marcellus as the woman bowed. They could not argue she had a point. Whatever the messenger had to tell them, it took precedence.

"Lieutenant General Reese sent me. We're stationed on the border in Raellwynt, and Athnaralan forces attacked us. On my ride north, I gathered more reports of attacks."

They felt the fury emanating from Eirian as she took a deep breath before asking, "Have we lost control of any sections of the border?"

"No, ma'am, we haven't lost control of the border. Thanks to the elves, we pushed them back. I skirted around the edges of King Paienven's forces, but it was his brother who saved our asses in Raellwynt. The few towns Athnaral took were being liberated when I left."

Marcellus murmured, "He ordered the attacks before you met with him."

"That was his plan all along. Thank the powers for King Paienven. I suppose we can assume the war is all but over," Eirian replied.

"I don't think it is." The messenger shook her head. "There was something else about the Athnaralans. Like some desperate madness was driving them to die at our hands, even after the elves arrived. They just kept coming and coming."

Eirian froze, color draining from her face, and she swallowed. "What did you say?"

"They fought like crazy men. Like they couldn't stop."

"Eirian…" Everett grabbed her arm.

It was obvious where her mind was going, but Everett doubted anyone would listen. He did not want them to think Eirian was going crazy like King Nolan had. Not with knowledge of what she could do. Catching Aiden's gaze, he silently pleaded for help.

Shaking him off, Eirian asked, "Tell me, did people complain about nightmares in your camp? Have you heard people on your journey complain about such things?"

One newly arrived officer commented, "War is stressful for everyone. People are having nightmares. It's only natural during times such as these."

"No, it's not the stress of war. There is something else going on that no sword can stop."

Sharing a look with Faolan, Eirian pursed her lips and contemplated her options. She had an idea that felt worth trying, but it was not something she could do alone. It was the only thing she could think of to find out if her suspicions were correct. The whispers told her to trust her instincts.

"Faolan, I need to borrow some of your people."

Whining, Faolan scratched the ground, and the gleam in his eyes told Eirian her request did not impress him. She suspected he feared her ability to draw on his fellow daoine. Turning to Aiden, she cocked her head to the side and watched frustration appear on his face.

"Captain, I want to ride away from the town, an area out of sight of the Athnaralans."

Taking a guess at where her thoughts were going, Marcellus asked, "Do you think it's related to the darkness?"

Eirian nodded, running a hand through the mane of brown hair that surrounded her face, pulling it from where sweat had stuck it to her skin. She did not think there was more rain coming for a few days at least, but it was difficult to tell.

"Yes, I think it's the darkness, and I fear our war has barely begun.

SEVENTEEN

Rows upon rows of tents covered the land, the grass trampled and lost to the mud. The legion from Onaorbaen had made themselves comfortable on the far side of Kelsby, away from the watching eyes of the Athnaralans. Scouts reported the opposing camp was breaking down, retreating to higher ground. Thinking about the last time he had stared out over that section of land, Aiden glanced at the keep towering above and smiled.

"Aiden."

"Why do you need to talk to me alone, Everett? I don't have long. Eirian is riding out with the Telmians to do whatever the magical thing is they have planned." Not looking at Everett, Aiden returned his gaze to the sea of tents.

Everett nodded, replying, "I'm aware. We needed to speak where no one could listen."

"That sounds serious. I'm not sure I'm interested."

"Aiden."

Hearing the frustration in Everett's voice, Aiden glanced at him. "You can't blame me. I've enough to deal with."

Rolling his eyes, Everett started sneezing and pressed his face into his shoulder. Watching him, Aiden shook his head and sighed.

"I think I might have the sickness going around," Everett told him between sneezes.

"I doubt that's the reason you needed to speak to me."

"No, it is not. Thanks for caring so much about my well-being, brother."

Rubbing his face, Everett pressed his fingertips into the flesh beneath his eyes, wincing at the pain. Cocking his head to the side, Aiden listened to the horns.

"You're not a child anymore, Everett. You don't need me to tend to you when you're ill. Find a nice young lady from among the ranks to rub ointment on you."

"You know you're respected, highly regarded even. No one questioned my decision when I chose you to be captain of Eirian's guards, not even my uncle."

"Thank you for the high praise, Your Grace. Why do I suspect my popularity has something to do with what you want to speak to me about?" Aiden asked, frowning.

"Because you're not an idiot." Shaking his head, Everett leaned back against the wall and closed his eyes. "I love you, Aiden. I thought choosing you was the best thing for both of you. That you'd protect her fiercely because she's family. That being her captain would make up for the promises our father made."

Crossing his arms, Aiden dug the toe of his boot into the dirt. "Get to the point, Everett. I'm short on time and patience."

Unresponsive, Everett opened his eyes and took in the camp of soldiers laid out before them. He had joined the ranks of those pressuring Eirian to attack the Athnaralans before Aeyren's reinforcements arrived. They wanted things to end sooner rather than later.

"People are noticing your ability to influence Eirian. I fear you may become a target for those who would use your ability for their means."

"Influence? What influence? If I had any ability to influence her, do you think that massacre would have happened? She would've gotten on her horse and left."

"You can't deny you have some small ability to sway her. Otherwise, she'd probably have killed you by now. I'm not the only one who has seen the way you two get with each other. I know I try to ignore it because she's my cousin, and you are my brother."

"You try to ignore a lot of things."

Everett shook his head and explained, "After the meeting yesterday, General Cameron suggested you have the support of the army and others. He wants you married to her."

Aiden arched a brow and replied, "That's hardly news. Cameron has been pushing it since before she returned from Riane."

"You know you're going to have to face the prospect of being legitimized. Cameron told me outright the majority doesn't care what Eirian wants. They intend to force her to marry you if the treaty with Ensaycal holds."

"Cameron vehemently opposed the marriage proposal offered by the Prince. He's loyal to Endara, and I understand why he prefers me."

Everett rubbed his face again and fought the urge to sneeze, pinching his nose to help. "I would've said the same about you, but it seems your loyalties are changeable."

"I remain loyal to Endara," Aiden grunted.

"I put you in this position and never considered you might develop an attachment beyond that of protector and charge. I certainly never thought you might become a liability to her."

Aiden had to agree with the sentiment. He was well aware of what people plotted behind Eirian's back. They had not excluded him from their plans, and the prospect was tempting. If things had been different, he would have embraced the task.

"Does it matter now? You'll be the king soon, thanks to her little secret."

Horns sounded again in the distance. Scowling, Everett pushed off the wall and approached Aiden.

"We're the only ones who know. Until then, remain alert, for Eirian's sake and mine. You're my only brother, and I don't want to see you dead because of my decision."

"Don't worry, Scrappy, I have my ways of finding things out. If anyone seeks to use me, they won't get far."

"The two of you are going to be the death of me!"

Aiden smirked. "Don't be so dramatic. If she wasn't half-duine, you'd be the loudest one supporting us. Be honest, you hoped for this when you made me captain."

"Do you love her?"

"As much as I believe I can love anyone."

Everett scoffed, "You've always been more like your mother. You love more deeply than anyone I know. Father knew it, but he could never beat it out of you."

Pulling him into a hug, Aiden smiled sadly. Grumbling, Everett let him have a moment before shrugging off the embrace.

"I've never regretted those beatings, and I'd take them all over again to protect you."

"You'd make an excellent king, and you're right. I'd support you. I might even think you're good enough for her. You're certainly better than the other Endaran options. Could you imagine Gallagher trying to court her?"

"I'd rather not." Feeling a stab of jealousy, Aiden shook his head.

Arching his brows, Everett chuckled, "Is that jealousy?"

"Captain!"

The sound of Kip calling for Aiden caused them to step apart. Turning, they regarded him standing a distance away with two horses. Seeing them look his way, Kip waved enthusiastically and remained where he was. He knew better than to approach without being summoned. Sighing, Everett nodded grimly and glanced at the sky with a frown.

"Just promise me you'll protect her, and you won't let your feelings get in the way."

"Don't worry, I will. Though I fear the greatest danger to Eirian is herself, and I'm not sure any of us can protect her from that. Now, as your older brother, I'm ordering you to get back inside and stay warm," Aiden replied with a wink and left.

When he joined him, Kip said, "Now, don't go killing me for being the messenger, but we're going to have to catch up."

Taking the offered reins, Aiden muttered, "She wouldn't wait?"

"Nope, Merle did his best, but uh… you know."

"That I do. Waiting wouldn't have made a difference, but that doesn't matter. She's angry with me. Come on, let's go."

Double-checking the tack before he hauled himself into the saddle, Aiden glanced at the sky. Then he peered at the horizon, where dark clouds gathered.

"Sooner she gets this over with, the better."

"Weather is going to turn again," Kip said in agreement.

Aiden nudged his horse into a canter, and Kip quickly followed. The group had not gotten far. Eirian was in the middle, guards and Telmians separating to give him a pathway to join her. Her eyes flickered in his direction long enough to take in the frustration on his face. On the other side, Merle leaned forward to grimace and shrug apologetically. Returning the gesture with a nod, Aiden said nothing and stared ahead at the road they were taking. In the sky, the familiar form of Saoirse circled.

"How far do you need to go?" Aiden finally spoke.

"Not far. Don't worry, Captain, we'll be near to Kelsby. We'll even keep our clothes on, so you don't have to kill anyone who stumbles upon their naked queen working magic."

Eyes widening, Aiden turned to stare at her and saw the slight smile Eirian wore as she watched the land they were passing.

"You're trying to annoy me, and I refuse to give you the satisfaction."

"I'm doing no such thing. If I were trying to annoy you, I'd have gone naked. Besides, I don't need you to satisfy me," Eirian replied.

"No, I'm sure you don't."

Her eyes closed briefly before Eirian pointed to the side. "That way."

The riders changed direction and left the muddy road to cross onto barely disturbed grass without questioning her. Nudging Halcyon, Eirian pushed to the front of the group to lead. Aiden did not follow, remaining beside Merle as he gave him a hard stare.

"How did your meeting with the Duke go?"

"Not the time or place. Has she given you any idea what she's going to be doing?"

"If she hasn't told you, what makes you think she's told me?" Merle asked in amusement.

Within earshot, one of the daoine pushed her horse forward and told them, "She's going to read the land and look for the darkness."

"I've seen her read the land before. She didn't need you to do it," Aiden stated, ignoring the way she looked at him.

"We'll lend her our strength if she needs it, and those who don't will be here to protect us if something goes wrong." Reaching out, she dragged a finger along his arm and said, "I'm sure you'd lend her your strength if you could."

Aiden exchanged a look with Merle and frowned at his barely contained laughter.

"How will she find the darkness?"

"It is unnatural, and she'll feel it."

"Sounds simple enough," Merle said.

He nodded at Eirian as they halted. She split from the group, holding her hands up to stop them as she tilted her head. They waited, watching her slip from the saddle to pace away from Halcyon, gaze directed at the ground. Then, tossing her head back, she turned and nodded. Aiden realized she only wore a gray tunic and trousers. Her weapons were missing, and he wondered why. Dismounting, the guards remained with the horses as the Telmians stepped forward to join Eirian. Aiden handed his reins to Merle to follow.

"For those of us who don't know what's going on, could you share some information?" Aiden asked.

Five of the Telmians split from the group and approached her.

Eirian explained, "With their help, I'll search the land for anything that doesn't belong. I'm relying on instinct to know what I'm looking for. It's not like searching for living things, so I'm not sure what I'll find."

Standing next to Aiden, Tharen said, "She's placing trust in her connection to the land."

"I see," Aiden muttered, crossing his arms.

"What do you want us to do?" A short, dainty woman asked, wide green eyes flickering between Faolan and Eirian.

"Slaine, wasn't it?" Eirian crooked her finger. "I want you to stand on my left, Muireann on my right, and the rest of you in a circle holding hands with them."

Following her instructions, they watched Eirian kneel between the two women. The magic was thick in the air, and Aiden swallowed back his apprehension. He felt her staring and met her gaze, frozen, as she lifted her hand to point to him. There was a tug at his belt, and scrambling to grab it, he watched his knife fly to her hand. None of them noticed it cut his hand as he tried to catch it, a thin line of blood welling up.

Tharen said, "You could've asked him."

"More fun this way," Eirian replied with a smirk.

She focused on her task and used the knife to cut her palms before placing it on the ground. The pain showed in her expression briefly, and Tharen quickly put an arm in front of Aiden as he moved.

"No, Eirian knows what she's doing."

"She cut herself!"

Planting her hands on the ground with the blade between them, Eirian looked at the women on either side. "I need you to put your hands on my shoulders and focus the power."

They nodded, slipping their hands under her tunic to touch her skin. Shivering at the coldness of their fingers, Eirian regretted not having a warm cloak to wrap herself in when she finished. Her magic wove around them, and Aiden wondered if it was his familiarity with it that made hers overwhelm theirs. Head tilted back, her face went slack as she took control of the power. The magic was everywhere, and it felt like his heart slowed to match it.

"Relax, Captain," Tharen said, watching Eirian. "Don't struggle. You'll distract her."

Shaking his head, Aiden dug his nails into his palm and hid the flinch when he felt the cut. "I understand the bloodlust, but this... this I don't understand."

"Close your eyes, breathe it in and let your body feel the power. Accept it. Eirian is more aware of you than she is of the others. Be her anchor when she needs it."

"I don't think I can do that."

Tharen replied coldly, "Then you shouldn't be here."

Scowling, Aiden rolled his shoulders and crossed his arms, staring at Eirian. Her brown hair cascaded down her back, a dark contrast to the gray of her clothing. Studying the details of her face, he watched her eyelids flickering. Then, glancing at the circle of Telmians, he noticed their eyes had shut. Aiden closed his eyes and concentrated on the tugging feel of the magic. It was a familiar whisper, persistent and calling to him with words he could not hear.

Eirian felt the land surround her like a blanket, a comforting sensation she loved. With the added power of the daoine, everything was clear in her mind, so she relaxed her control. Magic flooded through the earth, and, focusing on the flow, she directed it toward the Athnaralan camp. Passing through her people, she felt the thousands of heartbeats, like the vibrations from drums. It was a sound without being a sound, an ageless song that made her want to dance between them.

Letting their life forces surround her, Eirian relished in their strength, the vibrancy of their energy. It would be so easy to silence them, the delicate threads within reach of her fingertips. The desire to do so rose, but she pushed it away with help from the Telmians. Passing through the familiar earth of the battlefield, Eirian encountered the lingering touches of her magic. She knew the Athnaralans were close when she sensed the strangeness she had felt in Tomas and Aeyren.

The further she went, the more Eirian could sense the strangeness, a taste of fear brushing over her mind. It felt cold, like the darkest part of a winter night when the day would never come, and she remembered it. Halting her progress, she waited, visualizing herself standing where her mind was. While she lingered, she grew aware of Aiden's presence, realizing her power had drawn him in. Her own fear flashed through Eirian. She knew he was vulnerable without magic to defend himself in a place he did not belong.

"Aiden," Eirian called out to him.

Reaching out, she focused and drew Aiden's mind to her. It was a warm glow in his mind, and he welcomed her call. He didn't know if Tharen had realized this would happen, but he knew the next time anyone told him to accept her magic into his mind, he would consider slitting their throat. The experience was nothing like he had imagined, and to see the landscape the way her magic let her see it was as though he were in a strange dream. Aiden could tell everything apart, their different energies presenting as vibrant colors.

"Aiden."

The call came again, but Aiden's fear grew as he observed growing darkness behind the glow that was Eirian. He was desperate to shout at her to turn around. It appeared the shadows were going to attack when her power flared, blinding his senses. Yet, there was a feeling of safety, and it reminded him of being in his mother's arms, wrapped in blankets in front of a warm fire. Comforting memories coursed through his mind, and Aiden wondered if they were her doing.

Observing the darkness, Eirian did not move. She sensed the fear of the daoine connected to her and Aiden's terror at the void, but she forced them back with her desire to protect. The shadow was an old friend, every fiber of her recognizing it but unable to put a name to it. A name was on the tip of her tongue. If only she could remember it. Mocking laughter caressed her power, and staring into the darkness, she made out a form.

Eirian realized her suspicions had been right all along. There was something in the corner of her eye, just out of sight. The memories that scratched at her mind were not an illusion, but something buried deep. For once, the whispers of her magic were silent.

"You're weak in this form, my sweet little life," a voice told her.

Cocking her head to the side, Eirian peered at the constantly shifting figure and said, "You're frightened of me."

"You can't save them."

"I'd die to protect this land and its people."

"You will die, but not yet, and not by my hand."

"Would my death stop you?" Smiling, Eirian held out her hand. "Come, kill me."

She felt the darkness recoil, and the figure lost some form before it gathered again in a different place. Longing lanced through her, the emotion striking Eirian as strange.

"You'll watch all you love burn before the end."

"You couldn't defeat me last time, and I've no intention of letting you win," Eirian said, uncertain of where the words had come from.

"You're not her, nor do you have her strength. You don't know what you are."

"I'm the Altira. I have the strength of those who came before me. My blood and duty are theirs. My heart beats with the land."

Eirian lifted her hands high, feeling the power. She thought she felt the strength she spoke of and wanted to glance behind, half expecting to see others there.

Retreating, the darkness vanished, leaving her alone. In its absence, the longing returned, accompanied by the familiar whispers of magic. Knowing she was pushing the willingness of the Telmians, Eirian cast herself at the Athnaralan camp.

With a better understanding of what she was looking for, she found traces of the darkness everywhere, and anger filled her. Once finding the confirmation that she needed, Eirian drifted back over the land. Passing through her people, she found further traces of the darkness, her anger turning to grief.

When her eyes opened, it took her a moment to understand where she was. The feeling of disconnect made her lean forward on her knees and press her forehead to the ground. Staring at the grass, Eirian listened to the concerned daoine gathering around each other. Breathing deeply, she sat on her haunches and looked at the man crouched in front of her. Faolan held out his hands, waiting until she turned her palms up to face him. Frowning, he took hold of them and brushed the dirt away from where it had stuck to her blood.

"The cuts have healed," Faolan said, meeting her gaze.

Shrugging, Eirian took her hands back. "It would appear so, probably thanks to one of them. Our suspicions were correct."

"The darkness?"

"Yes."

"It was a void." Aiden's voice startled her, and Eirian remembered his presence. "A great void that wanted to consume everything, and it hates you."

Looking at Aiden, she realized he was sitting on the ground with Tharen hovering above him and asked, "How were you with me?"

"I don't know. Is that what the world looks like to you when you use your magic?"

Glancing between them, Faolan said, "What are you on about?"

"It would seem our dear little queen drew the captain into her read," Tharen explained.

"How?"

Leaning down, Tharen took hold of Aiden's hand where the knife had caught it. "A little blood goes a long way in magic."

Staggering to her feet, Eirian pushed away from the hands Faolan offered her and stumbled over to Aiden. Tharen released Aiden's hand, glancing between the two of them.

Eirian said, "He has Altira blood. Generations back, far enough that by our laws, his father could marry my aunt."

"You're certain it was the darkness?" Tharen asked.

"Yes."

Crouching in front of Aiden, Eirian stared at him, and he nodded in agreement. Frowning at the crouching pair, Faolan glanced over at his people in concern.

"What about the rest of you? What did you sense?"

Ilar leaned heavily on another man and said, "It whispered to me. I felt it calling my darkest desires forth."

"It was the same for me," another man muttered, shaking his head.

"There was only her standing between us, like a candle flame against the night," Muireann agreed.

Aiden was still pale, but he felt stable enough to stand. Glancing at his men, he saw them watching in concern.

He murmured, "A lover's caress, whispering it's okay to give in. Everything will be better if you surrender."

Remaining crouched, Eirian closed her eyes. "Don't let your thoughts dwell on it. Doing so will help it gain a foothold in your mind. It riddles the Athnaralans and many within our own ranks. I doubt most of them realize they're being used."

"What can we do to free them?" Slaine asked.

"Perhaps a cleansing would help, otherwise defeat the darkness and redo whatever they did last time. I wish we knew how to destroy it for good, but how am I to know if they didn't. How long until your king gets here?"

Forcing herself to stand, Eirian accepted Tharen's hand for stability. The two lords shared a look, and she understood its meaning. They did not know when Neriwyn would arrive. Approaching each of the Telmians who had helped, she lifted a hand to their faces and murmured her thanks. What they had done had cost some of their innocence. It had also cost Eirian's last fragments of hope that the warnings were wrong.

"Next time you ask for volunteers, remind me to say no," Ilar muttered, smiling faintly.

Nodding, Eirian replied, "I understand. Had I known what we'd encounter, I wouldn't have asked."

"You truly mean it. You'd give all you have before you used others. What a strange creature you are, Eirian."

"You're not the first to tell me that, Ilar, and somehow I doubt you'll be the last." Turning to Faolan, she said, "Take your people back to Kelsby. I need time to think."

"Saoirse will watch over you," Faolan replied.

The guards gave over the reins to their riders, moving out of the way as the Telmians mounted. Eirian watched them quietly, bending to pick up the knife from the ground where she had left it. A glance at the sky told her that more time had passed than she had realized. The sun crept toward the western horizon. Tharen was the last to return to his horse, his gaze lingering on Aiden before turning to leave. Merle passed the reins to other guards so he could approach. He observed Eirian and shook his head.

"Now, I don't know what happened, but you need to talk to her. She looks guilty."

"No, you don't know. I had my doubts about all this darkness shit. I thought the Telmians were inventing some magical enemy that would lead her away from us. That her father's madness made her all too willing—"

Merle argued, "You weren't the only one. We all did."

Giving him a pointed look, Aiden replied, "I'm aware. Just as I know that half my men have been feeding her information about nightmares and disappearances. The information she couldn't find out for herself because I don't let her."

"When your queen asks you to keep your ear to the ground and report what you hear, what are you supposed to say? No, ma'am, I can't do as you ordered because our captain thinks it would be a bad idea to entertain you. Yep, we'd keep our jobs after that."

Eirian turned to look at them, an eyebrow arched. "I can hear you."

"I didn't think you were listening," Aiden commented.

Moving, he held his hand out for his knife. Eirian glanced at the weapon and turned it in her hand, holding it out hilt first to Aiden.

"Clearly."

"You don't sound angry."

"Should I be? What you thought doesn't matter. All that matters is how I'm supposed to defeat something that wants to burn the world." Eirian turned her gaze to the guards, asking, "How do I fight nightmares and emotions? Something that invades the mind to take hold of the darkest thoughts hidden within. Can you tell me how I fight that? How do I stop it from destroying all of you?"

Staring at the blade in his hand, Aiden took in the flecks of blood dried on it and wondered which were his. "I don't know."

"Neither do I."

"But I do know every single one of us will have your back. Somehow, we'll defeat it together."

She whispered, "I'm sorry you experienced it, Captain."

Pursing his lips, Aiden slipped the knife into the sheath at his hip and ran a hand through his hair. "Sometimes things happen, Eirian, and we can't always explain why. You need to convince people the darkness is a genuine threat. The Telmians are no use to you, but I am. If I tell people it is real, and I've seen it, they'll listen to me."

"You saw it because of my magic and your Altira blood."

"You could try to show Everett or anyone with a dash of Altira blood, and they might see it, but it might also destroy them."

Eirian said, "You speak like you aren't at risk! The darkness could claim you, and honestly, you'd be a prime target for it. It would delight in taking someone so close to me."

Walking away, she found a clear patch of grass to sit on. Giving her a moment, Aiden glanced at Merle and shook his head. Then he approached and sat next to his queen. Her hands were in her lap as she stared at the horizon. Dark clouds hung in the sky, bearing down from the north, and Eirian wondered if the weather was typical for this time of the year. Studying her, Aiden saw the tiny bumps covering her skin and the tinge of blue discoloring her lips. He reached over to touch her arm and growled at her iciness.

"Does anyone have a cloak?" he called out.

"It's fine, Aiden," Eirian replied faintly.

Scowling, he shuffled closer and muttered, "It's not fine, darling. You're like fucking ice. The last thing we need is you getting sick along with everyone else."

"I don't get sick. I've never gotten sick, not even a little cold."

Fox approached with a heavy-looking cloak bundled in his arms, and Aiden watched as he shook it out to drape over Eirian. Two different furs lined the hood and upper section, her hands instantly reaching up to grasp at the edges as Fox pulled it over her head. Rubbing her cheek against it, a look of delight chased away the worry. Grinning, Fox finished wrapping it around Eirian and sat, earning himself an annoyed look.

"What's this fur?" Rubbing her fingers against it, she admired the spotted off-white fur.

He answered, "Northern lynx from the Fingers. It was my last hunt with my da before I left to join your guard. He figured it was time I went after the fiercest animal in the mountains. Said if I were going to be protecting the queen, I should be able to hunt anything."

Clenching his jaw, Aiden watched the way she relished the soft fur. "I've heard of them. How do you find them in the snow? I'd have a hard time spotting that."

"How do you find any quarry? Hunting isn't just sight." Grinning, Fox watched Eirian. "Don't start purring like a cat, ma'am, not sure the cap'n could handle it."

Realizing what she was doing, Eirian dropped her hands back to her lap and blushed. Her reaction made Fox laugh.

Eirian muttered, "Apologies. I'm half inclined to send you home to get me some. I can't believe how soft it is."

"I've noticed you like fur," Aiden remarked.

The faint smile that crossed her face at his comment made Aiden look away to stare at the oncoming storm. It was better if he did not think about Eirian and fur.

"As novices, we're not allowed luxuries like fur. Besides, it doesn't get so cold on the edge of the Yifthn Sea." Drawing the cloak closer, Eirian looked at Fox curiously.

"Yes, ma'am?" Fox asked.

"Is this weather normal?"

Shrugging, he picked at his teeth with a nail. "Some years are stormy. Others aren't. A few dry ones and then wet ones before a few more dry ones. It means winter will be harsh."

"So, you don't feel this is out of the norm?" she prompted.

"Nah. I'd have said sooner if I did."

She fell silent and retreated into her thoughts. Giving Fox a stern look, Aiden waited for him to get to his feet and return to the rest of the group. Staring over his shoulder at them, he took in the way they turned their backs. It was all the privacy they could give. Returning his attention to Eirian, he noticed she had turned her face into the fur-lined hood with her hand holding it in place. There were signs that warmth had chased the chill from her skin, her fingertips no longer a bluish-white. He wanted to sling his arm around her and pull her close, sharing his warmth.

"You didn't answer my question," Aiden said softly, tugging the hood from her face.

Staring at him over her hand, Eirian murmured, "What question was that?"

"Is that how you see the world? All those colors?"

"Short answer is yes and no."

"That isn't helpful."

"No, it's not. Yes, I see everything in those colors. But, no, those colors aren't colors like you think. They're the life force, the energy of things. Those others who can do it might not perceive life the same way. But, because I was the one in control, you received my perception."

Hoping her explanation was enough, Eirian uncrossed her legs and drew her knees up so she could wrap them in the cloak. She was still cold and wished she could curl up in his arms. Her thoughts reminded her of how warm he could be.

"Do you make yourself appear the way you do? So bright and the purest white I've ever seen." Closing his eyes, Aiden recalled her appearance.

"I make nothing appear the way it does. If you saw me as white energy, then that's the color of my life force. When I pushed you back from the darkness, what did you experience?" Eirian glanced at him when she asked her question.

Opening his eyes again, Aiden noticed her lips were no longer blue. "I felt like comfort surrounded me, happiness, safety. At first, I thought I was wrapped in a blanket in my mother's arms beside a fire. Then other similar feelings from my memory followed. I don't know what happened between you and the darkness."

"I should've asked the daoine what they experienced."

"You protected me from the darkness. You made yourself weaker to protect me."

Aiden was angry with her for endangering herself, guilty that she had because of him. Propping her head up with her hand, Eirian regarded him in annoyance.

"Yes, I did. That's my job, so don't you dare get indignant! Not protecting you would've left me more vulnerable. I would've feared what it might do to you."

"If you hadn't taken my knife the way you did."

Recoiling from the accusation in his voice, Eirian looked away. She felt guilt over her actions and the danger they had put him in.

"You're right. It was my fault you were there. But, in my defense, I didn't know it was possible, and while part of me wants to explore what we can do, I won't endanger you."

Aiden rubbed his face. "Can I expect to experience anything else?"

"We won't know until something happens. You already seem like you can resist my powers. I remember on the battlefield, my bloodlust did not control you."

Deciding she had been there long enough, Eirian struggled to her feet and held her hand out. Staring at her hand, Aiden considered what she had said before he grasped it and let her help him up. Her hand was cold, and he wanted to hold on until it was warm.

"We should return to the keep. We don't want to get caught in any more rain with all the sickness going around. You've been cold enough today."

Flashing a cheeky grin, Eirian winked. "Yes, I need warming up. As do you, Captain, can't have your reflexes freezing. It wouldn't be very satisfying."

Watching her stride back to the horses, Aiden shook his head. "Bloody woman."

EIGHTEEN

Eirian stood on one side of a table with her arms crossed as she glared across it at Everett. "I'm going, and that's final."

Exasperated, Everett tossed his hands in the air and turned to Marcellus. "Would you reason with her! I give up."

"I'm sorry, Everett, but I agree with Eirian. Right now, we're at a stalemate with the Athnaralans, and this is a new report. To have any chance of finding out if the darkness is causing the crop failures, she needs to investigate one."

"Exactly!" Eirian said.

"Besides, Aeyren wouldn't expect her to go riding off to a farm to look into a crop failure. He'll expect Eirian to remain here, so she's safer going."

"She won't be alone. Half the Telmians are coming, all of her guards, several other nobles, and we have a company of soldiers for protection," Gallagher commented.

Hovering behind Eirian, Gallagher looked like a hopeful child. At the other end of the table, Cameron sat studying a pile of reports. He had kept out of the argument, more concerned with troop movements and the reports outlining attacks to the south.

"We can't afford to run short on supplies. If the darkness is behind it, then it's an excellent strategy. Wouldn't you agree, Captain?" Cameron asked Aiden.

Aiden kept his hands behind him as he attempted to hide in the corner. He agreed with Everett, but Eirian was in no mood to hear it when they had already argued about it.

"Yes, sir, I agree. We can't ignore a potential food shortage while at war."

"Do you agree the Queen of Endara should be the one to investigate if there is magic involved with the crop failure?" Everett asked pointedly.

"It's not my place to have an opinion. I follow the orders my queen gives me." Rocking on his heels, Aiden avoided the annoyed look Eirian sent his way at his use of the words she had yelled at him.

Eyes narrowing, Everett declared, "Obviously, I'm the only one with any sense. If I can't convince you to remain here, then I'll come with you."

"No," Eirian told him sharply. "You're to remain here. Should Athnaral make any moves while I'm absent, you're in charge."

"Are you sure, ma'am?" Cameron glanced up from his work.

"Yes. The Duke is my heir."

Bowing his head, Everett understood her reasoning. "As you command."

Eirian stepped away from the table and told Aiden, "Give the orders, Captain. We depart as soon as everyone is ready."

Nodding, Aiden slipped from his corner and out of the door. Watching him go, Cameron's aides exchanged sympathetic looks before continuing with their work. Gallagher bowed to Eirian, leaving the room to prepare himself and the handful of nobles going. They expected to be gone for a few days, and most were glad for the excuse to get away from Kelsby.

"Do you have any orders regarding the enemy?" Cameron asked.

"I should think it's obvious. Don't let them pass. We have the greater numbers right now, and we must hold out. Eventually, Aeyren will realize there's no way for him to take Endara." Making her way to the door, Eirian stopped and told Marcellus, "If he comes to the negotiating table, offer Everett up as a husband to Princess Ayelian."

"You can't make that decision!" Everett shouted at her in frustration, his voice hoarse from the illness plaguing him.

Smiling at him coldly, Eirian replied, "Yes, I can. I'm the queen of Endara. If I order you to marry a milkmaid, then you'll thank me for my choice and marry her."

Opening his mouth to argue, Everett shut it when Marcellus shook his head. Arching a brow, Eirian turned to the door and left the room. Two of her guard squads were waiting outside, and Merle handed over her cloak. Accepting it, she tossed it around her shoulders and secured the buckle with quick-moving fingers. While ensuring it would not catch on her swords, she thanked him. He grunted, unwilling to test her mood by speaking. After the encounter, no one knew what to expect from Eirian from one moment to the next. Even those she rarely got frustrated with had been victims of her mood.

"I presume the others will be outside with the horses?" Eirian started down the corridor, the men moving out of her way.

"Yes, ma'am," Merle responded, maintaining his spot half a step behind.

People moved out of the way, saluting as the group passed. Eirian had paced the keep often enough to know which way to go. When they stepped through the open doors into the sunlight, her hand shot out to catch the apple Gabe tossed at her. Slipping into the group, he matched her stride and watched from the corner of his eye as she bit into the fruit.

"They lost their last-ditch attempt to stop you going."

"Yes, they did. Thank you for the apple. You always know what to get me."

Gabe smiled, replying, "You're always hungry. The boss man said he'd have the horses ready and waiting outside the gates."

Pausing her stride mid-bite, Eirian looked at him. Gabe shrugged, glancing at Merle.

"That sounds more prepared than I expected."

"Yeah, we figured it would put you in a better mood."

Several guards groaned quietly at the comment. Eirian's eyes narrowed, and she continued to eat the apple. The crunching of her bites was the only sound they paid any attention to. Gabe was the only one unbothered by the way she regarded him, and his gaze flickered to where Aiden was waiting. Noticing his change of focus, she finished eating and turned to continue her path toward the gate. Lingering until he was at the back of the group, Aiden joined Gabe.

"She's under stress." Shrugging, Gabe eyed Aiden and said, "You can see it."

Huffing, Aiden ignored the worried looks his men gave him, replying, "She's insufferable, and she knows it."

"Are we sure the darkness can't influence her?"

"Lord Tharen doesn't think so."

Hand reaching for the knife secured at the small of his back, Gabe asked, "What do we do if it has compromised her?"

"I don't know, but I also don't think it'd come to that." Aiden looked at where Gabe's hand had gone. "Would you kill her?"

"Absolutely. All that power under the influence of something that wants to destroy us? Can't say it's a prospect I care to entertain. She'd expect us to do it."

Grunting in agreement, Aiden stared at the back of Eirian's head. Outside the main gate, the company of soldiers waited in tidy rows while the gaggle of nobles, Telmians, and guards milled in front of them. Spotting Brenna and Isabella on their mounts, she sighed and made her way to where Fisk stood with Halcyon.

The horse tossed his head, nickering a greeting, earning himself a warm smile and the apple core. Scratching behind his ear, Eirian ran her hands over him before going through her usual routine. Noticing her bow, she glanced over her shoulder at Aiden and inclined her head. He did not respond to her acknowledgment, moving to his horse in a hurry. Approaching, the lieutenant escorting them saluted. His fist remained on his chest longer than necessary.

"We're ready to leave, Your Majesty."

"Thank you, Todd. Anyone not here can either catch up or miss out." Looking at the Athnaralan camp, Eirian grumbled, "I don't want to waste any time."

Saluting again, Todd replied, "Yes, ma'am. I'll give the orders."

While he returned to his company, Eirian checked her bow to ensure she could pull it easily from the quiver. Testing the draw, she grunted in appreciation of whoever had taken the time to string it. Then, slipping it back, she turned her attention to her ladies and saw Faolan with Muireann.

Todd called out, and the company of soldiers started moving. Nudging Halcyon, Eirian headed to the front with her guards following. Settling into position, she let the gelding have his head and relaxed into the sway of his movements. With the passing of the last storm, the days had taken a warm turn, and she hoped it was a sign there would be no more rain. She knew it would make the passage of troops easier, but the rain had taken a toll on everyone.

"Ground's sodden," Gallagher grumbled, bringing his horse up alongside.

Eyeing the road, Eirian replied, "What do you expect? It's only been a few days since the rain stopped. I don't think we need to tear up the ground, so we'll take it easy."

"A fine idea. War does enough damage, though I suppose you can repair some of it."

"I could, but I wouldn't unless I had to. I've upset the balance enough recently."

"You know, I understand what you mean by balance, but I don't."

"The balance is life," Faolan answered.

He glanced at him. "So basically, the natural order?"

Nodding, Faolan moved up and explained, "Those with magic have to learn when it is appropriate to use their powers, and when it isn't. Your queen can do a lot with her magic but doesn't because there is no need."

"Or because it's frivolous," Eirian added.

In front, Aiden glanced over his shoulder and quipped, "You mean like making things move just because you can? That's pretty frivolous to me."

She sneered at him, making a rude gesture.

Faolan watched Saoirse gliding above them. "When will we reach this farm?"

Eirian answered, "Late tomorrow, but it should be a pleasant ride so long as the weather remains with us."

Gallagher gazed at Saoirse and sighed in appreciation before looking at Faolan. "Forgive my impertinence, but I don't know which form I admire more. Lady Saoirse is magnificent."

"I'll tell my sister you said so," Faolan chuckled.

Glaring at the back of Aiden's head, Eirian dug her nails into the reins. He sensed her stare, glancing over his shoulder with a smile.

"Is it possible for non-daoine to learn to shapeshift?" she asked.

"If it was, wouldn't they teach it in Riane?" Gallagher said.

Faolan arched a brow at Eirian, knowing why she was curious. "The gods tied the ability to our magic, which, as you know, differs from that of humans and elves. Besides, the years we take to master the pain of the transformation are greater than your lifespan. Though it is easier for some."

Startled, Gallagher gasped, "Pain?"

"Yes, in the beginning, it's excruciating. Every part of your body is shifting and changing. Your bones and muscles, your organs, your flesh. It all transforms. It takes time and discipline to overcome, something not all of us can do. A broken limb can trap us in either form. If poorly healed, we can never shift again."

"What decides your animal form?" Isabella asked.

"Mostly your traits, the things that define you. A basic example would be that Saoirse is a solitary person. She prefers to stalk her prey from afar. She is observant and capable of great patience, but she can work with others when the need calls for it." Glancing up at his sister, Faolan chuckled.

Aiden commented, "She's also very opportunistic."

"That she is, no denying it."

Giving Eirian a cheeky grin that made him look even younger than he was, Gallagher inclined his head at her. "What do you think Her Majesty might be if she could do it?"

Several of those listening gasped at his words, eyes darting to Eirian. The question had Aiden looking back, an eyebrow arched in surprise. Faolan chuckled, shaking his head with a grin, and waved at Aiden.

"I don't know. What do you think, Captain?"

"I think I value my hide enough to keep silent," Aiden replied.

Bringing his horse in closer, Fox rubbed a hand on his cloak and said, "Northern lynx."

Surprised, Faolan looked at him, and his eyes went to the fur that Fox was caressing. "Really?"

"Yep. Fierce, solitary, deadly, and you don't see them coming until it's too late. They'll shred you. When needed, they'll work with others but prefer being independent."

"All valid observations, but I'm not sure they apply to Queen Eirian. One of the biggest aspects of her identity is that of a protector. Do you disagree?"

"I've seen a female lynx defend her den and kittens."

"All creatures protect their young," Brenna observed.

Eirian did not look at them, saying, "Honestly, I'd probably be a wolf, like Lord Faolan."

"Really?" He contemplated it and admitted, "I could see it. I'm having difficulty picking a single animal that would suit you. It's the self-sacrificing part that throws me."

"I'm sure individual wolves do what's needed to ensure the survival of the pack. Just like I'll do whatever I have to do to ensure the survival of my people."

Nudging Halcyon forward, Eirian did not wait to hear a response. Her guards did not move to follow her, Aiden signaling to them to remain where they were.

He said, "For the sake of our sanity, we should let her be."

Left alone to ride on the outskirts of the group, Eirian monitored the land. She did not know what to expect, a niggling feeling at the back of her mind warning her to keep watch. Letting her magic drift, she closed her eyes and trusted Halcyon not to put a hoof wrong while she meditated. The whispers of her guards and people had not escaped her notice.

She could admit it was increasingly difficult to control her mood. When she slept, her nightmares plagued her, so she tried to avoid sleeping. It had occurred to Eirian to speak to Tharen and seek his help in freeing herself from the dark thoughts. Every time she convinced herself to seek him out, her courage failed. It was not only the spiral of dark thoughts that bothered her. Her magic had been as erratic as her mood, the whispers worsening.

"Your Majesty," Todd spoke softly, curious but reluctant to disturb her. "It's getting late. There's a suitable spot to camp approaching."

Opening her eyes, Eirian blinked a few times before looking at Todd riding beside her. She still felt disconnected, shadows dancing around the edge of her vision.

"You know the region. I'll take your recommendation."

"Do you mind if I ask what you were doing?"

"I was—" she stopped speaking as she caught sight of the lone hill ahead.

Following her gaze, Todd said, "Cynwrig Tor. We'll camp on the other side of it near the Arianell. There's a farm there, and I sent a rider ahead to seek permission from the family. I'd rather not scare them by camping two hundred people on the border of their land."

"The Arianell?"

"Aye, it's a stream that runs from the Fingers to the Efa." Gazing at the hill, he shrugged. "I forgot you haven't seen this part of Endara. The appreciation in your eyes reminds me how beautiful my home is."

Sighing, Eirian continued to stare at the view. Todd had seen it before, preferring to take in the admiration he saw on her face.

Eirian murmured, "I think it would take a hundred lifetimes to see every beautiful thing that Endara has to show us. More than that to contemplate the rest of the world."

Todd patted the neck of his horse "I suppose you're right. Most people stop thinking about the view because they're too busy surviving. They rarely leave the area they were born in. Seeing the world is the joy of wealthy people and soldiers."

"And mages, if they bother to leave Riane."

"There are more mages out there than you realize, ma'am. I don't know what they teach you in Riane, but most are open to those with magic. Now, I'd best be returning to my place."

Saluting, Todd kicked his horse forward and left Eirian in silence. Halcyon tossed his head, reminding her he was behaving. Leaning forward, she scratched a spot under his mane.

"I know, my love, you want to run. So do I. Let's go."

Looking over her shoulder, Eirian took in the distance to her guards before turning to assess a path through the others. Chuckling, she settled into the saddle and nudged the gelding. His ears pricked, snorting as she guided him to the edge of the line and did her best to make it look like she was joining Todd. Then, relaxing her hold on the reins, she signaled to Halcyon that he could run, and kept her eyes on the looming hill.

"Fuck!" Aiden cursed.

Taking off after her, the guards ignored the looks they received. Eirian was making a direct line toward the hill, and Aiden hoped her horse had more sense than she did. The ground was rough, and they dared not put their mounts at risk of a broken leg. Her gaze picked up the stream further on as she got closer to the hill, and she hesitated. Halcyon slowed, allowing her guards to catch up. Bringing themselves in on either side, Merle swung forward and grabbed the reins while Aiden reached for her arm.

"What the fuck do you think you're doing?" Aiden growled.

Eirian did not answer, her magic drawing her gaze to a neat stack of stones set into the side of the hill. Scowling, Aiden looked at what had drawn her attention and shook his head, letting go of her wrist. Nodding at Merle to release the reins, he watched her move forward. Getting as close as possible on horseback, Eirian ignored her guards. Dismounting, she rubbed a hand on Halcyon's neck before carefully picking her way up the grassy slope toward the odd formation.

Aiden asked, "What is it?"

"I don't know."

Clambering up the last part, Eirian reached for the stack and touched it. Her magic reacted to the wards worked into the stones, and she had to fight not to double over in shock. Stumbling back, she almost knocked Aiden over, but he caught her. Looking at her with concern, he kept his grip tight.

"What was that?"

A shrill cry pierced the air, alerting them to Saoirse gliding down to the ground. Watching the eagle transform into a woman, Eirian kept glancing at the stack of stones. Her magic had settled but remained ill at ease with whatever the stones guarded.

"It's a cairn. I've been here before, a long time ago." Red hair tumbling down her back, Saoirse gazed up at the hill and said, "This is a place of great sorrow."

"What are those wards?" Eirian asked.

Looking to Eirian, Saoirse said, "You don't know."

"Obviously not."

"This is where the last Altira rests."

Aiden tightened his grip, pulling her against him as she stiffened, and he asked, "What do you mean, this is where the last Altira rests?"

"What did I say that was confusing?"

Arching a brow, Saoirse glanced past them at Faolan. He shook his head at her.

"I didn't realize we were coming near here. Otherwise, I'd have warned you. To the south is where the darkness was last defeated. They brought the Altira here."

Elbowing Aiden, Eirian freed himself from his grasp. "Is she the only one?"

"Many mages fell during the war, and while they returned some to their homes for burial, they lay most to rest in mass graves further south. Including our own."

Pointing to a location in the distance, Faolan stared at it in sorrow. Saoirse touched his shoulder, eyes filled with sorrow.

She said, "We argued with King Neriwyn. We wanted to take them home, but he said they belonged here now."

"All of you leave," Eirian commanded. "I don't care if you want to stand around watching me from a distance, but I don't want any of you near me right now."

Meeting Faolan's gaze, Aiden saluted her and turned to pick his way down to his men. Shrugging, Saoirse spread her arms and transformed, hopping across the ground briefly before her wings lifted her into the air. Lingering, Faolan pursed his lips, considering what to say.

"I can't tell you what answers you might find."

Kneeling by the cairn, Eirian waited until her senses told her she was as alone as she was going to get. Better prepared, she reached out and touched the stones, allowing the magic of the wards to wash over her. There was a familiarity she could not place. Magic swirled, and she wondered if she should have left things alone. Closing her eyes, Eirian's mind filled with a bright white light, and she felt it chasing her shadows away.

"I see you've met my daughter," a woman whispered.

Opening her eyes, Eirian stared at the strange apparition crouching beside the stones, watching her. "What are you?"

Cocking her head to the side, the woman frowned and reached out to touch Eirian's cheek. It was a cold sensation that was not a genuine feeling, and she shuddered.

"She hid the memories of your meeting. I can undo that. To answer your question, I'm your ancestor. Only an Altira could disturb me."

"The ancestors are real?" Eirian asked.

"What do they teach you if you don't know about your ancestors?" Wonder crossed her face as she stroked her hand over Eirian's cheek, murmuring, "It's like staring at a mixture of my daughter and my greatest friend. How could this be?"

Trying not to flinch from the cold sensation on her face, Eirian pursed her lips. "How did you defeat the darkness?"

"She has returned?"

"Yes."

"Shianeni warned me our efforts wouldn't banish her forever. It is unnerving. You look like her, but I don't know how that could be possible. Perhaps it's the longing that makes it seem so. How many years has it been?"

"They say a thousand years have passed since the end of the mage wars. What is the darkness?" Eirian asked. "And how do I defeat her?"

Leaning back, the spirit sighed. "The darkness is a god. You don't defeat her. Banish her, yes, but you can't defeat something that exists in everything. They're all co-dependent, good and evil, light and dark, thought and feeling, war and peace. There can't be death without life. So with my life and my death, I created the ward that imprisoned her."

Her heart sank, and rubbing her face, Eirian glanced over her shoulder at her guards and said, "A god? I thought they all left?"

"They didn't leave. They're out in the world doing their own thing, keeping themselves from mortals. I don't know if she was always the darkness or if something made her that way. Shianeni couldn't tell me. Or rather, she wouldn't."

"How do I remake the ward?"

Staring past her living descendant, the spirit observed the men. "I can't tell you. You'll know when the time comes, and you'll know the price. Perhaps you already know what it will take. You'll need all the support you can get."

Eirian whispered, "Then I'm right in suspecting I'll die."

"Death is the least of what it will take. Remember, acceptance and balance. The darkness is an extreme unbalance."

"I have a darkness of my own. I've killed hundreds who may not have deserved it."

"And I killed thousands. I created weapons out of stone and living wood and sacrificed my brethren and mate. I scorched land so badly that life could never again grow there, rendering the earth a wasteland. The darkness that stains you is nothing compared to mine." Standing, she said, "I'll release the memories my daughter hid. Tell Shianeni I miss her."

Frowning at the figure, Eirian shook her head. "Who is Shianeni?"

"The darkness is free, and you don't know Shianeni? She is the first, the queen of Telmia. She should guide you as she guided me."

"The Queen of Telmia has vanished. Neriwyn is coming, and I hoped he could help me." Watching grief appear, Eirian wondered how the dead could still feel emotions.

"Then I'm sorry, girl, so sorry. I fear you may die in vain, for I had her power to help me, and she was the most powerful in existence. She was life, and I loved her greatly, though few could resist loving her." Reaching down, her hand touched Eirian's cheek again. "Before I leave, what is your name?"

"Eirian Altira."

Chuckling at the name, she faded. "We come a full circle, and my name becomes yours. May the darkness always fear an Eirian Altira."

Overwhelmed by a sudden pain in her head, Eirian cried out and clutched it. The memories of her night in the tomb of her ancestors flooded back. Curling in on herself, she sobbed. She was unsure why she cried. There was no relief in the tears, simply despair. When arms wrapped around her, she did not need to look to know who it was. Inhaling the scents of horse, leather, eucalyptus, and sweat, she tried to find comfort in his embrace. Aiden had tucked her head under his chin, a hand stroking her back gently to calm her, but his actions only made Eirian feel worse.

Hearing her sobs become whimpers, Aiden continued to stroke her back. "I don't know what caused this, but I think you needed it."

"She said my death might not be enough. If it's not, then it will have been for nothing. You might die for nothing," she whispered and rubbed her face, trying to banish the tears.

"Who told you?"

"The last Altira, the one buried here. I disturbed the wards, and she appeared to me. I don't have the help she had to banish the darkness."

Aiden grunted and pulled her away slightly to kiss her forehead. "You'll have all the help you need, darling. If I die serving you, it'll be the death I wanted. More so if it means you can save everyone else."

Eirian murmured, "I'm tired of death, and it's barely begun. How much more will I have to face? How much can I deal with before it breaks me?"

Meeting his gaze, Eirian blinked furiously to fight back the fresh tears that threatened. Lifting a hand to her face, Aiden brushed away a tear with his thumb.

"It might break you for a time, but then you'll remember why. You'll remember children playing, men and women working hard to make their lives, your family, friends. The princes. Me. You'll remember every death and what they died for. Only then will you find the deep well of strength you possess, and you'll keep fighting. The world could fall apart, and you'll keep fighting. We all will."

She knew he was right, even if she did not feel that way. The mixture of memories and new knowledge sat uneasily in her mind. It made Eirian more aware of the clamoring memories that had demanded recollection all her life.

"I don't want more death. I understand my own is the price, but—"

"We're soldiers, as are most of those you worry over. Do you doubt we know our lives are a price to pay when required? That we don't accept our death serves the same purpose you believe yours will? If I must die to save a family, then I'm at peace."

"I'd never be at peace with you dying for me. Or Merle, Gabe, and the rest, even that fool, Fionn. I never want to see your corpse in front of me."

Closing her eyes, Eirian turned away. Resting his cheek on her head, Aiden stared at his men. He had sent half of them to the camp. She had ordered that they travel light, so there were no tents to put up. Knowing her, he understood she wanted a few nights without the confines of walls around her and nothing but clear skies. He could appreciate it, but he had doubts it was what she needed.

He whispered, "I'd never be at peace with outliving you."

"Don't say that, Aiden."

"Why, Eirian? Because you're reminded that you're loved? You disrespect the people who'd grieve your death."

Ashamed, Eirian struggled to her feet. Her knees protested, and she realized she had been kneeling on stones. Adjusting her belt and weapons, she did not look at Aiden.

"We should join the others."

Watching her, he said, "As you wish, ma'am. We should get you some baldrics."

"I'm happy with the way I have things."

Offering him her hand, Eirian did not smile. She had baldrics tucked in her chest in Kelsby, but she did not mention them. Checking her feet were stable before he accepted her help, Aiden frowned at the blood stains on the knees of her trousers and touched her leg.

"You're hurt."

"What?" Stretching out a leg, she peered at her knee and grunted, "Huh. There must have been a sharp rock. It's nothing, but I'll ask Muireann to look if you wish."

"You need to stop offering your blood." Taking her hand, Aiden stood with a groan.

Arching a brow at him, Eirian chuckled, "You're getting old, Captain."

The look he gave her made her laugh, and it pleased Aiden to see her smile chasing away the tears. "I'm only five years older than you."

"See, old! You're over thirty now. It must be time to retire."

"I'd offer to prove to you I'm nowhere near ready to retire, but you have—"

Eirian held up a hand to silence him, and Aiden looked at the group of guards where a rider was approaching. Carefully picking their way down the side of the hill, she did not meet the concerned stares of her protectors as they drew closer. His eyes narrowed at the sight of Devin waiting to the side with a worried look.

"What happened?" Aiden demanded.

Devin saluted, saying, "The lieutenant and Merle sent me. There's news."

"What news?" Eirian prompted, leaning against Halcyon.

"The rider sent ahead to speak to the farmers has returned. They're all dead, and it isn't pretty. The lieutenant and others have gone to investigate, Merle included. He thought you'd want to know and left the rider to tell you what she saw."

No one responded, and the two on foot hauled themselves into their saddles. Then, pulling on their reins, they followed Devin. What little good humor Eirian had found vanished at the thought of an entire family dead. Her mind ran through all the possibilities. She doubted it was the Athnaralans, but she knew there was the possibility some had slipped past. When they reached the camp, Fionn and his men were waiting with a pale woman who Eirian doubted was over sixteen years.

"Your Majesty." She saluted, and they saw she had been crying.

"What did you see?" Eirian asked gently.

Wide eyes stared in horror as she recalled, "They were all dead, even the little children and the baby. I did a quick search for anyone else, but it was obvious they'd been dead for a bit. Dead in their beds, throats slit like cattle."

Eirian's gut clenched at the thought. "Is it hard to find? I'll not ask you to return."

"I have to take you. If I can't face it again, then I don't deserve my place." Clenching her fists with determination, the young woman glared at the solemn guards.

"Let me assure you, there's a world of difference between death in battle and what you saw. Even the most experienced officer will tell you that dead children haunt you," Eirian said.

"Have you seen dead children before? Killed in their beds?"

"I have. So, I tell you again, I'll not ask you to return. There's no dishonor in choosing not to, and if anyone says otherwise, tell them your queen herself said it."

Glancing at her horse, the soldier shook her head and said, "I can do it. Not because of what others might think of me but because I'll think worse of myself."

Aiden grunted in approval. "Good girl."

NINETEEN

Eirian could not decide if she had ever visited a place more disturbing. Spread out around the area, many guards and soldiers looked sick at what they had viewed. She had not gone inside the main house, and she was unsure she wanted to. The smell of vomit assaulted her nose and drew her gaze to a young nobleman retching off a pathway. Glancing at Aiden, she could tell he had withdrawn behind a wall in his mind. Returning her stare to the house, Eirian took a deep breath and started off toward it. Merle stood beside the door, watching the area angrily.

"Your Majesty, I'm not sure you should see it," he said, not looking at Aiden.

"It's okay, Merle. I can handle it." Brushing past, Eirian found Todd sitting at the table inside the kitchen area with his face in his hands. "Lieutenant?"

Lifting his head, Todd mumbled, "I'm sorry, ma'am, but I knew these people. They were good people."

She leaned against the table. "I understand."

"I have people scouring the area for any evidence of what happened. There are no signs of fighting… I can't… you should see for yourself. They're all in their beds… even the little ones," Todd replied, glancing at Aiden.

Taking a long look around the kitchen, Eirian prepared herself for what was to come. Her eyes lingered on the pots hanging from heavy beams. The fireplace had gone cold. Cups sat on a bench beside a stack of plates, and a moldy mound on a heavy wooden board was all that remained of a loaf of bread. A slatted window allowed light into the room, and she wondered if the family had left it open. The view was of a grove of fruit trees, chickens scratching around the fallen fruit. Staring through the gaps, Eirian decided generations must have spent hours watching children run around and play beneath the shade of the trees.

"Ma'am, it's going to be dark before long," Aiden said.

Giving the grove a last glance, Eirian turned and followed him into the hallway. Gabe was waiting, leaning against a wall and looking bored. He had not waited when he arrived, going straight in to look at the bodies. A staircase led to the second floor, and a soldier was hovering, his face grim. The slight breeze coming through open windows did nothing to chase away the smell of death and decay that filled every space.

Going into the first room, Eirian ignored the guards and let her magic swirl around her. Beams of light showed the flecks of dust floating in the air and gave enough illumination that she could take in the two beds on opposite walls. Tiny figures lay on them, looking almost peaceful in the positions they had remained in. Dark stains surrounded them.

Approaching a bed, Eirian stared at the young boy in sorrow. Brushing the hair from his face while studying the gaping wound at his throat where someone had slit it, she wished she could use her magic to undo senseless deaths. Gabe moved in to stand beside her, and she looked at him. There was a disinterested look on his face, and he leaned down to peer closer at the wound for a second time.

"Whoever did it knew what they were doing. Clean, one cut from above. Right-handed. They would've stood here to do it," he commented. "Quick. The boy wasn't expecting it."

"I agree. There is no hesitation, one quick cut. Sleep relaxes, so minimal need to counter resistance," Eirian murmured, turning to look at the other child.

Leaning in the doorway, Aiden had no interest in a closer look and asked, "Have you examined many dead? I understand his observations."

Not looking at Aiden, Eirian pulled back the sheet covering the second boy. "No other injuries. They were sleeping peacefully before being killed like cattle and left to bleed. I don't think I need to look at the others if they're all like this. How many adults are there?"

"Five, and they're all the same. There is one you should see, though. One of the green-faced officers told me they found a knife on the floor next to him. He's the only one I haven't checked because I was waiting for you."

Gabe cocked his head to look at the carved figures of animals that sat on the windowsill. Looking between them, it disturbed Aiden how easily they moved around each other and discussed death.

Nodding, Eirian replied, "Well, let's get on with it. Show me the body."

Pointing back the way they had come, Gabe said, "Downstairs and at the back of the house. They said it looked to be a workroom with books and similar."

Dragging her hand along the wall, Eirian felt like they had invaded the house and wondered what the family would have thought about their queen being under their roof.

"Records for the farm?"

"That'd be my guess."

"Can you sense anything with your magic?" Aiden asked.

Eirian shook her head. "Not really, but I haven't tried. I don't need daylight to use my magic, but I do to look at the bodies."

Bowing, Gabe let her go into the last room first, and Aiden thought he saw him smile. Stopping inside the doorway, Eirian looked over the shelves that lined one side of the room opposite where a small desk sat beneath a window. Books and objects filled them, organized chaos that told of generations of use. A long bench stretched from one wall to the other, a fine layer of dust settled on it. Folded neatly, a pile of fabric sat beside a dark wooden box that Eirian suspected contained sewing equipment. The room felt practical.

When Eirian finally drew her gaze to the chair in front of the desk, she stared at the floor. Blood had dripped down the arm hanging over the side, pooling around the knife that lay where it landed. Swallowing, she took in the way the older man's head had flopped, specs of blood blackening the gray hair. Then, stepping around, she leaned back against the desk to stare at the wound in his neck. It was not as clean as the two boys, and her eyes flickered to the knife.

"He did it."

Less fussed about getting close to the body, Gabe prodded the dead man and examined the wound. "No hesitation, but he struggled to get it done. It took him multiple passes. He suffered, but he didn't leave the chair or stop himself."

Curious enough to look, Aiden frowned, asking, "What would possess a man to keep going after the first try? Surely instinct would kick in?"

"You're right. It would take something else to keep going," Eirian confirmed.

Looking at her, Gabe grabbed the gray hair and forced the head back. Aiden flinched at the action, his gaze darting to Eirian, expecting her to be uncomfortable. But he saw disinterest on her face.

Gabe commanded, "Look in his eyes and tell me what your magic sees."

Crossing her arms, Eirian arched a brow. "Magic doesn't work like that."

"Way I see it is if there's darkness involved, your magic will find it. Isn't that the whole point of this little expedition?"

"No harm in trying," Aiden said.

Sighing heavily, Eirian dug her nails into her arms and directed her magic toward the body. It felt like it did every time her magic touched the recently dead. There were traces of life that remained for days before fading, traces that left her uncomfortable. It was not like the bones in the tomb where life had long vanished. Eirian could taste the lost potential. She ignored how her skin prickled and her magic protested, focusing on the task.

Eirian stopped fighting her power and let it go, closing her eyes as it spread. Shadows marred the landscape in her mind, seeped into the earth, and she understood what had made her magic unsettled from the moment she arrived.

It tainted everything. A flicker of life caught her attention, and drawn to it, she felt its desperation and fear. Knowing it was not a soldier, Eirian opened her eyes and stared at the watching men.

"There's a survivor."

"Where?"

Aiden started moving to the door. Shifting around the body, Eirian followed him and pointed in the direction her magic had guided her.

"That way."

He was almost running as he strode down the hallway, shouting for Merle and the others, his commotion attracting the attention of Todd. Eirian's directions led them to the barn, and a group of soldiers stood outside looking confused.

"There's nothing in there but supplies and equipment," one of them said.

Looking at Eirian, they waited for her to say something. Shaking her head, she hushed them and signaled for them to wait outside. Going through the opening, she took a moment to adjust before trusting her magic to guide her. Faint and terrified, the spark of life drew her up a ladder to the hayloft, and Eirian had to duck to avoid hitting her head. Creeping along carefully, she came to a wall and glanced across the loft, seeing it stretch from side to side.

Running her hands over the timber, she tried to peer between planks to see if it was the back of the barn. Her magic told her what she was seeking was close, adding to her doubt that it was the outer wall. Sitting on her heels, Eirian stared and waited for inspiration to strike. She put herself into the mindset of a farming family living close to the border and figured someone would have built an escape hole. Eyes drifting over the timber, she contemplated where she would place a hidden trapdoor.

Eirian knew it needed to be big enough for an adult, but not so big it would stand out. Crawling to where the roof and floor met, she glanced back and assessed that it was a straight line from the stairs. Pushing against the planks, there was a scrape, and she smiled. Opening the little door, she crept through, keeping her head low so she could protect it if the person on the other side attacked her. The space was wide enough for an adult to lie down and touch a hand to each wall. Staying crouched by the door, Eirian spotted a small figure huddled in the corner. Not wanting to scare it more, she kept her back against the door to let in light. Her magic filled the area, and she did her best to make it a calming force.

"Hello there," Eirian spoke softly.

It moved, and she saw eyes stare back at her. "Please don't hurt me."

Biting her bottom lip, Eirian swallowed. The voice was faint and fearful.

"I'm not here to hurt you. They sent me to find out what happened. Can you tell me?"

"Ol' Pa hurt them. He tried to hurt me, but I ran away."

"Are you hurt?"

A tiny arm lifted. "He got me."

Eirian did not move, continuing to let her magic wrap around the child, encouraging them to trust her. "You did the right thing running and hiding. I know you can hear lots of people outside, but I promise it's safe to come out. They serve the queen."

The child replied, "Ol' Pa said the Queen couldn't save us from the bad."

"She knew something was wrong. That's why she sent us. I'm sorry we came too late, but we're here now, and if you come with me, I can help you."

There was the sound of shuffling as the child crept closer. "My mama said the Queen must be beautiful. Have you seen her?"

Looking down, Eirian said, "I've seen her, and she is pretty. My name is Eirian, but you can call me Ree. What is your name?"

"I'm Ona. You have a pretty name. My name is not pretty."

"I think your name is beautiful. Ona, will you come with me? It's getting dark outside, and I'm hungry. Are you hungry? I bet you're hungry."

The little head nodded. "I'm hungry. I don't want to go back to the house. What did you do to Ol' Pa?"

"You don't need to fear him. It's safe now." Shifting, Eirian moved to go through the door. "I'm going to crawl out. Can you follow?"

"Yes. You sure it's safe?"

Remembering the dead man in the room, Eirian replied, "I promise you're safe, and I won't let anyone hurt you."

"You promise?"

"Yes, I promise, and if anyone hurts you, the Queen will punish them. I'm the special envoy she sent to check on your family, and she made me promise to look after you."

Watching Eirian crawl through the doorway, Ona followed slowly. The light was fading fast, and they crawled to the ladder. She glanced back at Ona and noticed a makeshift bandage wrapped around her arm. Peering over the edge, she debated what to do next. Eirian heard talking outside, her magic confirming they were the only people in the building.

"I'm going to climb down first, okay? That way, I'll be there to catch you if you have trouble. You watch me go so you can see me all the time."

Wrapping her arms around her knees, Ona nodded, mumbling, "Okay. You promise you won't leave me?"

"I promise." Swinging her legs around, Eirian held on tightly to the rungs as she went. "See, I'm right here, and you can watch me. I won't leave your sight."

Climbing slowly so she could keep her eyes on the small face, Eirian was careful not to miss a rung. She did not fancy slipping and slamming her face into the timber. She did not step away from the ladder when she felt solid ground under her feet and held her hands up.

"I'm down. Your turn."

Ona clung to the ladder tightly as she climbed. Surprised by how tiny she was, Eirian closed her hands around her when she came into reach and helped her finish the distance. Clinging to Eirian, Ona stared wide-eyed at the barn doors and the fading light beyond. Ruffling Ona's messy blonde hair, she noticed the slight curve to her ears that suggested elven blood and frowned. Then, dropping into a crouch, she offered her hands to Ona and nodded at the doors.

"There are lots of scary people out there, but it's okay. They only look scary. They're soldiers and guards, and they won't do anything to hurt you because they obey me."

"Because the Queen sent you?"

"That's right."

Standing, Eirian held on tightly to the small hand and wondered how she would stop Aiden and the others from giving her away. Standing close to her leg, Ona nodded and did her best to look brave. She did not understand why she trusted Eirian to protect her, but her presence made her feel safe.

Ona declared, "I'm not scared!"

"It's okay to be scared." Chuckling, she ruffled Ona's hair again and smiled before calling out, "I found a girl, and we're coming out!"

They heard someone issuing orders to back away. Outside, Aiden and her guards waited with Todd, the lieutenant looking baffled at the sight of the child. Shaking her head, Eirian met Aiden's gaze and hoped he could understand the plea in her gaze.

"Maj—" Todd started, but Aiden smacked his back, making him cough in shock.

"How about we let her explain?" Aiden said.

Frowning, Todd muttered, "I intended to."

Giggling, Ona stared up at Eirian. "They aren't scary!"

"I told you, the Queen sent them. She wouldn't send scary people to rescue you. That's why she picked me." Winking at Aiden, she pointed and said, "He tries to be scary, but he's a big doll."

Aiden arched a brow. "I'm sure there's an excellent explanation, and we'd love to hear it."

"How come his sword is longer than yours, Ree?" Ona asked, looking between them.

Choking back laughter, Merle shook his head, muttering, "That's the start of a terrible joke."

Scratching her head, Eirian grinned at Ona. "Well, he's a normal guard, and as I told you, I'm a special envoy for the queen. What makes me special is I have magic, and I fight differently. I use two short swords, and they mean I kill more bad people than him."

Nodding, Ona looked at Aiden with an air of superiority that only children could manage and told them, "My papa has magic."

Understanding dawned on Todd's face. "You're Nina's child! Where's your ma?"

"Mama and Papa brought me here and left me with Ol' Pa because they had to go away. They had orders." Clinging to Eirian, she stared up and asked, "You can find them? The Queen will let you take me to them?"

"I'm sure the Queen will do everything she can to help you get back to your family," Aiden stated in amusement.

Hearing Ona's stomach rumble, Eirian nodded toward the horses. "How about we return to camp? I'm sure we could all do with some dinner."

More familiar with children, Merle approached Ona and crouched to introduce himself. "Hey there, I'm Merle. Would you like to sit on my shoulders? I have a niece your age, and she loves to be up high above everyone. She pretends she's a queen."

Grinning, Ona nodded and let Merle lift and swing her around. He settled her onto his shoulders with ease. Remaining where she was, Eirian watched them head to the horses, ignoring Aiden as he crossed his arms and stared at her.

"Special envoy to the queen?" Aiden asked.

"I promoted me!"

"And the child?"

Shaking her head, Eirian waved over her shoulder. "She was hiding in an escape hole. I presume the old man was her grandfather. She called him Ol' Pa and said he did it, but she ran away and hid from him. Is her father an elf?"

Realizing the question was for him, Todd replied, "Yes, he is. Nina met him when she was first sent to the Ensaycalan border. She always wanted to see more and joined the army as soon as she was old enough. That's how we met. I courted her while we were training, but she wanted to leave, and I didn't. I didn't know she had a child."

Relieved Ona had not lost all of her family, Eirian left a weight lift before her mind returned to what she had sensed. "I'm sorry, Todd."

"Why would Aaron do this? He loved his family, and he was not a violent man. By the powers, he'd give thanks and apologize to the animals he killed!" Filled with sorrow, Todd asked, "How do I tell Nina that her father killed her family?"

"I'm still stuck on the special envoy part," Aiden grumbled.

"I didn't want to tell a terrified child that the woman rescuing her was queen, so I said the Queen sent us because she knew something was wrong. Aaron? You said it was Aaron? Well, he told them I couldn't save them from the bad." Eirian sighed in defeat. "And he was right. I couldn't save them. Or any of the others who've died so far because of the darkness. But I'll do everything I can to save who I can."

They stared at her.

Gabe murmured, "Yeah, I thought you might say that."

"You're telling us this darkness made Aaron kill his family? How is that possible?" Todd stared in disbelief.

"The darkness is... evil magic. Ancient evil magic that caused the mage wars."

Eirian dared not utter the word god. None of them would understand.

Aiden explained, "Way I understand it, it gets into your mind and makes you think differently. Makes you go mad. If your friend was being terrorized by the darkness, he might have thought that killing his kin would protect them. Or the madness told him to do it. There are many possibilities."

Approaching Todd, Eirian put a hand on his shoulder. "Give them a respectable burial, including Aaron. I know you want to blame him, to be angry with him, but I swear to you that none of this is his fault."

"Can you stop this darkness?" he asked seriously.

"Yes." She hoped he could not see the doubts she harbored.

Nodding solemnly, Todd signaled for some of his people. "I'll remain here and oversee the graves. We'll be late returning, but I'll be there to lead you to our destination."

Stepping around him, Eirian ignored the appraising looks directed her way by Aiden. She was silent, mulling over her thoughts as she walked to the horses. Hearing a high-pitched giggle, she watched Merle entertaining Ona and smiled sadly.

"He comes from a big family." Aiden said, "For a child who has been through a harrowing few days, she's coping well."

"I might not be a blue, but I have some tricks. If Ona's parents are soldiers, she might find it reassuring to be around soldiers. There's damage to this land, and I suspect when we get where we're going, I'm going to find it's the same."

Grabbing her wrist, Aiden frowned. "Can you fix it?"

Letting her gaze flicker toward him, Eirian shook her head. She wanted to tell him everything the spirit had told her, but the words died in her throat. They were not words she could speak where others would hear.

"Maybe. I'd need time to understand how the darkness damaged the land before attempting to undo it. And time might not be something I have. I need to focus on defeating Athnaral and then the darkness. For all we know, defeating the darkness might fix it."

"You told the lieutenant you can stop the darkness. I understand why you lied."

"Do you?" Arching a brow, Eirian inclined her head at Merle and the child. "Because I'll be honest with you. If I can't stop the darkness, then we may as well kill everyone now."

Looking at the child, he said, "While you live and breathe, you are hope."

Gabe chuckled, "Listen to you being all positive and uplifting."

"Somebody has to be." Scowling, Aiden snapped, "Move your asses."

Looking at Eirian, Ona beamed and pointed at Halcyon. "Merle said that's your horse. Can I ride with you?"

"Sure."

Waiting until Eirian had hauled herself into the saddle, Merle lifted Ona off his shoulders and onto Halcyon. Settling her in front of Eirian, he arched a brow.

"You're full of surprises, Ree."

"Thank you, Merle. I enjoy surprising people." Wrapping an arm around

Ona, Eirian winked, adding, "Make sure you tell our queen that."

Laughing, he slapped a hand to Halcyon's flank, and the horse snorted. "I'll try to remember next time I see her."

While they waited for those returning to camp to mount, Eirian studied the sky wearily. The last rays of light cast a fading glow through the clouds scattered over the horizon. The trees loomed ominously, and several horses showed signs of spooking. She sighed heavily and stroked her free hand over Ona's hair. Peering up at her, Ona blinked curiously.

"What kind of magic do you have? My papa makes things with metal. He has a yellow ring and always tells me that when I meet a mage, I have to look for their ring, but I can't see what color yours is."

Glancing down, Eirian replied, "I'm a purple mage. I can do lots of things with magic."

"Like what?"

"I can fight and kill bad things. I can make things grow and search over great distances in moments without moving from my place."

"Is the Queen a mage?"

The question was innocent. Arching a brow, Eirian glanced at Merle. He smirked at her, remaining close as the group moved off. They did not want to risk going any faster than a walk with night encroaching. Not answering Ona, she returned her free hand to the reins and reassured the horse beneath them.

Tugging at her sleeve, Ona continued to peer up, asking, "Are you the queen?"

Chuckling, Aiden leaned forward to shake his head at Merle. "I bet she was waiting to see who ruined it first."

"Yes, I am, Ona." Nose flaring in annoyance, Eirian glared briefly at Merle.

"Oh." Looking at the withers of the horse, Ona sighed, "That's why you're special? Because you're queen?"

Squeezing Ona gently, Eirian looked up at the stars appearing in the night sky. "No. No, it's not. I'm special because I have lots of magic."

"That's one way to put it," Aiden said.

Confused, Ona frowned. "But aren't queens special?"

Holding up a hand, Merle shook his head in amusement. "Don't look at me, Your Majesty! I'm just a normal guard, like the captain."

Rolling her eyes, Eirian did not need to glance at Aiden to know he looked equally amused. "Well, yes, queens are special, but they're a different special. Being a queen is like being a mother. You must look after lots and lots of people, make sure they have food, a roof to live under, things to do, and rules to follow. I bet your mama gets very cranky when you're naughty."

"Papa says she doesn't get mad enough. Like the time I broke her bow."

Leering at Aiden, Merle teased, "Sounds familiar."

"Be quiet, Merle," Eirian chided. "Sometimes it's hard to get mad at people when they do the wrong thing, especially if you care about them. Another thing queens and mothers have to do is to protect people."

"You know a lot about what mothers do for a woman who doesn't want to be one," Aiden commented with a smirk.

Sucking in a deep breath, Eirian pushed her annoyance aside. "It's hardly a mystery, Captain. I spent a lot of time imagining what having a mother would be like."

Fidgeting in her spot, Ona patted Halcyon. "Why are you queen?"

"Because my father was the king."

"Why?"

Unable to resist laughing, Merle wished he could see the look on her face and said, "Welcome to children."

"He was the king because his father was the king before him."

Not satisfied with the answer, Ona persisted. "But why?"

Closing her eyes, Eirian considered the question and what answer she could give to satisfy Ona. "Well, an old man told me the reason my family rules over Endara is that we come from the first humans the gods made. That makes us a little different from other humans. It's the same with the family of the elf king your father serves. They come from the first elves, so they're different from the other elves."

"Oh." There was a hint of surprise in Ona's voice, and she was silent for a moment before asking, "What are the gods?"

"Yes, ma'am, what are the gods?" Gabe chuckled.

His question made Merle and Aiden burst into laughter. Grinding her teeth, Eirian decided she would make the three men pay.

"I'm afraid I can't answer. No one knows what the gods are. All we know is that they're powerful because they made our world. We exist because of them."

Aiden asked, "But why? Where are they?"

"She's going to kill us," Merle muttered.

"Well, Captain," Eirian said through clenched teeth. "I don't know where the gods are. They left us. However, I know where my boot is going to be."

Ona giggled, "Up his bum?"

Eirian spluttered, "Where did you hear that?"

"Mama says it to Papa sometimes when he makes her mad, but he laughs and kisses her." She looked at Aiden with a grin. "Are you going to laugh and kiss Ree?"

The guards burst into laughter again, and Aiden was the loudest. Groaning, Eirian squeezed her eyes shut and reminded herself that Ona did not understand why her comments made the men laugh. She wondered if it was punishment. Giggling as well, Ona wriggled around and accidentally elbowed Eirian in the side, causing her to grunt in discomfort.

"I'd ask what's so funny, but I'm more interested in where you found a child." Appearing in the darkness, Fionn brought his horse alongside Aiden.

"Survivor," Aiden replied.

"I see... and you thought it was a good idea to let the child-fearing queen look after her?"

"I'm not afraid of children," Eirian muttered.

Reaching out, Ona held onto the reins next to Eirian's hand. "You don't like children?"

"I like children. I'm just not very good with them."

Her answer received more laughter. Cocking her head to the side, Eirian frowned in the dim light cast by the many campfires.

"Can I hear music?"

Groaning, Merle slapped his face, causing everyone to look at him. "Congratulations, ma'am, you're about to find out what it's like going anywhere with northerners."

"Aren't you a northerner, Merle?" Fionn asked cheekily.

"I'm not that north. We have Onaorbaens surrounding us. You'll probably find Fox and Mac off somewhere drinking. Dancing. Singing. It's torture. Why do you think I found my way south?"

Astounded that people could play music and dance when they had just discovered a house full of dead people, Eirian growled, "Unbelievable! Have they no respect?"

"This is their way of showing respect. They'll raise a few drinks in memory of those who have died." Aiden spoke softly, "Let them be, Your Majesty, and show them you respect their ways."

"Can I go see the music?" Ona asked hopefully.

Willing to put up with the music for the sake of the girl, Merle said, "I'll take her, and we can find some food while we're at it."

"No, I'll come. Knowing Aiden, we're right in the middle of it all."

Shaking her head, she halted Halcyon and waited for one of her guards to dismount to help Ona off before she slid from the saddle. Feeling the brush of magic, Eirian turned with a smile and bowed her head to Muireann as she approached.

Muireann said, "I had a sense you might need me."

"Ona, would you let this lady look at your arm? She's a healer."

Wide-eyed, Ona stared at Muireann. "What's a healer?"

"Someone who helps hurt and sick people."

"Oh. Like you? You help people. Can't you heal me?"

Exchanging a look with Eirian, Muireann smiled calmly as she crouched in front of Ona. "Her Majesty isn't a healer. It won't hurt anymore if you let me look at your arm, and once I look, I'll take you to see the dancing and the music. I like music, do you?"

Pulling a brave face, Ona held out her arm while clinging to Eirian's leg with the other. "I like music!"

Carefully unwrapping the makeshift bandage, Muireann maintained her smile as she ran her hands gently over the cut. "Who bandaged this for you?"

"I did it myself!" Proud of her effort, Ona gave a toothy grin. "Mama always wrapped up hurts like that."

"You did a good job, and it was clever thinking. Now, this will feel strange, but it won't hurt."

Letting her magic thread its way through Ona, Muireann felt Eirian watching. Sensing the early stages of infection setting into the wound, she worked through what supplies she had to use with her powers to combat it. It was early enough that it did not concern Muireann, but her magic told her something fatigued Ona, her stress levels far higher than they should be. She did not know what Ona had been through, but she would leave asking until the day. There was enough anxiety rolling from Eirian that she did not need to ask to know the answers would not be good. Letting the information flow over the link she shared with Faolan, she finished healing Ona's arm and settled on her heels.

"Your Majesty, she has an infection beginning, but I have what I need to tend to it."

"I'm not surprised," Eirian said.

Letting go of Eirian's leg, Ona grabbed her hand and offered the other to Muireann. "Can we go now? I'm hungry."

Wrapping her fingers around the smaller ones, Muireann chuckled, "I smelled something delicious. It might have been close to the music."

Ordering some of his men to deal with the horses, Aiden followed. The guards kept watch, concerned about drinking soldiers. They had built a large fire near the middle of the camp, casting light over the surrounding people. It was beside this fire a group of soldiers stood playing their instruments. Others clapped and sang, setting the beat for those dancing. They passed flasks among the bystanders, hunks of bread and meat going from hand to hand. Leaving them, Muireann spoke a few soft words to another before she returned with some food.

Taking the offering, Ona wasted no time in eating. She watched the spinning dancers, the firelight casting shadows over them as they moved, and Eirian remembered bonfire nights on the beaches of Riane. Women spun between partners, heads tossed back with smiles and laughter, and it did not take her long to realize the Telmians were among them. Their grace set them apart from the humans.

Turning her stare to the musicians, Eirian took in their instruments. Several fiddles accompanied the whistles and flutes. Saoirse was among the singers, her voice rising clear and beautiful above the others. It tugged at her mind, the whisper of memories telling her she had heard Saoirse sing before. Grunting, Aiden stood at her side and watched with a hint of boredom.

"You've not seen any country dancing before, have you?"

Glancing sideways at Eirian, he cocked a brow before looking back at the dancers. She chuckled, resting her hand on Ona's shoulder as the girl ate.

"I've seen similar. In Riane, we have bonfire nights on the beach where we dance and drink until the sun rises over the Yifthn sea." Breathing deeply, Eirian told him, "I prefer this type of dancing to the ones expected at court."

"Why?"

Smiling wistfully, Eirian closed her eyes and listened to the music shift to a haunting melody. "It's more alive."

Bowing gracefully before Eirian, Faolan offered a hand to Ona and said, "Hello, little one. Would you like to join us?"

Quickly shoving the last bit of her food in her mouth, Ona looked at Eirian. "Can I?"

"Of course, you'll be safe with Lord Faolan."

Letting her hand drop, Eirian watched Faolan lead Ona away. The dancers welcomed them into their midst, and Ona laughed gleefully. Watching, she realized Ona must have joined in on such dances before. Lifting her gaze to the sky, she took in the moon, creeping higher, three-quarters full and casting a silvery glow over the people. It mixed with the yellows and oranges of the firelight, giving the daoine an ethereal quality that caused them to stand out among the darker tones of the humans. Muireann hummed along to the music, earning appraising looks from the guards.

"Is this how your people dance?" Eirian asked quietly.

Looking surprised, she replied, "Of course, dancing is an expression. Your body knows what to do. Just trust it to feel the music. Don't you dance?"

Chuckling, Merle stepped out of Eirian's reach and said, "No, she doesn't dance because of clumsiness."

"Perhaps you need to find the right beat or simply the right partner." Smiling, Muireann accepted the hand of a soldier who approached and let him pull her into the swirl.

Offering Eirian his arm, Aiden said, "Come on, ma'am, we're hungry, so let's find somewhere quieter to eat and rest."

Ignoring the arm, Eirian shook her head. "I'd rather stay here."

"Why?" Gabe asked.

"The next person to say why is going to regret it."

The men laughed.

Sighing, Gabe said, "I'm genuinely curious."

Letting her gaze follow the dancers, Eirian told them, "Because their energy, their passionate desire to live, is a soothing balm right now. You don't feel it like I do, and right now, I need this to chase the shadows from my mind."

Staring at her, Aiden understood what she was not saying and stretched his arm out, offering his hand with a smile. In this crowd, no one would care if he held her a little too long or if his hands strayed. There was not enough light for anyone to notice if his lips brushed her skin.

"Let me teach you the steps."

TWENTY

It surprised the farmers when Todd introduced Eirian, their first instinct sending them to their knees in front of her. Biting back a sigh, she smiled patiently. Standing beside her, Ona looked as self-important as a child could manage, her chin high, glaring at the children gathered behind the adults. Putting a hand on Ona's shoulder, Aiden leaned forward to whisper a suggestion that she go play, but she shook her head.

"Please, there's no need for that."

Eirian ignored a snicker behind her. She knew Aiden would deal with the laughing guard later. Todd nodded reassuringly to the people kneeling, and they stood.

He told them, "My apologies for the surprise. I thought my messenger told you Her Majesty was coming."

"They did, but we didn't believe it." The head of the family, an elderly woman, looked anywhere but at Eirian. "We're not worthy of your presence, Your Majesty."

Biting back another sigh, Eirian maintained her smile. "You couldn't be more worthy, and I'm grateful to be in the position to investigate your crops."

The matriarch bowed stiffly, offering her hands. "I'm Glynn, Your Majesty, and this is my family's land. We thank you for coming and the honor your presence brings us."

"I hope I can help. Unfortunately, this is the first chance I've had to attend a farm where crop failures have occurred. But don't worry, the crown won't abandon you. I'll ensure we take care of you and the other farms for as long as necessary."

Taking hold of the toughened hands, Firian lifted them and kissed the backs, receiving gasps from the farmers. Regarding her curiously, Glynn glanced at Ona beside her.

"Thank you. We feared we might need to leave before winter if we didn't have enough stores."

"While we're here, should you need any help with repairs, the good lieutenant can organize people to assist. Just ask."

"You are too generous, Your Majesty."

Letting go of Glynn's hands, Eirian ruffled Ona's hair, earning a grumble from the child. "Ona, why don't you play with the other children. Merle and Isabella can go with you."

Aiden grunted, sharing a look with Merle that clearly said he was glad it was not him, and Merle grinned at Ona as she turned to look at him crankily.

Ona whined, "But I don't want to."

"I think it could be fun, Ona," Isabella said, offering her hand. "Don't you want to run around for a while? Trust me, it gets boring watching Her Majesty do mage stuff, and you won't miss anything. We could make Merle take turns giving rides on his back like a horse."

Turning to her kin, Glynn pointed to one of the older children. "Sally, why don't you show them the swings in the orchard."

Staring at Eirian in awe, Sally replied, "Yes, Grandmother."

"Go on, Ona, have some fun."

Giving her a little push, Eirian smiled at how she sulkily took Merle's hand and dragged her feet. Waiting until the children and several adults left, Brenna looked at Glynn.

"Perhaps this family would be open to the girl remaining here until her parents are located. It would be a far safer option than returning to a battlefield with us."

"It is true then? We're at war with Athnaral?" a man asked.

Inclining her head, Eirian replied, "Sadly, yes, we are. However, you need not fear, Ensaycal has come to our aid, and together we'll defend Endara."

Glynn's eyes narrowed at the swords hanging from Eirian's belt. "We'd be happy for the child to remain here. War is no place for children."

"I'll consider it, but I suspect Ona would run away to look for us. Now, the day is getting on, and I'd like to see your failed crops."

"May I ask what you hope to learn that others could not?"

The quietly chatting voices hushed, and the eyes of nobles, guards, and officers focused on Glynn. Clearing his throat, Todd thought it would be best if he answered.

"Her Majesty is a mage."

Turning, Glynn said, "About bloody time one of those was in charge. When I was a child, there was a mage living nearby. A good healer who helped a lot of folks and livestock."

Smiling, Eirian was pleased to hear another person saying positive things about mages. It served as a reminder that so much they had led her to believe was wrong.

"I know of masters in Riane who wish to see mages living among the people. Perhaps after the war, we'll see changes. Mages don't serve their purpose if they're not helping others."

"I hope I live to see those changes. The fields are this way."

Beckoning over her shoulder, Glynn ignored the number of people who followed. Moving out of the way in confusion, the family lingered on the outskirts of the group, watching the heavily armed people cautiously. They had never seen so many soldiers, the weapons more intimidating than Eirian's presence. The eldest son quickly moved to his mother's side, but Glynn shooed him off with a wave of her hand. Chuckling, Eirian matched the woman's stride and tried not to tower over her, opting to offer her arm without a word.

"How many generations of your family have farmed this land?"

Shading her eyes with her other hand, Eirian could make out the faint rise of mountains in the far distance and made a note to ask Fox if they were the tip of the Fingers.

"Six. It will be seven soon enough, I suppose. I've got a grandson who'll be old enough to look for a wife one of these days. He's a good boy, sensible head on his shoulders, unlike some. My great-grandfather earned this land by serving an earl. I've quite forgotten what he did, but we have his sword in the house. One of my sons left to join the army and wanted to take it with him, but I wouldn't let him. Caused a bit of a row."

Despite her age, Glynn set a fair pace, and they arrived at the edge of the fields. No one spoke as the visitors stared at the remnants of a wheat crop. Instead of green, the stalks were black, and Eirian's attention went to the ground at their feet. Her eyes took in the soil, a frown creasing her brow as she turned to stare at the well-worn path.

"Forgive my ignorance, but is the soil normally that color?" Eirian pointed at the ground.

One of the younger women said, "No, it's not."

"I thought that might be the case. Tell me what happened."

Blowing air through her lips, Glynn shrugged. "We don't know. One day we had fields of healthy wheat, as normal, and then the next morning, my boy came in all panicked because it looked like this. Nothing else, it was just the wheat."

Rubbing her chin, Eirian looked up at the sky, where Saoirse circled. "When did you notice the soil changing color?"

"Day or so after we got over our shock and started trying to work out what happened. We thought maybe some sort of poison, but none of us has heard of anything that fast."

"Have you been watching to see if the change is spreading?"

A man held up a hand, saying, "I thought it might be a sign of poison, so I dug holes at regular intervals over that way."

"And has it been spreading?" she asked him.

"Ma'am, none of the other reports have mentioned anything about the crop death spreading." Gallagher said, "There haven't been reports of farms side by side being affected. It's random."

Eirian did not look at him, keeping her attention on the farmers. "Forgive me, Lord Gallagher, but what do you know of farming and soil changes?"

"I see your point."

Gallagher shared a look with one of the other nobles. Shaking his head, the man shot a look at his mother, and Glynn nodded.

"No, Your Majesty, it hasn't spread. Not that I've seen," he said.

She cocked her head at the field, circling the air with a finger. "Have you been checking on all sides?"

"No…" Embarrassed, he looked down at his feet. "I didn't think to check on all sides. I worried about it getting closer to the house and the paddocks with our livestock."

"And that's a fair concern. Don't worry, I don't think poorly of you for not considering it. You needed to make sure your family wasn't at risk, and I would've done the same. However, I want you to take some of my people with you, show them what we're looking for, and then check those sides." Turning to Aiden, she instructed, "Send a couple of your men."

Aiden nodded in agreement and signaled several he knew had grown up in farming areas. "You heard what she wants."

Glynn observed Todd selecting people to go with her son and nodded approvingly. "You don't waste any time, do you, Your Majesty?"

"No, I try not to," Eirian chuckled.

Searching through the gathered people until she spotted the distinctive red hair, Eirian waved at Faolan.

"Gar, take the rest of them with you. They can show our visitors where to go. Make yourselves useful," Glynn directed her kin.

Faolan cast a look up at Saoirse and asked, "Do you need her or me?"

"Both. I want to know what she sees, but I'd also like to know what your people feel." Tapping her fingers against her bent thumb, Eirian considered her options. "I'll do my usual tricks, see if I can't bring life back into this."

Faolan stared at the dead wheat. "I think that's beyond your scope. Sometimes the only thing is to cleanse and start again."

"I'm not overestimating my abilities. Just monitor what you feel from me."

"I understand," he murmured and waved at the wheat. "Saoirse says she can't see any obvious differences in the land."

"Well, it was worth asking, so thank her for me."

Watching him slip away, Eirian noticed the numbers surrounding her had dropped. Many wanted to help the investigation, opting to go with the farmers to look around. Others had split off to explore while the rest remained to see what she would do. She sensed the expectation in the air as they watched, and it made her nervous. Moving away, Eirian held up a hand and shook her head at Aiden when he moved with her.

Scowling, Aiden crossed his arms and glared as she crouched at the edge of the field. Digging her fingers into the soil, Eirian rubbed it between them and stared blankly at the black stalks. She felt the magic of the Telmians as they began doing what they could. A niggling voice at the back of her mind warned her to wait until their activities died down. Deciding there was merit to the idea, she settled on the ground in a more comfortable position.

"Ma'am?" Aiden spoke.

"Hmm?"

Resting her chin on her hand, Eirian gazed at the dead plants in front of her. Aiden cleared his throat, signaling he was waiting for her to say more.

"I'm waiting on the daoine to finish what they're doing."

John grunted, "Right."

"Do you think there's anything you can do to save this crop?" Kane asked.

Eirian shook her head, admitting, "No. Despite how it appears, my powers have limits. But there's no reason I can't do something about the next. If there's the seed."

"May I ask what you mean?" Glynn remained at a distance.

Aiden looked grim. "Her Majesty can make plants grow. She's saying that if you have the seed, she'll grow a fresh crop in place of this one."

Eyes filling with a mixture of skepticism and awe, Glynn turned away. "We have some spare seed. I suspect there's little to do except watch."

"Thank you, Glynn, that'd be very helpful."

Eirian continued to stare at the field. Approaching cautiously, Aiden knelt and leaned in.

"While I applaud your enthusiasm about growing them a new crop, there's the minor issue of what to do with this," he murmured.

Glancing at him sideways, Eirian smiled in amusement. "Why, Captain, you don't think I haven't got that covered as well?"

"I dread to ask."

"Don't worry, Aiden, I know what I'm doing."

Opening his mouth to speak, Aiden quickly shut it and held up a hand. Eirian watched the emotions cross his face while he organized his thoughts.

He said, "I want you to promise me you won't be putting anyone at risk."

"If everyone follows orders, then no one should get hurt."

Ignoring Aiden's groan, Eirian reached out and scooped up a handful of dirt. He watched it trickle through her fingers.

"I suspect the earth has changed color because of whatever the darkness did to the crop," she mused.

"No offense, Eirian, but that's stating the obvious."

Choosing to ignore his flippant comment as she had ignored his groan, Eirian continued, "I'm going to read the land. Don't let anyone disturb me unless it's a duine, and they seem concerned. If they're concerned enough, you might finally get to follow through on that threat of knocking me out."

Biting the insides of his cheeks, Aiden looked at the sky and watched the circling eagle. He asked the powers to give him the strength to deal with her.

"Do you plan on explaining what you intend to do?"

"Maybe. It all hinges on this land not being toxic to life."

"And how will you work that out?"

Eirian swept her gaze over the area. "I need a seed. Any seed will do."

Covering his face, Aiden sighed, "You're lucky Fionn didn't hear that."

"Huh?"

"Don't worry. I'll go find you a seed. There's bound to be a weed around here somewhere." Pushing himself up, Aiden said, "Just focus on what you need to do."

Huffing at him in annoyance, Eirian wiped her hand on her trousers. Relaxing her hold on the magic, she sensed the Telmians had ceased their activities. It meant she could begin her efforts. Glancing over her shoulder at the watching people, Eirian reminded herself they expected her to produce answers. Dreading the disappointment if she failed to meet those expectations, she closed her eyes and allowed her magic to show her the land.

Giving herself a moment to enjoy the energy of the living, Eirian ignored the shadows dancing at the edge of her awareness. Acutely aware of her, the Telmians warded themselves. Buoyed by the energy, she pushed her focus into the land that had once teemed with life. Drawing herself deep into the ground, she found flickers of life and gave thanks. She fed power to the earthbound creatures as she worked her way up through the layers. The closer Eirian got to the surface, the more aware she became of the death lingering in the grains of dirt.

Her mind tugged at her magic, forcing it to examine the shadows. There was a sense of familiarity, the whisper that she knew what it was if only she would remember. Eirian noticed how similar aspects of her power were to the god who had become the darkness. Fear and relief chased through her, fighting for dominance, and her grip over her power wavered. Feeling the shadows creep closer, Eirian reminded herself that she did not destroy for the sake of destruction. Tightening her control, she focused on her task and attempted to feed life into the crop. When her magic failed, she opened her eyes.

"I expected it to take longer." Sitting on the ground beside her, Aiden cocked his head to the side as she looked at him. "I owe Merle a silver piece."

Blinking at him, Eirian dropped her gaze to the dandelion in his hand. "Perfect."

Handing it to her, he chuckled, "Told you I'd find a weed."

"I'm rather fond of dandelions, or did you forget? Watch!"

Clasping the stem, Eirian leaned forward and blew on the yellow flower, transforming it into a cloud of white seeds. Her breath sent the seeds twirling through the air, and Aiden watched her face as she tracked their progress. Then, feeling her power flare, he turned to look at the dead crop and sighed at the sight of vibrant green shooting up among the black. It was the green of hope. Brilliant yellow flowers burst into bloom, and cheers rose loudly from the onlookers.

"You can save these people from hunger this winter," Aiden commented. "And no, I didn't forget."

"So, it would seem. But first, I must cleanse this field."

Stretching, Eirian did not meet his gaze. A niggling suspicion told Aiden he would not like what she had planned.

"Can I say no?"

Shrugging, Eirian got to her feet and turned to the jubilant people behind her. Glynn stood with several of her kin, all of them regarding Eirian in amazement. Meeting Faolan's gaze, she cocked a finger at him, and he approached confidently.

"If anything is to grow here without my magic fueling it, then I need to cleanse the field of the contamination," Eirian said as soon as Faolan was close enough.

Nodding, he glanced at the sky. "We can do that."

"No, I will. Can you help contain it? I'd hate for a spark to cause problems."

"By cleanse, what do you mean?" Aiden pushed for an answer.

Ignoring him, the two regarded each other, Faolan looking amused. "You want to make a show out of it, don't you? It would fuel the rumors about your powers, but what about the itch?"

Eirian replied, "I know, that's the point. I learned something today, and I want to send a message to the darkness. As for the itch, I can cope."

"I'll make the arrangements. You should prepare your people." Turning, Faolan winked at Aiden, chuckling, "Looks like you're in for a show, Captain."

Pinching the bridge of his nose, Aiden sighed. "I won't like this, will I?"

"There are parts you might like." Focusing on the sun, Eirian pursed her lips and contemplated what to tell him.

"You won't tell me, will you?"

"Not at all. If I don't tell you, you can't stop me."

"Well, I can, actually. I could knock you out, as you so helpfully suggested.

However, you want to help these people, and I can't stop you from doing that. Just... no one will get hurt, will they?" Aiden asked.

Shaking her head, Eirian put a hand on his arm and offered him a small smile. "Aiden, trust me. So long as everyone follows my instructions, no one will get hurt. Including me, before you ask."

Covering her hand, he ignored the prickle of her magic over his skin. "Have you done this before?"

"Yes. Now, I should tell everyone what I've learned." Drawing her hand away, Eirian moved toward the waiting crowd with a smile.

Glynn said, "Impressive, instead of wheat, I have a field of weeds."

"The land is not dead, only the crop. It will support life, but first, we need to chase the shadow from it. Tonight, we'll banish those shadows, and tomorrow, it will be wheat again."

People stared at her in confusion.

Gallagher said, "What do you mean?"

"We're going to burn the field."

"Isn't that risky?"

Licking her lips, Eirian chuckled, "Only if you're stupid enough to walk into the fire."

"You're going to burn my field of dead wheat and then make a fresh crop grow. How?" Glynn asked, taking in the confused faces of her family.

"Magic did this, dark magic, and magic can fix it. I can fix it. All I ask is that everyone withdraws to a safe distance and doesn't approach the field while I work." Eyes narrowing, Eirian gave the guards a knowing look.

"Well, in that case, it's a good thing we have spare seed."

"Thank you."

Moving away to stand on her own, Eirian felt the daoine working to lay wards. She wondered if anyone realized the extent of the bonfire she would create and, frowning, let doubts flutter through her thoughts. Quashing them as quickly as she had allowed them, Eirian rolled her shoulders and rested her hands on the hilts of her swords.

"Is there anything we can do?" Todd asked curiously.

"Actually, yes, while my people are busy preparing what they need to do, it would be useful if you set up small fires along the boundaries of the area. Unlit, for now," Faolan answered as he returned to the group, green eyes gleaming with amusement. "Unless you can create fire yourself, little Queen?"

Eirian shook her head. "No. Good thinking, wolf."

Uncrossing his arms, Fionn was the first of her guards to break his silence. "You're going to make a huge fire? A damn pity we don't have more ale or wine with us."

"He has a point," Devin grumbled. "At least we'll have music."

Drawing Eirian a little further away, Faolan inclined his head toward her people. "You realize they won't react well."

"I know. They'll get over it. The night is approaching, and I thought you could light the fires as the sun sets," Eirian suggested.

"Why? You could get on with it now."

"Symbolism. My father once told me I'm the light in the darkness."

There was a grim set to her gaze, and Eirian looked at her people. Faolan followed her stare, his gaze settling on Aiden.

"So, let me be their light in the darkness, and I will shine."

He murmured, "No, it's not about them. I understand you feel you've let people down, that you've failed to protect them, but walking into a burning field won't banish those feelings. Though, the itch might."

"Ah, wolf, you're reading into things." Eirian arched a brow at him.

"I have my moments where I do my sister proud."

Unable to resist chuckling, she glanced at the descending sun. They stood in silence, watching the sky.

Eirian murmured, "You're right. It won't banish—"

"Then why do it?" Faolan did not let her finish.

"I was getting to that. It won't banish those feelings, but it might help me feel like I can do something. That I'm capable of the task ahead."

Sensing the approach of another daoine, they turned to watch Muireann moving toward them with her hands wrapped around a cloth bundle. Much of the crowd had dispersed, the prospect of a fire sending soldiers and nobles alike to where they had set up camp. Eirian knew they would take advantage of it and pass what little drink they had around as they made merry. Taking in her guards, she ignored Aiden and let her eyes linger on Gabe. He returned her stare with a slight smile and a wink that felt familiar.

"I brought you food. You need to eat and rest while you can," Muireann said.

She was not as intimidating as Tharen, but she didn't need to be. Following her softly spoken command, Eirian accepted the bundle. Unwrapping it, she found some meat and cheese. The sight made her acknowledge her hunger.

"Thank you."

"I can do this." Muireann sat beside her, shooting a look at Faolan. "You don't have to."

"Thank you for your offer, Muireann, but this is something I need to do. Perhaps the next one can be yours."

"You realize you're going to let several hundred of your people see you naked."

"I do."

Faolan spread his hands, muttering, "She's a mage, and she doesn't care. It's only them that will care. I've got my spot planned for the show."

"Don't aggravate my captain," Eirian growled, pointing at Faolan.

"You wound me." He mockingly covered his heart. "As if I'd do such a thing."

Eirian glared at him.

"I wouldn't!"

"Yes, you would. Tell me again how Aiden found out about my scar?" she reminded him.

"I meant to ask," Muireann muttered. "But I forgot. Why wasn't it healed properly?"

"Punishment for stupidity. They left it to heal naturally."

Disgusted, she screwed up her nose. "How barbaric!"

Finishing her food in silence, Eirian pulled her legs up and wrapped her arms around them. Her mind drifted to Riane. Resting her head on her knees, she closed her eyes and thought of the great cliffs overlooking the sea. The garden there had been her sanctuary, a quiet place she could find solitude. Eirian pictured every stone, every variation of color, the waves crashing on the rocks at the base of the cliffs. She tasted the salt, felt the wind stinging her face, and longed to be there, leaning against the wall and watching the sea beneath a sky that never ended.

"Eirian." Faolan touched her shoulder gently. "I'm sure whatever you're thinking about is wonderful, but you have a job to do."

"I know." Lifting her head, Eirian stretched her legs before accepting his offered hand.

Tilting his head toward her guards, he said, "Everything is ready."

Sucking in a deep breath, she let it go slowly. There could be no hesitation.

"Okay, I can do this. Just make sure my guards don't hurt themselves."

"You didn't tell your captain?"

"Don't be silly. Why would I do that?" Eirian flashed him a grin. "I wanted to provide you with some entertainment."

Faolan did not look convinced. "Right."

Slipping the rings from her fingers, Eirian secured them in a pouch before unbuckling her belt. Then, carefully wrapping the leather around her weapons, she handed them to Faolan.

"Oh, you of little faith."

"While I appreciate the wicked side of you, this is not the time or place." Cradling the weapons in his arms, Faolan grumbled, "And you have ladies for this."

"True, I do. I also have guards, but you're here. And you're prettier."

Watching her unlace the front of her leather jerkin, Faolan sighed and turned to glare at her guards. Chuckling, Eirian shook her head and waved over her shoulder to summon one of the watching men. She knew it would be Aiden, and did not meet his frustrated gaze when he came to stand at her side. Handing him the jerkin, she moved to lift the haubergeon over her head while he bundled up the armor in his hands.

"Why are you taking off your armor and weapons?" Aiden asked.

Meeting Faolan's reluctant gaze, Aiden did not look at her.

Eirian explained, "I don't need it for what I'm about to do, and I don't want to risk damaging it."

She ignored the little choking sound Faolan made.

Aiden growled, "What have we said about being honest with each other?"

"I'm going to be performing this task as a mage, not as a queen."

Dumping the weapons on the growing pile held by Aiden, Faolan bowed out of the conversation. "I'm going to make sure my people are ready."

"Coward," Eirian hissed at him.

"Yep, that's me." Waving his fingers at her, he turned swiftly on his heels and strode away, singing, "Lord Faolan, the coward wolf."

Huffing, Eirian focused on her bracers, fingers working at the cords that held them tight around her wrists. "I need you to trust me, Aiden. This is where magic can be wonderful or terrible, depending on the actions of those around the mage."

"Now see, when you ask me to trust you, I want to hit you over the back of the head and drag your ass away," he answered.

Adding the bracers to the pile in his arms, Eirian sat to remove her boots. "Maybe one day you can do that, but not today."

Feeling a flutter of magic, Aiden turned to watch Saoirse stalking toward them with a determined smile. "Wonderful, here comes the bird."

"I know."

"I'm not missing this!" Saoirse declared in delight as she took in the feelings surrounding the duo. "Faolan said you haven't told them, so there's no way I'm missing this."

Eirian tossed a boot at her, groaning, "Oh, for the love of life."

"At least you took the time to put some clothes on," Aiden muttered.

He gave Saoirse a dark look as she kicked the discarded boot in his direction. Then, grinning, she flicked a lock of hair over her shoulder.

"I didn't want to be a distraction."

Tossing her second boot at Aiden's feet, Eirian stood and removed the rest of her clothes. "Of course you didn't."

"Your Majesty..." Aiden took a deep breath to calm himself. "Ma'am, why are you taking off your clothes?"

Staring at the dropping sun, Eirian felt the chill of night creeping in. "Because they put me at risk of being burned."

"Your Majesty!" Brenna hurried over, her voice a higher pitch with shock. "What are you doing?"

Finished with her task, Eirian added the garments to the pile in Aiden's arms and turned to Brenna. Her hands freed her hair from the cord binding it, the strap joining everything else.

"Your Grace, could you and the good captain please go over there?"

"No!" Brenna shouted.

"I'm a mage. Sometimes we need to be naked, and this is one of those times."

Furious, Brenna reached for the clothes in Aiden's arms, lecturing, "You're the queen of Endara, and you will put your clothes back on right now!"

Saoirse watched in amusement, chuckling, "I knew I didn't want to miss this."

Gathering her magic around her, Eirian stood straight, brown hair tumbling over her shoulders. The look on her face encouraged them to take a step back.

"That was not a request! That was an order. Saoirse, make sure no one comes past the wards," Eirian commanded.

The sound of shocked chatter rose loudly as the people observed their queen walk naked toward the dead wheat. Eirian felt their agitation. Stepping into the field, she flinched at the feeling of the crumbling stalks against her skin, the lingering shadows like an ooze creeping over her magic. Taking a moment to stand there, she allowed herself the opportunity to accept the sensation rather than fight it.

"I think now is the time you tell us what she is about to do," Aiden demanded.

He wanted to refuse the ushering motions Saoirse was making to send them toward the staring crowd.

"She's going to burn the field. The magic will protect her, but anything that isn't of her body will catch alight and put her at risk." Standing with her arms crossed, Saoirse glared at the worried guards. "Just do what you've been told."

Horrified, Brenna gasped, "She's going to be among the flames?"

Joining them, Faolan said, "I told her to tell you, but she wouldn't listen."

Staring at Eirian as she moved through the stalks, Aiden wanted to dump her things on the ground and storm after her.

"She gets very stubborn," Aiden commented, forcing himself to remain.

"Captain, what would Everett say?" Hand on her hip, Brenna pointed at him.

"I can already hear him yelling at me, at her, at me, at you, and then at me again."

Aiden was not lying when he said he could already hear in his mind what Everett would say. Studying him, the conflict on his face did not disappoint Faolan.

"Just shut up and watch, forget her state of undress, and marvel at the display of magic Eirian's about to give you. A cleansing on this scale is spectacular."

Knowing it was time, the Telmians lit the small fires spread outside the field and retreated until they were safely on the other side of their wards. Eirian turned to face the watching crowd and held her arms wide for the show. Her magic spread until it reached the wards, filling the space. Then, feeling the spark of energy the fires gave off, she wrapped her power around it. Even at a distance, she felt the heat, the dancing of the flames.

Tilting her head back and closing her eyes for focus, Eirian drew the flames to her. The image her powers provided allowed her to see the shadows, a sense of anger coming from them. She knew the darkness was aware of her and heard the defiant whispers along the edge of her consciousness. The flames danced higher, and Eirian pulled the cleansing energy into her, feeding it through her magic to chase away the shadows.

"Captain!" Merle panicked, taking a step toward the burning field. "Aiden, she's in the middle of that!"

Putting an arm in front of the guards, Faolan said, "She's perfectly safe. Just watch."

People were pressing forward, and the wards flared to stop them from going closer. Shouts of fear rose, demanding for someone to do something as the flames raced toward the woman in the middle of the field. Clinging to her things, Aiden stared at Faolan while his men and Brenna panicked. Glancing at Eirian, he wondered if she could hear them and hoped they were not creating a distraction that could cost her.

"Enough!" Faolan bellowed, his power flashing through the crowd and bringing them all to silence. "Be quiet! Your queen is safe. She knows what she's doing."

"If you're wrong, wolf, and she gets hurt," Aiden said, giving him a look that promised no mercy.

The fire swirled higher, and they could no longer see Eirian. In the middle of the flames, she fed the energy through her magic. It had consumed the wheat, nothing remaining of the devastation the darkness had caused. Shadows darted through the flames, and she smirked, her magic capturing them. Doubts and fears arose in her mind, prompted by the lingering darkness. Eirian welcomed them, accepting them as hers as she drew the shadows into her reach. She used her power to banish them altogether, and a brilliant white light spilled over the field, flaring within the borders of the daoine wards.

Almost blinded by the flare of light, everyone turned their faces away, covering their eyes. Gasps of shock came from the red-haired siblings as they felt the wards crumble, Eirian's magic washing out over the crowd. They could not stop it, the power beyond anything they could control. They felt their fear banished and knew she was chasing any lingering remnants of the darkness from those watching. It lasted mere moments, but it felt longer before the light retreated. White fading to the normal range of colors the fire had possessed, they turned their gaze back.

"By the powers," Saoirse murmured, reaching out to Faolan.

Grasping her hand, Faolan had to agree. Eirian was striding toward them, the fire moving out of her path. Behind her, the sun had set, and the field continued to burn, the flames no longer reaching high into the air. She glowed with her power. Most people dropped to their knees in awe when she stopped halfway between them and the fire. Shoving Eirian's things into Brenna's startled grasp, Aiden ignored the protests and hurried over. Her eyes settled on him as he approached her, and the shine of magic within them almost made Aiden stop.

"Do not touch me!" Eirian said, holding up a hand as he drew closer.

Swallowing back his fears, Aiden walked around her, the light from the fire more than enough to examine her. Thankful to find Eirian unharmed, he stared at her face. He had thought the storm's effects had been beautiful, but they did not compare.

"I don't know if I should be angry at you or happy you're intact."

"I told you I'd be fine."

"Well, I'm sorry if we doubted your word when we watched you walk naked into a field and set it on fire."

His sarcasm made her smile. "I suppose I deserve that. The flames will die before sunrise. Now, I need somewhere to rest."

Offering his hand, he did not miss the way her lip curled in a slight sneer at it, and he said, "You need clothes first."

"Nothing is touching me until I say otherwise. I mean it, nothing. Magic has a cost."

Joining them, Saoirse pointed at the farmhouse. "Come, this way, the orchard is ideal."

Watching in confusion as the two women walked away, with Brenna following like a faithful hound, Aiden turned to Faolan. "What's going on?"

Faolan answered, "The itch. Ask in the morning. For now, take your men and guard her, but don't touch her. Speak only if she invites you to."

Holding his hands up, Faolan turned to the crowd while Aiden and the guards hurried off. They stared at him, waiting for an explanation of what Eirian had done.

"Let's not waste a bonfire! Your queen is hale, so raise a toast."

Explanations could come later.

TWENTY-ONE

The fire had died, the glow no longer visible from where Aiden leaned against a tree. Scattered around the orchard, his men kept curious people away. Saoirse had led Eirian into the trees, where she had settled in the middle, careful not to touch anything except the ground. Muireann had joined them during the night, the healer sitting opposite Eirian. They had not spoken a word, and the guards remained silent. Though her magic had faded, she still glowed similarly to the daoine. Every time he glanced at her, Aiden wondered if it was a sign of her heritage showing.

Aiden's ears pricked at the sound of footsteps, and pushing away from the tree, he turned to face the approaching person. "Fox? I thought you were around the other side."

Fox flashed a grin in the darkness. "I was, and now I'm not. Cap'n, I'm going to offer my cloak."

"I don't think that's a good idea. They said not to go near her." Glancing at the bundle of fur and fabrics draped over Fox's arm, Aiden frowned and said, "I'm sure she'd appreciate the thought, though."

Shrugging, Fox stepped past. "It's nearly dawn, and she's still naked."

Letting him go, Aiden followed a few steps behind. A weary glance at the sky through the trees told him it was growing lighter. The two Telmians glared at the guards, but Fox ignored them, holding his cloak out in front of him as an offering. With her eyes shut, Eirian did not seem to notice them. Aiden stared at her face, trying to ignore her state of undress and the fact the other guard could look. It made him clench a fist in frustration.

"If you scowl any harder, Captain, you might forget how to smile," Eirian murmured.

Opening her eyes, she looked past Fox at Aiden.

"You must be cold, ma'am." Fox showed her the cloak. "I thought you might like my cloak since the fur is so soft."

Shifting toward Fox, Muireann reached out and ran a hand over the fur. She smiled, making a noise of appreciation that had Fox grinning.

"That is lovely and soft. Are you ready for anything to touch you?"

Lifting her arms stiffly, Eirian ran a hand over the opposite arm and flinched. "Barely, but it'll have to do. Thank you, Fox. You're right, I'm cold, and your lynx fur is wonderful."

Her movements were slow as Eirian carefully accepted the cloak from Fox and draped it over herself. The discomfort as it settled against her skin was obvious, and Aiden wondered why the magic had affected her so. Satisfied, Fox moved into the shadows of the trees, leaving him with the women. Aiden felt Eirian staring at him intently, and he looked at her. Then, following a lock of dark hair over her shoulder, he looked away quickly when his mind reminded him of the feel of skin.

"Good grief, Captain, what are you thinking?" Saoirse chuckled.

"I beg your pardon?" Bristling at her laughter, Aiden crossed his arms.

Eirian smiled, chiding, "Saoirse, don't tease him."

Laughing again, Saoirse lay back on the ground and propped her head up with a hand. "He jumps from emotion to emotion. It's making me dizzy. I wish you'd let me play with you, Captain. All those bottled-up feelings."

"Saoirse."

There was a hint of warning in Eirian's voice, and Aiden looked at her, seeing a frown. He wondered if he would have seen jealousy if there had been enough light.

"Well, you're not playing with him," she said petulantly.

He sighed. "Dawn is coming, Your Majesty."

"I know," Eirian responded tiredly.

Aiden stared into the darkness. Better he stared at shadows than at her.

"Ma'am, dawn is coming. Don't you think it's time you put some clothes on and prepared yourself for the inevitable onslaught of questioning?"

Stretching, Eirian surrounded herself in the cloak. He noted hesitation in her movements.

"Why, Captain, you sound concerned about everyone seeing me naked. Again."

"While I enjoy the sight, it's not one I care to share."

Saoirse rolled flat onto her back, cooing, "So possessive, Captain. Be careful of those feelings because they could get you in trouble."

Ignoring them, Eirian said, "I'll dress. Just don't touch me, please."

"I don't understand, but I'll make sure no one touches you," Aiden replied.

"Except you," Saoirse said, laughing.

Bowing, Aiden returned to his spot. He refused to give Saoirse the satisfaction.

"The sensitivity should have faded by now," Muireann commented.

She got to her feet and located the bundle of clothes and weapons, bringing them over to Eirian. Reluctantly pushing the cloak from her shoulders, Eirian carefully sorted through her things, finding the cord to tie her hair back first.

"I know. I suspect it's because it wasn't a normal cleansing. The darkness left traces that didn't appreciate my efforts."

"My brother is most disturbed that you obliterated our wards while not losing control of the flames," Saoirse commented, staring at the fading stars.

"I was chasing those traces, and I didn't want them to find purchase in anyone. The wards would've been fine if I hadn't been so determined. But, at least I was gentle about it." Dragging her clothes on slowly, Eirian bit her lip at how rough the fabric felt.

Incredulous, Muireann said, "If you call that gentle, then I'd hate to know what you consider rough."

"I hope none of you ever have to see me get rough." Working on her boots, Eirian realized how sensitive her feet were and sighed.

Saoirse chuckled, "Ticklish feet?"

"There's nothing you can do to help me?"

"Not magically, but I have herbs that will help numb things a little. However, I wouldn't advise it until after you've finished with the field," Muireann informed her.

Rolling over, Saoirse suggested, "You could do it, Muireann. It's not a big area."

"I offered. Eirian refused."

Shrugging, Muireann wondered if she had changed her mind. Shaking her head, Eirian confirmed the refusal.

"No, I'll do it."

Bundling her armor and weapons together, Eirian left them on the ground. Growing bluer with every moment that passed, bands of pink and orange spread across the sky to herald the rising sun. Devoid of clouds, the day promised to be a fine one, and she felt the vibration of life. Birds flitted from branch to branch in the trees looming above, singing their tunes with merriment. In the distance, kookaburras mocked them with their laughter.

Her skin felt like it was burning, the rub of fabric making Eirian want to tear the clothes off. Lifting Fox's cloak, she carefully draped it around her shoulders and wrapped it close, hoping that warmth would help. The fur against her face was as soft as she remembered. But it was not the pleasure she wished it were. Getting to her feet, she ignored the scrambling women and peered into the fading shadows at the figures of her guards.

"Captain?" Calling for Aiden, Eirian kept one hand clasping the cloak.

Aiden broke away from his tree and approached her. "Yes, Your Majesty?"

Waving her free hand at the pile on the ground, Eirian watched his eyes narrow at it as she said, "I'm not ready for anything more than this."

Looking her over, Aiden was thankful she had put her clothes on. "I see. It would be nice if you gave me some sort of explanation."

"Have you ever been burned?"

"I have."

"Do you remember how painful it was and how sensitive the new skin felt?"

"But you weren't burned." Cocking his head to the side, Aiden admitted, "I don't understand."

"Without magic, it's hard to understand, and I don't know how to describe it adequately. When we perform a cleanse, we pull the energy of the fire into ourselves and then back out again to destroy whatever it is we are cleaning. While my physical body was unharmed, my magic was burned," Eirian explained, her frustration showing.

"And each of you has done this?"

"I love it," Saoirse replied, sauntering over to Aiden to run a hand over his arm. "You can't imagine what it feels like to enjoy the company of another when you're so sensitive. Even more so if they're magical. It magnifies every brief touch."

"You are a strange, strange creature," Aiden muttered, stepping away from her.

"The last time I did one, I couldn't tolerate shifting for days, even though I felt fine outwardly after a few hours," Muireann informed them.

Lifting her hand to cover her face, Eirian stopped short when her mind reminded her how it would feel. "I've never met a mage who can't do this. Riane teaches everyone once our control is at the right point. And before you ask, no, it can't be a weapon."

Aiden's brows rose in amusement. "I wasn't planning to ask. The prospect of a naked person walking into a battle to burn everyone alive is not one I wish to entertain. Besides, you'd probably tell me it's because you kill everyone, friend and foe."

"It can clean up after a battle. Most frequently, it's used to dispose of the dead during plagues. It burns more effectively than ordinary fire."

"Fair enough. Why didn't any of you do it after the round with Athnaral?"

Directing his question to the ladies, Aiden caught sight of his men surrounding them. Eirian followed his stare, watching as the guards glanced away from her attention.

Saoirse walked away, telling him, "We figured you'd want to deal with the dead in your way. Perhaps next time I will, and you can entertain me afterward."

"Or someone else could do it, not you," he muttered.

"You're no fun, Captain." She called, "Come, Muireann, we have work to do."

Left with her concerned guards, Eirian sighed softly and clung to the cloak tighter. "I suppose you think I'm a little insane."

Picking up her things, Gabe snorted. "Well, insane doesn't fit. We saw you walk through the fire, unharmed."

Shushing him with a wave, Fionn asked, "So, that scar?"

"Training accident."

"With a whip?"

She dismissed the question, hiding her face in the hood. Then, hearing a pained grunt, Eirian glanced back at them and saw Fionn rubbing his shoulder with Merle glaring beside him. Merle bowed his head, his eyes flickering to where Aiden stood. Facing her guards, she let go of the cloak, spreading her arms instead of putting them on her hips like she wanted to. They stared at the bored look on her face and collectively glanced past her at Aiden.

"No, don't look at him." She commanded, "Look at me!"

"Ma'am?" Merle asked tentatively.

Shaking her head, Eirian held up her hand for silence. "If you think I'm bothered you saw me naked, then you're wrong. Please get the silly thoughts and comments over with so you can move on and do your jobs. You're not the first group of people to see me naked, and I highly doubt you'll be the last."

"I just wanted to know about the scar!"

Fionn shrugged, earning himself another punch in the arm from Merle. Snarling at them, Eirian spun around and stormed past Aiden, who gave her an amused look.

She muttered, "Honestly!"

"You heard your queen." Shaking his head at his men, Aiden followed Eirian, hurrying to catch up with her. "You realize you're going to get comments about it for a long time."

Shooting him a dark look, Eirian hissed, "And if you can't keep yourself and your men from being part of it, then perhaps you don't warrant your position."

"Always with the threats. You're not getting rid of me that soon, darling."

Smirking, Aiden reached for her arm and stopped when Eirian skittered away, his smirk fading. The look that flickered across her face made him feel terrible.

Aiden whispered, "I'm sorry."

"Good morning, Your Majesty!" Todd's voice boomed, and they stopped staring at each other to turn in his direction.

Todd strode toward them, a hand on his sword as he regarded Eirian and her guards with a neutral expression. Several other officers and nobles followed, a mixture of emotions on each face. She wished she had forced herself to don her armor and weapons, the lack of them leaving her feeling exposed.

"Good morning, Lieutenant." Keeping her voice even, Eirian smiled at the group.

Looking her over, Todd smiled broadly. "Forgive me, ma'am, but you're bloody amazing."

She stared at him before glancing at Aiden, seeing the shock on his face. Holding a hand up, Eirian opened her mouth, then shut it, working through her response options before settling on something.

"Thank you... I think."

"We weren't present on the battlefield, so it was quite the spectacular treat to watch you walk out of a burning field unharmed. Once we got over our shock, we raised many toasts in your honor."

He did not mention the unending bawdy jokes that started before consuming said toasts. There was no need to provide fuel for the rumor mill by giving Aiden a reason to come to blows with anyone. Not with the whispers that he would be king after the war.

"Having witnessed both, I suppose you could call the fire a spectacular treat," Aiden commented, comparing the two events in his mind.

Eirian knew which she preferred and redirected the conversation. "I need the seeds for this crop brought down to the field and sown."

Raised on a farm, Todd arched an eyebrow in amusement. He was not the only one, even Merle chuckling behind her.

"While the field looks as though it hasn't been burning all night, there's more to it than cleaning away the old and sowing fresh seed."

"Perhaps normally," she said, a knowing smile curling her lips. "However, there's nothing normal about this."

"That's fair. Everyone wants to know what exactly you did last night with the fire."

There were nods and murmurs of agreement from the people with him. Turning her face to the sky, Eirian took in the mixture of colors that lingered after the dawn.

"It's quite simple. Corruption killed the crop, and with a combination of magic and fire, I burned away the corruption."

"All right then." Nodding, Todd signaled to a young woman hovering on the outskirts of the group. "Let the good people know Her Majesty wants the wheat sown."

Tilting his head to the side, Merle regarded Todd with a baffled look. "That's it?"

"Yes, that's it. Some of us don't feel the need to question our commanders. Our queen obligingly gave us a basic explanation, and we accept it. We're not mages, we don't need more information, nor would we probably understand it."

Todd gave the guards a disapproving stare. Grinning, Eirian felt the annoyance coming from her guards.

She said, "I think I like you, Todd. You could teach my guards a few lessons in keeping their mouths shut and following orders. If you ever fancy joining the royal guard, I could free up a captaincy for you."

He grinned, enjoying the dark expression on Aiden's face. None of the guards looked impressed by the implication of Eirian's words.

"I'm full of questions, but I know it's not my place. I'm just a lieutenant, and you have nobles who'll demand answers. Though you make a very tempting offer," Todd said and winked at Aiden.

"Have you seen the Earl yet this morning?" Reminded of Gallagher, she felt the need to ask after him.

"Yes, he never left the field. Most left and returned to camp to sleep after a few hours of merriment, but not him."

Knowing the Earl was a faithful ally, Eirian nodded her thanks and turned her gaze in the field's direction. "He finds magic fascinating."

"Rightly so." One of the lesser nobles in the group said, "Magic is very fascinating."

"I should get on with it. For those who've traveled with me from Amath, this won't be a new show."

"You can make sure it's just the wheat, can't you?" Gabe asked.

He was not the only one recalling all the times she had sent things into overgrowth. Shrugging, Eirian waited for the group in front to move.

Devin chuckled, "Isn't this where she normally says, 'I'm good but not that good,' or did I miss it?"

"Shut up, man. I don't want to get in trouble later," Kip grumbled, waving at Merle.

The rest of the walk to the field was quiet, Eirian disinterested in talking, and no one willing to press for more information. Most of the guards were still bristling from the insult thrown their way by Todd, and Aiden was sullen, shooting angry glances at her. When they arrived at the field, Gallagher and Brenna were standing together. Brenna's hands waved around furiously as she argued with him. Clearing his throat, Gallagher directed her attention to the silently observing Eirian.

"Your Majesty."

Brenna took in the distance between Eirian and her guards. She saw the way Eirian clung to the cloak hanging around her like it was a shield and the bundle of weapons and armor that Gabe carried.

"Good morning, Your Grace, Lord Gallagher." Eirian's eyes skipped past them to the cluster of approaching daoine, and she added, "Lord Faolan."

Faolan skipped the pleasantries and asked, "Are you sure you can do this?"

"Of course."

"You can barely tolerate anything touching you. I know this is only a small area compared to what you can do, but to use that much power when you're still so sensitive? I don't think it's a good idea, and if Tharen were here, he'd agree."

Looking confused, the Endarans were unsure if they could say anything to help either side. Grunting, Aiden shook his head, pushing his anger aside to let concern take precedence.

He murmured, "If the wolf doesn't think you should, then perhaps it's time to put aside your pride and let someone else do it."

Grinding her teeth, Eirian glanced at him before returning her focus to Faolan. "I appreciate your concern, Faolan, but I assure you, I'll be fine. Muireann is preparing something for me to take afterward. Besides, I'd hate to deny my guards a chance to protect me. They get so few opportunities."

Snickering, the soldiers within hearing did not hide their amusement as the royal guards looked unimpressed. Crossing her arms, Brenna stepped closer and shook her head in frustration.

"If there's no need for you to do it, then allow someone else the opportunity."

Eirian understood their concerns and appreciated where they were coming from. However, knowing they were right made her more determined to go ahead. Refusing to answer, she slipped around the people and headed to the field. There was no evidence of a fire, no crumbled remains or ash coating the earth. All had burned, leaving only dirt and footprints where people had walked to reassure themselves their eyes did not lie. A magical fire consumed everything and left nothing. She felt traces of her magic, but unlike the day before, the field felt clean. There was no lingering evidence of the darkness.

Sensing Faolan behind her, Eirian said, "You can't convince me otherwise."

He rolled his eyes and huffed, "I've gathered. Stubborn woman."

"I can't show weakness to the darkness."

"Delegation is not weakness."

"It is when dealing with a god!" Rounding on him, Eirian growled, "If the darkness thinks for a moment that she can overwhelm me, we're all lost."

Eirian's words forced Faolan to confront the reality of how much he had forgotten over a thousand years. "What did you say?"

"What part?"

"How do you know the darkness is a god, and I don't? I'm fifth among my people! I should know the darkness is a god."

Incensed by his reaction, her magic gathered around Eirian in a cloud of frustration, but her voice remained low. "This is not about you. If you want to rage, question your competence, or any other petty thing, then turn and walk away right now. Otherwise, I require you to join the crowd, smile and pretend I've said something reassuring, and have absolute faith in my ability to do this minor task."

Faolan stared at her in amazement, replying, "I see. And despite it being a minor task, the likelihood of everything being overwhelming afterward is?"

"Irrelevant," Eirian said icily. "Irrelevant, because I can handle it. Just like I've always handled it. Just like I'll always handle it. Because that is what I do!"

"By the powers, you're so stubborn, Eirian Altira, and it'll be your bane."

Magic remained curled around her, and Eirian blinked before turning to note Glynn and her family standing with everything they needed to sow the field. Watching her walk toward the crowd, he took a deep breath to calm his frustration.

Spreading her arms wide, Eirian smiled at the farmer. "Good morning, Glynn. Let me get out of the way, and you can teach me how to sow a field."

"Teach you?" Glynn said, "Please, Your Majesty, you've given us more than anyone in our position could ever expect from their queen."

"Of course, I'll remain out of your way."

The matriarch smiled thankfully, waving a hand at a woman who bore a strong resemblance to her. "Thank you. My daughter made you something for breakfast. Unfortunately, we can't feed everyone, but it would be remiss if we didn't feed our queen."

Stepping forward, the woman held a tray between her hands with an elegantly embroidered cloth covering it. "It is nothing fancy, but we hope you find it acceptable."

Flattered by their generosity, Eirian murmured, "Thank you. I'm sure it'll be wonderful."

Giving a signal to her kin, Glynn watched as they lifted the bags of seed and several members of Todd's company moved to join them. Eirian did not pay attention, maintaining her focus on the proffered tray and its mysterious contents. Reaching out, she traced the intricate pattern of swirls and realized it was a mountain scene, clouds crowning the peaks. It held her focus, Eirian studying each little stitch and admiring the hard work that had gone into the creation. She wondered which of the women had done it.

"Ma'am?" Aiden prompted her.

Shaking her head slightly, Eirian smiled faintly and turned the cloth over. It covered several small rolls of bread, the different colored swirls making her look questioningly at the woman holding them.

"I bake things into the dough." She explained while pointing at each roll, "These have herbs and tomato, and these have wild garlic and onion."

"Really?"

Eirian's eyes went wide with delight, and she reached for a roll. Peering past her, Merle grunted in appreciation.

He said, "My mother does things like that."

Biting into one of the tomato rolls, Eirian tuned out the conversations. Her stomach welcomed the food, her nose enjoying the smell of fresh bread and herbs. She decided they could easily replace the fresh berry pastries she loved. It was a savory combination so delicious that she did not understand why it was not more commonly made.

"That's the face she makes for pastries," Isabella said and giggled. "I think you've pleased Her Majesty greatly."

Brenna pursed her lips, agreeing, "Indeed, they smell delicious. Thank you, Glynn."

"I can't take credit when it was Aimee's idea. She loves cooking and can make a feast out of almost nothing," Glynn told them.

Beaming at Aimee, Glynn showed her pride. Pausing in her slow consumption of the food, Eirian looked at the woman with a smile.

"If you ever want a job, I wouldn't say no to these."

Blushing, Aimee replied, "I couldn't leave my family. Your kitchens don't make these?"

"They make pastries and things, but I've never had flavored bread." Eirian gasped, "Oh, oh yes! Tell me you've made ones with cheese through them?"

"I have. It's a good use of old cheese."

Holding up a hand, Eirian sighed. "I'm going to hold on to that thought, and one day, someone will make it for me."

"Ree!"

Turning at the sound of the little girl, Eirian watched Ona skip toward her. Merle was quick to scoop her up and onto his shoulders before she could wrap her arms around Eirian.

Giggling, Ona pulled his hair, squealing, "Put me down!"

"No can do, chicken. The boss lady has things to do."

Merle kept a tight grip on her scrawny legs, winking at Eirian. Selecting a roll, she offered it up to Ona.

"Later on, Ona, when I'm less busy."

She tore at the roll, and Merle felt crumbs land on his head as she said, "Okay."

"Thank you, Aimee. This was what I needed." Eirian turned to watch the field.

Observing the line of people pulling plows along, she followed the ones behind them with her eyes. They were scattering the seed, and her magic registered the potential as each landed on the ground. Slipping in beside her, Brenna cast a look over her shoulder at Merle carrying Ona on his shoulders.

"She should stay here."

"I won't abandon that child after what she's been through. Ona remains with us until we find her parents," Eirian responded sharply.

Brenna sighed in frustration. "Eirian, we're at war. You might have brought us time for reinforcements to arrive, but we're still at war. Do you think the safest place for that innocent child to be is at your side? You can't protect Ona by taking her to a battlefront!"

"She's right," Aiden commented.

"I understand you feel an obligation to Ona because you think you let her down, that you could have done something about what happened to her family. But you're wrong."

Closing her eyes, Eirian thought back to the sight of Ona huddled in darkness and terrified for her life. "She comes with us. You leave, so does she. The rest of the time, Ona can learn to fight back."

"You'd have that little girl taught to fight?"

"Why not? She's no different from noble-born or mage-born children who have swords pressed into their hands from early on. Unlike them, though, Ona needs to know she can defend herself if she is ever in danger again."

A person scattering seed turned and started back to the watching bystanders. Brenna knew she had lost her chance to convince Eirian to change her mind, but she understood her reasoning. Stepping around her guards, she avoided any accidental brushes against anything as she moved. It had been difficult to hide how much eating had affected her. Instead, she dredged up every fragment of determination that she possessed. Releasing her tentative grip on her magic as she walked, Eirian felt it spread eagerly.

"So it begins," Fionn chuckled.

They watched greenery shooting upward as they reached for the source of magic.

Kane laughed, "Got to admit, it's incredible to watch. I mean, she walks, and plants just grow. Do you think that's what it was like for the gods?"

"What are you on about, idiot?"

People turned to look at him, and Tyler slapped a hand to his face, scolding himself for speaking. Deciding he might as well expand on his comment, Kane continued.

"Well, the gods made everything, right? Do you think they could walk around, and things just grew as they do for her? It makes sense to me."

Frowning, Faolan dwelled on what Eirian had said about the darkness being a god and said, "That's a simplified view of what the gods did, but understandable."

The soldier bowed and waved a hand over his shoulder at the lines working. Eirian stood at the edge of the field, ignoring the dandelions around her feet.

"They finished sowing, but there's not enough for the entire field," he told her.

"That's fine, so long as there's enough to see them through winter."

Green shoots had already appeared, steadily covering the field. Eirian was thankful her magic was doing what it always did without her control. A glance told her plants were growing, the bright yellow dandelions blooming like happy drops of sunshine. Scattered among the greenery were tiny little white flowers that resembled upside-down horns. Eirian stared at them, taken in by the delicacy of their appearance.

At the other end of the rolling wave of green shoots, farmers and soldiers were staring in wonder at the slowly growing grain. Eirian gathered her focus and magic, concentrating on the sprouting seeds. Keeping her magic controlled, she raised the wheat to the same stage as the dead crop. Watching the grain reaching skywards, she understood the people's amazement.

The spark of life always made her magic happy, but Eirian was eager to finish. The moment it resembled the image in her mind, she withdrew her magic and clenched a fist in front of her stomach. The bite of her fingernails did not help the way her skin crawled like ants covered it. It gave her something to focus on, and she breathed deeply. While making the wheat grow, she could ignore the increasingly dreadful feeling creeping across her skin.

Avoiding the stares of the approaching people, Eirian kept breathing slowly and lifted her gaze to study the sky. Scattered across the blue expanse were fluffy white clouds and no signs of rain. Turning, she kept a blank expression, hoping Faolan would hold back his comments. Glynn had tears in her eyes, and she held a hand to her mouth. Beside her, Aimee wore a similar expression, but her hands were gripping the tray tightly.

Aimee cried, "Thank you! Thank you!"

"It's the least I could do. I want you to tell Todd what else you need to make it through winter and get a start on the new year. I'll have no one forced from their homes because of the plague upon our existence," Eirian spoke steadily, though her heart raced.

"We can't accept more from you, Your Majesty," Glynn replied, lowering her hand.

Tilting her chin forward, Eirian squared her shoulders and did her best to look commanding. "Your queen will have no arguments on the matter. The throne must care for the people of Endara, and your family won't starve this winter. Please excuse me."

Ignoring everyone, Eirian headed back to the grove of fruit trees. It offered a semblance of sanctuary to hide in until Muireann brought the concoction to help. Withdrawing into herself, she kept her head down and paced the orchard while waiting. She knew her guards were watching in concern and expected Aiden to storm over to her to demand answers.

Faolan's magic made the feeling of crawling over her skin increase. Lifting her gaze, Eirian swept it over him as he stood glaring at her with his arms crossed before dropping it back to the ground as she paced. It was clear he was doing it on purpose, knowing how much worse it would make her feel.

"You didn't even make a show of it." His voice was bitter. "Are you pleased?"

"Why don't you take your self-righteousness, turn around, and leave," she snapped.

He smiled faintly, purring, "What does it feel like? Ants? Spiders? Grass seeds caught in the fabric of your clothes. Is it scratching at your mind, driving you to distraction yet? How long before you rip at your skin? Will we need to bind your hands to stop you from harming yourself? The good captain might like that."

"What are you on about?" Aiden asked, walking over to stand next to Faolan.

"What she's experiencing right now."

Flicking a hand at Eirian, Faolan glanced over his shoulder to track the approach of Saoirse and Muireann. Aiden took in the cup Muireann grasped.

"Why is she feeling those things?"

Faolan replied, "She explained to you about the sensitivity. Well, we avoid using our powers while we recover. Without the recovery period, the use of magic isn't the smooth thing it normally would be. It's more like walking on a broken leg. Magic has a cost. Most of the time, it's just hunger."

"But why? I've seen her do many things with little recovery time."

"Not like this. The fire burned Eirian's magic and like flesh, and it needs to heal." Keeping his eyes locked on Muireann, Faolan sensed the palatable relief pouring off Eirian at the offered cup.

Aiden frowned, murmuring, "Magic is part of your body. Like an extra limb. You need to fuel it and care for it like the rest of your body."

Shooting the men an amused look, Saoirse waited for Eirian to down the drink. Her face screwed up in disgust at the taste. Lifting her hands, Saoirse disregarded the weak protests from Eirian and cupped her face. Arching a brow, Faolan took a step toward them, opening his mouth to question Saoirse, but halted when he realized what she was doing.

"Just breathe in, Eirian. Breathe in my power and relax. Let me calm your mind."

"What is she doing?" Aiden asked.

"Saoirse is like those you call blues. She's using her power to calm the Queen, so what Muireann gave her can work," Faolan explained.

"Can she ride?"

"That's a question for Muireann. I don't know how strong her mixture is. If I could influence any decisions, I suggest we remain where we are until tomorrow."

Nodding, Aiden turned, saying, "I'll speak to Her Grace and the lieutenant. I don't believe there's any rush to return to Kelsby."

"That'd be a good idea. Eirian won't thank us for it now, but she will when she feels better. Or she won't."

"No, she's too damn stubborn."

Giving Eirian a last look, Aiden strode off to the soldiers and nobles beside the field. Relaxing into Saoirse's power, she was vaguely aware of him leaving. Saoirse felt different from the influence of blues she had let in previously. It washed away the crawl of her skin as long as she kept her eyes on Saoirse. Eirian saw her mouth moving, but did not register the words, nodding in agreement. Her mind grew foggier, and her magic attempted to push out the influence, but the herbs had taken effect.

Letting Eirian crumple, Saoirse turned to the guards as they came running. "She's going to sleep for a while. I think Muireann must have made her mixture a little too strong."

Humming in agreement, Muireann chirped, "Sorry, my bad. I must have miscalculated the blend. Oh well, I guess she has no choice but to rest."

Bending to pick up Eirian, Merle gave them a wry smile.

Twenty-Two

"Tell me what I'm looking at."

Leaning forward in the saddle, Eirian shaded her eyes and peered into the distance. Halcyon shifted and strained his head to reach for a clump of grass, his tail swishing. Beside her, Todd was staring similarly.

"I don't know, ma'am. It looks like Athnaralan troops to me."

Grunting, Aiden agreed, "A wild assumption, but I'd say reinforcements arrived."

Taking a deep breath, Eirian muttered, "Yes, that's what I thought. We've had no messengers alerting us to their arrival or that they are outside Kelsby. Unless you've been keeping secrets, Lieutenant."

They were far enough away that it was difficult to estimate how many soldiers there were. However, from what Aeyren had said, Eirian knew it would be another legion. Running a hand through her loose hair, she tuned out the buzz of conversation. She had hoped for more time before the Athnaralan reinforcements arrived. Casting a glance skywards, she saw Saoirse had circled away from the enemy and could not resist a brief smile.

"Ma'am, are we going to proceed to town, or are we going to stay here and stare at the enemy?" Gabe questioned, leaning forward in his saddle.

Kyson laughed, "Maybe if she stares at them long enough, they'll vanish."

Shifting her gaze to the sea of tents between them and the walls of the town, Eirian knew Todd needed to update his commanders. "Lieutenant, thank you for accompanying us."

He saluted with a grim smile. "It was an honor, ma'am. However, we're going to the same place."

"I know, but we don't know how things might be, and I thought I'd thank you now. After all, Lieutenant, you've got a company to command."

"And Her Majesty has an entire kingdom to offend," Fionn quipped.

"Defend," Kip corrected.

Shaking his head, Fionn grinned at the scolding looks directed his way and said, "No, definitely offend. It's Athnaral, and she offends them by breathing."

Not bothering with the banter between her guards, Eirian cast a worried look at Brenna and Isabella, taking in how Brenna held Ona close. "I want you to remain here until we can organize someone to escort you to safety."

"Of course, Your Majesty," Brenna replied, keeping a protective arm around Ona. "We'll remain at a safe distance."

Ona blinked up at Brenna. "What's wrong?"

"The bad people have come back, and our queen needs to leave some of us behind where we're safe," Isabella explained in a soft voice.

"Can I go with Ree? I want to see the bad people."

Giving Ona an affectionate smile, Eirian said, "No, Ona, I need you to stay with Brenna and look after her. Can you look after Brenna and Isabella for me?"

Chewing her lip, Ona whined, "But I want to come with you."

"I'm sorry, Ona, but you can't. I don't want you, Brenna, or Isabella to get hurt, and if you come, I'll be so worried about you that I won't be able to be the queen. You want me to protect everyone, don't you?"

Ona pouted. "Yes, Ree."

Feeling bad for her, Aiden said, "Don't worry, chicken, if we have to fight the bad people, she'll leave and find you."

"Yes, that's right," Brenna said with a smile. "She'll join us and leave the fighting to the soldiers."

There was a prickling to the back of her neck, and Eirian turned slowly, looking in all directions before glancing skywards. No longer in sight, she wondered where Saoirse had drifted to before looking back at Ona and her ladies. Her magic whispered, warning her to prepare.

"Of course, I know what I have to do. Look after Brenna and Isabella, Ona. That's your task as ordered by your queen."

Her words made Ona perk up with self-importance. "Yes, Ree, I'll miss you."

"I'll miss you too, Ona."

Exchanging a silent understanding with Brenna, she decided not to linger and touched her heels to Halcyon. Shouting commands, Todd signaled to his soldiers to follow. Half the nobles remained behind, their desire to avoid risking their lives overriding any interest in finding out what was happening. The prickle of discomfort across the back of her neck remained, and Eirian tightened her grip on the reins, picking up the pace.

Halcyon's long stride covered ground swiftly, and Eirian enjoyed the smoothness of his canter. Soldiers lined the road as they passed the camp, cheers rising to greet their queen. Then, spotting a line of riders waiting for them outside the walls, she drew the big gelding back down to a walk. Her gaze settled on Everett, and Eirian lifted her hand in greeting.

"Your Grace, it appears you have a minor problem."

He arched a brow, replying, "Apologies, Your Majesty, I know I was filling in for you, but apparently, I'm not as intimidating."

"We knew they were coming, Everett. When did they arrive? Have you met with Aeyren?"

Nudging his horse forward, Marcellus looked for Brenna while explaining, "Yesterday, and no, we haven't met with him yet. Where's my wife?"

"She remained back, along with many others. Why was no messenger sent ahead to warn us? Have there been any communications?"

Marcellus and Everett exchanged pensive looks, and she ground her teeth, nodding. Everett took the moment of silence to respond before she could speak again.

"Their demands have changed. Marriage is off the negotiating table."

"The elves?" Gallagher asked.

"If we can buy a few days, they'll be here. A legion, including mages and the Prince."

Taking a deep breath, Eirian turned her mount from the gate to go around the outside to get a good look at the enemy forces. "It'll be enough. We'll make it more than enough."

"What she means to say is she'll make it more than enough." Aiden realized she was leaving and growled, "Where do you think you're going?"

Pushing Halcyon into a canter, Eirian led them around the outskirts of the town until she saw the Athnaralans. Halting, she leaned forward in the saddle to stare at the lines of soldiers. Then, casting a look upward, she took in the archers positioned on the top of the wall, watching for any movement.

Releasing her magic, Eirian sent it outward to establish if mages had joined them. The traces of what she had done had faded, but the land remembered her, welcoming her power. She felt others on the outskirts of her reach and, turning her focus from the army facing them, stared in a new direction. There was something familiar about what she sensed, the whispers in her mind growing louder.

"Faolan," she called, letting go of the reins to lift her hand and shade her eyes.

Her guards let Faolan through, his hair gleaming like coppery blood in the sunlight, and he asked quietly, "Your Majesty, how can I be of service?"

"Where's Saoirse?"

People looked to the sky for the eagle, and Faolan shifted nervously in his saddle. "She's gone to greet the others. They're out riding. Did you learn anything?"

Pursing her lips, Eirian debated about letting him keep his secrets and decided it was best to do so for the moment. "Well, I hope they have a delightful ride. And yes, I learned something, but I suspect I don't need to tell you."

His eyes narrowed, and he murmured, "I suspect you're right."

"Everett, Marcellus, when did you exchange messages last?"

Returning her focus to the more imminent problem, Eirian tugged at the buckle securing her cloak and shifted to free the trapped fabric. Scratching his chin, Marcellus shrugged.

"I'd say this morning."

Clearing his throat, Gabe pointed at a group of riders departing the enemy camp. "Did they know Her Majesty was away?"

Watching the fluttering white flags above them, Marcellus said, "I'm fairly sure everyone knew Her Majesty was absent."

Eirian kicked Halcyon into motion and headed toward the approaching riders, disregarding the people surrounding her. She heard the startled shouts of her guards and nobles as they followed. Seeing her coming in their direction, the riders halted. Unhappy with stopping again, Halcyon tossed his head and reared, making Eirian chuckle. Patting his neck, she made soothing noises. Slipping from the saddle, she threw the reins to a scrambling Kip.

"Eirian!" Everett dismounted and hurried after her, stopping himself from grabbing her arm. "What are you doing?"

Holding up a hand, Eirian cast a smirk over her shoulder. "I'm making a demonstration while receiving their message."

"I'm sure whatever she's about to do will pale next to walking through a burning field naked," Todd commented, earning exasperated looks from those who had witnessed the act.

Rolling her eyes, Eirian strode toward the waiting messengers. Releasing control over her magic, she took in how the Athnaralans shifted uncomfortably at the sight of everything growing. It was one of those times when she was thankful she could make a display without effort. Grass and wildflowers grew thick and fast, bursts of color scattered throughout the lush greens.

Pushing her cloak over her shoulders, Eirian let them get a good look at the twin swords hanging at her waist. Sweeping her gaze over them, she was pleased to see the general was not present, her dislike for Tomas so strong it made her fingers itch to hold a weapon. She did not need to look to know Aiden, Merle, the two dukes, and many officers were barely three strides behind her and doing their best to behave as though everything was normal.

"I see the Ensaycalan army on my borders hasn't changed your king's mind." Waving at them, she asked grimly, "Does King Aeyren have so little regard for your lives?"

They exchanged glances before one of them said, "It pleases King Aeyren that you've returned, and he hopes you have the answer he expects."

Blinking, Eirian waited a moment before bursting into laughter. Her magic responded to the newcomers in the distance, and she enjoyed the feel of their power brushing back.

"Oh, yes, I've such good news I can't wait to share. So why don't you go tell him? He won't want to put it off."

"You... you do?" The man looked surprised, stammering his question, and his companions blanched. "We'll return and inform His Majesty you wish to meet."

"As soon as possible."

He nodded enthusiastically, gaze shifting to a vibrant purple flower that had grown beside Eirian. "Of course, as soon as possible."

Waiting for the Athnaralan group to turn their mounts around and ride back to their camp, the Endarans stared in amazement at Eirian. She did not face them, her hand reaching to pluck the flower leaning against her thigh. Six delicate purple petals encircled a pale-yellow center. Twirling the stem in her fingers, Eirian turned. Catching the concerned stares of Everett and Aiden, she dismissed them as she leveled her focus on Faolan.

"Lord Faolan, would you like to tell me who is riding toward us?"

Her words shifted the focus to him, and the nobles broke into chatter, asking questions for themselves. Faolan clasped his hands behind his back, regarding Eirian seriously.

"I wanted to prepare you, and if you had proceeded into the keep, I'd have had the chance. I'd also like to point out that you shouldn't be using your magic like this. You're still recovering."

"That doesn't answer my question."

"What are you on about?" Marcellus asked.

Cocking her head to the side, Eirian arched a brow at him daringly. "Yes, Lord Faolan, what am I on about?"

He shook his head slightly before answering, "I told Her Majesty that King Neriwyn was on his way. It would appear he has arrived."

Silence fell over the group, and Eirian crossed her arms. "If Aeyren interprets my words the way I hope, then his timing couldn't be more perfect."

"You hope Aeyren will come and meet you as my king arrives with his troops."

Mentally kicking himself for not seeing her intentions, Faolan respected her manipulation. He suspected Neriwyn would find it hilarious when he found out. It was the sort of thing he would do.

"Precisely."

Foliage continued to creep upward as she twirled the flower. Then, flexing her control, Eirian withdrew her power and stopped the growth. A light breeze made the tall grass bow like a wave, flowers bobbing merrily in the sun as she tuned out the burst of conversation. The accusatory tones coming from many of the nobles told her Faolan had kept his news to himself. She wondered how her people would handle so many daoine.

Holding up a hand, Eirian silenced them. "How many is he bringing?"

"Enough for what you want."

"That doesn't answer my question."

Faolan sighed. "At least a legion. He desires this conflict over."

Running a hand through his hair, Everett looked pleased before realization overcame him, and he grimaced. "I'm not sure we can accommodate thousands of Telmians and their interests."

There were a few knowing snickers in response, and Eirian sighed heavily.

"Well, with a legion of elves and a legion of daoine, we should present a formidable opponent. Let's hope Aeyren sees sense."

"But thousands of daoine warriors." Gallagher groaned, "Thousands. A handful is hard enough to cope with."

"Thank you," Faolan muttered.

Eirian watched the Athnaralan camp, and her twirling of the flower became an erratic action. A petal had fallen, leaving a gap in the bloom. The stem was ratty, no longer the firm green stalk it had been. Sensing his stare, she glanced at Faolan and shrugged, stepping into the grass. It moved with her, separating as she walked, heads of seed brushing on her clothes and sticking to the scabbards that hung from her belt.

Trailing her hands over the tops, Eirian ignored the prickle that told her the Telmians were getting closer. Whispers grew louder in her mind, begging her to remember. There was movement in the opposing camp, riders gathering and horns blaring in the distance. Halting, she looked over her shoulder to watch the approach of more officers, General Cameron leading them.

"Greetings, Your Majesty!" he called out, lifting a hand in salute.

Waving, she smiled. "I see you've kept my kingdom intact, General."

Grinning, he clapped a hand on Everett's shoulder and laughed, "Of course. This one has a good head on his shoulders."

"It's no wonder people want him as king." Eirian turned back to the Athnaralans. "Here he comes. I can smell the darkness."

Watching the riders leave their camp, Eirian plucked a vibrant orange flower and slipped it behind her ear. Grumbles told her Aiden and Merle were fighting with the long grass, the plant life not parting for them the way it did for her. Standing on either side, they stared blankly at the Athnaralans as the horses drew close. Aeyren remained mounted, glaring at Eirian, while Tomas sneered at Aiden.

"I see you've given up the pretense of being a respectable woman. No filthy pet today?" Aeyren did not bother with niceties.

Eirian smiled and ignored his reference to her clothing, holding up a finger. Surprised by her response, Aeyren and Tomas exchanged looks.

"Wait, let me call him. He's over there." Turning, she whistled. "Faolan! Here, boy!"

Faolan shook his head, asking, "Do I need to change in front of all these people?"

"I don't think that's necessary," Aiden muttered with his hand on his sword, not turning to see if Faolan was stripping.

Aeyren glanced at Faolan, scornfully asking, "Am I supposed to laugh?"

"You asked about my wolf. I was attempting to explain him."

Continuing to smile, Eirian released her power and took delight in the startled looks as the grass grew. The whispers in her mind were persistent, urging her to kill them.

"And you expect us to believe your pet and that man are the same?" Tomas laughed mockingly.

"No, believe what you like. I understand your mind is too narrow and incapable of comprehending anything beyond your small beliefs."

Everett choked, spluttering at the condescending way Eirian spoke. "Your Majesty!"

"How dare you speak to me like that!" Tomas spat.

Taking a deep breath, Eirian smiled serenely and lifted her hands, holding them out. Around them, the field withered, seeds scattering in the breeze. Shocked gasps and shying horses greeted her display, and her smile grew wider. The flower tucked behind her ear remained unchanged, and, plucking it free, she let it rest on her palm before blowing on it for show.

It became a head of seeds, and her breath sent them into the breeze, where they were the first to become green and growing when they hit the ground. Horns sounded shrilly in the distance, the rumble of hooves making everyone turn to look. A quartet of riders approached, and Aiden touched a hand to Eirian's arm to direct her attention. The wave of power that hit her was more overwhelming than she had expected.

Mounted on a massive dapple gray, a man cantered toward them. Eirian knew it had to be King Neriwyn, and a glance at Faolan confirmed her suspicions. She thought she felt familiar magic, but the intoxicating level of power swept it away. Distracted by the screaming of the whispers, she did not realize the field had regrown, and flowers were blooming brightly around her.

Halting his horse, Neriwyn regarded the two groups while leaning forward in his saddle. Eirian was unsure what she had expected, but he was nothing like she thought he would be. Short black curls framed a face that seemed neither young nor old, and piercing dark eyes lingered on each person as he took them in. Gazing at him, Eirian battled with the tugs on her mind that told her she knew him.

He wore leather armor, contrasting colors layered on top of each other, and they saw the hilt of a sword at his back. A second sword and an axe hung at his waist, while a strung bow sat against his horse's flank, similar to Eirian's. Feeling Aiden shift beside her, she spared him a reassuring glance before spreading her arms with a welcoming smile. The Athnaralans murmured in confusion, none of them sure of what was going on.

"Warmest welcomes, King Neriwyn. Your presence here honors us. I'm sure it also honors King Aeyren," Eirian said, bowing to avoid meeting his gaze.

Slipping from the saddle, he strode toward them, stopping beside Faolan, who dropped to his knee. "You've done well, my wolf, thank you."

"King Neriwyn? The King of Telmia?" Aeyren sounded strained, and Eirian winked at him. "I didn't believe you had an alliance with Telmia."

Noticing the surrounding foliage, Eirian debated cutting the flow of her magic and decided against it. She wanted them to deal with the constant reminder.

"Why would we lie about our alliance?"

Chuckling, Neriwyn closed the distance between them. "Queen Eirian Altira, it's wonderful to meet you. You don't know how long I've waited for this moment."

"Oh, I have a fair idea. I'm going to say about a thousand years."

Her eyes met his, the familiarity striking her again, and Eirian let him lift her hand, placing a kiss on the back. Feeling an agonizing jolt at his touch, she flinched when memories tugged at her. The shadows lingering at the edge of her vision twisted.

"Something like that." Turning to Aeyren, he arched a brow in amusement. "You're meeting with the queen of Endara, and you couldn't bring yourself to dismount?"

General Tomas said, "That's correct."

It felt like the temperature dropped, and Neriwyn let Eirian's hand go to move toward the Athnaralans. Their horses skittered, and she felt the wrap of magic around them.

"And you think you're superior to the Altira mage? She, who is first among all humans? What do they teach you these days?"

Watching them struggle to control their horses, Eirian commented, "Your Majesty, you can't blame them for not knowing what the Altira mage is."

"Indeed."

Amused, Neriwyn glanced at her, and the magic faded, allowing them to regain control of their mounts. Making moves to recover their discussion, Eirian addressed Aeyren.

"We don't have to end things negatively. I remain open to negotiations between Athnaral and Endara. We need not enter a war you can't win."

Aeyren's eyes narrowed, and he replied, "There will be no peace."

"Keep your eyes on the horizon, little human, because over seven thousand of my people are about to appear. Have you ever fought against the daoine? No, of course, you haven't. No one has, not since the last Altira mage." Neriwyn pointed at Eirian. "Her ancestor ended the mage wars and defeated the darkness. You're familiar with her. She whispers sweet nothings so very well, and the stench of her is thick on you."

Aeyren shook his head with a sneer, but those watching him closely saw a flicker of something in his eyes. "You withdrew for generations and now think you can prance among us and issue threats? Return to your isolation, King Neriwyn, and let us deal with each other."

"Don't be mistaken, little human. I've missed nothing. I know many things people would keep secret. I even know the truth behind your family, General Tomas," Neriwyn said.

"You know nothing," Tomas snarled.

Lifting his hand, Neriwyn flexed his magic, and the vast field of greenery that Eirian had grown died. Her breath caught in her throat at the display.

"Queen Eirian is not the only person here who can wipe out large quantities of people with little effort. If our combined forces aren't enough to make you agree to negotiate, then perhaps you need reminding of what happens when you come against magic like ours."

One of Aeyren's advisers quickly declared, "King Aeyren will withdraw to consider negotiation. I'm sure we can find something to make everyone happy."

"That's all we ask," Everett answered. "Our kingdoms have enjoyed a sort of peace for many years. We wish for that to continue and have no desire for war."

"As do we." The nameless man cast a silencing glare at Tomas.

Eirian nodded. "Go, consider your options. I want our kingdoms to be friends."

Regarding her with distaste, Aeyren looked like the words were turning sour in his throat. "I'll consider my options."

Watching the Athnaralans return to their camp, the Endarans and their ally remained silent. Tomas lingered a moment, his glare settling on Aiden.

"I've not forgotten you, bastard. You will die on my blade."

Aiden chuckled, "You first, General."

Spitting at him, Tomas wheeled about and kicked his horse into a canter. Sighing, Eirian rubbed her face and withdrew her magic to cut off the growth. Then, turning to Aiden, she jabbed his chest in annoyance.

"Do not aggravate that man."

"I'm not letting you have all the fun, ma'am," he responded in amusement.

Shaking his head, Marcellus bowed to Neriwyn. "I'm sure this wasn't how you expected your first meeting to go, Your Majesty. I apologize for the way our queen handled things."

Laughing, Neriwyn grinned, and it reminded Eirian of Celiaen. "I can't accept your apologies, Duke Raellwynt, because, as I recall, I hardly helped matters. You waste your breath trying to negotiate peace when they're firmly under the grasp of the darkness."

"He speaks the truth," Eirian said. "We have much to discuss."

"Indeed, we do, more than you realize."

He met her eyes, taking in the hint of accusation that lingered in them. Grunting, Cameron turned in his saddle to look where the Telmian forces were due to appear.

"We need to accommodate your troops."

"I'll have my commanders liaise with you and your officers as to the best place to set camp. It is a great deal of work to situate so many." Offering Eirian his arm, Neriwyn waved at the three hooded figures. "However, I believe introductions are due."

Curious, she let him lead her toward them, and her people followed a few steps behind. Faolan grabbed Aiden briefly and leaned his head in with a worried look.

"I couldn't have prevented this. You mustn't let your feelings impede your duty."

"What do you mean, wolf?" Aiden's eyes narrowed.

Faolan cast a sad look at Eirian, murmuring, "She's about to reunite with a friend."

Seeing Neriwyn approaching, the riders dismounted and walked to meet them halfway. Eirian felt the prickle of familiar magic, and it drew her gaze to the figure on the left. Pushing their hoods back, they allowed everyone to see them. A man as dark as Tharen was light dominated the trio. Everything about him suggested danger. On his right, a woman with short coppery red hair wore a broad, disarming smile. The last man had familiar golden curls and smooth confidence Eirian recognized instantly.

"Gal!" she screamed his name and dropped Neriwyn's arm, breaking into a run.

Galameyvin laughed, catching Eirian to swing her around in the air. She wrapped her arms around his neck and kissed him, with no regard for the people watching them. When it ended, he buried his nose in her hair, feeling like he was home as he inhaled the scent of flowers.

"I wasn't expecting you to be this happy to see me, Ree."

Confused, her nobles exchanged looks before Marcellus asked, "Who is that?"

Understanding what Faolan had tried to warn him about, Aiden crossed his arms and put on a blank face. "I believe that's Prince Galameyvin, nephew to King Paienven."

"That's him?" Everett questioned.

Marcellus demanded, "You knew?"

"Only a little and fairly recently."

Brushing hair away from her face, Galameyvin studied the lines of stress that were apparent around her eyes. Seeing Eirian had confirmed how much he had missed her, but she was not the same woman he had said goodbye to in Riane.

"Congratulations. I wish I could've been there, but my uncle had other plans for me."

Reminded of what Celiaen had done, Eirian pushed her anger down before it could dampen her happiness. "Telmia has always interested you, so I know this appointment would've been a dream come true. So many things have happened."

"I know, and we'll have time later to tell each other everything, but right now, people are growing impatient."

Taking hold of her arm, Galameyvin turned Eirian to face her people and Neriwyn. There was a mixture of opinions on the faces of the Endaran nobles, and she regretted her excited greeting. Not daring to look at her guards, she focused on Neriwyn and the two newcomers flanking him, with Faolan hovering close by. They were heavily armed, and Faolan looked worried, but she could not ask why.

"I'm glad I insisted they wait until after the Athnaralans departed," Neriwyn chuckled, eyes glittering with mischief. "I thought you might appreciate this gift. Just remember he's mine until his king says otherwise."

"Thank you."

Bowing her head in genuine appreciation, Eirian turned her focus to the dark lord beside Neriwyn. His power was familiar, and she wondered if they had crossed paths previously. He met her gaze, smiling slowly, and it reminded her of a predator. Galameyvin cleared his throat as a distraction, allowing her to look at the dukes. Everett was curious, but Marcellus had his arms crossed and a look of anger as he flickered his gaze between his queen and the prince behind her.

"My lords, General, may I introduce Prince Galameyvin of Ensaycal. Emissary to Telmia, and probably the primary reason I didn't get myself killed growing up. Gal, these fine men are my dukes, Everett and Marcellus, and General Cameron, commander of the Endaran army."

Turning to Neriwyn, she waved to show she was waiting for him. Mischief faded into seriousness, and Neriwyn turned to the man beside him first.

"Lord Vartan, my right hand and most trusted advisor, and the Lady Healwen."

Vartan reached forward and caught Eirian's hand, bowing his head over it to murmur, "My Queen, it's been a long time."

Eyes wide, she glanced at Faolan and hoped he had told Neriwyn that her blood status was a secret. Like when Neriwyn had touched her, Eirian felt a jolt at Vartan's grasp.

"It's an honor to have such a renowned warrior among us, Lord Vartan."

"And it's my honor to serve you in this battle." Releasing her hand, he nodded to the nobles. "General, I believe we need to discuss encampment?"

Nodding, Cameron replied, "Of course, straight to business. I respect that."

"It helps that daylight is not on our side."

"Your Majesties, if you'll excuse us?"

She nodded, telling him, "Of course, he's right. There's not much light left."

As they spoke, the first lines of Telmian soldiers appeared in the distance. Eirian took them in and wondered how she would keep her secret. Meeting Everett's stare, she knew the same question was on his mind. It occurred to her to re-evaluate her plan before things unraveled. A calm settled over Eirian, and Galameyvin brushed his fingertips against the small of her back. It was a subtle reminder that he could read her moods as easily as a book. She welcomed his power, letting it soothe her.

"If you let us know how many are in your immediate party, sire, we'll do what we can to find rooms for you in the keep," Gallagher said.

Neriwyn shook his head. "No need. I'll remain with my people. Faolan and his companions may choose to join us. It's their decision."

Bowing, Faolan glanced between Eirian and Neriwyn, conflict showing on his face. Trying to take control of the gathering, Marcellus lifted a hand and pointed at the town.

"I recommend we reconvene inside the keep. Your Majesties have both had long rides today, and refreshments wouldn't go amiss."

"Of course, Your Grace, that's a marvelous idea. I think it's safe for Lady Brenna and the rest to join us," Eirian said with a smile.

Staring at the Athnaralan camp, Neriwyn murmured, "That would be wise. The darkness is unhappy with my arrival, and I fear what she may do."

Those on horseback turned first and headed into the town. Most people were quick to hoist themselves into the saddle and follow, but Eirian did not move. The daoine, her guards, and the dukes remained with her. Sighing, she glanced at Galameyvin over her shoulder and shrugged, walking toward Halcyon. Then, halting before she covered the distance, she squared her shoulders and turned around.

"Your Graces, please continue without me. King Neriwyn, may I speak with His Highness?"

"Eirian, this is not the place," Everett said, giving her a knowing look.

"I'm only asking for a moment to speak to him. My guards will be right there. Please, show His Majesty around Kelsby, and I'll join you shortly."

Clapping a hand to Galameyvin's shoulder, Neriwyn chuckled, "A moment."

Waiting until they were as alone as Aiden would allow, Eirian ran a nervous hand through her hair and smiled at the man she had loved for so many years. "I missed you."

Ignoring the murderous glare directed his way, Galameyvin cupped her face gently. He wanted to show her how much he had missed her.

"I know, Ree. I missed you too. I heard what happened with Celi."

"You did? I suppose I'm not surprised." Closing her eyes, Eirian welcomed the familiar influence of his power. "Did you know?"

"Of course, everyone did. I always thought you knew, but I gather it was a complete surprise. Celi loves you, Ree, completely and maddeningly."

"He wants to give up his right to the throne and remain in Riane."

Shrugging, Galameyvin said, "He's been talking about it for decades."

"He spoke the truth," she mused. "I wasn't sure I believed him."

"Eirian, we cannot go back to the way things were."

Rubbing his thumbs over her cheeks, Galameyvin glanced at the staring guards. Nodding slowly, Eirian smiled sadly, leaning into him. Her magic was calm, the whispers silent like they always were when he was there.

"I know, but not for the reasons you think."

"You're the queen of Endara now. What other reasons could there be?"

She kissed him softly, taking her time. Eirian did not care if her guards saw when they had already witnessed the previous one. She just wanted to feel his lips against hers.

"More than a few, and I'll catch you up. Now, before my captain loses his mind, we had best join everyone else."

Catching her hand, Galameyvin stopped her from leaving. "You need to be careful of King Neriwyn. He's more powerful than he lets on, and there's something about him."

"I know. My instincts tell me I should trust Neriwyn as far as I can throw him," Eirian replied, winking at him.

"I dread to ask what you've been up to."

Looking out over the battlefield of flowers, her brown eyes darkened, and Galameyvin sensed the grief. He recognized the taste of it, and that was all he needed to know.

"Best not to then. I've heard enough about it to not want to hear you scolding me."

"Don't turn your back on Lord Vartan either."

Giving him a knowing look, she said, "Come on, my guards are getting agitated. I'm not in the mood for my captain yelling at me today."

TWENTY-THREE

Leaning against the rooftop wall, Eirian stared at the Athnaralan camp and mulled over what might happen. Even with the Telmian forces, she expected Aeyren to push for battle. Messengers from the south reported his legions continued to attack despite being defeated.

"Eirian?"

Aiden crossed over and leaned against the wall with his arms crossed and eyes locked on the door. It had been a rough few days, and he knew Eirian had little chance to stop.

"You're worried. You know you can talk to me."

Glancing sideways at him, Eirian chuckled, "I've got a king determined to wage war on my kingdom. There's over seven thousand daoine camped alongside a similar number of my people. Plus, elven troops are on their way. Am I worried? Damn right, I'm worried."

"I'm worried about you. Tell me what I can do to make you feel better."

Her jaw dropped in surprise, and Eirian turned to face him as she murmured, "Why, Captain, what a rare offer. Normally you'd rather try to beat my worries out in training."

He did not smile. "I know, but that's not what you need. Right now, no one else is around, just me, and I'd never think poorly of you for feeling. You can trust me."

"Aiden," she huffed and tilted her head back in frustration. "Neriwyn is on his way up, and I'd appreciate it if you and your men were on the other side of the door while we talk."

"Are you sure that's a good idea?"

Shrugging, Eirian returned to staring at the enemy. "No, frankly, I'm not, and I don't trust him. But I want answers."

"Your mother." Realizing exactly what answers she was after, Aiden nodded. "I'll make sure you're undisturbed."

"By the way, Aiden, if you thought I missed your bout of jealousy yesterday."

Glancing at him, Eirian smirked when he bristled at her comment. Pushing away from the wall, Aiden could not resist crowding in and running a hand down her side. They had not been alone on the roof since the day in the rain, and he wanted to remind her.

"How did it make you feel?"

"King Neriwyn is almost here."

"And your point is?"

Rolling her eyes, Eirian slipped from his grasp and tutted, "Captain, you've got a job to do."

Scoffing at her scolding tone, Aiden made his way to the door. "As you command, ma'am."

Neriwyn was leaning against the wall when he pulled the door open, staring blankly at the guards lingering on various steps. They looked uncomfortable, and a glance further down told him why. Vartan perched on a ledge with a leg swinging back and forth while playing with a knife, threatening energy oozing from him. Despite the charming smile Neriwyn wore, Aiden understood he was by far the most threatening person they had come across. More dangerous than Eirian. It made him uncomfortable to let Neriwyn have time alone with her.

"Her Majesty is ready for you."

Stepping up to Aiden, Neriwyn put a hand on his shoulder. "Don't worry, Captain, your queen is perfectly safe. I'd never harm her. You don't know how precious she is."

Bowing, Aiden replied, "She doesn't enjoy waiting."

"No, I imagine she doesn't."

Chuckling, he slipped through the door. Turning around at the sound of footsteps, Eirian took in Neriwyn. He bore no weapons. Instead, he wore a deep green tunic, a leather vest instead of armor, and a long black coat embroidered with an intricate pattern of swirls. The sun caught his hair, giving it an almost blue sheen and reminding her of Celiaen. He grinned, and she felt the urge to smile back. But, staring at him, Eirian felt the familiar whisper of memories she could not touch begging for recollection.

"Good morning, Your Majesty," she said, leaning against the wall.

Cocking his head to the side, Neriwyn looked at the camp in the distance. "Have you come to any conclusions?"

"Aeyren won't stop, not until he's dead, or I've locked the darkness away."

"Unfortunately, you're right. I understand you learned the truth of what the darkness is. Faolan accused me of manipulating my people."

Eirian took a deep breath and let it out slowly, counting the beats silently to quash her desire to echo the accusation. "It seems like a strange thing to forget."

"I didn't deny the charge. It's better if Faolan believes it was me. You, however, I'll tell the truth because you must know. The manipulation was not my choice, nor was it my action, though I complied with it."

There was a seriousness in his expression that had Eirian straighten and run a hand over her hair. Intensifying, the whispers told her Neriwyn spoke the truth.

"There was only one person who could perform such a feat."

"Your wife?" she asked.

"Your mother."

Going still, Eirian stared at him. Her mind whirled, but no words could come to her. Neriwyn stared back, waiting for the initial confusion and shock to wear off. Pacing, she wrung her hands and attempted to organize her mind so she could continue the conversation. Talking was the last thing Eirian felt like doing. She wanted to scream and tear at him, to demand he take it back.

"My mother was the queen of Telmia?"

Neriwyn said, "Among other things."

Biting her lip, Eirian closed her eyes. Pressing at her mind, the whispers urged her to believe him, and she wished they would be silent.

"I don't understand how my mother could be the queen of Telmia."

"Because she had to be."

"Had to be?"

Leaning against the wall, Neriwyn watched her pace and hated the lies he was telling. "She had a vision after the last war that told her the darkness would return. Another told her we could defeat it by combining the bloodlines. For years, she searched for answers, guided by her visions, until she had a plan. It took more years for her to put that plan into motion."

"And you let her?"

"No one ever let your mother do anything. She was life. I didn't want her to do it, admittedly for selfish reasons, but my desires don't matter when the fate of the world is at stake. Should I have stopped her and doomed us all?"

Closing her eyes, Eirian sighed. "She knew she'd die. You knew."

"Yes."

"Why did she make your people forget the darkness is a god?"

He had practiced the lie enough that Neriwyn almost had himself convinced it was the truth. "She thought it was better they believed the gods left. It was easy to make history for humans and elves. The cycle of life and death manipulates the truth with time."

"The amount of power it would've taken to do what she did... I don't understand how I could be more powerful than she was. Why would she sacrifice her life to have me?" Eirian asked, trying to imagine how powerful her mother had been.

Arching a brow, Neriwyn chuckled, "It's understandable you doubt yourself. You aren't less powerful, but your perception limits you. We don't intend for you to defeat the darkness alone."

"My perception? I don't think my perception changes what I'm capable of. I mean, I certainly couldn't manipulate the memories of an entire race!" she said, voice rising.

"Have you ever tried?"

"No, of course not!"

Smiling at her mockingly, he replied, "Then how would you know?"

Opening her mouth to respond, Eirian stopped and sighed. Everything he was saying only made her hate her power more. The shadows flickered at the edge of her vision, whispers telling her that Neriwyn was speaking in half-truths.

"You're right. How would I know? And before you ask, I won't try."

"Why would I? You don't need to do it, unlike her. Everything she did was for life."

"I cannot help but resent her. For what she did to my father, her people, me. If she knew so much, she would've known the position this would put me in. Did she know I would lose my father to madness?" Angry, Eirian pointed at him, snarling, "After she died, you could've come to my father! You could've told me the truth!"

His smile faded to grief, and Neriwyn murmured, "I could have, yes. But do you think your father would have wanted to talk to me? I was created for her, and we were together for eternity. Your father loved her, but he was not me, and he knew it."

"I'm a bastard. I have even less right to the throne than I thought."

"No, by your laws, you're legitimate. I'm surprised that's where your mind went."

Glancing at the sky, she studied the clouds. "It seemed the less distressing route to go. My father never stopped grieving her death. I'm sure you can appreciate it."

Walking over to her, Neriwyn touched the side of Eirian's face gently. He felt her agony and the conflict tearing at her. It made him want to tell her the whole truth. Closing his eyes, he considered the options and weighed up if sticking to the plan was the best choice.

"Letting Shianeni go so you may be born and knowing she would give her life to you... nothing has ever hurt so much. When she passed, the pain was..." He sighed, saying, "I wanted to let the bond take me, but I couldn't. I know I have a part to play, and your brother didn't need to lose both of his parents."

"I have a brother," Eirian whispered, covering her mouth.

"Yes, you do, and he looks forward to meeting you. Emlyn could not be the brother he wanted to be while you grew up. It took all of his love for life to leave you, but he has always watched from afar. He loves you dearly and has done so since before you were born."

The thought was enough to make Eirian crumple, covering her face while she sucked in shaky breaths. Moving to offer her comfort, it surprised Neriwyn when she shoved him away, her magic a swirl around them. Her mind lingered on how different things would have been if she had known the truth, and her rage sparked. Letting her hands drop to her sides, Eirian clenched her fists and growled.

"How dare she play with our lives like that! I have mourned the mother I never knew for as long as I can remember, but she doesn't deserve my grief. How could she do what she has done to her children?"

"Don't think she did it lightly! Shianeni was life, and she couldn't deny you a chance to live. Nor could she deny the chance of life to countless others who would never be born if you weren't. All those people who'd die if you never lived. Would you not do the same if presented with such a reality?" His voice rose, a hint of anger in it.

"I…" Frustration and despair kept her frozen in place, words lodged in her throat.

Reaching out, Neriwyn put a hand on her shoulder. "It's the truth. You're her daughter, and you always choose your duty to life first. You're more than you know."

"And did she know I'd die to fulfill this duty? I know what the cost is to stop the darkness."

Shaking off his hand, Eirian glanced at him over her shoulder, and he saw tears in her eyes. Her rage remained, but the whispers in her mind told her she could not fight him.

"What a sorry state of affairs."

"It may seem that way right now, little Queen, but I believe you'll see things differently soon."

Eirian slumped, sighing. "Yes, given time, I might feel differently, but right now? It's my right to feel angry, and hurt, and disappointed. I'm allowed to feel it toward her, toward you, and toward whoever else was complicit in the whole fucking situation."

"I encourage you to feel. Feeling is good. It means you're alive," Neriwyn said.

"How do I defeat her? You said the bloodlines need to combine."

"That I don't know. All I can surmise is the solution somewhere within you, and it's up to you to find it. As for combining the bloodlines? You've taken the first steps."

"The bond."

"Yes."

Nodding, Neriwyn felt her rage rekindle, and stepped back in surprise. Clenching her fists, Eirian recalled the events surrounding the bond being forged.

"Has nothing in my life been by chance? Have you planned my every step?"

"Eirian—"

"No! Damn it, no! Just no! I don't know what you expected, but I know this conversation could've gone differently. You could've broken the news to me in a kinder way, prepared me for it, given me some background. Anything but like this."

Lifting a hand, Eirian pointed an accusing finger at him. Her magic crackled through the air, and Neriwyn wondered if she knew she was glowing. Briefly, he saw a shadow of Shianeni, his heart clenching with grief. He picked the threads of stolen Altira magic woven through the power Eirian had gained from her mother. The contrasting elements blended so completely, it took his breath away. Dropping to a knee, Neriwyn knelt, and she faltered.

"What are you doing?" Staring at his bowed head, Eirian lowered her finger and felt foolish as she asked, "Why are you kneeling?"

Lifting his face to gaze at her, Neriwyn smiled sadly. "I kneel because you are life, and you're glorious. I kneel because one day you'll be the greatest of us all, and I kneel because I want to."

The magic fizzled out as Eirian turned away and walked over to the wall. Staring at the growing camp, she ran a hand over her forehead and sighed.

"I'm not my mother."

"No, you aren't. Your mother was many things, and I'll never stop loving her, but she made mistakes. Her mistakes aren't yours."

"You say I'm not her as though it is a weakness."

Remaining on one knee, Neriwyn looked at the sky and let himself enjoy the warmth from the sun. While her rage had died, the twist of her magic remained, and he wanted to bask in it.

"That wasn't my intention. You don't want to be. A lot depends on you being better. Now, you need some time alone, even if you haven't said it out loud."

It was hard for Eirian to resist laughing at the obviousness of his statement. "Some time? That's an underestimation! I could have years and still feel the way I do right now."

"You'll always have whatever help I can give. I understand how you feel, never forget that. Some Telmians are likely to consider you their queen should they discover your mother was Shianeni." Pushing up, Neriwyn took a moment to steady himself. "It should remain a secret. I understand why you don't want people to know."

"Thank you."

"I'll leave you to your peace."

Striding to the door, Neriwyn did not bother to bid her farewell. He knew she did not want to hear it. Vartan was still sitting on his perch and tormenting the guards in the corridor. The only one of them who looked unbothered was Aiden, his attention focused on the door. Neriwyn paused beside him, glancing out of the corner of his eye to watch his focus shift.

"If you value your life, I wouldn't go out there. I know you think you have a way with her, but right now, she has no desire to see anyone."

Aiden said, "What did you say? We felt her fury."

"I only told her the answers she sought."

Waving at the men, Vartan grinned. "That was fun. We should do it again."

Once they were far enough away from the royal guards, Neriwyn paused and glanced over his shoulder, telling Vartan, "I've sent for the Prince."

"She took the news that well?"

"Eirian has her mother's temper, and you remember what that was like."

"Oh, yes, I remember it well," he chuckled.

Aiden was unsure how long he had waited at the door, hoping for a sign it was safe when he felt calm spreading through him. Turning, he watched his men relax as Galameyvin casually strolled up the stairs with his hands clasped behind his back and a disarming smile. They could not resist his power. Arching a brow at Aiden, Galameyvin's smile faded.

"She's out there?"

"Yes," Aiden replied, looking at the door fondly.

Staring at him, Galameyvin realized the truth and muttered, "Figures."

Pushing past, he nudged the door open and took a glance at the rooftop before slipping through. Eirian had her back to him, but Galameyvin knew she was aware of his presence. Slamming the door, he pressed a hand to it and cast wards to keep anyone from disturbing them. He did not push his power toward her. He simply stood watching and waiting for her to turn.

"I know what you're doing, Gal."

"And what is that?"

"You want me to acknowledge my feelings and welcome your influence. You don't enjoy trying to force it on me, even when you've felt it necessary."

Nodding, he wandered the edge of the roof, gazing out at the view. "True, I suppose it's because it's easy for me. Almost as easily as you make everything grow."

"There's a reason they say you're the most powerful blue alive. It's why you were Celi's blue."

Feeling him step around her, Eirian turned in expectation of him stopping. But Galameyvin continued exploring.

"No, I was his blue because, well, family. If things had come around in a different order, the council would've assigned me to you. Speaking of, I haven't met your blues yet."

Pursing her lips, she said, "They didn't assign any. You could say they hope things go drastically wrong and I'm forced to return to Riane. They want me to be the grand mage."

"Ah, that," he muttered in frustration.

"So much has happened, Gal. So much has changed in a short amount of time."

Galameyvin chuckled, "Well, yes, of course it has. For a start, you're a queen now. Did you think things would always be the same?"

"I liked things the way they were. At least I was happy sometimes. Now I'm perpetually anxious. I'm facing a war because of an ancient enemy, and the fate of the world is on my shoulders. I barely sleep."

Huffing, Eirian slid down the wall and sat with her back pressed to the warm stone. She stared at the sky, and Galameyvin felt the swirl of her emotions. Biting the inside of his cheek, he pushed away his concerns and reminded himself he was with her again.

"Not to point out the obvious, but it would seem the fate of the world has always been on your shoulders. The difference is now you know." Walking over, he sat beside Eirian and poked her arm, asking, "Isn't it better to know?"

She gave him a look that made his smile fade. Galameyvin had seen the gleam in her eyes before, and he wanted to chase it away, but he sensed the shields Eirian had erected to keep him out.

"You'd think so, wouldn't you?"

"What is it, Ree?"

"I don't know where to start."

"Try the beginning. That's the logical place."

Resting her head against the wall, Eirian gazed at the sky and counted tufts of cloud, whispering, "Would the beginning be before I was born or?"

Shaking his head, Galameyvin was not sure how to answer. "Okay, wherever you think you should start, go from there."

"My father was going mad before I left Riane, and they thought it was a good idea to keep it a secret from me. And then, because I barely knew him, I didn't see the signs."

"Like you said, you barely knew him. How could you realize there was anything wrong? I doubt anyone thinks poorly of you for not realizing. However, that doesn't stop you from thinking poorly of yourself. You've always been one for feeling guilt when the guilt is not yours to feel."

Nudging him with her shoulder, Eirian said, "That's occurred to me."

Grinning, he nudged her back. "I know, but sometimes you need reminding."

"Baenlin tried to convince me to return to Riane. They sent him to offer me the grand mage position. I made a deal with him, but I think it's moot now."

Cringing, Galameyvin whistled. "What sort of deal?"

"Oh, the sort where if I'm not the queen of Endara, I have to return to Riane. If I try to do anything else, go anywhere else, he gets to come and fetch me."

"You are very fetching. I always enjoy fetching you." Winking, he asked, "Why do you feel the deal is moot now?"

Taking a deep breath, Eirian questioned what she should tell him first. She figured either option was likely to shock him.

"Because I'm fairly certain the battle with the darkness will kill me and because my mother was the queen of Telmia."

Puffing his cheeks out, Galameyvin held his breath while her words sunk in, and he contemplated which revelation to respond to first. Then, deciding to follow her lead, he reached over and grabbed her hand, squeezing it tightly.

"You've never feared giving your life to the right cause. Life matters the most to you, not yours, but everyone else. When you aren't shielding your magic, you shed life everywhere you go. You breathe energy into those around you. I think it's pretty telling about what your purpose is. Unfortunately, there is always a cost, and someone always has to pay."

"Wow." She blinked, murmuring, "Are you saying I'm okay with dying so long as I win?"

"Yes, Eirian, and you know you are. You're always the first to dive into a fight, the first to defend others. You give your energy to those who need it even when you have none to spare. If it needs the surrender of your life to ensure that the rest of us survive, you'll do it."

Deflated, she drew up her knees and wrapped her arms around them. "You're right."

"Then what's bothering you about it?"

"I wish I wasn't this person, and that I didn't put everyone else first. I wish I could free Celi from our bond because I don't want to drag him down with me."

Lips thinning at the reminder about their bond, Galameyvin said, "I understand. Perhaps not quite the same, but I have my share of things I wish were different. Celi loves you, he always has done, and if you thought for a second that he wouldn't be by your side fighting until the end, then you'd be wrong."

Turning to stare at him, she laid her head on her knees. Galameyvin gazed at the tumbling brown hair he longed to bury his hands in. It was thick and wild, reminding him of the growth Eirian could cause.

"If you've known all along that he loves me, why did you let me into your bed?"

"I'm only a man, Ree, and I saw the same things he did. You're incredible. How could we not love you? Not to mention the man on the other side of the door is also very much in love with you."

"You know Aiden loves me?"

He shrugged, muttering, "You sure pick them. He's as possessive as Celi."

Eirian chuckled, "You have no idea. They hate each other."

"I wouldn't be so sure about that. You and Celi share the same type."

"I love you, Gal. When he told me he'd gotten his father to send you to Telmia, I was so furious I told him I couldn't forgive him. I thought I'd never see you again, and I'd never get to tell you how I felt, and I regretted it."

"Ree—"

Lifting a hand from her leg, she waved it to silence him. Galameyvin arched a brow in amusement, content to let her carry on for the moment.

"No, Gal, please, let me finish. Someone recently pointed out that I have a type, and perhaps the reason I love you is that you're not like them. You are my calm in the storm."

"Ree—"

"And I do need that. I need the calm you give me. You soothe the constant conflict I feel, you give me peace, and I crave it. It's easier said than done to stop feeling for someone, but I've been trying to put it into perspective. You're my friend, a confidant, a lover, a rock to cling to when the landslide threatens to sweep me away, but—"

"Eirian Altira!" His voice was stern, and she stopped speaking, allowing him to say, "I've always known you love me. And you're right, you crave what I give you, but you also crave what Celi gives you. Remember, you're two sides of a coin, and those sides need different things to balance them. One day, when you're older, you'll figure out how to calm the constant swirl of conflict that wants to create and destroy. I think when that happens, you'll be the scariest damn mage alive."

Smiling faintly, she asked, "When did you get so wise, Gal?"

Leaning against her, Galameyvin rested his head on her shoulder, muttering, "I've always been wise. You're just too stubborn."

"I love you."

"I love you too, but you also love Celi."

"Yes, I do, but long before either of us were born, the powers bound Celi and me. Maybe I've always known we never had a choice, and that made me rail against it."

Lifting her head from her knees, Eirian bumped it against him. Then, frowning, he moved away to peer at her in confusion.

"Come again?"

Spreading her hands nonchalantly, Eirian said, "You never believed us when we said the bond wasn't on purpose. We didn't choose it. It was our fate. I wonder if it had to be Celi or if it were an accident of birth that determined which one of your family it would be."

"I think I'm missing a key piece of information here, and I suspect I need to direct the conversation to the matter of your mother."

"Good point. So, I found out my mother was a duine. Father knew because she told him things. They married, and I was born. She made him promise to keep it hidden. Nolan knew before I was born that I'd be a mage. They knew she'd die. During his madness, he mistook me for her and revealed the truth. Celi was the only person I told."

Taking a deep breath, Eirian closed her eyes and shook her head. Her mind was strangely silent. The whispers faded beneath the conflicting swirl of her thoughts.

"When we got here and engaged with the Athnaralans, I pulled power from the daoine without their permission, and I had to reveal the truth to Faolan. I told Aiden and Everett because I don't have a right to the throne."

He pursed his lips thoughtfully. "I see. The daoine don't share power, and you taking it from them would've been a great shock."

The comment made her laugh bitterly. "Not as great a shock as it was for my people to see me kill hundreds and turn them into husks."

"I heard. There are some among the Telmians who can do it, it's considered a dangerous gift, and they encourage those with it to become healers and nurturers."

"Which is understandable. I've always meant it when I've said it's the other side of my ability to give life. Not my red skills. They're different." Stretching her legs, Eirian crossed them at the ankle and sighed.

"Did your father know who he married?"

Mulling over Galameyvin's question, Eirian recounted her conversation with Neriwyn. "I suspect he did. Shianeni would've needed to convince him to go through with it. But, despite the reasons she came to him, Nolan loved her."

Shifting away from the wall, Galameyvin turned to face her and crossed his legs. "Eirian, from what little I've learned about her, Queen Shianeni was a very charismatic woman. Her people loved her dearly. I don't know how much of it was her magic. But, knowing you are her child, I think some of it was her power. You have a way of attracting people to you."

"She was a manipulative woman who made her entire people forget what the darkness is. I also suspect she made them accept her absence. I mean, why would anyone just let their queen go missing without turning over every rock and leaf to find her?"

"I admit I found it strange none of them knew when she left. They're very hazy on the subject, and Neriwyn forbids discussion about it. You realize many would suggest you have a more legitimate claim to the Telmian throne than Neriwyn."

Scowling, Eirian shook her head. "I don't understand why. I have an older brother."

"Telmia is matrilineal." Galameyvin shrugged, waving at her as he said, "As the daughter of Queen Shianeni, they could rank you higher than her son."

"I barely want to be queen of Endara. I certainly wouldn't want to be the queen of Telmia. But to the point, she specifically chose my father because of who he was."

"Well, she could hardly marry and have a child with your aunts." His flippant comment earned him an awkward kick. "Sorry, Ree, but it's true. You're the combination of the Altira and Malfaer bloodlines... oh."

Eirian stared at Galameyvin as he slumped. "What?"

"Celi is the heir of the Kaetiel line. So perhaps it's not you who has to fight. What if our assumptions are wrong?"

"You're suggesting I'm supposed to have a child with Celi, and our child is the one who'll fight the darkness?"

"It makes sense to me."

"That would suggest we're going to lose this war, and the darkness will spread over the lands until said child grows up."

Nodding, Galameyvin looked pensive, murmuring, "Sometimes hope only comes at the darkest point when all seems lost."

Holding up a finger, Eirian screwed up her face. "There is just one problem I would like to point out."

"Yes?"

"I'd have to have sex with Celi and conceive."

Snorting, Galameyvin gave her a look that was a mixture of amusement and mocking. "I fail to see the issue. The last time I checked, you both have the necessary parts. Unless something has changed recently. I mean, I could imagine Celi cutting off his balls in a fight."

Fighting to keep a straight face, Eirian covered her mouth and giggled, "Really, Gal?"

Taking advantage of her mirth, he reached forward and tickled her as best he could despite the armor she wore. "Yep, really."

Laughing, she wriggled away from him and said breathlessly, "What have I told you about tickling?"

"When have I ever done what you tell me?" Galameyvin asked, wriggling his brows.

"In all seriousness, Gal, I don't know what to do."

Shifting his legs around, he considered her statement. "Yes, you do. You always know what to do, but you never like to admit it. You think it makes you look better if you pretend to need time, advice, and other people's suggestions."

"I don't think that!"

"Don't be argumentative. You know exactly what I'm talking about. What I'm trying to say is in this fight, you already know what you have to do."

Leaning against the wall, Eirian stared at the sky, whispering, "My life has never been my own. My thoughts and decisions were determined by absentee creators who left their mess for us to deal with."

"Absentee creators, I like that." He nodded in agreement. "But how is the darkness their mess?"

"Because the darkness is a god."

Galameyvin rubbed his face, sighing. "Of course it is. However, if there is still one god here, then what about the others? And how do you destroy a god?"

Going with the first thought that came to her, Eirian kept watching the sky. "Only a god can destroy a god."

"Were you told that or?"

"The gut instinct you told me to listen to."

"That would explain why the bloodlines needed to come together. They say they're the descendants of the first three people created by the gods. The templates for the three races and the first they gave magic. I'd say that's pretty significant." Glancing at the door, he said, "They want you."

Dropping her shields, Eirian let his power sweep away the feelings of anger, betrayal, and grief she had clung to since her conversation with Neriwyn. "I know, and all I want is to shut out the world and lay here with you."

Scrambling to his feet, Galameyvin stretched to chase the stiffness from his joints before he offered his hand to Eirian. "We can't. I don't want to confuse you any further."

Gripping his hand tightly, she let him hoist her up, and the contact helped his magic soothe her. "I can't pick between you. You and Celi make two sides of a coin."

Feeling her love through his magic, Galameyvin did not let go of her hand as she stepped in close, murmuring, "I suppose we are."

"Maybe it's supposed to be that way."

Lifting her free hand, Eirian stroked the side of his face gently and brushed the hair from his eyes. She wanted to cling to Galameyvin and let his kisses chase the world from her mind. He could make her forget.

"Maybe it's why we always found it so comfortable to be together."

Groaning, Galameyvin turned his face into her hand and kissed her palm. It was clear what she wanted, desire rippling through her magic.

"Ree."

Maintaining a tight grip on her hand, Galameyvin snaked his around her waist and pulled Eirian against him. Their magic swirled comfortably around them, so completely familiar with each other that her power did nothing to keep him from her mind. Happiness bubbled through her. She did not know if it was her emotion or his, but she did not care.

Reaching up to kiss him, Eirian buried her hand in his hair. Pulling back, Galameyvin opened his mouth to say something when the sound of horns filled the air. Their focus shifted, and she realized her bond with Celiaen was pulling her. He was calling, and she felt his desperation. Letting go, Galameyvin did his best to look neutral, but he could not stop the flicker of frustration he felt.

Moving to the edge of the roof, he looked out. "Negotiations are about to get serious."

"Celiaen has arrived."

"He certainly has perfect timing."

Crinkling her nose, Eirian chuckled, "Yes, I was about to change your mind."

Arching his brows, Galameyvin replied, "Well, you were going to try."

Twenty-Four

"They're in the hall," Fionn said when they came through the door.

"Thank you for controlling your magic," Aiden grumbled at Galameyvin.

Nodding, Galameyvin apologized, "I'm sorry. It's a habit when around warriors. But, don't worry, I do it to Ree as well. It makes her cranky, and I find it amusing."

Scowling, Eirian started down. "If they're already waiting, let's not make them wait any longer than necessary."

Once Galameyvin had withdrawn his magic, all of Eirian's anxiety came flooding back. The anger she had let him banish was simmering below the surface, encouraged by the whispers. The guards cleared out of her way before looking at the two men. Shrugging, Galameyvin moved to follow, but Aiden blocked him. A simple look had the other men scrambling down the steps. Cocking his head to the side, he waited patiently for Aiden to speak. He knew where the conversation was going from the emotions surrounding Aiden.

"I don't know all the details, and I don't care, but if this little triangle between you, Eirian, and Celiaen endangers her…" Aiden's voice trailed off, leaving the threat unsaid.

"Ah," Galameyvin chuckled. "I wouldn't describe it as a triangle. But tell me, Captain, where do you factor yourself in it?"

Swallowing, Aiden muttered, "I don't know what—"

"No need to play coy, Captain. I'm a blue. Not just any blue, but the one Ree lets in. I know exactly what you feel for her, and she for you, for Celi, for me. Before concerning yourself with what risk we pose, consider what risk you do."

"I've met other blues, and they're not like you."

Smiling darkly, Galameyvin said, "No, they're not. You've never met a blue like me."

Torn between reaching for a blade and a desire to avoid Galameyvin's influence, Aiden bit the inside of his cheek. "I thought Soren was a terrifying prick."

"Yet compared to Ree, I'm a kitten." Starting down the stairs, he snapped his fingers. "Well, come on. Don't you want to protect your queen from my cousin?"

Following several steps behind, Aiden admitted, "I know about the bond."

"Interesting. Who told you?"

"Celiaen did. They had an argument, and Eirian said she regretted it."

Cursing himself, Aiden tried to stop telling him what had happened. Mouth curling in a smirk, Galameyvin cast a glance over his shoulder. He could feel Aiden's attempts to resist.

"Oh, I'm sorry, Captain, just a little longer. What else do you think I need to know?"

"She's under orders to marry him if it looks like Paienven will withdraw support."

It was worse than Eirian's bloodlust, and Aiden could not push past the influence. There was a strength to his attempts at resisting the compulsion that had Galameyvin curious. It reminded him of Eirian.

"And who are you?"

Swallowing, Aiden answered, "My father was the Earl of Tamantal. Duke Everett is my half-brother. I knew Eirian as a child."

Galameyvin withdrew his power, laughing, and Aiden was glad the compulsion had ceased. Remaining silent as they circled their way down the stairs, he was quick to slip past when they reached the ground level. His men and Eirian were out of sight, driving his need to catch up with them. He wanted to be there before Galameyvin, to see the look on Celiaen's face when he arrived.

Endaran nobles and officers crowded one side of the chamber, while Neriwyn and his closest had the other. Everett and Marcellus stood at the head of the room, heads bowed as they talked to Eirian and General Cameron. Heavily armored elves dominated the remaining space. Celiaen was at the front with his arms crossed and at an angle to watch the main doors.

Aiden was not the only one looking forward to the two princes' reunion. Eirian knew when Galameyvin appeared, and Aiden watched her face as Celiaen turned to face him. He could tell it worried her, but she did not stop speaking. Anger was apparent for a moment before Celiaen forced a smile in greeting. Looking over his shoulder as he hurried to join his men, Aiden took in the amusement on Galameyvin's face. Saluting Eirian, Aiden flicked a glance at Gabe, taking in the delighted smirk he wore.

"Cousin." Galameyvin extended a hand to Celiaen. "It's good to see you."

Taking the offered hand, Celiaen searched the blue eyes that reminded him of his father. "I hope you've enjoyed your time in Telmia."

Catching a hint in Celiaen's stare, Galameyvin knew he had something he needed to tell him. "We can swap stories with wine and fair company."

"I'll bring the company." Celiaen did not need to say it aloud to know he understood.

"I'll bring the wine."

Eirian spoke loudly, "Welcome, Prince Celiaen. I hear you bring gifts and reinforcements."

Looking at the officers lined up, Galameyvin swallowed when he saw who Paienven had sent. General Darragh looked bored, a disinterested stare directed at Eirian. He knew the general would not have accompanied Celiaen unless his master had special orders he wanted seen to. When Paienven had dirty work that needed doing, Darragh was the man who did it.

"Indeed, Your Majesty, we picked up some strays," Celiaen replied.

Gabe shifted, his delight obvious, and Aiden realized what was going on. The elves had prisoners. Watching the set of Eirian's shoulders, he suspected what was on her mind, and a quick look at the princes told him they knew as well.

Nodding, Eirian said, "I presume you've something in mind to make them talk. Your army should force Aeyren onto the back foot, but I doubt he'll agree to peace."

"Then we wipe them out." Darragh glanced at the Telmians. "We outnumber them. So, let's get on with it."

Taking a deep breath, Eirian forced herself to keep a friendly tone. "While I appreciate the suggestion and acknowledge you're right, I'm not willing to sacrifice so many lives."

"General Darragh."

"I know who you are, General, and it's wonderful to have another experienced tactician here to give informed advice. Especially one so highly regarded by his king."

Recognizing the suspicion in her eyes, Celiaen wanted to divert the conversation. "We'll have the prisoners placed in the holding cells."

Shooting a silencing glare at Celiaen, Darragh stepped forward with a hand on a hilt. "My informed advice is to wipe them out. They're continuing to attack up and down your borders, and the only way to stop it is to cut the head off the snake. You want to save lives? Then give the fucking order."

Lips pursing, Eirian knew all eyes were on her and held up a hand to keep her advisers quiet. "I appreciate the suggestion, but we're not there yet. Aeyren isn't the problem. He's merely a puppet of our real enemy."

"Cut the strings."

"Not yet."

"Ma'am, he has a point," Cameron murmured.

Eirian took a deep breath and glanced at Neriwyn, who was subtly shaking his head. "I said no. What I want you to do, General Darragh, is stand where the Athnaralans can see you and look pretty."

Darragh looked her over with a trace of amusement. "I don't stand anywhere and look pretty."

"Fine then. Prince Celiaen can stand there and look pretty while you pull his strings. Because that's why you're here, isn't it? I know exactly who you are." Her tone continued to be friendly, but those who knew Eirian well knew it was a tone intended to threaten.

"Come now, Your Majesty, we're all friends," he said, chuckling. "How would you apologize to King Paienven if his eldest son ended up dead?"

Eirian said sweetly, "I know his other children, and it wouldn't be a drastic loss."

Groaning, Celiaen pinched the bridge of his nose, and Galameyvin snorted.

The sweet tone faded, and Eirian continued, "Don't presume you can come here and give me orders masked as suggestions. Because let me tell you now, no one gives me orders."

There was a pause as everyone waited for Darragh to respond. Nodding in appreciation, he stepped back beside Celiaen and clapped a hand to his shoulder, squeezing tightly.

"I see why people compare her to your mother. Fine, have it your way, Queen Eirian. However, I've orders from my king to do what is needed to safeguard Endara."

"If it comes to it, then do what you must." Glancing at the crowd, she sighed. "Have your prisoners secured, and I'll meet with you. I want to hear your news, Your Highness."

Arching a brow, Celiaen said, "I have a lot of news. Once we're settled, we'll talk."

Waving at Vartan, Eirian pointed at Darragh. "Lord Vartan, you may wish to coordinate a meeting with General Darragh and General Cameron."

"As my queen commands." Vartan bowed, and she gave him a contemplative look.

Clearing his throat, Cameron stepped forward. "I'll supervise the transfer of the strays. If you'd excuse me, ma'am, I'll go with the general."

"Of course, Cameron, please make sure they're tended to."

"I'll get you caught up on our dealings so far," Cameron said to Darragh.

Saluting Celiaen, Darragh gave Eirian a calculative look before following Cameron. Splitting away from Neriwyn, Vartan prowled after them. Her eyes followed him while Eirian wondered how much of the truth he knew. Then, catching Celiaen's gaze, she nodded, and he returned the gesture.

The Ensaycalan party filed out, Galameyvin lingering. He was torn between going with Celiaen and staying in the hall. Shooting looks between Celiaen and Neriwyn, he waited for a signal that he could go. Neriwyn lifted two fingers, and Eirian watched relief cross his face before he turned, negotiating his way through the lines.

While she waited for the elves to be out of earshot, Eirian studied the light filtering through the top windows behind her. The windows were small, but they illuminated enough to draw her attention to carvings in the ceiling.

"What are you looking at?" Everett peered upward, his brow creasing with concentration. "Oh, aren't they pretty?"

Marcellus followed suit, saying, "I hadn't noticed them."

Chuckling, Eirian rolled her neck and felt it pinch. Some carvings were familiar. They stirred the shadows at the edge of her mind, leaving her unsettled.

"They're an oddity. I'm not sure why I haven't noticed previously."

"Why would anyone carve knotwork into the ceiling?" Everett asked.

"It's not just knotwork. Look, that symbol there. It's the quaternary knot. There's only one place I've seen it other than in books," Eirian said.

Her gaze dropped to Gabe, and he shrugged, mouth twisting in amusement. Seeing them made Eirian determined to remember to ask him about it. Squinting, she pointed at several spots where it looked like the work was a distinct style.

"I'd be curious to know how much they've changed over the years."

Everett stated, "You're stalling."

Giving him a somber look, Eirian glanced around the hall before murmuring, "Regarding those strays. I'd like to be there when they're questioned."

"Are you sure that's what you want?" Eyes flickering sideways, Marcellus recalled the reports from her hunting trip.

"No!" Everett declared, "You're the queen! Queens don't interrogate people."

Biting her lip, Eirian said, "I'm effective."

"Technically, they're Ensaycal's prisoners, so you'd need to convince Prince Celiaen and his general to let you anywhere near them. And speaking of the general, I take it you know something about him?" Marcellus crossed his arms.

"I know what I've been told. Darragh is uncompromisingly loyal to his master. If he's here, then Paienven and Celiaen didn't see eye to eye. He'd have orders to keep the Prince in line and doing what his father wants him to do."

"Is he dangerous?"

"Absolutely. Celiaen has no authority over him. However, I have a plan that may win me a shred of respect. He's a red, and there's only one way to determine the pecking order for reds," she told them, touching a hand to the hilt of one of her swords.

Rolling his eyes, Everett sighed heavily. "Is that a good idea? He's far more experienced than you. If you lost—"

"I won't lose, and I might make it interesting."

"How so?" Marcellus asked.

"If I win, I get to interrogate the prisoners."

Unable to resist chuckling, Marcellus clapped a hand to her shoulder. "That's how you expect to get us to agree. Well, I know you can floor me in a heartbeat, so I'll reluctantly give my permission to avoid the embarrassment."

Reminded of his single attempt to spar with her, Eirian gave him an apologetic look. "I only go easy on one person."

Behind her, Aiden muttered, "Keep telling yourself that, ma'am."

She was about to respond to him when a little voice squealed her name and Ona came skipping toward her. Aiden smirked, thankful for the timing.

"I thought you were with Isabella and Brenna?" Eirian asked, ruffling Ona's hair.

Wrapping her arms around Eirian's legs, Ona giggled, "I gave them the slip."

Pursing her lips, Eirian bit back a snicker because she knew her guards were listening. "Now, Ona, what have I told you about giving people the slip?"

"Don't get caught, and don't tell anyone."

"That sounds right!" Laughing, Marcellus looked for Brenna. "If that's what you're teaching this child, perhaps we should be thankful you don't want any of your own."

Offering a hand to Ona, Eirian winked. "I'm teaching her valuable life lessons. Come on, Ona, let's go watch the elves. Perhaps we'll find someone you know."

Watching her walk out of the hall hand in hand with Ona, Everett commented, "It's only been a few days, but it feels like the girl is good for her."

"I'll try to keep her away from General Darragh," Aiden replied.

"Aiden, is she okay?"

"Honestly? I don't know. She was in private audiences with King Neriwyn and Prince Galameyvin before the Ensaycalan legion arrived."

Hearing the unspoken words, Everett glanced at Aiden with a frown. "Send for me tonight."

"The two of you are keeping secrets from me, Everett, and I'm letting you, but if they endanger Endara, I won't be forgiving," Marcellus said in warning. "Right now, I'm trusting you have the best interests of the kingdom in mind. Don't make me question that trust."

"As soon as I feel it's no longer in everyone's best interest, I'll tell you."

Saluting the two dukes, Aiden hurried after his men. Eirian was meandering along and pointing things out to Ona. Soldiers saluted as she passed, earning smiles from the queen they worshipped. He found it amazing how proud they reacted to receiving a brief look and smile. The town was busy, an increasing mix of humans, elves, and daoine roaming the grounds. In the sky, multiple daoine circled in their bird forms, the keen eyes of the raptors able to see further. Word of the stalemate had spread, and many townsfolk had risked returning. They did what they could to assist the army defending Kelsby.

"Ma'am, where are you planning to go?" Aiden asked.

Directing a slight smile at him, Eirian pointed her chin to the open gate and the spreading sea of tents. "I'm going to admire our superior numbers. Enjoy the sunshine, the smell of thousands of people gathered in rustic facilities. Perhaps play a trick or two."

Excited, Ona squealed, "Can you make the flowers dance?"

"Maybe, I'll think about it."

Squeezing the little hand, Eirian kept walking. Peering up at her, Ona gave her a wide-eyed look that earned a chuckle.

"Please?"

Catching her other hand, Aiden swung the skinny limb into the air. "Stick that bottom lip out a little further, chicken, and she might give in."

Letting her legs give out, Ona forced the two adults to catch her weight, and Aiden winked at Eirian, prompting them to swing her up. Laughing, Ona grinned happily, swinging between them. The gate loomed, and Eirian's gaze settled on the crowd. Turning at the sound of the child's laughter, the generals and their officers watched the Queen of Endara approaching.

Celiaen was with them, and the sight of her with a young girl surprised him. He had seen Eirian with children before. The older novices were required to work with the youngest, and he had seen her as a reluctant teacher, terrified of the children she had no clue how to deal with. Beside him, Galameyvin chuckled softly and prodded his side.

"It's a surprising sight, isn't it?"

"Who is the child?" he asked quietly.

"Her ward," General Cameron answered, a hand gripping the hilt of his sword as he glanced at Celiaen. "Her Majesty rescued her after her family died in an attack by the darkness. She'll remain until such a time as we can reunite her with what remains of her family."

Remaining shocked, Celiaen shook his head. "I never thought I'd see the day Eirian Altira would take a child under her care."

"Your Highnesses, Generals, fancy finding you here," Eirian said.

She let Ona have one last swing before gesturing for her to be still. Darragh regarded her thoughtfully, eyes darting to Ona briefly and taking in the curve of her ears.

"You knew exactly where we were."

Eirian batted her eye. "Of course I did. I was feigning surprise for their sake."

Waving at her guards, Eirian ignored their looks in return.

"What can we do for you, Your Majesty?" Vartan inquired, his dark eyes studying the lay of the land before him.

Crouching in front of Ona, Eirian brushed her unruly hair away from her face and smiled. Raising a brow, Celiaen looked at Aiden questioningly, and he shrugged.

"Now, chicken, I'm going to talk to these good men, so you need to be quiet and listen."

Nodding, Ona stopped smiling and pulled her version of a fierce look. "Yes, Ree."

"That's my good girl." Standing, Eirian returned her focus to the amused men. "Now, it's the minor matter of those strays you picked up, Celi."

Celiaen shook his head, replying, "I know what you're thinking, Ree, and we have people who are very skilled at doing it. It's part of their job."

"You want to question them?" Darragh laughed. "I'm tempted to agree so I can watch a little girl like you try to get information out of a seasoned officer."

Groaning, Galameyvin recognized the delight in Eirian's. "That didn't come out the way he intended it to, Eirian."

Lifting a hand in his direction, Eirian clicked her tongue in a scolding manner and shook her head slowly at Darragh. He had said exactly what she wanted.

"Oh, no, it came out exactly how he intended it. So, how about we make a bet?"

Arching a brow, Darragh crossed his arms and stared at her challengingly. "You have my interest. What are your terms?"

"One round in the square, and if I win, I get to play with your prisoners."

"And if I win?"

"Then we'll attack the Athnaralans."

"Hand to hand or with weapons?"

"Eirian, don't do this," Celiaen pleaded, taking a step toward her.

Pursing her lips, Eirian shrugged. "Both sets. Luckily, we have sweet little Prince Galameyvin here to check my influence."

"You have a bet. I'm looking forward to proving the stories about you wrong."

Uncrossing his arms, Darragh offered her a hand, and Eirian grasped it with a grin. Then, letting a trickle of her power creep over him with a wink, she nodded at the camp.

"Oh, they're certainly stories. It's hard to express the truth accurately."

Celiaen held up a hand and growled, "As your Crown Prince, I forbid this course of action, General Darragh."

Fearful gazes flickered between Celiaen and Darragh as Eirian let go of his hand and stepped back. Chuckling, she nodded to Vartan and Cameron, the Telmian watching the exchange with disinterest. Behind her, the royal guards looked dumbfounded, Aiden holding onto Ona's hand with a blank look. Shrugging, she turned and walked toward the camp, power trailing her.

The newly arrived elven officers watched her go, flowers bursting into bloom as she moved. None of them had seen such a display before. Following, the guards were careful to avoid stepping on the flowers, but Ona kept stopping to pick the ones that caught her eye. Her tiny fingers worked at weaving them together, slowly crafting a wreath.

"Gal, would you talk sense into that bloody woman while I deal with the general?" Celiaen shot Galameyvin a look that sent him hurrying after Eirian. "General Darragh, she's taunting you. You don't know what she's capable of."

Confident, Darragh laughed, "Boy, she's cockier than you, but I answer to your father and not you, so there's nothing you can say to stop me from teaching her a lesson."

Stepping up to Darragh, he sneered. "And you call her cocky. I'm going to enjoy watching her wipe the floor with you. You'd better hope she's learned some restraint because I've seen what's left of those she questions, and it's rarely as pretty as the flowers she's throwing around for your amusement."

"I don't suggest you keep her waiting, General," Vartan commented and started after Eirian and her guards.

Keeping stride with her, Galameyvin kept his power in check. "Ree, what do you think you'll gain from this?"

"Respect."

"As a warrior or as a queen? Because they're not the same thing to him. Darragh serves my uncle and no one else, not even my father."

"I don't need his respect as a queen or as a warrior, but I want to question those prisoners. To do that, I need him to respect that I'm not—"

"Not what? A delicate woman? Intimidated by a little pain? But, Ree, I've seen you when you use those abilities. It's, by far, the darkest part of you. Do you want to open yourself to it right now?"

"He has a point," Aiden grumbled.

She felt the watchful stares of the soldiers bustling around the camp. The magic whispered in her mind, dragging tendrils of rage to the surface.

"You don't get to comment, Captain. As for your concerns, Gal, I'm more than capable of protecting myself."

"As the closest thing you have to a blue, and considering how you were feeling just a little while ago, I have to disagree. You don't get to take your frustration out on prisoners," Galameyvin said.

Clamping down on her desire to fight with him, Eirian resumed walking toward the nearest training square. Galameyvin knew what it meant when she did not answer. Feeling Celiaen's anger approaching, he rubbed his face and waited, curious about what had set him off. Spotting Vartan first, he nodded, and Vartan glanced him over as he passed. It was near impossible to miss Eirian's progress toward the training area, off-duty soldiers making their way alongside, hoping to see their queen in action.

When Celiaen reached him, he asked, "Celi, what's wrong?"

Stomping past, Celiaen muttered, "He's as bad as her. I'm going to enjoy watching Darragh get his ass handed to him."

"What did he say?"

"That he was going to teach her a lesson."

Falling silent for a moment as he walked, Galameyvin looked at the sky and sighed. "We need to talk, but by we, I mean all three of us."

"You have no idea, Gal, no idea at all." The response was so quietly spoken that Galameyvin nearly did not hear it. "She can fight him today, can't she?"

"She has a lot of rage. I was with Ree when you arrived. She let me calm her for a while. We had better hope he doesn't push her, or we may need to stop her from killing him."

"I hate to say it, but killing him may be in our favor."

Eirian stood in the middle of the marked-out square while unbuckling her belt. Beside her, Ona eagerly held the weapons. She watched in fascination as Eirian unlaced and pulled the leather jerkin over her head. Guards exchanged banter with the growing crowd of soldiers surrounding the square. Aiden was silent and hovering, waiting to take the armor. Galameyvin's breath caught at the sight of her standing there, full of confidence.

The mail haubergeon Aiden had commissioned was no longer hidden beneath the leather. Pulling the mail over her head, Eirian dumped it in his arms and left herself with no armor. Taking the belt and weapons from Ona, she secured them around her waist. Sunlight caught her hair as she unwrapped a leather cord from around her left bracer, and spotting the two elves, Eirian smiled slowly. Crouching, she allowed Ona to work her fingers through the tresses, coaxing them into a messy braid and tying it off with the cord.

"She's changing," Celiaen said sadly, and Galameyvin glanced at him.

"We all change as we need to, and she certainly has a need. By the way, where's Tara and the others?"

"Setting up camp."

The rest of the Ensaycalan group arrived, Darragh strutting into the square with confidence vibrating through his magic. He did not make a move to shed any of his armor. Shooing Ona and Aiden away, Eirian stood opposite him, completely relaxed, her confidence showing through. Rather than joining his men, Aiden approached the two princes with a furious gleam in his eyes.

"I hope you two can stop this nonsense."

Shaking his head, Celiaen replied, "We can intervene. Galameyvin is more than capable of stopping the general."

"That's not the answer I wanted," he muttered, turning back to the square. "Bloody manipulative woman, she set this entire thing up."

Checking her weapons, Eirian crinkled her nose at Darragh. "Standard rules?"

"Of course. First blood?"

"Not this time."

His eyes gleamed, and he purred, "You're keen for a lesson."

"Oh, don't worry, General. I won't go easy on you."

Bowing, Eirian stepped back and turned to the watching Endarans, lifting her hands. All focus settled on her, the soldiers keen to hear her words.

"What do you say? Shall I help this general understand why he should fear Endara?"

Cheers rose, and the elves looked around in surprise. Glancing at Celiaen, Aiden shrugged. If the circumstances had been slightly different, he would have enjoyed the expression on Celiaen's face.

"It's become a thing for her to make rounds of various training areas and work with the soldiers."

"Earning their respect," Celiaen said.

"Maintaining it. She earned it when she slaughtered hundreds of Athnaralans on the battlefield. But there's now a greater number of people here who didn't witness it and only have the stories to go off," he explained.

Celiaen choked, "She did what now?"

Unimpressed by Eirian's words and the response of the audience, Darragh remained in his spot, taunting, "It's not too late to change your mind, little girl."

Drawing her blades, Eirian lifted the hilts and bowed, touching the pommels to her forehead. "Likewise, General. Remember, I was the first choice for the next grand mage."

"That means nothing in a fight."

Mimicking her actions, Darragh held his blades with the confidence of hundreds of years of experience. Knowing what they needed to do, the handful of blue mages let their calming influence spread out over the crowd. It was necessary to prevent the soldiers from being affected by the two fighters. Galameyvin kept his magic close, ready to intervene if it looked like the duel was going badly.

They touched blade to blade, saluting each other before beginning. Remaining out of reach, Darragh prowled, watching her move to get a feel for her. She had dropped all of her shields, allowing her magic to fill the air, and Celiaen felt the simmering rage through their bond. Casting a wink in his direction, Eirian's lips curled into a determined smirk as she purposefully dropped her guard.

Seeing her distracted, Darragh went on the offense, hoping to end the fight quickly. He ignored her magic. His control was one reason he had excelled to the point of becoming a general. Before he could land a blow, Eirian moved, delivering a taunting slap to his ass with the flat of her blade. Spinning to locate her, Darragh recoiled in surprise when she met him with a fist to the cheek, and he felt blood.

Laughter rose from the watching Endarans, the soldiers whistling and jeering. Catching sight of Eirian standing a distance away, Darragh proceeded with more caution and the intention not to let her get him a second time. Crouching, she watched him circle with the keen precision of a predator sighting its prey. When he struck, she toyed with him, parrying his blows effortlessly.

The ring of steel rose above the din of the audience, strikes and counterstrikes coming fast thanks to the magic driving the fighters. Waiting for Darragh to think he had her, Eirian dove to the side, hooking a foot around his knee and tumbling him to the ground. Tossing her swords to the side, she landed on his back before he could right himself, driving him face-first into the dirt. Feeling the hand buried in his hair yanking his head back, the prick of a blade on his throat startled Darragh.

Eirian straddled him, leaning down to purr, "Now, what was that about a lesson?"

Grunting, Darragh glared at her from the corners of his eyes, angered by the taunting smirk on her face. "You got lucky, girl."

"You're welcome to try again, but I wouldn't drag it out a second time for your pride," she replied, withdrawing her knife and shoving his face into the dirt before getting off.

Enraged, Darragh rolled over and went for her back. There were shouts of warning, and Eirian sidestepped his forward motion, thrusting her elbow into his face with force. He swore loudly as he hit the dirt a second time, feeling his nose break. Standing above him, twirling the knife in her hand, she sighed.

"You just couldn't stay down, could you?"

Wiping blood from his face, he snarled, "You broke my nose!"

Shrugging, Eirian sheathed her knife and offered a hand. He was lucky that was all she had done. The whispers had wanted his blood.

"Yes, I did, but what did you expect? You should pay attention to the rumors. Hardly any of them are lies."

Giving her hand a dismissive stare, Darragh studied her and saw a hardness he had not expected to see. "So, you can kill dozens without ever lifting a blade?"

"Hundreds. Did you lower the number on purpose or have the stories of my abilities shrunk instead of magnified?"

"I did."

Darragh accepted her hand and winced in pain when his nose started throbbing further. Chuckling, Eirian put a hand on his shoulder and peered closely at his face.

"Sorry, it looks like I caught you with my seal. You've got a bit of an imprint on your cheek. I guess you're mine now."

"Do you put all of your allies through this?" he asked.

"Only the ones who give me a hard time. Though I'm not foolish enough to take on someone I can't defeat, otherwise I'd go a round or two with Lord Vartan. I mightn't be as old as you, General, but I'm not a girl. I'll do whatever it takes to win this war."

Letting her magic swirl around them, Eirian gave him a glimpse of the darkness she hid. Knowing what his orders were, Darragh wondered what Paienven would say if he were in the same position. Doubt filled him, and he glanced at the watching princes.

"I believe you. I underestimated you, ma'am. I won't do that again."

Eirian let go of him and stepped back with a grin. "People constantly underestimate me. It gets tiring. Remember, those prisoners are mine to question."

"I'm looking forward to watching you work."

Picking up his swords, Darragh kept a careful watch as Eirian did the same. Focusing on the crowd, she slid her swords into their scabbards and held her hands high. She felt their energy, and the whispers urged her to give them more.

"I'm sorry that ended so quickly, but I hope you enjoyed it. My thanks to General Darragh for letting me kick his ass for you."

They responded to her words with cheers and whistles. Looking around at the faces watching them, Darragh understood what she was doing and accepted Eirian was far more dangerous than he had given her credit for. The Endarans adored her, and he wondered what they would have done if he had defeated her. Bowing, he turned and strode over to Celiaen.

"Your Highness, I owe you an apology. I shouldn't have dismissed your warning."

Amazed, Celiaen accepted the apology. "That's alright, General. I've trained with her a lot over the years, and I know how she gets."

Lifting a hand to his nose, Darragh glanced at the swords hanging from Celiaen's belt, knowing they were a match for hers. "Well then, perhaps you should see if you can't convince her not to play with the prisoners."

Hearing his words, Eirian laughed, "Oh, General, I think your prince is feeling off his game today. His confidence in being able to knock me down is failing him."

Flicking a look at Galameyvin, Celiaen murmured, "Do I risk it?"

"She's performing for her people, so I wouldn't unless you're confident you can beat her."

Bowing stiffly, Celiaen said, "Your Majesty is correct. I'm feeling a bit off my game today."

"Well then, we'd best let these good people return to their day!" she replied.

Ignoring the shouting crowd, Eirian strode from the square. Surrounding her, the guards kept the soldiers from crowding in. Ona clung to her and, concerned they might injure the girl, Eirian lifted her onto her shoulders. Giggling, Ona waved at people with one hand while clinging to Eirian with the other. Cameron and his officers joined the guards, escorting Eirian through the camp while the elves trailed behind.

Waiting until they were free of the camp, Darragh allowed a healer to tend to his nose and the cuts on his face. Breaking away from Eirian and her guards, Cameron joined him.

"One day, your queen will be something entirely else," Darragh told him.

Chuckling softly, Cameron said, "She's going to unite a divided world. Just look around you, General. She's already done more than anyone could have imagined."

"Who else has brought humans, elves, and daoine together in a thousand years? I hope she doesn't bring us all down in a rain of fire first."

"After one of the recent displays of her power, it wouldn't surprise me if she could rain fire down on us."

"Is it possible to control her?" he asked quietly.

Cameron shrugged and pointed at Celiaen. "There's a chance he could."

"I was afraid you'd say that."

TWENTY-FIVE

Removing the stopper, Galameyvin lifted the flagon to his nose and inhaled the sweet scent of the Telmian wine. He had carefully hoarded several types, his favorite blackberry hidden away for future consumption. Pouring the contents into the two cups, he pushed the stopper back in and turned to look at Celiaen sitting on the rug in the middle of the tent. The Telmian tents were decadent, much like everything had been in Ashendon. Galameyvin suspected it was part of their frivolous guise. Holding out a cup, he waited for Celiaen to take it before he sat, leaning back against a pile of cushions.

"It's potent stuff," he cautioned as Celiaen lifted his cup to take a sip.

"I'd apologize, but I suspect you've enjoyed yourself. Saoirse speaks highly of her time with you."

Chuckling, Galameyvin lifted his cup in a mocking toast. "That I have. Yet, for all your hopes, you didn't achieve what you wanted."

"Are you planning revenge?" Despite the sweetness, the wine left a bitter taste in Celiaen's mouth. "She loves you. All it would take is a word, and I'd be out in the cold again."

"Considering recent information, I believe I'd risk the future of everyone if I did so. But that's not my news to share. You, however, carry a fear that has me concerned. Celi, what has happened?"

Sitting forward, Galameyvin stared into the dark eyes he knew so well. Exhaling heavily, Celiaen tightened his grip on the cup.

"It's Paienven. His ambition has expanded."

"Endara."

"Yes, he has a long-term plan to absorb Endara into Ensaycal, and it starts with this war. First, I convince the nobles there is no other option than for us to marry. Meanwhile, our forces will help people rebuild. They'll provide supplies, protection, encourage them to view us as the answer to all their problems, and demand a union between our kingdoms."

Nodding slowly, Galameyvin saw where he was going. "And you'll be the consort to their queen, the king the young will grow up knowing. He thinks you can take the kingdom when she... dies... offering continuity."

"I'd unite Endara and Ensaycal by being the king of both." Swigging the wine, Celiaen snorted. "It's never going to happen."

"No, it's not, but you cannot tell him."

"You know, don't you? I didn't miss the emphasis you placed on die."

Giving him a knowing look, Celiaen glanced at the tent's entrance, expecting Eirian to materialize. Galameyvin leaned back and stared at the roof, watching the way the flickering flames made the shadows dance.

"That she won't die of old age?"

"She told you?"

"Oh yes, I can tell you all the fine details. I mean, we were busy reuniting, and then you arrived, which interrupted us, but still..."

Grinning, Galameyvin knew he was goading him. Jealously lanced through Celiaen, and he glared into the deep red wine, swirling it carefully.

"Oh, I'm already aware. I felt Ree's happiness and sensed your influence. Congratulations, Gal, how does it feel knowing all you have to do is to appear for her to be yours?"

"Would you believe me if I told you it doesn't feel as good as you think it does?"

"No."

Sipping his wine, Galameyvin sighed. "I suppose you wouldn't. It's Ree, and the powers know how long you've loved her. She loves you too."

"Invoking your privilege as a blue?"

"If it helps you move past your jealousy toward me, then yes. We're bound to the same woman, and for her sake, we need to be a team again." Shaking his head, Galameyvin said seriously, "We can't ask her to choose."

Rubbing his face, Celiaen did not know how to respond. "Why not?"

"Because she can't. Ree needs every bit of strength she can get, and we can't do anything to weaken her. When everything is over, if you want me to, I'll leave, and you can spend the rest of your life wooing her without me."

***

Securing the cloak around her shoulders, Eirian lifted the hood and pulled the wool close. Then, activating the wards worked into the weave of the material, she crept to the door of her chamber. There was only a single squad of her guards on watch. Merle and his men split between the antechamber and the hallway. A pang of guilt hit as she slipped through the door, her magic hiding her actions.

Reassuring herself that she would be back before they noticed her gone, Eirian crept along the wall, keeping a watch on the men sitting at the table. The door was open, and she was thankful she did not need to use more magic. Glancing both ways along the hall, she located the rest of the squad and planned her route. By the time she was past them, the guilt was sitting heavily in her gut, and she considered returning to her chambers.

Face hidden by the shadow of her hood, Eirian dropped her wards and did her best to avoid notice. The late hour meant there were very few people patrolling the halls. Gazes slid past, assuming she was another officer making her way to her post. She could almost taste the freedom when she reached the keep's lowest level and kept a tight grip on the cloak.

"I hoped you wouldn't do this, Eirian."

Peeling away from the wall where he had waited, Aiden blocked her path. Startled, Eirian stared at his boots before lifting her face to meet his disappointed gaze.

"Fancy meeting you here, Captain."

Disappointment morphed into fury, and Aiden shoved her back, snarling. "You promised no more sneaking out! But here you are, slipping out of the keep without your guards. For what? Which prince are you sneaking out to visit?"

"I was planning on meeting both," she replied, letting go of the cloak to ball her fists.

His lip curled into a sneer. "I wouldn't have guessed you liked it like that going from how the Crown Prince carried on."

Eyes narrowing, Eirian stepped up to him and tilted her head back. "Throw whatever insults you fancy at me, but I need to talk to them. I've been keeping my promise, but now I need to break it."

"No, you don't." His voice was low, an attempt to avoid attracting attention. "You're so fucking predictable. I watched you all evening, and I thought to myself, she's going to give us the slip tonight. I knew you'd break your promise to me. After everything!"

Magic swirled around her, and Eirian trusted her abilities enough to let the hood fall back from her face, growling, "Don't you dare! You don't know how guilty I feel."

"Feeling guilt would suggest you know it's wrong. So why are you doing it?"

"Because there are things I need to tell Celi." Glancing away, Eirian felt him shift to prepare for a blow she had no intention of delivering. "And I need to forget all of this for a little while. I want to sit with my friends, drink wine, make jokes, and pretend nothing has changed."

Aiden took in the pleading look on her face and relaxed some tension in his stance. "I understand, but I can't let you do it. It's my job to protect you, Eirian."

"I'm sorry, Aiden."

"Your apology won't change my mind about dragging you back to your quarters. I should have tripled your guard."

Clicking her tongue, Eirian said, "I wasn't apologizing for sneaking out. I was apologizing for what I'm about to do to you."

She grabbed his arms and leaned in to kiss him. Surprised, Aiden pushed her away when he felt her power rush through him. Keeping her grip tight, Eirian pressed him against the wall and drew a trickle of energy from him. Overcome with drowsiness, Aiden realized what was happening and stared at her in shock over the betrayal.

"Eiri—"

Stroking his face gently, Eirian guided him to the ground, murmuring, "Hush, Aiden, you're going to have a little sleep. Don't worry. You can scream at me in the morning."

Crouching, Eirian sighed and propped Aiden against the wall. Working wards, she ensured no one would find him, knowing his embarrassment if they did would do further damage to their relationship. The guilt returned as she stood and looked at him, mixing in with the regret that it would be unlikely he would trust her again.

Lifting the hood back over her head, Eirian turned and resumed her path. The town was dark, the only light coming from torches along the wall. Squads of soldiers patrolled the streets, and she did her best to maintain the appearance of being one of them. Stars blanketed the sky, but Eirian did not spare them a glance. She felt where Celiaen was, the bond calling.

Skirting the edge of the camps, she listened to the laughter of the soldiers gathered at campfires and the faint thrum of music. Magic was thick in the air as she crossed into the Telmian camp, the sound of music louder than it had been among the humans. The tents were different. Even in the faint light, she could tell there was an opulence to them.

Gritting her teeth, Eirian shook her head and followed the pull. She strode the pathways that wove through the sea of tents, carefully avoiding ropes and wandering daoine. Occasionally, a stranger sauntered toward her, confidence fading the moment they caught a flash of her power. When she located the two elves, she stopped outside a tent and looked around curiously.

Lingering, she wondered if the princes knew she was there. She sensed a haziness through the bond and suspected they were drinking. The faint murmur of voices within had her ears straining to make out their conversation. Looking up, Eirian drew peace from the spill of stars, admiring them while taking deep breaths of the cool night air.

Hearing laughter inside, she decided it was time. Parting the canvas, Eirian slipped into the flickering shadows of the tent and turned to secure the fasteners that kept the door shut. Pushing the hood from her head, she moved to face the two men sprawled out on a pile of cushions, cups in hand, and a leather flagon on the floor between them.

Grinning at her wide-eyed expression, Celiaen took a sip from his cup and winked at Galameyvin. "I told you she was outside."

"No, I'm pretty sure I told you."

"Nope, I told you. I could feel her. Bond and all that."

Crossing her arms, Eirian glared, demanding, "How much have you had to drink? I hoped to talk."

"We're sober enough." Celiaen held his cup in her direction and patted the cushions. "You'll like this. It's very sweet."

Galameyvin chuckled, "She does like sweet things."

"Well, aren't you two all friendly with each other again?" she muttered, not moving.

Rolling his eyes, Celiaen drained his cup and laid back. "Make yourself useful, Ree. There's bread and cheese on the table."

"I could go with something to eat," Galameyvin said in agreement.

Sighing, Eirian uncrossed her arms and undid her cloak. Bundling the garment up, she dumped it on the chest and made her way to the table. Celiaen had spoken correctly. A tray with half a loaf of bread and a wedge of cheese was the only thing occupying the surface. Picking it up, she passed it to Galameyvin and sat on the edge of his bed. Pouting, Celiaen grabbed the bread and broke a chunk off.

"Take off your weapons, Ree. Relax and have some wine. Unless you ask, we won't bite... you're welcome to ask, I won't say no."

Studying her, Galameyvin asked, "What's wrong? Something is bothering you, and it isn't us."

"I wouldn't exclude you from what's bothering me, Gal," she replied shortly.

"So, share with us. That's why you're here, isn't it? You knew where Celi was and that he'd be with me."

Annoyed by the hint of condescension in his words, Eirian's lip curled. "I'm here to talk to my friends because I missed them and thought they had missed me. But you know what I did to come and see you? I gave my guards the slip when I'd promised not to."

Giving her an amused look, Celiaen finished the bit of bread he had broken off. "If you don't stay too long, you can get back to your cage without them ever knowing. I promise I won't tell. Can't say I expected the captain to have put his leash on you."

"Aiden knew I'd do it, and he was waiting for me when I got to the main doors. I left him sleeping soundly in a nook, and when I collect him, I'll pay for my choice. There's no way he's going to forgive me, let alone trust me again." Pointing at them, she said, "You two had better be bloody sober enough for this fucking conversation."

"He matters a great deal to you, doesn't he?" Galameyvin turned his gaze to Celiaen, saying, "He loves her."

Nodding, Eirian tugged at a loose strand of hair that hung down the side of her face. As much as she did not want to say it, she had to be honest with them.

"I know he loves me, and he'd do anything to protect me. Aiden is a good man. I find myself perpetually surrounded by good men who believe they love me. Present company included. He knows I'm half-duine, and he doesn't care."

"How did he find out about your duine heritage?" Celiaen asked angrily, picking up the container of wine and ripping the stopper out to top up their cups.

"I told him. During the battle, I pulled power from the daoine. My actions understandably caused upset and confusion. I had to tell Aiden and Everett. Honestly, I felt I owed it to them. I know they're always going to be on my side." Her words had the two elves sharing looks.

"I haven't told Celi," Galameyvin said gently. "This is news for him."

Exhaling, Eirian stretched her legs in front of her and shifted uncomfortably. She felt Celiaen staring and knew she had to tell him about her mother before they went any further.

"King Neriwyn told me who my mother was this morning. To say it was a shock would be an understatement. She was Shianeni Malfaer, the Queen of the Telmia."

"Well, fuck." Peering into his cup, he huffed. "How much wine do you have hidden away, Gal? Because this isn't enough."

"I'm not letting you drink all my wine."

"Is that all you have to say?" Eirian asked.

Cocking his head to the side, Celiaen blinked. "What else am I supposed to say? You just answered every question anyone could ever have about your powers. It explains everything."

"I was planned a long time ago. Our bond was no accident, either. There was no way to avoid it except not to have met."

Speaking before Celiaen could, Galameyvin said, "How does that make you feel? I know you've wondered how things would be between you if the bond hadn't happened."

"Shut up, Gal," they snapped simultaneously before sharing a smile, and Eirian chuckled, rubbing her face tiredly.

"I loved you before the bond, Ree, and I'd still love you if we were no longer bound. They couldn't have foreseen that. Being bound to you isn't a burden, and I wouldn't change it," Celiaen said, sitting up and crossing his legs. "Look, I know you don't see the bond the same way, and I expect finding out the powers intended it has only made you detest it further. But we're creatures of duty."

She arched a brow. "You're telling me our bond is part of our duty?"

"Our duty to life itself, I can make the connections. You're the Altira mage.

You're destined to defeat the darkness, but you can't do it without me. The bond must be important for defeating the darkness. Otherwise, why would it exist?" Waving at Galameyvin, Celiaen frowned. "I know he's more powerful than me, but I'm the Kaetiel heir."

"Celi, I've learned a lot recently and have had little time to process it. The darkness is a god. Somehow, I must defeat a god, and I believe it'll cost my life. But I have hope now. Neriwyn survived my mother's death, and they bonded at creation."

Galameyvin grunted and held up a hand. "You hope you can protect Celi from your death. But may I point out a flaw? Your bond is incomplete."

Her eyes narrowed in his direction, and Eirian muttered, "I know."

"I stand by what I said, Ree," Celiaen spoke decisively.

"What are you talking about?" Galameyvin asked.

"Celi won't complete the bond until I stop regretting it and admit I love him and have loved him all along," Eirian explained. "He's romantic. Wants the whole declaration."

Smirking, Galameyvin gave Celiaen a look. "I already broke privilege once."

Pointing at him, Celiaen grumbled, "You think she'll forgive you?"

"I know she'll forgive me." He continued to smirk. "She always forgives me. It's you she gets cranky with."

"What did you say, Gal?" she demanded.

"I told our beloved Celi that you love him."

Angry, Eirian sighed and lay back on the bed, staring at the roof of the tent. "Why are you interfering, Gal?"

His magic flared, calming influence settling over the two warriors. Intoxicated, Celiaen did not fight it, and Eirian considered the consequences of what would happen if she set a drunk red off. Closing her eyes, she took a deep breath and let the calm work through her. With her eyes closed, she picked up the sounds from outside the tent once more, laughter and singing in the distance, bringing a faint smile to her lips.

There were other sounds Eirian did her best to tune out, not wanting her mind to linger on them. Hearing movement, she cracked her eyes open a little and stared at Galameyvin, his hand held out. Swinging a hand to grab him, she pulled herself back into a sitting position.

"Remove your weapons, Ree, and come talk to us. Cry if you need to."

"No more wine."

"For now. Celi has news for you that may make you want to drown your anger in a drink or two," he said.

Pulling Eirian to her feet, Galameyvin clasped her hand while she steadied herself.

"It's going to be a long night, isn't it?"

"As long as you need it to be. Now come and relax. Pretend we're back in Riane." Stroking his thumb across the back of her hand, Galameyvin cooed,

"We're back in Celi's quarters in Zarthein house, talking and laughing."

"I know what you're doing, Gal."

Pushing the image his words conjured in her mind to the back of her thoughts, Eirian pulled her hand from his grip. She unbuckled her belt, carefully bundling the weapons with the leather. Stilling her hands, Galameyvin took the swords and knives from her to place them with Celiaen's.

"Forgive me, Ree. I was trying to help you relax. It's only us, and you have nothing to fear."

Looking from him to Celiaen sitting on the floor, Eirian murmured, "I think I have a lot to fear from you, but that's neither here nor there right now."

"The cushions are rather comfortable, Ree." Returning to the spot he had vacated, Galameyvin picked up his wine. "The Telmians do like their luxury."

"They're not the quick tumble in an alley sort," Celiaen chuckled.

He uncrossed his legs and shuffled out of the way to make room for Eirian to sit with them. Giving Celiaen a dark look, she dropped to her knees and sat, eyeing the cushions like they were a trap.

"We're well aware you're fond of alleys, Celi."

Baring his teeth at her, he said, "Only when I'm frustrated with you."

"Give her your news." Directing the conversation back on track, Galameyvin sniffed at his wine but did not drink.

"My father has rediscovered his ambition. He wants Endara. I have orders to defend your position, destroy Aeyren, and convince your council to overrule you. He wants you surrounded by people who answer to him while your people view us as benevolent saviors."

"Wait—"

Celiaen kept talking. "Then, while we rule side by side for years to come, I'm to make myself the preferred option for continued stability once you die. I'm to capture you without it ever appearing as though you're my captive."

Watching the flicker of rage spark in Eirian's eyes, Celiaen glanced at Galameyvin and took in the way he stiffened as his influence over her faltered. Galameyvin reached for Eirian's hand, knowing she had a harder time resisting him when they were touching.

Galameyvin spoke soothingly to distract her from his actions. "Ree, he has no intention of doing what Paienven ordered."

She thought about pulling away, but meeting Celiaen's worried eyes, she let Galameyvin wrap his influence around her. It was easy to surrender to him.

"That's why he sent Darragh, to make sure you did as ordered. When I abdicate, and he finds out you knew the truth all along... what will he do to you?"

"I hadn't thought that far ahead yet."

"Liar."

Bowing his head, Celiaen replied, "I dread his fury. Perhaps I'll run away before he finds out."

"Your mother is an even greater hunter than Baenlin," Galameyvin commented.

"Yes, but I'm her precious firstborn."

Rubbing her face, Eirian said, "Or he finds out who my mother was, and suddenly his desire to see me controlled by people of his choosing increases. You could have brought yourself some favor and told him about our bond. It would've suited his ambitions."

"I'd never betray you, Ree. Never." Celiaen was adamant. "I told you from the beginning that you could always trust me. Remember the first time we met in the garden on the cliffs. You showed me you could make things grow and die, and I promised you could always trust me."

"What do we do?" she asked. "I suspect you have a plan."

"I do. You say yes to me. We make Darragh think I'm doing as ordered."

"And we do our best to make sure he doesn't find out you knew about my heritage. When the time comes to reveal it, I'd best manage a convincing lie to cover up that some of us have been keeping this secret since shortly after my coronation."

Giving her an amused smile, Galameyvin said, "Your father kept it from well before you were born. If anyone makes too much of a fuss, just tell them that. They can be angry with the man who knew all along and never said a word. The man who married the Telmian queen in the first place and kept her secret."

"He has a good point. Just remind them King Nolan knew and still intended for you to be his heir." Celiaen supported the idea.

"So, I need to behave like you're finally winning me over. I suppose that includes allowing you, and General Darragh, to guide the war efforts." Offering him a wry look, Eirian murmured, "You may have to scold me for making a spectacle of your general."

His lips twitched, and Celiaen fought back a grin. "Yes, I should scold you, but I'd rather reward you for kicking his ass so magnificently."

Arching a brow, Eirian did her best to look mystified. "There's no need for a reward. The pleasure I gained from having his face in the dirt beneath me was ample."

Tightening his grip on her hand, Galameyvin clicked his tongue at them and increased the strength of his influence. "Now, children, none of that when we're supposed to be having a serious conversation. So, if Celi's plan for keeping Darragh happy satisfies you, then we should move on to the bigger topic. How do we defeat a god?"

"A god?" Celiaen took a calm sip of his wine.

"The darkness is a god. We assumed Eirian is the key to defeating it, but maybe it's the two of you together."

"Or three of us," she murmured.

Celiaen's eyes narrowed, and the strength of his jealousy broke through the fog of calmness. "Three of us? You're including Gal?"

"I don't know what he told you when he broke privilege, but I've realized many things recently. I love you. I've always loved you, and the more I thought about what could happen, the more I realized nothing terrifies me as much as the thought of living without you." Looking away, Eirian sighed heavily. "You're a part of me, Celi, but so is Gal. I'm in a constant state of conflict, and it is with both of you I find peace."

"Eirian… I…"

Turning to Galameyvin, Celiaen pleaded with him silently to release them from his influence. Hesitating, Galameyvin let go of her hand and withdrew his power.

"Don't make me regret this, Celi."

Finding a safe spot for his cup, he put it down before scrambling to Eirian. She held her hands up to stop him, but he grabbed her wrists and pulled her into a tight hug. Meeting Galameyvin's eyes over her shoulder, Celiaen inclined his head, signaling him to join them. Wrapping his arms around her from behind, Galameyvin caught the smile appearing on Celiaen's lips.

Stiffening briefly, Eirian closed her eyes and breathed them in. It made her relax, curling into Celiaen's chest while wrapping an arm around each of them. They made her feel safe, as they always had done. Her magic wrapped around them, and she sensed their power mixing like it had so many times in the past. Feeling wetness on her cheeks, Eirian turned her face into Celiaen's shirt to hide her tears.

"I don't know what I'm doing, but I can't do it without you. You give me strength."

"No one ever really knows what they're doing, Ree. Life is all about stumbling along, trying to make the best of our decisions without knowing everything that is to come," Galameyvin told her.

He pulled out of the hug and stroked her hair gently, staring at Celiaen. Nodding in agreement, Celiaen planted a kiss on the top of her head.

"And because Gal said it, we know it's true. We'll face the darkness, and we'll defeat it together. You can always count on us to be there for you, no matter what."

"I fear the only way to defeat the darkness is with my life," she mumbled.

"Then we go down fighting until the end, and we'll make it glorious. The darkness will rue the day it came back."

Rolling his eyes, Galameyvin chuckled, "Such a red thing to say."

"Speak for yourself. I don't recall you ever backing away from a fight. You're half red and probably would've been if you weren't so bloody good at being a blue."

Giggling, Eirian pulled herself away from Celiaen's chest. "I have seen you kill. Your swords aren't decoration."

"And there was that time you started a brawl. Now that was some good fun. Ree ended up with broken ribs, remember?"

Scowling, Galameyvin shook his head. "So, in your wondrously tactical mind, Celiaen, do you have a plan for taking on a god?"

"About that." Tugging Eirian into his lap, Celiaen cupped her face so he could maintain eye contact. "How did you learn the darkness is a god? The gods left. Or so we're taught."

Blinking, she replied, "I had an encounter with an ancestor bound to her grave. The last Altira mage who defeated the darkness. She told me Shianeni helped, but I didn't know at the time she was my mother. There's no killing the darkness. We must lock her away."

Eirian left off the part where she had been told completing the seal had cost her ancestor her life. She hoped Celiaen could not see she was not telling him everything. However, he dashed her hopes when his fingers dug into her cheeks.

"That's why you think you're going to die. It took her death to seal the darkness away. You didn't plan to share that bit of information, did you?"

"No, I thought I'd shared enough for tonight."

"Valiant Eirian, first to fight, first to defend those who can't defend themselves, to pick them up from the ground when they're knocked down. That's why you've spent so much time thinking. You were told the price of defeating the darkness, even if you weren't told how." Closing his eyes, Celiaen sighed.

Galameyvin stretched out to retrieve his cup and the flagon of wine. Removing the stopper, he topped up the contents and pressed it into Eirian's hands, bidding her drink.

"I think it's time you had some of this. He'll just finish it once you leave."

"Who said she was leaving?"

Momentarily petulant, Celiaen let go of her face and wrapped his arms back around Eirian before she could roll out of his lap. Burying his face in her hair, he inhaled the sweet scent of flowers. He did not want to let either of them out of his sight.

"She did. Just a wee matter of her dear captain."

Reminded of Aiden, Eirian lifted the cup to her lips and drank a swig. "I doubt I'll live to see the dawn once I wake Aiden up."

Chuckling, Celiaen tucked a stray lock of hair back behind her ear and encouraged her to take a second swig. "I can sympathize with him."

Grinning, Galameyvin wriggled his fingers at Eirian and asked Celiaen, "Do you think he's discovered how ticklish she is?"

"I should bloody well hope not. Sometimes it took all my control not to skewer her flings when we returned to Riane. Especially Rylee."

Choking on her swig of wine, Eirian glanced between them, wide-eyed. They stared at her, and she wanted to shrink away. Instead, tightening her grip on the cup, she tipped her head back and drained the contents. Plucking it from her hands, Galameyvin shook his head in amusement while Celiaen scoffed.

"You know, we're still no closer to a plan to defeat the darkness than we were when I walked into this tent," Eirian said, feeling the effects of the wine hitting her.

"No, we're not. We don't have enough information. You need to find out what you can from Neriwyn and Vartan. They're the only ones who'd know what Shianeni did to help the last Altira," Galameyvin commented, and glanced at the door contemplatively.

Rubbing his chin, Celiaen asked, "Do you think you could speak to your ancestor again? Knowing what you do now, you could give her those facts and see what she says."

The idea forming in her mind had Eirian feeling like a giddy child. "I could find a horse right now and return to the grave. Come with me, just like we used to, the three of us giving your minders the slip. Tara could compete with Aiden to see who yells the loudest."

"I forgot what a lightweight drinker she is." Peering at the cup he had taken from her, Galameyvin snorted. "Ree, you're not thinking straight. Sneaking off is too dangerous."

"For whom? There's enough magic sitting around that I could probably wipe out all of Aeyren's forces without breaking a sweat."

Not amused by her suggestion, Celiaen grumbled, "I'm not letting you deny me a fight. However, I agree with Gal. You can't just go sneaking off, not even with us. This isn't Riane, and things aren't a game anymore."

"I snuck off to come and see you," she muttered sulkily.

"Yes, and we're glad. The difference is, here, you're surrounded by your soldiers and those of your allies. You're close enough that the bond would alert me should anything happen."

Silent for a moment, Eirian drew her knees up and wrapped her arms around them. "Fine. I won't get a horse and sneak off on my own."

"Another thought occurs to me. We need to know what information they recorded in Riane." Galameyvin bit the inside of his cheek before asking, "Who can we trust to send?"

"Tynan would be our best choice, or maybe Kenna. Tara or Alyse would be better."

Blinking at Celiaen, Eirian realized she had not seen Tynan. "Where is Tynan?"

"He's here, back in our camp. There was no need for him to accompany me tonight. If Gal is at my side while we deal with Athnaral, Tynan will do this task for us."

Eyes gleaming with mischief, she glanced at Galameyvin. "Who said anything about Gal being at your side? You have a blue, I don't. Maybe I'll convince Neriwyn to lend him to me."

"If you think I'm leaving you alone with Gal for extended amounts of time when we're supposed to be courting." Celiaen arched a brow, purring, "Then you'd be mistaken."

"Don't I get a say in this?" Galameyvin asked in amusement.

"Of course." Eirian winked.

Shaking his head, Celiaen disagreed, "No, not at all."

Deciding to settle the discussion, Galameyvin said, "Tynan is the best choice. He knows you well enough to know what is at stake. He's trustworthy. You could ask Tara or Alyse, but I think I can hear their mocking laughter and the sound of Tara's hand connecting with your head. Cai would work, but the council has no respect for them."

Shrugging, Eirian unraveled and scrambled to her feet, feeling her head spin. When it settled, she located her weapons.

"Alright, like you said, he knows a lot already, and I trust him. Ask if he'll do this. I feel there might be something in Amath as well, but I wouldn't know where to look. Tynan might convince Baenlin to get him access, especially if he says I'm going to abdicate and the archmage thinks he's won our deal."

Celiaen got to his feet and stretched. "You'd mislead my uncle for your benefit? If he found out."

"By the time he found out, we may well be dead."

Her response made Galameyvin chuckle, "He'd bring you back to kill you again."

Giving him an amused grin, Eirian picked up her cloak and wrapped it around her shoulders. "I'm counting on it. Good night, Gal, don't let Celi get too drunk."

Following, Celiaen halted her outside, grabbing her hand to murmur, "I'm owed a kiss."

"Are you? That's news to me."

Letting him pull her in, Eirian rocked forward on her feet and slung an arm around his neck, meeting his kiss eagerly. With the wine in her system and the whisper of the bond, she did not want to let Celiaen go. The whispers told her to go back inside with him to Galameyvin and stay the night wrapped in their arms.

Resting his forehead against hers, Celiaen sighed. "Thank you."

"For what?"

"Taking what I said seriously. For reaching some level of acceptance. For a lot of little things that all add up." Kissing her again, he let go and stepped back, saying, "For opening those pretty brown eyes of yours. I love you. Now, go wake up your captain, and take your lecture like a good little queen."

Chuckling, Eirian nodded and pulled the hood over her head. "I love you too. If I don't see you in the morning, assume Aiden has locked me up or killed me."

Turning, she slipped into the darkness and left Celiaen standing outside the tent. A glance at the stars confirmed it was later than Eirian expected, the hours till dawn short. No longer filled with the faint sounds of laughter and music, the camp felt still. A prickle at the back of her neck told her she was being watched. It was not a surprise. She knew the daoine were aware of her presence among them.

Hurrying, Eirian returned to Kelsby, hoping the brisk pace would help clear the fogginess from her mind. The wine had left her feeling warm, a reminder of why she rarely drank more than a sip. Lifting her hand to salute the guards watching over the gate, she joined the squads patrolling the town, keeping her head bowed and hood shadowing her face.

Slipping into the keep, Eirian made her way to the nook where she had left Aiden. Her wards remained in place, and he was unmoved. Leaving them, she melded in and crouched beside Aiden. Putting a hand on his shoulder, she took a deep breath before she fed her magic into him.

His heartbeat sped up as she banished the sleep from him. It took a moment, but Aiden soon jolted, eyes flying open and hands grabbing her furiously. Not moving, Eirian watched him blink away any confusion that had been present as he narrowed his eyes at her, rage filling them.

"You need to give me one good fucking reason not to lock you in your chamber and throw away the key."

She said sweetly, "Good morning, Captain."

Twenty-Six

Rubbing his eyes blearily, Everett followed a solemn Randolph. His guards grumbled as they trailed behind, clueless why the Queen's Guard had come knocking in the early hours of the morning. Everett had tried to convince him to explain what was going on, but Randolph had remained tight-lipped. When they reached Eirian's quarters, the first thing he noticed was the increased number of guards.

Signaling his men to remain in the corridor, he exchanged a look with the squad leader. He nodded, trusting his men to find out what information they could. Merle and his squad were inside the receiving chamber, a mixture of anger and frustration thick in the air. Staring at Aiden leaning against the door to Eirian's room with his arms crossed and a murderous glint in his eye, Everett finally realized what was going on.

"What did she do?"

"Ask her yourself."

Aiden pushed himself off the door and opened it, waiting for Everett. The fire was lit, and Eirian was in front of it. Straddling the chair backward, she had her arms crossed over the back and chin resting on top while she stared into the flames. Glancing over his shoulder at Aiden, Everett walked over and cleared his throat tentatively. Lifting her head, she turned to look at him, the apologetic expression on her face morphing into anger when she spotted Aiden.

"Get the fuck out of my chamber, Captain," she snarled.

Glaring, he crossed his arms stubbornly. "You brought this on yourself, Eirian."

Sucking a breath in through his teeth, Everett looked between them. "Would someone explain why I'm not in bed?"

Leveling a finger at her, Aiden spoke first, "Your queen used her magic to sneak out tonight to visit her precious princes."

"She's given you the slip before. Did you always react with this much anger?" Slightly less confused, he told Eirian in concern, "You know better, Eirian."

"No, the part he's angry about is he had a suspicion I would. When he confronted me, I made him take a nap and left him hidden until I returned." Eirian licked her lips. "And right now, I'm tempted to do it again."

Nodding slowly, Everett understood why Aiden was furious. "You know I support Aiden in this matter. There was no need to sneak out, and it was a reckless, idiotic thing to do. What if there'd been an Athnaralan spy wandering around? They could've killed you."

"You know your brother far better than I do, Your Grace. So, tell me he wouldn't have prevented it if I'd asked Merle and his men to escort me to the princes."

Knowing she was right, Everett looked at Aiden, saying, "She has a point."

"Of course," Aiden muttered, his arms remaining crossed.

"However, I need to ask what was so important you needed to speak to them privately at such a late hour."

Her mouth twisted. "Neriwyn revealed my mother's identity."

They stared at her, and Aiden's arms dropped to his side. "I waited for you to tell me, but clearly, it was more important to tell them."

"And you call me a petulant child." She arched a brow.

"I gather she wasn't a random Telmian." Everett ignored them glaring at each other.

"No. No, she wasn't. She was their queen. My mother's name was really Shianeni Malfaer, and while we know about Neriwyn, she was their actual ruler."

Stunned, Everett covered his mouth, walking over to sit on the edge of the bed. "I don't know what to say."

"She manipulated things to ensure I'd be born. Nolan knew everything. I even have my very own half-brother."

Chuckling at the irony, Aiden said, "So technically, you're a bastard."

"Technically not." Eirian did not look at him, explaining, "Telmians don't marry. Though bond mates, Shianeni and Neriwyn never married by your standards and therefore, when she wed King Nolan, everything was legitimate."

"Your standards? Are you thinking of yourself as one of them already?" Everett asked, scratching his cheek.

Taking a step, Aiden pointed at Everett and hissed, "I said you needed to tell him."

"For the love of... what else is there?"

Closing her eyes, Eirian dropped her head down. "You're trying to cause fights, Aiden. I'm sorry you're furious with me. I'm sorry I hurt you by betraying your trust. But please, either shut up and let me explain or get the fuck out."

"I'm not leaving you alone. I told you the cost of your decisions," he snarled.

"Then shut up!"

"You know, if anyone ever said the two of you had killed each other, it wouldn't shock me." Shooting a frustrated look at Aiden, Everett placed his hands in his lap. "Shut up, Aiden, and let Eirian speak."

"Thank you, Everett. There's a magical act forbidden by Riane. It's not taught, and it's barely spoken of. A magical marriage binding the powers and life force of those involved. A reason it's forbidden is that the death of one often causes the death of the other. It can also create an imbalance of power. If you bind two of the most powerful mages together…"

"I see." He did not quite grasp the implications, but Everett would not admit it.

Eirian stared into the fire sadly, continuing, "There are restrictions to it, of course. It's not breakable, so only those who truly love each other would undertake it. Or those intended by fate to defeat an enemy far more powerful than them."

"Your mother loved Neriwyn enough for such a binding, but left him to marry your father. To what, give birth to you?"

Breaking his silence, Aiden grumbled, "That's not the binding to worry about."

"It isn't?" Everett looked troubled, asking, "What have you done, Eirian?"

"The powers bound me to Celiaen years ago."

She lifted her head and unfolded her arms, pushing herself from the chair to walk to the window. Everett mulled over her statement, trying to make sense of it.

"We didn't ask for it or do it ourselves. It happened. We never understood how, and Celi has never complained about it."

"How does something like that happen?" Everett asked.

"It was a bit of a crazy situation. Rebels ambushed us while roaming the countryside. Celi and I had our fun slaughtering those who had hoped to kill him, which somehow triggered the bond. Gal stopped us from completing it, and we returned to Riane. The next day, they left, and we didn't see each other for a couple of years."

"I see."

"In recent days, we've been made aware of certain things. Shianeni Malfaer married Nolan Altira so she'd give birth to the next Altira mage. A child combining two of the three original bloodlines. But that left the Kaetiel line. We've worked out they intended our bond to bind the three original magical families with one purpose."

"Fight the darkness."

"Yes."

Leaning forward, Everett scratched his forehead. "Well, no one could deny you were born a queen."

"Everett, Paienven wants to absorb Endara. Celi has orders to convince you to overrule my decision not to marry him. He didn't tell his father I intend to abdicate or about our bond. We've agreed to court for the sake of his orders. General Darragh is Paienven's enforcer, and we need to make sure he believes Celi is following orders." Glancing over her shoulder, she explained, "When this is over, he plans to abdicate his position. Celi wants to remain in Riane and aspires to the high council."

"Then why didn't he tell his father?" Aiden snapped. "He could've done that instead of trying to marry you and making himself a threat to Endara."

"He's risking a great deal to help us protect Endara. Paienven is not someone to cross, Celi fears him, and we should too."

Her lips thinned, and her gaze switched to Aiden. Standing, Everett paced across to the fire and stared into the flames.

"Let's do it now. We'll convene the present council members and announce you're abdicating. If you explain that yesterday Neriwyn told you your mother was duine and you cannot in good conscience remain queen, Darragh may believe Celiaen didn't know."

"It might protect you from accusations you knew all along," Aiden said.

Eirian replied, "I don't know what legal basis I have to abdicate because, to be honest, my mother being duine isn't good enough. While we agree it's not ideal, it's not against our laws. If it were, the question of marrying Celiaen wouldn't have come before the council."

"Legitimacy, say you're a bastard. Marriage is marriage, and your mother married Neriwyn. Fuck your technicalities."

"Aiden, you're saying that because you want to hurt her," Everett spoke softly. "Your jealousy is speaking. I said your feelings for Eirian would cause you pain."

Turning around, Eirian hoisted herself up to perch on the windowsill and looked from one man to the other. She knew what she had to do.

"No matter what we do, this is going to cause chaos for Endara. Right now, I'm the queen, and I'm asking you to remain silent about this. I might not need to abdicate."

Hearing the coldness in her tone, Everett shifted around to stare. "What do you mean you may not need to abdicate?"

"The darkness is a god, and last time we battled her, the price of victory was the Altira mage. I'm saying, Everett, that the most likely outcome of this war is my death. All we can do is hope I succeed and save you all."

"No!" Everett protested, shaking his head angrily.

Smiling sadly, she nodded. "Yes. I hope it doesn't because I'd like to spend years discovering everything this world offers."

Eyes searching her face, Aiden growled, "You're resigned to dying."

"I accept it. My greatest weakness is duty. I always put it first. Sure, sometimes I kick, scream, and fight, but in the end, I do it."

"I won't let you kill yourself for this." Taking a step toward her, Aiden snarled when she lifted a hand and stopped him with her power. "Eirian!"

Behind Eirian, the light appeared on the horizon, heralding the dawn. He stared, watching the early rays illuminate her skin.

"I'm not sure where you got the idea you could change anything, Captain."

"You made me a fucking promise, right here in this room. A promise for after the war when you were no longer the queen."

Unsure of what Aiden was saying, Everett shook his head. "She's right, Aiden. We must stop the darkness, and if she doesn't do everything she can, we may all die."

Exhaling heavily, Eirian stared at Aiden, saying sadly, "Aiden, I've made you many promises, and I already suspected this fight would kill me when I made that promise. I'm letting you walk away. I'll legitimize you today, and Merle will be the captain of my guard. Everett will be the king when this is over, and you'll be earl."

"I don't want you to legitimize me."

"Your other option is to refuse the chance to leave my guard. In which case, you'll watch me accept Celiaen. You'll stand in my shadow while another man takes what you desire. Do you want to do that?"

Aiden glanced at Everett and saw pity in his eyes. "You don't love him."

"You're wrong, Aiden. I always have. The thing is, it's possible to love multiple people, so I won't lie and deny my feelings for you. That's the only solace I can offer."

Releasing him from the grip of her power, Eirian slid from the windowsill and spread her hands. Aiden wanted to go to her, but Everett cleared his throat.

"Please take my offer, Aiden, do the right thing for yourself."

Everett grunted, "Do it, Aiden. I know I'm only your younger brother, and you like to think you know better, but I'm telling you, take it. Take it and run. Go home."

"No."

"I won't make the offer again, Aiden."

Clenching his fist, he pointed at Eirian furiously. "Your promises might be worth shit, but mine aren't. I'm the captain of your guard, and I'll remain so until you're no longer the queen or I'm dead. I'll always protect you."

With a nod, she dropped the matter. "Right then, we have work to do, and I want to move fast to take advantage of the Ensaycalan legion. Everett, gather Marcellus and the rest and join me on the ridge overlooking Aeyren's position. Bring a tent."

"What is your plan?" he asked.

"I've been playing the queen for Aeyren. Now I'm going to play my actual role. It's about time everyone met the Altira mage."

A coldness to Eirian's smile left the two men uncomfortable. Bowing stiffly, Everett eyed the door in the corner of his vision.

"I'll do as my queen commands. Are we at least allowed breakfast?"

"No, you can starve," she chuckled, arching a brow at his startled look. "Of course you can have breakfast. What do you take me for?"

"Right now, I don't know. If you'll excuse me, I'm going to go dwell on my thoughts while I organize things for you."

"By the way, Everett, I'm going to make another trip. There's something I need to do, and I can't do it here."

He paused in front of the door. "Dare I ask what?"

Thinking of the cairn on the side of the hill, Eirian wriggled her hand. "We'll call it communing with the ancestors. I recently learned that if you're a mage, it's possible."

"What can't you do. No, that wasn't a question."

Pulling the door open, Everett stepped through and yanked it shut behind him. Then, looking at the angry guards, he sighed.

"Your captain is a fucking idiot."

Staring at her, Aiden waited, but Eirian remained silent, dodging him to cross to her chest of belongings. He walked over to the chair, dropping onto it wearily. Crouching, she lifted the bundle of weapons from the top of the chest and placed them on the floor before rummaging through for the gray garments. Pulling the linen out, she rocked back on her heels and stared at the crinkled fabric, rubbing a thumb over the purple stitching. Placing it down, she added other clean garments she needed.

Glancing at Aiden, Eirian sent her hand into the chest and closed her fingers around the rolls of leather tucked into a corner. The cold iron of the buckles dug into her palm, and she felt the wards worked into them. The familiar hints of Fayleen's magic made her smile. Dumping the leather on top of her weapons, she rummaged for one last item. Pulling the silk pouch out, she assessed the object's weight and pursed her lips thoughtfully before closing her hand around it tightly.

Shutting the chest, Eirian left her hands on top and stared at the wall. "I'm going to need you to leave the room, Captain."

"And if I don't agree?"

"You told me you'd give me privacy when required. I plan on changing my clothes before going out there and being the big, bad mage I need to be."

His eyes raked over her. "I've seen you naked."

She sighed tiredly. "I take it you want to sit there and stare while I strip. Don't you think that's rubbing salt into your wounds? All that looking without being allowed to touch?"

"Fine, but I'll be on the other side of the door waiting for you."

Getting to his feet, Aiden gave the pile of items on the ground a curious look as he walked to the door. Waiting for the thud, Eirian started picking up her things and laying them out in order. Once satisfied, she pushed herself up and stripped off her armor. Placing the leather on her bed, she peeled off the clothes she had been wearing and dumped them in a pile where she knew Isabella would deal with them.

There was a small bowl of water on a table with a neatly folded stack of cloths for washing, and plucking the top one from the stack, Eirian dipped it in the bowl. She rid herself of traces from the day before, then tossed the wet linen onto the pile. Taking her time to dress, she considered what she would do and questioned at what point to draw the line.

Smoothing her hands over the gray linen she had adorned for the first time since leaving Riane, Eirian felt confidence fill her. Deep purple embroidery ran along the hems, signifying her order. Picking up the jerkin, she pulled it on and tightened the cords, making sure her tunic sat comfortably beneath it. The bracers followed, and Eirian flexed her hands and wrists as she walked back over to the chest.

Unraveling the leather straps, Eirian slung them across her body and worked to position them and tighten the buckles. The wards helped to keep them supple. Then, extracting her belt from the scabbards, she wrapped it around her waist and connected the straps to it, ensuring they would remain in position. Walking around, she stretched and shifted, reminding herself what it felt like with the extra straps before adding her weapons.

Recalling Aiden's offer of baldrics, Eirian chuckled at the thought of his reaction when he saw her. Selecting the swords, she secured them across her back and took several attempts at drawing. The motions came easily. Years of practice had ingrained them into her muscles. Her knives were next, the two smaller blades nestled at the small of her back as usual. Glancing around the room to locate her bow and quivers, she smiled.

Separating the quivers, Eirian tipped the arrows out and adjusted the straps. She positioned it on top of the bow quiver before attaching it to the belt at her waist. It felt odd having it there, and she allowed a moment to reacquaint herself with it. Then, picking up the bow, she slid it into the quiver before adding the arrows. Knowing it had been months, Eirian went through the motions repeatedly until she was sure she wouldn't fail in drawing her weapons.

The last thing on the top of the chest was the silk pouch. Picking it up, Eirian untied the string to tip out the diadem that had belonged to her mother. Staring at the twists of silver and emeralds, she debated securing it among her hair. She had intended to but contemplated if it was too much. Huffing, she glanced at the windows and the growing light, hearing a knock.

Remaining as she was, Eirian ignored the knocks and bit her lip. Giving in, she untangled the diadem and lifted it to secure the gleaming jewels in her hair. Satisfied, she turned to the door, moving to let the knocker in. She fully expected it to be Aiden, and her expectations were correct. Smiling, her gaze flickered past him to take in the guards in the second chamber.

"Where did you?" His shock faded, and Aiden walked around her in a circle, examining the crisscrossing baldrics.

"You look fierce, ma'am," Sid observed.

Lips twitching in amusement, Eirian admitted, "Fierce was my intention."

"You didn't answer my question," Aiden said and stopped in front of her, eyes narrowed while he lifted a hand to touch the top of her bow.

"I've had it all along." Sidestepping him, Eirian headed for the door. "Well, come on then, I haven't got all day to wait for you to finish gawking."

"Hey, Captain, have you ever seen someone wearing a bow like that?" Gram asked as they followed her.

"I have," Fisk muttered, knowing they would ignore his opinions.

Aiden shook his head. "Most archers I know use longbows, not a recurve. But we don't utilize mounted archers."

"Perhaps we should," Eirian chimed in, glancing over her shoulder.

"I'd like to see you have a company of mounted archers recruited and trained before you need them."

Laughing, she ran a hand over the smooth timber at her side. "I wouldn't bother when our forces aren't accustomed to fighting alongside mounted archers. But you know that and were attempting to bait me."

Scowling, Aiden ignored the snickers from his men, muttering, "I'm glad to see you're not dulled by the lack of sleep. Or the lingering effects of wine."

Her laughter made his scowl deepen. The corridors were bustling, soldiers moving out of the way with salutes as they observed their queen. People were flowing in and out of the great hall, the occasional daoine and elf mixed in among the humans. Eirian paused outside, peering through the doorway to assess if she wished to go in there. Not spotting the people she was looking for, she met Aiden's gaze and shook her head.

"Where would Cameron be?"

"Side chamber under piles of reports."

She knew exactly which room he referred to and spun on her heels. "Sometimes I wonder if he sleeps."

"Sometimes sleep gets harder when you're old," Aiden replied simply. "Even more so when you carry the weight of a kingdom's army on your shoulders."

"I know."

Eirian sensed Darragh and Vartan inside. With so many magical people in the area, it was harder to pick out individuals at a greater distance. When she stepped into the chamber, they glanced at her, and the handful of officers lining the walls were the only ones who openly stared. Barely looking at Eirian, Vartan pointed at something on a map.

"Good morning, Your Majesty." Cameron glanced at her a second time, asking, "Did I miss something? Are we preparing for battle?"

"Maybe if I don't make my point," she replied, leaning on the table to peer at the map.

Darragh snorted, eyeing her curiously. "You almost look like a red."

Crinkling her nose, Eirian taunted, "Almost, but I'm too powerful. Do try not to forget, General."

"If you roosters have finished scratching up the dirt and squawking at each other, I'd like to hear what the plan is."

Finally looking up, Vartan stared at Eirian, and she watched his eyes widen briefly. The flicker of grief that passed over his face surprised her.

"Until now, we've focused on Aeyren and attempting to make him see reason. We've neglected the fact that he can't. I want to draw the real enemy out."

"By real enemy, you mean the darkness?" Darragh asked. "And how do you expect to accomplish that? Does it even have a tangible form?"

"Yes, tangible enough," Vartan answered.

"Tangible enough to stick a sword through?"

Eirian's lips thinned. "If a sword was all it would take to end this, it would've ended a long time ago, and we wouldn't be standing here having this conversation."

Cracking his neck, Cameron regarded Eirian. "Do you know what it will take?"

"Not exactly, but I'm hoping to figure it out soon. You know what they say about applying pressure to the right points to elicit the desired response."

Studying her, Darragh arched a brow. "You want one of our prisoners. Publicly."

"That's an extreme assumption!" Cameron quickly countered.

"It crossed my mind. I thought I could use my capacity for questionable choices to make the darkness focus on me. Then it occurred that nothing is stopping me from plucking her playthings where they stand."

The calculating gleam in Darragh's eye made Eirian uneasy. Stepping back from the table, Vartan shook his head. He did not need to confer with Neriwyn to know it was a bad idea.

"I would've thought your display in battle would've been enough to make that point."

"On the contrary, that was a rather big display of my value for life, not my ability to disregard it. Don't mistake me, Lord Vartan. I've no issues with torture, but it doesn't serve my purpose. The darkness doesn't care for my displays of life. They're utterly meaningless."

Vartan stared at Eirian, a muscle twitching in his cheek as his gaze flickered to the diadem nestled in her hair. "You want to make her come after you. If she thinks she has a chance at swaying you... this is a bad idea. Neriwyn would agree."

"Some days, I feel like I'm only getting a fragment of what is going on. I'm making decisions that affect every life outside these walls while you make plans that will trample them." Frustrated, Cameron slammed a hand on the table and pointed at Eirian. "This is what I want! I want to know the whole bloody truth. Because I'm not an idiot, Your Majesty, and I know you're keeping something from us."

Crossing her arms, Eirian inclined her head respectfully. "Cameron, I understand your concerns. I don't know how much General Darragh knows about the darkness, so perhaps it would be best if I give you both the truth."

"Thank you, ma'am," he replied gratefully.

"The darkness is a god."

The words shocked most of the room except Vartan. He took a deep breath and gave her a disapproving look, but Eirian smiled, batting her eyelids. It took longer than she expected for the exclamations and questions to pour from nearly everyone. Darragh was one of the few who did not speak, his mouth set in a grim line as he stared at her. Her guards remained silent, knowing they would have their opportunity to ask questions. Raising a hand for silence, Eirian waited for the voices to drop off. She nodded at Cameron, signaling for him to ask his questions.

"Are you sure?"

"She speaks the truth," Vartan answered. "It's been a long-kept secret for a good reason."

Eirian sighed. "I'm sure, Cameron, I had it from a reliable source. But before you ask, no, I don't know how to end this. However, I'm going to end it if it's the last thing I do."

"You're queen of Endara. It's not your job to die to protect us." Cameron was abrupt, his tone stern.

"I'm the Altira, that transcends being queen. If it was purely against Athnaral, I'd be the good girl you want me to be and sit back on my throne while letting you lot fight." Shaking her head, Eirian placed a hand on the edge of the table and said, "I need to draw out the enemy and see what weaknesses I can find. Because everyone has a weakness."

Mimicking her, Cameron stated, "That's a pile of shit if ever I've seen one. You're not the sort to sit back. You've made that clear. But let me make something clear to you, My Queen. Your priority should always be Endara, and if you can't do that, then we made a mistake."

Eirian understood what Cameron was telling her and gave silent thanks that her words had encouraged him to think that way. "I'll always do what I have to do to ensure the survival of my kingdom and everyone else."

"Why did we have to end up with a self-sacrificing, pig-headed mage as our queen?" he muttered angrily.

Rolling her eyes, Eirian turned away. "I'm done here. Make your strategies. That's your domain. You have my word, I won't interfere, but I will deal with the darkness."

Before they could stop her, Eirian pushed her way out of the chamber and plucked the offered bread from Wade's hands. He glanced at her weaponry briefly before turning to Aiden and nodding. Other members of the guard were sharing food with those that had not gotten the chance to eat something yet.

Chewing at the bread, Eirian pretended it was something tastier and wondered if the guard was punishing her. With all the forces surrounding Kelsby, the garrison kitchen had staff and supplies brought in regularly to feed the thousands. They monitored rations, but with the number of nobility and the Queen living in the keep, food had been less restricted, and she knew there were other options.

"Here." Pulling a carefully wrapped bundle from a pouch, Gabe offered it to her.

Folding the thin fabric back, Eirian smiled in delight at the sight of a handful of lilly pilly fruit, murmuring, "Where did you?"

Holding a finger to his lips, he winked. "I know a place."

"Thank you, Gabe, thank you so much." She popped one in her mouth and bit back a groan. "You always bring me the best treats."

"What did you give her?" Peering over Gabe's shoulder, Merle grumbled, "She doesn't deserve those."

Huddling over the fruit, Eirian shot him a glare. "Maybe if you gave me more treats like this, I wouldn't have given you the slip."

"It's true. She never uses her magic to get past me," Gabe quipped.

Walking along, the members of his squad voiced their agreement, earning shoves from their comrades. Aiden's eyes narrowed, looking over his shoulder at Eirian in the middle of the group. Taking her time to enjoy each lilly pilly fruit, she ignored the banter and focused on clearing her mind. She did not need to direct the guards. Aiden had already informed them of her intention. While she dressed, he had sent Fionn and Gabe's squads to organize horses and food. He had asked Merle and his men to get some sleep, but his stalwart second had refused.

"Why do you do it?"

Tuning back into the conversation, Eirian glanced at Paxton as he demanded an answer from Gabe. Arching a brow, Gabe smiled slightly, the look unnerving on him.

"One day, I'll ask Her Majesty to let me play with her, and she'll agree because I'm her favorite."

Snickers rose from the listening guards, and Eirian slapped a hand to her face, muttering, "I'm glad I know what you mean, Gabe."

"I know you do, ma'am. So do they, but they're idiots," he replied.

Their horses were waiting with the remaining guards. Halcyon greeted Eirian with a nicker, whiskers tickling against the exposed parts of her palm as she offered him the bit of bread she had left. Scratching behind his ear, she looked at Aiden while he checked his horse.

"I don't think we need them. We can walk where we're going, and it saves having them waiting around and taking up space. Merle and his men can return them to the yards, then get some rest. They've been up all night, and I don't need them and everyone else that will be there. In fact, I think it's for the best if you and your men join them, Captain. Gabe and Fionn will be more than enough."

"You can think what you like. I'm not fucking doing it. Where you go, I go," Aiden responded gruffly. "Or didn't I make that clear enough?"

Stroking a hand over Halcyon's neck, Eirian sighed. "Fine, but Merle, his men, and the horses are going. That's an order. We walk to the ridge."

Answering quickly, Merle accepted the order gracefully, "Yes, Your Majesty. We'll take care of returning the horses and then get our rest. Captain."

Feeling the familiar pull at their bond, she ignored the hand taking the reins from hers. They were close enough to the gate for her to watch Celiaen and his companions arrive, Galameyvin at his side. Similarly dressed and armed, Celiaen wore more armor. She had seen him wear the layers of leather countless times before. Even envied the exquisitely crafted armor that transformed him from a light-hearted young man to a serious warrior. It was more beautiful than the plate he wore in battle. Smiling warmly, Eirian took several steps away from her guards and the horses to greet him.

"It is a lovely morning, Queen Eirian."

Bowing, Celiaen returned the smile and offered his hand to her. Placing her hand on his, Eirian glanced at Galameyvin a few steps back as Celiaen kissed the purple band encasing her finger.

"You seem in much better sorts than I expected this morning, Your Highness."

Smiling wider, Celiaen did not let go of her hand. "It just so happens that I do still possess a grain of sense. We stopped drinking after you removed your fair company."

"I'm glad to hear it. I often doubt your sense." Extending her other hand to Galameyvin, Eirian waited for him to take it. "You're just in time to join us."

"Are we now? Join you at what exactly?" Kissing her hand, Galameyvin glanced at Aiden, observing his furious glare.

"I fancy a walk and a picnic overlooking the beautiful land I rule. You can join me if you wish, but I intend to depart now."

"What are you planning?" Celiaen inquired quietly.

Eirian plucked her hands from their grasp and smiled mischievously. "I'm going to taunt the darkness."

Twenty-Seven

Walking along the ridge, Eirian watched the enemy camp. At her side, Celiaen remained silent, busy with his thoughts and happy to stroll without speaking. She drew comfort from his presence and the occasional touches of his hand. Stopping, she tilted her head back and gazed at the circling forms of the daoine. The broad wingspans of shape-shifted birds cast shadows whenever they drifted across the sun. Despite it being early morning, the summer sun was harsh.

"They don't stop being impressive." Celiaen did not need to look to know she was watching the daoine. "Have you considered trying to learn?"

Shrugging, Eirian rolled her neck and stretched, replying, "I have, but it's not a priority. If I survive, there will be plenty of time to find out."

"I'll be jealous if you can."

Smiling, Celiaen flicked a hand at her bow, and Eirian shrugged.

"I know. I should string it before our friends appear."

Scrunching his nose, he shook his head. "That's only half of what I meant. When was the last time you wore it like that? If you need to draw quickly, will you be able to?"

"Are you doubting my abilities, Celi?" Raising a brow, Eirian sounded amused.

Leaning in, he nudged her shoulder with a grin, purring, "Oh, always."

Fishing a string from their spot, Eirian pulled the bow from the quiver and carefully pressed one end of the limb into her leg while she strung it. He watched in amusement.

"You don't even have a bow, so you're not in a position to doubt me."

"You know I prefer to be face-to-face when I kill someone."

"Or it's because you're not that good at hitting your target," she teased.

Pulling the string, Eirian tested the draw before sliding the bow into the quiver at her hip. Celiaen smirked, and the gleam in his eyes promised he would make her pay.

"Oh, dear heart, I can hit my target perfectly. Come to my tent tonight, and I'll show you."

Hearing a cough, they turned to look at Aiden, and Eirian rolled her eyes.

"You make such a compelling argument for yourself, Your Highness. How could I resist?" She scratched her cheek. "Wait, yes, there it is. I'm not charmed by you."

"Yes, you are. You just like to pretend you aren't."

Celiaen took a step back from her with a wink. Returning her focus to the Athnaralan camp, Eirian rested one hand on her hip and pursed her lips.

"How long do you think it'll be?"

"Well, if it were me, I'd make you all sit here until mid-afternoon at least. I'd find a nice shady spot to watch you sweat it out."

"It wouldn't be the first time someone called you a sadistic son of a bitch."

Laughing, he agreed, "My mother would be flattered. How much patience do they have?"

Stroking her chin, Eirian tilted her head to the side for a moment before answering, "I don't think Aeyren is very patient. He has been quick to respond previously."

"That was before the rest of us arrived, and he thought he had you in his grasp. It surprises me they haven't turned tail overnight."

Aiden grunted. "He's too proud to do that."

"Better a wounded pride than the wholesale slaughter of your forces. Aeyren can't expect to live if he's taken captive," Celiaen replied. "When the odds are this far against you, a retreat is the only logical response."

"It's not pride. I've read the reports and heard the accounts. I think she's driving them to their deaths. Because Celi's right, any of us would've retreated in his place." Eirian sighed and looked at the increasing number of people gathering around the shelter. "It's one thing to face unbeatable odds when you're desperately defending your lands and people, but another when you're the invading force."

Giving her an unreadable look, Aiden said, "They weren't unbeatable. You just let us think they were."

"Would you have believed her if she had told you?" Galameyvin asked, approaching with his hands grasped behind his back.

"I don't know."

"It is often easier to ask for forgiveness than permission."

Dropping the hand from her hip, she said, "If I hadn't been there, they would have been."

"You have some inquisitive people waiting to find out what you have planned." Galameyvin studied the lay of the land. "They were at a disadvantage attacking from their position. The stupidity of numbers, I suppose."

"I thought you were a blue. What would you know of battle strategies?" Aiden muttered snidely, and his men flinched at the look that appeared on Eirian's face.

Magic flaring with her anger, Eirian crossed over to Aiden. Before he realized what she was doing, she had her bow knocked and drawn, with the arrow pointed at his throat.

"Watch your words, Captain."

Leaning toward Galameyvin, Celiaen fought back a smile. "Are you going?"

Galameyvin walked over to Eirian and put a hand on her arm gently, murmuring, "Ree, relax. The captain isn't to know."

"No, he's being an ass and picking at anything he can to irritate the fuck out of me," she snarled, refusing to lower her bow despite the strain of holding the draw.

"Damn straight I am." Aiden tilted his head, taunting, "Are you finally daring?"

Dropping her arm, Eirian slipped the arrow back into the quiver before swinging around and driving the lower limb into his stomach. Grunting with pain, Aiden doubled over, and shocked, Fionn went to his side to ensure he was alright. Returning the bow to its place, she stared at him expressionlessly. Everyone regarded her in horror, watching her walk to the tent. Still feeling the impact, Aiden straightened, pushing Fionn away.

"I'm sorry, Captain, her response was unacceptable," Galameyvin said with a frown.

"That wasn't a normal response for her," Fionn muttered, shaking his head.

Pulling a face, Celiaen commented, "Well, actually, it wouldn't be the first time she's done something like that, would it, Gal?"

Reminded of his encounter with her bow, Galameyvin flinched. "Either she's in a complete mood with you, Captain, or she thinks the darkness is watching."

Lyle pointed at Celiaen. "Why is it when you're around, the captain and Her Majesty end up fighting more?"

"Lyle!" Gabe scolded.

"I have nothing but the utmost respect for your captain," Celiaen replied, giving Aiden a knowing smirk. "Whatever issues there are between him and your queen are between them."

Shaking his head at Celiaen's back as he chased her, Aiden cast a look at his men. Galameyvin remained with them, unwilling to get between Eirian and Celiaen. Grabbing her arm, Celiaen forced her to look at him.

"What was that for? Your captain is irritating, but that was unnecessarily cruel to someone who cares for you."

Refusing to meet his eyes, Eirian said, "I gave him an out, and he refused."

"You're angry with each other." Celiaen ran a hand through his hair. "He's a good man, and he'll always have your back. What you did was unfair. You want to take out your frustrations, that's fine, but do it in the ring."

"Celi."

Running his hand down her arm, Celiaen curled his fingers through hers and lifted her hand to his mouth, murmuring, "You know I'm right. Those men respect you, don't do stupid things to make them stop."

"I'm going to force that damn legitimization down his throat."

"What legitimization?" Baffled, he arched a brow at her. "What are you on about?"

Her lips twitched in amusement, and she plucked her hand from his loosened grasp. "You didn't know? Your friend back there is the bastard son of Everett's father. So when I cease to be queen and Everett takes the throne, he'll be the Earl of Tamantal."

Celiaen was quick to correct her assumption. "No, I was aware of his lineage. Does that technically make him your cousin?"

"No! No. Definitely not. No."

"Say no again with a touch more emphasis. I don't think you were clear enough."

Chuckling, Eirian rubbed her face. "You're right. I overreacted, but I won't apologize. I told him I'm accepting you. Aiden's refusal has left me with no desire to apologize to him for anything right now."

"Gosh, I love the way you say accept me like I'm some sort of chore." Celiaen brushed his fingers over her cheek, murmuring, "Let me remind you what chores don't feel like."

He tilted Eirian's chin up and kissed her gently, bringing his other hand to her waist, pulling her closer. Returning it, her skin prickled with the knowledge they were being watched by people who served his father. Wrapping her arms around his neck, she deepened the kiss and hoped they were making a convincing enough show of it. Their bond pushed the concerns from her mind. It whispered sweetly, delighting in their contact, and Eirian felt the demand of their magic. She forgot where they were and pressed tightly against Celiaen. Dropping her lips to his neck, Eirian nuzzled his skin, inhaling the familiar scent of him. Whistles and jeers caused her to pull back with a blush.

"Still feel like a chore?"

Smiling, Celiaen tucked a strand of hair behind her ear. The bond called to him, and it tested his control. He wanted to grab Eirian's hand and lead her back to his tent.

"Oh, definitely." Winking, Eirian peeked a glance at the watching people surrounding the tent. "Let's hope your father's people brought it."

His smile faded. "I didn't kiss you for their benefit."

"I know. Neither did I."

"That was a nice show, little Queen."

Sounding cheerful, the familiar voice of Faolan made Eirian turn to watch him striding toward her with purpose.

"Good morning, wolf."

Eyes widening with shock, he stopped dead in his tracks and whispered, "Eirian... where did you get that?"

"Get what?" Celiaen asked.

Pointing at her head, Faolan gestured. "That!"

Lifting a hand to her mother's diadem, Eirian wondered if she had made a mistake in wearing it. "I think you already know, Faolan."

"No." Blood drained from his face.

Feeling concerned, Celiaen said, "Didn't you say it was your mother's?"

Closing the distance to Eirian, Faolan grabbed her hand. "Please tell me it isn't what I think it is."

"I'm sorry."

Devastation appeared on his face, and Eirian did not know what to do.

"I came to let you know King Neriwyn is on his way."

"Faolan!" Stopping him before he could back away, Eirian said, "He told me yesterday. He knew all along. You once told me you thought she might be dead because of her foresight."

Snarling at her, Faolan's power surrounded him, and Celiaen took a step back when Eirian's magic rose like a storm in response.

"You might result from her foresight, but you are not her."

"That's enough, Faolan!" Eirian snapped, raising a hand to silence him.

Celiaen commented, "Perhaps it'd be a good idea to remove it."

Glancing at the gleaming jewels in her hair, Celiaen felt the brush of Galameyvin approaching. Knowing his influence would have little effect on the two people facing each other, Galameyvin sighed.

"You're picking another fight already, Ree?"

"I'm not fighting," she replied. "Faolan is making his feelings clear."

Growling, Faolan spun on his heels and stormed off. She regretted his reaction as she watched his departure, hoping it would not ruin their friendship. Rubbing her face, Eirian turned to face Galameyvin and the circle of her guards. They stared as though they no longer knew her. Aiden looked concerned despite their encounter.

"This is not going how I planned."

"Knowing you, Ree, you didn't have a plan. You're notorious for making it up as you go."

"Shut up, Gal. I always have a plan."

Rolling his eyes, Celiaen agreed. "No, you don't."

"Ma'am, why was he so angry with you?" Gabe broached the subject.

"I imagine he thought her plan to confront the darkness is a bad idea," Aiden quickly answered, meeting her gaze and giving the slightest of nods.

Not satisfied, Gabe crossed his arms. "For the sake of your safety, Your Majesty, we'll pretend we believe the captain. We're aware something is going on, and if you don't trust us, well then, we might have a problem."

Murmurs of agreement came from the other guards, and Eirian replied, "When the time comes, you'll know."

"I'll hold you to that."

Exchanging looks, the three men who knew the truth were not sure what to say or if they should speak. A sigh saw Eirian turn away and walk to the tent. Sweeping her gaze over the people gathered there, she took in the mix of elves and humans. No Telmians were present, and it filled her with relief. Darragh watched with a smirk that made her uncomfortable.

Among the Endaran nobles scattered around, Gallagher was grinning and chatting to an elven woman who was nearly as tall as him with bright red hair. Eirian focused on him, feeling his happiness and admiration for his companion. A hand brushed against her arm, and she glanced sideways at Celiaen.

"A picnic, Your Majesty?" Darragh asked. "Dramatic on a battlefield."

"Yes. I have a flair for the dramatic when I feel like it. Don't I, dear heart?" Directing her question to Celiaen, Eirian smiled wickedly.

"I feel like that question is a trap," he replied.

Chuckling, Darragh arched a brow. "You learn quickly. She might let you keep yourself intact. It seems Kaetiel men enjoy pursuing ferocious women. Watch yourself, Prince Galameyvin, else you suffer the same fate."

Galameyvin slipped in on the other side of Celiaen. "I'll do my best to avoid loving the wrong woman."

"Tell me, Your Majesty, have the two of you always bantered so familiarly, or have you reconsidered the gracious proposal my king offered?"

Darragh's gaze dropped to where Celiaen's hand was holding Eirian's. Giving Celiaen a small smile, she shrugged and squeezed his hand.

"I've reconsidered it. I'm sure you can agree that facing a battlefield makes you contemplate your past decisions and where you would change things given a chance."

"They've always bantered that way," Galameyvin confirmed.

Laughing, Gallagher grinned. "That will thrill Sabine and the others."

Darragh's eyes narrowed, and he said, "Reconsidered, but you haven't changed your mind. So that was a kiss between friends?"

"Oh no, I was sampling the goods to see if they're worth the effort," Eirian replied. "I mean, it's him. Surely, he has something going for him. You know what I mean?"

His booming laughter filled the tent, and Darragh waved at her. "Respectfully, ma'am, you're not what I expected, and I find myself pleased by that. Perhaps I won't end up wanting to kill you before this war is over."

"No, trust me, you will." Marcellus joined the group and whistled at the sight of Eirian. "Good morning, Your Majesty. I hear you've been causing upset again."

She asked, "Would it be a good morning if I hadn't been?"

Opening his mouth to respond, Marcellus shook his head. "I won't touch that."

"Did you hear the news, old man?" Slinging an arm around Marcellus's shoulders, Gallagher waved at Eirian and Celiaen. "She's reconsidering his proposal."

"Yes, I've heard. Everett had me write a little something for you to sign later, ma'am."

"I'd have thought he'd want to write it himself." Knowing it was the legitimization he referred to, Eirian glanced over her shoulder at Aiden and took in the way his face paled.

Staring at Aiden, Marcellus replied, "He thought it was better coming from me. May I ask what brought it on?"

"You could call it punishment."

Intrigued, Darragh asked, "This sounds interesting. Do we get to hear more?"

They felt the approaching Telmians. Lifting a hand to her head, Eirian covered the diadem, exchanging a look with Celiaen. Looping his fingers through hers, he shrugged. A low curse from one of her guards and a tap on her shoulder from Aiden made Eirian turn around. Several of the guards pointed at the Athnaralans and a gathering group on the outskirts of the camp. Squeezing Celiaen's hand, she let go and moved into the sunlight, shading her eyes while she watched them. Darragh and Marcellus joined her, the general quick to stand at her side before Marcellus could.

"If I was him, I'd be copying your move and trying to make us go to them."

"Because we have the advantage."

"Yes, he'd want to inconvenience us. You realize this will turn into a waiting game?"

Sucking on her lip thoughtfully, Eirian glanced at him, saying, "I'm fine with it if you are. Or I could walk over there now and kill them all. There's enough magic here for me to draw on, and they wouldn't have a chance."

"I'd like to see you use that ability on a prisoner when we finish questioning them."

The thought made her sick, and she blanched. "I'm not comfortable with that."

"Yet you're happy to torture them?" Spreading his hands, Darragh stated, "In which case, I have no reason to believe you can."

Marcellus said, "Those of us who were here for the fight saw her do it. Nearly seven hundred men dropped dead like withered husks."

"Only that many? That's a drop in the sea of what Aeyren commands."

"I could have taken them all," Eirian whispered. "Every one of them and all of my people. But I stopped because I made my point, and they were retreating. I don't like killing people for the sake of it."

Darragh said, "Your mistake was stopping. This would be over, and you could be home in your castle."

Mouth curling in a sneer, Eirian squared her shoulders. Her magic whispered to show him what she could do. It would be easy. All she had to do was pick someone to kill.

"No, it wouldn't be over. The darkness would've found a new toy to use. Perhaps your king? What if she drove him to march on Riane? Or to turn on his brothers?"

Neriwyn's power slid over them, and Eirian did not dare turn to look at him. The whispers faded as a sense of peace settled on her. Her rage vanished, and her magic wanted her to go to Neriwyn.

"It's a lovely day for a picnic."

"We thought so too, and it's wonderful that you could join us. But, unfortunately, we neglected the picnic part," Eirian replied.

"Then it's a good thing I'm the king of picnics."

Clicking his fingers, Neriwyn signaled for his people to go around the crowd of elves and humans. They watched in amazement as the Telmians began unraveling brightly colored rolls of fabric on the flat land at the base of the rise. Others connected poles and further rolls of cloth, lifting them above to cast a shadow over the area. Darragh made a strangled noise when they started spreading cushions around, and Eirian bit back a giggle at how red his face became.

Standing close, Celiaen leaned in and murmured, "Now, this is a picnic."

She whispered, "I know what you're thinking, Celi."

"So I don't have to tell you what I'd like for lunch?"

Moving out in front of the watchers, Neriwyn held his arms wide. "You want to taunt the darkness? Well, I can do that. So, eat, drink, and be merry. All things that defy what she wishes us to experience."

"We're attempting to negotiate with Aeyren, and you want us to relax in front of them?" Darragh said.

Staring at Neriwyn, Eirian nodded slowly and admitted, "No, His Majesty has a point. My desire today is to draw out the master, not the dogs."

"Excellent. Come, let's find a spot to sit, and I'll treat you to a little Telmian hospitality."

Neriwyn glanced between Eirian and Celiaen with a knowing smile. Taking her hand, Celiaen led her down the slope to the picnic area.

"I'm keen!"

Looking over the people hovering around the outskirts, Eirian realized they were all young. Her power brushed over them, and she saw them watch her with awe. Their magic felt more than the average mage, but there was a youthful exuberance to it. She wondered if her magic felt similar to the older daoine.

Understanding how she thought, Celiaen selected a pile of cushions close to the front. Shaking her head, Eirian unbuckled her weapons and handed them to her guards. Aiden frowned at her actions before noting that others were doing the same, including the two princes. Already unarmed, Neriwyn joined them and gave Eirian a pointed look.

"You're certainly making trouble today."

"The captain would tell you trouble is all I'm good at."

Hearing a giggle, Eirian turned to see Saoirse approaching. She blew a kiss to Galameyvin and smiled knowingly.

"And that sweet prince would argue there are plenty of things you're good at. You've upset my brother, little Queen, and I don't like it when someone upsets him."

"Saoirse, enough," Neriwyn growled. "We're here to enjoy ourselves."

Giving him a defiant look, Saoirse sauntered up to Eirian and pressed a finger to her chest. Still affected by Neriwyn's power, Eirian's magic did not respond to her anger.

"You've no idea, little Queen. That pretty bauble in your hair? He made it. He served her, her loyal wolf." Her eyes darted to Aiden, lips thinning, and Saoirse said, "Her captain."

Stomach clenching, Eirian replied, "You're right, I didn't know, and I'm sorry I wore it. I'll remove it and return it to him."

"No, leave it on." There was a hint of regret in Neriwyn's voice as he spoke.

"You'll never be my queen," Saoirse snapped, turning to stalk off.

"I have no desire to be, Saoirse," Eirian called after her.

Touching her arm, Celiaen waved at the cushions. "Sit. I have a feeling there will be wine, and I think you need it."

"Too early to drink. At least wait until the sun descends." Everett joined them, watching Eirian drop onto a cushion as he said, "I didn't think this was what you intended."

"Thankfully, someone older and wiser than me changed my plan." Her mind was dwelling on Faolan, and Eirian barely glanced up at Everett.

Arching a brow at Neriwyn, Everett muttered, "Yes, we're very fortunate to have you as an ally, sire."

Sprawling next to Eirian, Celiaen grinned at Everett and waved. "Relax, Your Grace, find a spot and join us in waiting because there's little else to do. Unless you want to spend all day poring over reports?"

Resigned to sitting around and waiting for Athnaral to respond, Everett selected a position. Quick to take the other side of Eirian, Galameyvin ignored the knowing smirk that Neriwyn directed at him as he picked several cushions to lounge on. The guards remained standing around the outskirts, soldiers mixing in. Marcellus nodded appreciatively as he sat.

"My wife is going to love this."

"Brenna intends to join us?" Eirian kept her eyes on the Athnaralan camp, taking in the continued movement.

Nodding at Kelsby, Marcellus replied, "I suspect she will when she sees all this."

Looking at the people spread out and mingling, Eirian smiled. She saw the positive side to Neriwyn's decision, the chatter and laughter as nobles and officers got to know their counterparts. Meeting his gaze, she noticed a hint of sadness and, knowing it was her fault, turned to Celiaen.

He sensed her mood and patted the cushion beside him, encouraging her to lie on it. Deciding it would do her good to take the advice and relax, Eirian lay back and ignored the arm Celiaen quickly slipped beneath her. Watching the colorfully patterned fabric above them flutter in the breeze, she admired how it was thin enough to make the sunlight change the colors with every move.

"Ree!"

Chuckling, Celiaen rolled onto his side and stared at her, murmuring, "It seems your little ward has arrived."

Ona came bounding over and jumped across Everett to stare down at Eirian. She looked at Celiaen in wonder before putting her hands on her hips.

"Can we play chase, Ree?"

"Chase?" Eirian muttered. "You want to play chase?"

"Were you going to do grown-up things to Ree?" Ona demanded of Celiaen, causing the listening adults to chuckle.

Snorting, Galameyvin stopped talking to Marcellus and answered, "He wishes he could."

Rounding on him, Ona asked, "Are you going to play chase too?"

"Your Majesty, this is an interesting turn of events." Brenna stood behind Marcellus, hands resting on his shoulders. "Ona was very excited when she saw this."

Huffing, Eirian made herself sit. "Chase it is. Everett, I believe you challenged me a while back. Said you're faster than me."

Glaring at Eirian as she stood, Everett swallowed. "No, I have no recollection of such a challenge. You must be mistaken for someone else."

"No, I'm certain it was you." Touching his head as she picked her way out, Eirian waited for Ona to join her. "Brenna, you were there."

Grinning, Brenna agreed. "I was. You said you were faster than her."

Nudging Ona, Eirian inclined her head to the field in front of them. "You're it, Everett."

"You have to be joking," Everett groaned as everyone laughed at him while Eirian and Ona made a run for it.

"How about we make it a team effort?" Scrambling to his feet, Celiaen held out his hand. "There's two of them. Let's even the odds a little."

Accepting the hand, Everett arched a brow. "I take it you want to capture Eirian."

"No, that'll take both of us. She's fast."

"You want to run around like fools while our enemy is right there?" Marcellus looked at them in amazement.

Squeezing his shoulders, Brenna laughed, "Why not, love? We can have some fun and show the children we can keep up. Or do you fear you're too old to catch me now?"

"Those are fighting words, my friend. Are you going to let her challenge you like that?" Everett mocked.

He grunted, unamused. "Again, can I point out that our enemy is right there? What part of this is a good idea?"

Hiking her skirts up, Brenna sauntered away from him, declaring, "The part where having fun is the whole point of this endeavor. Or am I wrong, Your Majesty?"

Neriwyn nodded, replying, "You have a wise wife, Your Grace. The enemy feeds on the darkness within. Laugh, be happy, have some fun, and give your queen the energy she needs."

Following Brenna, Isabella grinned, telling Eirian, "They're going to team up on you."

Watching with interest as Eirian faced off against the dukes and a prince, the people still seated waited to see what was going on. Guards shifted nervously, Aiden shaking his head in disapproval. Hopping from foot to foot, Ona giggled excitedly, swinging Eirian's hand.

Crouching, Eirian leaned in to whisper, "If you get caught, kick them in the shin."

"Eirian!" Brenna scolded her.

"What?" Standing, Eirian held her hands up. "It's excellent advice. She's not tall enough for where I would've said. Do you think they're going to play fair?"

"No magic!" Marcellus called out.

"Deal!" she called back.

"I'll deal with my husband. Isabella, take Everett. Ona, help your queen." Used to playing with her children, Brenna issued directions quickly.

They waited for the men to make the first move. Laughing as she ran, Eirian kept a close eye on Ona. People had gotten up to watch the group chase after each other. Gallagher bumped fists with Everett when he joined his friend, and others followed. Bending over with her hands on her knees, Eirian grinned madly at Ona. The happiness on the girl's face was infectious. Looking over the collection of people facing off against each other in a strange game of chase, she spotted Neriwyn standing with Vartan.

"This is it, isn't it?" she asked Ona. "The whole point."

Ona screwed up her face. "What?"

Ruffling her hair, Eirian closed her eyes and soaked in the sunshine and the feelings coming from the surrounding people. "It's okay, chicken."

"Run, Ree!" Ona squealed, shoving her.

Letting Celiaen catch her, Eirian struggled to breathe in between laughing, "Run, Ona, it's too late for me! Save yourself."

Swinging her around, Celiaen grinned, purring, "Your cousin said I could have you."

"Did he now?" Arching an eyebrow, she watched Ona sneaking up behind him and asked, "Do you think you can keep me?"

Cursing when Ona threw herself at the back of his legs, Celiaen released Eirian, and she danced out of reach.

"That's not fair. I'm going to get you, little girl."

Watching him round on Ona, Eirian felt cold wash over her like someone had emptied a bucket on her head. Eyes widening, she saw the moment Celiaen sensed it. Turning around to look at the Athnaralan camp, she took in the single hooded figure approaching. As it drew closer, Eirian spoke in low tones to Celiaen.

"Take Ona away."

"Eirian—"

"Now, Celiaen!"

He hoisted the confused girl into his arms and said, "I'll see her away and come back. We face it together."

Letting her power surround her, Eirian drew on their happiness. She felt stronger for it and stepped forward, spreading her influence as she walked. But, unlike before, flowers did not bloom as she went. Coming to a halt, she watched and waited, staring into the shadow of the hood as it approached.

"Welcome, old friend. I've been waiting for you."

The figure stopped, and Eirian could not tell if it had a solid form beneath the cloak as it said, "You're so weak, my sweet little life."

"You've said that before, and I remind you of your fear of me."

"I don't fear you, Eirian Malfaer. You're weak, fractured. Incomplete. You'll be the downfall of all you seek to protect."

Tilting her head to the side, Eirian agreed, "Yes, I'm weak and fractured. But I'm learning and growing, and when the time comes, I won't be so weak."

"Perhaps," the voice whispered, and she started moving again, walking a wide half-circle to stand behind Eirian. "But what of them? Do they have the luxury of waiting? Do you think I'll wait for you to grow stronger before I destroy them?"

"Why do you hate us so much? You're one of the gods who created us."

"Such an ignorant child. Your minders know, and your mother was there. Where is she now? Gone because she couldn't bring herself to see this through. She left it to you. Left us to you."

Glancing over her shoulder, Eirian saw the two princes standing with Neriwyn and others. Thinking of the men she loved, she smiled knowingly.

"You're jealous of us. Did the other gods take away your toys? You're nothing but a child throwing a tantrum and destroying toys out of spite."

The hate and anger surrounding her were strong enough that Eirian feared she would choke on it. Refusing to close her eyes, she waited for the darkness to respond.

"Don't think you can trick me into revealing anything, little life."

"I'd never be so presumptuous," she replied with a touch of sarcasm. "But if I'm to die, I'd like to understand why."

"Who said you'll die? Perhaps I'll keep you caged, and you can watch in agony as I tear apart all you love with war and hate. Let you go mad with grief as every bit of life in this world ends. I'll be there whispering in your ear how it's your fault that you failed them. Maybe then, I'll let you be reborn."

Smiling slowly, Eirian chuckled, "They put you down last time, and we'll put you down again. I will destroy you."

Feeling an icy coldness against her back, she knew the mad god was close. Yet her magic did not falter, despite the ripple of pain that shot through her. Instead, it reminded Eirian that she knew her enemy, prompting a deep longing she could not explain. Like the memories she could never remember.

"You're not your mother."

"And you're not the one who created us."

"But I am."

"If you were, you would've simply destroyed us. They left us, and they left you. You want them to come back to save us. They won't because they don't need to. I'll save us." Eirian stared into the shadows. "You think you can make me doubt my resolve."

"You don't know the truth. They could tell you, but they won't, and neither will I."

"I might not know the whole truth, but you're wrong about one thing. I won't fail."

The god laughed mockingly, "I'm not wrong. You will fail."

Spreading her arms wide, Eirian smiled challengingly. "No, I won't. I'm not weak. I have more strength than you can comprehend."

"They're not untouchable. I took your father from you, and in the end, I'll take all of them. Who should I start with? One of your lovers? The golden one, perhaps. Your family? The child? I almost had her before."

"Thank you."

The darkness pulled back in surprise. "You're thanking me?"

Eirian's power surrounded her like a cloud, pushing the cold away. It spread out as a wall between the watching crowd and the god. There was a shimmer to it. A hint of the white light that those who witnessed her cleanse the field had seen.

"It's your fault I'm the queen."

"And you're thanking me?"

"Yes, because it suggests you couldn't allow something that would've happened if my father had grown old and died naturally. But see, when you try to force things to change, you often set yourself up for failure." Waving at the watching crowd, Eirian smiled. "Look what you've done. You've brought together elves, daoine, and humans for the first time in a thousand years. You united us, and doesn't that scare you?"

"You don't scare me."

"Yes, we do. Thank you for coming here to speak to me because seeing is believing, and now they all very much believe you're real. Which gives them the desire to destroy you."

Reaching for their bond, Eirian felt Celiaen's power joining hers. She thought she saw familiar blue eyes and gold curls inside the hood before the darkness vanished. Then, standing there facing nothing, her power still stretched out to protect them, she watched the people coming. The memories scratched painfully, and she tried to capture them, but they continued to elude her. Shifting, she stared at the Athnaralan camp with a determined look. Celiaen stood beside her, taking hold of her hand in silence.

"The war is just beginning, Celi."

He squeezed her hand. "The wall is a new trick. I think everyone saw it."

"I needed to make sure she didn't go after anyone. She will, though. She'll go after some of you and probably soon." Looking at their hands, Eirian sighed. "Being close to me is dangerous, Celi."

"We'll face it together, Ree."

Twenty-Eight

The stares of those who had witnessed her conversation with the darkness held a mixture of emotions. Eirian felt them following as she strode to the tent. No one spoke, but she knew there would be a barrage of questions. She needed to maintain control over the situation. Matching her stride, Celiaen looked grim. Cameron was waiting with several of his aides in the tent, a frown appearing when she halted.

"Can I assume that was our real enemy?"

"Yes." Eirian provided no more information, rubbing her face while listening to footsteps filling the small area.

He grunted. "There's no more doubting when it appeared in the flesh."

"I wouldn't say flesh."

"Then what was that?"

Dropping her hands, Eirian took in the staring faces and said, "That was… power. I saw nothing under her hood except the endless void of madness."

"But we all saw it!" Everett exclaimed.

Voice soothing, Neriwyn spoke, "That was what your queen wanted. Do any of you still doubt the darkness is real?"

"How do we know it's not some daoine trickery?" an elf demanded.

"We have no reason to do such a thing," Vartan snarled, locating the elf in the crowd to glare. "Our people have sacrificed more than you know."

An Endaran noble declared, "We all heard what that thing said."

"Indeed, we did." Commanding the people to quiet down, Darragh pointed at Eirian. "And before we rip apart every word exchanged, I'll ask one question. Why did it call you Eirian Malfaer?"

It felt like her heart was in her mouth, and Eirian stared at him as blankly as she could manage, replying, "I can't answer that."

He crossed his arms and turned, looking pointedly at Neriwyn. "And I think you can. There were some awfully specific things said about your mother. I imagine the intention was to unsettle you and to make us ask that very question."

"My father was Nolan Altira. I bear his name." Taking a deep breath, she admitted, "My mother, however, was Shianeni Malfaer, the former queen of Telmia."

"Wife to Neriwyn Malfaer," Darragh accused.

"No," Neriwyn responded. "Telmians don't marry, and I wasn't her husband. Malfaer was her name to give. Eirian is legitimate by Endaran laws and therefore the rightful queen."

Cameron showed nothing of his emotions and said, "Nolan's wife was Siani. What reason would the Queen of Telmia have to hide her identity and marry the King of Endara?"

"That's irrelevant!" Philip pushed his way to the front, glaring at Eirian in disgust.

"No, it's not irrelevant. So answer my question."

Shaking his head, Neriwyn answered, "She hid so no one would know what her child was. Unfortunately, the darkness has people who serve her, and Eirian needed protection. King Nolan and I were the only ones who knew. He knew everything from the beginning. Think how your king would've reacted, Darragh, if he'd known who Nolan married?"

"How long have you known?" Cameron asked, and Eirian glanced at Neriwyn.

"I told her yesterday. We met in private before the elves arrived, and I told her everything. Before that, she knew nothing."

Nodding, Eirian agreed with his statement and hoped that no one could sense her relief. "That is true. He told me the truth yesterday, and I'm still processing it. After all, it's not every day that you find out that what you thought you knew about yourself was a lie."

Breaking his silence, Everett added, "She met with me before dawn and told me what Neriwyn told her. We agreed it was better to let the truth continue to rest while we're at war. I believe the darkness has forced this revelation to cause disharmony among us."

"You're talking about a mixed-blood on the throne of Endara," Philip spat at him.

Clenching his fist, Marcellus snarled, "Now that's irrelevant! We were all for forcing her to accept Prince Celiaen as a husband, so none of us has a leg to stand on."

Regarding Eirian thoughtfully, Darragh turned to Celiaen, stating, "You knew."

Celiaen admitted, "She told me last night. I told her it didn't matter and that I still wished to marry her. I imagine my father would support unity between the three great bloodlines."

"Yes, he'd certainly see the potential." Darragh said, "Now, I'm just a general, but I don't believe there are any laws in Endara that contravene mixed blood from inheriting the throne. Else your council wouldn't have supported the proposal."

"You are correct. There aren't. Eirian's right to the throne depends entirely on the validity of the marriage between Nolan and her mother. We only have the word of King Neriwyn that he wasn't married to the late queen," Brenna answered, hands clasped behind her back.

Arching a brow, Neriwyn waved at the closest of his people, who were watching in silence. "Be my guest, question every single Telmian here. They'll tell you the same thing. We don't marry. Our lives are too long to bind ourselves to a single person."

Flinching as arguments broke out, Eirian swallowed, finding her voice. "Silence!"

They ceased arguing, and all eyes turned to her.

"I chose not to say anything because there is no guarantee I'll survive this war with the darkness. She is a god, and the last person to defeat her died. Why cause unnecessary issues when I could wait to see if I died first. Had I survived, I'd have brought it to the council and proceeded from there. Everett agreed it was the right course to take for the stability of Endara."

Nodding, Cameron said, "We could never say you're stupid. A mad king, an abdication, a coronation, a war, another abdication, and another coronation? Anyone with a grain of sense can see what that would do to the kingdom. Legally, you're the queen, and I doubt anyone could convince our soldiers that you shouldn't be. Personally? You're my queen. I respect you greatly, and I'll gladly serve you for as long as you'll have me."

"Thank you, Cameron," she said softly.

"I wouldn't be thanking me yet, ma'am. Your position is precarious."

The small amount of hope she had felt faded. "My thanks were for your respect."

"The small council has always supported you, Queen Eirian," Earl Kendall spoke.

Holding up a hand, Darragh told them, "Until I have word otherwise from King Paienven, Ensaycal recognizes Eirian as the rightful queen of Endara. I firmly doubt he'd change his stance on the matter."

"No, why would he if he thought he stood to gain from it!" Still defiant, Philip cast another disgusted look at Eirian.

"I don't know who you are, boy, but I'd have you hung if I had a choice." Darragh stood over him, growling, "Perhaps I'll do your queen a favor."

Agreeing with him, Marcellus scratched at his chin and waved at Philip. "He's a viscount of little importance but an overcompensating bark. We had him under guard, but he swore he'd behave."

"While he speaks aggressively and out of turn, Philip is still a viscount," Eirian spoke softly, giving him a kind smile. "And thus, deserves some respect."

"I don't need defending by some filthy mixed-blood abomination. I'd sooner kill you myself than see you remain on the throne," Philip spat at her.

Shaking his head, Cameron signaled to some of his officers. "Arrest the Viscount for threatening to harm the Queen."

"No!" She stopped them and took a step toward Philip. "Galameyvin, if you'd please keep him calm."

Moving swiftly, Galameyvin caught Philip's wrist and replied, "As you command."

"What are you doing? Release me!"

Philip felt the magic wash over him. He fell silent, staring into space with a blank expression. Few mages could resist Galameyvin, let alone those without magic.

"Majesty, what is it?" Gallagher asked.

Touching a finger to her lips, Eirian hushed him before placing a hand on the side of Philip's face. Her power chased through him, pushing Galameyvin out of its path. Knowing what to look for, she found tendrils of darkness woven throughout him. Reaching for Galameyvin's magic, she showed him what she saw. Letting go of Philip, they stepped back, and he looked between them with terror.

"He's tainted," Galameyvin declared. "Have him restrained where he cannot harm anyone or himself. We'll use him to teach what to look for and attempt a cleansing."

Bowing, Darragh signaled to a trio of his officers. "General Cameron, I hope you don't mind. I'd like some of my own to accompany him. They're mages, of course."

"That's a wise decision. But, ma'am, if the darkness has tainted him, then who else is vulnerable?" Cameron asked, crossing his arms to stare at Eirian with concern.

"I presume everyone is vulnerable, but she may be selective about who she influences. Galameyvin knows what to look for, and he'll show it to others." Sharing a look with Galameyvin, Eirian was glad he understood why she had shown him.

One of Cameron's aides pursed her lips, questioning, "How do we deal with it? We can't order everyone to line up and accept mages doing their thing."

"And the time it'd take to do that," Marcellus pointed out.

Standing behind Eirian, Aiden said, "There's no need. I've seen what Her Majesty can do, and she can read everyone at once. She showed me what the darkness looks like, fine twisting shadows that wrap themselves around a person until they overtake them."

"What do you mean? You're not a mage. So how could she show you?"

Darragh said.

"He may not be a mage, but he has Altira blood. It was unintentional, but a little blood mixing allows Her Majesty to do amazing things. I was there when it happened." Tharen's voice came from further back in the crowd, and Eirian wondered where he had been. "I'm learning there's a lot she can do. After all, they created her to be extraordinary."

Suddenly looking excited, Gallagher exclaimed, "You could do what you did in that field! You said you cleansed all of us, and since then, I've felt... lighter? Yes, that seems like the right word. Lighter. Free of the dark thoughts and nightmares that plagued me."

Going pale, Eirian muttered, "Nope. No. Someone else can do a cleansing. I need to pay someone back for drugging me, even if sleeping through the after-effects helped."

Understanding what she meant by after-effects, Darragh laughed, "It's good to know you're not so extraordinary that you don't feel the itch. Though, considering your power, I imagine the agony is exquisite."

Peering at the cringing faces of those with magic, Marcellus glanced at Everett and Gallagher. "Do you feel like this is an inside joke?"

"No, I saw how she was after she walked out of the burning field. I think she'd have ripped anyone's head off if they touched her," Gallagher replied.

"A burning field?" Hearing the comment, Darragh looked impressed. "On your own?"

"I had some daoine wards to contain it, but I may have ignored them. Well, more like flattened them like trees during a hurricane."

He glanced at Celiaen before nodding at her. "I think you may just be my new favorite purple."

"You had a favorite purple?" One of his aides asked in confusion.

"You're looking at them like they're fresh meat, and you're starving," Cameron said.

Cameron found it disturbing how Darragh continued to look between Eirian and Celiaen. Finally breaking off his stare, Darragh smiled at Cameron.

"I'm afraid the mage in me was imagining something incredible."

Everett flinched. "Dare we ask?"

"I imagined the potential of their children."

"Her Majesty doesn't wish to have children," Kendall pointed out.

Waving a hand, Darragh replied, "And she has to survive her fight with the darkness."

Clicking her tongue, Eirian said, "My fight with the darkness needs to be my focus. You're in command, Generals. I told you I wouldn't interfere, and I meant it. Everett will take my place. No doubt that'll mollify the council."

Everett disagreed, "Eirian, you're the queen."

"I know, Everett, but the council has the power to remove me. Better you take my place at negotiations than there be doubt over them. Anyway, you're a far better politician than me. You're less likely to kill someone."

Chuckling, Eirian watched a grin appear on Cameron's face, and knew he remembered their first meeting with the enemy. Supporting her, Marcellus put a hand on Everett's shoulder.

"She's right. Eirian, what do you need to do to focus on the darkness?"

Running a hand through her hair, Eirian replied, "I need to return to Cynwrig Tor."

"Isn't that near the last battleground of the mage wars?" Darragh asked. "There are a lot of graves near there as a reminder of what happens when magic turns on magic."

"That battle was the last time they defeated the darkness. Cynwrig Tor is where the last Altira rests. If you have enough power, you can make some dead talk."

Neriwyn said, "I'll accompany you."

"Sire, that might not be the best idea," Vartan protested, shaking his head.

"As will I." Celiaen added, "I'd like to see how it's done."

Seeing signs of fatigue, Marcellus asked, "When was the last time you slept, Your Majesty?"

Her brows rose, and Eirian glanced away guiltily. "Not recently."

"Eirian," he scolded. "How long since the last time you slept?"

"They drugged me for most of a day and night, then we rode for a day, camped a night. I was still tired and slept. Got back here in time to see the Telmian forces arrive, and then yesterday the elves." Pursing her lips, Eirian said, "So, I haven't slept the last two nights."

Unimpressed, Marcellus told her guards, "Captain, please escort the Queen back to her chambers and make sure she rests."

"Marcellus, I don't need—" Eirian argued, faltering at the look he gave her.

"That is an order, Captain. Drag her if you must." Marcellus looked over the people watching and noted their numbers had diminished. "The rest of you have duties to attend to, so I suggest you attend to them."

Putting a hand to her elbow, Celiaen murmured, "He's right, Ree. You need rest. Even Gal and I slept last night. I know you can go for days, but we need you to be at your best if we're going to defeat the darkness."

Moving to her other side, Galameyvin coaxed, "Come, Ree."

Huffing, she let them direct her out of the tent to return to Kelsby. "Fine."

"Captain, a word." Marcellus signaled for Aiden to stop and gave Everett a shrewd look.

"Yes, Your Grace?" Glancing anxiously after his men who had surrounded Eirian, Aiden's mouth twisted while he waited for Marcellus to speak.

"Congratulations are in order. I knew there was something more going on when Everett directed me to draft a declaration of legitimacy for the Queen to sign. If he becomes king, you'll be the Earl of Tamantal like your father always wanted."

His face went blank, and Aiden said, "It's not what I want."

"Rarely do any of us get what we want, Captain."

Keeping her head bowed as she walked, Eirian could sense the looks directed her way. The news of her mother would spread quickly. She wondered how long Cameron's assumption would remain correct that nothing could convince the soldiers to change their loyalties. Her guards were silent, their hands close to their weapons. Exuding his calming influence, Galameyvin spoke softly to Celiaen. When they reached Kelsby, Eirian stared at the lines of men and women waiting inside the gate.

Leaning against the wall, Todd grinned and saluted. "A good day to you, Your Majesty."

"Lieutenant." She arched a brow, nodding at the people.

"News travels fast in confined quarters, and we're here to hail our queen."

Laughing in relief, Eirian rubbed her face. "Indeed it does. Thank you, Todd."

"I watched you grieve farmers you never met, take a common child into your care, and walk through fire to ensure a family could survive. You are our queen. Never doubt it." Todd pointed at faces staring over the edge of the wall. "And a lot of them live because you walked through a battlefield risking your life to kill the enemy."

"You have a way of making a point, Lieutenant." Celiaen bowed his head respectfully.

"We thought she might need the reminder. Fuck the council. She's our queen."

Eirian felt like crying and ran her hands through her hair, gathering it over her shoulder while twisting it between fingers, confessing, "I won't forget this. If anyone ever questions my loyalty to you, you remind them I would die for you."

"I know," Todd replied and bowed, waving at the gate.

The people saluted while she moved between them. Offering smiles and nods to each, she listened to their words of support. Watching the interactions in amazement, Celiaen looked at Aiden questioningly and received a nod. The lines stretched through the town to the keep, and by the time they passed through into the slightly cooler building, Eirian felt energized.

"Have I told you today that you're incredible?" Celiaen said in amazement.

"Our queen has a way with the troops," Fionn chuckled.

Scoffing, Galameyvin admitted, "I used to worry about how you'd manage as the queen. You always seemed to rub people the wrong way in Riane."

Biting her lip as she walked, Eirian muttered, "I rubbed other mages the wrong way because I never behaved how they expected."

"No, he's right, Eirian. You've grown," Brenna said as she reached forward and put a hand on her shoulder.

"Brenna, what's going to happen?"

Waiting until they were inside the first chamber, Brenna stood in front of Eirian, placing a hand on each shoulder to stare into the wide brown eyes blinking at her.

"So long as you have the backing of the army and a third of the small council, no one can take the throne from you. The support of the army is compelling. However, what do you want?"

"I want Everett to be king, as he always should've been."

Beside her, Celiaen shifted. "But the queen is what you always knew you'd be. You've never questioned it."

"And that was burden enough. I'm responsible for every human, elf, and daoine. Being a queen is nothing compared to that." Pressing her fingertips into her closed eyes, Eirian felt a headache beginning and asked, "Where is Ona?"

"I sent her with Isabella when Celiaen brought her to me. She didn't need to be near that creature. She's been through enough." Brenna's lip curled with distaste.

The guards holding Eirian's weapons took them through to her chamber. Leaning against the wall beside the door, Aiden watched them thoughtfully before signaling his men. Giving orders for food and drink, he dismissed them.

"I think you need to sit, Eirian," he suggested, indicating the table and chairs.

Giving her a push toward it, Brenna agreed, "Honestly, not sleeping is foolish."

"I've been having nightmares," she admitted.

"Your nightmares are back?" Galameyvin asked in concern, taking a seat at the table.

Leaning on an arm, Eirian explained, "I suspect they come from her."

"But you bear no signs of her taint on you."

Huffing, Brenna clicked her tongue. "Driving Eirian to exhaustion would serve her purpose. If she can't get enough rest and attempts to fight, then it's a sure thing she'll fail."

"There's a reason we use sleep deprivation as an interrogation technique," Aiden said.

"I don't know about interrogation, but it certainly does something to you when you've got a newborn screaming."

Giving Eirian a look, Aiden shrugged and gave Brenna a response that only she would know to be a lie. "I suppose you're right. I was too young to remember my mother helping Tegan care for Eirian."

"If Everett becomes king, at least you'll be free to discover what sleepless nights with your own children are like," Eirian said, and dropped her head onto her arm.

No one else responded, and Aiden clenched his jaw, glancing at the lurking Gabe. Frowning sadly, Brenna stroked Eirian's hair and looked at Celiaen. She thought of Ona and wondered what a child of theirs would be like. It almost made her smile, imagining how troublesome Eirian's offspring would be.

"Your Highness, do you know how to defeat the darkness?"

Happily taking the change in subject, Celiaen shook his head. "No, I don't have a clue. But, hopefully, we'll get something from the last Altira."

"We should go as soon as we are able. I doubt the darkness will let us sit around on our asses for much longer. She'll want to end you before you can learn anything." Shifting his weight from one foot to the other, Aiden gave Celiaen an unreadable look, asking, "Are you sure you should come along?"

"Absolutely, I'd like to know what my ancestors did to help."

Eirian blinked at Aiden. "You watched last time. What did you see?"

Everyone turned to look at the captain, and he shrugged. "I'm not sure what I saw. You were kneeling in front of the rocks, and we watched through a haze. We could hear your voice, but not what was being said. Then it was over, you were crying, and I was comforting you while you told me we might all die."

"Maybe we should visit the other place," Gabe suggested.

"Where is it exactly? Gabe might be right, and it's worth a visit. Who knows what we could disturb?" Eirian glanced between Galameyvin and Celiaen with concern.

"Ask someone who was there," Brenna commented.

Nodding, Aiden turned his attention to the door when someone knocked. "A certain bird might know."

"I don't think Saoirse will talk to me now."

Lifting a hand, Eirian curled her fingers around the diadem in her hair and pulled it free. Walking in with a tray of food, Kane placed it on the table and bowed his head to Eirian.

"News is spreading, and they've dispatched messengers to Amath."

Ignoring him, Aiden scratched his chin. "You need to ask one of them. Neriwyn might tell you or that general of his. It's a matter of figuring out who'll tell the truth."

Closing her eyes, Eirian knew he was right and who she needed to speak to. "Aiden, dearest Aiden, I know you set me some new rules about going places, but I need to go somewhere tonight."

"Yes, to bed." He shot a look at Celiaen, observing his smirk, and added, "Alone."

Biting her tongue, she resisted the urge to roll her eyes. "I intend to, but I need to see someone. You can surround me with as many guards as you wish, so long as I can make peace and ask questions."

"I doubt he'll see you," Celiaen said with conviction, remembering the look on Faolan's face. "Not yet, anyway."

"He won't be able to resist seeing me, even if he won't speak with me."

Eirian turned her attention to the food on the table and sighed. Watching her pick at it, Celiaen twisted the red band adorning his hand.

"Ree, perhaps you should leave it for now and seek him tomorrow. You need to rest."

"You can tell me I need rest until you're blue in the face." She gave each of them a condescending look and said, "But how do you plan to stop my nightmares?"

"We can drug you," Gabe declared, and the others nodded in agreement.

Brenna was the only one who disagreed, "We can't drug her every night. It's not practical. What if something happens? I was there. I saw what they gave her. We couldn't rouse her until it had worked its way out of her system."

"We ask them for something weaker."

Studying her face, Galameyvin realized she was not telling them everything. "Oh, Ree, you still had them, but you couldn't break free because of the drugs."

Rubbing her face, Eirian gave him a half-smile. "You see through me, Gal."

"Sometimes you calm down and break free without waking," Aiden said, pushing off the wall to sit on the ground with one leg bent and an arm slung over it.

"And how do you know this, Captain?" Brenna gave him a shrewd look.

"You knew about them and said nothing?" Surprised, Eirian blinked at him before glancing at Celiaen, taking in the way he studied Aiden.

Nodding, Aiden explained, "Merle does as well. Unlike me, he's never willing to open the door and go over to calm you. You toss and turn, fighting something in your sleep, and you know me, I hate seeing you in distress."

Most of the nightmares seemed to blur into one in her mind, but Eirian knew sometimes they had left her. "Thank you, Aiden."

"So, what, someone sits with her while she sleeps and tries to calm her if she has a nightmare?" Grinning, Fionn winked at Aiden and quipped, "I think that goes against the whole alone-in-bed part."

"Ask Gabe how his black eye felt," Aiden growled.

Pensive, Galameyvin cocked his head to the side and stared at Aiden. "I don't think just anyone would work."

Celiaen and Brenna protested, but he raised a hand.

"Hear me out. I heard what Lord Tharen said. You two shared blood, and he is an Altira. What if it's why he can calm you? Just because he could, doesn't mean we could."

Clicking her tongue, Brenna pointed out, "I have Altira blood. Most of the nobility does."

"What Gal isn't saying is Aiden loves me, and that's what allowed him to calm me. He could be right. I've pointed out to the captain previously that he has an odd ability to resist my magic. It happened on the battlefield. While I drove everyone else to a killing frenzy, he was single-mindedly trying to get me to stop."

Not meeting Aiden's stare, Eirian resumed pushing food around the plate. She remembered the battle clearly.

Crossing his arms, Celiaen said, "Well then, I'll try. I'm your mate, and we've shared blood, a lot of blood."

"Mate?" Arching her brows, Brenna glanced at Eirian.

Selecting a piece of carrot, Eirian hummed, "He's getting all excited because I agreed to reconsider marrying him."

"Don't lie, ma'am." As much as he hated the situation, Aiden felt a desire to support Celiaen. "They're magically bound for life. It's confusing to explain and forbidden by Riane, could get them killed and all that."

"Captain," Eirian warned him.

"You know how I feel about it, Your Majesty."

It did not take Brenna long to connect it, and she said, "It all makes sense now, so much sense. I feel as though I'd have seen it sooner if I'd known it was possible to marry your magic."

Surprised, Eirian turned to stare at Brenna. "How?"

Giving her a scornful look, Brenna rolled her eyes before smiling. "Despite what my offspring might say about me, I'm not a silly old woman. You children think you can hide everything but a mother notices. I had my reservations when you first arrived in Amath, Your Highness, but it didn't take long to see the way you felt about her. Or the way her magic felt differently when you were near."

"I—"

Stroking Eirian's head, she chuckled, "And Eirian, you protested too much. The jealous glint in your eyes when you saw ladies fawning over him was a clear giveaway."

"My mother would probably look at us and say the same thing," Celiaen admitted.

"How does it work?" Curious, Fionn ignored the look on Aiden's face.

Sighing, Galameyvin looked between the two in question. "In their case, there was a lot of blood, and most of it wasn't theirs. In normal circumstances, it's like traditional marriage, but with an exchange of blood and magic instead of contracts. It's consummated as well, except I impeded that and continued to do so for years."

Spluttering, Brenna raised her brows at him. "I beg your pardon."

"Duchess, there are three men in this room who all deeply love your queen, and I'm the only one of them who'd give her up," he replied softly. "Though I'd rather not."

"And things just got very awkward," Gabe muttered.

Leaning toward him, Fionn pulled a face. "I feel like we should leave, but I don't want to miss anything. Merle is going to be so pissed he wasn't here."

Putting her elbows on the table, Eirian linked her fingers and pressed her lips to her knuckles, staring down at the timber holding her up. "I never asked for any of you, and I'll carry the guilt of it always."

"Did I ever tell you I was to marry another man?" Brenna asked, walking away with hands clasped behind her back. "Marcellus wasn't the one picked out by my parents. I never met him growing up because, as a younger daughter, they rarely took me to court. Then one day, he visited with my intended, and I knew he was the man I wanted to marry the moment I saw him."

Everyone stared at her in shock.

"My parents were furious that I'd dare demand they cast aside the negotiations they'd worked so hard on. We were a lesser family, and they argued his father would never agree to a marriage between us. The king's brother would not allow his son to marry the younger daughter of some viscountess."

Swiveling in her chair, Eirian gazed at Brenna in wonder. "Clearly, you succeeded."

Chuckling, she said, "Marcellus felt the same as me, and we began exchanging letters. We slowly hatched our plan in those letters, and it took two years. My refusal to see my original intended caused negotiations to break down. Finally, in frustration, my parents sent me away to stay with a relative."

"And?" Fionn asked.

"Conveniently, Marcellus was touring the border near there. I ran away. He found a reeve to bribe and had the marriage contracts drawn up. By the time our families tracked us down, I was pregnant."

Everyone's eyes went wide, and laughing, Eirian said, "Oh, Brenna, how rebellious! Why does no one speak of this? Marcellus is royalty. It would have caused a scandal!"

"Well, in those two years, your grandfather died, and your father became king. Nolan thought of Marcellus as a younger brother. He told everyone he'd given his blessing for our union and arranged everything. If there was one thing your father loved, it was love. So, no scandal, but in private, we were in a lot of trouble with our parents."

Cocking his head to the side, Aiden worked out the timeline in his mind. "You said you were pregnant?"

"I lost that child, the first of many stillbirths. Eventually, three lived, as you know. My point is, we don't choose who we love, and not everything is easy. Sometimes you must fight for what you want because you know with every fiber of your being that it's right for you." Brenna looked at Celiaen, then Eirian, saying, "And sometimes, no matter how hard you fight against it, things will happen you didn't plan on."

"Are you telling us to consummate our bond?" Eirian asked, still awed by the story.

Pursing her lips, Brenna glanced at the others. "Would I advise my queen to do something so improper? I've tried to make a lady out of you! The suggestion you sneak away to roll around in the hay with the man you've agreed to marry would never leave my tongue."

"Nah, we didn't hear that suggestion at all." Fionn cleared his throat, shooting a nervous look at Aiden.

"Riane." The one word from Aiden caused them to look at him sitting on the floor. "You need to go to Riane and ask for help."

Puffing out her cheeks, Eirian knew she was not the only one confused. "What?"

Galameyvin said, "We talked about sending Tynan to seek information."

"What if we don't have the time to spare?" Celiaen countered.

"Let's visit some graves, ask our questions, and go from there. We may not need Riane." Eirian ran a hand through her hair. "We aren't getting through this unscathed, and I must do what I can to minimize the chaos. Going to Riane would put Endara at risk."

"I understand that, Ree. I understand your desire to minimize the chaos your kingdom faces, but we need information," Galameyvin argued.

Agreeing with him, Aiden nodded. "He's right. No one will thank you if you miss out on an opportunity to learn how to defeat the darkness. A little chaos over leadership is fixable, but the kingdom in ruins? Not so easily fixed. We can get you to Riane quickly."

"If it comes to that," she answered. "Let's see what we find out first."

Standing, Galameyvin held out his hand. He saw the exhaustion in Eirian's eyes.

"Ree, you need rest. Would you let me help you? If you sleep now, I'm sure we could persuade your captain to let you out tonight to hunt a wolf. Isn't that right, Captain?"

Aiden responded, "Sure, get some sleep, and then convince me to let you free. No doubt we could work something out."

Twenty-Nine

Stars glittered brightly. Millions of little lights scattered over the dark sky. They taunted Eirian, something about them dragging at the memories. It had long stopped surprising her, but she could never shake the feeling. Staring northward, she tried to imagine how they would look from high in the Roof of the World. She had never been up a mountain, but Fox and Mac had told her it was clearer from there.

Laying on the damp grass, Eirian linked her fingers beneath her head. Her ears pricked at the surrounding sounds. The nearby stomp of hooves and the quiet chatter of her guards, the haunting howls of wolves in the distance she knew to be daoine. Closer than the howls, the hooting call of an owl caught her attention. Releasing her magic, her senses filled with life, and she breathed in deeply.

Restraining the urge to make everything grow, Eirian shut her eyes and flowed with the power through the ground until she found the pack running across the land. They confronted her with a wave of emotions that made her balk. Shining brightly in her mind, their energy was vibrant, and Eirian wanted to bathe in it. Most of them were unfamiliar, but picking her target out of the pack, she surrounded Faolan and let her power whisper to him.

She felt their paws touching the earth, the rhythmic beat of their stride like a dance. The lure of running with them was hard to resist. Eirian wanted to feel what they felt. Continuing for a little longer before she reluctantly withdrew, she turned in search of the owl. Locating the bird, she fed it a sliver of her power. Insects buzzed through the air, fireflies to her magic. Other sparks showed her where to find more. It was the part of her power Eirian loved most, seeing the energy of everything living.

Returning to herself, she opened her eyes to blink away the lingering flashes her magic left behind. Eirian had learned to hide the momentary disconnect she felt, knowing it made her vulnerable. Her mind adjusted to her physical senses, tuning into the soft thud of footsteps approaching. Turning her head, she picked up the shape of Merle looming over her and watched him walk around until he was standing at her feet.

"Any luck?" he asked softly.

"He's coming."

Grunting, Merle kicked at the dirt. "I'm sorry about being so angry over the whole sneaking out thing."

Eirian smiled sadly. "Don't be. You're right to be angry and disappointed. I don't blame you for it."

"Nah, way I see it, you shouldn't have felt the need. You should've felt you could trust us to take you. Gabe was right when he said you never do it to him. We should know it's important you see someone if you say it is. I mean, it's not like you sneak out for trivial matters."

"I'm not sure that's quite right."

"Back in Amath, you'd sneak out to release your magic because you were frightened of us. That's not trivial to me. We failed you. We should've made it clear your magic wasn't unwelcome. Most of us are normal folk. We like mages for what they can do for our communities, and we didn't communicate that to you. You shouldn't have felt the need to hide your magic or to hold back against the captain and pretend you're not as skilled as you are." Chuckling, Merle nudged her leg with his foot. "Maybe he wouldn't have been so stupid if you'd kicked his ass from the outset."

Not replying, Eirian contemplated him before saying, "That's not your failing. That's the failing of mages. Riane has withdrawn from society for generations, telling themselves that those without magic fear us. Unfortunately, Endaran nobility feels that way because of past Altira. My family is at fault, not you."

"Ma'am—"

"Merle, I'm serious. You have nothing to be sorry for. You've done your job to the best of your abilities, considering I haven't always been the easiest person to guard. I think highly of you, more highly than I think of most people who've crossed my path. All of you."

"We're not going to leave you."

"What?"

She frowned, shifting her arms from under her head to stretch them. Merle shrugged and looped his thumbs through his belt.

"We're not leaving you. What part of that was hard to follow? Thought you were smarter than that, ma'am."

Rolling her eyes, Eirian felt Faolan's approach and sighed. "I don't want you to give up your careers, the things you've worked so hard to achieve. But why follow me into death? No, I won't let that happen, Merle, so make sure you smack some heads together and get it through the skulls of any other fool thinking that way. You'll not be dying for me."

"Don't know that I can do that or that I'm willing to."

"Okay then, let me put it this way. You're loyal to your captain, correct?"

Merle agreed, "We are."

His answer made Eirian smile slowly. "Excellent. Because this is an order from me to you. When I cease to be queen, that'll mean Aiden is the Earl of Tamantal. I've signed the papers. He'll need loyal guards, and I'm charging you with being those guards. I can't imagine there's anyone he trusts more than you."

"Ma'am..." Merle looked away from her, shifting attention to the wolf prowling toward them. "I believe that's my cue."

"Wonderful talk, Merle."

Rolling onto her side, Eirian pushed herself into a seated position. Faolan sat opposite her and curled his tail around his paws. He whined, eyes filled with sadness. Nodding slowly, she looked at her hands in her lap and sighed. From her belt hung a pouch, and reaching into it, she pulled out the diadem. Letting it rest on her open palm, Eirian stretched out her hand, watching Faolan's stare drop from her face to the gleam of gems and metal. Baring his teeth, he growled and stood, stalking away with his head hanging.

"I'm sorry." She did not watch him circle her, turning her gaze to the sky. "I'm sorry she's dead because of me. I'm sorry she left you. But, most of all, I'm sorry I caused you pain."

He paced back and sat beside her, nudging her arm. Running a hand across him, Eirian wrapped her arm over Faolan's back and buried her face in his fur. Tears threatened, but she refused to let them fall. Sitting patiently while she drew comfort from him, he accepted what Eirian offered in return. Then, shaking her off, Faolan shifted into his natural form.

"I'm not angry with you."

"She died because of me."

He growled, and the sound was more threatening than when he was a wolf. "You're mistaken. She didn't die because of you. She died for you."

There was a hint of anger in her voice as Eirian said, "There are always other choices. She could've searched for another way to achieve her weapon against the darkness."

"She left us long before you were born, and I want to believe searching is what she was doing. Do you think she got to hold you before she died?"

"I don't know. Perhaps she did. She chose my name, after all. An ill omen to name me for her dead friend when she knew what my fate was."

Faolan bumped his shoulder into hers. "Or sentimental. You said Neriwyn told you? Did he tell you about her?"

"He told me of some of her actions, choices that made me feel poorly about her." Glancing at Faolan sideways, Eirian saw his flinch. "I know you blame him for things she did. He'd rather you blame him than realize she manipulated you."

"Me not realizing she was your mother speaks to the extent of her ability to manipulate us. When I reflect on it, the similarities between you are glaringly obvious. For her to do what she did?"

"She knew there was a lot at stake. I cannot criticize her as much as I desire to because I'm prepared to die to defeat the darkness. She made the same decision. I'm just one in a long history of people dying to protect others."

"As far as reasons to die go, it's a good one. Not as good as old age in the arms of the ones you love, but if you have to die, then saving the world seems like a damn good reason." Winking at her, Faolan leaned over and carefully picked up the diadem.

"You made that."

"I did. Would it surprise you to learn I'm one of the finest jewelers among my people? That Shianeni took this piece when she left and allowed it to come to you means a great deal to me. I know I reacted poorly to seeing it, and I regret saying you're nothing like her. You're her daughter, through and through."

"I handled it far worse than you did, but I was already in a foul mood."

"It didn't look like you were in a foul mood when you had your arms around the neck of your elf. I smelled what you were thinking."

Choking, Eirian shot him a look. "That was for show. His father gave him orders."

"Are you going to lie to me? With my nose?" Bumping her shoulder again, Faolan gave her a knowing smile. "You've finally admitted the truth. You love him. Yet another way in which you're just like your mother."

"I'm not sure what you mean," she replied in confusion.

Faolan glanced around, knowing exactly where each of her guards was standing. "Shianeni was a woman who had a lot of love to give. She loved Neriwyn and Vartan, but I suspect she loved your father. Like you, she inspired others to love her."

"And who are they in my story?"

"You don't need me to answer that."

Nodding, Eirian lay back on the grass. "Perhaps not. Your sister called you her loyal wolf, her captain. Besides being a talented jeweler, what were you to my mother? A lover?"

"Yes, I was her loyal wolf. I ran by her side, hunted and fought with her. Protected her. Shianeni was my queen, and yes, I was her captain. She was the first thing I saw, and, should I die, she'll be the last thing I see before I know nothing else," Faolan answered.

"What was she like?"

"Beautiful. Just being near Shianeni filled you with life. But she had a ruthless streak, and you didn't dare cross her. It was worse if you did something to someone she cared for."

"What was she like with her son?" Regretting it, Eirian knew the answer would hurt.

Taking a deep breath, Faolan stated, "You don't want me to answer that."

"Maybe not, but I guess I want to know if I missed out on something good. That if things had been different, they would have been different."

"Utterly devoted. For a long time, Emlyn was everything to her. But, knowing what I do now, I can recognize the signs of when she withdrew."

"You think she threw everything into him because she knew she'd never get the chance to with me?" Eirian said.

"Yes."

"Do you think he knew?"

Turning to lean over her, Faolan placed the diadem on her chest. "Our prince is his father's son. He plays his secrets close. So that's a question you'll have to ask him."

"Faolan, I have a different question for you." She ignored the weight of the object sitting on her. "The graves you spoke of from the last war."

"What about them?"

Raising a brow, Faolan waited for her question. Exhaling, Eirian wondered how many stars were in the sky. A whisper at the back of her mind told her she knew the answer.

"Is there a chance any had their bones bound? Could we call upon them for answers?"

"They may have been, but they couldn't tell you what Eirian Altira did to end it. Only she knew. And your mother, but we can safely assume no one bound her."

"It's surreal to hear her name spoken. I knew what it was, but that's the first time anyone has said it to me. I don't know how to fight this, and no one can tell me what to do."

Stretching out beside her, Faolan propped up his head and grinned. "Well, no, of course, they can't. Besides, what worked for her probably wouldn't work for you. Magic is like that. It's bound by personal strengths and weaknesses. The limits you'd go to are not the same."

"I'm willing to die to end this, and she already has. So I'd say the limits are the same."

Shaking her head, Eirian dropped a hand to the ground and tore a blade of grass from its roots, rubbing it between her fingertips.

"You plan to revisit her. Before you do, I'd prepare a list of specific questions. While I doubt she'd set you on the wrong path, she was a devious woman. She had to be to survive."

"And you don't think I'm devious?"

"Oh, little Queen, you're not devious. You're ruthless and determined, but you're honest, and you wear your heart so clearly."

"I know how to play the game."

Giving her a pitying look, Faolan sighed. "Yes, you do, and you play it adequately. However, and I'm being honest with you, you're not born to it like others are. Eirian, you're still a child, and you've determined you won't have the chance to grow up."

"If no one can give me another way to win that doesn't involve me dying, then what else am I supposed to believe?"

"My advice is to stop telling yourself what you can't do and imagine what you can."

Struggling into an upright position, Eirian ignored the diadem falling and stared at Faolan. "Imagine what I can do? If it were that easy, I'd end the war today."

"I'm completely serious, Eirian." Grabbing her wrist to keep her attention, Faolan said, "I saw her move water and earth, command animals, and never did I think I'd see someone who could come close. Then I saw you pull the power from a storm without thinking, and I bet if you'd wanted to, you could've used that power."

"I could have," she admitted.

"You reach into the earth, and you feel every grain, but have you tried to move it?"

Eirian's gaze flickered to her wrist, where he was holding tight. "No, but I know someone who can. For me, if it has the potential for life, for supporting life, I feel it. Sometimes it overwhelms me. I can touch a woman and know she's with child before she does. I can cause it to happen."

"You've helped someone with that in the past." Understanding crossed his face, and sighing heavily, Faolan released her. "It would take you no effort to quash something at the most fragile stage."

"You're right, no effort, but it cost me, even though I understood why I had to do it. All death costs me something."

"Eirian, you're as much Malfaer as you are Altira, and that might be what saves you."

Rolling away, Faolan stared into the darkness with his head cocked to the side. Eirian knew he was listening to something she could not hear, but she felt his presence.

"Faolan, I haven't said it to you before, but thank you for being my friend." Her voice was soft, and he glanced at her with a sad smile.

Bowing his head, Faolan said, "I know, and I value our friendship. By the way, if you think you're going to die, I suggest completing the bond. Don't abandon your mate to live on without the memory of being whole with you."

Rolling her eyes, Eirian watched him transform, muttering, "Cheeky fucking wolf."

Yipping, Faolan licked her face before bounding into the darkness. Remaining, Eirian pulled her knees up and wrapped her arms around her legs, resting her chin on a knee. She knew the real reason he left, and feeling the other duine prowling in the darkness, she waited. Hearing Vartan's approach, Eirian chuckled at the wards he had wrapped around himself.

"You put little effort in to avoid me detecting you, Lord Vartan."

Lifting her head, Eirian arched a brow as he materialized out of the shadows. Dropping the wards, he shrugged.

"You only saw the tail end of my efforts. They weren't for your sake. They were for his."

"Neriwyn?"

"He believes it's a bad idea for me to be around you." Standing over her, Vartan looked around and picked out her guards in the darkness.

Scrunching her nose, Eirian said, "Because he's concerned about how you might feel toward me?"

"You and your mother are more alike than you suspect. So yes, he has some concerns, but I think they're unwarranted."

"And why are you here?"

Moving away, he crossed his arms and kept his back to her, stating, "Shianeni wasn't present last time."

"My ancestor said she shared power with her." Eirian asked in confusion, "How could that happen without her being there?"

"Shianeni bound the Altira to the land with her blood and that of the Kaetiel. These lands weren't the ancestral home of the Altira family. While humans have always lived here, the Altira line did not." Rocking back on his heels, Vartan glanced over his shoulder at her thoughtfully. "Neriwyn doesn't want to tell you. He doesn't feel it's important, but I disagree."

"I feel the connection to the land. It recognizes me. Is that because of my Altira or my Malfaer blood?"

"That's your first question?"

"Seemed like the most relevant to me," she answered.

"Your mother gave you the stronger connection. She was life, something you inherited. The conflict between Endara and Athnaral began when the last Eirian Altira led thousands of humans, elves, and daoine over lands you no longer have on maps. Even the name Endara came from far away. As did Ensaycal, though Paienven doesn't know it. Ensaycal and Endara were once twin cities, on opposing sides of a great bay."

Closing his eyes, Vartan recalled the lines of people who had trekked across vast expanses to find the end of their war on the lands that had become

Endara. Rubbing her chin, Eirian could not wrap her mind around the prospect of even more lives depending on her.

"Vartan, are you saying people live in lands we haven't encountered in a thousand or more years?"

"Yes."

"Why are you telling me this?"

Turning to look at her, he said, "Because it's stupid not to. Did you think these lands are it? The world is a big place, and you're fighting for more than you know. Your mother led those people here. War ravaged the world, and your mother knew something about this place that changed everything."

"But you don't know what it was. That seems to be a reoccurring theme. No one ever knows anything. So perhaps I should face the darkness and hope to the powers my instincts guide me because, damn it, that's what it feels it'll come to."

Tired of hearing the same thing over and over, Eirian scooped up the diadem from the ground and tossed it at his feet.

"This is what I think. Shianeni Malfaer was a manipulative bitch who knew far more than she let on. She only shared fragments, and now I'm left with fragments of those fragments and not a fucking clue how to put them together."

"You aren't the only one who harbors a lot of anger for her."

Nudging the jewelry with his toe, Vartan picked it up. Rolling over, Eirian pushed herself onto her feet and stretched to chase away the stiffness from sitting for so long.

"Are you saying you're angry with her? Did she abandon you as badly as she did me?"

"She only abandoned one other person as you were, and he's not here. He'd like to be, but Neriwyn insisted he remain in Telmia, and he agreed."

"I don't understand why he'd remain behind instead of meeting his sister. Shouldn't he want to be by my side helping me?"

Staring at the mix of metal and gems in his hand, Vartan spoke softly, "He told me it isn't his time with you."

Exhaling heavily, Eirian approached him to take back the diadem. "Why are you so angry with her?"

"Because of you," Vartan replied, closing his hand to stop her. "Because she forbade me from being there to protect and teach you. I accepted her death. But I couldn't accept abandoning you to humans who didn't know what you were and then being sent away for training by those who didn't love you. Neriwyn knew, and he kept me contained in Telmia."

"You loved her." Eirian covered his hand.

Giving her a look filled with grief, Vartan said, "I suppose you could say I was her Galameyvin. Allowed to love her, but always giving her up to another. I told you, you're more like your mother than you could ever realize. Like her, you make people love you with no effort."

"I don't want them to love me. Love leads to pain."

"Yes, it does, sometimes unimaginable pain. But pain is not a weakness. It strengthens you. It's not your pain you fear, though, is it? You fear the pain you'll cause others."

Scoffing, Eirian pulled her hand away and turned her back on him. "You don't know what you're talking about."

Chuckling, Vartan opened his hand to stare at the diadem, murmuring, "Don't I? The last time I was with your mother, she was wearing this. I ran away to be alone because I was so angry with her, but Shianeni always knew where to find me. She came out of the mist, and I wondered, as I had so many times before, if she was a god. Shianeni wore the mist like a shroud, but it faded into a white gown as she drew closer. This was in her wild curls, and around her neck was the quaternary knot she always wore. I'd never seen her without it from the moment I opened my eyes to her face to the moment I watched her vanish—"

"Did you say quaternary?"

"Yes."

Rubbing her arms, she turned and peered at him. "And she always wore it?"

"Yes." Confused by her interest, Vartan cocked his head to the side. "Why are you so interested?"

Pursing her lips, Eirian shook her head. "Because the keep here has them carved into the stone in the hall. I haven't looked elsewhere, but it's a very obscure symbol these days."

"If it's so obscure, how do you know of it?"

"I found it in an old book when Fay and I were looking for decorative symbols to use in her leatherworking. She thought it suited me, and I felt drawn. Why did she wear it?"

"She always said it symbolized her bond with the others. You never saw it among the things left behind by her?"

Saddened, Vartan could not help but wonder where the necklace was. Frowning, Eirian dwelled on the symbol. An image of the one Gabe wore flickered across her mind, prompting the whisper of shadows.

"My father was careful with her things. You never saw her again after the mist?"

"No, never."

"I don't know why, but it feels important somehow. I'm sorry I interrupted your story. I think you were about to tell me about the last time you lay with my mother."

Vartan clenched his jaw, rolling his eyes skywards. "I was, but the point is lost on you."

Puffing her cheeks, Eirian muttered, "No, you were going to make a point about the pain of saying goodbye. Probably something about making the most of every moment, even though you know it'll hurt."

"You're right." Waving at her, he clicked his tongue.

"Now you're peevish with me. I apologized."

"Seeing you wearing this." Pushing the hand with the diadem in it at her, he growled, "It was like being run through. It forced me to see her in you, and it hurt."

Delicately plucking it from his grasp, Eirian slipped it into the pouch at her waist. She had no intention of wearing it again.

"I didn't intend to hurt you or anyone else by wearing it. Had I known its significance, I wouldn't have worn it."

"You don't understand, little Queen. You really don't."

"What don't I understand?" Eirian hissed, stamping a foot in irritation.

Not bothered by her attitude, Vartan crossed his arms. "That no matter how hard you try to avoid it, you will cause pain to the ones you love, and they will cause you pain in return. So accept it and find some shred of happiness while you can because that's what life means. It means you live, and you take whatever comes your way."

Anger deflated, Eirian looked at the sky. "What do you want, Vartan? I'm not my mother."

"No, you're not, and I'd never ask you to be." Unfolding his arms, Vartan reached out and touched her cheek, murmuring, "I want you to be who you are. In a few days, when you ride out to revisit the grave of the last Eirian Altira, I want you to take your time coming back and maybe swing northward. See the mountains."

"While I'm avoiding my fate and traipsing the countryside, what am I doing?"

"Finding strength and unity."

Opening her mouth to respond, she closed it again and slumped. Then, glancing over her shoulder into the darkness, she felt the guards watching and searched through her thoughts for the right question to ask.

"How did my mother make it work for her?"

His lips twitched in amusement. "Are you asking me how Shianeni juggled her lovers?"

"Well… sort of? I suppose I'm curious."

"I don't think our situation is quite the same. I wasn't just her lover, and I've remained his. We always return to each other. Is what you feel strong enough to ask. If they cannot be happy with a part of you instead of the whole, you won't find peace. Only conflict."

Running a hand through her hair, Eirian shook her head in surprised amusement. "I can't believe I'm contemplating it."

"It's the duine in you."

"It's a moot point. They'd never accept it."

Laughing, Vartan winked. "Well, I don't know about your captain, but I think the princes would surprise you, little Queen."

"Why do you all call me 'little Queen'?" she demanded in annoyance.

"I suppose it's half an insult intended to remind you how young you are, despite your lofty title. Perhaps it's to remind you that you're not the queen your mother was."

"Not the queen my mother was? No, I'm not, and I'll never be. When I face our enemy, it won't be as a queen."

"Eirian, you could sooner cut off your hand than stop being a queen. You could command all of us to lie down and die in battle, and we wouldn't be able to deny you. The land itself cannot deny you," Vartan said solemnly, staring into her eyes.

Searching his gaze for a hint of jest, Eirian ground her teeth. The whispers mocked her reluctance, telling her it was the truth.

"I wouldn't command you to do that."

"And you don't have to because everyone will do it anyway."

"Tell me about the other lands."

Chuckling, he arched a brow at her. "Great cities and kingdoms of daoine, humans, and elves all waiting to fall should you fail. She spreads her influence already, and war brews between neighbors. Magic turns on magic, and scholars whisper of dark times come again."

Fascinated, Eirian hooked her thumbs through her belt. "Do they know we exist?"

"No. Once there was trade, and people explored the world, but the last war lasted many years. Now, no one sails the seas. No one thinks there are lands beyond their own. Your mother made people forget. She compelled their focus to remain where they were."

"If I could go to one of these other lands, would we understand each other?"

"The gods only gave us one tongue with which to speak. Language can either unite or divide us. They wanted it to unite."

Stepping away, Eirian looked at the sky with a new perspective. "The world already felt so big."

"You, Neriwyn, and I are the only ones who know. I doubt the darkness would've told her minions. Her focus is on ending you. She doesn't need the Athnaralans to destroy the rest of the world, but she needs you out of her way."

"Because so long as I'm alive, I'm a threat. Why is the Altira line so much more a threat than the Kaetiel?"

Finally asking a question that had been bothering her, Eirian wondered if the stars were the same everywhere. Vartan paused, giving her a contemplative look.

"You haven't worked that out for yourself? Humans are powerful. Shianeni said humans exist to teach us how to live."

"But they have the shortest lifespan?"

"It's not the time spent living, but the quality of it. So often, it's the shortest spark that burns the brightest. The desire to make life count because it ends before they're ready."

Eirian felt foolish for not considering it. "Of course, that makes sense. Humans feel they've more to lose, and they fight all the harder for it. The daoine are mountains, tall and everlasting. While the elves are towering eucalypts, long-lived but end, eventually. Humans are a dandelion growing at the foot of them both, bright and stubborn, and keep coming no matter how hard you try to get rid of them. Just when you think you've done it, another has already spread its seeds to the wind."

Amused by her analogy, Vartan agreed, "Yes."

"Then why has the magic been fading among the humans here?"

"You know the answer."

"Because there was no Altira. The bloodlines are the heart of magic, aren't they?"

"They were the beginning of it, given straight from the gods," he answered. "The children of the gods, each tied to their creator."

"How angry is Neriwyn going to be?"

Smirking, Vartan wriggled his brows. "Don't worry about Neriwyn. I know how to soothe his anger."

"I don't think I want to know," Eirian muttered, pulling a face.

"And I wouldn't say because, unlike some of our people, I don't kiss and tell."

"I've been having a lot of nightmares recently," she said. "I barely sleep."

Frowning, Vartan replied, "I'm not surprised. Even if she weren't coming after you, your mind would be plagued by how she defiles the land. It'll get worse before the end."

Sighing, she nodded. "I know."

"All you can do is draw comfort and find peace wherever you can. If you were hoping I'd have some other advice for you regarding it, I don't. There's nothing I know of that will protect your mind from her."

"Good thing I wasn't hoping for something. Tell me, though, do the daoine have any secret means of travel that could get me places faster than a horse?"

His lips thinned. "There was a way, but the ability to do so vanished with the gods."

"How?" Demanding an answer, Eirian pulled her hair over her shoulder and twisted it in her hands as she joined him. "Vartan, tell me how they did it."

"There were great stone gateways, and we could walk through them to find ourselves in other places. Shianeni could control them, but no one else that I ever saw other than the gods." Knowing Neriwyn would be furious with him for telling her, Vartan rubbed his chin. "Eirian, I don't even know if they still exist."

Waving dismissively, she shook her head sadly. "It's fine. I was hoping for something else, but I suppose it can't all be that easy."

"Life isn't easy, and it's the challenges we face that help us find strength."

"I hadn't realized."

Leveling a displeased look at him, Eirian sensed Aiden. Glancing in his direction, Vartan gave her a wry smile.

"Speaking of challenges, I'll take that as my cue to leave. I hope you understand that I'd rather you didn't repeat certain things I told you."

Eirian nodded, agreeing, "You'll find I'm very good at keeping secrets."

"I'm not so sure about that."

"I'd try to assure you, but that would defeat the purpose." Giving him a slow smile, she looked at where Aiden stood. "It's been an informative night."

Vartan bowed, telling her, "The next time we meet, we might be preparing for a battle. I hope you can bring all your weapons to the fight."

Watching him turn, Eirian felt his magic wrap around him as Vartan faded into the darkness. Sighing, she shifted her focus to Aiden and lifted a hand to scratch her shoulder before tossing her hair over the other one. Hands on her hips, she waited for him to walk over.

"I thought you were planning to meet the wolf?" he asked before he reached her.

"He was here first. Lord Vartan was a welcome addition." Studying him, Eirian felt the weight of the advice given to her. "I wasn't expecting you to come out to fetch me."

Looking her over, Aiden did not appreciate the lack of weapons, but did not ask why she was unarmed. He knew she did not need them to defend herself.

"I believe we've had this discussion before."

Pursing her lips, she lifted her chin, murmuring, "Yes, I suppose we have. You're very fetching, after all."

"I'd say you're worth fetching, but I'd worry about my safety. Thankfully, you've nothing on you with which to land a sneaky blow."

"Aiden…" Sighing, Eirian dropped her hands. "I'm sorry for what I did, and I don't deserve your forgiveness."

He stared at her, taking in how she seemed to absorb the moonlight. "You took me by surprise. It was a reminder not to underestimate you."

"Why are you looking at me like that?"

"Because you're becoming more and more like them. Or perhaps you always were, and we couldn't see it. But it is increasingly obvious to me you're not like us."

"What makes you say that?"

"Right now, it's like you're bathing in the moon. I've noticed it a few times recently. Part of me is screaming that you're a creature far beyond my ability to handle, and I should run away from you, fast and far."

Brushing her hands over the wool of her trousers, Eirian swallowed. "You should."

Taking a step closer, he replied, "It's drowned out by the part of me that never wants to let you go. But I have to, don't I? I can't fight for your affection. To do so could ruin everything for everyone. The other prince knows it, and I'm not so stupid that I can't see it."

It hurt to make herself agree, and Eirian hoped it was the right decision. "Yes, yes, you do. I must have focus when I face the darkness."

"I meant what I said earlier." Lifting a hand to her cheek, Aiden shook his head, whispering, "I hate to see you in distress."

"That's not what you wanted to say."

Turning her face into his hand, Eirian felt the roughness of his fingers. She smelled the eucalyptus oil on his skin and knew he had been spending his time sharpening his weapons. It was challenging to resist kissing him.

"But it's the truth, darling, and I wish you all the happiness in the world, even if I'm not the one giving it to you."

"Why Aiden, I believe you're taking a page from my book of noble self-sacrifice."

Aiden laughed, "Can't let you have all the glory."

Meeting his gaze, Eirian said, "I hope there is an after the war."

THIRTY

"Have you seen her?" Fayleen asked Jaren as soon as she spotted him.

Shaking his head, he said, "No, but Baenlin nearly ran into her earlier, so Tessa is probably hiding. We're not so far from Riane that he wouldn't send her back in chains."

Flinching at the thought, Fayleen sighed heavily and looked at the sky. Colors mottled it, pale shades of yellow and pink blended with deep orange. The smell of smoke hit her nose, carrying the scent of cooking food to remind them they were hungry. Scratching her neck before shifting the quarterstaff secured to her back, Fayleen gave Jaren a frustrated look. He shrugged, glancing around at the tents being erected for the night.

"Why don't you get us some dinner while I find her?" he suggested.

"If you see Rylee and Luke, tell them what I'm doing."

Jaren kept his gaze on her back while Fayleen hurried off. He knew it was a matter of time before the masters and archmages leading the army would discover Tessa was among them. Her position as next in line to be grand mage was precarious, but the same laws applied to her that applied to the grand mage. Cursing, Jaren set off, searching for their tent, intending to remind Tessa what was at stake.

He did not begrudge her presence. If he did, he would not have helped her sneak out of Riane with the army after Queen Sannaeh had knocked sense into the high council. Leaving Tessa behind in the city without him to protect her was not an option Jaren would contemplate. Their father openly attacked her, while behind closed doors, their mother undermined her confidence, belittling Tessa with every other breath. It was why he had gotten her out of Riane the first time.

It was easy to find their tent tucked toward the outskirts of the camp. Tessa was particular about the location, not wanting to be too close to the edge, but not so far that it would be difficult to escape. Jaren did not blame her for keeping one eye on her back at all times. Even Archmage Calhoun and Archmage Azina had quietly admitted their fear her life was in danger from their father.

"Zach," Jaren greeted the man sitting outside the tent.

Glancing up, Zack replied, "She kicked me out."

"Why?"

"She wanted to play. Told me to keep watch. You know what she's like."

Staring at the closed tent flaps, Jaren pursed his lips and considered leaving her for a little longer. Tessa would either be making the earth move or throwing herself into one of her toys. Either way, if he disturbed her while she was in a foul mood, he would pay for it. Lifting a hand to the canvas, he glanced at Zack and took in the amused look on his face.

"Alright, what do you know?"

"Love, I know everything. Haven't you learned that yet?"

"Don't give me fucking blue riddles right now."

"Would I do that?" Zack chuckled. "She wasn't pulling out her toys when I left. However, I saw her gathering her books."

Hand falling away from the tent, Jaren understood what it meant. If Tessa had an idea in her head that she was trying to sketch out on paper, he would not get any sense out of her. She tended to hyper-focus, becoming oblivious to the world. There was no point going inside, so he sat on the ground next to Zack. Reaching for his hand, Zack squeezed it gently before lifting it to his lips to plant a kiss on the back of it.

"You're worried, my love."

"How long before we're found out? Tessa is a mess. Some days I'm convinced she has the strength to stand up to anyone, but other days…"

Squeezing his hand again, Zack said, "She can do it. All she needs is the opportunity to show them what she can do, and Tessa will believe in herself."

"I want to be angry at Ree for putting her in this position. Why couldn't she have just said yes?" Jaren groaned, "No, that's not fair."

"Ree turning down the grand mage position might be the best thing to happen to Tessa. Fuck, this war might be even better. It gives her a chance to show off to Baenlin."

Frowning, Jaren tried not to recall all the times Tessa had attempted to gain Baenlin's attention. He did not like to think about what might happen if her attempts came to fruition. Everyone knew Baenlin was only interested in people who furthered his power and influence. That he had dismissed Tessa for years before Eirian arrived in Riane only proved the effect of Hugh's claims about her. While Jaren respected Baenlin, he did not want him near his sister.

Jaren sighed. "I don't want her to show off to Baenlin."

"Don't get all overprotective. Tessa can hold her own. She just needs to figure it out for herself," Zack stated. "I know you love your sister, but sometimes I think you hold her back."

"You don't get—"

"Yes, I do. I'm your blue and your husband."

"Not yet, you're not. You've got to ask me first."

Fayleen appeared, holding a plate in each hand while her magic held two more in front of her. They blinked in surprise. Jaren quickly got up and took the ones floating in the air before she spoke. Blue eyes darting to the closed tent, Fayleen did not need to ask why they were sitting outside.

"Alright, I've got this," she drawled.

"She's drafting," Jaren explained.

Shooting a withering look at him, Fayleen snorted. "I said, I've got this."

Letting Fayleen enter the tent with the food, Jaren and Zack exchanged amused looks.

"She scares me."

"Really, Jaren? You're a big bad red, and you're scared by Fay?" Zack mocked him.

"Have you ever felt one of her knockbacks? They fucking hurt. Plus, she's the one who kept Ree under control."

Rolling her eyes at the comments, Fayleen carried the plates to the table and dumped them as loudly as she could manage. Tessa was leaning over sheets of paper, a pencil gripped tightly in her hand as she stared at a series of drawings. Her thick brown hair was pulled back in a braid and restrained by a bright purple ribbon. It hung over her shoulder, bow resting on the surface while she worked. Crinkling her nose, Fayleen glanced at them before plucking the pencil from Tessa's grasp. The contact startled her, and she lifted her head to blink.

"What do you want, Fay?"

"I want you to eat."

Tessa stretched her arms, rolling her shoulders to loosen the tightness she felt. Eyes shifting to the plates of food, she realized she was hungry and decided not to argue with Fayleen for disturbing her work. They were an army on the move, so the food was basic, but Tessa did not care. She hated eating at the best of times and wished it was possible to avoid it. Maybe if she could, her mother would be happier with her appearance. Waiting until Tessa had picked up a plate, Fayleen did the same.

"He didn't see you."

There was a brief look of disappointment before Tessa replied, "Good. Have you heard anything interesting today?"

"Messenger came from the north. They're in a stalemate at Kelsby. I don't know how much of it's true, but apparently, Ree did something big."

Watching Fayleen mop up stew with a piece of bread, Tessa asked, "Do you believe it?"

"Yes."

Chewing on the bread, Fayleen shrugged. She knew everything Eirian could do. If the reports stated she had stopped the battle and held off further attacks at her location, Fayleen believed it. However, Baenlin and the others had demanded answers from her, and she hoped her years of lying for Eirian had paid off. She considered telling Tessa the truth, but decided against it. Tessa had enough to worry about, and protecting Eirian was not her job.

"I should ask, but I don't know that I want to."

Fayleen arched a brow, muttering, "Worry about your own secrets, Tessa."

"I suppose that's your way of saying I should be thankful you're good at keeping secrets."

"You're my friend, Tessa. I'll protect you just like I protect Ree. Which is why I won't tell you. If I go down for being complicit in Ree's crimes, I'll not bring you with us."

Stirring the stew, Tessa gazed at Fayleen with curiosity. The fact she called them crimes suggested Eirian was hiding some terrible ability. She doubted Fayleen was the only one aware of it. Celiaen and his companions would be well and truly part of it. Glancing at the purple band on her finger, Tessa sighed and ate a spoonful of the warm food. Her mind swirled with the possibilities. It had been for too long that purples had felt a need to hide what they were capable of from the rest of the mages.

"Maybe that will be my fight."

"What?" Fayleen asked.

Tessa nodded at her ring. "We're an order of secrets. That's not right. We shouldn't have to fear what we can do."

"There's a bit of a difference between what you can do and what Ree can do."

"Why should that matter? We're mages. Our magic is a gift from the gods. If they didn't intend for people to do what they can, why make it possible? Eirian and I aren't the only purples keeping secrets."

She appreciated the frustration. Years of being in Eirian's shadow had taught Fayleen to pretend to be something less than she was. Unfortunately, people were content to believe it, dismissing her as nothing more than a lackey to a far more powerful mage. She was not sure Eirian was even aware of how others had treated her. Instead of dwelling on it, she wanted to uplift Tessa like Eirian had constantly encouraged her. Unfortunately, Tessa needed it far more than she did.

The stew was tastier than she expected, and between mouthfuls, Fayleen said, "True. The hardest part will be making those fuckers on the council listen to you."

Grunting, Tessa replied, "Won't happen while Hugh is an archmage."

"Your father is old. If your mother doesn't have him killed soon, I'll be surprised."

"Mother wouldn't do that."

"Tessa, your mother is the biggest cold-hearted bitch alive. Hugh will outlive his usefulness, and Riona will get rid of him," she argued, waving her spoon around. "She's probably picked out her next husband already."

Scowling, Tessa poked at a lump of meat in her stew and contemplated how to answer Fayleen. While she had a valid point, Riona was her mother, and Tessa needed to defend her. Even if it was undeserved. No doubt Riona would call her pathetic for trying. Glancing at the door to the tent, Tessa forced herself to finish eating without speaking. She saw Fayleen watching her closely with unmasked concern. With silence settled in the tent, they listened to the chatter of Jaren and Zack outside.

"He's worried about you," Fayleen murmured.

"Jaren always worries. I couldn't scrape a knee without him fussing over me as a child."

"It's sweet. My brothers are shitheads."

Snorting back laughter, Tessa asked, "Shitheads?"

"Yep."

"Really?"

"Truly. I don't think you've met any of them, probably for the best."

It was a lie. Fayleen thought the world of her brothers, even when they were complete asses. She knew they would come the moment she called if she needed them. That was what families did for each other, and she gave thanks every day for being part of two amazing families. Her birth family, and the one she had become part of with Eirian, Celiaen, and Galameyvin.

"Other than the news about the stalemate, did you learn anything from your day riding close to Baenlin?" Tessa inquired, setting her plate down.

"Nothing new."

"Oh?"

Fayleen shrugged. "Paienven is holding the border between Forrestfield and Riane. Apparently, he's sent General Darragh north with Celi. So, Ree will have help in Kelsby well before we get there."

"I'm surprised Baenlin hasn't stopped to assist with any of the Athnaralan attacks we have skirted past so far. Especially after he met with Yaernan."

"He wants to reach Kelsby."

Eyes narrowing, Tessa did not need Fayleen to say the name, to know why Baenlin was determined to make it to Kelsby. He was predictable in his pursuit of what he wanted.

"How's the stick going?"

Glancing over her shoulder at her quarterstaff, Fayleen answered,

"Working pretty well, actually."

"Good, because before you interrupted me, I was working on ideas for one of my own," Tessa said, flicking her hand at the papers.

"Need my input? I'm happy to look it over."

Cocking her head to the side, she joked, "Doubting my abilities?"

"You bet. Bloody purple thinking she's a yellow," Fayleen joked back. "But no, in all seriousness, if you need any help with it, just ask."

"Spoken to your irritating friend today?"

"Rylee? Haven't seen her since this morning. Baenlin has put pressure on her recently. I think he's trying to push her to be serious."

Tessa snorted. "I doubt she knows the meaning."

"That's not fair, Tessa," she scolded.

"You girls decent?" Jaren called through the canvas.

Neither of them answered, and Tessa sneered at the annoyed look on Fayleen's face. She did not care for Rylee or her attitude, even if Fayleen did.

"Well, I'm coming in, and I've got friends."

They turned to watch Jaren push through the door, Zack a step behind him, followed by Rylee and Luke. Carefully maintaining a blank expression, Tessa attempted to hide her frustration over the newcomers. Placing her plate on the table with the other empty one, Fayleen beamed at Rylee, but she did not smile back. Smile fading, Fayleen's eyes darted to Tessa.

"What's wrong, Rylee?"

Jaren muttered, "She wouldn't tell me."

"They know," Rylee stated. "A messenger came from Riane. They discovered your absence, Tessa."

Crossing her arms and smirking, Tessa said, "Took them long enough, but I suppose they wouldn't have looked for days after we left."

"Shit. Fuck." Looking around, Jaren hissed, "This'll be the first place they look."

"Yes. I came to give you a warning. Baenlin intends to handle it himself."

Exchanging looks, Luke and Zack felt concerned by the simmer of rage in Jaren's magic. Flexing her fingers, Fayleen moved to position herself between the entrance and Tessa.

"Thanks for the heads up, Rylee, but I think you and Luke should get out of here before Baenlin discovers you were part of it." Everyone gazed at her in surprise, and Fayleen smirked confidently.

Rylee asked, "Fay, sweet Fay, are you planning to stand up to Baenlin if he comes for Tessa? Because I just want to say what a terrible idea that is. He'll wipe the floor with your ass, and I'll have to explain to Ree why you're dead."

The confident smirk remained, and Fayleen replied, "He doesn't scare me. Hasn't for a few months now. If I can contain Ree, I can bloody well keep Tessa safe long enough to negotiate."

"If he doesn't order your execution for defying him—"

"Baenlin wouldn't risk doing that," Jaren declared. "Killing Fay would piss Ree off, and he doesn't want that. She'd never forgive him if he killed her friend."

"What do you mean, negotiate?" Tessa prompted.

"You want to go to war? Well, make him believe you belong there. Baenlin responds to strength." Fayleen shifted her stance to glance over her shoulder at Tessa. "You're the more powerful one. Remind him."

Looking at Jaren and Zack, Tessa frowned, considering what Fayleen had said. She knew the point was valid, and if she was going to be the grand mage once Mayve died, she needed to stand up for herself. Giving her a nod, Jaren silently agreed with what Fayleen said, and Tessa silently gave thanks for his support.

Jaren said, "You should go, Rylee. No point you burning your chances to advance. You have far more potential than I do."

"Like fuck I do," she snapped. "You're a fucking Valkera."

Screwing up his face, Luke muttered, "Well, I don't want to get in trouble. My archmages will have my hide for helping Tessa."

"He's got a point, Rylee. Hugh won't go easy on any blue caught helping me. I can fight my own battles. I don't need some bratty little red getting in the way."

"Bratty little red?" Rylee snarled. "You couldn't land a fucking blow on a scarecrow!"

Quickly getting between Tessa and Rylee, Jaren held a hand in either direction. "Now ladies, let's not fight with each other."

"It won't be much of a fight once I get my hands on her stupid ribbon."

Flicking the braid over her shoulder, Tessa sneered. "I'll show you what I can do with it."

Rylee's hand shot to a knife, fingers encasing the hilt in preparation as she mocked, "What, twirl it around—"

"Enough!" Fayleen bellowed.

They felt the impact of her magic before she finished turning around to face them. Frozen in place, the five mages stared at her in shock while she held one hand up. Curling her fingers, Fayleen regarded them with a furious expression, her power blanketing the tent.

"Are you a bunch of fucking children? Seriously! You're all decades older than me, but I'm the only one with any sense."

"I wouldn't be so sure about that," Baenlin spoke from behind her.

Still stuck, their gazes shifted from Fayleen to Baenlin, each of them aware of the danger they were in. His dark eyes regarded them coldly, and his coat did nothing to hide the arrangement of weapons adorning him. Keeping her hand in place, Fayleen looked over her shoulder, tempted to extend her magic to trap him as well.

"As soon as I heard, I knew you'd have something to do with it, Jaren.

However, I expected better, Rylee." Eyes narrowing in Fayleen's direction, Baenlin added, "I should have known you would be involved."

Her lips curled challengingly, and Fayleen said, "I'll take that as a compliment."

Baenlin lifted his chin, a flicker of rage appearing. Noticing Soren outside, Fayleen recalled what he could do. Next to him, Luke and Zack were inconsequential. Cocking her head to the side, she hoped Baenlin would remember her willingness to shield against him and moved a hand to the small of her back. Pointing roughly in Tessa's direction, she released her from the grasp of her magic.

Seeing Fayleen point at her, Tessa's eyes widened when she realized what was happening. Free to move again, she took a step in Baenlin's direction, keeping her shoulders square and head high. He scrutinized her, a hint of dismissal appearing on his face. Taking stock of it, Tessa reminded herself that he did not know what she was capable of. If she wanted to, she could put him on his ass without lifting a finger.

"What brings you here, Archmage?" she asked, keeping her voice calm.

He arched a brow, replying, "It appears I have an errant purple who thinks she can leave Riane whenever it suits her."

"Oh dear, that sounds like a terrible predicament. Whatever will you do when you find this errant mage?"

Jaren choked. "Tessa!"

"Be quiet, Jaren," Fayleen instructed.

"You want to know what I plan to do to you?" Walking toward Tessa, Baenlin growled, "First, I'll have you restrained. Then I'll make you watch while they flog your brother for his part in this venture."

Her veneer dropped, and Tessa snarled, "You won't lay a hand on Jaren."

"Careful, little Valkera, your claws aren't what you think they are."

Feeling a vibration in the ground, Jaren shook his head at Fayleen, hoping she would intervene. Ignoring him, she watched Tessa and Baenlin curiously, her blue eyes glittering with amusement. She knew she could step in at any moment to keep them apart, but first, she wanted to give Tessa a chance to find her confidence. Fayleen was the safest from Baenlin's wrath. He would not risk Eirian's ire by doing anything to her, and she did not intend to return to Riane. Not that any of them were aware of her plan.

Taking a deep breath, Tessa reminded herself to remain calm. If she showed her abilities off at the wrong time, they would not make the desired impression. She knew how to verbally spar. Riona had drilled her in it from the day she could talk. Baenlin stood over her, gazing down at Tessa in mild curiosity. He was not interested in seeing her become the grand mage, but he wondered if she might be useful.

"Why, Archmage, don't mistake my bark for my bite." Winking, Tessa purred, "You don't want to see my claws."

"Considering they're probably made from twisted metal and insane ideas, I'll happily pass on seeing them."

Her eyes slid to a carefully packed chest. Tessa had packed one of her latest inventions safely inside. With Fayleen's help, they had layered the glass orbs of combustible powder with wards to ensure they would not break or accidentally ignite. She planned to show them to Eirian, hoping for her support in using them against the Athnaralans as a trial to test their effectiveness. If anyone could appreciate their genius, it was Eirian. For all their rivalries in years gone by, they were both purples and understood how it felt to be dismissed.

Deciding to show one of her more harmless abilities off, Tessa dragged a hand over her face, imagining the shift of her features. Baenlin's eyes widened, watching her blue eyes become brown. Her hair darkened, and shaking her head, she tossed her braid over her shoulder. While he stared at the image of Eirian she had projected onto herself, it tempted him to lift a hand to touch her. He saw Fayleen watching in fascination, suggesting she was unaware of the trick Tessa had been hiding.

"How?"

"Uncanny, isn't it?" Jaren said, knowing precisely what Tessa had done.

Smirking, Tessa murmured, aware he would hear Eirian's voice coming from her lips, "Does this face suit you?"

"Can you—"

"Others? Of course. I simply chose this one to please you."

Rylee could not see what had Baenlin so entranced and demanded, "What's going on?"

"I'm showing the archmage why he won't send me back to Riane," Tessa answered. "Would you like to see another?"

Tessa repeated the process and applied her magic to her face a second time, giving herself Soren's features. Choking in surprise, Baenlin turned to look out of the tent at Soren before looking back. Her confident smile was out of place on his face, but he could not blame her for feeling it.

"It's a pity you're useless with a blade," he told her.

Growling, Jaren defended her, "Tessa isn't useless with weapons. I keep her training up."

Waving dismissively, Baenlin dropped his gaze down over Tessa pointedly. She had only changed her face, leaving the rest of her body as it was. Staring at Soren's face on the curvaceous figure was disconcerting. Chuckling, Tessa allowed the transformation to fade and lifted her hand to show Baenlin her empty palm.

"Well, Archmage?"

Smiling slowly, Baenlin told her, "I should send you back."

"Don't disappoint me," she replied. "I have such high hopes for our relationship in the future. After all, we'll be working together for a long time."

"How do you do it?"

"It's simple, really. All I have to do is manipulate the appearance of the particles. But it doesn't last as long as I'd like because the particles want to return to their natural state."

He regretted asking for an explanation; the words coming from Tessa's mouth barely made sense. It further reminded him of Hugh's claims that she bordered on insane. The rational part of his mind screamed at Baenlin to send her back to Riane, but curiosity got the better of him. Keeping her close would provide him with the opportunity to establish which of them was in control. Even though he clung to the hope of bringing Eirian back, Baenlin knew he could not afford to alienate Tessa.

"Can you do it to others?"

Tessa smirked. "Do you want me to make you prettier for an hour?"

"Just answer the question," he growled.

"No, I can't. Only myself."

Jaren swallowed nervously, hoping Baenlin did not detect that Tessa was lying to him. He was the only person other than Tessa who knew Eirian could do it with her help. It was something they had practiced previously. They employed the method to create a diversion, allowing Jaren to break Tessa free of the chamber Hugh had imprisoned her in. Eirian had worn Tessa's face, making sure to be seen before setting off one of Tessa's inventions. People had been so busy dealing with the mess to notice Jaren, Tessa, and Zack leave Riane.

"What a pity. You might've been almost useful to me."

Tessa wanted to tell him about her glass orbs. Her eyes went to the chest again, knowing that if anyone was going to appreciate their battle potential, it was the most feared red mage in the lands. Maybe if Baenlin knew what she could create, he would respect her. Noticing Fayleen shaking her head, Tessa pursed her lips and shrugged.

"Don't worry, Archmage. Get me to Kelsby, and I'll prove just how useful I can be on a battlefield."

Laughing, Baenlin said, "If you think I'm letting you anywhere near a battlefield, you'd be wrong."

"We'll see about that."

"Until we're back in Riane, you'll stay beside me. Guarded. Safe. As befitting the future grand mage. If you think you can defy my orders, I'll have you returned to the city in chains." Turning to Jaren, Baenlin added, "And you should count yourself lucky."

Rylee said, "I just want to mention that Luke and I didn't help."

Sneering, Baenlin asked, "Do you think I care? The only reason I'm going to let it slide is that you're one of my finest warriors."

"Thank you, sir."

"As for you," he spoke to Fayleen. "Just because we're on our way to find Queen Eirian doesn't mean you can defy me."

Smiling brightly, Fayleen fluttered her eyes and said, "Don't worry, Archmage, I wouldn't dream of defying you."

"You go where she goes."

Maintaining her smile, Fayleen hoped he could not tell how pleased she was by his decision. Remaining with Tessa was precisely what she wanted. It would give them time to discuss the final touches on the armor she crafted for Eirian. That, and they could talk about what Tessa wanted in a quarterstaff like the one she had designed for herself. She might be brilliant at creating new things, but Tessa was not a yellow.

"Of course, Archmage, as you command. I'll accompany Tessa wherever she goes and ensure she's shielded."

"Why does it feel like that's not a good thing?" he muttered.

"What about me, sir?" Rylee asked tentatively.

"Organize a guard to make sure the future grand mage remains where I can find her. You're in charge of ensuring Tessa doesn't do another disappearing act."

Licking her lips, Tessa stated, "I'm surprised you're not ordering I sleep in your tent."

Baenlin looked at her contemplatively. "Don't tempt me."

"It's a pity you still have your eyes on the wrong purple. You're a blind man, Archmage."

"And you're a fool, Tessa Valkera."

She hummed in agreement, approaching so she could look Baenlin directly in the eye. Unflinching, he ignored the swirl of magic around them. It lacked the murderous rage that drew him to Eirian's power, but there was a shift in the air he could not work out. Tessa's blue eyes gleamed with amusement, the tilt of her head almost challenging.

"I might be a fool, Baenlin Zarthein, but I'm not an idiot. I'm leaving that title for you."

Clenching his fist, he refused to let his anger seep through to his magic. Smirking, Baenlin stepped back, turning around to leave the tent. He paused at the entrance, glancing over his shoulder at Tessa.

"I'll see you for breakfast."

Releasing the others from her magic, Fayleen told Tessa, "Well done."

"Well done?" Rylee spluttered. "I'm surprised he didn't flatten her!"

Tessa slumped, confidence fading. Walking over, Jaren slung an arm around her shoulders and nodded at Fayleen.

"Fay's right. Well done. You've got to be bold, Tessa, and show everyone what you're made of. Don't let any opportunity escape you."

"And once we're in Kelsby, you and Ree can show the fuckers why they should fear purples." Fayleen smirked, adding, "Trust me, Ree will be down for that."

The two blues exchanged looks, concerned by the devious look on Fayleen's face. Equally worried, Rylee crossed her arms, glaring at her.

"I don't think I like the sound of this," she said.

"Rylee, you're not sleeping with Ree anymore, so I don't care if you like it or not."

Appreciating Fayleen's confidence in her, Tessa murmured, "Maybe Eirian and I can end this war together. I mean, why not? The future grand mage and the Queen of Endara. Two incredibly powerful purple mages united with one purpose."

Jaren chuckled, "Sounds scary. If that doesn't make King Aeyren back off, then he's the biggest idiot in the world."

Gazing at her, Fayleen said, "I think when you're working together, there's nothing you and Ree can't defeat."

"Well, I should keep working," Tessa replied. "Because we're riding to war."

Thank you for reading!

Go to 5310PUBLISHING.COM
for more great books you can read today!

If you enjoyed this book, please review it!

Connect with us on social media!
@5310publishing on Twitter and Instagram

Subscribe to our mailing list to get exclusive offers, news, updates, and discounts for our future book releases and our authors!

READ THE NEXT BOOK IN THIS SERIES: GRAVE OF DANDELIONS

JOYCE GEE

In the aftermath of the real enemy revealing herself, Eirian retreats from the allied armies to seek answers. Accompanied by Aiden, Celiaen, and Galameyvin, they are determined to confront the spirit of the last mage and face the dark god seeking their destruction.

With nightmares clawing at her fragile mind, Eirian embraces the whispers that have followed her for as long as she can remember. The fragments of memories inherited from her mother reveal more than she is willing to share with her companions. As many soldiers as they have, the Queen knows they do not stand a chance against the enemy while a god is driving them to madness. The price for victory is one that Eirian is willing to pay, even if her friends are not.

"Don't let them make me into a hero after I die."

Eirian knows what she is and what she must do to defeat the enemy threatening to destroy her world. With nightmares plaguing her nights, and the whisper of her mother's memories casting shadows over her days, Eirian must sort through the fragments to understand why everything has unfolded. Her life is not worth more than the lives of her people, and she will gladly surrender herself to save the ones she loves—especially when the gods of War and Death are planning to make sure she dies.

Eirian knows what it will take to defeat the mad god, but her companions refuse to accept her choice. Forced to keep her plan secret, Eirian intends to go willingly into a battle that might cost her life.

You might also like...
ARTIE'S COURAGE

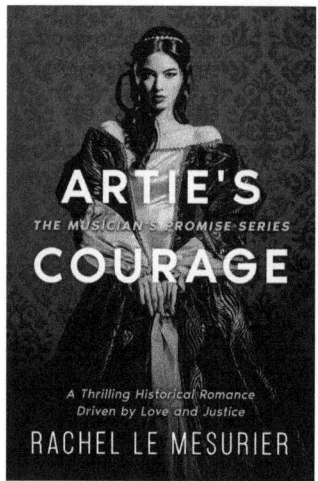

A courageous farm girl's life is changed forever when she falls in love with a charming street musician, opening her eyes to the cruel mistreatment of Mexico's mine workers and compelling her to stand with them against their oppressor - the man she is marrying.

Esperanza lives a charmed life. The daughter of a wealthy landowner, her family is thrilled when she attracts the attention of the handsome and mysterious Don Raúl, opening the door to a glittering life of opulence for them all.

However, a chance encounter with a charming street musician forces Esperanza to open her eyes to the cruel underworld of Mexico's mistreated working classes, and she begins to doubt everything she ever thought she wanted.

As the people begin to rise up in a bloodthirsty revolution against their oppressors, Esperanza is forced to make choices that she hoped never to face. Esperanza's decisions threaten to tear apart her family, her heart, and the country she loves.

In this brutal world where a few careless words can cost lives, will the price of freedom prove to be more than what she is willing to pay?

Led by strong female characters, ARTIE'S COURAGE turns the common damsel in distress trope on its head. Based on real historical events, this thrilling page-turner story of love and courage in the face of adversity follows characters on an emotional journey through laughter, tears, passion, and heartbreak.

"A rip-roaring, romantic adventure that is impossible to put down." —Starred Review

"A well-written and well-researched story against the background of early 20th century Mexico." —D. Wells, author

"Class intrigue, dynastic maneuvering, and dangerous politics against growing civil unrest in pre-revolutionary Mexico. Can an unlikely friendship blossom into more? I couldn't put it down, and nor will you!" —Jennifer Nugée, editor

You might also like...
LOST IN FANTASIA

When virtual reality takes over, it's hard to tell the difference between what is real and what is a part of a game. Having all memories of life before The Game erased, Tack's experience is altered when a glitch infiltrates her world. After her partner disappears, infected by the glitch, she is forced to find answers to the mysterious Game malfunction to determine if he is dead or alive.

Her home, partner, and game are seemingly destroyed. Glitched herself, Tack embarks on an adventure to unfamiliar and new worlds, including the largest Fantasy role-playing game, Fantasia. However, this glitch isn't like anything else the Gaming world has experienced. With no one respawning and the Game's Production team in a communication blackout, the lines between what is virtual and what is real are blurred even further. If Tack can't stop the glitch, she risks more than just losing her partner forever—everything she knows and loves might disappear.

Henry Fudders created the largest virtual reality game in the world, one that everyone experiences, whether they want to or not. The Game is praised for its adventure, creativity, and ability to blur the lines between reality and virtual reality. In less than one hundred years, the Game took over real life and built an experience indistinguishable from imagination—until a glitch began eating away at the core of Fudders' creation.

Fudders is dead, and those who know what to do to stop the malfunction are not doing anything to fix it. Struggling to survive in a world outside her own, she uses her battle tactics to make allies and progress in her quest to protect the world from the glitch. However, when confronted with the answers she's looking for, Tack is forced to choose between either saving the game or her newfound allies and partner.

"A surprising and engaging Lit-RPG adventure set in a future where gaming was so evolved (or decadent, depending on your point of view) that humans were employed as avatars... kept me involved in both the game world and the mystery."
—*Readers' Favorite Five Star Review*

You might also like...
BUT I'M NOT A HERO

High school sophomore Matt Pine always thought he'd grow up to be a superhero-after all, not everyone can move things with their mind. But he can only move small stuff, nothing big enough to matter; it wasn't big enough to save his mom from dying in a fire five years ago. Ever since he failed that night, he's been hiding from his Ability, and he's come to grips with the fact that superheroes aren't real. Now he just wants to get through high school in one piece.

But when a semi-truck smashes into a car right in front of him, and he watches the driver die, Matt soon discovers that the death was anything but accidental. The owner of the local auto parts factory, Seth Crossman, took the man out to cover up a defective product...and he's not done killing yet. And since everyone else in town is too scared to do anything, Matt decides it's up to him. That means learning to use this Ability he's been hiding from; and getting some help from Phillip and Tess, who have their own overlooked talents. But they're going up against brawn and bullets, so they'll have to pool everything they have to keep anyone else from getting killed-including themselves.

"A rare story that empowers kids from regular walks of life... Heroes are not just comic book legends defined by their powers, but everyday people who simply do what is right." —Early Reader Review

"When Matt faces trouble in his hometown, the teen and his friends soon find out they're not losers after all. In this young-adult gem, Demarest creates genuine characters whose loyalty and courage are tested. While doing the right thing isn't always easy, sometimes it's even dangerous." —Nicole Sorrell, author of *The Art of Living Series*

"The characterization of Tess, a non-speaking autistic girl, is not only extremely respectful and accurate, but something to be commended as an example as a superb representation of a capable autistic individual." —Early Reader Review

Milton Keynes UK
Ingram Content Group UK Ltd.
UKHW041845031123
431868UK00002B/14